Penumbra Database

**COREY PEARSON- CIA SPYMASTER
IN THE CARIBBEAN SERIES**

D1521406

Robert Morton

ISBN: 1542638402

ISBN 13: 9781542638401

Library of Congress Control Number: 2017901374

CreateSpace Independent Publishing Platform

North Charleston, South Carolina

Contents

Man's events

Great Abaco, An Out-Island in NW Bahamas
(GPS: 26°02'26.4"N 77°15'36.2"W)
Everything was quiet along the Great Abaco Highway (GAH) south of Marsh Harbor, the capital of Abaco, a 120-mile long, boomerang-shaped out island in the Bahamas. The GAH stretches from Walker's Cay on the northern tip, cuts through the central region where Marsh Harbor lies, then threads its way through heavy forest to the desolate southern end where it abruptly runs into the ocean at a remote village called Sandy Point.

Bolan Tougas maneuvered the Ford Expedition SUV in a feeble attempt to avoid a cornucopia of deep chuckholes lining the southern corridor of the GAH.

"Fuckin' potholes!" The left front wheel plunged into another deep rut. The highway became a narrow, limestone and gravel road south of Crossing Rock, a small fishing village south of Marsh Harbor. The region is desolate, populated by small villages whose inhabitants are descendants of fishermen and wild boar hunters. Nassau's glittery casino crowd, cabarets, and flowery-shirted travelers buying duty-free liquor and jewelry, and eagerly bartering for straw hats, mats, and dolls are absent here.

"Still, dis be better than the roads in Haiti...eh, Pierre?"

Bolan's assistant, Pierre Cherestal, also an illegal Haitian, grunted in agreement. He held a 9mm Beretta on the handcuffed passenger in the back seat, who wore an oversized scuba diver's wetsuit.

Both men fled the dismal life of Haiti and were flown into the Bahamas by an organization they didn't know much about...and still don't. Their illegal status was condoned by the Bahamian Agricultural Minister, who pulled a few political strings at the Department of Immigration. Both Haitians were granted Bahamian citizenship and alluring salaries by their enigmatic employer, unlike their illegal Haitian brothers and sisters who hopped into overloaded, decrepit vessels to endure harsh seas to reach the Bahamian out islands.

The Creole language permeated their basic English dialect, a second language to both. They were cousins, born several months apart upon filthy dirt floors in shacks outside of Milot, Haiti. They would have perished if not brought to a church-sponsored medical clinic, with placentas still attached. The final placenta separation was done properly to avoid infection by medical volunteers with good hearts.

As youngsters, hard labor and subsistence living permeated their lives. Under their parent's tutelage, they worked the eroding slopes of the Massif du Nord mountain range. The two families scraped the soil and grew sweet, miniature bananas called "figs," papaya, butter beans, and thyme. Chickens, a few mangy goats and an underfed cow scavenged freely around their adjoining mud shacks. The forests that covered the slopes of the Massif du Nord held the soil in check, but were ultimately ravaged and burnt into charcoal so people could enjoy cooked food. Electricity was an unknown luxury since the international trade embargo stopped fuel imports, thus raising the cost of fuel. They knew it was detrimental to cut down trees and farm on eroding hillsides, but poverty and hunger introduced an immediacy into their lives, negating the consciousness to contemplate long-range environmental disasters.

Neither Tougas nor Cherestal suffered malnutrition, thanks to food provided by the United Nations Relief Agency, along with their mother's ingenuity. Their source of protein was a seasoned paste, sometimes spread on bread when available but mostly eaten with bare fingers. Their mothers would pound peanuts and the roots of the vetiver plant with wooden mortar and pestle, then scrape the paste into jars and season the mixture with hot peppers. Their family size grew while global warming brought a yearly onslaught of hurricanes with hammering rains. It was a dismal combination of events. Soon, even growing peanuts grew frustrating as the hillsides were denuded of the precious forest canopy and erosion of good soil intensified.

Then, the 2010 earthquake...Haiti became a totally lost nation in twenty seconds. The epicenter was a mere fifteen miles from Port-au-Prince and the fifty-nine aftershocks, which were nearly as devastating as the initial impact, killed 250,000 people and leveled 30,000 commercial buildings.

Tougas and Cherestal were the oldest of many siblings and by the time they reached adolescence, they witnessed the symptoms of malnutrition seep the life out of their younger siblings: reddened hair, distended bellies, bony backs, stomachs growling in the dark of night...then death. Out of desperation, both young men fled the hillsides of Massif de Nord to make it on their own in the capital. They hoped to scrape enough money off the streets of Port-au-Prince to nourish themselves and bring back home whatever was left.

In the meantime, at least their families would have two less mouths to feed. Like young girls migrating from small Midwestern towns in the U.S. to Hollywood with idealistic dreams of reaching stardom, both young men trekked the market area in downtown Port-au-Prince with hopes of making money. Like seventy percent of their countrymen inhabiting this Caribbean isle of despair, they were illiterate, homeless and unemployed.

Apart from the dismal outlook, when opportunity knocked they were ready to open the door. The few well-dressed and brave tourists who ventured into the market square from the port area attracted their attention. Tougas and Cherestal brought a survival mentality from the countryside with them, a cleverness forged early in childhood, one indispensable for survival. They turned junk into cash by collecting beer cans and flattening them into trays and cutting discarded auto tires into sandals. The duo approached the rich tourists with their wares. One French couple felt compassion for the unhygienic pair donned in tattered jeans and grimy T-shirts. They donated 190 gourdes, about $11 U.S., for a pair of sandals, a voodoo doll made from scraps of material taken from the city dump, and several aged magazines lifted from the trash bin behind the Tiffany Restaurant. The Tiffany was an alien place to the impecunious pair who peeked through a back-alley window at waiters wearing black bow ties amidst aromatic whiffs of sizzling steak and seafood.

Miraculously, opportunity knocked twice. After a week of salvaging junk and turning it into marketable wares, an amicable man named Abner Orival approached them as they canvassed the Rue Marcajoux between the Cathedrale Notre-Dame and the port area. Orival was a paid recruiter for a Colombian named Virgilio Cesar Sandoval. He targeted vulnerable Haitians and conscripted them to work for Sandoval at a huge chicken processing farm on the out island of Abaco, Bahamas. It wasn't a difficult persuasion. Orival befriended them quickly, offering additional wares to sell for a sixty percent cut. The brothers were permitted to sleep in Orival's small backyard in the shantytown of La Saline, just north of Port-au-Prince.

The opportunity to become established marchands was too much of a temptation. A "Oui! Merci!" and energetic handshake solidified the business deal. Orival set them up with a rickety wooden stand laden with seashells, bamboo items, wood and stone carvings, leather work, baskets, pottery and fresh fruits. Tougas and Cherestal were permitted to snack on the cornucopia of mango, papaya, apricots, guava paste, pomegranate, yams, cassava and avocado piled high in woven baskets. They set up amidst the throngs of marchands lining the Grand Rue, often three columns deep.

Life was beyond fortunate. Compared to the man-made environmental squalor of the Massif du Nord hillsides, they considered themselves well-heeled in this city of over one million. No longer did their stomachs growl at night and their body weight gained twenty pounds since meeting Abner Orival. They bathed and brushed their teeth in the Bay of Port-au-Prince with soap and toothpaste and proudly sported their pepe', second-hand clothes purchased with their own money Neither would return to the wretched hillsides of Milot. They experienced classic post-traumatic stress disorder, Haitian style. The memories of people at the end stages of AIDS and cancer, dwindling away and receiving little treatment; bodies being Overtaken by parasites; their starving brothers and sisters…no wonder neither man discussed his past. Some things need to be forgotten.

One day, Orival drove them to the Hotel Montana for a visit with the man named Virgilio Cesar Sandoval. He talked with them privately on a patio surrounded by lush vegetation and offered a special deal. First, they must be trained in the art of urban guerrilla warfare by joining the Front for the Advancement and Progress of Haiti (FRAPH). Upon proving themselves, they would be employed as his personal bodyguards and become farm supervisors on a corporate chicken processing plant on Abaco, Bahamas. Their salaries would increase tenfold and each would receive full Bahamian citizenship. Tougas and Cherestal agreed. They would do anything for Sandoval, anything to distance themselves from the squalor and memories of Haiti…including torture and murder.

Bolan Tougas continued south on the Great Abaco Highway while Pierre Cherestal kept the Beretta stuck in the handcuffed man's abdomen. "If you try somethin' I gut shoot ya and you still be alive when ya meet Dagger Mouth."

The sandy-haired man in his late twenties, donned in the oversized wetsuit, slowly chewed on his bubble gum. He calmly replied, "Screw you, asshole."

Both Haitians laughed. Compassion never developed within their souls. Feelings of humanity vanished in childhood on the hillsides of the Massif du Nord. Sandoval satisfied their lust for economic survival with money and power and steered their absence of mercy, through fear, to a devotion only to him. He ordered the handsome, sandy-haired man to die unmercifully, and so it would be done.

The SUV passed the side road to Cherokee Sound, a small fishing village, and continued south for thirteen miles. They entered the secluded Bahamian Parrot Preserve, 20,000 acres of mature pine and palmetto palm forest in southern Abaco. Tougas braked and turned brusquely off the GAH onto a hidden pathway which ran for several hundred feet before abruptly ending on the Sea of Abaco. An endangered Abaco Parrot was eating the fruits and seeds in a thick grove of Madeira and Caribbean pine trees. The colorful bird rarely saw or heard human activity in his remote forest sanctuary. It retreated further into the treetop canopy upon hearing the approaching SUV scrape through the palmetto palm, wild guava and poisonwood saplings lining the hidden trail.

Tougas and Cherestal jumped out of the SUV, pulled their prisoner out, and mounted a video cam atop a tripod to record the pending horror. They viciously punched and kicked him to the ground, tied a chain to his ankles and dragged him onto a wooden dock jutting out into the Sea of Abaco. Cherestal sat on the dock, his Beretta still stuck in the hostage's gut.

Tougas dragged parts of a small mobile crane from the SUV and quickly assembled it. Then, he fetched a bucket of chicken parts and a jar of chicken blood from the vehicle and poured the contents slowly into the water.

"You 'bout to meet our friend, Dagger Mouth," Tougas said with a grin. He checked to make sure the video cam was recording, for Virgilio Cesar Sandoval enjoyed watching and listening to the screams of his helpless victims.

"Of course, if you want to tell us about who you work fo', we could set you free." He lied.

A few molecules from the chicken-blood slick floated through the turquoise and gin-colored waters, over the colorful stands of tube sponge, sea fans and elkhorn coral, then descended into a cavernous blue hole lying several hundred feet offshore.

The scent reached the tiger shark resting eighty feet below in the cooler waters. Millions of years of evolution caused its prehistoric brain to awaken when a minuscule amount of blood reached the cartilaginous beast. Its station-wagon sized body rose from the blue hole and tracked down the origin of the continuous blood slick. The dorsal fin protruded above the waves as it glided over the shallow reefs and approached the dock. Dagger Mouth grew energized as the blood trail grew stronger. Its electromagnetic sensors switched on to pick up any vibrations or minuscule electric fields generated from the source of the bloody fragrance.

"Here da monsta' come! Quick, Cherestal, let's make our friend more appetizin'. We gonna make you into chicken chumsicle, my silent friend who don't talk!"

Bolan began to laugh as he stuffed chicken parts into the oversized wetsuit, while Cherestal poked holes in it with his knife. The silent man finally spoke.

"I want you to tell Sandoval something. The organization I work for has resources beyond your comprehension. They will stalk you to the ends of the earth...and spend limitless resources to do so. They will exterminate Sandoval and both of you. You've made a grave mistake...your lives will go to the dogs after today."

Perhaps it was the somber tone, the unexpected confidence or the resoluteness buttressing their prisoner's last words that made them stop chuckling.

Cherestal blurted out, "Dis man should be beggin' fo' his life...not threaten us!"

Tougas yelled at his cohort, "Shut the fuck up! You forget we on video!"

Sandoval would view the video and hear the prisoner's words. The Haitian duo feared him more than this mystery man of mental steel. They hooked the ankle chains onto the mobile lift. Cherestal cranked the manual winch and the man in the bloated wetsuit stuffed with dripping chicken parts was hoisted upside down into the air and lowered to a foot above the water's surface.

The nineteen-foot shark glided in circles several times around the head of the sandy-haired man, who closed his eyes and remained silent. On the third pass, the 2,150-pound creature lunged. In an instant, Bolan and Cherestal stared at a severed pelvic bone and two legs dangling from the lift.

Tougas shut off the video cam. "I hope Sandoval not be angry at us. We couldn't get da brave man to scream."

Episode 2

An urgent call to come home...home to Key Largo

US
Key Largo, Florida
(GPS 25°03'52.5"N 80°28'17.8"W)
Corey Pearson sat at a table by the front picture window of the Key Lime Café in Key Largo, enjoying a conglomeration off the breakfast menu of steak and eggs, hash browns and grits, coffee and Key Lime pie. It was past 4pm, but with no time for breakfast or lunch, he didn't care about the unusual request. Neither did the waitress.

A customer decked out in cut-off jeans, sandals and a 'Wastin' Away in Margaritaville' T-shirt sat at the counter watching a small Motorola black and white TV, complete with rabbit ear antennae. The Parrothead wannabe sipped a Corona and snacked on a complimentary cheese plate which was frequented by flies. A large tarpon hung over the bar. Every picture and sign hung slightly askew, including a Karaoke poster that read, "No Refunds For Songs We Don't Play!"

Corey thought to himself. *Caribbean Basin Interdiction Force, CBIF, went all out acquiring this joint. Definitely doesn't draw the sport's bar, country western, college, punk rock, yuppie or corporate community. A class all its own*

The owner bragged to the Jimmy Buffett Parrothead about how he miraculously acquired a state liquor permit, his plans for a backyard patio for bands, and a remodeling of the downstairs bathroom.

I wonder how much the CBIF invested to take over this joint... and their reasons for doing so. The guy doesn't know he's working for them or that his newly-hired waitress is most likely a plant for the counterintelligence teams. Wouldn't be surprised if the Parrothead is, too

He gazed outside past the column of coconut palms and pink hibiscus decorating the front of the mom and pop bar and restaurant. It was Friday and an endless flow of traffic ventured west on US A1A, heading to Key West. The waitress tapped a series of buttons on the aged jukebox in the corner. It took a while for her selections to play, but finally a medley of Buffett tunes began, beginning with "Turnin' Around."

Corey noticed two men talking in front of a small grocery store across Highway 1 and wondered if they were agents of CBIF's counterintelligence (CI). *Probably not. They're too obvious. The real guys wouldn't be noticed. They're out there, somewhere, blending into the daily activities, invisible, and they tracked me since I left the Jamaican safe house*

He never had second thoughts about joining CBIF. Of course, no one "joins" CBIF. Many work for the organization without realizing it. Corey inadvertently became entangled in the web of the enigmatic group. He believed he worked for the CIA until he sensed something was out of the ordinary.

Initially, the CIA selected and trained him to be a Special Operations and Program Officer (SOPA) to plan and coordinate covert missions throughout the Caribbean. In that capacity, he earned approbation by setting up Operation Salt Flamingo in the southern Bahamas.

It was the portentous execution of "Salt Flamingo" that raised his suspicions. The resources available to accomplish each step of his covert plan seemed limitless: no red tape, cost restrictions or organizational bottlenecks from the Department of Homeland Security (DHS). CIA Case Officers keep their thoughts to themselves, so Corey's uncertainty about his true handlers went unspoken. He continued to do his job well, but privately questioned who his genuine employer really was. He wondered if his operations to build Caribbean spy cells were backed by the CIA...or someone else. Just a hunch, but his gut feelings eventually proved correct.

He sent detailed intelligence reports to CIA headquarters in Langley, but not one page ever reached the analysts there. All intel was furtively detoured to General Thomas Morrison, Director of Operations of the Caribbean Basin Interdiction Force (CBIF) command center in Key West, Florida.

Despite the deceptive hiring, Corey liked the pay increase and the feeling he got that his new line of work protected America's vulnerable southern flank and salvaged her democratic institutions and values. He didn't "interdict" drug smuggling shipments from South America as the title CBIF would lead one to believe. Instead, he hunted down terrorist cells throughout the entire Caribbean Basin, including Latin America and northern South America. The U.S. was at war, fighting an enemy that proved the orthodox methods used by law enforcement; i.e., the FBI and Department of Justice, to be ineffective. Corey's early intelligence training, in fact, was inadequate.

Corey didn't have second thoughts about coming on board with CBIF. His earlier years working homicide in the Miami Police Department, attending Miami University and graduating in forensic psychology, joining the FBI and specializing in Forensic Psychology and Profiling at the FBI Academy in Quantico, then entering the CIA's Clandestine Service Trainee Program left him ill-equipped to battle an enemy employing a world-wide, attack-oriented, team approach.

The Department of Homeland Security's umbrella cast a red-tapist, dark shadow over the seventeen intelligence agencies it governed. The mandarin system was unproductive in penetrating self-autonomous, stateless terrorist cells that stretched around the world and communicated via Internet, fax machine, encrypted cellular phone and courier to plan attacks and quickly swarm together to strike inside America. Only a totally black-funded organization like CBIF could uncover terrorist cells whose members believe martyrdom and certainty of paradise can be reached by detonating "dirty" radioactive bombs or biological weapons inside America.

A cell phone musical chime interrupted his thoughts. The waitress retrieved it from her apron and spoke guardedly while retreating to the back kitchen.

Hope this is the signal for me to come home. The counterintelligence teams must not have detected anyone tailing me from Jamaica Corey thought about the hectic day. He chugged down the iced tea, wishing it were a cold beer. An urgent call on his secure cell phone awoke him thirteen hours ago, at 3am.

"We need you to come home." Then, a click. CBIF never minced words. Agency protocol established what happened next: proceed immediately to the Montego Bay Sangster International Airport and check your locker.

Corey went on procedural autopilot. He threw together a few favored clothing items, electric shaver and toothbrush, then vacated the premises, leaving the rest of his belongings behind. As he backed down the driveway of the condo, he glanced down the street to see if the "cleaners" arrived. Yes, they were already there, parked a block away, waiting in a rusted-out, unobtrusive-looking, white van.

A few moments after Corey disappeared around a bend, the van pulled into the driveway. His temporary residence in Montego Bay was expertly sterilized in fifteen minutes. Before Cory reached the airport, the refrigerator, bed, ashtrays, wastebaskets, carpet, ceilings, walls and cupboards were vacuumed and cleansed with chemical amalgamations which left no residue behind. Marks, smudges…all physical clues that revealed Corey and his Jamaican cell chiefs had been there disappeared. Dishes and buffet containers with leftover Ackee and salt fish, jerk pork, curried mutton, Fricassee chicken and coco bread were tossed into a rubber trash can to be incinerated. The cuisine was delivered by a catering service named "Jamaican Cookery," which was owned and operated by CBIF.

By the time Corey retrieved plane tickets, a carry-on bag with fresh clothes, further instructions, and $5,000 cash from the airport locker, the "cleaners" vacated the safe house. No paper trail, fingerprints, hair follicles, or potential DNA samples remained.

Despite the 85-ton take-off weight, the American Airlines Boeing 737-800 rocked gently as it taxied to the main runway. The gentle motion lulled Corey to sleep. The pilot set the screw mechanism to extend the flaps and straps; the drilling sound further sedated him.

Met with Jamaican Cell Chiefs until 2am, then roused at 3...need sleep

He never heard the twin GE engines spool up into a high-pitched whine. The landing gear tucked into the belly of the behemoth ship at 6:48am. Before it completed the ascent to 32,000 feet above the sparkling gin and turquoise-colored waters off Jamaica, Corey's brain spiked out beta waves.

The roar of thrust reversers awakened him from a deep sleep as the Boeing touched down at Miami International at 9:42am. The 2½ hour slumber rejuvenated him. Thoughts of the three CBIF cells in Montego Bay and four in Kingston surfaced. It took years in the making, but the cell chiefs he so carefully recruited and groomed now worked alongside parliament members, banking executives, import/export tycoons, and high-ranking officials in the Jamaican Constabulary Force. Several of these assets were promoted to influential positions. Everything seemed to be going well in Jamaica. That is why the hasty call to come home to Key Largo puzzled him.

What's behind the urgent call? Can't have much to do with operations in Jamaica. No fresh intelligence twists or pressing problems surfaced recently. 'CBIF-Jamaica' is on track...secure

As instructed, Corey ended up at the Key Lime Café after climbing aboard an American Eagle at Miami International and flying to Fort

Myers-RSW airport, then catching a Cape Air Cessna flight which was forced to weave around a large flock of gulls before touching down on the tarmac at Key West International at 2:05pm. He climbed into a green Ford-250 pickup parked in log-term parkin space No. 43 and drove to this unpretentious eatery at mile marker 102.8 in Key Largo and ordered a meal, as directed.

I wonder how many CBIF counterintelligence agents have copies of my itinerary? Corey finished chugging down his iced tea and savored the last bite of Key Lime pie. The waitress reappeared from the back kitchen, stuffing the cell phone back into her apron. She walked across the peanut shell-littered floor to his table and laid a receipt on the vinyl, red-checkered table cloth. He stared at the blank tab and understood, handing her an arbitrary amount of cash.

"Keep the change."

She smiled and replied, "Thanks. Have a safe trip."

Corey returned the smile. "The pleasure's all mine. I must have a look at your wine list sometime."

In the pickup, Corey took a miniature penlight from the glovecompartment and shined it upon the blank receipt. Under the special UV light, the words *"You're cleared, come on home"* appeared.

Episode 3

The meeting

CBIF Safe House, Key Largo
(GPS: 25°01'54.1"N 80°30'08.6"W)
Corey pulled into the gravel driveway of the unpretentious Conch Inn Resort, a semi-private vacation complex with twelve cottages bordering the Florida Bay. The grounds were nestled in a mixed wood of coconut palm and Caribbean pine. He drove down the gravel cul-de-sac drive lined with cultivated allemande, bougainvillea and hibiscus and parked at the last cottage. It overlooked a small beach where children frolicked in the sand under the watchful eyes of their parents.

In front of the adjacent cottage, four men relaxed in lawn chairs, drinking beer and retelling fish stories. Graphite fishing rods with cork grips bristled from their open flatbed pickup truck, which stored life jackets, an electronic fish finder, Bahamas hats with large visors and back flaps, a large polypropylene tackle box, and a trailer tongue jack. Despite the high humidity and temperature, they wore meshed fishing vests with nylon shells and hand-warmer panel pockets, perfect for ventilation and freedom of movement while fishing...*and to quickly whip out a concealed CBIF standard issue Glock-30 and to store extra clips. Just a bunch of good ol' boys...right! These guys are even better than the Parrothead and waitress back at the Key Lime Café. A bunch of misplaced Shakespearian actors*

As Corey walked up to the cottage, a black sedan glided through the front gate and backed up to the vacant cottage across the way. Two men and a woman remained inside, observing him. He knocked on the cottage door. A voice beckoned him. He entered, unsure of what to expect. Corey paused momentarily at the entranceway. His jaw dropped slightly upon viewing the man seated at a desk...a man who meets secretly with the president in the Oval Office- General Thomas Morrison, age seventy-five, ex-marine and retired chief of the CIA's clandestine service. He was recalled back from a comfortable retirement to become the Directorate of Operations of CBIF. He reached over the desk and shook Corey's hand, motioning him to sit down. His presence meant only one thing...grave agenda was at hand. Morrison grinned, trying to ease the tension. "Corey, you look surprised to see me."

"Well, sir, that's an understatement. I don't know whether to be honored or alarmed. I was expecting a courier."

The general's grin vanished. "Before we're done with this briefing, I'm afraid you'll feel the latter. But, for now, let's review CBIF-Jamaica 7, our seven cells in Jamaica. The video and auditory feed from last night's meeting at the Montego Bay safe house didn't come through completely. We missed what cell chief Curtis Beacher said. Dam solar flare activity we've been experiencing lately. A geomagnetic storm from the sun screwed up the feeds covering the narcotics pipeline, so give me the details of what we missed."

The air conditioner mounted above the kitchenette window kept the ephemeral safe house at a comfortable seventy degrees, but Corey began to perspire...*What is the alarming news... let's start with that!* He gathered his thoughts about CBIF-J7 and last night's clandestine meeting with the cell chiefs. Everything had to be explained accurately, for his words are often repeated in the Oval Office during Morrison's undisclosed meetings with the POTUS.

"Curtis Beacher's shipping business is doing well. He employs sixty-five dockworkers and seventy-eight freighter crewmen…still imports bananas and citrus fruits from several CARICOM islands into Jamaica…"

"Which ones?"

"Antigua, Barbuda, St. Kitts, Nevis, Caymans and of course, Jamaica."

Morrison leaned forward. He didn't want to miss Corey's answers to the next round of queries. "The satellite feed scrambled on us. We heard him mention the Bahamas."

I knew they had the Montego Bay safe house bugged! "Yes. Beacher wants to cash in on their imports and exports. Eighty percent of the food eaten in the Bahamas is imported, almost half a billion dollars' worth. He wants a piece of their export market, too…crawfish, rum, salt from Great Inagua, and fruits and vegetables. Beacher mentioned the possibility of adding an additional ship to his fleet and adding several dozen crew members."

Morrison took the cigar from his mouth and blew a smoky cloud in the air. "We heard him, despite the chopped-up satellite feed, mention chicken production. The transmission grew garbled. What Bahamian out island did he mention?"

The opulent scent of the Montecristo Cuban cigar filled the room. Morrison always took a hefty puff from it when agitated. No one knew how he got a hold of them for free. They sold for over $600 for a box of twenty-five on the open market.

"He mentioned a large poultry venture on Abaco where broiler chickens will be bred, not just for domestic consumption, but for export to CARNICOM islands. The Bahamian Agricultural Minister gave the OK for production of a huge hatchery on Abaco."

The General reclined back into the chair and began grinding his teeth while thinking. Then, he inserted the Montecristo as a substitute. It was a standing bet amongst CBIF operatives that anyone who tracked down his Montecristo supply source would be awarded a night out of free drinks. Corey remained silent, whiffing the discharge of roasted nuts and hint of spice.

Morrison chewed the cigar as he spoke. "He's the dual national you recruited, right?"

"Yes, sir. His Father, John Beacher, was Jamaican and owned the shipping business. He married an American, Elsie Ring, in the 1980's and received U.S. citizenship. Senile dementia struck John Beacher at age seventy-seven, so Curtis and Elsie took over the company. She ran it until she passed away five years ago. Curtis inherited the entire operation."

"What about the drug shipments?"

"One of Beacher's ships, the *El Sea* which was named after his mother, moves narcotics into Jamaica from Haiti on the Port-au-Prince run. As you know, our moles in the DEA work undercover on the *El Sea* and keep tabs on the crew."

Morrison asked. "Your past intel reports stated that our DEA moles acting as crew members found out the drugs also pass through Cuba from Colombia?"

"Correct...only fifty miles of ocean separates Port-au-Prince from Cuba. The moles on the *El Sea* found out who the Haitian suppliers are and where they get the stuff from. This information is shared with Beacher."

"Is he worried about getting busted?"

"No, sir. I assured him that the head of DEA in Jamaica works with us and knows of the situation."

"A trusting soul. The coke is stored in his Montego Bay warehouse. He'd go away for life if busted."

Corey grew relaxed as the briefing progressed. "True, sir, but I took Curtis Beacher to a meeting with the regional and local heads of

DEA. We met at the DEA HQ at the U.S. Embassy in Kingston. They assured him he would be protected, even if Jamaican police raided the *El Sea* or the Montego Bay warehouse."

"Who were 'they'…any of the Jamaican forces attend the meeting?"

"No, sir. No chance of a local finding out about Beacher's cooperation with us. I drove him there by private car, tinted windows… drove into underground parking and onto a private elevator…no one saw Beacher come or go."

"The Jamaica Constabulary Force, Customs, and their Defense Force have good surveillance personnel and equipment, thanks to the U.S. I'm sure a good number of their agents are paid off by the cartels. The DEA estimates over 100 tons of cocaine passed through the area last year from South America to the U.S. That's a lot of bribe money. Good precautions, Corey. The meeting could have been monitored."

"Thank you, sir. And I know that our DEA friends in Washington are aware as well. The drugs come in on the *El Sea* from Haiti and are unloaded into Beacher's Montego Bay warehouse until another of his ships, the *Kingston II* makes the Ft. Lauderdale run. The crew is faithful. All unknowingly are paid informants of ours. Curtis pays them good wages, including large yearly bonuses that we cover…as long as he continues to give me useful information, that is."

Corey waited while Morrison paused to retrieve a black with gold-trimmed snuffer from his shirt pocket and unscrew the end of the tube. He watched as the general slid the burning Montecristo into the tube and threaded the end back on, creating an air-tight chamber.

"Yes," Morrison said, "and CBIF will continue financing the operation. It's worth it. Any more indications of Middle East linkage to this Colombian-Fort Lauderdale pipeline?"

"I think so. The latest shipments contain half coke, half heroin. The heroin is top quality stuff, not from poppy grown in Colombia… most likely grown in the Middle East, probably Afghanistan."

"How can you be so sure it comes from Afghanistan?"

"Our informant in Haiti, Damballah Saint-Fleur, gave one of our DEA moles on the *El Sea* information about a Colombian drug smuggler named Virgilio Cesar Sandoval. His permanent residence is in Medellin, but he visits Haiti often and meets with the Minister of Parliament himself. DEA Medellin has photos of Sandoval meeting with Middle Eastern contacts."

Morrison frowned when Corey mentioned the name Sandoval. "Yes, I remember reading that in your report. They used commercial airlines to fly back to Afghanistan. Why would that be? Why not private jets supplied by the Colombians to avoid surveillance?"

Corey shrugged, "Maybe they were trying to blend in or think we're stupid. DEA and customs immediately got their flight schedules. They took off from three separate airports in Colombia...Medellin, Bogotá, and Barranquilla."

Morrison smiled. "CBIF performed a super-surveillance on them, including fingerprint and DNA sample collection."

"Yes, the operation worked well. A dozen agents from CBIF, DEA and customs posed as baggage handlers and air marshals. All their luggage was opened after they checked in and boarded...fingerprints lifted, hair samples taken..."

Morrison finished for him. "...and I especially liked how our men and women posed as federal air marshals, boarding the planes in Miami, London and Delhi. They took surveillance photos and tailed them in the airports during lay overs...all the way back to Kabul. Thirty-four hours of top-notch surveillance and intel-gathering."

Not to mention the DNA samples stored in a cooler and put into a digital format on computer along with the fingerprints, but he won't tell me that...only as much as needed. Why did he get uneasy when I mentioned Sandoval's name? Get to the finale...why did you call me home? Why did you show up, personally? I'll steer the conversation back to Sandoval. "Looks more-and-more like Virgilio Cesar Sandoval is a drug smuggler turned narco-terrorist," Corey said.

Morrison took his eyes off Corey, swiveled in his chair and peered out the tinted picture window. Children frolicked in the shallow waters of the Florida Bay while their parents watched from under a dense stand of coconut palms. Gazing out at the tranquil scene failed to hide his ill-at-ease. Corey knew Morrison well...a deep thinker with an enviable aptitude to collaborate bits and pieces of seemingly disparate information into an analogous gestalt. *Sandoval must be the reason for this urgent call to come home* Corey remained silent as the general assimilated the new information into his existing mental files of HUMINT culled from CBIF case officers and the assets they recruited throughout the Caribbean Basin. He thought about the people who would die if the information discussed during the past ten minutes fell into the wrong hands. The general's portable bug detector lay on the desk in front of him, its LED bar display and audio alarm indicated no wireless microphones or transmitters were eavesdropping in the vicinity. Wherever Morrison went, a continual electronic sweep preceded him.

Sailboats were moored offshore, prompting him to casually gaze around the cottage. *Must be a laser beam sensor hidden somewhere in the room. One of those boats could easily focus a hi-tech laser beam on the picture window and detect the infinitesimal vibrations emanating off the glass from our voices...our words could be recorded. Ah... the radio by the twin beds is probably housing it* He glanced back at the director of CBIF, who was still gazing out the window. Corey thought that Morrison was fitting all the new intelligence pieces together, but he wasn't. The director was considering whether or not to place Corey into a new assignment. He was mulling over Corey's past and if it would interfere with the new mission...if he was still consumed with thoughts of his wife Danielle who was murdered while on assignment with him in the very place where they first met and fell in love...a location he was about to assign Corey to return to. Would it reawaken dreadful memories that were best left forgotten?

Morrison swiveled his chair back and faced Corey. Life was full of decisions that weighed costs against benefits. Past memories better forgotten vs. a wealth of experience for this new, critical assignment. He decided in favor of the experience.

"Tell me about our informant in Port-au-Prince, Damballah St.-Fleur. Definitely giving us credible intelligence, is he? How do you know he's not working as a double for the narco-terrorists in Colombia?"

"I doubt it, sir. He's a devote priest, or houngan as they refer to him. Damballah practices Voodoo as his father did. He has a large following of Haitians who believe he has direct contact with the spirit world. His heart lies in revenge against FRAPH, the Front for the Advancement of Progress of Haiti."

Morrison looked skeptical. "Corey, we've spent millions to build an army of paid informants throughout the Caribbean Basin, our southern flank. Why doesn't Damballah ask for monetary gratuities? I like informants who give us intelligence out of commitment to their homeland and family...they're more committed. They hate those who spoil the dreams they have for their loved ones. They're more reliable than paid informants, but are you sure there's that much hatred for the FRAPH squad who murdered his parents? How do you know the Colombians or Cubans aren't giving him cash and using him as a double?"

"General, I believe he is a credible asset. The hatred runs deep. His father indoctrinated him into Voodoo. As a youngster, Damballah learned the chants and the art of entering the trance-like state. He believed the vodun or spirit entered him through his father...and so do his spiritual followers who number in the thousands. I observed a worship ceremony with Curtis Beacher outside Port-au-Prince. Damballah had at least 6,000 followers chanting and dancing to the drumbeats all night until sunrise."

General Morrison remained suspicious. "I just don't want our operation to be neutralized. You remember that the U.S. supported the Haitian regime that committed the atrocity. How do you know he doesn't harbor deep hatred toward *us*?"

The Director of CBIF had a point, but Corey knew Damballah's voo-doo-driven vow to avenge his parent's murder was intense.

"I understand how he *possibly* could despise us. But, the atrocity committed in front of his home in the early morning hours trounces any anti-American sentiment. He was only twelve when Aristide's hench-men came. From the time of the 1991 coup that ousted President Jean-Bertrand Aristide until 1994 when the U.S. finally invaded Haiti, the Haitian Armed Forces maintained power through FRAPH and...." Morrison interrupted. "...and three years of hell fell upon those Haitians who supported Aristide. Your intelligence maintains that his father supported Aristide."

"Yes, sir. His father was an outspoken and powerful houngan who supported Aristide during the 1990 presidential election because of the economic plans in his campaign platform. But, Aristide changed and became brutal. Damballah's father started preaching anti-Aris-tide messages. A FRAPH squad raided their home in the early morn-ing hours of 1992. They dragged him and his parents out into the street. Damballah and his mother were bound and forced to watch the torture, which took a half hour before death fortunately arrived. Then, they tortured, raped and slit the throat of his mother. Damballah saw it all and is resolved to find and murder every member of this murderous FRAPH squad, which still exists today."

"Sounds like our man in Haiti is on a personal mission of ven-geance."

Corey agreed. "Yes, he has a score to settle...it's a voodoo spiri-tual mission of death...which entered his body from his deceased father's soul. At least that's what he believes."

The General soaked in Corey's words. "I can see why he hungers for our intelligence as to the names of the FRAPH executioners... and not our money."

"That's the way I see it, sir."

General Morrison agreed that Damballah St.-Fleur was the per-fect asset in Haiti and was pleased with Corey's work in Jamaica.

"It looks like J7 is on to a narco-terrorist connection. The DEA brass promised to leave the pipeline open, for now. If the Haitian traffickers are busted along with Virgilio Cesar Sandoval, the cartels would quickly find another kingpin to do his dirty work. The Middle East terrorist connection would go underground. You've done well, Corey."

"Thank you, sir." Corey felt uneasy as he gazed at the *Miami Herald* lying on the desk. The headlines read:

> Heroin Flooding into SE Florida. Governor Walter
> Demands Inquiry. DEA Remains Dumfounded

Morrison held the paper up in display. "I'm thinking your thoughts, too. I don't like looking the other way as the traffickers fill our streets with smack. But, it's a cost vs. gain decision. A bust would prevent us from uncovering a Middle East terrorist-cell connection. We'd never get a hold of their money or identify and kill the bastards. They'd go underground and regroup."

Corey nodded. "I realize that. They'd eventually hit us again. I can't get over the 2018 attack, when al-Qaeda took thirty-five kids hostage in that elementary school in Boston. Kept them in the gymnasium for a week, taunting their parents and all of us… then blowing them up after leading us to believe negotiations might work. None were U.S. citizens. They all slipped through our borders. It was a well-funded sleeper cell… fuckin' bastards."

"It was worse than the Orlando gay nightclub and the Sandy Hook Elementary School massacres combined…even surpassed 9-11 due to the week-long tormenting." The hardened general shook his head in disgust. "Ruined America's psyche. I still see the anguished faces of the parents, then the looks of hope as the terrorists negotiated with the FBI, leading us all to believe a compromise was possible."

"That's why CBIF sprung up out of the CIA's Clandestine Service and the reason we must keep the Jamaica-7 operation alive. We've got to wipe out the narco-terrorist connection throughout the Caribbean."

The Director of CBIF retrieved the black, gold-trimmed snuffer from his shirt pocket and unscrewed it. The raison d'être for CBIF was overpowering. They couldn't afford to lose once. They had to hit a homerun every time. He remained silent for a while, then asked, "Is our plan working?"

Corey continued. "With the pipeline left intact, we can continue gathering intel. Damballah is our ticket. A dozen of his Voodoo followers work at the Port-au-Prince dock area. They tip him off about Sandoval's every move. But, we need you, general, to continue supplying the names of the FRAPH squad members who murdered his parents. As long as I supply their names to Damballah, he'll continue relaying information to us about Sandoval."

Morrison stuck the Montecristo back Into his mouth and chuckled. "Sounds like we're being blackmailed by Damballah. How much more detailed intelligence on Sandoval can Damballah give us?"

"Well, sir, last week I gave him the name of one of the squad members you released to me, the one who murdered his mother. In return, he assured me that he would keep us informed as to when Sandoval arrives and departs, where he beds down, who he meets up with, places he frequents, and his ground transportation. Sandoval arrives by private helicopter at the dock area, not at the Port-au-Prince International airport."

Morrison blew a smoke circle into the air. "How accessible is the helicopter? Can we get close to it?"

"Damballah said that some of his voodoo followers work at the port warehouse and Sandoval actually pays them to guard it. They wheel the chopper into the warehouse and store it there until he leaves. Sandoval has two bodyguards who follow him around. He also revealed that a government limo picks them up at the dock area and takes them to the Hotel Montana. Nice place. Rebuilt after the earthquake. Private with gardens, but with his money I don't understand why he doesn't buy a plush condo."

The general replied, "Maybe he doesn't want to appear obvious or have a high-profile. At any rate, he behaves too routine, too careless. Let's find out more about him. I'm putting more resources into Haiti, but not to bribe or recruit more paid informants. Damballah's role won't exceed supplying us with intel about Sandoval's activities. I'm going to plant several CBIF counterintelligence teams into Haiti and set up a synchronized HUMINT and technical intelligence operation. I don't want Damballah to know what we're up to. Eavesdropping equipment will follow Sandoval everywhere he goes."

Corey grew a bit reflective. "I guess 'Salt Flamingo' was a good investment."

"Yes, it was. Our recruitment of Damballah and the entire Haitian connection were expedited by 'Salt Flamingo'. You planned and executed it well."

Corey remembered "Salt Flamingo," code name for Damballah St. Fleur's mysterious recruitment. In September 1994, when 21,000 U.S. troops invaded Haiti in Operation Restore Democracy, Jean- Bertrand Aristide was restored to power. After years of despotic leadership under Jean-Claude "Baby Doc" Duvalier, Haiti welcomed Aristide. In their first Democratic election, swarms of poor, starving Haitians flooded to the polls and elected their only chance of hope, the *Titid* Aristide. After winning, the Haitian military was disbanded and the most corrupt and barbarous officers were banished into exile.

But, a covert CBIF operation transpired just prior to the first U.S. troop assault on the Haitian beaches. Unbeknownst to the U.S. Congress and the news media, a force of fifty special op troops arrived at Keesler Air Force Base in Mississippi at 2am. They came from parts unknown with proper paperwork for admittance into the base. The elite group leaped off two troop transport trucks and double-timed it up the aft loading ramp of a waiting C-130 Hercules. Corey believed this Air Force Reserve Command wing in Mississippi would be ideal to stage "Operation Salt Flamingo" because the famous 403rd maintains a dozen C-130 Hercules transports and a dozen WC-130 aircraft equipped with special weather-gathering instrumentation. They were the original "Hurricane Hunters" and flew routine missions over the Caribbean Basin.

No one paid much attention to the newly arrived C-130, nor did the control tower take much notice when it was cleared for takeoff at 2:20am, a week before Operation Restore Democracy commenced. Several hours later, the commandos parachuted from 500 feet above ground and, in a few moments, all fifty commandos touched down on the remote, forty-nine square-mile, sweltering southern Bahamian island of Little Inagua.

Corey was there to greet them. For several weeks, he had been surveying the remote island, using his usual cover as a marine biologist conducting reef surveys and monitoring reef fish populations. When he wasn't scuba diving and recording fish populations, Corey explored the island. Little Inagua provided a harsh environment... a tourist "un-friendly" one. Development avoided this place of little rainfall or fresh water. Constant trade winds made airplane landings and take-offs treacherous. It was isolated and close to Haiti, a strategically perfect home base for Operation Salt Flamingo.

Corey thought he worked for the CIA at the time, but his intel reports were rerouted to General Morrison who shared them with CBIF's moles at the Pentagon. Corey recommended that Little Inagua be the staging area for Operation Restore Democracy. In return, the Pentagon moles leaked to Morrison when the U.S. military would begin rolling. CBIF had to get in and get out of Inagua secretly, before ground forces set foot on Haitian soil.

The CBIF moles relayed to Morrison that the military brass planned to send the 189th Corps Support Battalion Task Force from Fort Bragg to Fort Eustis to load its equipment onto landing craft utilities, and then proceed to Little Inagua. The invasion of Haiti would need combat service support units to provide a constant supply of water, oil, lubricants and petroleum. Little Inagua would be the support staging area.

All the while, Corey thought he worked for a splinter group within the CIA, not for an organization with secret agents implanted inside the Pentagon, divisions of the CIA, and within the sixteen other agencies comprising the U.S. Intelligence Community. He believed he was gathering intel for a narrow and specific covert operation and that his intelligence reports were sent to the Director of Clandestine Operations at the CIA, not to General Morrison of CBIF. In fact, he had no idea CBIF existed.

CBIF eschews discernibility, so before the U.S. combat support forces arrived, the fifty-man special ops force stealthily landed in the uninhabited wilderness and inhospitable pothole terrain of the tiny Bahamian islet. Only Corey, a few fishermen who came ashore that night to rest before heading home to Great Inagua, and sea turtles that came ashore to lay eggs on the deserted beaches witnessed the eerie night parachute drop.

The next day, Corey shook hands with the special op leader, bidding him good luck. Both men related well to each other. They liked the excitement on the ground, in the trenches. The middle-aged special ops warrior refused a desk assignment, and Corey refused a teaching position at the new CIA training school.

Both men enjoyed action, but for different reasons. The mature warrior had it in his blood, ingrained in heritable DNA strands. Most of his current family and ancestors were warriors as well. Earlier in his career, he successfully apprehended Serbian President Slobodan Milosevic who, in 1999, through fear and executions, forced 740,000 Kosovo Albanians to depart.

Likewise, Corey enjoyed the thrill of the chase, the battle of intellects with some physical clashes as well, but he was driven by love of country… and anguish over his wife's murder.

The lethal force leaped into five UH-60L Blackhawk air assault choppers. Corey hoped for their safe return. Their mission was to bring back a revealing collection of files and documents, and to extricate a Haitian spy recruited by Corey. They soared 200 feet above the Caribbean Sea and sped toward Haiti at 165 mph. Two AH-64 Apache attack choppers, heavily armed with laser-designated Hellfire missiles joined them for backup.

In addition, Corey acquired three UH-60Q Medevac choppers, which trailed the air-assault armada. Each Medevac transported two surgeons and four surgical RN's, on-board cardiac monitoring and medical suction systems, oxygen generation, and IV solutions. A total of eighteen severely wounded commandos could be treated. The only thing the flying medical staff lacked was information on where they were going, the purpose of the mission, and who their employer was.

Thirty minutes later, the deadly private army swooped down upon a police station on the outskirts of Port-de-Paix in northern Haiti. They met little resistance after shooting dead two Haitian policemen who fired at them. The remaining police officers fled while the special external antennas on the Blackhawks intercepted and jammed their portable radios so they couldn't call for help.

In twenty minutes, the warriors leaped back into the choppers with thousands of paper documents, video tapes, DVD's, audio recordings, and a CBIF mole named Gesner Verdieu. Verdieu hid in the basement of the police barracks holding a transmitter that guided the helicopters in. Corey recruited him a year before from within the Haitian FRAPH police force. Five minutes passed…they touched briefly down at a remote Haitian farm and snatched up Verdieu's wife and four children. A half-hour later the air armada landed safely back on Little Inagua.

General Morrison interrupted his thoughts. "You know, Corey, recruiting Verdieu and bringing him back to the U.S. proved very useful to us."

"Is he still residing in Virginia?" Corey asked.

"Yes. His family assumed a new name. They fit in well. The neighbors suspect nothing. We gave him enough seed money to start a new life after he passed the polygraph tests. He examines the mounds of data we seized in the FRAPH police barracks raid. His children attend public school. Bright little kids who learned English quickly. He's on our payroll as a consultant for Haitian affairs. Sometimes, I pour through the FRAPH documents with him. They're awful... videos and memos detailing rapes, arson, extortions, murders, tortures... sick cookies they are...just like ISIS. I agree with you on Damballah's loyalty. He needs us to complete his mission of revenge."

Corey smiled whenever he thought about Operation Salt Flamingo. "I knew Verdieu could help us find willing spies in Haiti. He recommended I target Damballah St.-Fleur and recruit him."

Morrison spoke emphatically. "Yes, and as Verdieu continues siftng through the Haitian documents we learn more. If we continue get- ting critical intel on Sandoval's activities in Haiti from Damballah, I will continue supplying him with the names of the FRAPH execution squad that still exists today, the one that executed his parents, years ago, before his childish eyes."

Corey sensed CBIF-J7 was going on some sort of offensive and the reason the general appeared in person was about to be revealed. "Yes, general. The info we get from Damballah's dock workers in Port-au-Prince and from Curtis Beacher and his crew should enable us to pinpoint Sandoval's every move and uncover the specifics of the narco-Middle East terrorist link. The agents you put in place on Haiti will know exactly where to position the eavesdropping equipment."

Morrison stuck the Montecristo back into his mouth. It was time to divulge the real reason he called Corey home...intelligence from the CBIF cell in Nassau...news that will deeply sadden and distress the master spy seated across from him.

A moment of silence followed. The general puffed on his Monte Cristo, then dropped the bombshell. He looked Corey square in the eye

"An alarming event has happened. In the documents taken in Operation Salt Flamingo was a man that Verdieu identified as a Haitian FRAPH squad member, the same execution squad that murdered Damballah's parents years ago. We have identified him as Bolan Tougas. Duane Collier met this man and partied with him at a night club…the night he turned up missing. We haven't heard from Collier since yesterday."

Corey rose halfway out of his chair. "What! That's impossible! I personally trained Duane on how run the seven cells in Nassau. What was he doing in a fuckin' nightclub in Haiti with a FRAPH member? How could he be missing? He knew the check-in protocol and back-up system. There was supposed to be people shadowing him and taking pictures of every contact meeting he had. What the hell was he doing in Haiti…way out of his element?!"

Morrison grew more somber. He knew Duane Collier was like a son to Corey. Duane's father, Drew Collier, was a lifetime friend of Corey's and one of the 125 killed at the Pentagon on 9-11. After his wife Danielle was murdered, Corey had difficulty fulfilling his assignment as CBIF case officer of the seven cells he created in the Bahamas, code-named CBIF New Providence-7. So, he ordered him to train Duane Collier to take over the operation. The reason Corey was taken out of Nassau and inserted into Jamaica was to help him forget the past and to start anew.

Morrison understood Corey's exasperation. "I'm sorry, Corey, but Collier wasn't in Haiti." He slid a photo over the desk. "This was taken at the Hard Rock Café in Nassau. Bolan Tougas was the last person Collier was seen with. That's why I called you home…to speak to you personally. This Haitian pipeline reaches farther and deeper than we realize. You won't be returning to Jamaica. You're heading to Nassau…tonight. Agent Duane Collier's missing and you're going to find out what happened to him."

Episode 4

Betrayal

Hart Senate Office Building
Washington, D.C.
Senator William Warren sat at the end of a thirty-foot table in room SH-219, a dark-wood chamber in the innards of the Hart Senate Office Building. It was a room where many esoteric discussions are held concerning U.S. intelligence matters. As Chairman of the Senate Select Committee on Intelligence, he kept tabs on the finer details of intelligence activities conducted by the government. The committee embraced both political parties equally; any decision made was passed by majority vote of the eight Republicans and eight Democrats who at- tend the regular meetings held every other Wednesday of each month. A quorum was needed to vote on matters and Warren calculatingly scheduled this closed-door meeting at a time inconvenient for three members. Warren learned through unscrupulous inquiry that the trio had to be in the Senate to vote on matters of prime importance to their constituents. If present, the two Democrats and one Republican would likely vote against today's committee proposal or form a committee to inspect the matter further.

More than a third of the members sat before him, listening to Colombian Army General Manuel Castano's long testimony draw to a close. He pleaded for more sophisticated weaponry for his militia. Warren knew the majority of the quorum would vote for today's proposal, which would make him a richer man.

Castano wound up his 1½ hour presentation, "… and in conclusion, I tell you we no longer exercise sovereignty over our own country. FARC, the *Fuerzas Armadas Revolucionarias de Colombia* controls the countryside while the *Ejercito de Liberacion Nacional* or ELN as you Americans name it, has several urban fronts. They are ruthless and extract 'war taxes' from our people. 'Necklace bombs' are strapped around the necks of the loved ones of those who don't pay. Just last week, our bomb squad worked for three hours trying to remove one from the neck of a young boy whose father refused to pay this tax to them. It detonated, killing the boy and two of my brave bomb squad officers. So, I plead with you to pass this measure. We need sophisticated weapons to continue the war against a hard-hitting enemy. I thank you and will take any questions you may have." Lieutenant General Castano sat down at the opposite end of the table from Senator Warren. Several minutes of silence ensued as the intelligence committee members perused the classified documents before them that listed all weapons the U.S. currently supplies the Colombian military with. The documents were retrieved from a secure storage area and could be examined only in this room. No copying, editing, or removal of secure documents was permitted from the Select Intelligence Committee chamber or antechamber.

Senator Warren sat comfortably in his specially-ordered, ergonomic executive chair crafted in premium Italian black leather. He eyed the less significant members and glanced at his luxurious Cartier pasha Chronograph watch, which hid wrist scars from a childhood he resentfully journeyed through.

Finally, the Honorable Republican Senator Ruth Winstrom from Rhode Island fidgeted, then spoke from her uncomfortable vinyl and cloth chair. "You're very convincing, general. What type of weaponry are you asking for? And, why aren't the weapons already supplied to your forces sufficient?"

"Please do not get me wrong, Honorable Senora Winstrom, I appreciate the weapons you supply us with. Without what you've furnished, the lives of many of my brave soldiers would have ended. But, things happen in warfare that no one can foresee. The Gau-19 Gatling machine guns you equipped our drug-fighting helicopters with actually threw them off-balance when fired. They're expensive to operate and maintain, and are so heavy that they tip our helicopters dangerously forward and we lose air agility when trying to avoid ground fire from the heavily armed FARC. Still, without them many of my brave soldiers would have perished. I know the powerful people in the company that makes these fine machine guns and two key House Republicans in the district the company is in say that it was our faulty installation and misuse of them that caused the problem and…"

Senator Winstrom interrupted. "But, general, don't the Gau-19's rapid fire and fifty caliber rounds penetrate the thick jungle canopy? Remember, you told us that you needed heavy fire power from the choppers …that your weapons were just noisemakers that only scared away crows? We spent millions arming your choppers with this weapon, which you now tell us was a waste of money. I again ask you, what new weapons system are you asking for? And, how can you assure us we won't be wasting the tax payer's money again?"

The general stood back up and responded to the concerns of the female clandestine meeting member. "Your honor, Madam Winstrom, we must retool our forces to get back on the offense. We must conduct more ground assaults on the guerrilla strongholds in the countryside. I must give you proper feedback for things that work…and those that don't. The sixty Blackhawk and Huey choppers dealt a deathblow to many terrorists in my country, despite the inadequacies of the Gau-19's mounted on them.

But, we need a new generation of mortars, along with RPG's and hand grenades. We plan to mount relentless operations to fight FARC close up, hand-to-hand if need be. We need hi-tech mortars with laser guidance and grid switches to launch precise firing missions. With these modern weapons, my forces can launch a surprise reign of terror upon their encampments and clandestine cocaine laboratories.

Our change of strategy from air to ground operations requires this avant-garde, hi-tech weapon system. The terrorists would never hear or see us coming until it was too late. We must keep trying until we find the things that work well. Again, I thank you for allowing me to speak before you."

The General sat down. Several moments of silence again ensued as each member assimilated the past several hours of lecture.

Senator Warren piped up. "I think we've read and heard enough input to vote responsibly. If there are no more questions for Lieutenant General Castano, I'd like to propose that we recommend funding for the hi-tech mortar system, earmarked for the Colombian Army. The cost will be a drop in the bucket, considering this year's aid package to Colombia is $2.5 billion."

A Democratic member from Kansas eyeballed his Wal-Mart wristwatch with impatience, then raised his arm, exposing a functional suit that seemed glued together compared to Senator Warren's camelhair and cashmere apparel. He spoke from his vinyl seat. "I motion that we fund a shipment of fifty of these mortar batteries with laser-guided, precision homing devices. I believe the nickname for them is the 'advanced 140mm mortar bomb'. Feel free to correct me if I got the name wrong."

Another member added, "I'd like to include in the motion that General Braddock, Commander of the U.S. Southern Command, be notified immediately upon this resolution's passage. He will decide which base the shipment goes to. In fact, Lieutenant General Castano, I also move that you meet with him and work out the details, including when the weapons will be shipped."

"I would be more than happy to meet with the U.S. general," Castano quickly replied.

Senator Warren chipped in. "I also recommend that General Braddock keep this committee informed as to when and where the weapons are transferred inside Colombia. His strategy to create smaller bases and decentralize our presence throughout Latin and South America makes it difficult for us to keep tabs on things."

Senator Ruth Winstrom looked troubled by Warren's remark. She chimed in. "True, my dear friend, Senator Warren. But, we must remember the local leaders throughout Latin and South America were reluctant to house large U.S. military bases in their respective countries. Now, we're more welcome. In the long run, this new 'deconcentration' strategy helps us protect our southern flank."

Beyond the politically correct parlance, the female Senator didn't consider Warren her friend, nor did she trust him. His demeanor concerned her. The Chairman of the Senate Select Committee on intelligence usually knows, in general, what the seventeen intelligence agencies are up to. But, his thumbs were on everything... micromanaging them. She sensed his intense scrutiny of the Intelligence Community was spawned by alternative motives. She trusted her gut instincts. After all, she conquered many opponents in her lifetime of political scuffles, using calculated and precise campaign tactics, all of which hinged on visceral feelings.

Hence, she was dubious of Warren. Beyond the obvious arrogant and disrespectful choice of meeting room furniture which raised his stature above the other members...she felt this narcissistic man who needs to create illusionary images of superiority to hide a low self-esteem or short penis (as she jokingly said to her staff) should not have been entrusted with overseeing America's Intelligence Community.

"I do stand corrected, Madam Winstrom. A good point." Warren fought back the anger the female senator spawned within his easily-threatened psyche. The members stared at his laser teeth-whitened smile and celebrity hair style with natural-looking flaxen hair that veiled graying locks underneath. Senator Warren hid his narcissism well, for he had much practice.

Years ago, at the urging of a Princeton political science professor, he sought help through psychotherapy. It was to no avail, for he couldn't face his insecurities stemming from childhood. Instead, Warren demeaned the psychoanalyst. After all, the mental health professional was starting to detract from his sense of mastery and omniscience. Throughout his middle-aged life, the senator grew obsessed with fantasies of success, power, and special treatment. At the same time, he learned social suitability by being a bystander to normal people...observing them in social situations... learning how to display proper emotions at the appropriate time even though he couldn't feel the emotional link between them. He was a genuine sociopath who wrapped himself around the American flag.

And so it was, here in this secretive room SH-219, in the bowels of the Senate Hart Office Building, that no one noticed the sudden surge of anger. *How dare someone, especially a woman...rectify me!* He quickly forged ahead. "Since there's no further questions, let's formulate a motion to vote on the 140mm laser-guided mortar bomb for the Colombian Army."

Episode 5

Operation Coral Reef

CBIF Safe House, Key Largo, FL

General Morrison remained patient as Corey assimilated the bad news and persisted with his questioning.

"A Haitian FRAPH member at the Hard Rock Café in Nassau…it's hard to believe Duane Collier could be kidnapped! He knew how to use the backup system and the protocol to follow. It would've been impossible for him to leave the club with this Haitian FRAPH killer… Bolan Tougas. There would…or should…have been agents outside the club in communication with the ones inside, who should have had concealed cameras. Collier was a case officer… that I personally trained!"

The deputy director of CBIF slowly pushed a sealed manila packet across the desk. The label read CBIF *New Providence-7: Operation Coral Reef, Top Secret.* That's why I'm sending you there…to find out the answers to those questions. I have your replacement for CBIF Jamaica-7. As we speak, he's landing in Montego Bay. You're going to Nassau… immediately."

A few moments of silence transpired as Corey stared at the table, allowing for the initial shock to simmer down to mere anguish. Finally, Morrison calmly said, "The answers to some of your questions are in this intel packet. I want you to stay here and read it thoroughly for the next hour. You will make contact with your original cell manager number four of the Potter's Cay cell."

"Darnell Ferguson?" Cory asked soberly. "I haven't talked to him since I left the Bahamas a decade ago."

"Yes, your old friend Ferguson in Nassau. It's all in the packet. The buddy system *wa* in effect at the Hard Rock Café. Darnell and three of his Potter's Cay fishing boat crew *were* covering Duane Collier's club meeting that night. The Haitian arrived with a limo driver who turned out to be the driver and bodyguard for the Bahamian Minister of Agriculture. Darnell will brief you on the information he has. You are to meet him at the Poop Deck Restaurant on Bay Street in downtown Nassau tomorrow at noon. The cleaners are on the way here, so at 7pm leave and drive back to Key West airport. Your plane tickets, passport, and $5,000 in Bahamian currency are in the packet. You already have $5,000 American cash from the Montego Bay Airport locker. You'll take American Eagle to Miami, then Bahamasair for an 11:37pm touchdown in Nassau. Wear the clothes you've got on so our taxi driver will recognize you at the airport. He'll drive you to the Hibiscus Beach Inn safe house outside Nassau."

General Morrison rose from his chair. On the way out, he put his hand on Corey's shoulder. "We're at war and you're one of our best foot soldiers. I've never forgotten that fact. That's why I called you home. You're a seasoned spymaster who created the Nassau cells. No one would be in a better position to find out what happened to Collier than you. No shiny medals or ticker-tape parades when you return from a successful mission… you operate under a cloak of darkness. I know Duane Collier was like a son to you and you taught him well to take over the Nassau cells. That's why we recruited you from the CIA. You're greatly appreciated by all of us…including the POTUS."

"Thank you, sir."

"Study the CBIF New Providence-7 folder, leave it on the desk and depart here at exactly 7pm. That will give you enough time to be at the Key West Airport by 8:30. You'll assume the usual cover of marine biologist. Your luggage, diving equipment and research materials are packed in your truck outside...find out what happened to Duane Collier."

Morrison walked out of the cottage and Corey perused the intel report. At 7pm, after digesting every word in the thirty-page folder marked *CBIF New Providence-7: Operation Coral Reef, Top Secret* he vacated the safe house and climbed into the Ford 250 pickup. He paused to gather his thoughts. The resort almost seemed abandoned. The three agents in the black sedan across the way and the jovial good ole' boys next door were gone.

A quiet serenity enveloped the place, like the calm before an ominous storm. Only the distant laughter of children and gentle breeze gingerly lifting the palm fronds up and down were discernible. He gazed through the coconut palm and Caribbean pine toward the beach. The children were still playing in the waters of Florida Bay under the watchful eyes of their parents who were oblivious to the clandestine meeting that just transpired in their midst.

Why did Danielle and I fall in love... two case officers assigned together...I guess CBIF thought it would make the perfect cover for the Bahamas. Who murdered Danielle? Someday, I will find out

A squeaking noise disturbed the natural rhythm of the resort and interrupted Corey's reverie. Three women dressed in pink cleaning uniforms with monogrammed *Conch Inn Resort* insignias pushed a large cleaning cart up to the cottage door and entered without knocking. *The counterintelligence cleaners* He set the Ford 250 in gear and sped to the Key West Airport.

Episode 6

Treason in action

Hart Senate Office Building
Washington, DC
(GPS 38°53'33.8"N 77°00'15.5"W)

As expected by Senator Warren, the Senate Select Committee on Intelligence voted and the motion to release the hi-tech laser-guided mortar system to the Colombian army passed. Warren bid farewell to a beaming Lieutenant General Castano and exited the top-secret committee room. He strode past a pair of young marines guarding the antechamber entrance and classified documents section. They snapped their heels and skillfully saluted, but Warren merely grunted and returned a lukewarm salute, withholding eye contact or any customary acknowledgement.

He didn't go to the garage, since his Chief of Staff Mark Serwin was waiting for him outside. He walked down six flights of stairs and through the main floor atrium, admiring the suspended sculpture, nicknamed the "mobile." Warren paused to gaze at the four organically-shaped clouds hanging from a single shaft suspended from the building's roof. He always stopped to reflect on this moving structure which dominated the nine-story-high atrium. The largest cloud was forty-three feet long and weighed 4,300 pounds. A warm appreciation filled his body, not for the beauty of the masterpiece... it was simply another affirmation of his importance.

Warren strutted out of the northeast side of the Hart Building and through a small grove of trees onto Second Street, N.E., where Serwin waited for him in an idling Mercedes-Benz SLR McLaren. The senator quickly inspected his vehicle, checking to see if any nicks fouled the seamless silver sides of the $467,000 coupe, which the bank held a title to.

Mark Serwin greeted his boss as he climbed in. "How'd the meeting go?"

"As expected. Your inquiries into the schedules of the few non-compliant members of my committee, who rarely see eye-to-eye with me worked quite well. None were present. You are quite deft at finding things out about my opponents."

Serwin revved up the supercharged V-8 engine and kicked the McLaren into gear, unleashing the 671 horses under the hood. "It was easy, sir. You legislators wouldn't believe how your staffs mingle and talk. Over a few drinks at the Georgetown University tavern, I told each of them you wanted to talk to their boss man, and found out when they were free...and weren't. Process of elimination."

"Whatever. I'm pleased. You did well for me."

"So, Lieutenant General Castano's gonna get his military equipment?"

Warren smiled triumphantly. "Yes, and that means the National Zoo drop. Onward, Mark."

It was five miles to the National Zoo and Warren made sure his seatbelt was securely fastened. Mark Serwin couldn't shake his experiences in the skies over Viet Nam. His road-driving habits verged toward the skills needed to dodge SAM missiles and to survive a dogfight with a Mig-17. The Mercedes elbowed its way into a roundabout and miraculously nuzzled in between two cars, abruptly passed the car ahead, and zipped back into the outside lane, missing the overtaken car by three inches, just in time to rocket off the first exit onto Pennsylvania Avenue.

Warren opened his eyes to look at the Peace Monument. The two women statues mourning the loss of seamen during the Civil War zoomed past.

"You know, my dear friend Mark, you're the only one I trust driving this beautiful motor vehicle, but it's not equipped with afterburners."

"Sorry about that...keep thinking I'm in a cockpit. I'll slow down a tad."

The Senator tolerated Serwin's addiction to fast driving, for it was a symbol of how the two men became associates, not true friends... just opportune acquaintances. Warren needed power, not affiliations. Besides, it would be difficult for anyone to tail them without being obvious.

The duo took a left onto Constitution Avenue NW and traveled straight on US-1 (50), passed the National Archives on the right and the National Museum of Natural History on the left. Warren constantly viewed the rearview mirror for a tail.

"Slow down briefly," Warren instructed. He inspected the parking lot at the Natural History Museum. If a green van with a white cloth hanging out the passenger window was there, he was to proceed. If not, the drop was called off. The van was there, and a man talking on a cell phone was standing next to it.

"What was that all about?", Mark asked.

Warren glanced over at him. If looks could talk, it would have told him to mind his own business. "Proceed as usual, Mark."

Mark happily accelerated to eighty-five mph, then rocketed half-way around Dupont Circle onto Connecticut avenue NW. An undiagnosed and untreated ADHD adult, he processed information simultaneously, all at once. He hated the sequential world; reading and writing and sorting out information letter-by-letter, word-by-word was a laborious task.

In his younger days, he made it through the air force academy and kept motivated by keeping the end in mind, dreaming of the long lines of camouflaged F-4 Phantoms at Luke Air Force Base in Arizona. The textbook memorization and essay demands of the Officer Training School were difficult for him, but his dreams got him through. Upon graduation from OTS, he was promoted to lieutenant and stationed for a year in a replacement training unit (RTU) at Luke Air Force Base. When F-4 pilots completed their tours in Viet Nam, his unit replaced them.

Two months later he was soaring north of the DMZ with two F-4 escorts when five Mig-17's closed in. His quick reflexes and impulsiveness paid off. Mark Serwin flew into a thick cloud formation a mile away, turned sharply, then roared in behind two Migs, firing a heat-seeking AIM-9 Sidewinder that locked in and blew the tail off one. Then, a MIG came straight at him. Its nose lit up as cannon shells tore past his cockpit. Serwin pulled up and vertically soared into the heavens. He switched on afterburners and brusquely veered earthward sharply to the left in a rolling scissors motion, ending up closing in behind two MIGs at 600 knots airspeed. Another short-range Sidewinder blew a second MIG into small pieces. A blip on his radar pinpointed another MIG several miles away. Lieutenant Mark Serwin fired a long-range Sparrow missile, and in several seconds the third MIG exploded.

Then, his radar lit up. Over a dozen MIGs were bearing down on him. He retreated south into a fog bank above the rice paddies and ignited his afterburners. An F-4 couldn't outmaneuver that many MIGs, but it could outrun them. In the veil of fog, only 150 feet above the rice paddies, Serwin eluded the hungry pack and headed south toward the DMZ at the speed of sound.

The Mercedes-Benz SLR McLaren sped over Rock Creek which borders the National Zoo. The senator interrupted his top advisor's thoughts. "Pull in here at the western entrance by the visitor center."

"Yes, sir." Serwin braked and turned into the zoo entrance. He drove slowly, steering among the parked cars. The senator motioned him to maneuver under a broad oak tree.

"Stop here," Warren said. He handed his chief of staff a small microcassette containing Lieutenant General Castano's speech. "I want you to cruise around the zoo perimeter. Drive by the visitor's center at exactly 4:50pm. I'll be behind it by the cyclone fence bordering Connecticut Avenue. If I'm not there, I want you to pass by every fifteen minutes until I show up. When you see me, pull over on the berm and I'll tell you where the rendezvous is. Drive the speed limit from now on until you reach it, meet the contact, give him the cassette, take the money, then come back to this exact spot at 6:45pm."

Warren stepped out of his cherished Mercedes and began a casual stroll along Olmsted Walk while Serwin exited the park. He stopped at the Cheetah Conservation Station. A crowd was observing a mother Cheetah with a sizable litter of five cubs. He knew the Colombian drug traffickers were highly organized and carry out their business with extreme detail. They almost certainly were observing him, making sure he wasn't being tailed. At 4:40pm he was to sit on the right side of a park bench opposite Gibbons Ridge, place his right arm on the arm rest and gently probe the underside for the encryption card.

Warren walked further down Olmsted Walk and stopped at a kiosk. The National Zoo was jam-packed with visitors on this weekday afternoon. If American counterintelligence was on to him, the crowds would obscure their presence...they knew how to blend in. Of course, the people he dealt with were deft at counterintel as well, and would surely notice their presence.

It made good tradecraft to create unnatural movement patterns for those who may be tracking him. He purchased a Fuji Quick Snap camera and some souvenirs, then quickly retraced his steps on the Olmsted Walk. After several minutes, he abruptly turned and revisited the kiosk, as if he forgot something, then proceeded further on to Gibbon Ridge.

He caught sight of the designated bench a hundred feet ahead. A man of Middle Eastern decent was seated there, wearing sunglasses and a pulled-down cap, talking on a cell phone. As Warren approached, the man calmly rose and walked away.

The senator sat down and played out the game plan. His fingers felt a putty substance with the cryptic card stuck to it. He carefully palmed it and kept it hidden while retrieving a paperback book from his suit coat pocket. Warren slowly unfolded the card and laid it down on the book page.

Fifteen vertical up and down zigzags were etched out across it with dots at each apex and bottom. To unlock the code, Warren took a bookmark from the paperback. It had the alphabet letters from lower case a-z printed from top to bottom. The key to unlock the zigzag message was the spaces between the alphabet letters. His contacts had a Xeroxed replica bookmark key with the exact gaps between each letter. While pretending to pleasure read under the shade of ginko trees, on a relaxing park bench at the National Zoo, the Chairman of the Senate Select Intelligence Committee positioned the bookmark key along the side of the graph-like zigzags. He aligned each dot with a parallel letter on the bookmark.

At 4:50pm, Serwin obediently drove past the visitor center on Connecticut Avenue. Senator Warren stood behind it, close to the chain-link fence, snapping pictures of an ornamental shrub with the cheap camera. The ex-jet fighter slowed down and rolled past him on the berm. Without looking up or taking his eyes from the view finder, Senator Warren said loud enough for Serwin to hear, "Nanny O'Brien's Pub."

Episode 7

Missed contact

Poop Deck Restaurant & Pub Nassau, Bahamas
(GPS 25°04'28.1"N 77°19'03.5"W)
Corey Pearson sat on a barstool at the Poop Deck Restaurant & Pub sipping a Goombay Smash. General Morrison scheduled the rendez-vous with Darnell Ferguson at noon. It was 12:30pm... a no-show. A lone man entered the restaurant, drawing Corey's attention. His behavior was dissimilar to that of a typical customer. He sat at a ta-ble overlooking Nassau Harbor and nervously glanced at Corey and the other bar patrons, then at the entrance doorway and around the open-air restaurant. Whoever it was he expected to meet made him uneasy. Corey made a quick mental note of the man's physical ap-pearance and exited the restaurant.

CBIF protocol dictated the next step. He proceeded west on East Bay Street toward the backup rendezvous, the Bullion Bar at the British Colonial Hotel, the old "BC" as the locals nicknamed it. Corey footed it quickly down East Bay Street for an eighth of a mile until he reached Potter's Cay, a conglomeration of open-air venders and fishing boats underneath the Paradise Island bridge. Once there, he glanced over his shoulder to determine if the uneasy, thin, mustached man in the Panama hat followed him out of the Poop Deck.

Checking his back too quickly would be a subtle give away that his presence in Nassau wasn't merely for duty-free shopping, espe-cially if this atypical man was well-trained in foot surveillance. The noonday sun beat down relentlessly. Fumes from the jitney buses, taxicabs, delivery trucks, rental cars, mopeds, and a plethora of limousines rose from the pavement in a shimmering, gaseous cloud. *It will be a hot trek to the 'BC.' Does Darnell Ferguson's no- show at the Poop Deck have anything to do with the jittery man there? Darnell's got info about Duane Collier's disappearance and I've got to talk to him. Can't afford any delays. What made him terminate our meeting?*

Remorse, a tinge of guilt, lack of adequate sleep and anguish consumed him since General Morrison called him home to Key Largo. CBIF policy requires case officers to check-in twice a day, but it has been two days since Duane Collier's last contact. *Things don't look good. Duane is in serious trouble...or dead. No! I'll assume he's alive...we will find him. It was me who persuaded CBIF to take him in...I trained him to become case officer of New Providence-7.*

Denial of reality cushions the effects of apprehension. Corey pressed on to the backup location at CBIF Cell-02, the Bullion Bar at the old "BC." If Ferguson couldn't make this second rendezvous, then he would inform Milo Symonette, the bartender there. Milo "The Messenger" takes messages that cell managers call in for various reasons, including a missed contact meeting, to set up an alternative location.

A young Bahamian boy worked the corner where the Paradise Island Eastern Bridge slopes over Nassau Harbor onto Bay Street on the Nassau side. The span was a lifeline connecting the rich real estate of Paradise Island to an older, poorer and dirtier downtown Nassau. Regardless, the capital city, with its historic government buildings and British architectural style, retains the true Bahamian spirit. To Corey, Paradise Island was an alien intrusion, an artificial theme park atmosphere which invaded the Bahamian culture. It was a knife jabbed into the traditional Bahamian's soul.

The boy searched the crowds for gullible tourists to bargain his wares. At the tender age of eight, he was a skilled salesman and readily charmed the sightseers. He snorkeled off Arawak Cay and Saunders Beach, just west of downtown Nassau, gathering several dozen small, orange-red starfish from the shallow sea grass beds. He dried them in the sun and hoped someone would take pity on him and rationalize a good reason for forking over $2.50 apiece for the slightly malodorous ocean creatures. The boy was deft at reading people's responses and the timing of his sales pitch was perfect. If they hesitated or were about to decline a sale, he would commence singing a cute Bahamian children's song:

Morning, good morning, how are ya this morning?
It was a rainy day!
That's what the froggie say!"

More often than not, they'd reach deep into their pockets. The olfactory sensation was slight enough to go undetected until his customers were back resting in their cramped cruise ship cabins.

The young boy spotted Corey walking apart from the throng of normal wayfarers, a lone stray apart from the herd...an easy catch. He approached this fast-past man, but stopped. This potential customer appeared to have an agenda beyond that of a mere tourist on a shopping spree. The intense face and purposeful stride differed from the ambling gaits of the cruise ship hoards. He let him pass by.

Corey noticed the Bahamian boy's retreat as he continued on his mission to the old "BC." *That kid's reaction to me...not good...I look out of the ordinary...my facial expression...my manner...as if some urgent business was on my mind...blend in with the crowd...follow procedure... don't react as you feel...act the opposite.*

He slowed down and began feigning an interest in Bay Street's surroundings. Worrisome thoughts kept resurfacing. *Why didn't Darnell Ferguson make the Poop Deck rendezvous? Was he tailed? Did something spook him? Was it the ill-at-ease man? What additional details does he have on Duane's disappearance?! Don't fret...*

procedures are in place...if anything's amiss, he'll leave a message with Milo, 'The Messenger.'

Corey passed the entrance to Potter's Cay, the soul of Nassau, the location of Ferguson's Cell No. 4. It was an amazing place at the east end of Nassau Harbor, under the Paradise Island Bridge. He paused and glanced down the cement roadway and dockage area, hoping to see Ferguson. No luck. A few pleasure boats docked there, along with the out-island mail boats and fishing trawlers.

A half dozen potcakes scavenged among piles of discarded conch shells and rotting fish innards. They growled menacingly as he passed by. The fetid odor was overwhelming. Nassau changed little since he created the seven CBIF cells a decade ago. The Bahamian public illegally discarded household appliances and garbage in the dumpsters, leaving the fruit, vegetable, fish and conch vendors with little alternative but to pile their garbage on the hot pavement. The dumping laws weren't enforced a decade ago and still aren't today, to the chagrin of the Minister of Tourism.

A symbol of the new Bahamas. Under a bridge leading to the multibillion-dollar Atlantis Resort lies a breeding ground for rats, flies, and feral potcakes. The tourists with fat wallets, Gucci watches and handbags, decked out in threads from lofty-named clothiers ignore this unsightly place. To them, Potter's Cay must be a hellhole subsisting beneath a bridge of gold, a monument to a third world country surviving among billions of tourist dollars. It sure brings out the economic and cultural abyss between impoverished locals and well- heeled, transient visitors He couldn't see Ferguson tinkering around his boats. Duane's life was in peril and an urgent rendezvous was missed. He continued down East Bay Street, approached Parliament Square and entered the plush shopping area of downtown Nassau where high-priced jewelry and emeralds changed hands between local shopkeepers and foreigners. Corey concealed his frustration and emulated a fun-seeking tourist. He paused again halfway along the two-mile trek from the Poop Deck to the Bullion Bar and pretended to gawk at the lavish storefront window displays. He observed the throngs of passing human reflections to see if the nervous man in the Panama hat was tailing him.

Affirmative. He was on the sidewalk across Bay Street, pausing to window-shop after a fast stride from the Poop Deck, which Corey forced upon him. *Unsystematic behavior...incredulous for a tourist or local...got to get a make on this guy* Corey turned and gazed across Bay Street, directly facing the back of the man tailing him. The fast stride didn't tire the athletic forty-year-old spymaster, but he pretended to succumb to the heat and fumes. Corey removed his hat and wiped a sweaty brow, then leaned against a pole and detached a metal Voyant Sports Bottle from his belt. General Morrison made sure it was packed with his luggage in Key Largo. Corey twisted the cap a quarter turn, pulled up the retractable plastic drink straw and took a cool sip of ice water.

He wished his unskilled pursuer would turn around. A horse-drawn carriage toting tourists approached and Corey pretended to show interest as it passed by. The brightly colored metallic sports bottle housed a miniaturized, digital video camera, transmitter and batteries.

The hoofs clopped down loudly on the narrow East Bay Street, echoing against the duty-free liquor, perfume bar, and jewelry store-front windows. His target grew impatient and turned around just as the carriage passed by. Corey lifted the sports bottle and took another refreshing sip. Passing tourists, fresh off the newly-arrived cruise ships docked in Prince George Wharf, were unaware that Corey was snapping digital photos of the man. He screwed the top back on, hooked the sports bottle back onto his waist belt, and continued down East Bay Street.

He strolled past East Street and approached Bank Lane. The British Colonial Hotel rose majestically above the end of East Bay

Street in the distance. Corey didn't glance back, assuming the persistent but callow man in the Panama hat was still tailing him.

Suddenly, approaching on the opposite side of Bay Street, a familiar face emerged from the shopping crowds. A decade had passed, but the face was unmistakable. It was his old friend and the manager of the Potter's Cay cell...Darnell Ferguson.

Episode 8

A betrayal of trust

Connecticut Ave., NW Washington, D.C.

Mark Serwin approached the entrance to Nanny O'Briens Irish Pub. He paused and glanced down Constitution Avenue toward Warren's parked Mercedes-Benz SLR McLaren. No suspicious movements among the multitude of pedestrian traffic. He switched on the remote security system, which armed the Mercedes' audio alarm, hidden video and GPS device which could track the vehicle if someone was foolish enough to steal it. He entered the legendary pub.

Several lone patrons sat at barstools propped up to the aged bar running down the right side of the place. Everyone sipped properly-prepared Guinness drafts. Traditional Irish music flowed from the jukebox. To the left, age-old wooden booths and tables set around a small stage where Irish folk sang, fiddled and strummed away during the evening hours. A bodhran goatskin drum, bagpipe, fiddle, flute, traditional string guitar and mandolin lay idle in the nearest booth.

It was the perfect meeting place, a neighborhood pub and pastoral escape from the congested environs just outside. His contact sat at the far booth.

Serwin walked up to him as he gulped down a Smithwick's. "Kind of funny seeing a Colombian gobble down Irish corned beef and potatoes, washing it down with an Irish red ale. You think you're in Kilkenny County?"

"Ah, me amigo. Hola Mark. Dis beats jerk pork and coco bread.

Sit yo' ass down."

Serwin slid into the booth and faced the man with dark complexion donning a three-piece, pinned stripe suit and sporting a pair of bloodred tears tattooed under his left eye. The two didn't shake hands. They wanted their meeting to look like two habituated friends imperturbably meeting for just another inconsequential chat. The jukebox music, which the tattooed man loaded up with two albums, muffled their voices.

"I'm doing quite well, my old friend, Virgilio Sandoval. The last time we met was at the orgy with your Colombian whores at the chicken processing plant on Abaco."

"Yeah, and you be there with da big-headed fool you work for, Senator Warren...dat mon addicted to putas."

"Putas?"

"Yeah, putas...ya know...whores."

"True, Virgilio, he is an arrogant SOB, but he pays me well and lets me drive how I want."

Virgilio Sandoval gulped down the remaining Smithwick's and set the bottle on his empty plate. "He dun not pay ya as much as ya made when we first meet...when you work for Royal."

Serwin eyed the expensive business suit. It clashed with the red teardrop tattoos and unrefined language. He knew Sandoval was skillful at smuggling cocaine and heroin for the narco-terrorist cartel... and would murder with zest anyone threatening his empire. He remembered those days following his return from Viet Nam, ending his career as an ace Phantom jet fighter pilot. He could have re-enlisted and lingered awhile longer in the air force, but the pay offered by commercial airlines overpowered his will to remain. Serwin preferred chattel over patriotism.

For several years, he flew commercial airline flights out of Miami international Airport to the Caribbean, earning a third more yearly income than the air force paid. But, his nice salary wasn't enough to supply his craving for riches. Gambling and heavy drinking increased rectilinearly to his escalating personal debt. After skipping out for a scheduled flight and appearing in the cockpit a second time with alcohol breath, he was fired on the spot. Having lost his plush home and Mustang GT, he holed up in a motel by Miami International and frequented a nearby tavern. That's where he met Virgilio Cesar Sandoval who, after listening to his Viet Nam and commercial airline experiences, offered him a job flying for Royal Airlines.

Serwin made twice as much flying Royal than he did flying for the commercial airline that canned him. Of course, nice offerings come wrapped in bad packages with strings attached. The Royal Airlines fleet consisted of a dozen prop planes. He piloted an aged DC-7 that was owned by American Airlines in the 1950's. When the jet age arrived, the old bird was sold to the Moroccan government to fight a locust scourge. It was converted to a sprayer and outfit- ted with a huge internal tank to haul insecticides. After a decade of service, mechanical problems cropped up, so the Moroccans sold it to Royal Airlines, who regularly bought planes no one else wanted. Serwin recalled the thrill of juicing up the revamped DC-7. It started with a slight detonation rather than a revving up sound because Royal used engine parts from a mothballed military C-121 Super Constellation and other rusted-out military surplus planes to overhaul the DC-7 engines.

It didn't bother Serwin that commercial airline pilots referred to the cluttered and segregated Royal Airlines section of Miami International bordering NW 36th Street as "Corrosion Corner." He laughed all the way to the bank.

The barmaid interrupted his thoughts. She shouted over to them from the bar. "You guys want anything else?"

Serwin ordered a pint of Guinness. Sandoval opted for another Smithwick's.

Sandoval asked, "You like flyin' dat rickety plane and you knew what was in da insecticide tank too...didn't ya?"

"Yes, to both questions. I take it the pipeline you currently run remains comparable to the old days?" Serwin knew it probably changed from top-to-bottom.

"What comparable mean?" "The same."

"Oh...yeah...no changes. Ya rememba da routine, when ya take off from dat dirt airstrip in Colombia, then use Cuban airspace and waters to dodge U.S. and Bahama agents? We still use aircraft and land in Nassau or some remote Bahama out island. Easy to pay-off out island customs people, but we do as can do at Nassau Airport."

"How so?" Serwin asked. He knew Sandoval was lying to him and that much had changed since his old days of smuggling with Royal. "Well, at da Nassau airport we pay off da police dog units dat sniff for da drugs. They look da other way. We move mucho coke through airport to southeast U.S. using Bahamian air carriers." Sandoval started laughing, then continued. "But, if da airport authorities watch too much... we air drop loads up to 600 kilos to go-fast boats at last minute."

Sandoval switched the conversation to a more innocuous topic as the barmaid approached with Serwin's properly-prepared pint of Guinness and his Smithwick's.

When she left, Serwin commented, "Yes, it was quite a time with Royal, and it doesn't surprise me tactics haven't changed much. I guess because the Bahamas are too inviting, being on air and sea routes between Colombia and the U.S."

"Yeah, and when heat gets on da air route, we use da go-fasts... even pleasure boats, even big containa ships with big secret compartments headin' to Nassau or Freeport. So many ports of entry into Bahamas...over seven-hundred islands, and not 'nough men to watch dem all. Da custom guys who watch too good...we pay dem off."

Serwin took a gulp of his Guinness. "Sounds like not many of your men get caught."

"Oh…dey get caught now and then. We got trouble tryin' to pay off office of Public Prosecutions, but dey still don' prosecute my men even though dey try…'cause of weak drug laws and jury corruption. We pay off da jury membas too…threaten da honest ones."

"How do you intimidate the honest jurors? Beat them up?" "What intimidate mean?"

"Scare them."

"We dun have ta scare dem. Just call dem up and say what dere kid was wearin' on way to school dat mornin'…dat get dere attenciones!" Sandoval roared in laughter. Dey end up takin' bribe money. What a poor Bahama mon don't do when I offer dem $15,000 to not convict? Plus, we got IBC and bank secrecy law in Bahama. My bossman pay fo' good defense attorneys. Dey delay drug cases for years."

Serwin thought about the IBC's, the unregulated business corporations. "And on top of it all, the IBC's and secret bank accounts make it easier to launder your money."

"Si, dat's right. It all be prime for us. And, if my men get sent up to da Fox Hill Prison or Carmichael Detenciones Centre, da lawyers wid fat wallets get dem out on bail and declare mistrial. It all start ova again. What's more… U.S. can't extradite my men 'cause da case lie 'round foreva in da Bahama court."

Serwin took a last swig of Guinness and looked at his watch. "Well, my old friend, I must pick up the senator in fifteen minutes." He withdrew his right hand from the tabletop, revealing the microcassette tape of Lieutenant General Castano's speech. "Here's a present for your bossman… from Senator Warren."

Sandoval chose a booth where no one could see the tabletop. He placed two envelopes on it. "And here be for you and da big-headed boss you work fo'. His be on da left…it got $50,000 in big bills…da other foe you…it got $25,000…all da bills big…got faces a' men name William McKinley and Grover Cleveland on dem."

Corey felt relieved after spotting Darnell Ferguson on the opposite side of Bay Street in downtown Nassau. Ferguson scratched the left side of his forehead with his left hand. *The spy craft begins. Ferguson was a quick learner when I taught him foot surveillance tactics.* The gesture indicated that he spotted Corey, who adjusted the left side of his waist belt, signaling that he had a tail. Ferguson signaled back that he understood.

Moments later, Corey veered off his steadfast westward course by crossing East Bay Street to the opposite side, passing over Ferguson's eastbound footprints and continuing in a westward direction. Upon reaching Bank Lane, he strolled south into the south side of Parliament Square. Corey paused to admire the government's Senate and House of Assembly buildings, just long enough for Ferguson to cross Bay Street and do a U-turn and pick up Corey's westbound trek.

Ferguson quickly detected the curious thin man who pursued Corey. He saw Corey stopped ahead, as if sightseeing, and scanned the corner of Bay Street and Bank Lane, where Corey just vacated. There the target was... standing motionless, stalled for no apparent reason. Ferguson knew it was Corey's amateurish tail. A thin man with a Panama hat, apparently waiting for Corey to resume his walk.

Few changes occurred on Parliament Square from a decade ago. The quasi-Caribbean, old-world, colonial architecture complete with Flamingo-pink walls, white pillars, and dark green shutters remained. Despite a few shutters hanging slightly askew on rusted-through hinges and several yellowish-brown window shades stained by years of cigar haze, the structures maintained the grace needed to offer a panegyric salutation to the white statue of Queen Victoria, which they clustered around.

The noisy traffic on East Bay Street flowed past while Corey allowed several uneventful minutes to drift by. *Ferguson should have spotted my careless follower by now* He continued his surveillance tradecraft, knowing Ferguson was familiar with the cat-and-mouse game. An excellent location for foot reconnaissance was nearby, an observation point where he could see all without being seen. *It's time to turn the tables around* He walked briskly off Bank Lane onto the Parliament Square south grounds, passed the front entrance to the Bahamian Senate Building, rounded its northwest corner and quickly strode south down a broken ceramic and brick pathway which hugged the west wall. He trekked through a small park behind the senate where young Royal Palms were recently planted and approached the Supreme Court, which graced the southern border. He strode past several Royal Bahamian policemen positioned in front of the Supreme Court, nodding politely to them as he past. They smiled and wished him a good day. Corey rounded the beautiful building, briefly returned to Bank Lane which bordered the Supreme Court's eastern side, then headed diagonally through the Garden of Remembrance behind it.

He stopped momentarily at the cenotaph, a carved stone honoring Bahamians killed in World Wars I and II, then glanced back down the path toward Bank Lane. No one in sight, except for a lone surrey carrying sightseers. He continued down the park path through a mature stand of towering, majestic Royal Palms and marched up the narrow entrance steps to his strategic objective: the octagonal-shaped Nassau Public Library.

The ancient steps creaked as he hastily climbed to the third floor, disregarding the historical prints, colonial documents, ancient books and Lucayan artifacts enshrined in narrow spaces that used to be jail cells. The place was built in the late 1700's by an English Loyalist and resembled an old munitions storage facility, with a good 360-degree view to spot approaching enemy soldiers. Corey took advantage of the design, exiting the top floor onto an outside wraparound balcony set amongst the treetop canopy of the Royal Palm grove below.

He peered down through thick cover of palm fronds toward Remembrance Park at the southeast corner of the Supreme Court Building, which he just rounded. He hoped to see the thin man carelessly following his trail with Ferguson imperceptibly lagging behind.

Neither prey nor predator appeared. In the distance, the colossal platforms of cruise ships nestled in the Prince George Wharf rose above the downtown skyline. Corey walked around the balcony, checking out Shirley Street, which runs east-west and marks Parliament Square's southern border. Nothing.

He bent down and duck-walked around the octagonal balcony to observe the west side. There the thin man was, baffled that his quarry eluded him, pacing up and down Parliament Street, which runs parallel to Bank Lane.

Where the hell is Ferguson? Peering over the balcony railing, he noticed a slight movement to the right. It was Ferguson, calmly pretending to admire the stone cenotaph in the Garden of Remembrance. Both men would remain in their positions until their pursuer gave up his amateurish pursuit, then they would become predators, stalking him for the remainder of the day. They would uncover his connections, which may lead to Duane Collier's disappearance. Places where he dined and bedded down would be recorded, his residence would be bugged and his telephone tapped. Personal conversations within and calls to and from his residence would be dissected for any connection to Collier's disappearance. The contents of his outside garbage cans would be inspected. Everybody he met, talked to or looked at for more than a few moments would be video-taped and logged into CBIF's main computer terminal to be cross-referenced with trillions of bits of stored, world-wide intelligence data.

Ferguson continued his watch, occasionally glancing around to catch a glimpse of Corey. A little help was in order. Corey crept further around the balcony to a small break in the treetop canopy. The opening revealed his head to Ferguson but not to the thin man. Ferguson spotted him and scratched the left side of his forehead with his left hand. Corey pointed his finger at him, then to their prey's location, indicating for him to continue the tail. Ferguson knew Corey would fall in a short distance behind him. But, the thin man remained stationary, hoping Corey would reappear.

Moments later, two motorcycles sped up Parliament Street close behind a car with a noisy muffler. The entourage slowed down for the red light at the Shirley Street traffic light. Three muffled "pop-pop-pop" sounds barely permeated the traffic clamor, a seemingly low-profile sequence of events ignored by pedestrians and motorists. To Corey, the almost inaudible reports might as well have been artillery shell bursts. He scrambled back to the balcony's eastern overlook. The thin man lay face down on the sidewalk of Parliament Street, his hands and feet quivering...then coming to rest. Corey noticed two blood spots on the upper torso of the man's white shirt, and an en-larging red pool as the fluid of life seeped out of his head onto the sidewalk. *Seal Team 6 couldn't have done better...a very professional hit, indeed*

Episode 9

Milo "The Messenger"

Milo Symonette wiped off the mahogany bar top at the British Colonial Hotel's plush Bullion Bar. He gazed out the picture windows past the lush tropical gardens, watching Darnell Ferguson proceed down the walkway and sit at the Patio Grill & Pool Bar. Ferguson alerted him that he missed a meeting with his old friend Corey Pearson at the Poop Deck and that Corey should be along shortly.

Milo "The Messenger" knew exactly what to do and placed a large vase with ornamental reeds at the end of the bar so it would be easily visible from the hotel lobby. It was a signal to Corey that the coast was clear and his missed contact is present. He surmised there was a connection between their canceled clandestine meeting at the Poop Deck, the police cars with sirens blaring that sped past the old "BC" toward Parliament Square minutes ago, and the backup rendezvous meeting about to take place.

The only thing he knew about his role in the organization he worked for was that Bullion's was used as a contingency site when scheduled contacts between members were cancelled. Milo wondered what happened to Duane Collier, who had been absent for a long while. He recalled, years ago, both Collier and Pearson meeting together frequently.

He muttered to himself while cleaning the bar and waiting for Cory. "Then, Pearson vanish with his wife Danielle…and Duane Collier take over. Now… Collier vanish…and Pearson, he be back." Milo knew not to ask questions, just take and deliver messages... then walk away and forget everything.

His life improved since Pearson walked into his vendor's stall a decade ago at Cable Beach, outside downtown Nassau. Unlike the monogrammed, colorful silk shirt and Tommy Bahamas pants that he puts on proudly each morning, he once wore a soiled T-shirt and second-hand jeans. Corey Pearson was curious about the piled conch, sea shells, and stacked starfish Milo Symonette sold under a sign that read, "TRESHURES OF THE SEA: I sell purfek conch shels w/no hole & fish souvenirs, too."

Milo recalled how interested Corey was in his life as a straw market vendor and how he listened to him vent about how miserable the working conditions were. He told Corey how the big fire forced him and hundreds of other vendors to vacate the Bay Street Straw Market by Prince George Dock, where the cruise ships docked: "So, I go open up at Cable Beach. The Govament do nothin' ta help."

A decade ago, he lamented to Corey how the filthy bathroom facilities and lack of electricity forced him to close his stall at night for fear of being robbed, and that the lack of running water and garbage-infested surroundings at Cable Beach kept tourists away.

Corey visited him daily and bought his wares. They talked more and Corey learned about his wife, who was a laid-off hotel worker. They had two boys attending Nassau's A. F. Adderley High School and a growing pile of bills. He remembered how Corey took a liking to him and two months later got him into a bartender training program at the Hibiscus Beach Inn.

Milo had no idea the inn was a CBIF safe house, run by a middle-aged Brit code-named Nigel, who retired from MI6 with an impeccable background. Nigel walked away from MI6 after twenty-five years of service with three intelligence medals pinned on his lapel. As an operations officer, he collected critical intel for the home office at Vauxhall Cross in London. Nigel's intelligence-gathering capabilities overseas saved the United Kingdom's national security and economic well-being a half dozen times. CBIF hired him on as the proprietor.

The Hibiscus Beach Inn reflected classic CBIF policy: open to the public and seemingly transparent, blending into everyday life. After a half-year of training and working as barkeep at the inn's pub, Corey made sure that Milo was hired as a full-time, professional bartender at the Bullion Bar while his wife was employed as a maid at the Hibiscus Beach Inn. Both their boys graduated from A.F. Adderley HS and were accepted into the cadet-training program in the Royal Bahamas Police Force (RBPF).

Milo restocked the beer cooler while thinking how his life improved after meeting Corey Pearson. The mounting pile of bills vanished. Of course, neither he or his wife realized that Corey got them their re-spective jobs and that he also did some political maneuvering with a CBIF asset who held the position of Deputy Commander in the RBPF, which resulted in both their son's acceptance into the cadet program.

A calm voice interrupted "The Messenger's" thoughts. "How's my old friend Milo? Long time no see."

He looked up from the beer cooler. A swell of emotion took over him. He spoke softly but passionately, "My Lord...Corey! So glad to see ya! It's been so long a time!" He embraced his old friend.

Episode 10

Clandestine contact

Corey walked out of the Bullion Bar into the "BC's" tropical gardens after Milo proudly told him that both his sons were promoted to detective rank in the RBPF. He didn't tell Milo that they unknowingly work for CBIF. Deputy Commander Ellison Rolle of the RBPF was one of Corey's paid informants and received a hefty stipend for elevating both boys to be detectives. The Deputy Commander sends them out, on occasion, to stakeout individuals of interest to CBIF.

He found Darnell Ferguson perched on a barstool, savoring a Yellow Bird in the shade of the Patio Grill & Pool Bar. The steady but gentle breeze from Nassau Harbor and Paradise Island felt good.

"Mr. Ferguson, I presume?" Corey inquired.

"Yes, sir, and you must be Mistah Pearson, the man who want to rent my boat to do reef fish survey."

"One and the same." The two shook hands. Several other patrons warmed nearby barstools, uncomfortably close, gulping down Kalik beers and snacking on complimentary conch fritters.

Corey said, "Why don't we both discuss our plans for the survey on the patio table, in the shade of a nice royal palm. By the way, call me Corey."

Ferguson played along, feigning a first-time business meeting between total strangers. "And, you can call me Darnell."

Corey unrolled a map of the reef systems around New Providence and Paradise Island, pinning it down on the table with salt and pepper shakers and a reference book entitled, "Reef Fish Identification: Florida, Caribbean, Bahamas" by Paul Humann. They were far enough from the patio to not be overheard. The music and people frolicking in the pool blocked out their conversation.

Corey didn't bother to rehash old times and went right to the chase, zeroing in on Collier's disappearance. "The man shot and killed was at the Poop Deck. I take it there's some connection to his murder, your 'no show', and Duane Collier's abduction. Did you know him?"

"Dun know his name o' face. He come lookin' for me at Potter's Cay. I be layin' down inside the *Conch Queen I*, takin' nap. One of my crew be on deck when da man come askin' fo' me. As instructed, he tell him dat I be at da Poop Deck meetin' an American marine biologist for business talk. Then, I begin tailin' da thin man as he walk out of Potter's Cay. I follow him to Poop Deck, where you be. I thought it best to go to Bullion to tell Milo what's up. Den I head back down East Bay Street, hopin' to catch ya bein' tailed, which you was."

Corey said, "Good choice to walk back toward the Poop Deck, knowing that I'd be heading to the Bullion Bar after a half-hour wait. Your foot surveillance tactics worked perfectly."

The Potter's Cay cell manager beamed with pride. "Your organization, whatever it is, train me well. Dat's what my plans be. Dat poor man got no surveillance skills at all."

"Yes, a nervous and frightened man carrying a secret for you. But, why did he want you? What secret did he want to unload?" Corey asked himself as well as Ferguson.

"Like I say, I dun know. But enough of a secret to get bumped-off fo'." Ferguson held up his empty glass of Yellow Bird, motioning to the bartender. "Might as well make our meetin' bona fide."

Corey continued his prodding. "We have to see if there's a connection between his execution and Duane Collier's disappearance. You spent much time with Duane, correct?"

"Yes. We was close. Spend much time helpin' him out with underwater archeology. Store his equipment on da *Conch Queen I* He dives much around New Providence, explorin' Blue Holes and underwater caves. Found Lucayan artifacts. He even speak to classes at University of da Bahamas."

Maybe that's why the man ended up tailing me. He must have known Ferguson and Duane were good friends. At the Poop Deck, he was easy to spot...the poor guy...bungling and nervous...a man who got mixed up with the wrong crowd and who knew too much. A man who knew he was being hunted down...one without hope...afraid to go to the police...must have thought the people after him had influence with the higher-ups, so he avoided going to the RBPF. We're dealing with people of money, power...trained hit men...possible connections with Middle Eastern terrorists.

Darnell grew nervous. He knew the questioning would soon focus on Duane Collier's abduction and what went wrong. He looked solemnly at Corey and said, "Ya know it was a good hit...no mugga off da street blow dis guy away...dey be professionals."

"Tell me about the abduction. I read my organization's report." *The CBIF New Providence-7: Operation Coral Reef, Top Secret' folder Morrison gave me at the Conch Inn Resort safe house in Key Largo* "You and four of your crew kept tabs on Duane at the Nassau Hard Rock Café when he was abducted. You reported that he was socializing with two men, one appeared Haitian and the other was the limo driver to the Agricultural Minister."

"Dat be right. One guy... he have definite Haitian face. No doubt. I can spot Haitian a mile away, standin' sideways. They either do nuthin' or do somethin' a Bahamian not want to do...filthy work. My boats see dem comin' in sloops all da time, overcrowded...must be bad time fo' dem in Haiti, to come to Abaco and stay in plywood houses at da 'Mud and Pigeon Pea' town in Marsh Harbor...no electricity...no runnin' water...no job...no nuthin."

Corey started to connect the dots, links which he would never disclose to Ferguson or to the managers of the six other Bahamian cells he created a decade ago. Even though Ferguson passed the yearly polygraph test with flying colors, he was given intel on a "need to know only" basis.

The bartender appeared with another Yellow Bird, decorated with mango and coconut slices. Corey ordered a Bahama Mama and assumed his deep cover while the barkeep tidied up their patio table. "So, Darnell, I plan to use a camcorder with underwater housing to record and document the size of the remaining groupers off New Providence. I'll also count species' populations, particularly the dwindling numbers of Nassau Grouper..." The bartender left to fetch Corey's drink. He displayed calm on the outside, despite his mind going in several different directions. *Bahama Mama...our favorite drink...Danielle and I used to visit this very same place. Why did she have to die...I know her murder was linked, somehow, to our mission in the Bahamas* "Illegal Haitians flock to this settlement in Abaco... what's the name of it, again?"

"Mud and Pigeon Pea town. They risk dere lives comin' to Marsh Harbor, da capital of Abaco. Dey be in high demand to do grubby work and get paid nuthin' fo' it. A Haitian...he can live on a loaf a' sweet Bahamian bread for a whole week. Must be much misery in Haiti...dey leave any way dey can."

Corey's Bahama Mama arrived. *The Haiti/Ft. Lauderdale drug pipeline must involve Abaco. What did Duane Collier stumble onto? The Bahamian out island of Abaco comes up again! General Morrison was curious about Curtis Beacher's interest in expanding his Jamaican shipping to Abaco and Beacher mentioned the Bahamian Minister of Agriculture OK'd the huge chicken processing operation in Abaco. Duane was last seen with the Agricultural Minister's limo driver and with the Haitian Bolan Tougas. Tougas' photo was taken by Ferguson inside the Hard Rock Café and was identified by Gesner Verdieu as a new member of the FRAPH squad that murdered the parents of Damballah Saint-Fleur in Port-au-Prince.*

"So, tell me how this Haitian man and limo driver got Duane out of the night club. How did they get past the four of you?"

Ferguson knew he'd be picked apart on the abduction. "Well, they be drinkin' at da Hardrock and…"

Corey interrupted. "Hold on. Let's start at the very beginning. Tell me about the approach. Where did you meet Duane and start surveillance backup?"

Darnell pointed past the beach, towards Prince George Wharf. "We park over dere by cruise ship dock…"

"What time?"

"At 8pm, as Duane told us to do. He already park his car dere and signal us to follow him on foot. He get out of da car and walk west down Woodes Rogers Walk to Charlotte Street…den he turn right and head south to da Hard Rock Café."

"What did you see then?"

"Well, there be a line at da Hard Rock…Duane stand in line… twenty people ahead o' him. Three of us wid da digital videocams hidden in our shopping bags get in line four people behind him, so nobody know we were associated wid Duane. I contact two otha of my crew to walk from Bay Street up to da club, so dey could wait outside."

"Duane Collier told you he'd be meeting with the agricultural minister's limo driver…right?"

Ferguson felt a bit threatened by the questioning, which he knew would be in much detail…and was being recorded for further polygraph testing. "Yeah. I leave two o' my crew outside to watch tings goin' on. Then, I go through the line behind Duane wid two of my men. Then go in. Duane didn't hook himself up so we got no audio feed, just the video."

Corey digested Ferguson's description of the tragic night. *Duane didn't wire himself…no audio feed…didn't want to be caught wearing*

*a concealed microphone...must have been in the beginning stages
of probing...he was on to something big and didn't want to blow it.
He had a gut feeling about something and was trying to ingratiate the
limo driver and the Haitian Bolan Tougas.*

"Where did he meet them inside?"

"Both men be sittin' at table by da stage. Duane walk right up to
them. The limo driver smile and shook his hand, den introduce him
to da Haitian. Den, they begin drinkin'. Me and my two crew, we sit
several tables away but could hear nuthin' cause a loud calypso steel
drum band wid fire-eatin' and limbo start up."

"How long were they drinking? How much did they have to drink?"

"That just it, they stay for less than an hour and have only two rounds
apiece. Duane could not a been dat smashed...but he act like it!"

"OK, this is important so try to answer it as best you can. How did
they sneak past you? There were three of you inside and two waiting
outside...five men they got by?"

Ferguson drained his Yellow Bird. Corey knew he felt bad about
his failure to protect Duane Collier.

"Dey didn't sneak past us. It happen sudden-like. All three o' dem
get up and stumble out o' da place. Duane, he seem more drunk den
da others. My men an' me...we only put down two drinks apiece, but
we feel drunk...but it was hard day o' work...we just tired. We get up
and be right behind dem when dey go downstairs and out da front
door. We wasn't goin' ta let Duane out o' our sight. But, a half-dozen
men bump into us outside on Charlotte Street...we start shovin' back.
Duane didn't put up no fight. I see da Haitian guy and two other guys
shove him into the limo and roar off afore we could do sumthin'."

Corey recognized Darnell felt sorrow and guilt. "You did the right
thing, Darnell. You ran back in and checked Duane's chair and table
in case he left anything behind, like a note written on a napkin, and
you collected evidence for us, their drinking glasses and the cigarette
butts left in the ashtray."

"Yeah...and I give dem ta Pinkston at da Hurricane Hole Marina on Paradise Island. People inside da Hard Rock watchin' all dis goin' on...dey think we be crazy, 'specially me and my crew when we run back inside and scoop up cigarette butts and half empty drinks. Even da steel drum mon stop playin' in disbelief."

Darnell held his head down, shaking it with humiliation. "I hope nobody recognize me dat night."

Corey patted him on the forearm. "You did what you were trained to do. And, it wasn't your fault that Duane was abducted..."

Ferguson interrupted. "But, how can you say dat, mon? There be five of us and we all be in good shape...strong as lions...and we let Duane get taken away."

The spymaster thought about how to give comfort without disclosing too much. He placed his hand on the distressed cell manager's forearm. "Listen to me. Don't beat yourself up over this. You're still with us...the organization. We'll find out what happened to Duane and you won't be blamed for it. Everything is still in place. I'll conduct reef fish surveys...the same deep cover with you as my guide. That's all you have to know for now."

With that said, Corey stood up, smiled and shook Darnell's hand as if a business venture was consummated. As Ferguson walked back through the lush tropical gardens, Corey gathered his navigation map and reef fish identification manual and stuffed them back into his attaché case.

Still nursing his Bahama Mama, he walked down the stone steps that he and his wife Danielle once wandered down to reach the old "BC's" small, private beach overlooking Nassau Harbor. A cruise ship bellowed its arrival as several tugboats raced out to guide it into Prince George Wharf.

He stretched out on a lounge chair under the shade of a thatched palm-leaf shelter. The intense sun disappeared behind dark clouds rolling in. Visions of his wife surfaced. She was making sand sculptures.

That was a decade ago. They used to look out at the amazing colors of the ocean.

The storm grew closer, the skies darkened and the turquoise, dark-blue, lime green and gin-colored waters faded until the ocean grew as murky as the sky. *It's beginning to piece together. I wish I could have told Darnell that his efforts weren't in vain, that his retrieval of Duane's glass and delivering it to Pinkston...a seemingly trivial act in the heat of battle... actually provided critical evidence. Pinkston rushed it back to the U.S. where it was analyzed at CBIF's clandestine forensic lab. Duane's drink was laced with Versed, the drug used for conscious sedation before surgery. It's quick acting and backs up Darnell's description of how 'they all three got up quickly and stumbled out.' The limo driver and Haitian had to act fast and get him into the limo so he wouldn't pass out inside the Hard Rock Café. The new generation of Versed is tasteless, water soluble, and impairs memory. A perfect drug for the occasion. As the three exited the place, an anesthetized Duane was held up by his captors, who feigned drunkenness themselves in the crowded nightclub, holding him up while quickly leaving. The new generation of Versed has an amnesiac effect, and Duane... wherever he is right now...probably remembers little of the incident... if he's still alive* Corey gazed out into the harbor. The bright white Hog Island Lighthouse at the tip of Paradise Island, built in 1817 and one of the oldest lighthouses in the West Indies, offered a stark contrast to the darkening sky behind it. He attempted to reason out the mayhem thrust upon him since yesterday's three am telephone call in Montego Bay, ordering him to come home to Key Largo.

The tropical storm neared and birds sought shelter in the palms overhead. Their songs grew subdued. A couple of lovers strolled down the beach to an isolated section and sought shelter inside a gazebo. A two-masted schooner with an American flag flapping off the stern glided past and moored among a dozen other yachts.

The peaceful surroundings were suitable for a man living a life of quiet desperation. It helped Corey analyze, deduce, and sort through the disorder, to reshuffle madness and turmoil into stability and pre-dictability. *I wouldn't be surprised if Ferguson and his crew members inside the Hard Rock Café were drugged as well. A worker in the nightclub must be on the payroll...but whose? Darnell and his crew are hardened seamen...powerful men. The five of them could have easily fought off the attackers and saved Collier. It was a setup, an expert abduction...just like the proficient execution of the amateur thin man on Parliament Square. What was he trying to tell Ferguson? I've got to find out who that man is and what he knew. Duane Collier stumbled onto something big and unexpected. How is Bolan Tougas linked to all this? It must be linked to the Haitian pipeline through Jamaica into Ft. Lauderdale*

The wind grew brisk out of the northwest, making the flags flutter on the fastened-down boats. The vessels tugged at their moorings and swung around simultaneously to face the storm bearing down upon them. The spirited wind bowed the overhead palm leaves and produced ripples on the protected waters of the inlet. The few remaining sunbathers hastily retreated back to their rooms. Corey remained calm, developing a game plan.

Whatever Duane stumbled upon was bigger than he thought... beyond a drug trafficking operation. Duane would have simply notified our moles inside the DEA if that were the case. Something drove him to take a huge risk

The sun cast a faint hue of light through the approaching clouds. The palm fronds intertwined in the thatched roof above him began vibrating and rustled in the steady breeze. Grains of sand lifted off the beach and stung his face. Discarded plastic cups blew across the sand. The ocean grew darker, the temperature dropped quickly, and the cool wind soothed his suntanned face.

We're at war with an unseen enemy...radical Middle-Eastern terrorists who wear no soldier's uniform...aren't associated with an official government, country boundary or demilitarized zone. They target Westerners, particularly Americans...their soldiers are obscure, non-state actors who infiltrate the West via sleeper cells... France, Germany, England, Spain, Sweden, and throughout the Caribbean islands... including the Bahamas. No wonder General Morrison stresses HUMINT, human intelligence. Whoever kidnapped Duane Collier and executed the amateur thin man operates with boldness, a paranoid devotion and...

"Excuse me, sir. I'd like to talk to you."

Corey leaped from his lounge chair and wheeled around. A plain clothes detective stood before him. Two uniformed RBPF officers stood ready at his side with their hands palming holstered handguns. Corey caught his breath. "Oh, sorry! You guys startled me. Is anything wrong?" His heart beat quickly and labored breathing gave him away. He was relieved to see the well-pressed, white jackets and wide, red strip running down each navy-blue pant leg. *Shit...I thought I was meeting my enemies earlier than expected...kidnappers and assassins*

The detective was direct. "You have something to be startled about, mon?"

"No, nothing at all. It's just that..."

The young detective interrupted. "A man was shot to death by Parliament Square today. Were you in the vicinity?"

"Well, I was sightseeing around Parliament Square, but I didn't see or hear any shots." Corey lied.

"You were more than in the vicinity. The librarian at the old Nassau Public Library said a man of your description was there, acting suspiciously. Two policemen at the Supreme Court building said a man of the librarian's description passed them shortly before entering the library, at the time the murder took place. It was also reported that you took off quickly after the shooting. I'm afraid we'll have to take you in for further questioning."

The young detective stepped back and the two uniformed officers instructed Corey to turn around. They padded him down for weapons and cuffed him, escorted him through the tropical gardens and front lobby of the old "BC," then placed him in the back of a patrol car.

Corey looked out at the tourists who stopped to watch the proceedings. *I can't believe it. I managed it so Milo's two sons got into the RBPF cadet program…then manipulated things so they were promoted into the detective ranks…and I was just arrested by one of them.*

Episode 11

CBIF Key West HQ

General Morrison sat at an open-air table at the Turtle Kraals restaurant, munching on crab cakes topped with mango chutney. It was an historic place where in years past kraals were used as holding corrals for green turtles before they were made into turtle soup. Perfect location, he thought- a funky old place on the waterfront and only a five-minute stroll back to the clandestine CBIF HQ where he lived on Eaton Street in Key West's Historic Seaport District. He loved crab cakes, having dined on them for years when living in Severna Park, Maryland during his tenure at the CIA HQ in Langley. Bigger crabs in Maryland, but Turtle Kraals mixes them with chutney, making the cakes larger. Morrison thought they tasted better in Key West, despite the smaller size.

A DIU (Daily Intelligence Update) from Corey Pearson was expected and Morrison kept his lightweight, secure cell phone at ready in his shirt pocket. It only weighed four ounces, but used a large bit encryption on either end to prevent eavesdropping. Several "businessmen" with briefcases sat at a far table. They were part of Morrison's counterintelligence crew and swept the open-air café for video or telephone microphones and remote-controlled transmitters. He continued ingesting the scrumptious crab cakes, wondering what Corey uncovered about the missing case officer.

The Florida Keys made an ideal location for CBIF HQ. The Atlantic, Western Caribbean Sea and Gulf of Mexico converge into the archipelago of hundreds of islands strung out over 130 miles. Morrison liked the fact that Key West was closer to Cuba than to Miami and US 1 was the only land-bound entrance and exit.

The counterintelligence (CI) crew blended well with the customers who shared the café with them. Morrison watched the 130-foot schooner *Western Union* slowly edge its way out of the Key West Bight into the Gulf of Mexico. A hundred tourists were aboard, watching the experienced crew raise the towering sails. In the dock area, pelicans and cormorants waited patiently for arriving fishermen to toss fish innards to them.

Morrison's secure cell phone vibrated. He nonchalantly withdrew it from his shirt pocket. "Go ahead."

"It's Pinkston. Much has happened down here since Pearson arrived. He's been arrested as a murder suspect. Milo delivered the message to me. Corey talked with Darnell Ferguson for about an hour. Then, after their meeting at the British Colonial ended, a detective and two RBPF officers arrested Corey on the beach and hauled him away." "Don't worry. I'll take care of it. Send in a burst transmission to Jeannie with the details." Morrison returned the secure cell phone to his shirt pocket and motioned the waitress for his bill. CBIF's mainline computer was code-named "Jeannie" after the 1960's sitcom "I Dream of Jeannie."

He casually strolled out of the café onto Margaret Street, crossed over Caroline Street, then turned right onto Eaton Street. Morrison's gait increased. He passed several dozen renovated historic homes of tropical West Indian architecture before reaching CBIF headquarters, which was a refurbished bed and breakfast bought from a fourth-generation family member who had proudly managed it. CBIF offered him a monetary deal he couldn't refuse.

A peaked-roof cistern on the side of the nineteenth-century home collected rainwater off the roof. Two Key West cats sprawled in a wicker couch on the front porch. Morrison walked up the front sidewalk to the spacious white house with red shutters. It was two stories

with a large attic room at the peak. Refurbished, smaller conch houses set on each side of the unpretentious HQ, both owned by CBIF and
inhabited by counterintel teams.

Three neighbor men sitting on the front porch of one bid him a
hello through a jungle-like tropical garden of palmetto palms and
tree-dwelling orchids growing in the taller coconut palms. Whimsical
polyester wind wheels of tropical fish were stuck in the front yard,
along with a hand-painted pink sign that read:

Some people like lemons, others like limes

Key West embraces and provides refuge for gays and lesbians.
Morrison thought they played the part well....so well that he sometimes wondered if they weren't acting. He didn't care; they were well-
versed in tradecraft and protected him well. Nothing else mattered.
Two wore baggy pants and T-shirts advertising the Green Parrot Bar
and Hog's Breath Saloon. The third wore a see-through net shirt. He
waved back to his three greeters, aware that fully-loaded Glock 30's
were stuffed in their pants and 12-gauge shotguns loaded with slugs
and Ingram Mac-10 submachine guns with plenty of 30-round clips
were just inside their front door. He didn't care if they were pretending
to be gay...or not.

The General retrieved a keycard from his wallet, making sure his
thumb and index finger contacted both sides of the bottom portion.
He inserted it into a door slit and briefly glanced at the peephole installed in the age-old front door made from polished cypress planks
while saying "Hello" to the two lounging cats. They stared back indignantly. The key card, miniaturized video installed in the peephole
and hidden microphone activated Jeannie's ID database. Instantly,
Jeannie recognized the keycard's magnetic strip and compared it to
his two fingerprints, voiceprint, and facial and iris configurations. In a
split second, Jeannie instantly resolved that it was OK for him to enter
the premises.

The cats met his greeting with a glance bordering somewhere between supercilious and scornful. It was clear that he forgot to feed them that morning. His fingerprints were automatically wiped off the keycard upon withdrawal from the door slit. Morrison pushed down on the brass latch and entered.

He advanced toward the basement War Room, as he nicknamed it, walking over creaking pinewood living room floor boards past a Louis XV caned eighteenth-century chair with a leather embossed portrait of Louis XIV hanging behind it. The back-dining room was furnished with a rare Italian Rococo Giltwood console and five-piece Puerto Rican nineteenth-century caned mahogany salon set. Unbeknownst to the neighbors, the time-honored walls had been dismantled so reinforced steel plates and bullet-resistant Kevlar could be installed from floor-to-ceiling. Then, the original walls were painstakingly reassembled back into place.

The priceless furniture collection justified to nosy neighbors the need for a most atypical front door keycard lock. In a bland corner of the dining room, set amongst celebrated antique surroundings, he unlocked a pine door in need of a paint job. It was located in an inconspicuous corner- Morrison planned the look of insipidity, for the door led to a basement bunker which housed Jeannie and her priceless two-way, high-speed internet connection to CBIF's private satellite communications system.

Once in, Morrison entered a large, soundproof space with one-way visibility and bulletproof glass walls. He sat down in an ergonomic chair with high back and pillow for comfort. Separate computers and keyboards encircled him on three sides. With a gentle leg push, Morrison effortlessly floated in his chair on reinforced casters from one to the other. Shelves of classified USB flash drives towered over each computer terminal. Little wonder his "gay" neighbors watched him constantly from their front porch, with concealed weapons. They could summon a dozen of their heavily-armed colleagues in less than one minute.

Morrison typed in his PIN number and password, then inserted the key card while stating his name. Jeannie allowed him access to her vast online files and satellite communications. He sat patiently, waiting for Pinkston's burst transmission to come through. Looking out through the sound and bulletproof diaphanous walls that enveloped him, he fretted over the arrest of Pearson...for murder. A cell phone couldn't permeate the reinforced steel plates, which covered the basement ceiling, walls and floor, so a small radio transmitter hardwired to a concealed outside antenna lay nearby. An electronic device to detect odorless gas was mounted on the ceiling and a gas mask complemented the security measures.

All three computer screens lit up a pale blue, flickered, then Pinkston's burst transmission appeared on the lead screen. Morrison eagerly read it:

(DIU) CBIF- Nassau Cell No. 6 Case Officer

Pearson arrested by RBPF detective and two uniformed constables after his meeting with Duane Ferguson at British Colonial. Called in by Milo "The Messenger" to me while Pearson being handcuffed on beach at 17:25 hours. Milo reported the detective was his son. RBPF escorted subject into patrol car 17:31 hours. Assumed taken to Nassau RBPF Downtown District Headquarters for further questioning.

Morrison retrieved his regular cell phone and typed in some numbers. A voice answered, "Royal Bahamian Police Force, Deputy Commander Ellison Rolle's office. How may we help you?"

"Let me speak to the Deputy Commander."

"I'm sorry, sir. He's in a meeting right now. Allow me to take a message and he'll call you back."

"Interrupt his meeting and tell him it's the organization Corey Pearson works for. We're concerned about his arrest. Have the deputy commander call me back ASAP." Morrison disconnected his modified regular cell, which didn't have a GPS tracer.

One minute later, the secure cell phone vibrated. "Morrison here." "This be Deputy Commander Rolle callin' you back. I had to excuse myself from a meeting. What be the emergency?"

"Corey Pearson's been arrested at the British Colonial Hotel. He's on the way to District HQ in downtown Nassau for interrogation."

Rolle replied, "We had murder by Parliament Square, so my detectives must suspect Mistah Pearson. Don't worry…I take care of it."

Episode 12

The interrogation

Carmichael Detention Center
Carmichael Road- Nassau, Bahamas
(GPS: 25°01'04.8"N 77°22'58.0"W)
Corey was puzzled as to why Detective Symonette and the two uniformed constables pulled up in front of District HQ in downtown Nassau, then transported him to the Carmichael Detention Centre after receiving a call on their radio. New Providence has several police divisions, each headed by a commander and deputy commander, and downtown HQ is where Deputy Commander Ellison Rolle's office was. *The call must have been from Rolle. Why would he, the RBPF mole I recruited years ago, order them to bring me here...to this decrepit place?*

The detention center was situated in the middle of a sunbaked, treeless field outside Nassau and surrounded by razor wire with guard towers at each corner. His arresting officers marched him through the overcrowded prison area that housed illegal Cuban and Haitian immigrants. Each one wore an orange tank top and swimming trunks. Corey passed a crowded jail cell warehousing a half dozen inmates sharing four beds. The stench of human sweat and feces was strong. Most compartments had broken toilets and sinks. The prison guards were armed with pepper spray, batons, stun guns, and 9mm Berettas.

His escorts took him up to the second floor into a sweltering office and ordered him to sit down.

An hour passed while he waited for whoever to come and begin the interrogation. The ceiling fan spun slowly while an aging air conditioner rattled and spewed out a paltry amount of cool air. He was hopeful that Milo notified Pinkston the moment of his arrest, who would send a burst transmission to CBIF HQ in Key West. From there, General Morrison would notify Rolle in Nassau on his secure cell phone. *Hopefully*

Suddenly, his three keepers seated on a bench outside the door rose and saluted. Rolle saluted back and entered the room with a manila folder, sat behind an old desk and ordered his constables to wait for further orders downstairs. He waited until their footsteps faded away before speaking.

"Well, Mistah Pearson, we do meet again…after ten years." Corey rubbed his manacled wrists against his knees. The handcuffs were put on tightly. "It's been a while, deputy commander. I see you've come up through the ranks quite impressively from the time you enlisted in the RBPF. Street constable, promoted to corporal, sergeant, inspector, then chief inspector…finally deputy commander. Lots of promotions in a short time." *All because of my help…you're indebted to me and you know it*

Rolle tossed a small handcuff key to Corey. It landed on his lap. "I take it your organization taught ya how ta uncuff yourself. You know lots 'bout me. Must be thick dossier 'bout me at the organization you work fo'…whateva and whereva it be."

"Well, thanks for the key, but I always carry a No. 1 size paper clip in my shirt pocket, bent just right to open these." He couldn't rotate his wrists to unlock the triple-hinged American made Hiatt heavy-duty cuffs, so he clenched the cuff keys in his teeth and promptly unlocked them.

The RBPF official smiled at Cory's resourcefulness. "Could you a done dat with da paper clip?"

"Yeah."

"Dey sure teach ya to be resourceful." Rolle cut to the chase. "We got lots to talk 'bout, Mistah Pearson, beginning with da shootin' on Parliament Square."

Corey rubbed his bruised wrists. "You know I didn't shoot that man, so why did you have me arrested?"

"Don't jump ahead 'o me. I know you did not shoot da man. Our investigation show bullets enter from street level angle. Accordin' to librarian, you was on da balcony o' da library. But, I want to know the extent of you bein' involved." Rolle slammed his baton on the table top. "And don't tell me you have nuttin' ta do wid it! Da cuffs can be put back on and you be takin' downstairs to stay for a few more days. Want to share cell wid our Haitian friends down dere?"

"No." Corey knew Rolle was bluffing, but decided to play along. As in their past symbiotic dealings, each could do much for the other. Rolle was a religious man who possessed integrity. He walked the talk and backed up what he promised. Corey targeted him because he had access to intelligence that CBIF needed...police files and information on narco-terrorists. He wouldn't be enticed with money, sex, or drugs and was so clean that bribery wasn't an option. Corey used Rolle's love of the traditional Bahamian way of life and a yearning to save it from crumbling to recruit him a decade ago.

Corey amassed a thorough bio on Rolle which was stored in Jeannie's "Caribbean Asset" digital files in the War Room: devout Baptist with a degree in Theology, old Nassau Guardian newspaper clippings announcing his "acceptance of the Lord as Savior," attended the Bahamas Baptist Bible Institute, taught Sunday school, sang in the church choir.

Rolle spent his boyhood growing up on Great Guana, a seven-mile-long cay off Great Abaco Island. He attended the Guana All-Age School and absorbed the out-island moral fiber and honest lifestyle which he brought to the corrupt streets of Nassau at age fifteen when his parents relocated there to work in the hotels.

Corey targeted Rolle for recruitment, over a decade ago, by attending Sunday services at his Baptist church. He sat in the back pew, for few white people attended the sermons. Rolle was just promoted from constable to sergeant in the RBPF. Corey introduced himself to Rolle, using his deep-cover identity as a marine biologist studying reef fish populations around New Providence.

Rolle taught Sunday school at the church and tried to instill the out-island moral fiber in the students he taught. Corey offered to provide snorkels, fins, and masks along with boat rides to the offshore reefs so the children could learn more about the inspiring underwater Bahamas that surrounds them.

The program took off, with over sixty children from the church participating. CBIF funded the project called "Reef Awareness" and Rolle was appointed director. He handled the funds and every penny was accounted for, thanks to his integrity. More CBIF funds flowed in for new church sound and lighting systems, and to equip its Boy Scout troop and Brownie pack with uniforms and camping gear.

Additional CBIF funds enabled Rolle to help Nassau's youth resist the "devil's temptation" of making quick money from street drug peddling. Every young person caught dealing was sentenced to jail, but upon release entered a court-ordered youth computer literacy training program, youth marching band, or a sport teams. The sports teams became very popular, so Corey suggested to Rolle that he form a youth partnership between the RBPF, his church, and the schools.

Nassau's youth were kept so busy in football, tennis, and track & field that the delinquency recidivism rate declined. Funds to pay teachers and coaches to make extracurricular stipends flowed in freely from "Mistah Pearson," as Rolle referred to him. Corey told Rolle that he had some very rich friends back in the states who always were willing to fund special projects throughout the Caribbean. He wasn't exactly lying.

Sergeant Rolle grew suspicious of Corey's true identity after the six-teen-year-old daughter of a parliament member was attacked at her home when both parents left to attend a fundraising gala. The unfortunate teenager didn't get a good look at the assailant who broke into the house. The would-be rapist wore a ski mask. She fought hard, kicked and scratched his face and T-shirt, and wrestled a baseball bat from his hands. She whacked him on the head with it. Due to the ferocity of the girl's resistance, the man fled with the bat, leaving no semen or noticeable clues behind.

The Bahamian Investigative Unit was baffled by the attempted rape and had few clues to follow. Corey struck while the iron was hot and told Rolle he had colleagues back home who could bring in high-tech equipment that could reveal overlooked microscopic bits of evidence.

Two CBIF forensic scientists arrived the next morning and inspected the home with ultraviolet light, which gave a fluorescence to certain body fluids. The reagents leuco-malachite green and or-thotolidine were gently sprayed over the crime scene. Even though the assailant's head barely brushed the armrest of the living room couch after she clubbed him, a heretofore invisible trace of blood turned bright green under the light from the chemical's influence.

They found four Rothman brand cigarettes in the backyard, behind some bushes where the assailant apparently lay in waiting. The cigarettes and blood patch were analyzed four hours later at CBIF's forensic lab. DNA matched the dried saliva and sweat from the Rothmans to the trace bloodstain found on the couch.

Corey handed over the detailed forensic report to Rolle, who presented it to the girl's father, the Nassau Guardian newspaper, and to his investigative unit. CBIF advertised a $3,000 reward for the arrest of the suspect in the Nassau Guardian and sent the earmarked reward money to Rolle's office under the name "Anonymous." The would-be rapist was arrested within two days. Even though Rolle was promoted to the rank of inspector, then to chief inspector, he remained suspicious of Corey's true identity. Marine biologists usually don't have the type of "friends" that Corey had.

Corey massaged his bruised wrists. "Well, commander, I'm glad your investigators ruled me out as the killer. OK, I did witness the shooting. I can help you solve this crime, but I need to know some things, too. Yes, I'm back after a decade to study reef fish populations and…"

"Mistah Pearson! Dun hand me no lies. What are you *really* here fo'?"

"I can't tell you."

"How do you know he be tailin' ya? And, where was you when you notice him?"

Corey didn't want to mention the Poop Deck, where cell chiefs often meet their CBIF handlers. He wanted to keep Darnell Ferguson's name out of the investigation, too. "I cannot tell you that, either."

Rolle grew restless. He had a murder to solve, one that occurred in Nassau's historic Parliament Square, the symbol of the Bahamian way of life. He knew Corey's organization was fighting for a worthy cause and its resources seemed limitless. Being a religious man, he was frustrated by the drug smuggling and Haitian influx, watching the religious and Bahamian culture he knew from childhood disintegrate. His lifelong Christian mission was to save the Bahamas from the devil cloaked in the form of drug smugglers and veiled in the swarm of Haitians illegally migrating via rickety, overloaded boats into the Bahamian archipelago. Rolle knew Corey could help him achieve his God-chosen mission in life.

"I tell ya what, Mistah Pearson." Rolle took off his deputy commander's hat and leaned backward in his rickety chair, wiping the sweat beads off his forehead. "Not only do I tell you the identity and background of da man who tail ya, I help out with whateva else you be investigatin' here on my island. I know whateva reason you be here is for da protection of your America and you won't be bringin' evil to

New Providence. Ya know my resources be made available to ya, but I need some favors from you...and from your rich friends."

"Name them and I'll be honest in telling you if I can be of assistance."

Rolle lifted his plump body out of the chair and checked to see if anyone was poking around by the open door. The hallway was empty. He checked the overworked air conditioner to see if it was turned on high, then gave it a whack to make the rattling noise subside. It didn't. He sat back down. "First, as ya know, we have big Haitian problem here. You see the topsy-turvy downstairs. Last week our defense force intercept thirty-foot sloop carryng 247 Haitians...just five miles west 'o South Beach. Dere be sixty-seven women, forty children and nine infants among them. Da boat was dangerously overcrowded, so our patrol boat tow it to da Coral Harbour Base and hand ova' da whole bunch to immigration. Dey bein' processed as we talk. But, afta dey decide who get political asylum and who get deported, the deported ones come here to Carmichael, and dat be most o' them.

Corey asked, "Why don't you deport them all at once so you don't have to house them here?"

"Good question, Mistah Pearson. Simple answer...we dun' have 'nough money cuz' my government dun want to spend da money. Parliament pays out half million ova' last five months deportin' da Haitians, but more illegals sneak in all the mo' faster. Human smugglers demand 5,000 dollars for passage to da Bahamas in rickety, homemade boats. Most slip under our radar. Dey end up in ramshackle villages outside Nassau...no runnin' water, no electricity...no jobs. Our schools, hospitals, and social services be swamped."

Corey sensed his exasperation. "It seems like you can't stem the tide. If people are miserable enough, they'll leave anyway they can. Still, I don't see how I can help you."

Rolle leaned forward, looked Corey squarely in the eyes and solemnly stated, "We can control Haitian problem with more patrol boats. With larger fleet we can interdict dem comin' our way *and* deport dem as well...before dey reach heah."

"Deport them...back to Haiti?"

"No, Mistah Pearson. I know dat not possible. I be thinkin' of transportin' dem down to remote island in south Bahamas at place called Devil's Point on Great Inagua island. From dere, we can pay smugglers to run dem back to Haiti. We pay each Haitian sizable amount o' money before dey depart to help dem relocate back in dere homeland. Kind a' reverse repatriation program. Would be cheaper den what we be doin' now, with immigration costs, housin' dem, payin' for da crimes dey commit."

Corey detected an urgency in Rolle's words. It sounded like a political speech. *I can turn this into a win-win situation. CBIF has long-range plans to entice him to run for a Parliament seat, and back him financially. Spearheading a drive to stem the tide of illegal Haitians would be a huge plus in his campaign...the Bahamian's tolerance for illegal Haitians has run thin. That, plus his background of service to church and community would make him a formidable candidate in the battle for a Parliament seat...hell...even to run for prime minister. He wants more patrol boats...I can use this to kill two birds with one stone...he can aid us in covering our southern flank from terrorists trying to sneak into the U.S. from the Bahamas...I'll offer him...*

Corey's mental plotting halted when the electricity went off for the second time that day. An enervated feeling fell upon the two men as the room grew dim, the ceiling fan creaked to a halt and the rattling air conditioner hushed. They sat in silence, staring at each other. The distant grousing of captive Haitians crept into the room. "No see ums," the barely visible bugs that tormented tourists, immediately invaded the place. Both men started scratching their legs as the quick-crawling pests attacked.

Rolle reached in the top desk drawer and retrieved two containers. He rolled up his pant legs and sprayed 100% Deet on both lower legs, then rubbed in *Skin So Soft*. He tossed the spray can to Cory.

"They not be as good at fightin' 'no see ums' as my father's bush medicine on Guana Cay. When I was a young boy, he go brew parts of aloe plant and bloodberry berries with roots from a plant he'd neva tell no one 'bout. His secret brew drove 'no see ums' away fo' days. Now, tell me Mistah Pearson, do ya' think ya' could be of assistance to my idea of stopping' dis Haitian exodus at da source...to stop dem before dey get anywhere near New Providence?"

Thanks to the power outage and "no see um" invasion, Corey had time to complete his thoughts. "Yes, I have a plan that could work. DEA confiscated dozens of drug-smuggling, high-performance go-fast boats. They're over forty-five feet with triple diesel engines. It's highly likely, with my organization's contacts, that I can have them renovated and fitted with high-tech radar to interdict Haitian boats. We could train our constables on how to use the equipment."

"How much dey cost?"

"Millions, but it would be a donation to you and the RBPF from my organization."

"What type equipment you talkin' 'bout?"

Hi-tech stuff to help the U.S. stop terrorist cell infiltration from the entire Bahamian archipelago. "Bullet proof vests, fingerprinting equipment, blood-sampling kits for DNA analysis, body bags in case anyone died in transit, night vision binoculars and goggles, microcassette recorders, secure cellular phones and portable radios, un- secured VHF radio, digital camcorders and cameras, computers and scanners, ion scanners..."

Rolle interrupted. "What da hell we need all these 'tings fo'? I just wanna turn back da Haitian tide, not invade da country...what da hell is an ion scanner?"

He can't refuse the offer I'm giving him...too much for him to gain... more work, yes...but CBIF can covertly train his men. "Ion scanners enable you to search concealed compartments, especially on larger vessels. There could be humans or drugs in sealed crates or cubicles on board, especially on cargo ships." *Or concealed terrorists and weapons being smuggled up through the Caribbean to the Bahamas, then into America. The bio-metric data collected would be sent to CBIF's forensic lab for analysis*

Rolled looked pensive. He eased back in his chair, rested his hands on the top of his head and stared at the ceiling. "You talkin' 'bout a dozen go-fasts, hi-tech equipment, men to train...I'd be in charge of a small navy."

Corey offered reassurance. "My organization would provide the training through the DEA offices in Nassau and Freeport. You would oversee the entire operation, but there are some strings attached. You will no doubt turn the flood of illegals into your country into a trickle, but each adult must be fingerprinted, photographed, and have blood samples taken. We can place several DEA agents on each vessel to assist in the field training." *A CBIF mole posing as a DEA official, that is.* "The data will be turned over to my organization. We'll run the bio-metric data through our database and notify you if you apprehended a maritime drug smuggler, fleeing drug kingpin or international fugitive." *Like a Middle Eastern terrorist hell-bent on killing Americans* "Of course, Deputy Commander, you will get all the credit for each arrest. My organization shuns publicity."

"Hmmm...I do like this sweepin' idea. It would help our homeland...beyond catchin' illegal Haitians. I wonda how I could approach da politicians...and parliament...with dis idea?"

Corey grew excited at the thought of having an undercover flotilla of go-fast boats searching through the 700 islands of the Bahamian archipelago for terrorist cells attempting to infiltrate north into the U.S. from Haiti, Cuba, and the Dominican Republic. He pulled his chair up to Rolle's desk. "You're sure no one is listening in on us?"

"Positive. Why you think I call the constables after dey arrest you and order dem' to take ya away from district HQ an' bring ya here? Dis second floor hallway be vacant. My men be downstairs."

Still, Corey continued to talk in a hushed voice. "You and your men will be thoroughly trained to operate the intercept boats and communication, surveillance, and navigation equipment. It will be done at the DEA offices in Nassau and Freeport. We will secretly fly you and your men to a secret base in the U.S., without a visa or passport required. *I wonder if he's heard of the secret 5,000-foot airstrip at the CIA's the 'Farm'.* You will be at this secret location for further training and indoctrination."

Rolle was growing hesitant at the 'too good to be true' offer. "Indoctrination … fo' what? I thought I be da one in charge?" "You will be totally in charge. The main goal of your operation is to interdict illegal Haitians....*and terrorist cells.* The only requirement is that you collect biometric data on every person you catch being smuggled into your country. It will be helpful to both you and my organization. DEA agents on each go-fast boat will help with the field training and digitizing the data. When we receive the digital data and compare it to our intel base and to Interpol's, we will let you know of any bad guys you've nabbed trying to enter your country. That will be a great selling point to your parliament members."

The Deputy Commander remained a trifle skeptical. "This be a very expensive undertakin', Mistah Pearson."

"Yes, it will be. But, you will be helping both my country and yours and it will be funded by my organization. We'll send you to a normal drug course sponsored by the Federal Law Enforcement Training Centre in the U.S. There, we'll work out the details of the operation with you, including selling points which you can share with your commander upon arrival back in Nassau. But, since you went through the seminar and 'persuaded' U.S. officials to go with *your* plan, the U.S. will insist that you will be in charge of the operation, which *you* conceived. I'll make sure none of your higher-ups takes over the operation and gets all the credit." *Like the FBI does to CIA and CBIF undertakings* Rolle was convinced. "So, it really ain't no drug interdiction operation at all…it's for findin' human smugglers."

"Yes, in a way." *And terror sleeper cells bent on sneaking into America*

"Count me in…Mistah Pearson."

The hefty police official glanced at his watch. "I now go to late lunch meetin' wid my detectives. Be back in an hour to drive ya back to your hotel." He slid a dossier across the desk, "I dun' know what yo' organization be up to or why dey send ya back here, but I sure da reasons be respectable ones. Here be info on da unfortunate man who tail ya. He go by the name o' Sidney Fowler and he work fo' our Agricultural Minister supervisin' da huge chicken farm operation on Abaco. Happy readin' til I get back."

Episode 13

CBIF stealth satellites

CBIF HQ- the War Room
Eaton Street, Key West Florida
(GPS: 24°33'38.7"N 81°47'50.6"W)

An assemblage of nine CBIF new generation reconnaissance satellites flew in orbit over the Caribbean Basin. No one, save General Morrison and CBIF technicians, knew when or where they would be overhead. Their orbital patterns couldn't be detected, tracked or predicted, making it difficult for terrorist cells to conceal their communications and travels. The operation to develop and fly the stealth birds was code named Operation Invisible and cost a whopping $15 billion.

General Morrison knew Corey would contact him after his release from RBPF custody. If he remained under arrest, Deputy Commander Ellison Rolle would update him. Either way, he kept Jeannie honed-in on the broadband wavelength used by the communications satellites. While looking around the HQ fortified basement, he recalled how adamant Senator William Warren, Chairman of the Senate Select Intelligence Committee, was of Operation Invisible. He tried to kill the proposed financing measure for it, but Senator Ruth Winstrom argued against his wishes to both the House and Senate appropriations committees. Senator Warren's veto was overridden and Operation Invisible commenced. Stealth technology that cloaked fighter aircraft from enemy radar was used to create three communications intelligence (COMINT) satellites that hovered unseen over the Caribbean

Basin. They provided Morrison with two-way e-mail, cell phone, and voice-over Internet and fax capabilities through secure channels.

Morrison had instant communications with ground stations throughout the Caribbean, providing high-speed internet connectivity to several thousand CBIF undercover case officers, cell chiefs, and counterintelligence agents.

A year later, three stealth IMINT (image intelligence) satellites were launched over the Caribbean. They began transmitting aerial photography to the Key West HQ War Room. If CBIF operatives reported questionable activities, the IMINT satellites would be sent hovering over the suspicious area and photograph high resolution, color images of the events taking place.

CBIF operated eight safe houses in Key West. One housed satellite image interpreters, who masqueraded as drywallers. They often frequented the HQ on Eaton Street, posing as casually-dressed friends to Morrison or as laborers dressed in jeans and T-shirts, toting putty knives, a wallboard saw, sanding blocks, fiberglass mesh tape, and paint sprayer. Their van, with the logo "KW DRYWALL" was often seen parked outside the headquarters.

Not only did they provide satellite IMINT interpretive assistance to Morrison, their work van was often seen parked outside the other seven safe houses in Key West. The KW DRYWALL agents were skilled at searching for small electronic listening and recording devices that could be planted in a room and monitored from afar. To make things look aboveboard, besides sweeping rooms for electronic bugs, they actually performed drywall services to businesses and private homeowners throughout Key West. It looked good on their W-2 forms.

The last three espionage satellites were secretively launched, not by roaring rocket engines blasting them skyward, but by gently pushing them into space from the large cargo hold of the Space Shuttle Endeavour during an ordinary and unrelated mission. The astronauts were specially trained for the Operation Invisible missions and tossed specially manufactured debris into the heavens to confuse snooping ground radar. They were SIGINT (signal intelligence) satellites and began eavesdropping on all airwave communications throughout the Caribbean Basin. Operation Invisible was complete.

Morrison waited in the isolated War Room. He could never understand why Senator William Warren was so opposed to the stealth satellite operation, which protected America's southern flank. He was thankful for Senator Ruth Winstrom, the House and Senate appropriations committees, and the CIA for conducting a cost/benefit analysis which eventually helped override Warren's objections.

Episode 14

Rolle's interrogation continues

Corey finished reading Sidney Fowler's dossier that Deputy Commander Ellison Rolle gave him. Rolle returned from lunch and silently watched as Corey poured through the file on the naïve shooting victim who had no experience in foot surveillance. Fowler worked for the Minister of Agriculture as a supervisor at the immense chicken operation on Great Abaco Island. Fittingly named Abaco Poultry, LTD, it employed over a hundred workers and spread out over 150 acres south of the capital, Marsh Harbor. Fowler was a native Bahamian, born and raised on Abaco. He was forty years old, never married, deeply religious, and received a degree in agriculture at the College of the Bahamas in the School of Natural Sciences and Environmental Studies.

The Minister of Agriculture pops up again. His limo driver took part in the abduction of Duane Collier from the Hardrock Café in Nassau

Rolle interrupted his thoughts. "So, Mistah Pearson, my question to ya is why would a man who spend time on Abaco supervisin' da huge chicken farm be so interested in you?"

Corey lied and didn't mention that Fowler was trying to find Darnell Ferguson, not him. "I honestly don't know." *Did Fowler see something at Abaco Poultry that nauseated him, something so contrary to his religious beliefs that he had to tell someone? If so, why did he seek out*

Ferguson, chief of the Potter's Cay No. 3 cell? How did he know to tail me when Ferguson didn't show up at the Poop Deck Restaurant and Lounge? Has the cell been compromised? "Where was Fowler last seen before his murder?"

"Just yesterday he be on Abaco. I call my constable in Marsh Harbor, Cecil Turnquest, and ask 'bout Fowler. Interestin' enough, he saw Fowler eatin' breakfast at da Conch Inn Marina. Cecil always eat dere and he seen Fowler eat dere often. I have not put that data in the dossier yet. Funny thing is…Cecil said dat Fowler seem nervous 'bout something' when he ate dat morning'."

Corey noticed a tinge of anger in Rolle's eyes as he spoke of the slain man. He gently asked, "Sounds like he was in a hurry to get to Nassau?"

A cop's passion to solve violent crimes is ubiquitous. The Fowler murder upset the deputy commander, for it happened on his turf…in the heart of Nassau. He took it personally. Cops own the streets…not the criminals, and this happened on *his* watch.

Rolle picked up the baton and slowly tapped the desk top with it as he continued. "He ate quick breakfast then left Conch Crawl and drove to Marsh Harbor airport. His car still be parked there. I check da plane schedules. He pay $200 for Bahamasair flight 136 out o' Marsh Harbor at 7:25am and land in Nassau at 8am. Den, he begin tailin' ya from somewhere you won't tell me 'bout and end up bein' put to da death on Parliament Square four hours after he touch down in Nassau. He tail ya to tell ya somethin' and someone be tailin' him ta kill him." Rolle slammed the baton atop the desk. "And you say ya don know nuthin' 'bout it!"

Cory watched the veins almost pop out of Rolle's neck. *Look submissive…look down…wait for him to calm down. The cost vs. gain will win out…he's got too much to lose. We can make him prime minister someday, and he knows it. Wait a bit and to get back on track*

After the veins shrunk back into Rolle's neck, Corey spoke. "You're a loyal professional officer of the RBPF. I know that from our past dealings that go back over a decade. I can assure you that I do not know why this man followed me. But, I can tell you with confidence that my organization will find out why. I give you my word, as I have done in the past. When we find out why he was killed and by who... you will be the first to know. In return, I would like to know about any information your detectives uncover."

The robust Bahamian police official knew Corey always delivered on his promises. He swiveled in his chair, stared out the window at the thick canopy of palm tree and Caribbean pine forest beyond the razor-wire fence while patting the palm of his hand with the baton. He recalled his promotions from street constable to his lofty position in the RBPF, the church youth programs he directed, solving the attempted rape crime of the teenage daughter of the parliament member...and now, he was about to become the commander of a fleet of high-performance go-fast boats. He wondered how many of these endowments were attributed to Corey and his organization...or to God. No matter, he thought to himself...God meant things to be and it was by *His* design that Corey and him were brought together.

Rolle swiveled the chair back around and scrutinized Corey. "Mistah Pearson, I call you Corey now. I always wanted to ask you something'. Rememba, many year ago, when ya began attendin' Sunday service at my Baptist church?"

Where's he heading on this new line of questioning? "Why yes, of course I do?'

"I must know what draw ya dere. After all, you be da only white person in attendance, sittin' in da back pew...can ya tell me what brought ya to da church?"

Rolle's a devout Baptist...he seems to be contributing our meeting to some preordained, spiritual happening. I'll play along. "Well, I don't know. I felt an urge to attend...don't know where it came from. I was on New Providence for weeks, knowing few people, when a strong desire to connect to something or someone overcame me. Other than that, I have no idea why. It was a craving I could never explain." *Actually, the intel file I built up on you at CBIF HQ made you a prime target for recruitment. That's why I "accidentally" bumped into you at the church. But, I'll settle with a predestined meeting planned by the big guy upstairs. Any explanation to get you to help me hunt down Duane Collier's abductors*

As if from a higher order, a warm, pious smile appeared on Rolle's face. "It be agreed, my friend. We help each other out on da murder. There be much good come to me, my family and da community since we meet. I believe it be a blessing from the Lord and not a trick from da devil. I trust you and da organization dat pulls your strings. You represent da good, not da evil. It be ma duty to cooperate wid da good in life and not wid da devil. My heart tells me ya organization is up to nuthin' but righteousness. Its main purpose be ta help da U.S., but in doing' so, it helps da Bahamas, too. I give you the full cooperation o' da Royal Bahamian Police Force resources to help in any way I can."

Corey listened patiently to Rolle's righteous analysis of how their relationship came to be. Suddenly, Rolle's pious demeanor transformed into a sinful manifestation. "So, by default, ma friend, I have 'nuther matter to discuss. It be eatin' away at me fo' over a year now and has great consequence for me and my family. You, along with the Almighty, might be able to help."

I was waiting for this one. The New Providence-7 file General Morrison gave me at the Conch Inn Resort safe house in Key Largo included a brief on Rolle's daughter. Her fiancé was a Bahamian Customs agent who was murdered by a drug smuggler last year. He supposedly fled the country. Another act of kindness from CBIF is about to be granted

"Sounds grave. How can I help?"

"My daughter, she now be twenty-two years old. I think you rememba her from long ago."

"Yes, she sang in the church choir and participated in the Girl Scout Troop you created through your church. She was an only child back then. I believe her name was Shantel." *That's her name accord-ing to the files Morrison gave me*

"You got good memory, my friend. Shantel be ma only child. My wife and I, we do everyting' we can fo' her. She graduate from college and work as bank manager in downtown Nassau. Den, she meet and get engaged to da right man…she meet him at our church. His name was Bernard Knowles and he be a newly hired customs officer. Such a nice young man. Dey be much in love."

Rolle's eyes teared up. "Da weddin' planned in July at da church neva happen. He be gunned down by drug smuggler. He be trained to clear private planes flyin' into our country at isolated station at Sandy Point…remote place at end o' Great Abaco Highway. Has runway three thousand feet o' packed coral and limestone. No nightlife ta speak of down dere in southern Abaco, but dun matta to Bernard. He be homespun boy who meet da wrong people in his job. Private planes from U.S. don have ta clear customs when leavin', but dey must have passport ready when touchin' down in da Bahamas at any point o' entry. Some bad people decide ta make Sandy Point dere point of entry. He would a made good husband fo' ma Shantel and good son-in-law ta me."

Rolle took out a manila envelope from his uniform, which was graced with epaulets and hanging medals for community service and bravery. "Please look through dis. I Xerox it from da killer's dossier. No pictures, but sketches of man made from whateva Sandy Point villagers could rememba of his looks. We got no more leads 'bout dis man…'cept what's in dere."

Corey slid out the contents on the desk top: a sketch of the face, general declaration and cruising permit cards, passport, special landing reports, copies of his aircraft registration, airworthiness cer-tificate, pilot's certificate, and a recent medical.

Corey asked, "Why did Bernard make copies of these items? It wasn't necessary for him to do so."

"'Cause he grow suspicious o' dis man after he make 'bout a half-dozen flights from the U.S. Bernard take it on himself to do so. He was a thorough young man who take pride in his job. He told da man it was new procedure...dat everybody had to."

"I take it all these documents are fake? The cruising permit would enable him to fly from airport to airport anywhere in the Bahamas with just one of them."

"Yeah. Bahama customs pretty consistent in da paperwork requirements."

"Any indications he flew to other places in your country?" *So CBIF could track down others in his narco-terrorist cell*

"No, he always stay on Abaco and leave his plane docked at Sandy Point airport. He call taxi in from Marsh Harbor and go dere and rent a car. Must o' been expensive to do dat...Marsh Harbor be fifty miles to da north, nuthin' but dense forest the Great Abaco Highway cut through. Da killer usually stay on Abaco fo' a week, then he fly out agin'. No one know what he do or where he stay. He write on da immigration Arrival/Departure card dat he be stayin' at da Conch Inn Marina in Marsh Harbor, but turn out he pay cash fo' room dere but neva use it. He stay someplace else."

Cory continued inspecting each document. "Any car rental, credit card charges, restaurant, hotel, gas station receipts?"

No. Like I say, he pay cash for everyting' but nobody eva see him eatin' anywhere or out in bar wid friends. We dun know the where, what or who 'bout dis killer."

This drug smuggler/murderer had a place to stay no doubt... someplace private ...a friend's house... wait a minute. "Where is the Abaco Poultry, LTD operation?"

"Halfway to Marsh Harbor from Sandy Point...off a da GAH. Why ya ask?"

Bingo! I'll bet this motherfucker's connected to the poultry operation along with the minister of agriculture and his limo driver who helped abduct Duane Collier from the Nassau Hard Rock Cafe. "I'm just curious. Sorry to hear about your son-in-law. He sounded like a dedicated young man. Tell me more about the killer…when did things go sour?"

"Well, dis man start doin' nice tings fo' Sandy Point and da customs office and da airport down dere. He install tie-downs by the runway so planes don' get blown into da ocean. When da wind kick up down dere…it be bad. Summer afternoon thunderstorms sweep through southern Abaco and da winds…dey can blow small planes over. Everyting' seem fine, but den friends o' dis man start flyin' in wid dere own planes, a half dozen planes flyin' in at one time. Turns out, one o' dis killer's buddies start bribin' da other customs agent who work at Sandy Point. Bernard find out 'bout it and report it to his higher ups. Dey wire Bernard up and he pretend to take bribe, too. Den, big court case set to prosecute Bernard's dishonest custom partner an' da' drug smuggler who bribe him. Bernard also recorded da man offerin' to bribe him, too… to not testify, and he report dat too. Next day, da lead smuggler man in da sketch you be lookin' at show up and shoot Bernard's head off wid a high-powered handgun."

Corey turned the sketch around so Rolle could see it. "Look at that face. It isn't Cuban or Haitian. It has the appearance of a Colombian, possibly mestizo. There's a good chance this man is Colombian. What are these symbols the artist sketched, just below his left eye?"

"They be pair o' teardrop tattoos…bloodred teardrops."

Episode 15

The DIU

Morrison sat in the Key West HQ War Room. He knew that CBIF's mole inside the RBPF, Ellison Rolle, would take care of Corey's arrest. Upon his release from custody, he would send a burst transmission of his Daily Intelligence Update (DIU) of what he's learned about Duane Collier's disappearance. Pearson always seemed to be at the right place at the right time, or wrong place at the right time...or maybe the wrong time. Regardless, Pearson had a gift for recruiting spies for CBIF after win-win agreements were negotiated...a truly diplomatic case officer.

After Rolle drove him back to the Hibiscus Beach Inn safe house, Corey voice-recorded a burst transmission onto a miniature tape and boarded a jitney back into Nassau. He walked into the Bullion Bar at the old "BC" and left the burst with Milo, then walked across Bay Street and watched Pinkston enter the British Colonial Hotel to retrieve it. As instructed, Milo had called Pinkston on the secure cell phone after Corey left.

Pinkston gulped down a cold Kalik in the bar and retrieved the tape, then walked out the front lobby door and returned to his PT boat. Corey nonchalantly followed him back to the Paradise Island Hurricane Marina, making sure there was no tail. *Pinkston will insert it into his computer. The computer algorithm will encrypt my spoken DIU and relay it to the CBIF stealth communication satellite, which will transmit it at 290 times normal speed to Jeannie's radio monitor. Jeannie will decode the indecipherable message into legible words, which will appear on Morrison's computer screen. Shit! Just arrived here and in a day and a half, a murder...then I'm arrested...I'll wager Morrison is sitting in the War Room right now...waiting...chewing on his cigar*

For an hour, all three computer screens in the War Room remained a lifeless, pale blue. The general jerked slightly when they flickered and Corey's burst transmission came through. He eagerly read the DIU:

DIU CHECKABLES- WHAT WE KNOW

(1) Duane Collier abducted from Hardrock Café in downtown Nassau. Don't know if any of New Providence- 7 cells have been compromised.

(2) Man named Bolan Tougas led the abduction. Darnell Ferguson took photos from inside Hardrock Café. Bolan Tougas identified by Gesner Verdieu, Operation Salt Flamingo's mole exfiltrated from Haiti. Verdieu reports that Tougas is newer member of same FRAPH squad that executed Damballah's parents years ago.

(3) Limo driver to Bahama Minister of Agriculture participated in abduction. Collier drugged and pushed into limousine outside Hardrock Café. A professional job. CBIF forensic lab analyzed drink residue/tainted with surgical sedative. Highly suspected that Ferguson and his men were drugged inside the Hardrock Café as well.

(4) Curtis Beacher reported Bahama Minister of Agriculture OK'd development of large chicken Processing operation on Abaco.

(5) Sidney Fowler supervised the Abaco Poultry, LTD and was murdered while tailing me; works for Minister of Agriculture, who OK'd the large poultry operation to be developed. Fowler

hurried to Nassau to Contact Darnel Ferguson at the Poop Deck rendezvous, but was gunned down in downtown Nassau (Parliament Square). It was professional hit- two motorcyclists behind truck with noisy muffler, excellent marksmanship.

(6) Deputy Commander Ellison Rolle perplexed about illegal Haitian problem throughout Bahamas, New Providence in particular. I offered his RBPF one dozen go-fast boats. Recommend we train his men to pursue drug smugglers and illegal Haitians. Could place two CBIF agents on each boat posing as DEA to keep eye out for terrorists. Told Rolle that we would train him and his men to use high-tech equipment and ion-scanners. Estimate 40 of Rolle's RBPF constables to operate go-fasts. Could covertly airlift Rolle and crew on non-scheduled flight to the 'Farm' airstrip. Our man Rolle would be likely to win parliament seat with this under his belt.

(7) Deputy Commander Rolle's future son-in-law, Bernard Knowles, as noted in CBIF files, murdered by drug smuggler. Rolle gave police report to me. Looks like Colombian, possibly mestizos. Has two bloodred teardrop tattoos under left eye. Escaped Bahamas and is possibly inside U.S. Rolle requests we search him down and deport back to Bahamas. Would be good favor to Rolle to keep him as a strong asset.

End of Transmission

The computer screen to Morrison's right flickered, then Corey's face appeared. "Can you hear me OK, sir?"

Morrison tapped a code into his desk drawer console. It opened and he retrieved a secure internet crypto-telephone and plugged it into the computer. Corey did the same on his end, onboard Pinkston's PT boat. Their words would be encrypted during satellite transmission.

"Well, I'm glad to see they didn't bruise your pretty face during the interrogation."

Corey wanted to chuckle, but couldn't. Morrison usually faked humor during CBIF's many misfortunes, but even humor can't wring joy out of irritation. He faked a chuckle, "Yes, sir. I'm quite alright. Uncovered some compelling stuff."

Morrison got to the point. "I read the seven checkables on the DIU. Item No. 1 concerns me. Duane Collier, if he underwent torture, may have revealed our seven cells in Nassau."

Corey sat in the bowels of Pinkston's PT boat. It was docked in the Paradise Island Hurricane Hole Harbor Marina. He spoke into the cryptone cell phone. "Yes, we can't discount that possibility. Should I order polygraphs on the cell chiefs?"

"Yes, immediately. If any of the seven cells were exposed by Duane, they may have bribed one of our cell chiefs or cell members. I'll notify our contacts at CIA that nonscheduled flights will start arriving at the 'Farm'. Let's begin tomorrow evening at 20:00 hours. That OK with you?"

"Sounds good. Probably should start with Darnell Ferguson, since we have to run a poly on him about the nightclub abduction anyway." Morrison retrieved the black snuffer with gold trim from his shirt pocket, unscrewed the end of the tube and stuck the Montecristo Cuban cigar between his teeth. "OK, beginning with Ferguson, all seven cell chiefs will be flown to the 'Farm' and undergo initial inter- rogation, separately of course. If all goes well, they should all be back in Nassau by noon the next day."

"I'm sure Ferguson will pass with flying colors."

"We'll see. By the way, where's Pinkston? He can't overhear our conversation, can he?"

"He left wearing swimming trunks, sir. Probably in the Hurricane Marina pool." *The general operates on a "need to know only" basis. Pinkston is totally trustworthy...but the 'trust no one' motto is strictly enforced...information dispensed to as few people as possible*

"Good. Keep this conversation confidential. In the meantime, Corey, have your cell chiefs keep a close watch on their workers. One of them could have been identified and turned by Collier's kidnappers... if Collier broke under torture, that is."

Perish the thought "Always a possibility. When all cell managers are cleared at the 'Farm', I'll have them keep an eye open for unusual behaviors that indicate a compromise from a bribe. The cell workers seem to be satisfied so far, what with the yearly bonuses, family medical cover- age, good hourly wages, and whatever needs to be done to help them out in case of a family emergency."

Morrison took the Montecristo out of his mouth. "Thanks to us." Corey agreed. "So true. Still, any unusual travel patterns, sudden purchases of expensive items, new acquaintances...We'll keep an eye out on this end."

Morrison watched Corey's brow furrow slightly on the screen. He respected Corey's instinctive counterintelligence ability. "Our agents at Langley will be waiting for the flight to arrive. Any further suggestions about DIU item No. 1?"

Corey replied, "Yes. If someone's been bribed or somehow flipped into being an informant, he or she may feel isolated and guilty...a bit anxious. They'd probably want to confide in someone...spouse, husband, friend, brother, sister...anyone close to them. Going against your country or an organization that takes good care of you can be a nerve-racking experience. They may spill the beans to someone as time passes. So, let's wait a while after all the polygraphs are completed, then offer a $5,000 reward for the double agent, if one exists, just to be safe."

Morrison stuck the Montecristo between his teeth again. "Why not do it now?"

"Sir, like I said. If a double exists, he or she may not have spilled the beans, yet. An immediate bounty would scare them off. If we wait a while for them to confess to someone, then the reward money would motivate his confidant to snitch on him. A friend, even spouse, may not remain loyal after they find out that what he's doing can hurt the Bahamas...plus the $5,000 would...".

Morrison interrupted. "A mix of guilt, patriotism, and greed, eh?" "Yes, General. That's why when the reward money is announced to the crews by the cell managers, it should be stated in broad terms that they're fighting an enemy that can harm the welfare of all Bahamians."

"Corey, your plan sounds good. Interrogate and administer polys to all cell chiefs at the 'Farm'...observe for behavior changes among their crew and identify any of their workers with relevant behavior changes...then after some time, offer the reward."

"I'd also recommend that if our enemy's double agent does exist and if we catch him, or if he turns himself in, that we grant him immunity from prosecution. Then, we could use him as a triple agent."

"Good point. Let's skip to DIU No. 6. You're talking about some large expenditures for a go-fast fleet. But, the DIU mandates we go to *Obscure Transgression* (OT) level. That should negate any appropriation squabbles. This whole affair of finding out what happened to Duane Collier will delve into black funding. Once OT is declared no member of congress, not even the Senate or House select intelligence committees will know where the funds come from or where they're going. Your request to supply Commander Rolle with one dozen go-fast boats and to train his men shouldn't be a problem."

"Great, general. So far, we've done much to insure Rolle's advancement to deputy commander. I can see him winning a parliament seat in the near future. Milo's two sons are detectives and will become chief detectives. We can have Ellison Rolle's detective unit investigate people of interest to us and we can gain access to classified information."

"Your penetration into the Royal Bahamian Police Force, the RBPF proved very beneficial. I might add, Corey, that you must have ESP."

Corey looked surprised on the screen. "How so, General?"

"Your idea for a go-fast fleet will carry out a goal I've been working on with CIA, DEA and Coast Guard Intelligence to catch terrorists moving north from Venezuela and Colombia to Cuba and Haiti, then slipping into the U.S. through the Bahamas. The fleet, commandeered by Rolle, will accomplish that goal. That's another reason why I doubt funding it will be a problem."

"If I may pry, sir, will the boats and training take place at the Miami Beach Marina?"

Morrison chuckled. "Very funny. You remember our past conversations about my boyhood dealings with the CIA station in Miami. Yes, the training will take place there. What type of equipment and personnel would you request for this operation?"

"I talked with Deputy Commander Rolle at the Carmichael Detention Center outside Nassau about the hi-tech equipment. He was initially a bit timid about the spy gear, but I convinced him to agree."

"I can only guess at the win-win discussion you had. What will we be training him and his men to use?"

"All the usual stuff. Bulletproof vests...because of the heat and humidity, I recommend the Kevlar-based bulletproof vest. I found it best down there... only weighs 2½ pounds with the new material they use. We can train them to use our fingerprinting equipment, blood sampling kits for DNA, body bags, night vision binoculars and goggles, micro-digital cassette recorders, both stationary and portable GPS systems, handcuffs, secure cellular phones and portable radios, unsecured VHF radio, camcorders, digital cameras, computers and scanners, ion scanners...I also mentioned we could provide training through the DEA office in Nassau. But, if we do the training through Miami, that would be fine, too, probably better because..."

While listening to Corey's plans, Morrison's mind floated back to his youthful days when his father worked for the CIA in a Miami River boat yard. It was used to stage speedboat infiltrations into Cuba. During the pre-Bay of Pigs era they lived in a nice home close to the Coral Gables waterway. Each morning, his father would drive to the Miami Beach Marina, where the 150-foot Explorer II was anchored.

Sometimes, he'd go with him, but was never allowed on board. Still, fishing off the pier beat staying home alone. His mother worked twelve-hour shifts as a surgical RN at Miami Mercy Hospital. He listened to his father discuss the ship with curious neighbors at backyard BBQ's, relating how it was engaged in "oceanographic research" for Florida Atlantic University in Boca Raton.

Young Morrison could never understand why he wasn't allowed inside the ship and why his father never showed him the research equipment onboard. It was later revealed by the news media that the Explorer II was a mother ship that supported speedboat infiltration missions into Cuba. His father directed a team which planned and implemented the insertion of Cuban exile teams and weapons into Cuba in the dead of night. At age seven, Morrison yearned to work for the CIA.

"...so, that's about it, general. Once you give the OK, I'll notify Rolle that the dozen go-fast boats will be transferred to his police unit and marine interdiction training will begin for him and roughly forty of his top RBPF officers in Florida, compliments of CBIF. Will the go-fasts be ready to roll?"

Corey's question stirred Morrison away from his boyhood flashback. Jeannie was recording the entire conversation and he planned to scrutinize it later.

"They'll be ready. The coast guard, customs and DEA confiscated them during a raid along the mangrove inlets along Colombia's Pacific coast last year. Made a huge bust...twenty-two boats and thirty tons of coke."

"Whew! That's a lot of nose candy. A record bust, no doubt." Corey remembered his stay in the area over a decade ago after training Duane Collier to take over CBIF's New Providence-7 cell network after Danielle's murder. He was temporarily reassigned to Colombia before being relocated to Jamaica. He met many peasant farmers who grew coca plants throughout Narino province along the Pacific coast in southwest Colombia.

He recruited some of the farmers, who provided him with intelligence on the Revolutionary Armed Forces of Colombia (FARC). Corey learned which plantations FARC controlled and the locations of their clandestine labs where they purified coca leaves into cocaine. He spent four months at the U.S. Coast Guard base at the mouth of the Mira River, about twenty-nine miles southwest of Tumaco, Narino's largest coastal town. For several hundred miles, a few inland roads and miles of isolated waterways crisscrossed the mangrove forests. The region was a smuggler's paradise.

Morrison said, "Yes, it put a big dent in the pipeline. Thanks to the intel you got from your recruited assets down there, we knew where to strike. The raid was unexpected and happened so fast they didn't have time to burn the boats or haul the coke away. CBIF requisitioned the go-fasts and lifted quite a few fingerprints off them, too."

Corey added, "As I remember, the go-fasts had satellite cell phones stashed with the coke in the bows. They were built in a clandestine jungle factory that one of the farmers told me about. It was hidden under the forest canopy in Narino province."

"We will put them into good use in the Bahamas. Each boat has hi-performance engines."

Corey asked, "How many horsies we talking about?"

"Over 850 HP. They go like bats out a hell...sixty-five miles per hour top end with a full load. The Bahamians will like them."

"What about the GPS waypoints found on their cell phones? What destinations were set in them?"

Morrison knew Corey was probing. He decided to tell him some of the dots to connect. "Remember our conversation at the Conch Inn Resort in Key Largo? We talked about the Colombian drug smuggler named Virgilio Cesar Sandoval, who visits Haiti often."

"Of course, sir."

Morrison inserted the Montecristo into his mouth. "Well, here's what I didn't tell you. When we discussed that DEA Medellin had photos of Sandoval meeting with Middle Eastern contacts, I didn't tell you that the meeting took place on a string of cays off the southern coast of Cuba, called Jardines de la Reina."

Corey asked, "You mentioned that CBIF agents tailed the Middle Eastern men back to Afghanistan after that meeting, and that they flew back out of Colombian airports."

Morrison chewed on his Montecristo. "DEA reported that Sandoval flew them back to Colombia in his helicopter after the clandestine meeting in Jardines de la Reina. We found out…"

Corey connected the missing dots. "You found out about Jardines de la Reina because it was positioned in the GPS longitude/latitude coordinates on the cell phones confiscated from the drug bust in the mangroves off Narino's coast. Then, you had CBIF agents go there undercover and keep it under surveillance. That's how you got the photos of Sandoval and his Middle Eastern friends."

"Correct."

Cory heard "Balls" growl on the deck above him. It was one of Pinkston's six potcakes. "Balls" sits in the captain's chair and faces off with anyone trying to board the PT boat. The dog was trained to guard the boat and to warn Pinkston of anyone's approach. If a person approaches on the dock, it growls. If they behave like they're going to touch or board the boat, it growls menacingly and snaps. If they board the boat, "Balls" earns his name.

He heard a voice. "She's OK, 'Balls'." *That's Pinkston. He must have picked up a woman at the pool. Better end this DIU quick*

"Well, sir, the Colombians know how to make go-fasts seaworthy. I'll relay the good news to Rolle so he can deliver a report to Parliament. If they're built for smuggling drugs, they're perfect for interdiction as well." *Capturing terrorist sleeper cells trying to sneak into the U.S., that is.*

"So true, Corey. Tell Deputy Commander Rolle that his fleet will be a stealth one, so to speak. The Colombians installed four 200hp engines and made them quiet. The hulls are low profile and painted blue to avoid surface radar and to blend in visually with the sea. They even have automatic roll-over, sea-blue tarps. When a U.S. Customs plane is in the area, they cut the engines so no wake can be spotted and sit with the tarp pulled over to avoid visual detection. Pretty sneaky, those Colombians."

Corey heard Pinkston and the woman laughing on the top deck. "Balls" stopped growling. "Yes, they're a sly bunch. Sir, if you notice No. 7 on the DIU. I know there's really nothing in it for us, but I think we owe it to Rolle to help him out here, too."

Morrison chewed on the Montecristo while speaking to the screen before him. "Yes, I agree. Too bad about the murder of his son-in-law. You mentioned the killer's sketch in the RBPF files looks Colombian, possibly mestizo."

"Yes."

Morrison chewed harder on the Montecristo. "You also mentioned the killer had two red teardrop tattoos under his left eye?"

"Yes, sir."

He bit through the Montecristo. "The photos of Virgilio Cesar Sandoval meeting with his Middle Eastern contacts on Jardines de la Reina...they show he has two bloodred teardrop tattoos under his left eye."

Episode 16

Stacey at NSA

National Security Agency (NSA)
Fort Meade, Md.
(GPS: 39°06'31.8"N 76°46'18.2"W)

Stacey walked into security clearance at the NSA. She differed from the other highly-trained and indoctrinated ECHELON signals intelligence analysts, for her illusory employer was CBIF. She logged onto her computer terminal and entered a personal code.

Her assignment was to hunt down a terrorist, code name "Radical Archer." He had purchased shoulder-firing missiles that were stolen from a British army unit outside London and reportedly has many friends in Tunisia, including black-market arms dealers.

If knowledge is power, Stacey was about to become the most powerful person in the world. She revved up a mighty program code named "Dictionary" and tapped in four-digit codes for the Tunis, Tunisia locale. Names and subject headings and internet addresses, along with telex, cell phone, and fax numbers used by individuals, businesses, government offices and private organizations associated with "Radical Archer" appeared on the screen.

She pressed ENTER and connected to a synergistic, global interception and relay espionage system that pries into private and commercial communications. Stacey's classified Dictionary program stores shared data from the other ECHELON agencies from around the world- if she intercepts a keyword that's registered in Britain's

Dictionary program, her computer would pick out and record the intercept, then send it to Britain's spy headquarters, and vice versa. Ground stations in the U.S., UK, Australia, Canada, New Zealand and in other nameless locations place their interception systems at each other's disposal.

Stacey cracked her knuckles and began vigorously typing away. *Carpal tunnel be damned...'Radical Archer', I'm going to hunt your ass down* Using this worldwide network of massive ground-based radio antennae, she effortlessly infiltrated the group of Intel satellites encircling the earth used by telephone companies. It enabled her to pry into maritime communications off the Tunisian coast.

She entered other codes into ECHELON's Dictionary, which enabled her to sift through millions of simultaneous phone calls, fax, and ninety percent of the world's private e-mail addresses. All key words and data linked to "Radical Archer" would be filtered out of them in order to find his whereabouts.

Stacey tapped in other ground-station codes, gaining access to Russian, Indonesian, and Latin American satellites. Amazingly, she intercepted thousands of phone calls to and from Tunisia that were transported by cables under the Mediterranean Sea. A shadowy branch of CBIF's special forces that was hand-picked from the Navy Seals secretly installed intercept devices on the cables 300 feet down. Anyone or anything that CBIF grows suspicious of becomes an ECHELON target. There is no medium of transporting information that Stacey cannot listen in on. She operates in a legislation-free environment, above the law, and effortlessly invades family homes and businesses. She's accountable to no one. Her name, position, and salary remain nameless and traceless, for her funding resources are buried deep within the Pentagon's procurement budget and is also concealed in the stock market under a street name account held by CBIF.

Suddenly, a red light glowed, signaling a "hit" from the U.S. Embassy in Tunis, Tunisia where CBIF secretly installed sophisticated microwave receivers and processors. A phone call was intercepted from a hotel in la Goulette, a seaside town on the Mediterranean Sea outside Tunis. The complete, two-way phone conversation was printed out in English translation.

Then, another hit! Stacey's heartbeat quickened. Dictionary keywords snatched information from an innocent-looking, redbrick building at eight Palmer Street in downtown London, England. Every telex passing in and out of London is intercepted by ECHELON computers operating within the walls of this charming, petite building with daisy-filled window boxes.

Stacey alerted her station chief, who analyzed the intercepts, voiceprint matches, and subject matter with intel from the Fusion Center in Trenton, NJ.

A half-hour later, halfway around the world, a dozen armed men from CBIF's Dirty Tricks division accompanied the local CIA station chief into the hotel lobby in La Goulette. They could recognize "Radical Archer" by sight and would receive $10,000 for interrogating him and an additional $20,000 for finding out where the missiles were. Then, they would receive a $10,000 stipend for murdering him...but only in that order.

The team quickly found their target and kidnapped him from the hotel. The leader of the Dirty Tricks division was a large man named Oppressor, who sported a snarling werewolf tattoo with blood dripping from its mouth. He specialized in enhanced interrogation techniques. After an hour of grilling, "Radical Archer" divulged where the shoulder-firing missiles were...in a New Jersey warehouse.

Interestingly enough, CBIF and CIA counterintelligence agents had already been observing the warehouse owner in New Jersey, whom they deemed suspicious. Stacey passed the new intelligence on to them and a brief meeting at the Trenton Fusion Center was held. It was determined that the time for surveillance was over...it was time to strike.

An hour later, surprised passersby watched as the warehouse was raided by 185 local police and FBI agents along with a dozen unidentified men and women wearing head and face scarves to cover their identities. The shoulder-firing missiles were recovered and the New Jersey warehouse owner and his brother were taken away in handcuffs.

Stacey stared at her computer screen and breathed a sigh of relief when the ordeal was over. She was pleased with how former spymaster Charlie Anton's pioneering concept of Fusion Centers healed the fissure between the two worlds of law enforcement (LE) and counterintelligence (CI). The CI surveillance way of life now coexisted alongside LE's criminal arrest culture...they knew when to observe and gather intelligence, and when to slap the cuffs on. Lives had been saved today.

A day later, a Tunisian fisherman found a body floating in the Medjerda River that was about to be swept into the Gulf of Tunis. It was identified as "Radical Archer."

Abaco bound

A pause followed after Morrison mentioned Sandoval bore bloodred teardrop tattoos under his left eye. Corey talked first. "I guess there is something in it for us. Deputy Commander Rolle asked me to hunt him down and deport him back to the Bahamas." *After the Dirty Tricks division waterboards him all afternoon*

Morrison agreed. "Yes. There's probably a connection with this killer and Duane Collier's disappearance. I'll contact our moles inside ICE. It'll be a top priority. Just tell Rolle we're honoring his request to apprehend him."

"Will do, sir. He'll be glad to hear it. There's a link between Sandoval, the ex-Haitian FRAPH member Bolan Tougas, the agricultural minister's limo driver, and Collier's abduction from the Hard Rock Café. Curtis Beacher's report of the Minister of Agriculture's support of the chicken operation on Abaco and Sidney Fowler's flying from Abaco to Nassau to tell Ferguson something...and his execution on Parliament Square...it's time to connect the dots, sir."

Morrison began chewing his Montecristo again. "Yes, and doing so will lead us to the who and why of Collier's disappearance. He uncovered something big...larger than a mere drug smuggling operation."

"I'll fly to Abaco ASAP. Also, I request we begin immediate surveillance on the Minister of Agriculture, his limo driver, and the operators of the Abaco Chicken Processing operation."

"Yes, immediately. Can you use the same cover you're assuming now?"

"No, the Nassau Grouper survey won't do there. But, it's pretty much common knowledge that I'm a marine biologist. Remember when I studied the pod of Atlantic spotted dolphins on Abaco years ago, when I created CBIF New Providence-7?"

"Yes, of course."

"I can assume that same cover in the guise of a follow-up study." Morrison swallowed a few bits of saliva-soaked cigar. "Sounds logical... convincing. We'll place an article about your dolphin venture in the Abaco newspaper. We are officially going to *Obscure Transgression* level. I'll activate the Dirty Tricks division and the counterintelligence teams you requested from the Turks & Caicos, Nevis, St. Thomas, Dominican Republic and the Florida Keys. They'll be arriving in Nassau and Marsh Harbor, Abaco over the next few days."

"Will the Dirty Tricks guys and gals be using the usual cover?"

"Yes, crew members on Darnell Ferguson's ship, the *Queen Conch II*. I've already notified him and he agreed to lease us the ship, again."

"Thanks for calling in the CI teams I requested."

"They will immediately be reassigned to you in the Nassau/Abaco, Bahamas sector."

Corey asked, "Should we communicate by the secure satellite phones? There will be much HUMINT, human intelligence, collected."

"Yes, but via our satellite system. I've ordered our image interpreters to reprogram one stealth IMINT and one COMINT satellite to hover over Nassau and Abaco. We'll eavesdrop in on the Parliament Building in Nassau and on Abaco Poultry, LTD in Abaco. As intel is gathered, Stacey, our mole inside NSA will register it into the ECHELON database. We'll be able to tap in to what they do and say."

Corey never liked the miscreants working in the Dirty Tricks division, but realized their mission was a necessary evil. "Some interesting individuals will be landing in the Bahamas."

"Yes, indeed. Keep safe on Abaco."

"Yes, sir." *OT level...Obscure Transgression. From here on, the end justifies the means. The CI teams I've trained will be arriving shortly in the Bahamas... to operate under deep cover, above the law, and beneath the radar of government and law enforcement. They're financed through black funding and leave no money or paper trails behind when they leave. Duane's abductors... murderers...will be ferreted out, observed for a while to increase CBIF's intelligence data base...then exterminated*

Episode 18

The *Gang of Six*

CIA HQ, 7th floor
Langley, VA
(GPS: 38°57'08.1"N 77°08'39.9"W)

It was four hours since Corey and General Morrison discussed the DIU and made the decision to go to OT level. Things moved swiftly. Corey was on his way to Abaco Island where the riddle to Duane Collier's disappearance lay. His cover was marine biologist conducting follow-up dolphin research, and as his Bahamasair flight lifted off the tarmac at the Lynden Pindling International Airport in Nassau, General Morrison pulled into CIA headquarters in Langley, Virginia in an unmarked car. The counterintelligence agent/driver knew the general adulated soft-rock, so pre-recorded songs of James Taylor, Fleetwood Mac, The Eagles, Journey, and America flowed from the car's sound system.

An interruption came on the car's audio system, which picks up publicly-announced terrorist alerts from the DHS's Twitter and Facebook pages: "Homeland Security elevated the terrorist threat in the New York/New Jersey sector from 'Guarded' to 'Imminent'. This heightened alert is due to increased worldwide chatter among terrorist networks. Local and federal authorities raided undisclosed locations." Then, the sound system resumed playing a Joni Mitchell anti-war ballad. Morrison knew Stacie at NSA uncovered the chatter, for he was alerted earlier before leaving Key West HQ.

A CI team picked Morrison up at Washington's Dulles airport after another CBIF counterintelligence team drove him from Key West HQ to Ft. Lauderdale airport, making sure he wasn't shadowed on Route A1A. Meanwhile, Corey would touch down in Marsh Harbor Airport on Abaco in thirty-four minutes.

The agents drove Morrison into the basement of the CIA HQ in Langley. He exited the car and was greeted by four security guards who escorted him into a private elevator and taken to the seventh floor. There, he entered a soundproof, glass-enclosed room. One of the senior guards paused before closing the door. He smiled at Morrison and said, "Welcome back, sir. We all miss you here."

The general smiled back, thanked him and sat down at a solid Cherry rectangular table with a three-inch thick top. No tape recording devices or microphones were permitted in this special room. The six-foot long conference table was the smallest at the CIA, with six chairs positioned around it. Only a minimal "need to know" number of participants ever entered...the *Gang of Six*

Soon, his five associates entered the room. Everyone appeared solemn, as if attending a funeral. The ex-Department of Homeland Security's Assistant Secretary of Intelligence and Analysis, Maxwell Gordon, briefly acknowledged General William Morrison, "Bill."

Morrison replied with a head nod and they shook hands across the table. Their connection went back a long way. Max performed so incredibly well in the high-ranking DHS position that he was appointed Director of the CIA's National Clandestine Service and took over clandestine collection of foreign intelligence. Max works undercover and is never named in the news media or outside the walls of the CIA. Only the POTUS and members of the Senate and House Intelligence Committees are aware of his position.

"I wish we could meet for other reasons, Max," Morrison said. "It's been a while since CBIF went to *Obscure Transgression* level."

Morrison shook hands with the other four men- Dr. Alex DuRoss, Director of the National Security Agency (NSA); Colonel Brent Burkin,

Director of the Defense Intelligence Agency (DIA); Roger Hart, Deputy Director of the National Reconnaissance Office (NRO); and Walt Mason, Director of the FBI.

The six men were key to implementing CBIF's missions when they went to the *Obscure Transgression* (OT) level. The previous U.S. president OK'd the creation of CBIF in response to the increased terrorist attacks within America. Over half had been perpetrated by radicalized U.S. Muslim citizens born and raised inside America, but who had strong links to their radicalized brothers and sisters overseas.

The FBI and its counterterrorism division had been ineffective in stopping the escalating attacks. A strong counterintelligence operation was needed, one unhindered by the constraints placed on law enforcement. So, CBIF was created along with the *Gang of Six* to conduct its clandestine operations. General Morrison was appointed Director of CBIF and assumed chairmanship of the group. He reports to the POTUS regularly.

The *Gang of Six* will pool their resources to hunt down whoever abducted Duane Collier and preemptively destroy any related threats to America's national security. The six men formed a stand-alone entity, unacknowledged, a sleeper cell within the seventeen agencies which comprise the U.S. Intelligence Community (IC). They are accountable only to themselves. No congressional oversight or executive orders delay or obstruct their operations. Their purpose is to maintain national order and tranquility in a chaotic world through robust counterintelligence methods and direct and preemptive action.

General Morrison embedded CBIF moles in each member's respective intelligence agency. The five men seated around him were aware of some of the moles, but not all of them. Only U.S. President Robert Rhinehart and General Morrison knew who the undisclosed moles were and where they operated. Paradoxically, this concealment protected the privacy and liberty of the American public while protecting them from radical jihadist.

The 2015 Charlie Hebdo satirical magazine office massacre in Paris signaled the beginning of a new era in radical Islam's offensive against the West. It was a new wave of jihad, marked by increased harmonization between heretofore disparate terrorist factions who conducted recurring attacks on soft targets throughout the West. More innocent Westerners were killed and maimed and an overwhelming uneasiness permeated the psyche of Europeans and Americans alike. It became obligatory for the U.S. Intelligence Community to create CBIF, the *Gang of Six*, and the ability to operate at an *Obscure Transgression* level when the need arose.

The Department of Homeland Security (DHS) got off to a rocky start after 9/11, but due to a man named Charles "Charlie" Anton, who was Max Gordon's predecessor, things began to turn around. Max learned much from Anton's implementation of "Fusion Centers," which were hybrids of Britain's MI5 domestic spying model. CIA and CBIF operatives were stationed at hundreds of these centers throughout America's heartland and seacoast cities. They learned to cooperate and share timely overseas information with federal, state and local law enforcement officials.

Still, a rift continues to exist between the two worlds of law enforcement (LE) and the CIA's counter intelligence (CI). The FBI and local police departments are geared to conduct short surveillance and arrest criminals, or terrorists, as soon as enough evidence is gathered to hold up in court for a conviction. After all, FBI agents and local patrolmen are promoted in the LE system depending on the number of arrests they make.

Charles Anton's Fusion Center concept encouraged the two cultures to pool their resources and try to collaborate and work as a team. The hope was that the two disparate cultures would realize their symbiotic relationship and eventually complement each other. After all, that's what the distinct terrorist factions and their splinter groups around the world have learned to do amongst themselves.

The transformation wasn't easy. CI chooses to sit back and be patient, to observe and learn as much as possible about the jihadist suspects they target. CI doesn't have arrest powers like LE does and thinks globally, not locally. When CIA and CBIF operatives and their foreign assets discover overseas plots to harm America, they monitor and observe the enemy's attack plans abroad. Through intense surveillance, they eventually uncover direct contacts and associates who reside inside America.

Oftentimes, overseas-based CI agents find the locale inside America where a strike is planned to occur. Then, the CBIF and CIA operatives stationed at the closest Fusion Center share the overseas intel with the local FBI and police officials.

Gradually, LE began to accept CI's point of view and they began to work together. LE delayed slapping the cuffs on prematurely and allowed CI agents to continue domestic surveillance. Both disparate worlds fused together by better understanding each other's needs.

When Max took over the aging Anton's place, he continued implementing the concept of Fusion Centers. Anton was Max's mentor and, in the beginning, he witnessed much infighting between LE and CI. But, Max persisted in forcing them to mix. For America's sake, he remained determined to make the CI surveillance way of life exist alongside LE's criminal arrest culture.

Max asked General Morrison to bring into play his secretive CBIF network due to its seemingly unimpeded funding and resources and the fact that it worked alongside the CIA. Neither had domestic arrest authority like the FBI and other law enforcement agencies, but they fought domestic terrorism smarter, for it's more difficult to conduct secret, sophisticated surveillance on an intelligent radical Islamist than to arrest a dumb crook.

Many believed that the fusion of such disparate cultures would never work and it was difficult for Max Gordon to accomplish after the legendary Anton retired. He felt like he was training an NFL team to win a MLB game. The skills needed for CI weren't understood fully by LE. But, Max persisted.

Then came the merger with CBIF. The money poured in to the Fusion Centers for purchases of hi-tech surveillance equipment and continual life-long, career training. Gradually, the law enforcement mentality and counterintelligence mindset seemed to edge closer together...they discovered common ground.

Over a beer, Max was told by the special agent in charge of the St. Louis FBI unit, "You know, Max, this is beginning to work. My agents still get recognition and advancement depending on how many arrests they make. They brag about how many criminals and terrorists they arrested and sent to prison. But, they realize that their surge in arrests and successful convictions depend on the CI community. You guys observe and amass a huge amount of intelligence on suspected radical jihadists, including their connections, equipment purchases and links to financial supporters and sympathizers. Law enforcement is finally catching on."

Max was pleased with the direction the DHS was heading. When it's time for an arrest, the CIA and CBIF agents give their intelligence to the FBI and local police departments. The CIA and CBIF agents often participate in the raids, wearing balaclavas. The FBI gets all the credit and the public remains ignorant of the effort that CBIF and CIA operatives expend to gather foreign intelligence with domestic links.

That's the nature of CI- you remain concealed, invisible. Having deep undercover operatives exposing their disguise by appearing in court to testify during a prosecution case is nothing short of ludicrous.   It would alert sleeper cells inside America of the overseas methods and sources CI agents use to track them down. The LE-CI merger was easier because the FBI and local police departments got all the headlines and glory.

The symbiotic relationship was akin to the "glass ceiling" concept. LE remained the arms of, and supervised by, our judicial system while CI remained recluse and self-driven. CI operatives now covertly work inside the U.S. through Fusion Centers, and many terrorist attacks have been thwarted. Since CIA and CBIF agents working inside America and throughout the Caribbean Basin have no powers of arrest, they aren't pressured by judges and prosecuting attorneys, especially in re-election years, to prematurely step on people to get short-term results.

Historically, law enforcement realized they can't catch all the common criminals and can never totally stamp out crime. However, they learned they could come closer to doing so by working alongside CI via Fusion Centers. Dozens of terrorist attacks in America's heartland, which were planned and funded overseas, were thwarted. LE discovered the global reach and persistence of Middle Eastern terrorists and finally came to grips with the knowledge that their efforts must lead to a 100 per cent arrest rate...*before* a crime was committed. They couldn't afford to miss one, since terrorist attacks are so lethal and wreak havoc on America's economic well-being and emotional psyche. Such a perfectionist arrest record could only be accomplished through preemptive and deceptive CI techniques...inside America's borders.

The FBI learned the benefits of not arresting too early to obtain news media coverage, recognition, and job promotions. CBIF convinced federal judges and prosecutors, during election years, to ease off from pressuring law enforcement officials from making premature arrests so they could campaign on a "hard line against terrorism" stance. LE held back and allowed CI to keep suspected terrorist cells under surveillance longer. Ironically, working alongside CBIF and CIA operatives throughout the Fusion Center network resulted in the FBI making larger and more extensive arrests and prosecutions.

Counterintelligence tactics and methods uncovered homegrown terrorist sympathizers and financial backers who were, heretofore, beneath the radar of LE. No longer did LE simply slap the cuffs on when enough incriminating evidence accumulated for a successful court prosecution. The balance between observing, analyzing and gathering additional intelligence as opposed to rushing in and arresting seemed to be in equilibrium. Max continued the fusion between the two disparate worlds to insure this delicate balancing act endured.

The five men listened intently as Morrison described the abduction of Duane Collier, Corey Pearson's DIU, the proposed Bahamian go-fast fleet, the murder of Deputy Commander Rolle's future son-in-law, and Virgilio Cesar Sandoval's narco-terrorist linkage. When he concluded with his briefing, Gordon, Burkin, Dr. DuRoss, Hart, and Mason looked at each other and nodded in agreement.

Max said, "Let's make it happen."

Colonel Burkin added, "We have at least twenty billion hidden deep in the Defense Department procurement budget. Should be no problem funding this OT operation. I'll notify my men at the Pentagon to clear $10 million for starters. Bill, send me a list of equipment needed for the go-fast fleet and an estimate of the cost for training the Bahamian crews."

Morrison replied, "Will do."

Dr. Alex DuRoss said to Morrison, "I'll alert your CBIF mole, code-named Stacie, in our NSA satellite monitoring and ECHELON division. She can maneuver one of our satellite birds to sweep over the Bahamian Nassau/Abaco region and link up with your stealth satellites. Stacie can set the Echelon Dictionary program to eavesdrop on the fax, e-mail addresses, cell phone numbers, code words...whatever is used by the bad guys that your CBIF ground agents collect."

The unanimous response pleased Morrison, even though it was expected. "Great, gentlemen. I'll give the go-ahead for my people to proceed to Nassau and Abaco."

Morrison then turned to Dr. DuRoss. "Alex, our top operative, Corey Pearson, is now on Abaco. He'll establish collection priorities for the arriving agents. They're very skilled in what they do."

"I've heard good things about his recruiting abilities." DuRoss said.

"Yes, indeed. Pearson requested that I activate these particular agents for this mission. He recruited them in the Caribbean through the years and all went through extensive training at the 'Farm'. They will gather much ground intelligence which I will forward to you at NSA so Stacie can constantly upgrade her Dictionary program."

Alex replied with a silent nod, eased back in his chair and rested his chin in a pensive manner upon clasped hands. It was an unstated understanding.

Morrison thought it ironic how the most profound statements were often made in silence. Alex knew how the game was played at OT level...they all did. They were silent warriors and another asymmetric clash with radical jihadists was underway. Going to *Obscure Transgression* (OT) level was a necessary evil, always necessary but never good. Peace for America since 9-11 remained elusive. Even though furtive on-the-ground HUMINT intelligence-gathering was integrated with elaborate space-born technologies, the art of asymmetric warfare remained simple: gather and analyze intelligence on a nationless and obscure enemy, go from the known to the unknown... remain invisible, blend into the background...know thy enemy... then strike them stealthily and hard.

For several moments, the room remained quiet. Finally, Max broke the ice. "We all know what we have to do to support the battles our General "Bill" Morrison gets us into!"

The group released a loud guffaw. An absence of humor would make their line of business nearly intolerable.

Still chuckling, General Morrison reached into his briefcase and took out five satellite cell phones. "Yes, once again...I've dragged you all into another one. And as good little warriors, you know we must communicate well." He passed the phones around.

"These are the usual high-security ones with voice scrambling, but they're a bit different. You can use them on either a landline or cell phone. The portable telephone scrambler is embedded in the bottom with a unique security code to use when you call me or vice versa. My man in Nassau, Pinkston, built them in his workshop on the PT boat."

"Oh, you mean the genius computer hacker you saved from a prison stretch?" Burkin asked with a wide grin.

"Yes, the one and only. Thank God, he's on our side. Pinkston created a twelve-digit code that uses a digital encryption algorithm. When you enter the code, an algorithm he invented rolls the scrambling code over 50,000 times. We can talk all day long on these babies in complete secrecy before the pattern repeats itself."

Dr. DuRoss asked, "Bill, I take it we only use them to call another of these cell phones only and not call a landline or regular phone with a separate scrambler?"

"Correct. Only call one of these other five phones. We can talk to each other singly or have conference calls and communicate simultaneously anywhere in the world. Never use them to call each other at our desk phones, even though the lines are secured. I realize they have scramblers too, but Pinkston installed a joint tactical devise that neutralizes all wiretap or electronic eavesdropping methods. If the code is ever encrypted and broken, we would waste mental energy and time tracking down anyone in our offices with knowledge and access to our desk and personal cell phone scramblers."

Maxwell Gordon couldn't resist it, "Do you mean I can't use it to call Domino's pizza and order a home delivery?"

General Morrison replied with a polite "Ha, ha", then retrieved a file marked *Top Secret- Nassau/Abaco Sector* and handed it to Dr. DuRoss.

"Alex, here's some beginning intelligence data for Stacey to enter into the Dictionary program."

DuRoss replied, "It'll be put in ASAP. I hate to hand-deliver it to her. I want to stay as distant from her as I can. I don't want to arouse suspicion in the NSA that she's a mole for CBIF."

"No need to," Max Gordon chipped in. "I'll call downstairs for one of the CIA couriers to do that."

Dr. DuRoss asked, "Wouldn't that be a bit risky...to send a courier to the NSA? I know their honest, but who knows?"

Morrison grinned slightly. "Don't worry we have special couriers inside CIA that specialize in delivering CBIF-related materials."

"Good grief...you guys are everywhere!" Roger Hart of NSA said. Brent Burkin of the DIA made light again. "Oh, I didn't realize the CIA had employees at the E-7 level."

Burkin's ribbing once again eased the tense atmosphere a bit. Couriers must have an E-7 grade or above and carry Armed Forces Courier Service ID cards. A select few were recruited into the ranks of CBIF for further specialized training to handle documents like the one Morrison handed to DuRoss. It would be kept safe and sound during physical delivery to Stacie at the NSA, locked in a special case that was handcuffed to the courier's wrist. If the case traveled more than ten feet from the courier...it would self-destruct.

Max replied, "Very funny, Brent. At least the CIA and CBIF aren't considered oxymorons, like 'military intelligence' is."

A few nervous chuckles ensued, then Max turned to Morrison, "You'll also have the full cooperation of the analysts downstairs...the ones who specialize in Bahamian political history and culture."

The atmosphere turned sober quickly after Brent's attempt at humor. Morrison took out his Montecristo and inserted it between clenched teeth.

"I appreciate that, Max. Gentlemen, we all know what we have to do. I'll keep you all updated on a regular basis. May the hunt for Duane Collier's abductors and the terrorist plot he almost certainly uncovered begin."

The six silent warriors rose from the table and hastened back to their respective agencies.

Four hours later, General Morrison sat alone in the basement computer room at CBIF HQ in Key West. The meeting with the executive brass from the National Reconnaissance Office, Defense Intelligence

Agency, National Security Agency, FBI, and the Central Intelligence Agency ended at 2:45pm. He felt uncomfortable flying directly into Key West after leaving the OT level meeting at CIA, so he made the 2½ hour flight from Washington Dulles to Miami airport, where he climbed into a waiting SUV. As usual, a CI team discreetly followed him to the Florida Keys where three additional CI teams monitored his return along Highway 1 from Key Largo to the Key West HQ. There were no tails.

Inside the War Room, Morrison inspected the list of special CI agents that Corey requested for this OT level operation. Each one had special talents apposite for the first wave of the operation to find Duane Collier's killers. He programmed Jeannie to summon the silent warriors. It was now 7:45pm…he pressed the send button. They would impalpably slip into the Bahamas. The battle has begun…at the *Obscure Transgression* level.

Episode 19

CBIF mole inside the NSA

*We live in a dirty and dangerous world ... There
are some things the general public does not need
to know and shouldn't. I believe democracy
flourishes when the government can take legitimate
steps to keep its secrets and when the press
can decide whether to print what it knows*

Katharine Graham

NSA Headquarters
Fort Meade, Maryland
(GPS: 39°06'31.8"N 76°46'18.2"W)
"Are you Stacie?" a voice behind her asked.

Startled, the CBIF mole turned around to view two uniformed men. One carried a briefcase shackled to his wrist.

Two NSA security guards armed with standard 9mm Berettas stood behind them. They met the two uniformed visitors at the front security gate, required them to park their SUV far from the NSA main headquarters building, then drove them the rest of the way in their H2 Hummer.

"Yes, I am."

The man with the briefcase held up an Armed Services Courier Service ID card close to her face, then unlocked the cuffs and opened the special envoy case. He defused the automatic self-destruct mechanism, handed her the folder inside, stepped back, then was escorted away.

She opened the folder marked "Top Secret" and pulled out a single-sheet letter:

Attention Code Name "Stacie"

You have new CBIF assignment. The NRO's satellite "Evening Star" will be repositioned to fly over sector Bah 444-9477. First flight over Nassau/Abaco sector at 18 hours, 13 minutes, 34 seconds EST tomorrow, crossing Bahamas at GPS Geographic coordinates: 25° 5' N 77° 21' W

Evening Star to communicate with one (1) CBIF IMINT and one (1) CBIF ELINT satellite already in geosinc orbit over this sector. These two stationary CBIF satellites will relay HUMINT (human), IMINT (image) and ELINT (electronic) intelligence to Evening Star; i.e., "Mother Ship," which will relay all intel to you. You will filter all intel through Dictionary program to retrieve relevant data. You will promptly expand Dictionary data foundation base as CI ground officers and HUMINT agents in Bah 444-9477 sector collect critical intel.

Special note: Focus on communications between above sector with Middle East sectors, particularly Afghanistan/Lebanon.

Begin new Dictionary program for Bahamas sector Bah 444-9477 with following foundation data gathered by agent in place:

*Duane Collier *Cory Pearson *Bolan Tougas
*Nassau Hard Rock Café *Darnel Ferguson *Curtis

Beacher *Sidney Fowler *FRAPH *Deputy Commander Ellison Rolle *illegal Haitian *Bernard Knowles- son in law to Rolle *Virgilio Cesar Sandoval *red teardrop tattoos *Alfred Moss- Bahamas Minister of Agriculture *Dona Anani Guanine *Abaco Poultry, LTD

Report to your regularly scheduled Employee Performance Evaluation in my office tomorrow at 08 hours 30 minutes. Will discuss details of this operation at that time, in private. We are at OT level. As usual, you are bound to secrecy.

Dr. Alex DuRoss
Director of National Security Agency
Nation Security Agency Branch

Stacie read through DuRoss' orders then opened up the Dictionary program and began imputing the new intelligence. CBIF's HUMINT case officers and their recruited agents would collect fax, cell phone, e-mail addresses and computer codes that their targets send and receive... anything connected to the CBIF operation will be placed into her database.

With CBIF's stealth satellites linking with the "Mother Ship," millions of ELINT data bits will be sucked up by CBIF stealth satellites in the Nassau/Abaco sector, like dust swept up from a carpet into a vacuum cleaner. It will be relayed to the Mother Ship; i.e., "Evening Star" as she passes over in her polar orbits.

CBIF's IMINT satellite will relay visual images it takes as well. If any electronic communications anywhere in the world remotely relate to the Dictionary database produced in the Nassau/Abaco area, she will be alerted.

In twenty minutes, she finished imputing the data into Dictionary. She sat alone staring at her computer screens, once again contemplating her role in the scheme of things. She thought about her position as a mole for CBIF, in the bowels of the NSA, and of her worldwide capabilities of spying on everyone's computers, cell phones, faxes…whatever travels through the airways. She wondered if ECHELON would someday be used for corrupt purposes or if another sociopath like Adolf Hitler would ever rise to power within America. Would Edward Snowden's NSA leak back in 2013 ever be considered an act of heroism?

Stacey returned her thoughts to the present and wondered how many lives she saved after "Radical Archer" was captured. The surveillance power of ECHELON made it all happen. She was glad CBIF was created…she thought that there's some things the general public, even those in power… do not need to know.

Episode 20

A recruited asset from Andros, Bahamas

Key Largo, Florida

Addie Kolmogrovov finished cleaning the CBIF safe house at the Conch Inn Resort in Key Largo. Like many Bahamians, her pure Bahamian blood didn't go back very far. Her surname originated when a Russian man settled in Kemp's Bay and married a Bahamian woman. The surname of her immigrant Russian grandfather was passed down on her father's side.

She took a breather from uninstalling the security devices in the room, sat at the desk where General Morrison spoke to her a decade ago, and looked out the one-way picture window. Children were playing in the warm waters of Florida Bay while their parents kept a watchful eye on them. She pondered on how she came to work for CBIF. It began when a man named Corey Pearson came into her life.

During her childhood, she moved from Kemp's Bay to Nicholl's Town on Andros, a large outer island in the Bahamian archipelago, and enrolled at Nicholl's Town Elementary School. Fortunately, the needy school received an entire library of textbooks from the U.S. Addie was fascinated by mathematics and proved to be a math whiz. In 3rd grade, she poured through the donated text books…geared to the high school level! Upon graduation from Central Andros High School, she was offered a U.S. government-funded mathematics scholarship to George Washington University in Washington, D.C. Unbeknownst to her, Corey Pearson scrutinized school records to find talented high school children on Andros, and she stuck out like a sore thumb.

Addie did not know the funding source that provided the stipend for her $3,000/month studio apartment in Georgetown, outside Washington, D.C. Life in plush and bustling Georgetown was incongruous to the simple, unruffled and tranquil existence of Nicholl's Town. She missed "Bossman," her pet potcake and celebrating the annual Junkanoo, Goombay, and Regatta events with her family and island friends. Whenever she left her Georgetown apartment to eat out, shop, or merely try an evening out, she felt the cultural divide.

She bridged the societal void by studying math intensely, readily absorbing advanced Algebra, Topology, linear Algebra and advanced Calculus. Despite the nostalgic island musings, her life in America was too good to be true...even in the midst of Georgetown's hurly-burly.

She sped through the curriculum and passed the Master's exams. The anonymous funding source sent her a letter which stated that further funding was available only for Georgetown University's computer science specialty and that she would be contacted by a representative to further explain the details. Addie was disappointed, for she wanted to pursue a doctoral degree in math. But, after meeting with the shadowy funding source's spokesperson, she couldn't resist enrolling in the computer science program. The full-funding would continue, including her studio apartment stipend, with the add-on that she could take five fully paid RT flights to Andros each year to visit her family, friends...and "Bossman."

There were some qualifiers, however. She had to go through the regular curriculum, but with emphasis on certain predetermined courses. Addie learned computer database management and informational retrieval. Her math expertise paid off and she ranked high in key courses: relational algebra, SQL query language, and advanced retrieval methods. Particular attention was given to deep data mining and data collection kept by large organizations and commercial enterprises. She quickly became skilled in data mining concepts and techniques and could find hidden patterns and relationships in massive amounts of structured and unstructured computerized data.

Lastly, her ethereal bursary stressed that she immerse herself in courses on defending computer networks against cyber attacks and malware used to harm them. She learned about network scams, viruses, worms, denial of service attacks, e-mail bombs, and how to buffer against overflow attacks. Two years later, she received her MS degree in computer science and...

Suddenly, her secure cell phone vibrated, interrupting her dream-like reminiscence. "Yes?"

It was a computerized voicemail from Jeannie. "This is an OT level alert. In several minutes, you will be replaced. We need you in the Bahamas." Then a click.

Addie looked out the picture window again, past the mixed woods of coconut palm and Caribbean pine. She worked for CBIF for several years without knowing it, all the time. She loved her Bahamian flag and what it stood for. She thought she was working for the U.S. DEA, prying into computer systems of drug smugglers and the illegal bankers who cleaned their money for them in Nassau. She covered as a cleaning lady for the *New Providence Cleaning Services, Inc.*

Then, one day she was "called home" to this unpretentious cottage at the end of a cul-de-sac inside the Conch Inn Resort. That's when she met General Morrison and another man she saw occasionally around Nassau, named Corey Pearson.

They told her she had been working for a secretive organization inside the U.S. Intelligence Community and that she had been helping them find narco-terrorist connections in the Bahamas. She didn't mind being deceived, for she loved her island nation and appreciated her scholarships to a higher education.

Drugs and terrorists bound for the U.S. were ruining the Bahamian culture and she would do anything to fight back. Besides, she sent a third of her salary back to her family on Andros. Addie learned that it was Corey Pearson who perused her Nicholl's Town and Andros High School records. He was searching for Bahamian school children who were gifted in math reasoning and problem-solving.

She recalled asking them, "I thought my scholarship was through a wealthy American who formed a fund called the Somerton Fund for Talent Development? It was set up to identify and offer high-achieving students in the Caribbean $50,000 to $150,000 scholarships per year in recognition for their expertise in Science, mathematics...anything outside the box."

She remembered the handsome man accompanying Morrison, named Corey Pearson, who told her the Somerton scholarship was a front financial organization...that it was spurious, but her education and diplomas were genuine.

She agreed to continue working for the mysterious organization, which was obviously embedded within the U.S. Intelligence Community (IC). After her consent, General Morrison and Corey Pearson assured her that her family on Andros would be taken care of if any need arose beyond what she could help them with. They were aware that she sent part of her income back to Andros to help her parents.

Addie heard an approaching car on the gravel driveway. Then, a knock on the cottage door. Another CBIF "housemaid" dressed in a similar pink work dress with a "Conch Inn Resort" insignia greeted her and handed her an envelope.

"Hi, Addie. Take my car back to your home in Key West. It's got everything you'll need in the trunk. You won't have to pack anything."

Addie switched car keys with the agent, then walked out of the cottage. In the car, she opened the envelope. Airline tickets to Nassau allowing her three hours before departure from the Key West Airport. Plenty of time. She drove down the gravel driveway past the row of cultivated allemande, bougainvillea and hibiscus and stopped to inspect the packet again before entering Route 1 to Key West. One sentence caught her eye: *You are to book into the Hibiscus Beach*

Inn upon arrival. Taxi driver will ID you by clothes you'll be wearing (laying on top of suitcase in trunk). Tomorrow at 1400-hours report to New Providence Cleaning Services, Inc. ...you will be briefed in detail on your mission... to infiltrate the office of the Bahamian Minister of Agriculture and plant audio bugs around his desk area and monitoring devices inside his computer and desk phone. General Morrison

Episode 21

Turks & Caicos honeytrap

Coral Gardens Beach
Providenciales, Turks and Caicos
(GPS: 21°47'07.5"N 72°12'16.2"W)

Dona Anani Guanikeyu was beautiful and she knew it. Still, she wasn't the least bit supercilious, due to her humble Tainos upbringing on Middle Caicos, the largest island in the Turks & Caicos chain. She sat at the Beach Café, a casual restaurant on Grace Bay listening to an American businessman tell her how wonderful he was.

A short while ago, he approached her while she strolled the adjacent thirteen-mile stretch of talcum-powder sand beach and said, "You're the most beautiful woman I've ever seen. Can I buy you a drink?" She smiled shyly and nodded OK.

So, there she sat, sipping a sweet Caribbean drink of mango and several other brightly-colored fruit mixtures to hide the deceptively generous amount of rum. She wanted a *Turks Head Stout* beer but her admirer insisted that he buy her a tropical drink. Dona was thankful that he dominated the conversation. She didn't like to speak of her deep cover unless it was necessary. It grew tiring when she had to lie about her classified career and life. But, that's what CBIF pays her to do...lie. Still, she enjoyed meeting visitors to Providenciales and learn about their lives in whatever country they came from. She gently stirred her rum drink while listening to this narcissistic man crow. At least he was devoted to her looks, in addition to himself.

Her beauty made men nervous and she thought it cute how he didn't stop talking. A pause of silence would have made him even more insecure, so he babbled on. Dona politely listened while the Grace Bay breeze gently carried the aroma of frangipani and pink hibiscus throughout the grounds of Coral Gardens.

Then, her secure cell phone vibrated. She opened it, pretending to read a text message. There was just a cryptic string of letters, numbers and shapes.

She interrupted the American. "You're a very interesting man, Mr. Smith...".

"You can call me Bill."

"OK, Bill. I enjoyed meeting and talking with you. Thanks for the drinks, too. Unfortunately, I have to get going. I just received a text message reminding me I have to get ready for an important business meeting. I've had so much fun talking with you that I forgot all about it."

Bill remained persistent, "How about we have dinner together at the Coyaba Restaurant? The blackened Mahi Mahi is to die for."

Dona finished her drink. "Well, Bill, you are so nice. Give me your telephone number and I'll call you if I get back in time."

He wrote his number down on a notepad, stuck it inside an envelope and handed it to her. "You are so beautiful. In case we never meet again...inside are free tickets for you to spend on yourself."

She thanked him again, rose from the table and glided out of the Beach Café. She was a half-inch under six feet tall and her long, black-satin hair tumbled around the knotted top of a semi-sheer lace swimsuit. The shirt coverup failed to conceal her bodily magnetism. Her long, golden-brown, tanned legs generated a stylish step that would rival a professional model's saunter down the runway. Bill and the other male patrons turned to view her one last time.

Upon entering her plush Coral Gardens condo, she hooked her secure cell phone to a portable scrambler and looked at the text message. The jumbled symbols reshuffled to read: *Home calling. CBIF at OT level. Carry-on briefcase switch at Budweiser Brew House at Miami International Airport, Concourse H. Open Bill's envelope. General Morrison*

Dona opened the envelope to find American Airline tickets to Nassau, Bahamas with a stop at Miami International (MIA). The flight departed in three hours from Providenciales International Airport. Instead of his phone number, Bill wrote "Good luck" on the note. Dona tossed the envelope on the kitchen table and cussed.

"Tickets to spend on myself...shit! I was looking forward to Mahi Mahi tonight."

Episode 22

An innocent victim

Great Abaco, a Bahamian out island
(GPS: 26°32'48.5"N 77°03'07.5"W)
Corey Pearson chugged down a cold Kalik beer at the outside patio Sunset Bar at the Conch Inn Marina in Marsh Harbor, the capital of Great Abaco Island. It tasted good in the 90-degree heat. He peered past a coconut palm into the Curly Tail Restaurant where, two days ago, Sidney Fowler ate his last breakfast before flying to Nassau.

A CBIF agent named Constance ran the Abaco safe house and worked across the street at Sappodilly's Bar. She told him that the barmaid at the Conch Inn Marina, named Shianna, was Fowler's younger sister. Thus, Corey chose to bed down at the Conch Inn. *No telling what little clue Shianna may reveal. She seems really down, depressed. Must have been real close to her brother. Why did Sidney Fowler tail me? What did he want to tell Darnell Ferguson? Who gunned him down on Parliament Square...and why? The answers lie somewhere here, on Abaco, along with the mystery to Duane Collier's abduction and murder*

"You want 'nuther Kalik, mistah?," the barmaid asked. "Sure, why not. You can call me Corey. What's your name?" "I be Shianna. You be the man studyin' our dolphin friends?"

Amazing how everyone knows quickly what everyone else is up to on these outer islands. "Yep. How did you know? I just got here."

"My aunt is da taxi lady who drove ya here from da airport. You say to her on the way what you do. Also, my boyfriend, he work at Cutter's where you rent the boat to do ya research. He tol' me he be busy pullin' out da old boat and motor you use years ago. Why you want that? Why don't ya want a new one?" Shianna asked.

Corey answered. "So the dolphin pod I studied will remember me." He didn't expect her to comprehend what he said.

"Oh…OK, Corey. Let me know when ya want 'nuther Kalik." The bereaved barmaid sat at the end barstool and stared wonderingly out into the turquoise and green waters of the Sea of Abaco. She seemed to be daydreaming…wishing for her older brother to return.

One of the waitresses stepped out of the Curly Tail Restaurant onto the patio. "I need two Goombay Smashes and one Yellow Bird." Shianna started to make the drinks, then began to sob. The waitress went behind the bar and hugged her.

"You poor lil' thing…your older brother be gone. He took so good care of ya."

Shianna said, "But, who eva want to kill him? Nobody hate him. He got nice job at da Abaco chicken farm. Nassau a bad place! Why he want to go there?"

The waitress replied, "I dunno why, hun. I serve him breakfast that mornin' before he fly out. He seem anxious 'bout somethin'… looked scared."

Shianna sobbed as she gathered the ingredients to build the exotic drinks. It was as if she were about to prepare a gourmet meal. While mixing the Gold Rum, Coconut Liqueur, and pineapple juice for the Goombay Smash, she retrieved coffee liquor, dark rum, and orange juice for the Yellow Bird. She continued on about her brother. "I know what you mean…the day before he go to Nassau, he out watchin' his Bahama Parrots south a' town. He always happy when he come back from dat, but not that day…somethin' he saw…I ask him if the feral cats ate mo' baby parrots, but he say no. I keep askin' him what upset him, but he not say anyting'. Then, suddenly he go buy airplane ticket to Nassau and go there dat same mornin' afta you serve him breakfast … and he get shot on Parliament Square."

Corey felt empathy watching Shianna suffer. *I hate it when the innocent become victims…wish I could tell her that whoever kidnapped Duane Collier probably killed her brother, and I will make certain they are exterminated. What upset Fowler so much while he was searching for the parrots? What did he see? It has to be linked to Duane Collier's abduction.*

The waitress hugged her again, placed the drinks on the tray and disappeared back into the restaurant. Shianna's boyfriend appeared and took over with the hugs. He looked at Corey over her shoulder. "Mistah Pearson, da old Boston Whaler you want…it be ready to go."

Corey thanked him, finished his drink and took a conch fritter off the plate Shianna set up for the patrons. *It's time to visit a pod of Spotted Dolphins in the Sea of Abaco. Will they remember me?*

Episode 23

The Beijing paradox

General Morrison waited for Hsin Chow's call on his secure phone. The Chinese operate a super-secret complex that eavesdrops on America's satellite-based military transmissions and on American home and business faxes, e-mails, and cell phones. When Corey Pearson began working for CBIF, he journeyed to Cuba to recruit assets who worked in Cuban hotels. A number of desk clerks were paid to monitor the hotel registers for a "hit list" of potential terrorists visiting Cuba.

Corey grew suspicious when large numbers of names like Yao Lee, Yo-Yo Quan, and Sin Ling suddenly booked in to hotels in Havana. Satellite imagery surveillance revealed a Chinese electronic espionage facility was being built…it literally sprang up in two weeks. In return, Beijing gave the Cuban government electronic countermeasures that blocked *Radio Marti* from transmitting pro-U.S. radio and TV broadcasts into Cuba from Miami.

A Chinese man named Hsin Chow registered at the Sofitel Sevilla hotel in downtown Havana. Corey discovered that he had an only son attending MIT in the states. In addition, his wife visits him in Cuba several times per year.

CBIF targeted Chow for explicable reasons, so Morrison had Corey register at the Sofitel Sevilla, posing as a French businessman. He "accidentally" bumped into Chow at the hotel's pool and fitness center. After several casual conversations, Corey laid out detailed plans on how Chow and his wife could defect to the U.S. when she came to visit him from China.

The spymaster assured Chow that CBIF's exfiltration team would fly them clandestinely to the U.S. and unite them with their son. The family would be given top-secret clearances, new identities, and $2 million cash. Chow was a priceless target for CBIF: a Chinese engineer who was a senior member of their SIGINT program. He was no less a genius and the Chinese surveillance satellites operating from Cuba were personally designed and built by him.

Upon defecting, CBIF planned to employ him as their mole at the National Geospatial-Intelligence Agency (NGA) in Washington, D.C. Chow's expertise in satellite surveillance technology led China to be a SIGINT leader in the Asia/Pacific region. He created dozens of SIGINT ground stations in mainland China which monitored signals from U.S. military units in the region. Before coming to Cuba, Chow devised a SIGINT operation at Hainan Island that monitored U.S. naval maneuvers in the South China Sea. It also eavesdropped-in on international communications satellites from SATCOM intercept facilities.

Hsin Chow was well known by CIA station chiefs throughout Asia, so when Corey identified him when he arrived in Cuba, General Morrison directed Corey to target and recruit him.

At the elegant, century-old hotel, Corey spent several weeks ingratiating Hsin Chow during poolside conversations, elegant dinners, and at the tavern sipping *Cerveceria La Tropicals*. One day, while they admired the photographic gallery lining the walls in the ceramic-tiled lobby, Chow turned to Cory and whispered, "These photos depict a Cuba with a past and present. My China is a communist dictatorship masquerading as a democracy. My son told me in private he no longer wants to return to China, even though he must. He is also in love with a fellow MIT student and they want to marry someday. You showed me a most detailed plan to get my wife and I out of Cuba and into the United States where we can begin a new life. I will do it."

Morrison recalled those earlier days when he realized Corey had the talent to become a first-class case officer for CBIF. Those were tumultuous times. True, there were terrorist attacks inside the U.S., but not at the intimidating level of today. Despite increased attacks by homegrown, radicalized U.S. "citizens", the ACLU and other civil liberties groups handcuffed law enforcement's attempts to ferret out diehard Islamic sleeper cells lurking in America's heartland.

How incredibly paradoxical, he thought. CBIF recruited Chow, who operated only a stone's throw away in Cuba, to conduct unrestricted electronic surveillance on America and share it with CBIF, since the CIA and NSA were not permitted to do so. CBIF actually outsourced domestic spying to China! He remembered planning out the venture with Corey, who returned to Cuba under the same deep cover to recruit Chow and to work out the details of the outsourcing. Corey and Morrison felt "What the heck!" Chow was already spying on the U.S. with greater fervor than the U.S. Intelligence Community was allowed to do, so why not have him spy FOR us, not ON us? The plan worked out well. Whenever Chow stumbled upon a homegrown terrorist in the U.S. contacting his jihadist cohorts in the Middle East to fine-tune their next attack plan, Chow would relay the intercept to Morrison at CBIF HQ in Key West.

The incongruity struck Morrison as somewhat comical. He smiled as he awaited Chow's call. He couldn't believe it was happening. Due to the ACLU lawsuits against domestic warrantless surveillance, CBIF actually farmed out the job to communist China's electronic spying facility near Bejucal, a small town south of Havana. Chow directed his technicians to reprogram the orbiting satellites and ground-based, state-of-the art signals intelligence hardware to pick up messages sent out from the U.S. to radical Islamic-friendly countries. CBIF had communist China spying for America.

In those earlier days of fighting radical Islam, Uncle Sam continued along a politically-correct but dangerous, self-governing, anti-racial profiling, anti-warrantless-snooping pathway to democratic preservation.

The top security telephone sounded. The general picked it up. "Morrison here."

A moment passed while the encryption algorithm transformed a scrambled voice into intelligible speech.

"It's me…Hsin Chow."

Episode 24

Dolphin encounter

The Dolphins' Way, In me
Aspirations of the living sea
The dolphins do move within me
The aura of their soul, I feel deep down
To be in the water and not on ground

Sifting through the ocean, an expressing show
Communication of a song and a blow
Protecting even those not of their kind
They ask nothing in return, they do not mind

The most gracious and unselfish of all that wander
I wish to swim with them, nothing could be fonder
The dolphins mean so much to me, you see
I need to thank them, for showing us how to be

Author unknown

Sea of Abaco
Abaco Island, Bahamas
(GPS: 26°31'59.6"N 77°00'29.1"W)
It was déjà vu to Corey as the restored, seventeen-foot Boston
Whaler cut through the Sea of Abaco. He headed southeast from
the Conch Inn Marina and stayed in fifteen feet of water to avoid the

shoals around Lubbers Quarters Cay. Upon reaching the southern tip of Lubbers, he slowed to a steady cruising speed of eight knots, a comfortable speed for spotted dolphins. He pointed the bow to SSW at 206 degrees M by 3.47 degrees NM and started the first leg of the triangular course...the same speed and route he used over a decade ago

I've got to stop thinking in human terms and start thinking like a dolphin. They live in an audio world...all our submarine technology is based on dolphin sonar. Our Navy guys can recognize a particular Russian sub by the sound imprint of its engine. The dolphins once pictured this same boat, with the same Mercury prop exhaust system sound, the same Verado 200 seventeen-foot Boston Whaler thumping sound as its hull cut through the waves...the same RPM's rhythmic hum at the same eight miles per hour cruising speed...the same triangular course. All sounds are turned into a visual image in a dolphin's large brain. I hope it arouses some stored memory traces. Will the pod recognize the boat and come to me...as they did a decade ago? Corey reached into a duffle bag and took out a digital camera equipped with 70-300mm zoom lenses and an underwater videography to record them underwater. He would take photos of the dolphin dorsal fins and tails and compare them with over 127 photos in an album he assembled years ago, with Constance.

General Morrison made sure the research package was stuffed inside his carry-on luggage before departing the Key West International Airport. It had photos and life histories of each member of the pod. The underwater video camera was equipped with a hydrophone to record their communications and sounding behaviors. Luckily, his prior dolphin study took place offshore to the newly-built Abaco Poultry, LTD, where the unfortunate Sidney Fowler worked. He planned to take photos of the shoreline and grounds for General Morrison's photographic interpreters to peruse. *This is great cover. I'll drop off the digital photos of the operation's dock area and shoreline and slip them to Constance at Sapodilly's. She'll download them at the safe house and e-mail them to Pinkston for a burst transmission to Morrison*

To the west was the 110-mile shoreline of Great Abaco Island. To the east was Tilloo Cay, one of dozens of cays lining Abaco's eastern coast. The cays protected the Sea of Abaco from the turbulent Atlantic Ocean. He stared down through the gin-colored water to the white, sandy bottom below. Patch reefs of colorful hard and soft corals slowly passed underneath, like oasis' in a vast sand desert. The red, yellow, green and blue sea fans and golden elkhorn coral grew from the hard-coral formations in the warm waters.

Corey knew that on the other side of the string of cays, the shallow reefs and sand flats abruptly end at a sheer drop off into 3,000 feet of water. It was like an underwater Grand Canyon, where the ocean current creates an eddy effect and water is pushed over the lip of the abyss, causing fish to congregate. The dolphins hunt along the chasm during the night and retreat to find shelter in the shallow Sea of Abaco during the day where the still waters and clear bottom enhances their sonar capabilities. They send out sonar and if nothing comes back, they know it's a safe place to rest and play.

Corey eyed the southern tip of Tilloo Cay and noticed the water rapidly growing shallow. *That would be the Tilloo Bank that extends west into the Sea of Abaco for two miles. Now for the second leg of my triangle. It'll bring me close to the Abaco Poultry, LTD shoreline.*

He turned due north. The huge chicken operation was directly west of his position. There was a large dock area and groves of thick Caribbean pine and palmetto concealed most of the buildings, including a large, stone mansion. Still cruising at eight knots, he reached for the digital camera and took shots with the zoom lens.

After several minutes, he took several hundred shots of the entire shoreline. The Bimini Top offered sun protection, but the heat bore down intensely. Corey wiped his sweaty brow and reached into the cooler for an icy can of Mango juice to quench his thirst while scanning the distant waters for signs of pod activity.

Then, he saw them. About 200 yards off the starboard bow. Half a dozen white breaks in the water, then more appeared. *They're staying visible, just under the surface. OK...they spotted me and seem interested. I won't rush over... must deal with them on their own terms. If they didn't want me to see them, they'd disappear, or never would have showed.*

Corey kept the boat on course. He recalled how the pod loved to play with this same boat years ago. It was like a magnet that drew them; he never needed to artificially feed them.

Suddenly, a large spotted dolphin leaped high into the air and landed on its back, making a cannonball splash. Then, the pod disappeared. In a few moments, they covered the distance underwater and appeared by the bow.

Just as he did a decade ago, Corey nudged the throttle to a faster speed. *I know what they want to do. Let's go surfing!* Several large adults started surfing atop the water thrust forward by the bow. Their tail fins weren't moving...they just relaxed and rode the artificial wave. He noticed a right tail fin with a shark bite gash. *My gad...it's 'Chop Tail'!* He grabbed the research packet and quickly scanned through the photos until coming to 'Chop Tail's' life history. At the time of the photo, he was estimated to be five years old, which would make him at least fifteen-years-old now.

Soon, half the pod members surfed on both the starboard and port sides. More congregated behind and began surfing in the wake. Some leaped out of the wake and did cartwheels and somersaults. *Yes! It's playtime.* He turned the boat in a circle, making the wake even bigger. Then, he slowed the boat down and stopped it, idling in the water. *Must be over forty of them! The pod's grown in size If they keep moving, they're not ready to play. I won't jump in yet...just let them check me out a while longer. If they come closer to me, that means they want to interact. Holy shit...'Chop Tail' is eyeing me from the water...he's swimming up to the boat... it's time to jump in.*

Even a protective mother dolphin brought her baby up to the boat for a curious look. Corey slowly lowered the anchor so not to spook them. He slipped on his mask, fins and snorkel, grabbed the underwater video camera and gently slipped into the water.

The older dolphins immediately drew near, albeit methodically and slowly. He videotaped them for identification of marks to compare with those in the photo album. Younger spotted dolphins kept in the distance until more trust was developed. The immature ones remain spotless, but upon reaching adolescence they gain more spots each year until the spots fuse and run together.

The adults eyed him from only four feet away. Corey saw in the distance the wary mothers, who guided their babies away to a safe distance. *Strange how the mothers will bring their babies up to the boat while I'm in it, but push them away once I slip into the water... kind of like deer watching you while you're in a car...but bolt as soon as the door opens*

Corey kept vertical in the water and submerged five feet. He remembered how the pod loved it when he went underwater. Now, the adolescents joined the older adults in observing him. He could hear the clicking and buzzing sounds of their sonar. A few sped away and returned with more pod members. *They're visualizing my heart beat... good grief! A few are by my left leg using their sonar to get a visual where the metal plate was put in. I can't believe the social interaction! They ran off to tell their friends...now their friends are back with them...they went right back to my left knee to get a sonar picture of the plate. I can hear them saying, "Hey, check out this dude's left knee." Incredible intelligence! I remember when I set up the Abaco safe house with Constance after I met her at Sapodilly's and recruited her years ago. She introduced me to this pod so I could conduct dolphin research as a cover. She hadn't been feeling well and had stomach cramps and fatigue. Constance taught me how to attract and interact with the dolphins. When we snorkeled, the pod members kept clicking their sonar at her belly. I remember laughing when several days later she went to the island doctor because the fatigue and headaches grew worse, only to find out she was pregnant...the dolphins knew before she did!*

When Corey surfaced, the free-roaming ocean mammals stuck their heads out of the water and murmured amusing noises to him. When he submerged again and spun around and floated upside down, they mimicked his every move. He swam in circles on the surface...so did they. When he shouted out on the surface, "Hello all you guys and gals!", they stuck their heads up all around him and chortled back. Some caught fish and played with them like a cat with a mouse, then returned to proudly show their snacks to him before gulping them down.

Corey frolicked with them for twenty minutes before noticing that he drifted far from the boat and the depth grew shallower. Suddenly, the pod pulled away from him, as if coaxing him to follow them in another direction. For some reason, they didn't want him to proceed. He gazed in the direction they seemingly did not want him to go and spotted a large blue hole on the sandy bottom a hundred feet away. He looked back at the dolphins...they had suddenly vanished. *A bad sign! Too rapid a departure. Why didn't I listened to them...they were coaxing me to follow them away from here, but why? This area around the Blue Hole made them uncomfortable...got to get back to the boat. I remember Constance warning me about this. To aliens visiting earth, all cities would look the same. They couldn't distinguish safe from unsafe neighborhoods. For reasons we don't know, there are some ocean areas dolphins feel safe to play in and some where they don't...even though humans can't tell the difference. I'm an alien in their world and don't want to run into whatever danger they sense.*

Corey began swimming away, looking quickly behind him as he did so. Then, he saw it. At first it looked like a huge torpedo coming straight at him. He dove to the sandy bottom and hid in the turtle grass. The mass of silver sped overhead just below the surface; it was thousands of silversides and mullet fish fleeing from the blue hole. He had seen them tranquilly feeding along the edge moments before. *Silversides ban together in a tight ball when they're frightened and race away. What frightened them!?*

The answer came too soon. As he rose from the sea grass beds, a huge shark rose from the blue hole and slowly but steadily headed straight for him. Corey saw the dark stripes on its gray back and sides...*tiger shark! Holy shit... it's nineteen feet long!* He chose to swim away from its path. *These monsters are scavengers and can't see well...throw a garbage can full of rubbish in front of one and it'll tear the metal to shreds and eat the garbage. I'll swim directly away. Hope it doesn't turn with me. Shit! Years ago, Operation Salt Flamingo on the out island of Little Inagua...last time I saw a tiger shark...it cut a large sea turtle in half with its serrated, cockscomb-shaped teeth.*

Corey swam sixty feet to the right, took a huge breath and submerged into a clump of turtle grass and held on. Mother Nature furnished the ill-sighted beast with multifarious equipment that atoned for its poor vision. It had little difficulty detecting Corey in the grassy sanctuary.

Olfactory sacs under the snout guided the beast along his scent trail to the spot where he first saw it rise out of the blue hole. It paused and circled slowly while Corey held on tighter to the clump of sea grass and hugged the sandy bottom. *I can hold my breath for about two minutes longer... then I've got to surface* His heart pounded harder. *I know this monster can sense vibrations...spear fishermen have been killed by them because the speared fish quiver and attract tigers from a long way off. I feel my heart pounding...can he, too? I hope not*

Unfortunately, Corey's brain was throbbing as intensely as his heart. Cortically, he was super-excited...desperately trying to formulate a mental game plan to win over the approaching beast. Adrenalin flowed. These human qualities, which put him on top in past encounters with terrorists, proved disadvantageous in the undersea world. He lay still. *In thirty seconds, I'll have to surface for air!*

The shark stopped its gyratory behavior and hovered, as if floating in space, facing Corey's hideaway. A feeling of helplessness overcame him as he peered at the wide mouth, broad nose and huge, barrel chest. His head and heart pulsated even more...*I've become a measly piece of protein at the base of Mother Nature's food chain.*

The motionless beast evaluated the minuscule feedback. Its lateral line sensed the minute vibrations emitted from Corey's throbbing cardiovascular system and leisurely glided toward him. It passed on the right of his sanctuary, then paused several yards away. *Got to stay still...my lungs are going to burst...need air!*

The tiger shark's electrosensory system detected the weak bioelectric aura emanating from Corey's stimulated brain. It spun around and bore down directly at him. Corey leaped from the shallows and surfaced, gasping for air. He began a fifty-yard freestyle race toward the Boston Whaler. *Should I ditch my underwater video camera? It's slowing me down...no...I can use it as a shield.*

The beast glided to his side, veered in quickly and prodded him with its snout. He slammed his fist down atop its immense head. The station wagon-sized shark veered away slowly but began circling as Corey hammered his flippers into the water. It approached from behind. Corey stopped. From an arm's-length away, the beast lunged.

He thrust the video housing into its jaws. The predator sheared the hard-plastic handle completely off the frame, then leisurely backed up and began circling again.

Corey continued his frantic swim to the boat. His index finger was cut, blood oozed out. *It bumped me...then lunged...one small bite... this monster's toying with me...sizing me up for a meal...it can swallow half of me and the camera in one bite.*

The heretofore sluggish shark ended its slow circling and attacked with amazing speed. Corey tucked his legs into his chest. He held the underwater camcorder and what was left of the housing up to his chest in defense. *Looks like Mother Nature is going to win this battle.*

Out of the blue, silvery forms streaked in from the left. It was 'Chop Tail' and three other adult males, plus four adolescents from the pod. The tiger shark cut short its final assault and faced-off with them. The eight dolphins rocketed over and under the beast.

Loud, threatening echolocation-bursts pierced the quiet waters. Clicking reverberations grew louder and rose to an intimidating crescendo. Corey felt like he was being scoured with a giant Geiger counter

The shark grew confused as the sonar blasts overwhelmed its keen sensory systems. Its fervor to devour Corey switched to a self-preservation mode. *Gotta use this opportunity to escape...I'll probably get only one chance. The pod resembles a SWAT team entering a room of an armed suspect...throwing in flash grenades to confuse him...then attacking*

The dolphins turned and charged. One adult feigned an attack on the shark's right side. The beast swiveled around to bite, leaving its left side vulnerable. 'Chop Tail' used echolocation to "see" the air spaces of the shark's lungs and cartilaginous rib cage, then rammed its snout into the exposed side. The hit was so hard that the two-ton predator bowed into a boomerang shape. The adolescents stayed a safe distance away, but besieged the shark's auditory senses with a cacophony of clicks, whistles and buzzes.

Corey stopped swimming away and stopped to witness the co-ordinated assault. He felt out of harm's way. Another adult dolphin slammed into the shark's left gill slits that provide oxygen directly to the eyes and brain. The beleaguered predator wheeled around to grasp the attacker, but to no avail.

Instantaneously, 'Chop Tail' smashed into the right gill slits while another adult simultaneously bashed into the Tiger's soft underbelly. The monster's eyes turned white, then it retreated back towards the direction of the blue hole. The mêlée was over in thirty seconds. As the defeated beast glided away on a tilt, the emboldened adolescents pursued it while the adults remained close to Corey.

'Chop Tail' approached and quietly eyed him, displaying an aura of calm and confidence. It positioned its snout a foot away and emitted a soft click and droning purr. Corey felt its sonar permeate his skin. His bones and muscles quivered like a tympanic membrane. He reached his arm out toward the dolphin's head...it didn't retreat. *My savior...I owe you my life. Maybe you were protecting the babies in your pod...maybe your intent was to save my life...maybe you remembered the times we had years ago...the sonar picture of the boat... of me...it never left your memory...I wouldn't be here right now if it weren't for you*

Corey's savior edged closer and made contact with his outstretched hand. A few unspoken moments passed, then 'Chop Tail' backed away and clicked. The adolescents returned from hassling the wounded beast. Corey swam toward the boat while the dolphins accompanied him.

Upon reaching the Boston Whaler, he paused and stared at them in silence. Eight dolphin heads protruded out of the water around him, watching in silence. A poem came to mind. *Protecting even those not of their kind...they ask nothing in return...they do not mind.* It was a surreal experience. He lifted his body over the gunwale and flopped onto the deck, then stood up to look out at his friends...they were gone.

Episode 25

Tiki Hut lunch

The Bahamas can get prickly hot during July, even with a gentle ocean breeze. Corey remained slightly shaken from yesterday's tiger shark nightmare, but he managed to chuckle after the astringently humorous episode in his life as a CBIF operations officer. Here he sat at the Tiki Hut, drinking a Kalik beer while waiting for Dillon to prepare his lunch of land crabs and rice.

A dozen times he was in life-threatening situations but avoided death through his own cunning. He'd been stabbed once and shot twice, but managed to survive. *Funny how life's events turn out. I've got bullet scars in my leg and forearm, a knife scar in my upper back, and a scrap of metal in my knee…and here I am, still alive. I just faced certain death, without backup…and along came the Lone Ranger on his white horse to save me…my savior, 'Chop Tail', with his pod of spotted dolphins!*

Dillon interrupted his thoughts. "I raise dees crabs in my own backyard. Pick 'em up along the road everywhere I go and toss 'em in da back of my pickup. Feed 'em coconut and table scraps. Before I bring 'em down heah, I get dem ready at home. I take off da claws and crack 'em with a mallet, den pull da bodies out from da back of the shell. Den, I scrape the fat off the da meat and from inside shell too." "Just like you did a decade ago, Dillon. It was my favorite meal then and still is now."

"Well, I thank ya, Corey. Ya know the trick? I prepare it at home, da night befo'. I heat big pot o' bacon, onion and celery, add tomata paste and mix it all together... da crab fat, claws and bodies with salt, pepper and thyme. Den, I pour in water, den da rice... presto! Twenty minute later it be done. I let it cool den put in refrig. Next day, I bring it heah and simply warm it up. Make it day before like dat and it got much more flavor."

It felt comfortable on the floating bar. The light wind blowing off the Sea of Abaco cooled the place a bit. The shade of the thatched palm roof and cold Kalik helped, too. Corey glanced out from the bar-stool beyond the open deck to the three sets of tables under luridly-colored umbrellas.

The table with the purple umbrella was still there, by the corner. That's where he first met Danielle. He envisaged both of them sitting there... drinking, laughing, pretending they weren't working coun-terintelligence for CBIF. *I still feel it! The love, the passion...then her murder. "Murder"... "homicide"..."possibly a serial killer or a home burglary gone awry" according to the police report. No clues, no leads to believe otherwise... except nothing was stolen from our house. Just the beaten-up body of Danielle lying face down in the living room*

"You awright, mon?" Dillon laid out a large plate of land crab, rice and Bahamian mac & cheese in front of him. "You didn't hear me ask ya if ya wanted the mac and cheese. It's on da house. For a second dere, you look like you was someplace else."

"I was. Just thinking of old times".

"I know what ya thinkin' 'bout. You was starin' at da purple um-brella table. Dat's where ya first met dat beautiful gal named Danielle. Every time you two come heah, you always sat at dat table under da same umbrella".

"Right on, Dillon. You're psychic...reading my mind."

"Sad thing dat happen to her. When I hear it on da news, I cry for ya, Corey. I jus' dunno know how someone can do stuff like dat to anotha human bein', specially to a gal like dat Danielle…so nice and sweet and all."

If you only knew what Danielle did…what I still do…the risks we took, the enemies we made. Play your alias to Dillon, just like you did to the Severna Park Police "I'm still not over it. There are serial rapist/ killers out there, Dillon. Danielle was at home, getting ready to fly back here to help me finish the dolphin research project. They still have no leads. The killer was good at what he did. No fingerprints, semen, hair follicles anywhere, so sign of struggle. Must have knocked her out with a stun gun."

"Well, I be sorry dat I prod into ya life. Ya always welcome heah, Corey. You jus' rememba dat."

A small skiff with two spiny lobster fishermen pulled up alongside the Tiki Hut. "Hey Dillon, look what we got for ya!" They raised a large screen cage with several dozen spiny lobsters inside, *crawfish* as the Bahamians call them. Dillon grabbed an old-fashioned kitchen scale and placed it on the deck railing.

As the fishermen handed up each lobster to him, Dillon quickly placed it on the scale plate, scratched down the weight, then tossed it into a large tub. At the Tiki Hut, tourists loved to choose their own dinner lobsters from the tub. Maybe it reminded them of some plush seafood restaurant in Maine. The local patrons could care less, whatever Dillon served them was always good enough.

Corey revered the Bahamian ability to reap out a living from the sea and land as he enjoyed another bite of succulent white land crab. A Bob Marley tune played from the kitchen area, causing his thoughts to bound back and reexamine the past… a yesterday without closure that still haunts him today. *Danielle enjoyed listening to reggae when in the Caribbean, especially Bob Marley. General Morrison recruited her directly out of the Department of Energy. She was a neophyte analyst at the DOE's Office of Intelligence and Counterintelligence. Morrison probably recruited her for her knowledge of nuclear proliferation. He assigned us to work together for good reason- she had the technical know-how...I had the spy tradecraft and counterintelligence savvy. Our assigned rendezvous was here...at the Tiki Hut...we sat at the table under the loud, purple umbrella. She told me how she collected and analyzed information about nuclear proliferation at DOE. I enjoyed discussing nuclear proliferation with her. She never told me why Morrison recruited her directly into CBIF and assigned her to work with me. Was there intelligence about terrorists using the Caribbean Basin as a path to smuggle nuclear material into the U.S.?*

Corey's reflections were interrupted by Dillon bickering over a price for the crawfish. "These look meaty 'nough. How 'bout fifteen dollars each?"

"How 'bout eighteen?," the fishermen yelled back.

Dillon offered them a deal they couldn't turn down. "Nope. Fifteen dollars firm...I'll buy all o' dem right now and pay ya $360 cash... right now!"

The fishermen smiled, "Dat be a positive! Let's finish up wid da weighin' in."

Corey returned to his ruminations. *Danielle's murder was too calculating, too professional. Burglars and killers make mistakes. Our home in Severna Park had layers of surveillance and security equipment installed, thanks to Morrison. The security cameras linked up to our TV, touch screen, iPhone, laptop computer...and to CBIF counterintelligence as well. Morrison, himself, could watch our property on his computer or cell phone from anywhere around the globe. Still, they slipped into the house undetected. The outside infrared cameras picked up nothing in the night, the wireless electronic dead bolt locks on the doors and windows weren't tampered with. Even the motion and heat sensors didn't pick up anything. If anyone was stalking outside or inside the house, their movements would have set them off... email and cell SMS alert text messages would automatically be sent out to me here in the Bahamas and to CBIF counterintelligence. But... nothing. No, a burglar or serial killer didn't enter the house and torture*

Danielle that night. I don't know the motive behind her gruesome murder, but it's connected to what we do. I'll find the connection, eventually, and...

The spiny lobster fishermen pushed away from the dock and yelled up to Dillon, "By da way, some dude from Albury Ferry tell us while we out in da Sea of Abaco dat the other ferry goin' from Guana Cay to Conch Inn find a tiger shark mostly dead on da water. Had fight wid dolphins...de dolphins won. Dey tie rope 'round its tail and tow it in. It hangin' by the Conch Inn dock. Da Albury Ferry man, he say a man be inside da tiger. Police all down dere investigatin' as we speak!"

"Yo ma! Naw, I believe ya." Dillon turned to Corey, "Corey, did ya heah dat? A tiger...." He stopped short, for Corey's place at the bar was empty, only a half-eaten meal and twenty-dollar bill wedged under the Kalik bottle remained.

Dillon shook his head. "Dat Corey. He always be in some kind a hurry."

Pandemonium set in on the dock at the Conch Inn Marina. A continual line of curious onlookers flowed in from Bay Street onto the large dock area. Royal Bahamian Police Force (RBPF) constables tried to conduct crowd control. It was nearly impossible to keep onlookers away as they performed their investigation. Corey squeezed through the throng, earning a couple petulant remarks.

Finally, he made it up to the front. The RBPF sequestered the dockmaster's boom and hoisted the mortally-wounded monster by the jaws to the boom's full extension of seventeen feet. Still, the tail and lower-stomach lay on the dock. It had to be over twenty feet in length. The two-piece boom had a recommended maximum of 2,400 pounds and the constables were worried it may snap and collapse on the crowd. The tiger shark must have weighed 3,000 pounds.

More RBPF constables arrived and began urging and prodding the crowd to move back. Corey took advantage of the commotion and advanced past them, pretending to return to his boat docked further down. He turned and snuck up behind a large trash bin to within eight feet of the boom. *It's the same monster that attacked me!* Large abrasions and welts were visible on the gill slits and stomach area where 'Chop Tail' and the other adult dolphins walloped it with their snouts. A doctor arrived from the local medical clinic and several ambulance personnel rolled a gurney onto the dock. Corey edged closer as the constables gently pulled the human corpse from the stomach. It was the upper torso- head, shoulders, chest, stomach and half a pelvis... all encased in a wetsuit. The hips and legs were absent. The constables stood by, snapping photos as the doctor put on latex gloves and gently wiped the stomach innards off the victim's face with antiseptic towelettes.

After the dolphin attack, the shark's digestive system pretty much shut down, leaving the face well-preserved. Corey crept closer and got a better look. His knees felt numb and he eased back onto a nearby bench. His eyes watered, a teardrop rolled down his cheek. *The light brown hair...the high cheek bones...the squared chin...it's Duane ... Duane Collier*

Episode 26

Meeting evil on the GAH

CBIF Safe House
Outside Marsh Harbor,
Abaco, Bahamas

Corey sat on the front porch of the Abaco safe house, waiting for Constance to finish her shift at Sapodilly's. He pondered over what his next move should be.

It was a single-level duplex with a large yard complete with a thick growth of tropical foliage. While eating a slice of sweet Bahamian bread with sea-grape jam spread over it, he gazed over the railing lined with empty conch shells. Constance loved gardening and the landscaping complemented her deep cover as owner of an outfit created by CBIF named *Natural World of Abaco*. A hedge of sea grapes full of dark-purple grapes lined the eastern boundary. *I wonder if Constance used them to make this sea-grape jam I found in her refrigerator? Tastes good on the bread. Probably so...she most likely baked the sweet Bahamian bread, too.*

Corey enjoyed the tranquility. He hadn't slept since seeing Duane's remains inside the shark's stomach. Twelve years ago, he recruited Constance while setting up the Abaco safe house. The duplex was suitable for hiding an agent or a recruited asset who was in danger and needed protection until CBIF's exfiltration team arrived. Surveillance equipment and firearms were locked in a state-of-the-art fingerprint electronic safe. Water was supplied from rain channeled off the roof into a 13,000-gallon cistern.

Duane Collier's body must be with Dr. Slesman by now. I hope Constance gets back from Sapodilly's soon...got to case out the area where Sidney Fowler hikes in the Parrot Preserve...it's close to Abaco Poultry, LTD ...I'll wager he witnessed Duane Collier's murder

Corey tasted the sweet bread and sea-grape jam. It was some rough and sleepless twenty-four hours. Collier's torso was removed from the tiger's huge stomach and the ambulance crew transported it to Marsh Harbor. He immediately contacted General Morrison on the secure phone, who in turn notified Deputy Commander Ellison Rolle of the RBPF in Nassau. Then, Corey contacted the consular at the U.S. Embassy in Nassau, telling him that CBIF would cover the cost for disposition of the remains and also notify Duane's family members.

In most cases, returning a body to the U.S. from the Bahamas is an expensive and lengthy process, but the U.S. consular and Rolle made sure the red tape didn't get in the way. Deputy Commander Rolle contacted Abaco constable Cecil Turnquest and told him that Corey Pearson was in charge of the corpse and to honor whatever he requested.

Corey had an ambulance transport the body to Marsh Harbor Airport where a waiting helicopter immediately packed it in ice. Collier's body was flown to Rand Memorial Hospital in Freeport, where the resident doctor prepared an official death certificate and faxed it to the U.S. consular in Nassau who used it to produce a *Report of Death* document. Normally, this official document is for- warded to next of kin in the U.S. for estate and insurance matters. Instead, the consular locked it in his private wall safe.

After the official paperwork was properly falsified and filed away at the hospital, police station, and U.S embassy in Nassau, Corey drove to Sapodilly's Bar in Marsh Harbor and told Constance to come directly home to the safe house, where he would be waiting. He planned to survey the 20,000-acre Abaco National Park and par- rot reserve where the late Sidney Fowler had witnessed something awful…probably the slaughter of Duane Collier. A Land Rover with *Natural World of Abaco* inscribed on the sides pulled into the gravel and coral driveway. It was Constance, his tour guide to the parrot preserve, which borders Abaco, Poultry, LTD.

FBI Forensic Lab Quantico, Virginia

Being the central area where packaged evidence from hundreds of law enforcement agencies arrives daily, the Evidence Control Unit (ECU) in the FBI's forensic lab was always busy, in a hectic sort of way. Dr. Slesman received a call on his secure cell phone, instructing him to be there at 1500 hours sharp with the rest of his team. They were all there by 1450 hours, waiting.

Slesman didn't know exactly who he worked for, but deduced it was some highly-classified, secret sector within the U.S. Intelligence Community (IC) that had priority over all else that came into the FBI's forensic lab. The message said that an agent was killed in a shark attack and he was instructed to determine if any foul play occurred. As he waited for the corpse to arrive, he reflected on how he became involved with his enigmatic employer.

Slesman had a long-standing reputation as being a magnanimous physician. Adopted by an elderly couple at age nine, he witnessed his guardians age and succumb to arthritis and heart disease. They both died in a nursing home during his senior year in high school. A brilliant student, he never forgot how their life's savings disappeared for nursing home care and insurance co-pays. He was determined to become a doctor, something his kind guardians always wanted him to be.

Finishing medical school a year early on a gratuitous scholarship, he began practicing medicine three days a week at the Detroit Medical Center (DMC) and sacrificed four days of his free time per week to work in inner-city Detroit where he treated elderly and poor patients at a free clinic. Two other doctors he befriended at the DMC volunteered their time, one day a week each, at the free clinic to help him out. Their fee was twenty dollars per visit, often waived. Dr.

Slesman's patient roster soon grew to over 1,200 at the clinic alone, not including his heavy load at the DMC. Low income people, the homeless, HIV patients, and quite a few Arab and Middle Eastern Americans, who number a half million in the Detroit area, benefited from his devotion and care.

A bachelor in his early thirties, he worked tirelessly and often slept overnight at the clinic, too tired to drive home to his comfy apartment. Things were going well for him and he earned the nickname "Father Teresa" by his fellow medical doctors at the DMC. As the years progressed, he befriended many of the Syrian, Lebanese, Iraqi, Palestinian, Jordanian, and Yemenis families who received his care at the free clinic. He learned that immigrants from the twenty-two Arab countries around the world share a common history, language and culture, but grew more diverse after living in the U.S. for a while. Many of his Muslim patients were not Arabs and not all of his Arab patients were Muslims, and the grandparents of quite a few arrived in Detroit in the late 1800's and early 1900's.

As the community began to trust him, he was invited into homes of Arabs who were Christians and members of catholic, protestant, and Methodist churches. He ate pork and drank wine with them at dinner. Even the more devoted muslims invited him into their households and he graciously ate Ramadan Kofta and Tandoori-style chicken along with them, minus the alcohol.

For a decade, Dr. Slesman held fast to his compassionate but exigent schedule. Unfortunately, Congress failed miserably to remedy the costs of Medicare and his reimbursements were cut by half. His liability insurance premiums quadrupled from $40,000 to over $160,000 per year despite never having a lawsuit filed against him at the DMC or free clinic. The salaries and health benefits he paid to the two RN's, three LPN's, and secretary at the free clinic also increased.

The coup de grace occurred one day at the Detroit Medical Center, when a lawsuit was filed against him by a patient's family who were overly-zealous to sue anyone. Despite the fact that the case was dismissed as frivolous, his malpractice insurance company increased his premium even more, simply because a suit was filed against him.

Despite his good intentions, it grew difficult to provide quality care to the families seeking medical care at the free clinic. He learned from his deceased adoptive mother that charity begins at home. She taught elementary school in Columbus, Ohio and her classes were mostly poor, inner-city black children and immigrant children from Somalia. Because of severe school budget cuts, she spent a third of her meager paycheck for proper instructional equipment. Dr. Slesman never forgot the lesson he learned from her: In charity, there is no excess, for true charity seeks needs, not reasons.

Despite his dedication, Dr. Slesman could no longer afford to operate the free clinic for his low-income patrons with zero or derisory health care coverage. He was forced to cut back services and let go half his staff.

His doctor friends from the DMC left, since their costs of operations increased as well. Things looked bleak until a man appeared at the clinic late one night while Dr. Slesman was locking up after an especially long and tiresome workday. The stranger introduced himself, stating that he understood the predicament the clinic was in and thought he could be of some help.

The next half-hour discussion changed Dr. Slesman's life. The abstruse man told him that he represented an organization that would acquire a government grant to fund the clinic $1.5 million a year for at least ten years. The funds would be earmarked for daily operations and to enhance services by providing three medical doctors. He could expand existing services and extend operating hours. The mysterious organization would guarantee the financing, but would select the three medical doctors and support staff.

There was also one more *major* caveat. The enigmatic man told Dr. Slesman that he'd have to gradually change his career to a related one. Even though he already completed medical school, he would spend two additional years in residency to obtain a Masters of Forensic Science degree. He could remain at the free clinic while taking the required courses online, which included forensic medicine, death scene investigation and clinical pathology skills.

The late-night visitor stated that his organization needed an expert in medicine who could diagnose the cause, time, and manner of injury or death of individual bodies brought to him. He wouldn't have to worry about meeting with the university's Admissions Committee for interviews or attending courses on campus.

If Slesman agreed to the offer, he would automatically be accepted into the program at a major university which would grant him the degree upon completion. During the training, he was assured that his work at the free clinic would not be compromised since he could pursue the forensic medical degree online. He would remain at the clinic, performing his usual work and supervising the three new doctors and their staff. All facets of the forensic schooling would be paid for by the organization. However, upon graduation, he would be required to relocate to a state-of-the-art facility in a beautiful rural area of Virginia.

Dr. Slesman's thoughts were interrupted as two men entered the Evidence Control Unit, carefully rolling a torso-sized package on a gurney. They bypassed the intake area and maneuvered the gurney into a room kept in reserve for Dr. Slessman and his assistants. They lifted the corpse from a chilled container and placed it onto a stainless-steel autopsy table that was perforated with small drainage holes and had a sink and faucet attached to the far end.

The duo signed a form then left, shutting the door behind them. The cadaver donned an oversized scuba diver's wetsuit. Slesman noted dozens of knife slits in the suit while unzipping the front of it. The slits rarely pierced the skin and he noted the fragments of chicken parts that were apparently stuffed inside. The head, torso, stomach, intestines, and top half of the pelvis were mostly intact. The pelvis was severed along a horizontal plane through the pubic bone, coc-cyx, and pelvic brim.

He put on a latex glove, slipped an interlocking stainless steel ringed glove over it, then put on another latex glove over the met-al glove. The three layers of gloves didn't interfere with his surgical dexterity.

Slesman told his two assistants to do the same, then said, "This unfortunate man was bitten only once by a very large shark. It severed the lower half of his pelvis from what's lying on the table. It was a de-liberate attack for food. Sharks will attack a swimmer multiple times, resulting in bites that aren't necessarily lethal because the shark per-ceives the swimmer as a threat. The wounds are usually small, like a dog nipping at someone who approaches its food dish. This wasn't an attack by a shark that was feeding in the area and feared this man was going to steal its meal. There wouldn't have been this much tis-sue loss…this single, murderous attack resulted because the shark wanted him a meal. Also, the knife slits in the over-sized wetsuit and visible chicken parts stuffed inside of it mean one thing."

One assistant asked, "What's that, sir?"

"Someone murdered this unlucky man in a most miserable man-ner. The shark had an accomplice. The organization I…and you two… work for will want to find out the circumstances. We'll be staying late tonight…a comprehensive autopsy is in order."

Great Abaco Highway
South of Marsh Harbor
Abaco, Bahamas
(GPS: 26°27'26.8"N 77°05'19.8"W)

The GAH was smooth until the Land Rover reached Snake Cay south of the Marsh Harbor Airport roundabout. It used to be paved all the way to its end at Sandy Point, but back-to-back hurricanes and lack of upkeep turned it back to its original condition: a limestone, gravel and mud corridor full of chuckholes. Two cars could barely pass each other and palm fronds littered the way; the once-mowed berm had reverted back to a thick jungle of palmetto palm and Caribbean pine. Corey sat in the passenger seat with binoculars while Constance maneuvered her Land Rover around rough spots. A backpack full of hi-tech spy gear lay between them.

Corey pulled out his GPS. "I marked the latitude where the tiger shark attacked me in the Sea of Abaco. According to our land map, it would be south of Crossing Rocks and north of the Abaco National Park where the parrot preserve is. We just passed the turn-off to Crossing Rocks, so I want to check out every path that leads off the GAH to the left, towards the Sea of Abaco."

Constance added. "If Sidney Fowler fled to Nassau to inform Darnell Ferguson of some awful thing he saw while bird watching in the parrot nesting area, it would be just ahead."

"How large is the parrot nesting area?"

"The park's 20,000 acres, but they nest in the northern section. Odd, but they nest underground, not in trees. Their nesting area has plenty of unripe Caribbean pine cones, poisonwood, pigeon berry, wild guava and gumbo-limbo for them to feed on. I bet Fowler was wandering around the nesting sites when he saw whatever happen that freaked him out."

"OK, let's go there. Is there a side road that leads to it?"

"No. It's pretty desolate. You have to hike about a quarter mile through the brush to get there. Fowler owns a red Ford Escort station wagon and usually parked it a few feet off the GAH, then hiked in. I've guided tourists there from the states and Canada, and Fowler sometimes came along."

"Any side roads nearby where he may have parked and hiked in?" Constance jerked the wheel to the right to avoid a deep rut. "Yes. The pines we see now are third generation. Years ago, lumber companies harvested the pine forest and plowed side roads about every half mile to pull out the timber. The original virgin forest was cut by the Bahamas Timber Company in the early 1900's. It sold out to a U.S.

company called National Container Corporation in the fifties. They shipped the pine logs to Jacksonville, Florida to make cardboard boxes. The second-generation Caribbean pine forest grew rapidly and Owens-Illinois came in years later. They built the main road we're on now, the GAH, connecting all the villages together. They also built miles of logging side roads deep into the forests...all connected to the GAH."

Corey remained silent for a moment, then replied, "Whew! Our search area is huge. Let's do what you suggested. Drive to where Fowler usually parked and we'll explore the nearby logging paths. Duane Collier's killers brought him to the Sea of Abaco from the Hard Rock Cafe in Nassau. The same tiger shark that attacked me was the one that killed him."

"It's about a half mile ahead."

Several moments passed, then Corey blurted out, "Wait... stop and back up!"

Constance slammed on the brakes and before she could shift into reverse, Corey jumped out of the Land Rover. He ran back a dozen yards, then followed a pair of faint tire tracks through the underbrush that led to a thick patch of palmetto palms and pines.

The branches parted easily, revealing an old logging road, completely overtaken by knee-high grass. Corey held the fronds partially open and yelled back to her, "Drive into the entrance and park here on the path. According to my GPS, this is almost the exact latitude where the shark attacked me."

She obeyed, then Corey grabbed the backpack and motioned her to follow. He whispered, "A vehicle drove through here recently."

Corey opened the backpack and took out two Glock 30, .45 caliber semi-automatic revolvers and handed one to Constance. The Glock 30 is standard issue for CBIF intelligence officers.

"This grass has been cultivated. It's Devil's Grass and doesn't grow naturally in the Bahamas. A disguised entrance off the GAH... we've got some exploring to do."

Corey made sure the Land Rover wasn't visible to passersby driving along the GAH. The pine and large palmetto palm leaves swayed back to their original position after the Land Rover pushed through them.

Constance was in a state of disbelief. "I've driven by here a hundred times and never noticed this old logging road. That's the weirdest grass...looks like a grayish-green carpet!"

Corey retrieved sound suppressors and King Tuk holsters from the backpack. "There's a regular magazine in the Glock and here's two extras with extensions, just in case. Put them in your cargo pants pockets."

"Shit! Will they fit? They're a foot long each."

"Yeah, no problem. Your CBIF-issued pants are tailor-made for them and have deep pockets. The extra magazines hold thirty-six bullets each. Screw on the suppressor and holster your gun. If we end up in a fire fight, I want both of us to make it out of here alive."

They tucked the Glocks inside their waistbands to conceal them in their pant legs, then pulled their loose shirts over the exposed grips.

Both agents advanced cautiously down the path. After a hundred feet, Corey pointed to tire tracks running through a mud puddle. He whispered, "Hand me the ruler and camera."

"Looks like a large vehicle," Constance said softly as she handed Corey the tape measure and digital camera.

"Yeah, probably an SUV of some sort, but we'll find out." Corey stood at a ninety-degree angle over the tracks and started photographing. He instructed Constance to toss the tape measure over both tire tracks. He wrote down each individual tire width, then the distance between them.

"The mud texture is perfect. Not runny but wet enough to leave a great imprint. Hand me the magnifying glass."

He got on his hands and knees and inspected the tire tracks up close. "One of the treads has a triangular-shaped stone wedged into it. It leaves a reverse mold in the tracks as the mud compresses into the tread and packs around the pebble." He found the next identical reverse mold several yards down and measured the distance between the two, determining the tire's circumference.

He took a close-up photo of the triangular stone mold and treads, then proceeded slowly down the grassy lane. They walked several hundred feet further until the path gave way to an opening on the Sea of Abaco.

Corey whispered, "It's like walking through a tunnel. The Caribbean pine overhang creates a complete canopy. This path of Devil Grass is invisible from the air."

Constance remarked, "It's so narrow. If I drove the Land Rover through here, the branches would scrape the sides. There'd certainly be scratch marks along the panel of whatever vehicle made these tracks."

They halted about fifty feet before the opening where the pine forest gave way to a clearing that was sparsely populated by palmetto palms. Corey motioned for Constance to sneak into the cover on her side while he noiselessly did so on his. Both crawled on until they reached the edge of the clearing.

Corey remained still, crouched down, surveying the open area of sand and coconut palms. A short, wooden dock jutted a dozen feet out into the Sea of Abaco. It was concealed by dense mangroves. *No wonder I didn't see it while doing the dolphin survey* They remain crouched, stock-still, and observed for five minutes until Corey signaled to move in.

Constance advanced to the dock and spotted a half-dozen cigarette filters scattered around. "Weird cigarettes. A big green "C" on the filters."

Corey identified them, "Comme il fauts…a Haitian cigarette, menthol." He thought about his past missions in Haiti...*you could buy them in Haiti for fifty cents a pack…the street vendors sold them to tourists.* He retrieved latex gloves, collection vials and tweezers from the backpack. After placing the Comme il faut filters into separate vials, he inspected footprints from the vehicle tracks to the dock, but the sand left them indistinct for individual analysis.

Then, he noticed dried blood spots and smeared blood, as if someone were dragged for several feet along the wooden dock to the edge. Corey took photos of the scene while Constance used a concave-shaped blade to thinly slice off samples from the blood patterns and placed them into vials, then label each specimen in accordance with each photo taken.

Corey recorded the GPS coordinates of the location, then they searched the area for additional evidence.

After fifteen minutes, Corey spoke. "OK, Constance, we've been here long enough. Let's get back to Marsh Harbor and send this off for analysis."

They retraced their steps along the abandoned logging path back to the Land Rover. Constance backed out onto the GAH while Corey remained hidden in the naturally-formed, concealed entrance. The palmetto palm and Caribbean pine branches gently swayed back to cover the opening.

Corey didn't reappear for several minutes while Constance waited in the car. When he finally got in, she didn't drive away. Instead, she turned to Corey and said, "You know something strange, Corey?"

"What's that?"

"That venture, finding Duane Collier's murder site, brought back old memories. We sure had some exciting times together a decade ago, before... you met Danielle."

"Yes, we did." *I cared a lot about you, Constance, before Danielle suddenly appeared in my life. Now, she's gone and even though I miss her, I find the former feelings I had for you resurfacing...maybe they never went away*

Corey didn't put into words what he was thinking, what he felt. After a few moments of silence, Constance put the Land Rover into gear and drove north on the GAH back to Marsh Harbor.

A minute of silence ensued before Corey finally spoke. "I think we're about to have another exciting time together."

"What do you mean?"

"Do you know anyone who drives a black Ford Expedition SUV?"

"Yeah, why?"

"Because they've been watching us since you pulled out of the abandoned logging road. I stayed hidden and searched up and down the GAH with these." He held up digital binoculars with 100x zoom. "About a quarter mile south, hidden in the brush. I could only make out the passenger side outside mirror, windshield, and rear panels, but it was a black Ford Expedition. A man stood half hidden behind it, watching us through binoculars. I could barely make him out, but he looked Haitian."

Constance abruptly steered around a water-filled chuckhole. "Not too many black Ford Expeditions on Abaco... one comes into Marsh Harbor now and then for groceries. Two men are always in it. They're foremen working for Abaco Poultry. A pair of mean bastards. We booted them out of Sapodilly's for starting one fight too many. Names are Pierre Cherestal and Bolan Tougas...both Haitians."

Corey gave Constance an admiring look. "Bingo! We're on to something."

"They've got something to do with Collier's disappearance?"

"Yes. Duane was last seen with Tougas at the Hard Rock Café in Nassau. I was sent to Nassau to find the bastard...and you just made it easier. The asset I recruited in Operation Salt Flamingo said Bolan Tougas was a new member to the infamous FRAPH squad that murdered the parents of Damballah St. Fleur when he was a child. St. Fleur is another of my assets in Haiti. Good job, Constance!"

"It ain't over yet!" Constance said while glancing in the rearview mirror.

Corey glanced out his side-view mirror, "Yeah, I see them. Their following us, but staying a good distance away. They're still doing surveillance, no aggressive moves, yet. Pull into that side road ahead on the right and jump out with your binoculars, as if we just saw a flock of Abaco Parrots fly by. Make sure your Glock 30's concealed…but be able to whip it out fast.

Constance turned abruptly onto the side road and pulled off onto the berm. Both quickly exited the Rover and held up their binoculars, pretending to search for the endangered birds that weren't there. Constance pulled down her waist band to insure the Glock remained concealed when she lifted her elbows up to gaze through the binoculars.

Moments later, the SUV swerved into the side road, almost fishtailing. Apparently, they sped up when Constance abruptly turned off the GAH.

Corey pointed to a line of Caribbean pine in the distance, as if to indicate where the parrots flew to. He lowered his binoculars and feigned a surprised look as Cherestal and Tougas skidded to a stop by the Land Rover.

"Everything OK?" Corey yelled out to them. He walked quickly towards them, but noticed their hands were not in sight, so he halted by the Land Rover in case he needed cover. Constance walked next to her vehicle and shouted out in a fake, concerned voice, "Do you need any help?"

Cherestal was the driver and he kept the engine running as Tougas rested his elbow on the open passenger side window. He stuck his head out. "It all be OK wid us, but not for you two. What da hell ya snoopin' 'round here for?"

Corey assumed the role of pissed-off tourist. "What the fuck are you talking about? I paid good money for this lady to take me on a parrot tour. I came all the way down here from Ohio to take photos of your Bahama Parrot and to meet the nice people of Abaco…and you barrel down the road and slam on your brakes, accusing me of snooping! I'm going to the police when I get back to Marsh Harbor and lodge a complaint." *I really want to pull out the Glock 30, blow your buddy's brains out, then stick it in your mouth and give you five seconds to tell me who gave the orders to kill Duane Collier*

Tougas didn't want to stir up trouble with the minister of tourism. Sandoval warned him to keep a low profile and not to do anything stupid...or else. "I guess we ova-react. Ya see, all dis land leased to da poultry farm and we protect it from unwanted visitors. Ya lookin' for da Abaco Parrot...eh?"

Corey walked nonchalantly up to the SUV while taking the Voyan Sports Bottle from his belt and unscrewing the cap a quarter turn. He pulled out the retractable plastic drink straw and took a sip. "Yes, we are. I guess I kind of overreacted, too...sorry for cussing at you, but we've been searching for the Bahama Parrot all day with no luck and, well, when you came screeching to a halt like that, you scared a flock away that we just spotted. You guys are just doing your job. The hot, sticky weather is getting to me. I'm just not used to it. If I see you guys in town, I'll buy ya a cold Kalik." *Then blow both your fuckin' brains out*

Constance casually rested her left arm on the hood of the Land Rover. She chuckled and asked, "Wait a minute! Ain't I invited, too?" Her right arm dangled behind her with the Glock 30 firmly held in it. If the killers made the wrong move, Corey would dive to the ground and commence firing upwards through the door panel while Constance fired over his head through the window. The maneuver was practiced many times at the 'Farm', the CIA's training facility in York County, Virginia.

Corey placed his hand on the SUV window, acting like a naïve and overly-friendly tourist. He told them about the secret logging road they found and hiked down in search of parrots, simply because he knew they were already aware of it. His acting performance seemed to work, for Cherestal inched the SUV forward, ready to leave. "OK, sorry for scarin' ya. Good luck wid findin' da parrots."

Corey smiled and waved at them as they pulled away. *Why the fuck didn't one of you make a wrong move...your time will come*

Episode 27

Autopsy discovery

After Dr. Milton Slesman examined the exterior of Duane Collier's remains, he used a scalpel to remove the wetsuit and store it along with the chicken parts in a side tub. Next, he cut a Y-shaped incision from each shoulder to the sternum, then cut down to the pubic bone.

He spoke into a recorder. "Note. Only four of the apparent knife slits in the wetsuit barely pierce the skin. Several dozen short, choppy stabs of approximately one-quarter inches."

With the aid of his assistants, the soft tissue covering the chest was delicately peeled back to expose the rib cage and chest cavity.

"A bruise on subject's skin over the right side of chest cavity and another skin bruise on lower right side of back. Will now inspect the chest cavity underneath."

Slesman took a saw and cut the Costal cartilage that joined the ribs to the breastbone, then removed both and inspected them.

"A slight fracture of left True rib number four and another in Floating rib number eleven, both directly underneath each surface skin bruise location."

He removed the heart and lungs, inspecting them. "Both organs appear normal. Taking blood sample from interior of heart." Slesman handed the heart to one assistant, instructing him to draw blood pooled in the left ventricle.

The CBIF-trained forensic medical examiner then took a scissors and dissected the abdomen. Slesman became engrossed in the stomach contents. "The stomach is bloated; it appears full of food." He was captivated with the stomach contents and immediately ordered his two assistants to remove the urinary tract and small intestines, pancreas, spleen, and duodenum, then to take samples of each for chemical analysis.

"Subject ate a bulky meal before his death. Stomach digestion is far from complete. Food type appears to be tomato-like sauce, possibly onions, some type of sea food, a sinewy…grisly meat…. perhaps mollusk, maybe conch, plus a bulky dough material."

With tweezers, he picked out each individual part and put them into a container. "Stomach contents will be analyzed, but it appears subject ate a full meal within two hours of death."

Slesman continued picking through the contents, and came across something odd. He lifted it out with his tweezers. "My gad… what's this?!" The two co-workers paused from slicing and storing samples and looked over at Slesman.

"Our deceased patient had swallowed a large ball of latex substance. It's a full inch in diameter. I'm dissecting it now…slowly, peeling away the layers…it must be gum, chewing gum…wait…there's a shiny…folded object…it's tin foil…tin foil scrunched up inside the ball of apparent chewing gum."

Slesman's assistants stopped their work and came over to him. "Here's a magnifying glass." one said.

"Hold it three inches over the foil." The doctor picked up two Hagedorn needles and leaned close. He gently unfolded the crunched tin, fold by fold.

"There's scratch marks on it…no, nicks…my gad, they're letters… faint alphabet letters."

He inspected them through the magnifying glass. "A sequence of capital letters…a word…It reads 'PENUMBRA DATABASE.'"

Episode 28

ELINT

Hibiscus Beach Inn
CBIF Safe House
Nassau, Bahamas
(GPS: 25°03'56.7"N 77°27'24.5"W)

Corey flew in from Abaco to CBIF's safe house in Nassau. The day hit a sultry ninety-two degrees. He sought refuge in the Hibiscus Beach Inn's pool by the main courtyard, several steps from his room. Two days passed since the altercation with Tougas and Cherestal along Abaco's GAH. The forensic evidence Corey and Constance collected along the abandoned logging road and dock was flown to CBIF's FBI attaché at the U.S. Embassy in Nassau, who immediately delivered it to a Cessna 208 Caravan parked in an unused section of Nassau's Lynden Pindling International Airport.

The single turboprop, fixed-gear plane made a great short-haul carrier between the Caribbean islands and the U.S. A single pilot crawled into the cockpit, revved up the engine and sped at   300 mph to the CIA's training facility, called the 'Farm', just outside Williamsburg, VA. The package was unloaded and delivered to an FBI facility nestled in a rural, picturesque area of Virginia. An hour later, Dr. Milton Slesman and his assistants at the FBI laboratory examined the contents.

Of the 500 scientific experts and special agents working in the state-of-the-art facility, Slesman and his special team handled top priority cases, and CBIF matters were one of them. He was grateful for the nameless organization he worked for, for it saved his free clinic in Detroit from folding.

The forensic examiner received a call on his secure cell phone and was told to drop everything he was working on, assemble his team, and process some incoming forensic evidence immediately. He and his assistants cut open the innocuous-looking package and retrieved Corey's photos of tire tracks, tape measurements of the tire widths and circumference, then opened the vials and extracted the cigarette butts and wood splinters with the bloodstains sliced off the dock.

Slesman called in two additional specialists to analyze the tire tracks and treads. When Corey walked up to the black SUV on the GAH, he took photos of Tougas and Cherestal inside and of the tires while pretending to sip from his fake Voyan Sports Bottle, which housed a miniaturized wireless camcorder. The team inspected the photos with magnifying glasses and recorded the tire numbers.

The facial photos of Tougas and Cherestal were fed into the facial recognition database operated by the FBI, which CBIF has access to. Called the *Next Generation Identification* (NGI) system, it is the largest facial and biometric recognition system in the world, containing over 200 million photos that were originally used for visa processing. CBIF has an expanding NGI algorithmic-connection inside Jeannie, and uses it for more than merely doling out visas.

Slesman applied the Chelex 100 extraction procedure to recover DNA off the cigarette butts and bloodstains. The hot, sweltering days on Abaco enabled him to detect the sweat and saliva that soaked into the cigarette filters. The DNA samples were amplified using a polymerase chain reaction technique and then typed successfully with a ground-breaking DNA Forensic Analyzer. It took only a few hours.

Dr. Slesman immediately wrote a top-secret report on the DNA and tire analysis results and handed it to the same men who delivered the forensic evidence to him four hours ago. They were instructed to remain at the lab until the analysis was completed and deliver the report directly to Pearson on Abaco.

He watched them walk quickly to their SUV and speed away. Slesman didn't know they drove from the 'Farm' to get to the lab. Once again, he wondered who his mysterious employer might be, an organization that brandished so much influence within the FBI and other government agencies. It did good things, like providing for three medical doctors and support staff, and guaranteed-funding to save his free clinic.

A short time later, the SUV cleared security at the front gate of the 'Farm' then sped onto the tarmac and rolled up to the same Cessna that arrived from Nassau only five hours before. The pilot already had both turboprops spinning. Two of the men boarded the plane with the packet and were airborne in less than a minute. The pilot flew a dozen Cessna's operated by HST Airlines and was accustomed to the chaotic flight schedule. "High-Speed Transport" was their motto and they delivered just about anything, anywhere, anytime, between the Caribbean islands and the U.S.

Like other CBIF operations, it was visible and open for public use but was haunted by a darker, furtive side that remained nameless and unidentifiable. HST Air deported Russian spies and other ousted foreign operatives, and transported abducted extraordinary rendition program captives to the 'Farm' or to Guantanamo Bay Detention Camp in Cuba.

With the upswing in terrorist attacks in America's heartland, the rendition program and enhanced interrogation techniques were reinstated whenever CBIF went to *Obscure Transgression* (OT) level. CBIF abducted targeted terrorists in the Caribbean Basin and loaded them onto an HST Airlines plane at some desolate island airstrip. Some were drugged, handcuffed, blindfolded, then transported by the Dirty Tricks division agents to an EIT room aboard Darnell Ferguson's ship, the *Queen Conch II*.

A gentle ocean breeze arose and the palm trees Corey pulled his lounge chair under began to gently sway. He lay there, blending in with the tourists, wearing a black Jimmy Buffett Parrothead short-sleeve shirt livened up with multi-colored images of parrots and toucans. Donning a straw hat and holding a Kalik, he looked like a man anxiously waiting for happy hour to begin at the nearest beach bar.

The lively tropical shirt was a deception. It hung loosely over drab cargo pants with four deep pockets. Two of them housed extended magazines filled with jacketed .45 caliber hollow points. His Glock 30 was concealed in a reversible holster held firmly by a metal clip onto the inside of the waistband.

He hoped Slesman's lab results would be delivered to him soon. His mind wandered and he began thinking about Milo "The Messenger" at the Bullion Bar in the British Colonial Hotel. *How time flies. A decade ago, I enabled him to escape the pandering life on Bay Street and take a bartender-training job here...at the Hibiscus Beach Inn. Now, Milo enjoys using his professional bartender degree at the upscale British Colonial's Bullion Bar, wearing Tommy Bahamas attire.*

His thoughts were interrupted. "I saw ya out here from da back-kitchen window. Dey told me you was comin' back and I was watchin' out fo' you. Welcome back, Mistah Pearson, and here be your favorite." *Speak of the devil. She remembers everything! What a kind-hearted lady Milo's wife is.* Corey took the Bahama Mama and set it down by the lounge chair, got up and gave her a hug.

"You've got a good memory, Chara."

"...Milo and me neva forget what you done fo' us. I know you had sometin' to do with Milo gettin' trained heah for da bartender job he got at da Bullion and me gettin' da maid job heah. I neva forget dem days...I was a laid-off hotel worker, Milo makin' nuthin' sellin' stuff to tourists on Bay Street...da bills piling up. Den, you come along and I get maid job heah at Hibiscus Beach...da pile o' bills disappear...

and now I manage the kitchen and specialize in Bahamian dishes. Ya gotta try my grouper stuffed with crabs one a deez nights."

"Most definitely will." Corey thought he'd pry a bit. "By the way, how are those two boys of yours? What are they up to?" *As if I didn't know*

"Lots happen since you leave. Dey both graduate from A.F. Adderely High School on da honor roll. Den, both get into da cadet-training program in da Royal Bahamas Police Force...now, dey both be detectives."

"Fantastic! Isn't it great how things turn out for the better?" *Yeah, I know about their detective ranks...one arrested me at the British Colonial Hotel as a murder suspect. It was me who got them into the RBPF cadet program and promoted through the ranks to detective class... by my maneuverings with Deputy Commander Rolle...our mole inside the RBPF*

"Yeah, wid God's blessing, we be pretty lucky couple...Milo and me."

"Well, hard work overcomes misfortune, too"... *and with the help of CBIF and me. My dear Chara...the Hibiscus Beach Inn is a CBIF safe house...the bonuses you and Milo got over the years...the schooling for your sons...their detective careers...all engineered and paid for by CBIF*

"Yeah...workin' hard plays a part in everyting' but God behind it all. By da way, Nigel told me to tell ya he want to talk wid you. He meet ya at da front bar in half hour." With that said, Chara walked back to the restaurant.

Corey sipped the Bahama Mama and enjoyed the refreshing ocean breeze. He hoped Nigel's reason for calling the meeting was because the FBI Lab results arrived from Virginia.

Much to think about! Addie Kolmogrovov, the Bahamian math genius he recruited in Andros and educated in Washington, D.C. was now posing as a cleaning lady for *New Providence Cleaning Services, Inc.*

He recalled recognizing Addie after the meeting with General Morrison at the Conch Inn Resort in Key Largo. After studying the *CBIF New Providence-7: Operation Coral Reef, Top Secret* folder the general gave him, he sat outside in the Ford 250 trying to regain his composure after hearing about Duane Collier's abduction. A cleaning lady wearing a *Conch Inn Marina* emblem on her maid outfit wheeled a pushcart past him and entered the cottage. It was agent Kolmogrovov.

He was glad Morrison agreed to send Addie to Nassau as part of the team, as he requested. It was 4pm. In several hours, she would gain access to the office of Honorable Alfred Moss, MP, the Bahamian Agricultural Minister in the Levy Building on East Bay Street in downtown Nassau. *Moss' limo driver accompanied the two men who abducted Duane Collier from the Hard Rock Café in Nassau. The pieces will fit together...Nassau is like the Beltway... 90 percent of the politicians give the other 10 percent a bad name. We'll find out what rock you crawled out from under, Mr. Moss... your link to Duane's disappearance will be uncovered, and you will pay.*

A half hour passed, then Corey walked up to the Hibiscus Beach Inn bar at the front of the property. It was 4:30 pm and no bartender was on duty, but it operated on an honor system. Corey grabbed a Kalik from the refrigerator behind the bar, filled out an *honor bar sheet*, then walked outside amidst the banana plants and sat down on a Caribbean pinewood swing. He admired the rows of green bananas on a single plant, all pointing upward and shielded by the broad, emerald-green leaves. A moment later Nigel appeared and sat on a wicker chair across from him.

He handed Corey a thick envelope. "Significant lab results. You and Constance gathered a lot of worthwhile evidence on Abaco."

Corey took the packet from the retired British spy, who was now on CBIF's payroll. It was unsealed, but Nigel was completely trustworthy. He retired from MI6 after twenty-five years and became the link between British intelligence and CBIF. He worked on cooperative operations with the CIA throughout the Caribbean. Vauxhall Cross in London, MI6 headquarters, agreed to have him work with CBIF and to assume proprietorship of the Hibiscus Beach Inn after "retirement," as long he passed on relevant information back to them.

During his tenure as an MI6 operation's officer, he "vacationed" frequently in the Bahamas with his family, making him the perfect candidate to oversee this CBIF safe house in Nassau.

"Who delivered it to you?" Corey asked as he eagerly began reading Dr. Slesman's lab results.

"The same Cessna pilot from HST Airlines who flew your forensic evidence to Virginia. Our shuttle picked him up and brought him here. Poor guy deserves a rest. Chara's preparing a Bahamian steamed lamb chop dinner and will deliver it to his room… compliments from us."

Corey bit his lower lip as he continued reading. *The DNA analysis of the cigarette butts and facial recognition results came up with zilch from the GNI terrorist database… dam!*

Then, the report found that the cigarette filter DNA collected at the dock at the end of the hidden logging road matched that on the cocktail glasses Daniel Ferguson retrieved off the table at the *Hard Rock Café* in Nassau.

Nigel said. "Read the vehicle description."

Corey read it aloud. "The tire track's width and circumference… the distance between the front and rear tires on each axle…67.2-inch rear track, 67.0-inch front track, 131.0-inch wheel base…the general size and all-terrain tire tread pattern…18 x 8.5 inch wheels, P275/65R 18 tires…all indications the vehicle was a Ford Expedition El King Ranch model 4dr SUV."

Corey smiled faintly and took a healthy swig from his Bahama Mama. "The vehicle Dr. Slesman's team identified drove down the hidden logging road to the dock where I collected the evidence. It matches the SUV model Cherestal and Tougas drove when they confronted Constance and me on the GAH!" *And, the same men who spiked Duane Collier's drink and abducted him from the Nassau Hard Rock Café...they will die for what they did to Duane. But, how did they get him from Nassau to Abaco? He wouldn't have gone with them without a fight...he almost seemed willing to go with them...what am I missing here!?*

He read the "stomach contents" section and looked perplexed as his MI6 comrade rose to get another drink. "Want another Bahama Mama? It's on the house."

Corey didn't look up. "No thanks, Nigel. I want to read this report with a clear mind." He continued to read in silence *Thick breading mixed with a spicy tomato sauce, onions, mozzarella cheese, sweet pepper and large amounts of conch bits.* Slesman's conclusion*: Most likely a pizza containing same ingredients. Aluminum foil gum wrapper with word "PENUMBRA" written with capital letters in manuscript on foil (photo enclosed). Digestion ceased two hours after consumption of stomach items, most likely at time of death.*

Nigel spoke solemnly. "Corey, skip to the last paragraph."

Corey cuffed through the pages until he came to the end *Dried blood spots taken from wood chips on dock were extracted and treated successfully for DNA analysis. They match with 99.9% certainty the tissue taken from individual killed by shark...also match with 99.9% certainty to the blood samples taken by CBIF agents from dock on Abaco...also 99.9% match with preserved blood taken at time of hire into CBIF and placed in agent-storage database. Conclusion: Greater than 99.9% match-up confidence with individual named Duane Collier* He looked up at Nigel. "I'll take that Bahama Mama after all...double on the coconut rum." *I found Duane Collier's killers...with 99.9% certainty ...and they're going to die*

Episode 29

Addie bugs Alfred Moss' office

East Bay Street, Nassau Bahamas
Near the Levy Building
(GPS: 25°04'35.6"N 77°19'50.3"W)
Addie Kolmogrovov inserted three quarters into the vending machine at the Texaco gas station on East Bay Street in downtown Nassau. She pulled the lever, a Bahamian coconut candy bar dropped down and she stuffed it into a deep pocket of her double-breasted house-keeping uniform, which had a *New Providence Cleaning Services, Inc.* logo sewed into the lapel.

A large purse dangled from her shoulder. A CBIF counterintel-ligence agent sat on a bench directly across Bay Street from the Texaco station, while and a man and wife CI team feigned win-dow-shopping a block further down, directly across from the Levin Building. All three agents toted cameras and camcorders, wore sunglasses and protected their heads from the intense sun with straw hats purchased from the Nassau Straw Market. They blend-ed-in well.

Moments later, a black Mercedes Benz S500L pulled into the Levy Building parking lot. It was followed by a Ford Explorer with two men in the front seat. The smartly-dressed Mercedes driver quickly got out and opened the rear door as Alfred Moss, the Minister of Agriculture, sauntered out the front door of his office building. He climbed into his $310,000 sedan and was driven away. The two men in the Ford Explorer followed.

The man and wife team watched the proceedings in a reflection from the storefront window, then signaled the sole CI agent across from the Texaco station that their target left. The solo agent folded his Nassau Guardian newspaper and placed it on the bench beside him. He removed his sunglasses and rubbed his eyes, a sequence of actions signaling that Alfred Moss just left his office.

That was Addie's clue. She stepped out onto the East Bay Street sidewalk in downtown Nassau, looking quite polished and professional in the fashioned housekeeping tunic. No one would guess her purse was filled with bugging devices. The traffic was heavy and exhaust fumes filled the air as she calmly walked to the next block and entered the front door of the Levin Building.

The CBIF counterintelligence couple walked west along East Bay Street, passing the single agent who walked east. They didn't acknowledge one another in passing. The woman agent smiled at her "husband" and said. "What a pompous bastard…a Mercedes S500L? I can see the Bahamian Prime Minister driving one of those…but the Minister of Agriculture?"

The partner replied, "Yeah. Surprised he didn't have 'PM Wannabe' vanity plates. The two men in the SUV escorting him were armed. Did you get good shots of them?"

The female agent held up her fake thermos housing a miniature high-definition, digital camcorder. "Sure did. Got Alfred Moss' ugly face, his limo driver, and the two armed thugs."

Her male partner said, "That's what bothers me…an armed escort. Moss' driver was packing, too. Did you see the bulge in his shoulder when he reached to open the rear door?"

"Affirmative…I have a gut feeling Addie's going to uncover some interesting items that may link Moss directly to Duane Collier's abduction and murder."

The "husband" shook his head. "I'm glad Pearson called us in on this one. I trained at the 'Farm' with Duane. He was a dedicated fella." Two fresh teams moved in to replace the three departing agents.

If Moss or any of his staff returned to the office for any reason that evening, Addie would be immediately alerted.

Corey finished the Bahama Mama Nigel brought him, then returned to his poolside room. He was grateful that General Morrison fulfilled his counterintelligence requests. All the intelligence operatives he wanted, he got.

Addie Komolgrovov arrived from Key West and assumed her house-cleaning cover. The beautiful Turks & Caicos woman, Dona Anani Guanikeyu, arrived and booked in at the downtown British Colonial. She would become a "honeytrap" when the need arose, but would remain a sleeper cell until then. Four CI teams consisting of a dozen agents were in place. Two teams posed as tourist couples aboard a cruise ship, another team of three assumed diplomatic cover in the U.S. Embassy on Queen Street in downtown Nassau, and the fourth team of five posed as scuba diver/thrill seekers aboard a yacht that cruised the Caribbean reefs.

Corey stared around his simple but clean and tidy room, complete with inexpensive furniture. It resembled a Holiday Inn Express. The air conditioner rattled slightly and the ceiling fan squeaked, but it was a perfect location for a CBIF safe house. Many travelers to Nassau and Paradise Island stay at plush hotels for four-day special deals. They don't want to spend exorbitant resort hotel rates for the extra days they stay in Nassau, so they book-in to inexpensive but clean and cozy places.

The Hibiscus Beach Inn meets their needs. Consequently, it has a high-turnover of passing day-trippers and longer-term lodgers who simply want to save money...a perfect backdrop for CBIF operatives to remain indistinguishable while intermingling in public view.

He talked to General Morrison yesterday on the secure cell phone. Morrison planted CI agents into Haiti as he said he would: three teams of four agents each, all posing as workers for a Caribbean NGO charity relief organization created by CBIF years ago. It was simply named Caribbean Relief. Damballah St. Fleur would notify them whenever Cesar Virgilio Sandoval arrived in his private helicopter at the Port-au-Prince dock.

The teams began a synchronized HUMINT and technical intelligence-gathering operation. Based on intel of who and where Sandoval met and visited in the past, they surreptitiously installed eavesdropping devices at predetermined locations.

The dozen CI agents had no difficulty moving around Haiti without raising suspicion. The dispossessed populace welcomed them. Haiti's fragile infrastructure and the inability of its government to cope with disasters transformed Caribbean Relief, nicknamed "CR" by the locals, into a coveted entity. Even though the earthquakes in Chile and Japan measured far higher on the Richter scale than the one that struck Haiti in 2010, the death toll of 230,000 deaths and 1.5 million Haitians left homeless required the largest emergency response ever. Thus, CR was a CBIF spy cell that helped the local people while providing cover for the counterintelligence teams.

Several Caribbean Relief members helped the Haitian children and their parents with educational expenses. The Haitians take pride in possessing official school uniforms, and the schools compete against each other for having the most unique attire. But, furnishing their children with a uniform is no easy task for poor Haitian parents.

Before school begins, the children have to go to their respective schools and pick up a piece of paper with a picture of the requisite attire drawn on it and a piece of material attached. Because the children won't be allowed to enroll in school without a proper uniform, the parents must take the sample to a seamstress and have the uniform made. To add further barriers, many schools require specific colors for school shoes, even for the ribbons that schoolgirls wear in their hair.

The CBIF agents helped the parents out by supplying them with free uniforms, complete with properly-colored shoes and ribbons.

They visited the Ministry of Education in downtown Port-au-Prince at the Palace of Ministries, and had no difficulty meeting with the education minister. He knew them well from past interactions with Caribbean Relief and was appreciative that they were willing to alleviate the uniform expense for many Haitians. The CI team left the ministry with hundreds of needy family names and addresses to drop the gifts off at.

The minister insisted they be given an extended Ford E-250 van with "Haitian Ministry of Education" logos marked on the side panels. He wanted to ensure that their mission of mercy was accomplished. Paradoxically, CBIF found the government van to be an effective stakeout tool, too.

The uniformed security guard motioned the arriving housekeeper over to his small metal desk in the foyer of the Levy Building. The desk was stored in a broom closet until he arrived. Then, he slid it out into the foyer. Addie noticed he was unarmed, but a walkie-talkie lay on the desk, no doubt hooked into RBPF dispatch. A stack of cheap magazines with shoddy-looking, naked ladies on the covers filled an open drawer. He looked at the credentials of the young lady, along with her work orders. "Addie Kolmogrovov. You must be new. Haven't seen ya before."

Addie switched over to her Bahamian accent perfectly. "Yeah, I be new tah *New Providence Cleanin'*…I be raised on Andros, but wanted da big city lights. So heah I be!"

The security guard handed her a set of keys and waved her on. He didn't bother inspecting her large purse, but thoroughly scrutinized her backside as she sauntered up the stairwell to the official offices. When she disappeared onto the second floor landing he reached into his desk drawer and retrieved a magazine he was looking at earlier.

The large, wooden door lock opened after some effort with the old-fashioned turnkey. She entered Moss' office and giggled to herself. *Piece of cake* It was a rather large, single-room office with a secretary's desk and greeting area in the front.

She scanned the room, finding no surveillance cameras mounted on the wall or ceiling. No surprise, since the security guard didn't have a monitoring screen by his desk.

Moss' desk was directly behind the greeting area, surrounded by file cabinets. She noted a landline phone, Rolodex file, family photos, and unfinished paperwork atop the desk. *Whew! What a smorgasbord ...where to begin?*

She took out a miniature digital camera from her purse, sat down at the minister's chair and began flipping through the Rolodex, photographing each card. Her training at the 'Farm' helped at this demanding task. In five minutes, she dexterously recorded all 256 cards into the mini-digital camera's memory bank.

Next, she photographed the paperwork left atop his desk and whatever was discarded into the wastebasket. Before moving to the landline phone, she ejected the camera's memory card and slid it into a secret compartment in her work shoes. A new SD card full of innocuous family photos was inserted into the mini camera.

She picked up the landline phone without dislodging the receiver and inspected its make and model number. *Perfect* It was an expensive business phone with all the bells and whistles, a feature-rich phone that provided space for bugs. *I can easily manipulate this* She inspected the plug-in adaptor socket that supplied constant electric power to the factory built-in microphone (the receiver) and speakers.

Addie installed an extraordinary bug into the receiver, one created by the CIA's Directorate of Science & Technology. The tiny device would route the electrical current, which airs the minister's phone conversation, to a small, flattened step-up radio transmitter that she glued underneath his desk top, to the back of the top sliding drawer. It would never be noticed. The end receiver was located on Pinkston's

PT boat. Pinkston would record everything and relay it to CBIF's stealth COMINT satellite.

Redundancy! Duplicity! Deception! Those words were repeated at the 'Farm' where she spent months training amidst mock-up offices of replicated businesses and simulated residential homes full of landline phones, answering machines, personal computers, cell phones, smart-phones, fax and dictation machines...even bedroom baby monitors. She could manipulate any device- wireless or plugged into a wall socket.

In one exercise at the 'Farm', her mission was to break into a house, find the computer of the target person and uncover all his friends on Facebook, Followers on Twitter, and contacts in his Gmail account. Addie accomplished the task in fifteen minutes, without leaving a trace of her break-in or machinations on the computer.

She checked under the desk where the landline phone connected to the wall, then retrieved a common dual modular adapter from her purse. After dislodging the one plugged into the wall, she cut through the threadlike wiring with a special scalpel and wired-in the replace-ment device via a two-way telephone line splitter.

Stepping away, she peered at her work. *Perfect...damn, am I good or what?* If the minister dropped something underneath his desk and looked at the wall jack, he would see a common adapter and never fathom that it monitored both sides of his phone conversations and transmitted them a half mile away to an FM receiver on Pinkston's PT Boat. The gadget used the existing phone line as both a power source *and* antennae

Even though she was anxious to start manipulating the computer, Addie stuck to the game plan. *Cell phones next.* Corey instructed her to find and compromise his cell phones, for a counterintelligence team tailed the Honorable Alfred Moss around Nassau on one of his shopping sprees. He purchased twenty-three cell phones from a doz-en different stores along West and East Bay Streets, then returned to the Levy Building. Since his two-man security detail followed him around, store-to-store, the CI team used much caution during the surveillance. One of his armed bodyguards accompanied him into each store while the other remained outside.

The CI team managed to photograph the men's designer bag he stuffed the cell phones into and gave Addie the photo and a description of it: a black leather 'lucrezia' model made by Givenchy with a square body and zip closure top.

Corey was particularly interested in this item and its contents because, upon leaving the Levy building for home that evening, Moss didn't carry it with him. Addie's directive from Corey was to find the bag and mutate the cell phones into intelligence-gathering resources... nonhuman informants, so to speak.

She pulled open the top desk drawers. They stored the usual office supplies. The bottom left drawer was locked. *Another piece of cake.* Applying her lock pic, it obligingly unbolted in fifteen seconds, revealing the Givenchy bag stuffed with unpackaged, new cell phones.

One-by-one, she opened them up and replaced each battery with a compatible one from her purse. Each innocuous-looking battery contained a built-in monitoring software program that would record calls and text messages sent and received by Moss. Every time he discarded one and made a call on a new replacement phone, its telephone number would automatically be recorded and sent to the CI team assigned to Moss. Then, the team would simply call the new number, but Moss' phone would not ring or vibrate. Secretly, it transforms into an eavesdropping device.

When Moss meets with anyone, anywhere, the conversation will be overheard by CBIF. Each battery also contains a GPS tracker which reveals Moss' whereabouts whenever the cell phone number is called. His location is instantly plotted on a computer map in the bowels of Pinkston's PT boat and relayed to General Morrison at CBIF HQ in Key West.

Now for the computer Addie inspected his desk computer. It was in the embryonic stage of development in an age of swiftly-evolving technologies in personal computing. Not wireless and without a battery, he unplugged it from the wall socket every night upon leaving the office. The bulky computer monitor weighed at least twenty pounds and was separate from the keypad and mouse. A passé computer tower rose two feet high beside the desk. *This guy is not as dumb as he is arrogant. A modern, wireless laptop with all the trappings can more easily be hacked than this historical artifact. I think our Mr. Moss may be storing and communicating about things on this dinosaur that he doesn't want anyone to know. Sorry, but you are about to meet the CIA's Directorate of Science and Technology wizards...may I introduce you to... "Cornucopia!"*

She lifted a thick CD Rom-shaped item from her purse and set it gently on the desktop, then opened the tower with a special tool. *I can't believe I'm manipulating a computer tower. The 'Farm' trained me to process these antiques and I thought they were crazy...right they were, wrong I was.* In less than five minutes, the Cornucopia device was hooked into one of the hard drives in the tower.

When the Honorable M.P. Alfred Moss, Bahamian Minister of Agriculture, plugs in and uses his desk computer, Cornucopia will relay many interesting things to Pinkston. His typed keystrokes, including passwords and usernames, will be traced. When the computer is turned on, any Facebook, Twitter, Chat site or Myspace activity along with emails and messages sent and received will be exploited.

Pinkston will transmit the Cornucopia-gathered information to the overhead CBIF COMMINT satellite, which will be relayed to Morrison at CBIF HQ. It will also be broadcast to NSA's Mother ship/Evening Star satellite, whereupon Stacey's Dictionary program will filter out relevant data.

Of particular interest to Corey were the domains that Moss seeks. Addie programmed Cornucopia to monitor what Moss searches for on Google, AOL, Yahoo, Myspace, ICQ, etc. By knowing the words and phrases he uses in the searches and on the websites he visits, Corey can gain knowledge about Moss' social life, political misdeeds, financial difficulties and a host of other scandalizing events that could be used to intimidate and pressure him to cooperate with CBIF. If Moss has financial difficulties, Corey would be more than willing to assume the "knight in shining armor" role and safeguard his pecuniary dilemma.

However, if it is revealed that the MP willfully participated in Duane Collier's murder, Corey will consult briefly with General Morrison... and have him exterminated.

Episode 30

Nassau British Colonial contact

In 2010, the British Colonial Hilton in downtown Nassau sunk $15 mil- lion into a major renovation. A large chunk went into fashioning the Bullion Bar, where Corey sat on a leather barstool with relaxing arm rests that blended perfectly with the leather-fronted bar. A young couple sat at the far end of the bar, talking to Milo "The Messenger." *Be patient... wait for them to leave.*

Corey feigned interest in the décor while slowly walking around the spacious room and admiring the black, lacquered credenzas and chandeliers hanging from the double-high ceiling. Satisfied that no one was relaxing in the leather club chairs that the pillars concealed, he returned to his plush barstool, admiring the herring-bone parquet floor on the way back.

His Bahama Mama was nearly empty, but he didn't want to call Milo over for a reload. That would interrupt the conversion and pro- long it further. He decided to listen in unobtrusively. The couple was in their mid-twenties, enjoying their last morning in Nassau. His eaves- dropping determined that a cab was going to pick them up in just over an hour and their suitcases were already stored behind the check-out desk.

The darkly-tanned couple was celebrating their first wedding an- niversary and it was no surprise to Corey when he overheard them say they were from Toledo, Ohio. Both wore bright and clashing combinations of hues and textures. A loud Hawaiian shirt hung over the husband's cargo pants and a barrette with huge tropical flowers fused to it sprouted from his wife's hair. She wore a breezy, semi-sheer Tommy Bahama shirt with bell sleeves and straight hem that hung loosely over her white, calf-length gabardine pants.

Good thing this place isn't open-air... they'd attract a swarm of bees Corey picked up the bar menu and acted as if he were interested in ordering an appetizer. The couple ordered another round of Bahama Mamas, slurring their words. While Milo mixed four ounces of Nassau Rum and four ounces of coconut rum with coffee liqueur, grenadine, orange juice, pineapple and crushed ice in the blender, the wife began complaining about their hotel room.

"You know, Milo, for the price we paid, I think our room could have been much better...it was pretty simple and smaller than I expected. The towels were thread-worn, the soap dish holder in the shower was loose and ready to fall off, and the drain was all rusty...even the shower door didn't close...and..."

The husband interrupted her. "But, honey, you have to admit that the staff is great here...and the food is top-notch."

Milo served them their drinks, garnished with mango and orange slices, slushy and high-powered. "Well, I will make sure I relay ya concern to da hotel manager, Missus Barkowski."

The wife continued as if she never heard Milo. She swiveled on the barstool and faced her husband, raising her voice just a bit. "You never listen to anything I say! Always disagree with me. You know dam well the carpet was stained, too!"

The husband took a gulp of his Bahama Mama. "But, Olga... someone must have spilled a drink. They'll replace the carpet."

Corey strolled out the back-patio door to the Bullion's outside terrace and dialed up his cell phone.

A melodious, easygoing Bahamian-accented voice greeted him. "British Colonial Hotel, how may I help you?"

Corey lightly wrapped a napkin around the phone's speaker. "Hello, this is Mr. Barkowski. What time did we schedule for the taxi pick-up?"

"An hour from now, suh."

"Oh no! I made a terrible mistake, but please don't let my wife Olga know about it. Our plane leaves earlier than I thought. Could you please have the cab pick us up right away? My wife and I are in the Bullion Bar."

"Right away, Mistuh Barkowski. It be between you, me and da fence post. You all checked out and set to go. Ya suitcases be right behind me at the desk and I'm watchin' them for ya. The taxi will be here shortly and we'll load them on it. I will call Milo when it arrives, so you just relax in the Bullion with Olga and enjoy the last of your stay here. We make sure you get to da airport on time."

Corey replied, "We had a wonderful time. Olga loved this place. We will return... thank you for all you've done for us."

Corey sauntered back into the Bullion Bar and held up his empty glass. "Bartender...Milo, isn't it? Could I have another Bahama Mama, please?"

Milo excused himself from the couple and began mixing Corey's drink. Their bickering somehow morphed into tribulations about finances and in-laws back in Toledo.

Milo set the drink in front of Corey. "Another day in paradise, eh, Milo?"

"The Messenger" chuckled and whispered. "Ya know, Mistuh Pearson, some people don't realize dat happiness come from da inside-out. When da American stock market go up, so do da numba of depression pills Americans gulp down. Ya got Walgreens, Rite Aid and CVS on every street corner now. I know, I see it wen I go ta da U.S."

Corey began with small talk. He didn't trust the young couple who were within hearing range. "Well, I'll self-medicate myself right here at the Bullion. You know, Milo, the Bahama Mama has a bit of history to it. It was born in the Bahamian heyday when your country was smuggling booze into the U.S. during America's Prohibition."

"I know dat personally. My granddaddy did a brisk whisky trade back then. But, funny, rum neva got popular til' the 60's."

Corey noted the couple began listening to their chat. "That's right...and guess what happened in the 60's?"

Milo knew the reason why rum became popular, but played dumb. "I don't know...what?"

"In 1961, the U.S. barred travel to Cuba, so millions began flocking to the Bahamas instead. Tourism and so much money flowed into the Bahamas that you were granted limited government and eventually, in 1973, you became a fully independent nation."

Corey smiled at the tourist couple, who seemed engrossed in what he was saying. He raised his drink to them. "And, that's why this beautiful couple here, and me, are sipping Bahama Mamas! We're enjoying this concoction because back then the Bahamians created it for thirsty tourists who wanted a cold, slushy and tasty rum drink."

The bar phone rang and Milo answered it. It was the front desk. Milo hung up and announced to the Toledo tourists, "Your cab be out front waitin' for you."

The husband paid the bar tab while Olga began complaining again. "It got here too early! I wanted another drink. Always slow as molasses down here when you're in a hurry, then they go on high-speed when you want to relax and...".

Her partner gently interrupted. "Well, honey, we don't want to miss our taxi." He helped her off the barstool and put his arm around her waist. It was a wobbly walk. He left his wife by the door and returned to the bar, slipping Milo a bill with Andrew Jackson's picture on it. "I'm really sorry, Milo. She gets this way now and then."

Corey peered through the wood venetian blinds to the lobby and noticed Darnell Ferguson stride past the young couple as they weaved unsteadily toward the front entrance. A net satchel full of conch slung over his shoulder. He exited the back-lobby doors and strolled through the spacious private gardens to the Poolside Bar & Grill.

As tradecraft modus operandi prescribes, Corey waited fifteen minutes before linking up with Darnell outside. He leaned forward and rested his elbows on the copper-topped bar, motioning for Milo "The Messenger" that it was OK to talk.

"Tell me, Milo, you ever heard of a man named Patrick Branaugh?" "Oh, you bet I have. He own da Irish pub jus down da street. It called Irish Frenzy and he got a brother heah in Nassau...a big banker with lots of money."

"What's his brother's name?"

"Da big banker...let me see...Sean, yeah, Sean...same last name... Sean Branaugh."

"What can you tell me about Patrick Branaugh?"

Milo leaned forward and spoke softly. "He come here when we got entertainment. A big womanizer. He wid a different woman each time. Can't keep his hands off pretty ladies, includin' those who work fo' him, even though he got a wife. My niece use ta work for him, but his hands be all over her all da time. He make Donald Trump look like a square. She be a pretty lady, my niece, but faithful to her boyfriend and God. She quit and sued him for sexual pesterin'...he even stalk her when she go home from work."

"I'd like to pay him a visit. You said the Irish Frenzy is close by?" "A five-minute walk from where ya sittin'. Jes' walk east on Marlborough Street for a hundred feet, den go right on Cumberland. His place be on da left."

"Give me another Bahama Mama. I'll take it out with me to talk to Darnell, and..."

"I know what you 'bout to tell me, Mistuh Pearson...part of my trainin'. I turn my back when pourin' da rum bottles to make people think you gettin' a full three shots, but dey can't see dat I only put in a half ounce. I don't know who ya work fo', but I do what I supposed ta do. Kinda fun takin' da secret airplane ride to somewhere in da U.S. every year. Dey hook me up and measure how truthful my answers are to all dem questions dey ask me. Dey seem ta like what I tell 'em... say I be an honest man."

"And that's why you're still working for us." *And still breathing.* Corey took the anemic Bahama Mama and walked out back to meet Darnell Ferguson. *Patrick Branaugh, womanizer, owner of an Irish pub in Nassau ... the man whose name was on the Bahamian Custom's form that the CI team discovered at the Hotel Montana in Port-au-Prince... the man to whom two cases of Arak, camel sweat, was being shipped to here in Nassau. General Morrison said the counterintelligence team in Haiti successfully replaced one of the bottles with a duplicate containing a transponder so we can track Abner Orival's smuggling boat from Haiti to Nassau. The ELINT satellite is programmed to pick up the transponder signal and guide the imaging, IMINT satellite in to take overhead photos of everything onboard the boat ...including any of the Middle Eastern men who had been sleeping on cots in Orival's backyard. Yes, I'm anxious to meet Patrick Branaugh and find out how he fits in to Duane Collier's abduction and murder*

The Poolside Bar & Grill was a perfect rendezvous point for an intelligence officer to blend in with the crowd. It set on lush, private grounds frequented by a steady flow of tourists and locals. The several guards that watched over the nine acres of gardens insured that vagrants stayed out. If a scruffy and disheveled local visited the BC gardens and solicited money or a favor, he would promptly be escorted through the lobby and out the front door.

The two bartenders admired the fresh conch Darnell delivered. One reached in the cash register, retrieved a handful of bills and inserted them inside a copy of the *Guardian*, then laid the newspaper on the counter next to Darnell. The other took the satchel into the back kitchen and began preparing conch salad.

Corey shook Darnell's hand. "Mr. Ferguson, so glad you could make this meeting. We have lots to discuss about the Nassau Grouper survey."

"You betcha. I got da boat all ready and your equipment's on board and locked up so's nobody can steal nuthin'."

Corey laid his shoulder bag on the countertop, took out his "Reef Fish Identification" book, authored by Paul Humann, and opened it to the back where he recorded fish sightings. Then, he laid down a map of the Great Abaco Barrier Reef system that runs along the many cays on Abaco's eastern shore.

"Here's the reefs that I want to dive for the survey." Corey circled a dozen spots with a magic marker.

"Oh, dey be beautiful reefs to dive in! Looks like you gonna have fun."

"I like to mix business with pleasure. You can approach each reef from the northeast. I'll dive in and swim southwest, diagonally, above each reef, fifteen feet off the bottom. I've got waterproof paper and an aqua pencil to record the grouper sitings."

"And, you want me to follow you, slowly from above, den pick ya up when you're done?"

"Exactly. If I see fish hiding in the shadows of a coral below me and I'm not sure if it's a Nassau Grouper, I'm going to dive down and shine an underwater zoom flashlight in whatever cavern it's hiding in. This is a scientific survey and I want to properly tally every grouper I spot on this diagonal grid. The coordinates of where I begin and where I finish will be duplicated in the future to measure the health of the Nassau Grouper population. I need to establish a baseline."

Ferguson looked puzzled. "The equipment I load on da boat fo' ya has a pole spear in it, too. What you gonna do wid dat 'ting?"

Corey nodded. "I plan to help out the Bahamian government with its lionfish problem. Whenever I see one, I will kill it."

Darnell smiled, "I'm glad. Dey invaded our waters. I see first one in 2005 and since then they be takin' over the reefs, crowding out our game fish."

"I'm glad to help out. And you're right, Darnell, it is an invasion. In 1992, Hurricane Andrew smashed an aquarium in Florida and a dozen lionfish washed into the Atlantic Ocean. Their populations exploded and the Bahamas got hit the hardest because of its proximity to Florida. They're native to the Indian and Pacific oceans and the spiny, venomous devils have no natural enemies here."

"I hope ya kill dem all, Mistah Pearson!"

"Well, I'll try to weed them out a bit. I'd like to start the survey at Hope Town Reef, then to Fowl Cay Reef and The Pillars on the first day."

A bartender brought them a bowl of conch fritters. "Sorry to interrupt, but I made dese special for you, Darnell, for bringing me da lobsters."

Darnell smiled broadly. "Why thank ya, Deangelo! It looks like your famous batch o' fritters...the one that the tourist people go nuts on."

"One and da same." Deangelo replied. "Dats why dey come here fo' happy hour. I beat a large egg with milk and flour, den put in ground pepper and Cayenne pepper, too. In dis batch I put in extra conch meat for you and your friend." He patted Corey on the shoulder. "Den, I finely dice da onion, green bell pepper, celery stalk, and cloves."

Corey stared at the scrumptious bowl of conch fritters, noting the large conch chunks. "Thank you so much, Deangelo. I've got to try one."

Deangelo smiled back as he returned to the bar. Tourists began to arrive and park themselves at the open-air seating. Happy Hour with free conch fritters was about to start. He yelled back, "Don't forget to dip dem deep in my sauce. I mix jus' the right amount o' ketchup, lime juice, mayo, and hot sauce togetha'...you will luv it. Tanks again fo' da lobster, Darnell."

They obeyed his orders and munched on the fritters, dripping with the special sauce and crammed with chunks of conch meat.

"Damn...these are good, Darnell. Best anywhere!"

"You betcha. You gonna like da Hopetown, Fowl Cay and Pillars... dey full o' elkhorn and brain coral. A big green moray eel... he be resident o' da Pillars Reef."

Deangelo came back and set a Yellow Bird decorated with coconut and mango slices in front of Darnell and gave him a wink. "Dat be on da house, too. Ya friend here want somethin?"

Corey replied, "Another Bahama Mama."

A few moments later the bartender brought Corey's drink. He took a swig. *Much more potent than Milo's version. Better pace myself. Time to discuss the reason Darnell called this meeting* "I forgot to mention, Darnell, I'll also be videotaping with that underwater camcorder you loaded onto the *Conch Queen I.*

A spray of water from the pool landed on the map spread out before them. *A good excuse to seek more privacy with Darnell.*

Corey wiped the water off. "Let's plan the grouper survey in a drier spot, shall we, Mr. Ferguson?"

"Sounds like good idea, Mistah Pearson."

They retreated to an adjacent tiled patio, well enough away from the pool and bar area. Corey laid the map and fish ID book down on a coffee table. "So, Darnell, what's come up?"

"I think one a' my crew is a mole. I did wat ya said to do...keep a close watch. He be actin' different. He act guilty...can't look me in da eye anymore. So, I ask around and find out he be spendin' lots a money...he buy a brand-new car, been gamblin' at da Atlantis casino on Paradise Island, puttin' down some big money playin' Blackjack, Craps and Mini Baccarat dere. I know cause a brother of anotha of ma crew deals at da tables dere."

"Which one is he?" "Devon Ledard."

"You told your crew about the $5,000 reward?"

"Yeah, I tell 'em, and dat's when da crew member turn him in...he tell me 'bout Devon's gamblin'...and somethin' more dat I think you'd be interested in."

Corey sipped his Bahama Mama. "And what was that?"

"He say dat Devon, when he go back to Abaco...he be sellin' drugs at Nippers on Guana Cay. He sell coke to da tourists."

"How often does he go back to Abaco?"

"Plenty a times. He only work fo' me part-time now. Says he misses his wife and kids. Dey live in da Great Guana Cay settlement and it's a stone throw away from Nipper's."

"Everybody know everyting 'bout everybody else on Guana. It be seven miles long and 200 yards wide wid only 150 people. Devon Ledard use ta be a God-fearin' man and now he wear fancy Tommy Bahama clothes, gamblin' lots a money at da Atlantis, drinks like a fish at Nippers and sells coke dere, too. He quit workin' fo' me full-time and goes to Guana for weeks on end to see his family, he say, but he nevah stays home when he git dere...he inta sellin' drugs big time."

"How did he react when you gathered your crew together and told them that they are all helping to fight an enemy that is harming the welfare of the Bahamas and you suspect one of them is a snitch for this enemy?"

"He *seem* guilty and dun look me in da eyes no more. Den, anotha crew memba give me all dis info 'bout his actin' different...it all add up...so I contacted ya fo' dis meetin'."

"I'm glad you did, Darnell. Here's what I want you to do. We're switching boats for the Nassau Grouper survey from the *Conch Queen I* to the *Queen Conch II*...and you know what that means."

Ferguson took a deep sigh and chugged down the remainder of his Yellow Bird, signaling Deangelo for a reload. "Yeah, mon... I know fo' sure. I dun like those guys who yo' organization hire to become my new crew members. They do peculia' stuff in dat locked room."

Yes, I don't like the Dirty Tricks division either. But, they have their function. "Yeah, I know, Darnell. Just ignore them. As in the past, you will remain the captain of the *Queen Conch II* and give your crew time off to enjoy themselves... paid time off, and my organization will reimburse you."

"Dat's one benefit o' me acceptin' the *Queen Conch II* from ya'll. Ma crew enjoy da paid time off. But, wat's in dat locked room? Wat do dey do to people that dey bring on board and put in dere?"

Easy with the questions, Darnell. Obscure Transgression level changes the picture. The room is used for Enhanced Interrogation Techniques (EIT's). But, I can't tell you that. The EIT equipment will be removed when the mission terminates and you can use the boat for normal fishing purposes again. Lots of benefits for you, my friend, to unknowingly aid CBIF in maintaining a mobile, maritime rendition black site...an illegal one at that, but necessary to safeguard the American public.

Darnell noted the annoyed look on Corey's face. "OK, I know, I ask too many questions...but I rememba hearin' the wailing and screamin' comin' out o' dat big room wen we be out at sea. Still, I keep ma mouth shut and enjoy da benefits a' havin' an extra ship."

"In the long run, Darnell, what goes on aboard the *Queen Conch II* is beneficial to the security of both the Bahamas and the U.S. We'll continue with the Nassau Grouper survey, although that will be a cover for the new phase of this operation. I won't be doing any surveying at all. In fact, the new crew arrives at the Potter's Cay dock tomorrow. They'll board the *Queen Conch II*, unlock the inner room and load it up with their equipment."

'Wailing and screaming'...CBIF needs to install more sound-proofing around the EIT room to muffle the noise even more. The Dirty Tricks division will bring their equipment onboard in innocuous-looking wax produce boxes with 'Fresh Produce' stamped on each one. The cartons house equipment to hold captives in prolonged stress positions, to subject them to deafening noises and sleep deprivation,

to waterboard and confine them in small, coffin-like boxes, and to expose them to extreme cold. No, Darnell, I don't particularly like your replacement crew either. But, I think back when al-Qaeda took thirty-five kids hostage in the elementary school in Boston, strapped explosive vests on them and kept them hostage for a week holding news conferences and taunting their parents and all of America... leading us to believe negotiations for their release might work...then blowing themselves and all the children up. A terrorist cell that slipped through our borders via the Caribbean... CBIF had to reinstate the extraordinary rendition program. America's psyche still hasn't recovered

"OK, I'll make sure ma real crew ain't dere when dey arrive. Mistah Pearson, dere's one other ting' I forgot ta mention."

Corey noticed his Bahama Mama was getting low. He motioned to Deangelo for another. "What's that?"

"My crew memba who turn Devon in, he say dat Devon meetin' up all da time wid two Haitian men who drivin' SUV on da Gran' Abaco Highway. Dey both work fo' the chicken farm on Abaco. And dat not all. He say dey take a Boston Whaler and dock off Nippers beach, pretendin' to fish fo' grouper and Yellowtail snappa'. He see Devon take money from da tourists at Nippers den go snorklin' out to da boat and da Haitian guys give him white stuff wrapped in ziplock bags."

The barkeep laid the Bahama Mama on the coffee table, then stepped down off the elevated patio. Corey waited for him to return behind the bar. "When is Devon returning to Abaco?"

Darnell was still working on his Yellowbird. "Day afta tomorrow.

He go every otha weekend...to Guana Cay and Nippers."

It's got to be Bolan Tougas and Pierre Cherestal using Devon as a mule. Sandoval lifted them out of the poverty in Port-au-Prince and satisfied their every need...except their greed. If Sandoval knew they were risking his operation by selling drugs on the side...he'd kill them. Shit! Devon is a fuckin' mole for Sandoval and a mule for Tougas and Cherestal on the side. I see a great opportunity here! Opportunity is about to knock and there's no door...I'm going to build one, fast.

Corey stood up suddenly and gathered his fish ID book and reef map. "I've got a plan to work out, Darnell. I want you to meet the replacement crew tomorrow and sail out the next day to Abaco. Moor in the Hope Town, Fowl Cay and The Pillars reef area. We'll carry on as if the Nassau Grouper survey is still going on. In the meantime, I've got another job to do. Contact me by regular cell phone when you arrive in Abaco."

Corey grabbed another of Deangelo's conch fritters, dipped it deep into the sauce and munched on it while walking away. Ferguson picked up the bowl and moseyed over to the bar to finish it off.

"Ya want 'nuther Yellowbird, Darnell?" Deangelo asked as Darnell finished the bowl of scrumptious conch fritters.

"No thanks. Gotta get back to Potter's Cay...expectin' visitors tomorrow mornin'. I don't want ta have no hangover wen dey arrive..."

Deangelo looked puzzled. "Why? Are dey important people?"

"No, dey ain't important ...to me anyways...it jus' dat I don't trust 'em and want to be on ma toes... dey give me da creeps."

Episode 31

Mata Hari

Irish Frenzy Pub Nassau, Bahamas Yesterday's receipts covered only a third of the day's expenses and it looked like today's proceeds would be as dismal. The thought of asking his banker brother for another loan repulsed him. Patrick Branagh peered out the door of his small office past the twelve empty barstools to the entrance door. Despite it being lunch hour, nary a customer entered in the past half-hour, save one couple who sat amongst the empty tables. They sat in silence, enjoying the famous Irish special- potato and leek soup.

He thought of the connection his brother had with the Abaco Poultry, LTD operation and the money that flowed his way because of it. Branagh smiled to himself in the small office, knowing that, despite his insolvent Irish saloon and restaurant, his skirt-chasing lifestyle would continue.

Just then, his way of life was about to change. The faint bell above the outside entry door tingled, signaling that a customer entered the tiny foyer. Branagh stared as the entrance door swung open and witnessed nearly six feet of natural beauty glide in and perch on a barstool. He remained in his office, peering at her. His bottom jaw dropped, his heart began beating quicker, and his breath grew deeper.

She sat sideways to him, revealing a flat stomach, long, beautiful legs and a face sculpted from the cover of *Elle* or *Glamour* magazine. A black, sheer thong swim dress slightly obscured the G-string bottom and string bra. Dona Anani Guanikeyu knew how to cover herself up and still reveal all. That's why Corey Pearson called her to Nassau from her plush condo and safe house at the Coral Gardens on Grace Bay in the Turks & Caicos.

Branagh recuperated physically and managed to walk up to her. The dimly lit atmosphere was slightly illuminated by the electric beer signs pushing Martinique's *Biére Lorraine* and Trinidad & Tobago's *Stag Lager.* The tall beauty with long, black-satin hair and golden-brown tan sitting before him added an extra glow to the surroundings.

"Welcome to the Irish Frenzy! Would you like to sample our lunch special?" He glanced at the barely discernible, upturned breasts underneath the swim suit. "If you'd like a cold beer, we have specials on the Bahama's *Kalik* Haiti's *Prestiqe*, Dominica's *Kubuli*

"I'll have a *Turks Head Stout* in a bottle, if you carry it."

"That we do." Branagh went to the freezer and got the stout and a frosted mug.

Dona took the cold *Turks Head* from his hand before he could set it on the bar, making sure her fingers touched his in the handoff. "I don't need a mug." She took a swig from the bottle while Branagh watched the dimples on both cheeks form as she sucked in a mouthful.

She noticed his shameless stare. Corey filled her in on Branagh's gluttonous sexual cravings, so she planned on using a direct, seductive routine. "I thought you'd ask me if I wanted a gin and platonic or Scotch and sofa...that's what the bartenders in the Turks & Caicos ask me. I usually choose the sofa."

It was lust at first sight for Patrick Branagh.

Episode 32

Danger lurks within America's southern flank

Dillon placed a can marked "100 percent Deet" on top of the Tiki Hut bar and Corey took advantage of it. He slipped off the Bohemian sandals and sprayed his feet, but to no avail. The itching continued as the inexhaustible supply of "no see ums" furtively crawled up the barstool legs onto his own.

Corey stopped itching and took another swig of Kalik. "I'll just ignore them as best I can. I remember they were just as bad a decade ago, eh Dillon?"

"Sure was and sure still are. But, we know how ta ignore dese sand fleas. I got da Deet dere to appease da tourists. Dats all dey know to use."

"Does that mean you have the real antidote to these biting, bloodsucking midgets behind the bar somewhere...hiding it from me?"

Dillon laughed and retrieved a bottle of aloe from behind the kitchen stove, tossing it to Corey.

With his right hand pouring the remains of Bahamian beer down his throat, Corey grabbed the airborne bottle of *Skin So Soft* aloe with his left. "You're a saint, Dillon. Do you share our anti-sand flea secret with the tourists?"

"Naw. The moe dey itch, the moe dey drink. I just let dem use up the Deet. Good for bizness...Deet and no see ums."

Corey couldn't help but laugh. He opened the bottle of *Skin So Soft* and rubbed healthy swabs of it into his feet, legs and arms. Immediately, the itching stopped.

He swiveled on the barstool and looked out across the Sea of Abaco. A gentle ocean breeze lifted the coconut palm fronds shading the patio and lulled him into a calm state of mind. Diminutive ripples gently lapped against the fifty-gallon drums beneath the floating deck. He stared across at the purple umbrella and table where he laughed with Danielle a decade ago. She was his counterintelligence partner, then friend, playmate, soul mate...and ultimately, murdered wife.

Thoughts of their Severna Park home in Maryland, the hi-tech security system penetration, and the skillful hit on her resurfaced again. *I will find out who tortured and murdered Danielle...and why. It's only a matter of time*

A dish of Land crabs with pigeon peas and rice appeared before him. "Here ya go, Corey. Hope ya stay dis time to finish it all. When da lobsta fishermen come last time and talked 'bout da man at Conch Inn Marina dock dat got eatin' by da tiger shark...you run off."

"Well, it's not every day you see a shark with a human being in its belly."

"Did ya know dat person?"

"No, poor fellah." *Time to change the subject* Corey ordered another cold Kalik. As Dillon opened the beer refrig, Corey pointed at the macaroni and cheese dish on the back counter. "Hey, Dillon, I can't believe I didn't notice your famous Bahamian Mac 'n Cheese back there. I'll take a plate."

"You'll love it...a meal all by itself. I cook elbow macaroni an' finely chopped onions, celery and green peppers...den add evaporated milk, bacon bits, crushed red pepper flakes and mild green chilies. Den, I shred da Daisy cheese wid mild cheddar, put in beaten eggs, den salt and pepper and put in oven for forty-five minutes and presto... here ya be." Dillon put a huge portion in front of him, next to the crabs and rice.

"My diet starts tomorrow, Dillon."

Just then, Corey's secure cell phone vibrated. It was a call from General Morrison, linked via satellite from CBIF HQ in Key West. Morrison had Corey replace his satellite cell phone with the same encrypted version he passed out to the *Gang of Six* during the secret meeting at CIA HQ in Langley. The phone was delivered to him at the Hibiscus Beach Inn safe house by special courier onboard CBIF's High-Speed Airlines (HST).

Seven people were now using the next-generation cell phone that Pinkston created: Corey and General Morrison along with ex-DHS Assistant Secretary of Intelligence Maxwell Gordon; Dr. Alex DuRoss, Director of NSA; Colonel Brent Burkin, Director of the DIA; Roger Hart, Deputy Director of the National Reconnaissance Office (NRO); and Walt Mason, Director of the FBI. However, only Morrison knew Corey Pearson used the seventh one.

Corey answered, "Hello, sir."

"Land crabs with macaroni and cheese...I see a stomach ache coming on. Listen, I got some critical updates to discuss. I know the Tiki Bar owner is trustworthy, but we can't take any chances. Some critical shit came in."

"Roger that." Corey walked away from the counter and sat at the table underneath the purple umbrella at the far end of the patio. "I take it that you've got the IMINT stealth satellite in operation, hovering over my head. Pretty good imaging for you to see what's on my food plate." Morrison chuckled and took a puff from his Montecristo cigar.

He stared at the computer screen in the War Room in the basement of CBIF HQ in Key West. Ten minutes ago, he was eating crab cakes with chutney at the Turtle Krall Restaurant & Bar in Key West's Historic Seaport District when a text message came in from Jeannie, code name *for* CBIF's mainline computer housed in the HQ basement on Eaton Street.

The pre-programmed message simply read, "Jeannie beckons." General Morrison left his meal unfinished and walked onto Margaret

Street, crossed over Caroline Street, then turned right on Eaton Street and strode past several dozen renovated historic homes of tropical West Indian architecture before arriving at the clandestine headquarters. Eight counterintelligence men and women prepositioned along the way watched over him.

He hurried into the basement and turned on the supercomputer. It was an intel report from the counterintelligence team he inserted in Haiti. After reading their findings, he contacted Corey without delay.

Morrison replied, "Yes, I *ca* see what you're eating. With one-foot optical resolution imaging, I can count the legs on those disgusting land crabs you're munching on. Not bad from 310 miles up. Your face fills up my computer screen."

"Incredible, sir. Operation Invisible was well worth the expense Glad you have them flying over the Abaco Poultry LTD farm, too."

"After your intel report came in from Abaco, I notified *Key West Drywall Company* and had them reprogram one IMINT image intelligence satellite from the Trinidad & Tobago sector to fly over Abaco." CBIF operates eight safe houses throughout Key West and *Key West Drywallers* is a business front for one of them, a team of IMINT satellite image interpreters who masquerade as drywallers.

"Yes, I know sir. Hope they like crabs with mac and cheese".

Morrison crunched down hard on his Montecristo. "I'm also watch-ing the chicken farm and tracking the Ford SUV those two Haitians fuckers drive around in. Wish you and Caroline blew them away when they harassed you on the GAH."

Corey took a swig of the cold Kalik. "So do I." *My opportunity will come... and I'll mention Duane's name as I put a bullet through their heads*

Morrison continued. "I'm also ordering a second IMINT and one additional ELINT, electronic intelligence, stealth satellite to back you up. They're so lightweight and agile that we can maneuver them quickly between Nassau and Abaco...in geostationary orbit, of course."

"Terrific, sir. With the ELINT, we'll be able to filter out any e-mail, cell phone, fax, walkie-talkie or short-wave radio signals that hint of Duane Collier's abduction and murder. We know who the killers are...I want to know who gave the order."

"And, so do I. We'll also have a constant flow of visual images coming from Abaco from that little bird flying above you. I'll let you know ASAP if anything worthwhile is picked up."

Corey gulped down the remaining Kalik and motioned for Dillon to bring him another. The general paused. His temporary silence usually meant he was gathering his thoughts before relaying crucial information. *What's the "critical shit from Haiti"...I want to end this intelligence-gathering phase and act on it!*

After fifteen seconds of silence, Morrison announced, "Our counterintelligence teams in Haiti were alerted by Damballah St.-Fleur that Virgio Sandoval's helicopter landed. As you know, Damballah's voodoo followers work at the port warehouse."

Dillon served his chilled Kalik. Corey waited until he retreated behind the bar before speaking. "Yes, his private helicopter lands at the Port-au-Prince dock area, not at the international airport. Sandoval pays Damballah's voodoo worshippers to guard the chopper for him."

Morrison added, "Yes. The CI team reported they wheeled it into the warehouse and stored it there. A government SUV picked him up and drove him to the Hotel Montana."

Corey asked, "What about Sandoval's bodyguards?"

"I knew you'd be wondering about that. Yes, Tougas and Cherestal got off the chopper with him... along with two Middle Eastern men."

Corey downed his Kalik quickly. "Those two fuckheads get around. Two days ago, they threatened Constance and me on the GAH, posing as security guards for the Abaco Poultry, Ltd. operation. Now, they land by helicopter in Haiti. That's 800 miles away as the crow flies."

Morrison munched on the Montecristo cigar. "They shadow Sandoval everywhere he goes. A dark government SUV with tinted windows picked them up at the Port-au-Prince warehouse and drove them to the hotel. Eight got out of the SUV and walked through the lobby to the outside patio...Sandoval, Tougas, Cherestal, the two Middle East men, and a Haitian government official with two uni-formed Haitian National Police officers."

"The HNP...were either of them one of my recruits?" "Unfortunately, no. The SUV belonged to the Haitian *Minister of Public Health and Population*, a guy named Laurent Rousseau. Our CI team got photos and audio tapes of their Hotel Montana meeting. They met a Haitian named Abner Orival, who turns out to be a recruiter and human smug-gler for Cesar Virgilio Sandoval."

Corey shook his head. "I bet he smuggled Tougas and Cherestal nto Abaco."

"Not only that, Corey, the two Middle Eastern men spoke perfect English. We didn't need an interpreter. They asked Orival how *their* men were doing."

"Meaning there could be a radical Islamic cell from the Middle East in Haiti?"

"Exactly." Morrison spit a diminutive piece of tobacco into the wastebasket beneath his computer desk. "When the meeting ended, several CI agents tailed Orival. He rode a motor scooter to a place he ownes in La Saline, a shantytown just north of Port-au-Prince. It's a small house, but had a good-sized backyard. A dozen men were sleeping in the backyard on cots. Couldn't determine how many were inside."

"Did they get facial shots?"

"Yes, close-ups. Wasn't easy because Orival grew a thick grove of grapefruit, orange and breadfruit trees around the yard. The team took their time, though, and got good shots whenever someone walked through an opening in the vegetation. At least a dozen of them were of Middle Eastern lineage. Our moles on the inside of NESA ana-lyzed the facial images of the two honchos that flew in with Sandoval.

Both were from the Middle East, but they said one was most likely from Afghanistan, the other appeared Lebanese."

Moles inside NESA...the Office of Near Eastern and South Asian Analysis... another obscure CIA department that CBIF penetrated. I wonder if the moles are the ones I recruited out of Trinidad and Tobago, years ago...a man from Pakistan and a woman from Afghanistan. CBIF gave them U.S. citizenship, new identities, and forty grand to entice them to come to the U.S. and work for the CIA.

Morrison chimed in, "Yes, your Trinidad recruits were the ones who analyzed the facial photos. Both of them are very useful to NESA... and to us. They provide much insight into the happenings in Pakistan and Afghanistan."

How did he know what I was thinking!? "I figured that's where they might end up, sir. What about NGI?"

Corey referred to the FBI's *Next Generation Identification* system that CBIF taps into. It is a vast database that includes digital recordings of fingerprints, DNA profiles, iris scans, palm prints, voice identification profiles, and facial photographs collected from state, county and school entities, and from roughly a million CCTV monitors placed along roadways, in shopping malls and on street corners throughout America.

Groups like EPIC and the ACLU tried to stop the government from using such technologies to fight terrorism, but the plethora of attacks within America's heartland since 2018 by homegrown radical Islamists hampered their efforts.

"We got NGI hits, Corey. Remember the photos taken by the DEA in Medellin that showed Sandoval meeting with three Middle Eastern contacts?"

"Yeah. They met in Medellin and flew back to Afghanistan on commercial flights. They departed from three different airports in Colombia...Medellin, Bogota, and Barranquilla. Your counterintelligence teams posed as Air Marshalls and luggage handlers. They opened their luggage after they checked in and lifted fingerprints as well as hair and DNA samples."

Morrison added, "Not to mention surveillance photos and voice recordings when they spoke on the planes and in airport terminals. As you recall, we had agents flying ahead on military craft and kept them under surveillance during layovers in Miami, London and Delhi airports. At the airport restaurants, the agents retrieved every plastic cup they drank from and cigarette butts they discarded in the smoking areas. All three landed in Kabul thirty-six hours later."

"Any of them arrive on the helicopter with Sandoval?"

"The NGI system got a hit on one of the two. Facial recognition from the photos and fingerprints lifted off the drink he ordered at the Hotel Montana."

The CI teams work fast! Corey decided to have a third Kalik. He motioned to Dillon across the patio. "Nice work. How did they get the glass? Pose as a waiter?"

Morrison replied with a bit of smugness. "Close guess. As they paid their tabs when leaving, a female agent distracted the waiter inside the Hotel Montana pub before he could collect the empty glasses and clear off the table. Another agent strolled past her to the outside gardens and quickly gathered up the cigarette butts and glasses used by the two Middle East men, packaged them and tossed them over the fence to others waiting outside."

"What was the NGI hit?"

"It spit out the name 'Batoor Emal'. Our NESA moles said it's a name of Pashto origin. They like to use first names representing some object or quality that they value. Last names are usually their father's name or the tribe they're from."

Dillon handed Corey his beer and quickly left. He sensed Corey was absorbed in the conversation he was having on the fancy-looking cell phone. Corey continued. "What does 'Batoor' mean?"

"Brave."

Corey took a big gulp of Kalik. "Great...wish it meant 'peace and harmony'. How did the NGI system connect his biometrics?"

"You won't believe this... he lives up to his name. As you're well aware, facial ID's and fingerprints, even eye scans, are taken routinely throughout Afghanistan and Iraq, particularly of men of fighting age."

"Yeah, and it took the U.S. time to convince the Afghan government to do so. The DOD threatened to withdraw our remaining 6,500 military advisors if they refused to. Last I heard, the NGI system has two and a half million Iraqis and over a million Afghan men in its database...all between the ages of fifteen and sixty-four. Anyone applying for a government job or at any American installation over there must submit to a biometric sampling."

Morrison continued, "All prisoners must do the same. Batoor Emal spent time in Saraposa Prison in Kandahar before the Taliban attacked it in June of 2008 and freed several thousand prisoners."

"And, our friend Emal was one of the escapees?"

"Correct. According to prison records, when arrested and charged he was ID'd as a Taliban fighter. During the prison attack, he escaped in the confusion and sped away in a minibus waiting outside. The fingerprints on the glass of Arak and facial photo taken at the Hotel Montana matched his NGI biometric sample taken in Afghanistan."

"What is Arak? I've been on every Caribbean island wider than fifteen feet across and never heard of it. Sounds like camel piss."

"Close, but no cigar. Arak is an Arabic word meaning 'sweat' and it's distilled booze from the Middle East. Analysis of the residual liquid in the glass after his fingerprints were lifted showed it's milky-white and has a high alcohol content of sixty percent."

"So, can we assume that the Hotel Montana orders this camel sweat for Middle Eastern visitors...specifically for Batoor Emal and his fellow radical Muslim militants?"

"Yes. The CI team found out that one of Damballah St. Fleur's voodoo followers is a waitress at the Montana. She dates the manager of the bar and did some checking for Damballah, at our request. Turns out her boyfriend was told to order two cases of the stuff from the U.S. It's illegal to export, so someone has pull".

"Probably Rousseau. He could sway Haitian and U.S. export and import regulations for a couple cases of Arak, being the Minister of Public Health and Population. Probably did it as a favor to Sandoval, Batoor Emal and the other Mideast guy."

Corey noticed a couple peddling past the Tiki Hut on a dual tandem bicycle with a large picnic basket attached to the handlebars. They stopped just down the way on Bay Street in front of the Union Jack Public Dock. He scrutinized them. *They're not trying to emulate the locals, like Abaco tourists usually do, by donning sandals, cut-off jeans and T-Shirts. They're wearing brand-name tennis shoes, polo shirts and car- go pants. They've got to be additional CBIF counterintelligence agents that Morrison sent...dressed too swanky for this section of Marsh Harbor. I've got to remind him that tourists dress differently in the out islands than they do in downtown Nassau, Paradise Island and Freeport.*

The couple parked the tandem and took photos of the dock workers loading boats. *They may get into problems at the Union Dock... and blow CBIF's cover* As if reading his mind, General Morrison replied, "Don't worry about those two on the tandem bike. They're one of us... keeping an eye on you. A picnic lunch isn't stored in the basket...but two Glock 30's with four extra magazines and stun guns are. I'm watching them, too, here in the War Room in Key West. They both have black belts in defensive Taekwondo and can handle themselves quite well."

Corey observed several drunk vagrants swigging cheap rum from brown paper bags. They eyed the couple through bloodshot eyes from a public shelter close to the dock. *Definitely not teetotalers*

A group of youngsters boarded a rental boat vacated by tourists who went for a quick shopping spree in nearby stores. The delinquents lifted an ice bucket full of beer from it and leisurely walked away.

"Glad they can protect themselves with their bare hands without re-sorting to the heavy artillery, which would definitely blow their cov-er... and our entire mission. Deputy Commander Rolle protects us only so much. What do we know about Emal's companion...the other Muslim?"

"A real mystery man. Photos taken at Hotel Montana matched facial recognition snapshots in the NGI database, but no name or biometric hits. He's referred to as 'John Doe-istan'. Agents took sur-veillance shots of him several years ago arriving at the Simon Bolivar Airport in Maiquetia, Venezuela."

Corey asked, "Arriving from Afghanistan?"

Morrison began chewing on his unlit Montecristo in the War Room. "No. From Tehran...as in Iran. They tailed him for two weeks through the Tri-Border Area."

"That's the region where Paraguay, Argentina and Brazil inter-sect ... with a large population of Lebanese immigrants. Iran's ter-rorist proxy, Hezbollah, operates out of there. I thought the guy was Afghanistani, like Batoor Eman."

"Apparently not...there's over 40,000 Lebanese Shiite's in the re-gion. Our Mr. John Doe-istan drove from Maiquetia to Argentina and holed up for two weeks at a home in Buenos Aires that's owned by a Lebanese businessman."

"Which verifies what our moles inside the CIA's NESA concluded from the photos...that this second man was from Lebanon. What we got on the businessman?"

"He owns a restaurant chain that was busted for funneling money to Hezbollah. Nothing much happened to him."

Dillon laid another Kalik down and retreated back behind the bar. "Not surprising...a lawless area. Iran's foothold in the Western hemi-sphere. I still can't believe the U.S. State Department thinks Iran's terrorist influence is waning in South and Latin America. Tell me, sir, what else did our agents uncover?"

Morrison answered. "They were on him like flies on a cow poo, DEA mostly, with a team of our guys. John Doe-istan drove back to Caracas, then flew back to Tehran after a stopover in Damascus, Syria with a fake Venezuelan passport."

Corey took a swig. He was prone to decant Kalik bottles expeditiously whenever Hezbollah activity is uncovered on his Caribbean turf. "I'm worried about Hezbollah and Iranian connections with the drug trade. Hezbollah are bedfellows with the kingpins."

"I'm afraid your suspicions are warranted. I think we've got real problems."

Corey took a lingering chug. *No shit*

Morrison continued. "This businessman, who John Doe-istan stayed with for two weeks in Buenos Aires, has an interesting story. In three years, his mom and pop operation exploded into a regional chain. He now operates eighty-five subsidiaries along the Colombian-Venezuelan border and throughout the Tri-Border Area."

"What type of business? I'm sure it's one that can easily launder large amounts of drug money."

"Exactly. He's opening up chain restaurants that offer budget meals. DEA and CBIF moles checked a dozen of them out. Best value in town...full of tourists, too. Waiters stride around the dining room with skewers of grilled sausage, chicken, beef, pork...you name it...and slice off as much as the customers want onto their plates."

"A cheap, fast-food restaurant with a high turn-over of merchandise equals easy money laundering."

Morrison continued, "No doubt. They even have a menu item called *Cupim*. It's a cut of meat from the hump of the Brahma bull that's bred in Paraguay and Brazil."

"What's the name of the chain?"

"'Don de dios'. It also has an Arabic word in parenthesis after it. I'll send it to you, since you know Arabic."

Corey looked as the Arabic symbol downloaded onto his cell phone. "It means 'gift from God', or allah...same translation for 'Don de dios'. Did the agents get any other link between this drug money- laundering prick businessman and Hezbollah?"

"I'm afraid so. Remember our recent meeting at the Conch Inn Resort in Key Largo, when I called you home from Jamaica?"

"Yes."

"You reported that your informant in Haiti, Damballah Saint-Fleur, gave one of our DEA moles aboard Curtis Beacher's ship, the *El Sea* info about the Colombian drug smuggler, Sandoval. You said that DEA Medellin took photos of Sandoval meeting with Middle Eastern contacts in Medellin."

"Yes, I remember. I also told you the shipments coming into the U.S. through the Colombian-Fort Lauderdale pipeline were half coke, half heroin. The 'H' was top quality stuff, not from poppy grown in Colombia. I suspected it came from Afghanistan."

Morrison began chomping on the Montecristo. "Our Mr. 'doe-istan' resembles one of DEA's photos of the Middle Eastern men who met with Sandoval in Medellin several years ago. The resemblance is hard to match due to his wearing a keffiyeh and he was sitting at a table in the shade."

"What about the photos taken yesterday at the Hotel Montana meeting in Port-au-Prince? Any good shots of John Doe-istan?"

"Excellent ones and I'm sending them to you directly. Should be downloading now."

Corey held the satellite cell phone closer to his chest with both hands blocking the screen as a safety measure. Three photos downloaded quickly. He studied them for half a minute, to make sure he wasn't dreaming. "Shit!"

"What's wrong?"

Corey polished off his Kalik. "General, have you entered these recent photos into the *Next Generation Identification* system yet?"

"No, but my men here in Key West are working on it as we speak.

Should be downloaded into the system within the hour. Why?"

Corey continued. "Because there will be a match. I recognize this man from photos taken by my cell chief in Curacao two years ago. And, the photos were cataloged into NGI."

"Who the hell is this guy?"

"Well, sir, he's a guy from hell. My man on Curacao had a crew of nine counterintelligence agents."

Morrison said, "Yes, I remember. I requisitioned them and sent them down there...at your request."

"It was good you sent them, sir. They monitored sixteen individuals linked to drug trafficking and money laundering. We put them under intense surveillance. It turned out that three were Curacaons, four were from the Tri-Border Area, four were Syrians, four were Lebanese nationals and one was a Lebanese American citizen."

"And you're going to tell me that Mr. John Doe-istan was one of them?"

"He was the ringleader and met often with Lebanese nationals linked to Hezbollah. Scratch off the name 'John Doe-istan' and write in Kassim Khoury."

"Is that his real name?"

"I doubt it. It was on a fake Venezuelan passport he used for several years before disappearing. Very crafty fellow. Bought a luxury chalet in Curacao, just outside Willemstad and used it as a safe house."

"Yes, I recall all that. Bought it with drug money."

Dillon looked over at Corey from behind the bar, wondering if he wanted another round. Corey waved him off. "Well sir, you recall how that operation ended on a sour note."

"How could I forget...fuckin' Walt Mason and his FBI goons. You and your CI team uncovered direct links between that Curacao cell and Hezbollah. They worked with Colombian drug lords and trans- ported coke to Europe and the Middle East. You were just about to uncover where they laundered all the profits before sending it back to Iran to fund Hezbollah cells in North America."

Bad memories! Corey's voice became a whisper. "Sir, why did your friend, Walt Mason, order the arrest of that one cell member... the Lebanese-American. We were documenting members of Hezbollah sleeper cells visiting that safe house. They came in from the Tri-Border Area...Argentina, Paraguay and Brazil...and we tailed them back and found out their Iranian contacts... we were about to smash a huge terrorist network...then Mason ordered a joint FBI and Curacao Police raid on the fuckin' place to arrest one fuckin' lowlife with a U.S. warrant for cigarette smuggling! How could the Director of the FBI be so stupid!"

Morrison extracted the Montecristo from his mouth and laid it gently on the computer desk top. "I asked Mason that same question. He never gave me a convincing answer and I never trusted him since. His nephew was a moribund FBI agent at best...and Mason assigned him to conduct the raid."

"I didn't know that. Nepotism...sir?"

"That, coupled with arrogance. As you know, the FBI's counterterrorism division is ineffective in stopping terrorist attacks in America's heartland. The Intelligence Community advised the president that a more robust domestic counterintelligence program was needed, one that law enforcement couldn't conceive of due to the legal restrictions placed on them."

Corey took another lingering gulp of the cold Kalik. "Too many constraints, plus the only way to rise in the ranks is to make an arrest as soon as enough evidence is gathered to prosecute."

"Exactly. His inept nephew was promoted to special agent after the Curacao raid. The counterintelligence and law enforcement cultures don't mix. We want to hold off on slapping the cuffs on...to continue surveillance and gain knowledge on the entire network. CIA and CBIF agents are promoted by the number of spies they recruit, by the number of moles they insert into terrorist cells...not by the number of terrorists prematurely arrested and sent to jail."

"Is that why you elevated me to special case officer of the Caribbean region?"

"No. I couldn't find anybody else who'd volunteer for the job. That's why you're sitting under a purple umbrella drinking cheap beer in sweltering heat at a second-rate bar that's bobbing up and down on empty oil drums. By the way, the live satellite feed shows that you're on your fourth Kalik. One more and it comes out of your paycheck."

Corey chuckled. "I enjoy your humor, General Morrison...laughter is better than booze or tranquilizers. It's cheaper with no side effects... and in this job, that you so graciously promoted me to, if we don't laugh then the wretched people we hunt down win."

General Morrison laughed quietly to himself. "So true. And laughter empowers me to endure the ineffectual capabilities of the FBI and law enforcement in battling global jihad that's knocking at our southern flank, the Caribbean Basin."

"Thus, CBIF was created by the IC and the POTUS."

Morrison's voice regained its formal and somber tone. "Yes, and we answer only to the president. We exist as a clandestine, cloak-and-dagger organization concealed within the seventeen agencies comprising the U.S. Intelligence Community...and American citizens don't have to worry about their civil rights and privacy being invaded."

Corey put his Kalik down on the table and itched his ankles. The "no see ums" found a trail through the thin layer of Skin So Soft. "Sir, I'm worried about Walt Mason being in the Gang of Six. Can you trust him? We have a Hezbollah terrorist cell leader, Kassim Khoury, alias 'John Doe-istan' returning after disappearing for two years. Cesar Virgilio Sandoval and his two Haitian bodyguards, who murdered Duane Collier, helicopter him in to Port-au-Prince with another wanted terrorist from Afghanistan named Batoor Emal. Then, Laurent

Rousseau, the Haitian *Minister of Public Health and Population*, picks them up in a government SUV and drives to Hotel Montana where they have a get-together with Sandoval's recruiter and smuggler, Abner Orival. *Then*, after the meeting ends your CI team trails Orival to his shack in some shantytown...and finds a dozen Middle Eastern men camping in his backyard."

"The short answer is 'No!', I don't trust Mason. In the world of es-pionage and counterintelligence, trust is the most important currency but if you trust too much, you may be deceived. We've been deceived by Mason years ago, during our Curacao operation...it won't happen again."

Corey's mind stopped registering the tingling sensation of "no see ums" crawling up his calf. "But, he's one of the *Gang of Six* and we're at OT level! What do you propose to do, sir?"

"That's why you're toting around the same military-grade encrypt-ed satellite cell phone that the 'Gang' is using...created by the innova-tive Pinkston himself. I will need instant feedback from you from now on. No more scheduled meetings...we will be in continual contact. Mason will remain oblivious to the Hotel Montana meeting. I will re-lease info to him that is innocuous."

"Glad to hear that, sir. If he found out about Emal, Sandoval, Khoury...the whole bunch, he would be itching to make multiple ar-rests. I can see him now, contacting his FBI legal attaches at the American Embassy in Santo Domingo and talking to President Rinehart about how inept the CIA and CBIF are for allowing these ter-rorists to slip through our southern flank. He'd make sweeping arrests throughout the Caribbean and..."

Morrison interrupted Corey as he began grinding the tip of his Montecristo. "...and then he'd appear on CNN, MSNBC, FOX, and every local TV station in all 50 states... probably be asked to run for congress...maybe make a presidential bid."

"Yes, and spoil any hopes of uncovering the network of terrorist sleeper cells on Haiti that are linked to more in Nassau and Abaco...

we'd never find out who's funding them and planning whatever attack they're setting up. It would be a repeat of Curacao." *I can't believe Mason made it to the top of the FBI...I guess dead wood drifts to the top*

Morrison agreed, then concluded the conversation. "There's one more thing before I sign off."

"What's that, sir?" *General Morrison always saves the best for last... drives me nuts!*

"At the Hotel Montana get-together, our CI team recorded them scheduling a clandestine meeting that all of them agreed to attend, and our two Middle Eastern friends said to make sure the two cases of Arak were there. The woman our CI team recruited via Damballah, the one who waitresses at the Montana and dates the manager of the bar...she snooped around for us and found the cases with two Bahamian Customs declaration forms filled out. Her boyfriend's name was listed as the sender."

"Was a receiver's name listed?"

"Yes...Patrick Branagh. They planned to send the Arak to him in Nassau, but the paperwork might arouse suspicion at customs. So, Abner Orival offered to smuggle the cases in on one of his boats."

Corey's face lit up. "I've got Dona covering Branagh in Nassau.

Can your CI team get a hold of a transponder?" Morrison seemed confused. "Why?"

"We can follow the two cases of Arak. It'll lead us right to where the meeting is. The satellite in geostationary orbit above me is an imaging one. But, you mentioned an ELINT satellite was going to be sent here as well."

"Yes."

"Perfect. If our CI team in Haiti can insert an automatic identification system transponder...AIS for short...into a duplicate bottle of Arak and switch it with one of their bottles, the ELINT satellite could track the electronic signal emitted. We would instantly be kept abreast of the position, course, and speed of Orival's boat and find out where the meeting place is."

General Morrison remained silent. He learned not to interrupt one of Corey's intuitive streaks.

Corey gazed skyward as if he could actually see the garbage can-sized satellite hovering 300 miles above him. "The ELINT satellite transponder feedback could be used to guide the imaging satellite precisely so it could photograph and record what and who else is on Orival's boat."

Morrison liked Corey's idea and finally spoke. "Like a dozen undocumented Middle Eastern men who slept on cots in Orival's backyard?"

"Precisely, although I think I know where the smuggling boat is headed."

"Where? The Customs Declaration Forms say the receiver is the man in Nassau who you unleashed Dona upon."

"Regardless, sir, I'll wager the final destination is the Abaco Poultry, LTD operation on Abaco... where Duane Collier's killers hide out. We're on to something big... I can smell it."

Episode 33

The Mata Hari honeypot

"This baby arrived yesterday at the 'Farm'. I've flown these Cessna 525 Citation's before. Goes like a bat out a' hell and great for island-hopping. It's got two turbofan jets."

Corey listened to the High-Speed Transport Airlines pilot brag about his new toy. CBIF acquired the new aircraft from the DEA after they confiscated it from a drug bust in Puerto Rico. He glimpsed at the seven leather seats, mahogany woodwork and refreshment center. A few bottles of rum, gin and vodka were fastened to the shelf above the ice chest drawer. *Tempting.*

One of the seats had an iridium phone port attached. *Hmmm. General Morrison would never allow any agents to use it... too easy to eavesdrop on. Must be bugged so CBIF can listen in when a passenger calls out...glad Edward Snowden didn't find out about it.*

"How fast we going?" Corey asked.

"490 miles an hour. We'll be touching down at Marsh Harbor shortly. I only need 1,300 feet to land this baby. Part of my training at the 'Farm'."

Corey made sure his seatbelt was snuggly fastened then peered northward out the window towards Grand Bahamas Island. The deep ink-blue of the Tongue of the Ocean grew lighter in color, transforming to lime-green as the ocean grew shallower. It abruptly ended in a thin strip of white formed from the talcum-powdered sand beaches lining Freeport.

It was a mysterious part of the ocean, a huge trench beginning at a depth of seventy feet off the eastern shore of Andros Island and plunging 6,000 feet. He glanced out the opposite window to view the sandy shallows off Spanish Wells in Northern Eleuthera. The swirling mounds of sand deceptively looked like submerged mountain ranges even though they lie in less than twenty-five feet of gin- colored water.

After the meeting with Darnell Ferguson at the British Colonial, he called Dona Anani Guanikeyu, CBIF's ultimate honeypot. He instructed her to target Patrick Branagh, owner of the Irish Frenzy Pub on Cumberland Street in downtown Nassau. He relayed to her what Milo said about the man, especially his weakness for women- a married man and ultra-womanizer who mingles with narco-terrorists.

A straightforward approach would work best, no need or time for a circuitous, relationship-building scheme with bogus convictions and phony flirtations. Branagh was historically unfaithful to his wife and treasonous to his adopted Bahamian nation that graciously granted him citizenship. He would turn his grandmother into ashes if given the right amount of money. Corey instructed Dona to establish a quick relationship and get as much information about him and his associates as possible.

The exotically-beautiful Dona would have little difficulty in her mission. He didn't code-name her *Mata Hari* for nothing. CBIF employs a dozen women throughout the Caribbean Basin as honeypots and Dona is, by far, the most competent. He gazed out the window again at the distant Grand Bahama Island and recalled her last honey-trap operation in Freeport. CBIF identified a major heroin trafficker named Diego who had close ties to Hezbollah agents operating in Colombia and Curacao.

CBIF booked Dona into a room at the Grand Lucayan Hotel where he was hiding out. By design, she bumped into him at the poolside bar and, the next day, lured him away from the hotel. She rented a car and they dodged his security guards, then snuck off to Gold Rock

Beach in the Lucayan National Park. Corey chose this area due to its isolation.

Dona and her terrorist-friendly drug trafficker pulled into a small parking lot in the park and walked a quarter mile along a trail through mangrove marshes to the beach. She feigned fascination with the starfish, stingrays, sea biscuits and sand dollars near the shore, then talked him into swimming farther out to where the snorkeling was much better.

Diego accompanied her on an exhausting swim to the pristine, gin-colored waters far off Gold Rock Beach. After fifteen minutes of snorkeling, she complained about being tired and waved for help to three fishermen on a nearby skiff. Once on board the boat, they jumped Diego, drugged him, then took him to Darnell Ferguson's *Queen Conch II*, which was docked a half-mile away. Due to its shallow draft, the boat was perfect for maneuvering the shallows throughout the Bahamian archipelago.

The CBIF's Dirty Tricks division posed as crew members on the *Queen Conch II* whenever CBIF went to OT level. Once aboard, Diego was taken to a large salon, galley and master stateroom which they customized into an enhanced interrogation area. After an hour of grilling, he spilled the beans and named four men who murdered a CBIF agent in Curacao four years prior.

The next day, Diego was found unconscious on a beach in Miami with three bulk amounts of heroine stuffed in a backpack, which he claimed wasn't his. The judge didn't believe him and sentenced him to ten years.

A week later, the four men on Curacao who murdered the CBIF agent simply disappeared one night and were never seen since.

Dona would have made contact with Patrick Branagh by now. Depending on how events unfolded, Corey thought of ways to employ her skills. For now, she'd be a classic honeypot, but if the need arose, she could lure him to a remote place on New Providence for an abduction. CBIF conducts government-sponsored kidnappings when at the OT level. There's an advantage to having enemy combatants vanish without a trace of wrongdoing, like Diego's disappearance from the Grand Lucayan Hotel in Freeport and his reappearance in Miami with lots of smack in his possession. Obviously, he tried to smuggle the "brown sugar" into Miami from the Bahamas on a go-fast boat. A clean abduction avoids pissing off the local authorities, like Deputy Commander Rolle. It also avoids risky diplomatic repercussions.

Corey considered further options, like using her to blackmail the swine. Digital videos of Branagh having sex with Dona could be arranged. Another option would be to drum up felony charges. Corey thought of the Julian Assange entrapment case. The founder of WikiLeaks faced charges of rape, sexual molestation and unlawful coercion when two Swedish intelligence honey-trap females accused him of such offenses. Corey suspected the women were planted into Assange's life after the U.S. government targeted him.

Dona would perform her magic on Mr. Branagh. A woman with her unique beauty and demeanor is rarely forgotten and may be recognized by the enemy in future operations. That was the danger she faced. She couldn't carry a concealed weapon, for it would contradict her deep cover. She portrays herself well as a single, profligate woman who chases after a self-indulgent lifestyle bordering on hedonism and call-girl immorality.

The trouble was, she wasn't acting. She traversed the Caribbean islands when CBIF went to OT level, hustling men. It was a necessary existence for her, a non-professional woman of monetary need who yearns to live a life of opulence- gorgeous looks, expensive clothes, and a plush condo at Coral Gardens in the Turks & Caicos with a Ferrari 458 Italia parked in the guarded garage. Honey traps like her who remain in the open always face danger.

That's why Corey placed a CI team in Nassau, posing as a married couple, at the Irish Frenzy Pub for lunch a half hour before she arrived. They carried concealed Glock 30's with four magazines of

Teflon-coated ammo. *The "bad guys" wear bulletproof vests nowadays. I hope Dona's never a victim of revenge...it's always a possibility, especially in her case...lots of enemies and a face and body that one can't forget. Despite an altered name, different island, and a fresh identity and cover, she'll need a well-armed CI team in her midst. But, there's another reason...I don't completely trust her*

A CIA psychiatrist told Corey, "Dona simply has no feelings of compassion." Corey had ambiguous feelings towards his Mati Hari creation and didn't need a psychiatrist to tell him she was a borderline sociopath.

Her association to CBIF began at age seventeen when she contacted the local authorities from a pay phone on Middle Caicos, the largest island in the Turks & Caicos. Her humble Tainos upbringing wasn't all that modest. In fact, her father collaborated with drug dealers and stashed huge amounts of cocaine and money in the basement. He looked the other way while they paid him a visit at all hours of the night to stash or pick up hundreds of kilos at a time.

Her father was drunk most of the time on his favorite beer, *Turks Head Lager.* The Colombian smugglers snorted coke at the kitchen table and guzzled down *Turks Head Lager,* which her father kept cold in a large refrigerator.

At age eleven, she'd listen from her bedroom to the night visitors seated around the kitchen table laugh as they chugged beer and snorted lines of *weasel dust,* a name her father nicknamed coke as. One night the Colombians stumbled into her bedroom and molested her. It continued for seven years. Dona recalled hiding under her bed, but they would pull her out by her ankles and sodomize her whenever the visited.

One smuggler she remembered in particular. He was a hideous-looking Paisa Colombian from Medellin. Knife scars creased his face and he smelled of musty perspiration and stale beer. He visited her Middle Caicos home every other Wednesday to drop off and pick up money and drugs... and to skulk into her bedroom later on in the night. Over a period of seven years, she was molested by the Paisas from Medellin, a Cachacos from Bogota, and a Costenos from the coastal areas of Colombia...she hated them all.

The horror ended on a Wednesday night, three days after her seventeenth birthday. She laid in wait for the scar-faced Paisa. Earlier that day she stole her father's fishing knife and spent the afternoon honing the twelve-inch blade on a whetstone coated with mineral oil. It was, literally, sharper than a razor. When *Scarface*, as she called him, lay on top of her, she thrust the knife from underneath her pillow deep into his side, then slit his throat with much delight and no regrets.

She crawled out her upstairs bedroom window and slid down a rope that she fastened to the bedpost, then ran to the airport in the nearby village of Conch Bar. There, Dona called the authorities and reported that she witnessed her father kill a man and that there were kilos of coke and hundreds of thousands of dollars in the basement. She gave the address, then ran and hid for several days in the many okra, cassava, guava, tamarind, sapodilla and sugar apple orchards that dotted the remote sections of Middle Caicos. With only several hundred residents on the forty-eight-square-mile island, she remained free for only a day before the Royal Turks and Caicos Police Force found her.

After the court case ended, her father and a Colombian man at the house were convicted of murder and drug-trafficking, then sent to the H.M. Prison- Turks & Caicos. Dona was only seventeen, so the courts allowed an American couple to adopt her. She became an American citizen and lived with her adoptive parents in a small town in upstate New York.

Her fresh start in a new life didn't go very well. She grew incorrigible and was ultimately diagnosed with an acute anti-social personality disorder. Dona defied the ethical, small-town moral code that her parents clung to. She caused them much chagrin and ignominy, especially since her adoptive father was the town's Methodist minister.

At age nineteen, her adoptive parents asked her to leave the home after she killed the next-door neighbor's cat and destroyed his BBQ grill. The police investigation revealed that the neighbor yelled at her after catching her stealing steaks off his grill. That night, she snuck back into his yard with a baseball bat and smashed the grill to bits after clubbing his pet cat to death while it slept on a nearby lounge chair.

She felt justified in doing what she did. Her statement to the police included, "...the man yelled at me for stealing a couple of stupid steaks off his grill."

After being booted out of the house, she waitressed to earn enough to rent a rundown apartment. Two months later, she was fired after a sizable sum turned up missing from the cash register.

Destitute, she hooked up with a young man and they lived together for eight months, but she left him when he proposed marriage. She could not form a romantic relationship, for it was impossible for her to feel fondness, let alone love, for anyone. In her childhood, such emotional attachments were never formed.

A year later, she applied for a job at the CIA. Watching spy movies fascinated her, particularly the ruses and deceptions that Hollywood attached to the CIA's clandestine service. A lengthy background check ruled out her admissibility; however, a CBIF plant in the CIA's recruitment department referred her to General Morrison, who hired her then and there for honey-trap assignments, working alongside the Dirty Tricks division.

Corey's musing was interrupted by the pilot, who announced through the open cockpit door, "We're coming up on the southern tip of Abaco. Touch down at Marsh Harbor in five minutes."

Corey acknowledged back with a head nod, then continued contemplating. The very reasons that made Dona so good at what she does could also compromise a well-planned operation. She engaged in daring activities and risky missions that didn't seem to bother her. In fact, she relished them, lied convincingly with much confidence, and trusted no one.

Being betrayed by her father as a little girl was the obvious reason. *At least our enemies won't be able to trick her into becoming a double agent... unless she approached them first...for a price...a walk-in. Is she the perfect honeytrap...my Mata Hari...or a loose cannon? She's a pure sociopath. What the shrinks at Langley told me about her struck me as very useful...that she is a bonafide sociopath and won't respond well to treatment that uses punishment...but she'll respond to incentives, ones that fulfill her wayward needs.*

The pilot interrupted Corey's thoughts again. "Sir, you wanted me let you know when we're approaching Sandy Cay. It'll be directly below us in one minute."

"Do me a favor and bank to the right. I want to look at the airstrip there. Then, if you can, bank a little more so I can see the GAH all the way to Marsh Harbor."

"No problem." With that the Cessna Citation tilted right for several moments, and then straightened out. The Great Abaco Highway and Sandy Cay airstrip were visible in the distance.

Incentives...wayward needs. Dona feels entitled to everything, both people and things...the Langley shrinks said she has an intense craving for authority and power... and revenge. These desires enabled me to recruit her easily. The plush condo on Grace Bay, the Ferrari, her use of counterintelligence tradecraft to bring down ruthless men... it all satisfies her needs for revenge, power, and to hurt back just like she was hurt when her childhood was stolen from her. No, I think she can be trusted...to an extent...but I'll always have a CI team in her midst, just in case

"There's the airport, sir, just ahead at ten o'clock."

Corey peered down at the Sandy Point airstrip where Deputy Commander Rolle's son-in-law was murdered by a man with a red teardrop tattoo under his eye, none other than Cesar Virgilio Sandoval. *Poor Bernard, a young Bahamas Custom agent assigned to this remote airstrip to clear private planes flying into the Bahamas. His only blunder was being honest. I promised you, my friend...Mr. Rolle, that I would capture Bernard's murderer...and that I will do. The airstrip used to be packed limestone and coral. Now it's paved! Who flipped the bill? It wasn't the Bahamian government.*

The village of Sandy Point lies adjacent to the strip, the last settlement at the southern tip of Abaco. He stared at the beautiful, deserted stretch of white beach. *It's pure paradise...proper name for the village...Sandy Point* Further north in the Caribbean Sea he recognized Disney's famous *Castaway Island*, named Gorda Cay by the locals.

As instructed, the pilot banked again to the right so Corey could view the Great Abaco Highway. It appeared as a narrow, white thread weaving through the dark, leafy-green canopy of subtropical forest. Moments later, they flew over the parrot preserve where he and Constance discovered the site where Duane Collier was murdered. Two SUV's were parked alongside the GAH near the hidden logging road. *I hope that's the cadaver dog team I called in. Morrison said he'd make it happen immediately.*

Episode 34

The body "snatchers"

Jenson readied his twelve-gauge pump loaded with slugs as he tried to keep up with the pack of six dogs. He looked up through the forest canopy as a Cessna jet zoomed low overhead. It would touch down at Marsh Harbor airport in several minutes. The sudden roar startled him, but he quickly returned to his mission. His two Bay dogs were of the Blue Lacy breed, specifically bred in Texas for hunting wild boar. He set them loose at the GPS coordinates that some guy named Corey Pearson gave to Victor. The location was a thousand feet south of the site where an agent met his macabre death. Of course, Jenson didn't know any of the details. His mission was to pose as a wild boar hunter from the U.S. while helping Victor recover a corpse.

The Bay dogs had incredible scenting ability and tracked a wild boar that passed through the location several hours before. Suddenly, they located the unfortunate pig and let out a distinctive howl, alerting the four burlier Catch dogs to take over the chase.

Jensen trained the four Catch dogs, all fearsome Dogo Argentinos. The pair of Blue Lacys followed the boar to a thick patch of palmetto palms and continued baying until the Argentinos arrived and charged through the palmettos without hesitation. They threw their muscular bodies against the wild boar and locked their massive jaws onto its neck, ears and face, pinning it to the ground and waiting for their master to arrive with the twelve-gauge to put a slug through it. All the dogs wore a cut vest to protect their vital organs and neck. The terrified and angry swine managed a swipe with its five-inch tusks before being overpowered. Blood seeped from an Argentino's unprotected face, the one clenching the hog's throat.

Jensen had a special license not to kill the boars, but to capture them. It was expeditiously issued by the Bahamian Ministry of the Environment and the Firearms Licensing Office. The firearm permits and hunting licenses took two days to process instead of the usual three months.

He rushed to his patient Dogo Argentinos and commanded them to continue holding the swine down while he bound its legs together. Then, he taped the muzzle shut and signaled the dogs to release their vice-like grip so he could slip a burlap sack over its head.

Upon immobilizing the hog, which he estimated to be just shy of 300 pounds, he retrieved a needle and thread from the first aid kit and began to sew together the tusk gash above the right eye of the Argentino. It would leave a bad scar, one complemented by other disfigurements left by past encounters with wild hogs, cougars, bears and by a knife-wielding man who made the mistake of attacking his master.

Jensen's cell phone rang. It was his hunting partner, Victor. "Victor, where you at? I just hog-tied a boar and need help dragging it back to the pickup."

"I'm about a thousand feet north of you. Just passed the clearing and dock area where the man we're looking for was murdered. Leave the hog and join me...my cadaver dogs are on to a scent."

Victor switched off the cell phone and watched the two cadaver dogs sniff around the short dock that Corey and Constance gathered evidence from. With noses burrowing into the sand, they trailed a faint ground indentation through the clearing into the palmetto palm and Caribbean pine forest. The dogs grew excited as they tracked the scent path where a bloody human corpse was dragged days before. He didn't wait for Jensen to arrive, for the dogs immediately reacted in their own unique ways whenever a decomposing body is near.

His female Blue Lacy showed avoidance by slowing down and growing cautious. She grew nervous and raised her hackles, then attempted to leave the area. He ran up and gave her verbal reassurance that all was OK and encouraged her to follow him. The male dog showed enthusiasm and charged into a small clearing in the dense forest vegetation that Victor would have easily missed if searching by himself.

He followed the canine into the clearing and witnessed the keener dog urinating on a pile of freshly-cut palm fronds that someone laid over a pile of leaves and pine needles. Throughout its training, the male Blue Lacy routinely pissed on every human corpse it located.

Victor laid the palm fronds aside, unfolded a tri-fold shovel and carefully scraped away the fresh debris. The serrated edge easily sunk into the coral rubble until it struck soft tissue a few inches under the soil. He didn't know the name of the decomposed person he found...that it was Duane Collier. His orders from Corey Pearson were to find the lower extremities of a male body, collect the surrounding evidence, package it and fly it back to the 'Farm'.

Six hours ago, he took off from the 'Farm' to land at Marsh Harbor airport. While in flight with Jensen and the eight dogs, he received an urgent call from Corey Pearson. Pearson gave him coordinates to a second location they were to search *after* first finding the lower half of a male body.

At the second coordinates, he was to search along a hidden, abandoned logging road that had been cultivated with Devil's Grass. It was the same concealed road that Corey Pearson and Constance discovered while searching for Duane Collier. If this second body was found, which Pearson said may be that of a middle-aged woman, he was to process and bring it back as well.

After both searches were completed, Corey instructed the two men and their dogs to move along the abandoned logging road to the disguised entrance and back onto the Great Abaco Highway where their pickup trucks were parked.

Then, they were to drive the pickups through the disguised entrance and down the abandoned logging road to retrieve both corpses. It woud all be monitored by CBIF's IMINT satellite.

Jensen arrived with the four Catch and two Bay dogs and commanded them to sit quietly with Victor's two cadaver dogs. All eight canines sat around the site, watching their masters go to work.

"We've gotta move fast, Jensen. Get out the digital camera and camcorders and shoot close-ups of whatever objects I point to."

Both men laid their backpacks on the ground and gently spread the forensic-collection equipment out before them. Victor slipped on latex work gloves for hand protection and began collecting potential evidence while Jensen recorded each item before it was touched. The smell was almost unbearable, even with nose protectors soaked in a strong peppermint-scented mixture. The head, arms and torso were missing, but Duane's pants were bunched-up above the knees, indicating he was drug there by his ankles. Unusual marks encircled both ankles, probably made from a chain instead of a rope.

Victor swept Duane's trousers with a filtered vacuum device to pick up any hair or fibers embedded in them, then used a magnifying glass and tweezers to remove remnant particles. He was puzzled over Pearson's urgent in-flight call, requesting him to search for another body at a second GPS position, that of a woman in her fifties. If found, he was to conduct a second collection and recording of insect activity on the woman's corpse as well. It seemed that finding and determining the time of the woman's death was of paramount importance to Pearson.

Although Victor had little training in forensic entomology, he was sure an expert would analyze the creepy-crawlies he and Jensen photographed and collected on and inside the malodorous corpse. Same with the woman, too, if they found her.

He knew enough to know why Corey wanted him to use the camcorder to film the insects and larvae on the body and in the soil around it, then to take zoom-in shots. In the "insect-cadaver interaction" workshops he took, Victor learned that insects begin colonizing a dead body immediately and in a predictable sequence. Blow flies visited the cadaver within minutes after it was dragged to this location. Then, flesh flies and house flies followed within the hour. Not long after that, a type of beetle arrived. He couldn't remember its name, only that taxidermists use it to clean flesh off skulls.

After all was photographed and recorded, Victor collected dozens of flies, beetles and maggots, dropping them into small vials. The entomologists would identify each species and determine the exact developmental stage of each maggot. He knew the blow flies and flesh flies were most important in determining the postmortem interval, or time of death. Flies, eggs, larva, larva pupating into flies...they'll find out the maturity sequence and work backwards to accurately estimate when this poor man's dead body was first colonized by the flying, crawling, pupating and wiggling creatures. In short, they'll narrow down to within minutes of when he was murdered.

An airtight body bag was unfolded and both men gently slid Duane Collier's remains into it. While they took a short breather before moving on, Jensen stared at the body bag and wondered what this unfortunate man got himself into. Half a body... severed through the pelvis. He knew the man was an intelligence operative, but nothing else was divulged about him.

How his shadowy employer operates always fascinated Victor. His secure cell phone awoke him yesterday at three a.m. A scrambled text message instructed him to report to the 'Farm's' secretive airport immediately with his two cadaver dogs.

He boarded an HST Airlines Citation jet, where Jensen joined him. Onboard, the pilot handed him a blank envelope with *"For Your Eyes Only"* written across the secured flap. Inside were two GPS coordinates: the spot where they were to park along the GAH and the location where he was to begin the search. He was to hunt in a southerly direction through a dense Caribbean pine and palmetto palm forest with his dogs. The packet also contained $10,000 in cash and keys to two pickups.

Upon landing at the Marsh Harbor International Airport just three miles southwest of Marsh Harbor, the Capital of Abaco, they bypassed customs and steered clear of the airport terminal. Chief Detective Milo Symonette, Jr. of the RBPF flew in from Nassau to meet Victor on the tarmac and escort him and Jensen along with the eight dogs to the two waiting pickups.

Detective Symonette handed Victor a sealed envelope containing two hunting licenses signed by the Bahamian *Minister of the Environment* and two firearms license permits from the *Bahamian Firearms Licensing Office*, signed by a Deputy Commander Ellison Rolle of the Royal Bahamian Police Force (RBPF) in Nassau.

The hog-hunting duo proceeded directly to the first GPS coordinate. Their mission was straightforward: to recover the bottom half of a male intelligence officer, then search for a female body, also presumed buried in the dense forest.

Victor often speculated about the organization he, and the dead agent before him, worked for. It was probably part of the U.S. Intelligence Community, but seventeen separate spy agencies operated under the IC umbrella. Which one was it? CIA? FBI? NSA? Maybe the Defense Intelligence Agency, the DIA? It was an enterprise that trained and paid him well, but remained a shadowy part of his life. He didn't think Jensen was formally hired by the same enigmatic employer as he, nor that he had any idea what was going on beyond simply having to help recover a few corpses during a wild-boar hunt.

It was a good cover story Corey devised: two rich guys from the states hunting boars with their trained dogs. He used Jensen to add credibility to Victor's masquerade. The bodies of Duane Collier and his mother could be recovered without exposing CBIF involvement.

Whatever the crisis, Corey remained level-headed and set up ingenious countermeasures to impending operational hazards. He instinctively recognized perils before they presented themselves and defied them by perceiving obscure connections of opportunity. By applying cunning tradecraft, CBIF was able to operate in the open but under the radar of enemy eyes.

The issuance of firearms and hunting licenses was expedited by Corey's passionate plea to Deputy Commander Ellison Rolle. He told Rolle that he was close to finding out who murdered his son-in-law and would give him the name as soon as he found out. He lied, of course, because he already knew who the killer was. But, if he divulged that it was Cesar Virgilio Sandoval, Rolle would immediately issue a warrant for him and blow the entire CBIF operation.

Rolle was hesitant to pull the strings necessary for the speedy license issuances, so Corey told him the go-fast fleet operation was ahead of schedule and the dozen boats were ready. He applied pressure mildly by reminding Rolle that forty of his RBPF officers would be flown to the Miami Beach Marina for training.

Corey knew that Deputy Commander Rolle was in the midst of the political battle of his life, one that could terminate his career and end CBIF's long-time influence with the Bahamian authorities. The RBPF Commissioner of Police had a nephew who was after Rolle's position. It was nepotism at its worse. His nephew was only two steps behind Rolle in rank and never had to climb the organizational ladder like Rolle did. From the lowest rank of constable, the nephew was reluctantly appointed Superintendent of the RBPF by the prime minister.

The Commissioner of Police exerted much pressure on Prime Minister Lightbourne. If his nephew wasn't promoted five ranks hastily, photos of Lightbourne having sex with a Colombian whore at the Abaco Poultry, LTD mansion on Abaco would surreptitiously arrive on the desk of the editor & publisher of the Nassau Guardian newspaper. The current Superintendent of RBPF was retiring in six months and if the nephew wasn't chosen as his replacement, the prime minister's masculinity would be the crux of chatter from Freeport to the southern tip of the isolated Acklins Islands.

Corey uncovered the plot to oust Deputy Commander Rolle through Addie Kolmogrovov's dexterous bugging of the office of the Honorable Alfred Moss, MP. In his desk wastebasket, she retrieved a discarded memo written by his secretary: He was to immediately call the police commissioner regarding his nephew. The urgent memo was a tip-off for CBIF to zero in on Moss' calls to the commissioner.

Addie had also inserted a bug into the receiver of Moss' landline desk phone and through the step-up transmitter she glued under his desk, Moss' entire conversation with the Commissioner of Police arrived at the end receiver a half mile away aboard Pinkston's PT boat docked in Hurricane Marina on Paradise Island.

Corey, Pinkston and the CI agents assigned to tail Moss sat in the galley of Pinkston's PT boat, listening to the entire conversation that Pinkston recorded. There was a pause in the telephone conversation between Moss and the police commissioner. Both men were apparently planning something.

Then, to Corey's dismay, the RBPF Commissioner asked the Agricultural Minister about the funds the Abaco Chicken Farm, LTD donated to purchase three patrol boats for the Harbour Patrol branch. He asked Moss to pull a few strings and allow his nephew to announce the christening of the patrol boats at the next parliament session. The Haitian problem would be brought up and the nephew would point out that just last week 198 Haitians were captured in the vicinity of Nassau Harbour, attempting to enter the country without proper documentation.

The Commissioner of Police wrote the speech his nephew was to give and faxed it to Moss, which Pinkston intercepted and printed out. The oration concluded with a summary of how inept Deputy Commander Rolle was in stemming the Haitian tide, which was more like a tsunami.

Corey notified General Morrison of the scheme and obtained his approval for a plan to save Rolle's career. He contacted the U.S. Embassy in Nassau and arranged for the dozen go-fast boats to be docked in Prince George Wharf in Nassau three days before the Commissioner of Police and his nephew met before the Bahamian Parliament. The US ambassador, along with Prime Minister Lightbourne, would announce to ZNS-TV in Nassau and Freeport, *Guardian Radio* in Nassau, and to the Nassau Guardian newspaper that, due to pleas by Deputy Commander Ellison Rolle to the U.S. Embassy in Nassau, *Operation Stop the Haitian Wave* (OSHW) was created. The public would be invited to view the go-fast fleet in Prince George Wharf and hear Rolle give a speech about how forty of his RBPF officers would be trained for the special police marine interdiction unit. Morrison agreed to have the officer training switched from the Miami Beach Marina to Nassau, where the fleet would be sent to at once.

After Corey explained his plan to Rolle, Rolle made sure Corey's request for two hunting licenses signed by the Bahamian Minister of the Environment and two firearms license permits from the Bahamian Firearms Licensing Office were on his desk, ready for his signature.

Victor didn't know all the details about the mission he was on. His thoughts about the human remains before him and his mysterious employer were interrupted by Jensen's pair of Blue Lacys. The dogs stood up, looked back at the clearing where Duane Collier was murdered, and began to whine. That kindled the killer instinct in the Dogo Argentinos. They rose, beefy bodies trembling, and began to growl.

Jensen pointed and blurted out, "Look, there's another fuckin' hog!" He wanted to give the sign for his dogs to chase after it.

Victor spotted the large boar sifting through the forest smorgasbord of food- wild berries, sugarcane, sapodillas, guavas, bananas and fallen coconuts.

"Calm 'em down, Jensen. Might as well tether them. Sorry, but our hog-hunting mission is over." He took out his android and tapped in the second latitude and longitude coordinates that Corey gave him. A satellite map appeared, showing their location and the spot where they had to begin the second search. It was 1,200 feet to the northwest.

"Let's go, Jensen. We've got to search for another corpse...that of a middle-aged woman."

Episode 35

Waiting game

Two small children frolicked in the deep end of the Hibiscus Beach Inn's pool as their mother watched over them. Both wore buoyant swim vests and enjoyed their daring venture into the "bottomless" marine environ of the cement pool. They grew tired after a while and crawled out of the pool and lay down on matching SpongeBob SqaurePants beach towels. The mother suggested they put on their sun hats and sunglasses, which they retrieved out of a tote bag adorned with a large SpongeBob face donning a toothy smile.

Chara, Milo "The Messenger's" wife, walked up to the family with a tray holding two gin and tonics and a large bowl of snacks. The couple thanked her. Then, she walked over to Corey.

"I know you didn't order this, my dear Mistah Pearson, but this be on da house." She handed him a Bahama Mama, then left. Chara sensed when Corey was deep in thought and he seemed more so today.

He sipped the drink while lying in the lounge chair, reading a book in the shade of palm fronds. He was waiting for a most important phone call. Onlookers could easily see the opened book partially hiding his face- "Reef Fish Identification: Florida, Caribbean, Bahamas" by Paul Humann and Ned DeLoach.

The call may solve the riddle of Duane Collier's enigmatic abduction. Corey recalled the high-level meeting with General Morrison at the Conch Inn Resort in Key Largo. *Morrison showed me a photo taken in Operation Salt Flamingo of a Haitian FRAPH squad member...* *a man newly-initiated into the death squad that murdered Damballah* *St. Fleur's parents before his very eyes... fuckin' Bolan Tougas. Why* *did Duane Collier meet with this murderous psychopathic Haitian at* *the Hard Rock Café in Nassau? Why didn't he put up a fight when* *Tougas abducted him?* The phone call may provide the answers to a hunch Corey had.

Similar to military protocol, when a CBIF agent dies in the line of duty, a Condolence Team (CTm) visits the home of a designated loved one. In this case, it was Joan Collier, Duane Collier's mother. His father was killed at the Pentagon during the 9/11 attack and he was an only child with no wife or children.

The CTm consisted of a CBIF psychiatrist specializing in grief counseling and a senior counterintelligence (CI) agent. They drove to Joan Collier's home in Severna Park, Maryland, knocked on the front door and readied themselves to be let in and seated in the living room. They would then announce, "Mrs. Collier, we regret to have to tell you that your son, Duane Collier, was killed in action while conducting a vital mission in the Bahamas for the United States Intelligence Community. We are in possession of his body and are preparing it for proper viewing. We will assist you in making funeral and burial arrangements."

In contrast to a U.S. military soldier killed in action, neither the psychiatrist or CBIF agent could reveal to Duane's mother how, why or specifically where he was killed. She would not witness her son's handsome casket, draped in an American flag, being wheeled down the ramp of an immense Air Force transport at Dover Air Force Base by fully-uniformed fellow soldiers. They would not reveal to her that Duane's autopsied remains lie frozen in Dr. Slesman's Evidence Control Unit (ECU) at the FBI's forensic lab in a remote rural area of Virginia.

Joan Collier never answered when the CTm repeatedly knocked on the door and rang the doorbell. They called her registered landline phone number, which clicked on an answering machine. A quick search revealed her car was left inside the garage. Thinking something was amiss, the CI agent used a lock pick to enter the back door. Inside, they found a very hungry Yorkshire terrier and Joan Collier's purse and wallet containing $278. Phone messages were backed up for a week.

Searching for signs of a break-in, they found a window at the side of the house that was hidden from the street and neighbor's view by a thick rhododendron hedge. The window stood inside the frame, a bit unsteady, for quick-drying insulation spray barely held it in place. The intruders cut a straight line across the middle of the window with a glasscutter and placed duct tape across the cut line. Then, they quietly gouged out black molding around the outside window frame and used a screwdriver to pry the bottom of the glass out of the frame. They gently karate-chopped the duct tape and the glass broke evenly, almost inaudibly, along the cut line. It didn't fall because the top of the window was fastened to the window lock. The bottom half of the window was gently swung open, allowing them to crawl into her house undetected. Before departing, they used the quick- drying insulation spray to hold the window fairly secure, then tore off the duct tape.

Corey took another swig from the Bahama Mama which Chara garnished with mango and orange slices. While pretending to study the reef fish identification book, he pondered the apparent break-in and disappearance of Joan Collier and what his next move would be if his hunch was correct. *When Constance and I searched the abandoned logging road, I noticed the SUV tracks we inspected veered off the trail and proceeded for about fifty feet into the brush. That's why I called Victor immediately after receiving General Morrison's call about Joan Collier's disappearance from her home in Severna Park, Maryland. I called Victor while he was in flight to Abacco from the 'Farm'. I gave him the second coordinates...to search for a second body.*

The non-secure component of his cell phone rang. It was Victor. Corey answered. "Keep it short and brief."

"Positive find at first location…lower extremity. Positive find at second location… woman, middle-aged, in her 50's."

Corey switched off the cell phone. Both corpses would undergo autopsies by Dr. Slesman in a few hours. But, it didn't matter. He did not need to wait for the results. His hunch was correct. The "lower extremity" and "middle-aged woman" were the remains of Duane Collier and his mother, Joan Collier. She had been abducted from her home in Severna Park, Maryland and brought to Abaco Poultry, LTD *Duane, no doubt, was shown a photo of his mother's terrified face with instructions to "do exactly as we say or she will be tortured, then killed"…or something to that effect.*

It explained why Duane didn't wear his GPS locator and arranged the meeting at the Hard Rock Café so hastily, why he failed to follow CBIF's check-in protocol and backup system, and why he didn't ag-gressively fight back when they abducted him.

Despite his cocktail being spiked with Versed, they took him out of the nightclub and into the limousine of Agriculture Minister Alfred Moss far too easily. The Versed was meant to throw CBIF off, to hide the driving force that led Duane to accompany his abductors into the limo. He wanted to save his mother from the agony of being tortured in some cruel manner, in a way that would make the CBIF Dirty Tricks division's use of Enhanced Interrogation Techniques seem pleasur-able in comparison.

Corey thought about his next move. *What do they want? What Duane and his mother must have gone through! Did they kill his moth-er in front of him? Did they torture her or threaten to unless he re-vealed all CBIF's New Providence-seven cells? The answer lies in the Penumbra Database…I've got to find out what it is!*

The children leaped from their SpongeBob towels when three Bahamian children appeared at the edge of the pool area. The parents smiled and invited them over. Corey watched them in action. They met the Bahamian kids while snorkeling off Orchard Beach, which was across West Bay Street from the hotel.

Both children faced their three Bahamian friends, but were a little unsure of what to say. The mother got up and hugged the three little guests and said, "I remember your names...Jimentia, Bernard and Keva! I'm so glad you came to visit us!"

The three smiled broadly at the friendly adult lady who came to their island. The mother continued. "And, we want to thank you for showing Bobby and his sister, Heather, how to snorkel in Orchard Bay. We will take home the shiny, pink conch shell you gave us. I'm glad you came to see us because I've got a surprise for you." She handed them three junior-sized snorkels and masks from her tote bag.

All five of the youngsters jumped into the pool and began an underwater shark-hunting expedition. Corey overheard the parents talking about introducing Bobby and Heather to conch fritters before they flew back to New York. She called Chara in the kitchen on her cell phone and ordered enough for all of them to munch on around the pool.

Corey watched as a bystander. The kids grew louder when the conch fritter party was announced. They began splashing and laughing loudly. *There is another world, another life that exists outside my reality. Maybe... someday, I'll experience a piece of it.*

Corey needed a tranquil place to calm down and plan his next move. He left the pool area and strolled along the limestone sidewalk through the plush grounds, stopping periodically to admire the banana and mango trees lining the path. One banana plant amazed him. It had several dozen rows of ripening bananas above a large purple inflorescence. The serenity aided his concentration.

The Penumbra Database...sounds like a computer file of some sort. Whatever secret it contains is of interest to Sandoval and his Middle Eastern contacts. Their tentacles reach far beyond Abaco Poultry, LTD. They have sleeper cells inside the U.S. that they can activate at a moment's notice. One abducted Joan Collier from her home in Severna Park, Md. and smuggled her to Abaco. Joan and my wife, Danielle, were best friends... Danielle wasn't tortured and murdered by a sloppy home burglar or serial killer as the police report suggests... there's a connection between the bastards who abducted and murdered Joan and Duane, and my wife's murder. Does the Penumbra Database hold the answer? I've got a game plan and will get Morrison to OK it...he'll meet with President Rhinehart in private to do so, which the POTUS will no doubt approve. No recording is made between Morrison and the president when CBIF goes to Obscure Transgression level...completely black funded... no paper or electronic trail of notes, memos, documents, emails, faxes or tape recordings for nosey members of the Senate or House Select Intelligence Committees or other congressional committees to subpoena. I have to find out what and where The Penumbra Database is. I'll start from the bottom and work my way up...Darnell Ferguson's crew member selling drugs at Nipper's on Abaco...muling for Bolan Tougas and Cherestal. I hope my plan works. It has to.

Episode 36

The terrorism battle

CBIF Headquarters- Eaton Street, Key West

Morrison finished the private conversation with Corey on Pinkston's twelve-digit algorithmic-encrypted phone. He OK'd Corey's plan, and knew Rhinehart would, too.

Corey had gone over the skillful and unparalleled, simultaneous abductions and murders of Duane Collier and his mother. He convinced Morrison to put the mission on fast forward, for the enemy violated a gentlemen's taboo among spy agencies...you don't commit assassinations amongst each other and you leave family members alone.

The conversation upset the general. He lived through the Cold War era where an understanding existed among spies, one that has been truncated by Middle Eastern terrorist groups in their jihad against the West. ISIS and other radical Islamists flout moral codes when they fight infidels...it is their duty to Allah.

Corey reminded the general that CBIF has its sense of duty and obligations, too. Not in the eyes of God or Allah, but in the name of the democratic preservation of liberty and self-determination. The unjust murders of Duane Collier and his mother were intolerable. CBIF must settle the score.

Radical jihadists view wickedness, depravity and deceit as righteous in the eyes of Allah when applied to nonbelievers. However, the narco-terrorists and radical Islamists involved in the murders of Duane and his mother miscalculated CBIF's devotion towards its foot soldiers. Those even remotely linked will be captured, imprisoned, tortured or murdered... with the blessings of President Rhinehart.

Morrison walked onto the front porch of CBIF HQ on Eaton Street in Key West and glanced at his three CI next-door neighbors who were reading magazines on the porch. A third agent ran surveillance from the oxeye window in the apex of their roof. The two cats he adopted lounged on his porch couch, ignoring him.

As he strolled down his front sidewalk, he thought about how vicious the jihad against the West has become. He would redesign CBIF's organizational structure, just like he did decades ago with Brewster Jennings & Associates. CBIF would replicate the appearance of a large corporation with Caribbean interests and be used as cover for Corey. Just like the BJ & Associates model, he would set up an office with secretarial staff, a listing on the Dun & Bradstreet database...the works.

He felt an intense burn in his gut when he thought of Valerie Plame, the classified CIA NOC agent who used his front company creation for her overseas cover. He still couldn't believe she was outed during the Bush administration...her covert identity published in a syndicated newspaper column by Robert Novak in 2003. He quickly gulped down several chewable Pepto-Bismol tablets and forgot about the incident.

The aging general needed a short break to dine. He'd been alone in the downstairs War Room since 5am. The three friendly next-door neighbors waved to the general as he strode past. He returned the greeting. Their home looked so peaceful, so elegant. No one would imagine 12-gauge shotguns loaded with slugs and Ingram Mac-10 submachine guns with 30-round clips stood just inside their front door. Nor would anyone expect Glock 30's to be well-concealed under their loose-fitting Jimmy Buffett shirts.

The fourth man came out of the house and sat with them after notifying the four other CI teams that Morrison was walking to the Turtle Krall Restaurant & Bar. During the ten-minute stroll, the general would pass two teams posing as ordinary natives going about their daily routines, while a third team would act like excited tourists. The three members of the fourth team were already seating themselves inside the Turtle Krall near Morrison's favorite table.

Morrison continued thinking about how he would revamp CBIF and the leadership role Corey would assume. He walked west on Eaton Street then turned right on Margaret Street, walking at a quick pace all the way to the Historic Seaport District.

He entered the Turtle Krall and a friendly waitress seated him at his favorite spot overlooking the forsaken kraals... now, merely of value to tourists. The waitress expected him to order his usual crab cakes topped with mango chutney, but Morrison surprised her by ordering the special- Yellowtail Snapper with sautéed Cuban-style black beans, grilled pineapple and pineapple mojo.

He looked out at the Key West Bight. It was still a working waterfront even though the shrimping, turtling and sponging industries left long ago. The docks now bustled with schooners, charter fishermen, and tourists who flocked to the seafood restaurants, laidback bars and nightclubs, and to the sign-up booths to go on dolphin excursions and sailing adventures.

The Yellowtail Snapper special arrived and Morrison dove into it. The meat was fresh and tasty; the catch most likely swam in the ocean that morning. The *Key West Historic Seaport District* acclimatized itself to a changing world. He would insure that his transformed CBIF and Corey's new role in it would do so as well. The circumstances surrounding Duane Collier and his mother triggered it. Corey Pearson would spearhead CBIF's rejuvenation in America's battle against radical Islam.

Hibiscus Beach Inn, Nassau, Bahamas

Four hours passed since Morrison OK'd his plan. As Corey meandered along the inn's woodland path lined with banana plants and Royal Poinciana trees, he thought out the final details. It would begin in twenty-four hours at Nipper's Beach Bar & Grill on Great Guana Cay off Marsh Harbor, Abaco. He had a plane to catch.

Episode 37

Controlled bust

The couple looked like something out of the 60's hippy generation. The man had long, silver-white hair with a pony tail. His female partner bore grey hair down to her waist. If Janis Joplin were still alive, they'd be a perfect match. The duo wore cut-off jeans, sandals and pot-leaf T-shirts that read "Rocky Mountain High = Colorado." Matching green Peridot Crystal marijuana-leaf rhinestone pendants hung from gold necklaces.

It was Sunday at Nipper's Beach Bar & Grill on Great Guana Cay. They perched themselves among the red, green and yellow stools that overlooked the talcum-powdered, white sand beach below. Boats moored offshore in the Atlantic Ocean and people snorkeled in the nearby coral reef, judged to be the third largest in the world. Guana Cay was seven miles long, but if you strolled the width of the island from Nipper's, you'd reach the gentle Sea of Abaco in two minutes.

Corey hid among the sea grapes and palmetto palms lining the hillside that overlooked Nipper's. His plan was unfolding. He scanned the tourist crowd through binoculars, hoping to catch a glimpse of Devon Ledard. They were helping themselves to the pig roast buffet that Nipper's held each Sunday. He observed a woman in a skimpy bikini line her plate with both roast and barbecued pork, peas and rice, Bahamian mac & cheese, Cajun coleslaw and custard corn bread. *How they hell can she stay so svelte eating like that?*

A voice sounded in his earphone. "Counterintel team two report-ing. Imagery satellite tracked two targets board targeted SUV at Abaco Poultry, LTD and drive to Conch Inn Marina in Marsh Harbor. Targets rented a Boston Whaler at marina and are now motoring across Sea of Abaco towards Great Guana Cay. IMINT satellite has picked them up and is beaming their route on channel six-two-nine. Over and out."

Corey switched the satellite phone to 629. An amazing and clear picture of the Boston Whaler appeared. By the length of the wake it was traveling top speed and heading around the east end of Scotland Cay, Guana Cay's next-door neighbor. *I wonder if General Morrison is watching this from the War Room at HQ in Key West? Probably is. The two killers, Bolin Tougas and Pierre Cherestal, will arrive shortly.*

The boat appeared in the distance, rounding the tip of Scotland Cay. *Come on, guys, come to papa...dock off Nipper's and make con-tact with Devon Ledard. Start selling the coke you steal from your boss, Sandoval. Come on guys...don't let me down*

Ledard suddenly appeared at the Nipper's tiki bar while the Boston Whaler made its way down the seven-mile strip of deserted beach that lined Great Guana Cay's eastern shore. It would moor off Nipper's in about a minute.

Corey observed the Dirty Tricks division aboard the *Queen Conch II*. It was anchored offshore. Two of CBIF's DEA moles occupied a rented Boston Whaler nearby. They pretended to enjoy snorkeling in the coral reef off Nipper's, but were prepared to photograph every-thing that Tougas and Cherestal did and audio-record everything they said.

Darnell Ferguson did not exaggerate about Devon Ledard's flam-boyant lifestyle. Decked out in Tommy Bahama shirt and pants and wearing a solid gold chain necklace, he strolled over to the railing that kept drunks from falling down the steep hillside to the beach below.

Shortly, the Boston Whaler moored offshore, Tougas tossed out the anchor, then took off his sunglasses and rubbed his eyes. It was a signal to Ledard for their coordinated coke-selling escapade to commence

Ledard walked down the wooden stairway to the beach and waded out to them. He rested his arms on the side rail and began what appeared to be a friendly conversation with the two murderers. They smiled and joked. *The DEA team's recordings will find out if your words are congruent with your friendly gestures.*

Cherestal slid something with his feet across the deck to where Ledard was holding on to the railing. Corey observed the stealthy maneuver through his binoculars, but couldn't make out what it was. Ledard rose slightly in the water as he reached down and picked it up off the deck and quickly stuffed it inside his loose-fitting cargo pants. Corey caught a glimpse of the packet. It was a clear bag of some type. Suddenly, his earphone sprung to life. It was from the DEA team. "We got nice close-up shots. Subject picked up large Glad Food Storage bag, the kind with a waterproof zipper. It has lots of smaller sandwich bags stuffed inside it, each one filled with white stuff...and I doubt if its baking powder."

Another CI team of three men and a woman slammed down rum drinks at a picnic bench on Nipper's large patio while listening to the famous Barefoot Man sing a song called "Layin' Low in Abaco." Each slat of their bench was painted a different coral reef color- turquoise, lime green, red, emerald green and yellow. A huge umbrella shaded the table from the searing sun, allowing the gentle ocean breeze to cool them somewhat in the 90-degree heat. The CI hippie-couple team sat at a nearby bench.

Corey spoke softly into his satellite phone, which connected to earplugs hidden in the sunglasses worn by each member of the four teams, fourteen counterintelligence (CI) agents in all. "OK, the targets arrived. Let's get to work."

Devon waded back to shore and climbed back up the steps to the patio where Barefoot Man was singing. His pants pockets were bulging as he maneuvered through the crowd of fans. He searched for potential customers and zeroed in on four young men sporting numerous tattoos with rings dangling from their ears, noses and eyebrows. They swayed to the Caribbean beat. He stepped into their midst and began dancing reggae, then stopped suddenly and whispered to one of them, "If you want some good icing on dat rum cake drink a' yours, I can accommodate ya."

The young man whispered something to his friends and they followed Devon into the men's room. Several minutes passed, then Devon came out. Soon afterward, the young buyers exited the men's room and returned to enjoy Barefoot Man, whom they seemed to enjoy even much more than before.

Corey patiently observed the environment for ten minutes. Devon inspected the crowd for more buyers while the Caribbean music artist sang about not having to be gay to ride the ferry to Nippers. No signs of local gendarmes or narcotics officers. It seemed right for the next move.

He whispered into the satellite phone to the four teams. "OK, it looks clear. Hippy team one, move in."

The Janis Joplin look-alike slid off her barstool and walked with an empty plastic cup back to the bar for a refill. Acting quite inebriated, she stumbled into Devon. "Oh, I be sorry, my good man." She smiled at Devon and actually moved her hand down to the bulge in his pants and patted it. "Either you be well-endowed, my Bahamian friend, or you're carrying something else down there I'd like to buy."

She was wired and Devon's voice was clearly heard. "I got some good shit down dere." He pointed to her pot-leaf T-shirt. "And it ain't dat stuff. It be white-icing."

The female CI agent feigned a drunken stupor quite well. She rocked back and forth while trying to maintain her stance. "How much we talking about?"

"This be good stuff. Cut just right. I askin' fifty dollars fo' a gram, but give ya two gram fo' only eighty-five dollars."

"I'll take two, but not here. I don't want my husband to see me buying hard stuff...he sticks to pot. Let's walk down the trail towards the settlement."

Devon followed her as she walked out the entrance to Nipper's and stumbled along a path that descended down a hill lined with parked golf carts. Not many cars traversed the single-lane roadways on Great Guana Cay. At the bottom was a cemetery with above-ground cement structures housing caskets.

Among the dead and gone, she stopped and turned to Devon. "I changed my mind...I'll take four grams." She took fifteen sawbucks out of her purse, with a nice pic of Alexander Hamilton on each, and handed the wad to him.

He handed her four clear sandwich bags. She quickly stuffed them into her shorts and said, "Later." Then she walked unsteadily back up the hill to her CI partner, leaving Devon behind. At one point, she teetered enough to practically fall down the hillside.

She turned back to Devon. "I think I might need some help getting back."

Devon didn't want the few authorities on Guana to find a tourist lady with four bags of cocaine stuffed in her pants. "Sure, ma lady friend. I getcha back up dere."

She rested a hand on top of his shoulder to steady herself. "Nipper's knows how to make rum drinks."

"That fo' sure. Taste like candy but sneak up on ya."

The hippie lady glanced up at the top of the hill to her teammate who served as a lookout. He adjusted his cap, indicating the coast was clear. Simultaneously, the three members of the CI team that were sitting on the multi-colored picnic bench passed him and headed down the hill. As they passed by the hippy lady, she reached into her purse and retrieved a harmless-looking key chain, then stopped walking, acting as if she were going to vomit.

Devon faced her directly. "Everyting OK?"

She immediately jammed the fake key chain Tazer into the most vulnerable part of his anatomy, just below the rib cage. A high-voltage, low-current electrical discharge overrode his body's muscle-triggering ability. Devon gasped slightly due to the sharp pain. The high voltage impaired, but did not harm him due to the non-lethal current.

He slumped to the ground as his muscles twitched uncontrollably. The hippie-lady along with the three CI agents stopped his fall. One of them injected a needle into his neck, causing Devon to immediately go limp...even the twitching subsided. Two of them slung his loose arms around their necks and seated the "drunkard" into the front seat of a golf cart parked beside the path.

Several tourists glanced suspiciously at them while walking past on their way to the pig roast.

One agent in the driver's seat held up a Kalik beer to the passersby and jokingly said. "Gotta get this guy home in one piece. Too much rum and don't want to read about him driving it into the Sea of Abaco!"

The tourists laughed as he started the electric golf cart and whizzed silently down the narrow, cement pathway towards Great Guana Cay Settlement. The road was actually a sidewalk, barely wide enough for two golf carts to pass each other. It forked to the right and led to the settlement, which has a rich English loyalist culture and architecture. The few loyalist homes that remain overlook the gentle waters in the protected natural harbor of the Sea of Abaco.

They veered off to the left onto a little-used path that followed the harbor to its end, only 400 feet away. The path ended by an abandoned stone structure that used to be a loyalist home. The front was overrun by black mangrove sprouting around a rotting dock that jutted out onto a tiny beach. The home was well-hidden by sea grape and golden trumpet vines.

They drove off the cement path into the backyard, then carried Devon's limp body through the back door into a room and seated him in a metal chair. His wrists were handcuffed to sturdy metal arm rests and a black nylon bag was slipped over his head.

One agent checked his stopwatch. "It's been five minutes since we put him under. Pearson will arrive shortly. Time to revive him."

He took out another needle, lifted the hood enough to expose Ledard's neck and injected a potion they nicknamed the "Narcon Cocktail." It was an effective mixture refined by the CIA's Directorate of Science & Technology and often used by the rendition teams.

In a few seconds, Ledard awoke from oblivion and tried to stand up. Both agents put their hands on his shoulders and ordered him not to move or speak. He obeyed.

A moment later, Corey Pearson walked through the back door into the room and ordered them to take off the hood. Devon blinked his eyes and looked around the dimly-lit room. The two windows were covered with black curtains taped over them.

He heard a boat growl to a stop outside. It was the two DEA agents who moored off Nipper's. They entered the back door and laid a laptop computer down on the table before him and opened a large seventeen-inch screen.

Devon began to panic. "Who be you people? You DEA or somethin'."

Corey stepped out of the shadows. The back door was left open a crack, letting a sliver of light illuminate the table area. Devon recognized him immediately.

"You be da man from dat organization in America that my boss Ferguson work for!"

"That's correct." Corey spoke in a calm but somber tone. "And you… in the next twenty minutes… have an important decision to make…one that will determine if you are sent to rot in the Fox Hill

Prison in Nassau for the next twenty years or..." Corey pointed to the slightly ajar back door... "walk out that door a free man."

"You got nuthin' 'gainst me. People I know got da local constable in dere pockets. His name be Cecil Turnquest...he be da Abaco Constable. He will make sure nuthin' happen to me!"

Corey snickered. "Perhaps you should watch a movie we made... you star in it. By the way, let's invite some others to view it with us. Deputy Commander?"

The door that led into the main house creaked opened and Deputy Commander Ellison Rolle and Detective Symonette, the son of Milo "The Messenger," walked in and stood behind Devon.

Rolle said, "Thanks for the inside scoop about Constable Turnquest. He may be sharing the Fox Hill Prison cell with you. Now, let's watch da matinee."

The DEA team played the video of Bolan Tougas and Pierre Cherestal arriving off Nipper's in the Boston Whaler and Devon Ledard wading out to them and retrieving the large bag of coke. The stream switched to the CI hippie-lady buying four grams from Devon by the Guana Cay settlement cemetery.

Corey tossed a paper on the table with a list of number/letter sequences. "These are the serial numbers of the ten-dollar bills the hippie-lady bought the coke with. Do you suppose they match the serial numbers on the wad of bills in your pocket? We also have a complete audio-recording of your conversation with Tougas and Cherestal and of your bartering on price with the hippie-lady...that green crystal marijuana leaf rhinestone pendant hanging from the gold chain around her neck was a video microphone."

Devon stared at the computer screen while the video streams of his selling coke played.

Corey said, "That video of you selling dope to the hippy lady and the 'bait money' in your pocket will put you in jail for a long time. One other thing, if you don't give me the info I want, Mr. Rolle and his constables along with the DEA team will arrest Tougas and Cherestal and tell them you ratted on them."

Devon bent his head down and replied, "OK, you got me."

Corey leaned forward and stared intently into Devon's eyes, "You also know what Sandoval will do to your wife and kids when he finds out."

Devon looked surprised. "Sandoval? I dunno no Sandoval."

Corey took out a photo of Sandoval talking to Devon in the driveway of the mansion at the Abaco Poultry, Ltd farm and tossed it on the table. It was taken by the CBIF IMINT stealth satellite.

"You're a lying sack of shit. I'm done with you." Corey nodded to the DEA agents and to Deputy Commander Rolle. "Take this fuckhead away and lock him up in the Fox Hill Prison. You DEA guys, arrest Tougas and Cherestal immediately. Tell them that you caught Devon Ledard in a drug sting and he ratted on them."

Detective Symonette unlocked Devon from the metal arm rest, lifted him up and handcuffed his arms behind him.

Corey calmly stated, "I'd hate to be in your wife and children's shoes. Sandoval will torture them to even the score for you ratting on his bodyguards. You fucked up."

Devon lost it and started crying. "Ok, OK...I tell you whateva you want to know...I promise!"

Corey motioned for Symonette to cuff him back to the chair. "That's good. First question...do you know who Duane Collier is?"

"Yeah. He hire Darnell Ferguson to take him on expeditions ta find marine artifacts. He be a marine archeologist."

"When did you first meet Mr. Collier and how often did you go on these expeditions?"

"Five years ago, I meet him and I go on every one."

Corey knew the time frame was right, for he helped Duane Collier implement his cover at that time. The Bahamas had plenty of underwater archaeological sites and they remain a mystery to archaeologists.

Duane Collier searched for the remains of advanced cultures, on the level of the Mayas, throughout the Bahama Banks. The theory was that they inhabited the Bahamas 10,000 years ago, at a time of lower sea levels. Since then, the ocean levels have risen and Collier searched for these ancient sites which now lay submerged.

"What locations did Collier go to?" Corey knew the answer, but wanted to get Devon talking with candor and truthfulness. A few innocuous questions would help before the cross-examination begins.

"We go through da Bahama Banks... 'Bimini Road' off Bimini and a place called da 'Temple' off Andros Island. Mistah Collier spend much time off Bimini and he find columns near da Bimini Road. He also find rows of stone blocks that stretch underwater fo' sixteen hundred feet off Paradise Point in North Bimini."

So far so good. He's telling the truth. At the time, I assigned Duane Collier to keep a narco-terrorist under surveillance who bought a plush home on North Bimini.

Corey switched the placid questioning into a grilling. "Now, tell me honestly... when you were at the Abaco mansion meeting with Sandoval, did you ever meet a man named Sidney Fowler?"

Devon grew fidgety, so Corey pointed to the sunlight beaming through the slit in the partially opened door and said, "And fucking remember, if you lie to me again that door to freedom slams shut. Deputy Commander Rolle will take you out of here in handcuffs and throw your ass in Fox Hill, the DEA agents will arrest Tougas and Cherestal and tell them you ratted on them, and your wife and children will be in grave danger. Now, tell me, did you ever meet Sidney Fowler?"

"Yes, I meet him many times at da chicken farm. I work wid him everyday dere. I do all the cleaning out of chicken shit and clean the chicken barns up."

Corey noticed Devon's breathing grew heavier. He placed his hand on Devon's chest, noting his heartbeat increased suddenly.

"Are you aware that Fowler was murdered in Nassau?" "Yeah, but I didn't have nuthin' to do with it!"

"Tell us what you do know about his murder. Do you know who murdered him?"

"I was workin' in one of da chicken barns and Sidney came in and looked upset. He nice man, fear the lord and all that...we talk 'bout religion a lot...he knows I stray from da lord too much and try to help me.'"

"When was that?"

"The day before he fly to Nassau and get shot. He told me he was out hikin' in da Parrot Preserve and dat he saw somethin' awful, someone gettin' murdered."

Corey lit up a cigarette. "So why did Fowler fly to Nassau? To contact the police?" *I know why he went to Nassau...to contact Darnell Ferguson, because Devon here told him to.*

"No! He go dere 'cause I told him to tell everyting' to Darnell Ferguson, my boss man at the Potter's Cay dock. Sidney Fowler is scared ta death of Sandoval and knows Cecil Turnquest, the Abaco constable, is paid off by him. I give him somebody to turn to for help. I know Ferguson got connections wid some powerful organization in America...and I also know you be part o' dat organization, too!"

Corey took a drag from his cigarette. "Did Fowler tell you who got murdered and who did it?"

"No to both questions, but I know da killers had to work fo' the chicken farm cause Sidney woulda gone to Constable Turnquest in Marsh Harbor if dey was anybody else."

"What happened next? It was you who told Sandoval that Fowler was going to Nassau to talk to Darnell Ferguson...it was you, wasn't it!?"

"Tougas and Cherestal drove back in dat big SUV and unloaded a portable winch and shovels. They come in da barn and see Sidney be acting nervous...real nervous. They know someting' was up wid him."

"What did they do then?"

"Dey go into the mansion where Sandoval was. Funny, dey got a camcorder out a da SUV… must a been makin' a video to show Sandoval."

Corey inhaled on his cigarette. A cloud of smoke hung in the room. "I asked you if you told them that Fowler was going to see Ferguson…I'm waiting for an answer!"

Devon looked Corey square in the eyes and his breathing remained calm when he replied. "Couple a minutes later Tougas and Cherestal come back into da barn…with Sandoval, who be totin' his .44 mag. Sandoval ask me why Sidney Fowler be so nervous and if he told me why he be so upset. I had to tell 'em! If dey caught me in a lie, dey would kill me on da spot."

"What exactly did you tell Sandoval?"

"I tell him dat Fowler come back from da parrot preserve and he saw somethin' that upset him a lot."

"Did you tell him that Fowler witnessed a murder?"

"Hell no! Sandoval woulda shot me wid dat big pistol right den and dere. I only tell him dat Sidney saw somethin' dat upset him and he should go tell him, Sandoval, or to tell Cecil Turnquest in Marsh Harbor. I tell Sandoval dat Sidney didn't want to tell nobody on Abaco, so I tell him to go to Darnell Ferguson and dat maybe he could help."

"Did Sandoval wonder why you told him to go to Ferguson?" "He know I work fo' Ferguson."

"Does he ask you about Ferguson…what he does? Where he goes? Who he meets?"

Devon grew nervous, again. "I ain't gonna lie to ya. Ever since da archeological missions began five years ago, when Duane Collier hire Ferguson to take him on dem, Sandoval been payin' me cash to tell him everyting' dat happen."

Corey blew a cloud of smoke in Devon's face. "So, you're Sandoval's mole in my organization and he knows Darnell Ferguson heads the Potter's Cay operation?"

"Yeah, beginnin' with Duane Collier, dey know all 'bout dat... for the past five years they know 'bout da mysterious American outfit you work fo'...with lots a money dat uses Ferguson and his boat to do their stuff ...whatever it is."

General Morrison and I made sure the stovepipe concept remains operational among the Caribbean cells. Darnell Ferguson knows nothing of the real objectives of our missions we hire him for...only the spurious facades we camouflaged them in. So, Sandoval knows nothing of substance about Ferguson's Potters Cay cell...or the six other cells in New Providence-7. Hell, even Ferguson doesn't know about the other CBIF cells.

Corey pressed on. "Do you know who killed Fowler in Nassau?"

"I think I do...and it ain't Tougas or Cherestal."

"Keep talking, you haven't given enough info to justify me letting you go free through that sunlit door...do you understand?"

Devon looked frightened. A tear rolled down his cheek. "I jus' want my freedom...and my family to be safe!"

Corey slammed his fist on the table. "What the fuck do you mean you *think* you know who killed Fowler? How do you know it wasn't those two zeros sitting in the Boston Whaler off Nippers Beach who you mule coke for?"

"Cause a what I see goin' on at da poultry farm. It weird as hell... men from Pigeon Peas, The Mud and Sandbanks come to da chicken farm all da time, but dey don't look Haitian."

Corey recalled his contact meeting with Darnell Ferguson at the Patio Grill & Pool Bar in the British Colonial Hotel's lush gardens in Nassau. *Darnell told me about the Haitian problem and how they congregated in the shantytowns on Abaco. Are Middle-Eastern terrorists hiding among them?*

"What do shantytown residents have to do with the murder...and what do you mean they don't look Haitian? They're all illegals from Haiti."

"Let me explain. Abaco got da biggest shantytowns in all of da Bahamas...The Mud has a thousand people livin' in shacks with out-side toilets. Pigeon Peas gots at least six hundred. Sandoval work it out wid da Minister of Agriculture and some banker in Nassau to hire dem to work on da poultry farm, to help ease the overcrowdin' and ta give dem jobs."

After taking another puff on his cigarette, Corey blew the smoke and calmly said to Devon, "You better start giving me some useful shit or this interrogation is over."

"At least twenty men arrive from da shantytowns. They stay in empty poultry barns, but they ain't Haitian-looking. A man who I know from Haiti brings dem dere by boat, but I don't know much else 'bout him. Dis man stay for a week at a time, then sail back to Haiti on his boat. He meets with Sandoval in his mansion, along with a banker from Nassau and a couple of men who look like the guys ya see on TV in Iraq and Afghanistan... Middle-East dudes."

Corey motioned for one of the DEA agents to hand him a manila folder. He took out a stack of twenty-five photos and placed them on the table in front of Devon, then uncuffed him.

"These men who you say look Middle Eastern. Are they in these photos?"

Devon calmed down and grew more cooperative. Corey sensed he resigned from trying to lie and barter his way to freedom. The only option was to tell the truth...or to be drugged, blindfolded and delivered to the Dirty Tricks division black site on the *Queen Conch II*, which was moored nearby off Nipper's. He'd be waterboarded for more information, then sent to Foxhill Prison to rot.

Devon wanted his freedom and family safety preserved. "I nevah forget a face. If they in here, I'll recognize dem."

Corey watched intently, looking for signs of recognition as Devon studied each photo. When Sandoval landed at the Port-au-Prince dock in his helicopter, the CBIF counterintelligence team photo-graphed him, Bolan Tougas, Pierre Cherestal, and two Middle Eastern men, Eamal Batoor and Kassim Khoury get off the chopper. They were picked up by a government SUV owned by Laurent Rousseau, the Haitian Minister of Public Health and Population.

The CI team followed them to the Hotel Montana and took video recordings and audio soundtracks of their meeting in the hotel's back courtyard. A man later identified as Abner Orival, a Haitian recruiter and smuggler for Sandoval joined the gathering. Orival owned the home in the shantytown of La Saline, where the CI team identified Middle Eastern men staying. Photos taken of each man at the Hotel Montana courtyard meeting were placed randomly in the mound of photos Devon was going through.

Suddenly, Devon began tapping his index finger on Batoor's photo. "He be there, definitely. I saw him a dozen times. I even served him a few of dat weird drink he likes. Yes...dis man be at da Abaco Poultry farm mansion."

"Describe the 'weird' drink," Corey said.

"I pour it from bottle dat Sandoval imports specially for da two Arab guys. It called Arak, and is like thick milk. I drink some behind dere backs and it be powerful...lots a alcohol...more den rum."

Corey took the photo and told Devon to keep looking. *Batoor Emal. Spent time in Saraposa Prison in Kandahar before the Taliban attacked and freed him along with 1,200 other prisoners.*

Devon examined the next three extraneous photos, then stopped. "Dis man is da one I was talkin' about. He bring da non-Haitian men from Haiti to The Mud and Pigeon Peas shantytowns, then dey come to da chicken farm. They all stay in da empty chicken barns and practice." "How many of them are there and what do you mean 'practice'... practice what?"

"Dere be dozens of dem and dey shoot pistols all day long in da barn... pistols wid silencers on 'em. They make a thump, thump sound, not a big boom."

Corey took the photo of Abner Orival, the Haitian recruiter and human smuggler for Sandoval. *Fuck! The CI team on Haiti spotted dozens of Middle Eastern men in the backyard at Orival's house in the shantytown of La Saline. He smuggles them into Abaco and holes them up in The Mud and Pigeon Peas, then takes them to Abaco Poultry, LTD...a human-smuggling pipeline for sleeper attack cells to sneak into America!*

Devon interrupted Corey's thoughts. "Dis be da other man from da Middle East. I dun like dis guy...he scary."

Corey took the photo and stared at it. Bad memories resurfaced. It was of Kassim Khoury, the Hezbollah terrorist cell leader, alias 'John Doe-istan', who CBIF had under intense surveillance two years ago, in Curacao. He thought about Khoury's link to Hezbollah in the Tri-Border Area and how he laundered drug money and used the profits to support Hezbollah sleeper cells throughout North America.

Devon held up another photo. "Dis man, I see him heah, too." Corey took the photo. It was Laurent Rousseau, the Haitian Minister of Public Health & Population. Rousseau picked up Sandoval and the rest at the Port-au-Prince docks when the chopper landed and drove them in his government SUV to the Hotel Montana.

"Tell me, Mr. Ledard, what exactly do you do for Sandoval at the Abaco Poultry, LTD farm besides clean the barns?"

"He hire me to tell him all 'bout Darnell Ferguson's going-ons."

Corey took another drag off his cigarette. "We know that. What else do you do at the farm. Have you ever been inside the mansion?" "Yeah, when dey have da big parties, I serve drinks and take care of dere needs. Dats why I know these pictures so well...I waited on these men at the last party."

Corey blew a swirl of smoke into Devon's face. "When was the last party?"

"About a month ago. Every one of dese men were dere. Sandoval bring up whores from Colombia. Dey service 'em all."

"Any other men, or women, attend these parties that weren't in the photos?"

"Fo' sure. Two men from Nassau...Irish guys. One owns a bar and da other be a big banker in Nassau. Constable Turnquest of Abaco show up, too... he like da Colombian whores. But...I don't think he be in his job too much longer." Devon glanced over at Deputy Commander Rolle, who stood quietly with a big smile on his face, nodding in agreement.

Corey persisted in his questioning. "What are the names of the Irish guys?"

"Sean and Patrick Branagh. Sean, he be da big banker and his brother Patrick, he own da Irish Frenzy Pub. Oh, I forgot...a real big wig from da U.S., a guvament big shot, but I dun know his name. He comes wid his aide."

"A U.S. government official...who brought an aide with him?"
"Yeah, dey come here too... fly in wid da Bahamian Agricultural Minister, da Honorable Alfred Moss."

"You say you don't know their names?"

Devon fidgeted in his seat. "No, I say I dun know da big, powerful guy's name, but I know his aide's name. We drive into Marsh Harbor one time to get a pizza that Sandoval wanted...he nuts on conch pizza. Da aide and I, we talk a lot and he told me his name when he was drunk...it be Mark Serwin."

Mark Serwin...holy shit! He's the chief of staff to Senator William Warren, the Chairman of the Senate Select Intelligence Committee.

Episode 38

The Cali exchange

Cali, Colombia

The full-size Ford Explorer SUV was rented for $178 a day, but the passengers would only need it for several hours. It took a circuitous route around Cali, a typical driving behavior of site-seeing tourists. With tinted windows, the occupants couldn't be seen until they pulled up to the Iglesia de San Francisco church in the central downtown area and the driver, aka "asesino rapida," exited and opened the back door.

General Manuel Castano climbed out and glanced at Cali's largest church, then strolled to a nearby plaza. His bodyguard followed slightly behind, concealing a machine gun pistol beneath a loosely-fitting, colorful shirt. Castano wasn't sporting his military attire with three stars to symbolize his teniente status, like he did inside the Hart Senate Office Building in Washington, DC when he spoke before Senator William Warren and the Senate Select Committee on Intelligence.

Today, he wore a small sombrero, slacks, and loose-fitting, long-sleeve cotton shirt that wasn't tucked in. Under the shirt, a M1911 semi-auto .45 was tightly fastened to the inside of his belt.

The duo strolled nonchalantly amongst the vendors, locals and tourists, blending in like a KKK clansman at a Martin Luther King rally. They feigned shopping while scanning up and down Carrera 5, Alvenida 6 and Calles 9 and 10. During their "sightseeing" circuit around Calle, Castano noted vehicles that looked even remotely suspicious, writing down license plate numbers and descriptions of the cars, vans, trucks and motorcycles that made irregular traffic maneuvers or simply followed them for an extended period. He took out his notepad and glanced at the list, but none were in the area.

So far, things looked secure for the exchange which was scheduled to occur in forty-five minutes. He was about to commit high treason. If caught, he would be executed or spend the rest of his life in the worst prison in the western hemisphere, Riohacha Penitentiary in Colombia's northernmost state of La Guajira. He knew the decrepit prison well, for he sent many traitors there.

The prison population exceeds the maximum capacity by 478 percent, the showers and toilets are deplorable, and the stench is unbearable. If caught, he would ask for the death sentence or commit suicide rather than being locked up inside Riohacha, where many of his adversaries, both guilty and innocent were imprisoned.

He bought a cheap pair of sunglasses and souvenir postcard of the Inglesia de San Francisco church from an insistent vendor, then checked his watch. A half hour before the meeting, time to proceed. Both men walked back to the SUV and drove toward the scenic drive that hugged the shores of the Cali River in the Penon neighborhood. One of Castano's spotters would be there, perched on a modern bronze sculpture of a cat.

Fifteen minutes later they were in the El Penon neighborhood and drove past the bronze statuette of a feline created as part of a renovation project. Both men glanced at the disheveled boy dressed in jeans and worn-out T-shirt, who lay propped against the sculpture, chugging down a bottle of 3 Cordilleras Mestiza in a brown paper bag.

The boy took off his sunglasses and wiped his brow, a signal that it was OK for them to proceed to the Cuisine Corridor for the luncheon date. The lieutenant general would soon dine with four other accomplices and discuss the pilfering, sale and delivery of U.S.

hi-tech 140mm mortars with laser guidance and grid switches for precise targeting.

The spotter looked to be around age thirteen. He was a youth member of the Urabenos criminal gang which Castano and his asociado Rojas supply military weapons to. A half dozen other gang members served as lookouts along the way to Cuisine Corridor. Castano supplied them with prepaid cell phones, which they would dispose of when the Cali exchange was completed. Meanwhile, he would receive a call from any one of them if anything looked suspicious.

The Urabenos operate intelligently. Unlike Pablo Escobar who made one-hundred percent of his money via trafficking drugs, the Urbaneos are diversified. Only half their profits come from drug sales. The remainder flows in from kidnappings, extortions, illegal gold mining, political assassinations, for-hire killings, and selling stolen military weapons that Castano and Rojas supply to them.

Several years ago, one of Lt. General Castano's technician soldiers was arrested for stealing pistols from the Cali armory. The day before his sentencing, the judge received a packet of $20,000 on his front door stoop, plus a note describing what his twin daughters wore to school that day. The case was dismissed.

Shortly after the signal to proceed, they drove into the Cusine Corridor, Corredor Gastronomico neighborhood and drove past famous restaurants. Castano decided to take one last excursion through the Granada and Paque del Corazon neighborhoods before advancing to San Antonio where he would dine at Platillos Voladores and make the exchange.

"Asesino rapida" slowed the Ford Explorer down to allow some children playing fuchi in the street to get out of the way. Castano watched them toss a beanbag, or fuchi, from foot to foot as they danced to the sidewalk, doing tricks as well. He remembered playing fuchi as a young boy growing up in Cali, the only positive remembrance of an otherwise ugly, poverty-stricken childhood spent in a survival mode.

His father was murdered and his sister was abducted and raped by the Colombian armed forces. He helped his mother survive by selling water door-to-door, hawking phone cards at traffic lights and selling fruit and vegetables that he stole from vendors.

At age twelve, he was arrested for theft and spent a few days in juvenile detention in Cali before an unknown source bailed him out. This man recruited him into the National Army where he was trained to fight alongside government soldiers in its war against FARC. By age fourteen, he was proficient in firing the Heckler & Koch MP5 submachine gun, M1911 pistol, and the U.S. M16A2 rifle with its M203 grenade-launcher attachment.

In boyhood, Castano learned that laws were made to protect Colombia's moneyed, while indicting its poor. He scoffed at the law prohibiting children under age eighteen to join the National Army. Hell, they recruited him at age twelve under a quid pro quo arrangement and provided clothing, meals and a penury monthly allowance, which he sent a portion of to his mother.

Several more years passed. Upon reaching age sixteen, the National Army of Colombia persuaded him to become an informer and to collect information while working undercover for a special operations unit that fought terrorist guerillas bent on overthrowing the government.

The unit trained him in clandestine spycraft needed to do special recon and to infiltrate the Urabenos drug-trafficking gang. He was successfully conscripted by the violent band and was able to give the special ops unit info on the locations of their cocaine labs, hideouts and day-to-day activities.

At age eighteen, the present-day Lieutenant General Castano officially joined the National Army of Colombia. He was assigned to the 3rd Division, which is based in Cali and has jurisdiction over southwest Colombia.

Since he was already well-trained in using the army's standard weapons and tactics since childhood, he advanced quickly from rank of soldier to second lieutenant, then to lieutenant, captain, major, colonel and ultimately to his present rank of lieutenant general.

It was time for the exchange. "Asesino rapida" steered the SUV up to the entrance of Platillos Voladores and let Castano off. He walked through the front foyer of the gourmet restaurant to the back patio, finding his table hidden amidst beautiful tropical vegetation.

Four men nodded to him as he sat down: Cesar Virgilio Sandoval, narco-terrorist drug smuggler; Juan Rojas, retired Colombian Army officer and arms dealer; Javier Sanchez, a higher-up in the Fuerzas Armadas Revolucionarias de Colombiationary (FARC); and Asif Qadeer Edhi, a radicalized jihadist trained by the Taliban in Pakistan's Federally Administered Tribal Areas (FATA). Edhi specializes in the formation and training of terrorist sleeper cells within the U.S.

Castano wasted no time. "Bienvenidos mis amigos. Vamos directo al grano..."

Asif Qadeer Edhi interrupted. "Before we begin, I do not speak Spanish well and none of you here speak my Pashto, so let's talk in the language we all share...English. OK?"

Castano felt his control of the meeting slipping away, but Asif held the briefcase stuffed with money, including thick wads of Colombian bills with a picture of Julio Garavito A. and the words veinte mil pesos printed on each one. If things go well, he would tote away a satchel worth $500,000 USD.

"Yes, you are right, Asif. We will speak English."

Edhi replied, "Thank you, Lieutenant General Castano. Now, tell me how these weapons will be delivered. I need a guarantee before the payments are made."

"The mortars are being disassembled as we speak in the military barracks here in Cali. The parts will be loaded onto a truck and transported to the Ecuador border. From there..."

Edhi interrupted, "Isn't that rather risky?"

Castano replied, "There's a slight risk to everything, but we take calculated risks when we smuggle weapons, quite different from being rash. Isn't that right, Juan?"

Juan Rojas, the retired army officer agreed. "Si, of course. The mortar parts will be loaded onto a military vehicle to avoid detection, a three-ton M35 cargo truck. The barracks has a fleet of them and they come and go constantly, delivering supplies to our outlying bases."

Sandoval chipped in. "Yes, and I have several drug pipeline routes that begin at the Ecuadorian border. Won't be no problem hidin' da mortars once da trucks get there. I got a hundred points along da border dat I use."

Rojas added, "And I use them, too, to ship stolen arms to narco-paramilitary groups. So far this year, I smuggled five-hundred automatic rifles through to Mexican and Guatemalan drug traffickers. Never been caught."

Castano continued. "At one of these remote points, they will be off-loaded from the M35's and manually carried over the border by Javier Sanchez' FARC soldiers and hidden in one of his camps inside Ecuador."

One of retired General Rojas' newly-bought cell phones chimed. It was a call from one of the soldiers at the Cali armory barracks. He listened for a few seconds and hung up. "My tech soldiers have disassembled the three mortars and are loading the parts onto the M35."

Castano smiled, "It won't be too much longer before they reach the Ecuador border. Let's eat."

With that, Cesar Sandoval signaled Bolan Tougas and Pierre Cherestal to summon a waiter. Both killers of Duane Collier flew with him from Abaco Poultry, LTD.

A nervous waiter arrived, alarmed by the bodyguards lurking about the restaurant and parking lot outside. "Hola! Gracias tan

Robert Morton

mucho por elegir Platillos Voladores para deleite de su paladar. Aquí están nuestras ofertas especiales..."

Sandoval interrupted the waiter. "Anybody want da special? I already know what I want."

Castano told the waiter they weren't interested in the specials and to leave the menus for them to look at. The server quickly glanced at Sandoval's two bloodred teardrop tattoos under his left eye, then obediently exited to the main restaurant/bar area.

Silence ensued for several minutes while they viewed the food items, then Sandoval motioned to Tougas and Cherestal to summon the waiter back.

In a half hour, an incredible epicurean feast arrived. During the wait, General Rojas received a second call, notifying him the hi-tech mortar parts were packed in crates, loaded onto the army transport trucks and hauled away.

Castano told Rojas to order the soldiers to drive the cargo to Ipiales, Nariño, Colombia on I-25. They would pick up a FARC revolutionary fighter at Route 10 Guaitarilla, who would guide them to a dirt road that led to the Equator border. The entire operation should take just under nine hours.

Asif Edhi enjoyed his plate of *sancocho de gallina*, a chicken stew mixed with banana, beef, onion, green tomao, spring onion and cassava. He licked the cumin, saffron and celery seasoning off his fingers and spoke while doing so. "OK, my friends, General Rojas and Lieutenant General Castano, I will pay you both half now and the remainder when the mortars reach the final destination in the U.S., as we agreed."

Sandoval glanced at his murderous bodyguards Tougas and Cherestal, nodding for them to make sure the waiter or wandering customers don't saunter by, then said to Edhi, "The exchange be OK ta make."

The Pakistani terrorist retrieved two satchels overstuffed with Colombian bills from his briefcase and slid them across the table. He then asked, "What's the chances of me getting some shoulder-firing missiles?"

General Rojas looked at Castano, who shrugged his shoulders and told him to tell Edhi what they have. "We do not have any shoulder-firing missiles, but have a Mistral missile, which is a man-portable launch unit that can be fired from armored vehicles, ships...even helicopters."

Edhi replied, "No, we need shoulder-firing missiles, man-portable ones... like the American Stinger. We want anti-aircraft, not anti-tank Stingers. What's the chance of you, Lieutenant General Castano, persuading that U.S. senator 'what's his name' to supply your forces with them?"

Castano replied, "He is Senator William Warren, head of the Senate Select Committee on Intelligence. I would have to justify why my army would need them. But, it could be done."

Sandoval chipped in, "If you give dis Warren enough money, he'd turn his grandma into ashes. I met his chief o' staff, Mark Serwin, at da Nanny O'Brien Irish pub in Washington and pay dem off for lettin' Castano talk to da Senate Intelligence Committee and to request dese mortars. I betcha he'd let Castano come and ask fo' the missiles, too."

"And how do I know this is true?" Edhi asked.

"Cause here's da proof." Sandoval took a cassette tape out of his pocket and plopped it in front of Edhi. "Dats a recordin' of Castano's talk to da committee, with the questions all the members ask him. Mark Serwin give me dis at Nanny O'Briens, a pub in Washington. You listen to it...Lieutenant General Castano could sway eskimos to buy refrigerators."

Edhi took the cassette. "Thank you for the recording, Mr. Sandoval, I will listen to it with my higher-ups. You also gave me this cassette to demonstrate that you played a part in acquiring the mortars, too. Am I right?"

"Yeah...it couldn't a happen in da first place if I wasn't involved. And, the delivery o' da mortars to the U.S. mainland ova my drug pipeline routes is anotha thing."

Edhi took out a third satchel and handed it to Sandoval. "We're well aware of that. Here's fifty grand, American. When you smuggle the mortars successfully to the hideout in the U.S., you will get three times that amount."

Castano said, "Getting back to the Stingers, if I could persuade the U.S. Senate Select Intelligence Committee...er, I mean Senator Warren ...of the Colombian army's need for them, how much would you be willing to pay."

"I'm the leader of the jihadi sleeper attack cells and am not involved in operational funding, but I'm sure it would be worth your while. My associates are planning simultaneous attacks on three American airports and they would do just about anything to get their hands on these missiles. I would guess a minimum of two million American dollars per missile. I know they want two Stingers at each airport, which they plan to fire from modified pickup trucks. We're talking roughly twelve million USD."

Castano nudged Rojas' shoulder, who was sitting next to him enjoying a plate of *arroz atollao*. Without looking up, Roja said, "I heard what our Pakistani friend said...you better start preparing your speech for Senator Warren, mi amigo."

Edhi chuckled. "Well, it's still a ways off. We have to case out each airport to identify the weaknesses in security, which is usually lax along the public roads below the jet final approach patterns. But, enough of our future plans...let's get back to the here and now. Mr. Sandoval, is your drug pipeline secure from the Americans? I'm hearing more and more of some organization called CBIF that operates in the Caribbean Basin. Should we be worried about them?"

"Yes, and no. We know CBIF gots agents all over da Caribbean and dey recruit locals to be informants. They have many counterintelligence officers, too."

"So, you're answer is 'Yes', they are a threat to our operations."
"Well, yeah, but 'no' also. We penetrate a CBIF cell in Nassau. It be under da Paradise Island Bridge. A man named Darnell Ferguson runs a fishin' boat charter and he work fo' dis CBIF and dey pay him well. One of his crew members, name Devon Ledard, tell us all about the cell's activities. It was controlled by a CBIF guy named Duane Collier...but I kill him."

Edhi, Castano, and Rojas were taken by surprise. Rojas spoke first. "Why the fuck did you kill an American agent who you suspect works for the intelligence services...this CBIF... whatever the fuck it is? They'll retaliate, the U.S. spy agencies are known for making somebody pay for harming their agents."

Asif Qadeer Edhi glared at Sandoval and said, "Suppose you tell us what's going on at that chicken farm on Abaco. Why, how, where and when did you murder this American spy?"

Sandoval's forehead began perspiring. "The corrupt Americano Senator William Warren come to da Abaco Poultry farm many times with his aid, Mark Serwin. He help out my drug pipelines from bein' uncovered. One day, he tell me dat a big fallin'-out happen between the FBI and da CIA regardin' domestic surveillance in da U.S. and dat CBIF got moles planted inside da FBI and otha spy agencies. One o' the moles worked at da Pentagon... named Drew Collier. He be da fatha o' Duane Collier, da agent I murder."

Javier Sanchez, the FARC revolutionary, had visions of American counterintelligence agents photographing him and his four luncheon buddies when they left Platillos Voladoreies. At times, he wished he never met Sandoval. "So, what was the purpose of murdering him?"

"I murder both him *and* his motha...let me explain. We got American higher-ups in our pockets. Dis American CBIF mole guy, Drew Collier, he be hackin' into Pentagon and defense department stuff for years and uncover FBI plot to undermine CIA takin' ova domestic surveillance. Big rift between CIA counterintelligence and FBI law enforcement ... different group of people they be! Big split between dem on how to combat guys like you, Edhi, inside da U.S."

Juan Rojas, Javier Sanchez, Asif Qadeer Edhi, and Castano stared at Sandoval in silence. The man with the bloodred teardrop tattoos under his left eye continued. "I know what you all thinkin'... how did I abduct a U.S. spy workin' for CBIF. Simple, I find out dat Duane Collier's mom has da database her husband gather 'bout plot between Senator Warren and da FBI against the CIA."

Rojas asked, "So, why didn't you target Drew Collier himself instead of going after his son and wife?"

"Cuz' Drew Collier, the CBIF mole inside da Pentagon... he be one a da 125 who got killed at da Pentagon on 9/11. His database was securely stored at da Pentagon, but the jet plane crash into his office and destroyed it. So, Senator Warren tell me when he come to da Abaco Poultry mansión dat everyting' Drew Collier collected against Warren and da FBI director was backed up on anotha database and dat a lady name Danielle Pearson, a good friend of Drew Collier's wife, may be hidin' it at her home in Sverna Park, Maryland. With da help o' da FBI official, me and my team bypass da home security and break into her home at three in da mornin'. We tie her up and sack da place but couldn't find nuthin'. So, we torture her some and make it look like a regular burglary. She didn't tell me nuthin'."

Castano thought about witnesses and asked, "Was she home alone? Didn't she have a husband, boyfriend or girlfriend?"

Dis Senator Warren, he tell me she married but her husband be a marine biologist and was gone studyin' wild dolphins in da Bahamas." "So, you couldn't find the database...what happened next?", Rojas asked.

Sandoval paused between mouthfuls of his dessert and calmly replied, "So, I strangle her ta death."

Episode 39

The chalk mark

Nassau, Bahamas

Corey flew back to Nassau from the Marsh Harbor airport on HST Air. He picked up his rattletrap car that he left at the Lyden Pindling Intl' Airport and entered onto John F. Kennedy Dr. He noticed a CI team began to furtively tail him. *Their good! Didn't notice them at the airport parking lot.*

It was a fifteen-minute drive to the Hibiscus Beach Inn CBIF safe house. Along the way, he reflected on how much was learned since being called home from Jamaica to meet with General Morrison at the CBIF Conch Inn Resort safe house in Key Largo. The intrigue surrounding Duane Collier's disappearance broadened into a global espionage and counterterrorism struggle.

The murder of Sidney Fowler on Nassau's Parliament Square wasn't done by amateurs- it was a hit, an assassination by the Haitians smuggled into Abaco's Mud & Pigeon Pea shantytown, then trained in military tactics at Abaco Poultry, LTD.

Sandoval's Middle-Eastern assassins tailed Fowler from Abaco to the streets of Nassau in his desperate attempt to contact Darnell Ferguson about the murder he witnessed. The link between Sandoval, his henchmen Tougas and Cherestal, the Agricultural Minister's limo driver and Sidney Fowler's frantic flight to Nassau was established.

Corey thought about Fowler's grief-stricken younger sister, Shianna, who bartends at the Conch Inn Curly Tails Restaurant in Marsh

Harbor. He would seek revenge for her and for Deputy Commander Ellison Rolle and his daughter Shantel. Bernard Knowles, the young customs officer slain by Sandoval at the isolated Sandy Point customs station would have made a wonderful husband and son-in-law. He couldn't forget Rolle's words at the Carmichael Detention Center: "My daughta, she meet Bernard at our church. He be a newly-hired customs officer. Such a nice young man. Dey be so much in love."

The strong connection with radical Islam bothered him. Sandoval's helicopter landed at the Port-au-Prince docks in Haiti with Batoor Emal from Afghanistan and Hezbollah terrorist cell leader Kassim Khoury, alias 'John Doe-istan' on board. Then, there was the Abner Orival connection, Sandoval's recruiter and human smuggler who hid undocumented, Middle-Eastern men at his house in the shantytown outside Port-au-Prince.

Corey thought about what the CI agents uncovered at the Hotel Montano- two cases of Arak to be shipped to Patick Branagh in Nassau. Devon Ledard reported that Patrick and his banker brother Sean both met with Sandoval at the Abaco Poultry, LTD mansion. He hoped his honeypot Dona uncovers communiqués between the two Irish brothers that establishes the time and place of their pending meeting with Sandoval, Khoury, and Eamal.

Now it was known why Duane Collier, skilled in spy tradecraft, hastily met with the murderous psychopathic Haitian FRAPH killer Bolan Tougas at the Hard Rock Café in Nassau, and why he allowed himself to be so easily abducted. His mother, Joan Collier, was snatched from her home and dragged to Abaco Poultry, LTD. Sandoval used her as bait to ensnare her son, Duane.

Corey imagined what must have gone through Duane's mind at the Hard Rock Café. He envisioned Tougas and Cherestal showing him a photo of his mother, bound and gagged, with bruise marks on her face, then telling him how they planned to torture and murder her if he didn't accompany them to the Minister of Agriculture's limo waiting outside. Duane's drink was laced with Versed, just in case he decided to fight back...which he didn't. He loved his mother too much. The drug made him appear to be an inebriated customer needing assistance from his "friends" as they left the nightclub.

It all came to a merciless conclusion when the cadaver dogs located Joan and Duane Collier's remains in the Caribbean pine and thatch palm forest in the huge parrot preserve south of Marsh Harbor. He entered the first roundabout and exited onto Prospect Ridge Road while thinking about Devon Ledard, who he flipped and turned into a double agent. Ledard would report all he sees and hears going on at Abaco Poultry. The CBIF stealth IMINT satellites monitor the property and photograph all ground movements. General Morrison instructed the team of satellite image IMINT interpreters at the *Key West Drywall* safe house in Key West to keep a close eye on the Middle-Eastern guards. Ledard said that they lodge inside one of the barns.

The IMINT interpreters reported the guards carry firearms and train in another barn at the poultry farm, the same building that Ledard said he heard subdued gunshots in. Corey verified that much of what Ledard revealed during the controlled-bust interrogation was true.

He went through the second roundabout and turned onto West Bay Street. The uphill driveway to the Hibiscus Beach Inn was just a short distance ahead. Corey glanced to the left at Goodman's Bay. The turquoise, dark-blue and gin-colored waters blended together nicely with the white sandy bottom. Vacationers staying at the Cable Beach Hotel jogged along the paths and snorkeled in the shallows. Children played on the beach, using pails of wet sand to create castles with windows made from sea shells. *I wish I had a family... a child. Maybe having a child would make what I do seem less cataclysmic. No, I don't think anything would. I wonder what it would be like to lead a normal life?*

An uneasiness arose. The clandestine intelligence-gathering phase of the mission was quickly merging into the action phase.

Armed clashes, arrests, a raid on the mansion, grillings and enhanced interrogations unauthorized by congress were approaching.

Sandoval transformed from a lowly drug smuggler into an international narco-terrorist. Well-funded sleeper attack cells of radicalized jihadists train at his poultry farm on Abaco. The financiers are Batoor Emal and Kassim Khoury. Sean Branagh, the Nassau banker and his brother Patrick Branagh launder and conceal the operation's money in illicit bank accounts.

Corey remembered the sixteen agents in his CI team that put Khoury under surveillance years ago. *Could Sean Branagh be the banker who laundered for the Hezbollah cell in the botched Curacao operation? "John Doe-istan," alias Kassim Khoury, snuck into Curacao from Venezuela with a fake passport and bought a luxury chalet outside Willemstad. Four of the cell members from the Tri-Border Area of Argentina, Paraguay and Brazil linked Khoury up with Colombian drug lords so Hezbollah could make millions smuggling Middle East heroin into Europe and Colombian coke into the Middle East*

Corey believed the huge profits were laundered by Sean Branagh and used to fund Hezbollah sleeper attack cells dwelling, lurking inside America's heartland. *We'll never know. Walt Mason ordered his moribund FBI special agent-nephew to preemptively raid the place and arrest one lowlife Lebanese-American "citizen" with an outstanding warrant for cigarette smuggling.*

The entrance to the Hibiscus Beach Inn appeared. He floored the rattletrap and made a shuddering sharp right off West Bay Street to generate enough momentum to make it up the hill. He hoped the bad brakes and bald tires would survive the steep incline. Glancing through the cracked passenger window at the hedge of pink plumeria and red hibiscus, he quickly checked out the "Welcome to the Hibiscus Beach Inn!" sign. In the lower right corner was a red chalk mark. It was left by his double agent, Devon Ledard. Red meant 'critical and urgent'.

Episode 40

Sleeper cell

Dearborn, Michigan

The densest Muslim population outside the Middle East resides in Dearborn. Most of them are Lebanese, but increasing numbers of Iraqis, Yemenis and Palestinians immigrate here as well. The city has demonstrated America's principle of acceptance and accommodation of foreigners- the local McDonald's and public school cafeterias serve halal meat, the businesses are bilingual, the restaurants serve hummus and the sight of women walking down the streets wearing head scarves are commonplace.

With Arabs making up 85 percent of East Dearborn and the entire Southside being 100 percent Arab, it's no wonder that four Arab-Americans were elected to the city council and the appointed police chief is of Arab descent. With the majority of Dearborn City Council being Arab Americans, it's also no surprise that America's right-wing evangelical Christians along with far-right politicians took a parody, lampoon-like article seriously when it announced that Dearborn became the first American city to officially implement Sharia Law. The fake news spoof also claimed that the hard-hitting new law overshadowed secular laws pertaining to crime, politics, economic matters, and personal matters such as sexual intercourse, fasting, prayer, diet and hygiene. When the preposterous article first appeared on the *National Report* website, the 50,000 Arab American citizens of

Dearborn endured the false claim and incidences of Islamophobia that ensued.

Those residents who frequented strip clubs and bought beer from the corner deli were certainly glad the Sharia Law rumor was untrue. Unfortunately, the Intelligence Community estimates that half a percent of American Muslims dwelling in Dearborn sympathize with and support radical Islam, and Asif Qadeer Edhi sat in a comfortable chair in the living room of one of them. A radicalized jihadist trained by the Taliban in Pakistan, he managed sleeper attack cells hiding out in America's heartland.

Edhi was exhausted after the long, meandering trip to Dearborn from South America. After the meeting in Cali at the Platillos Voladores gourmet restaurant and paying off Lieutenant General Castano for the laser-guided mortars, Sandoval drove him to the Simón Bolívar International Airport in Caracas. Upon arrival, they stopped for a rest at La Estancia restaurant and ordered their famous steaks, purportedly the best in Venezuela.

Edhi recalled seating himself at a corner table of La Estancia, facing the wall with his back toward the entrance. Sandoval sat opposite him and kept a close eye on the customers who entered. Seated at the table next to Edhi was one of his long-time associates, Francisco Cadenas of SEBIN, the Servicio Bolivariano de Inteligencia Nacional. It was Venezuela's premier spy agency.

With the help of SEBIN, Edhi's sleeper-cell members could enter Caracas and travel throughout the Caribbean using fake passports, credit cards, and immigration documents. His sleeper agents flew circuitous routes from Afghanistan and Pakistan to the Simón Bolívar International Airport, then disbursed to the Tri-Border Area and stayed at jihadi safe houses in Paraguay, Argentina and Brazil. Most of the safe houses were operated by Lebanese immigrants who sympathized with Iran's terrorist proxy, Hezbollah. With impeccable fake documents, Edhi's agents also enter Canada and the U.S. from Caribbean airports.

Francisco Cadenas was a master forger. He finished off his T-bone steak, gulped down the remainder of his expensive wine and briefly glanced at Edhi, who then looked across at Sandoval. Sandoval scanned the entrance and inspected the other diners, then nodded. With that, Cadenas rose and slipped a packet upon their table as he passed. He also picked up an envelope Edhi placed by the edge that contained large bills totaling 50,205 Venezuelan bolivars, worth about $8,000.

The one-hour flight from Caracas to Willemstad's Curacao International Airport went down with no complications. Edhi retrieved his small suitcase from baggage claim and took a taxi to the historic section of Willemstad, where he switched the documents Cadenas forged for him with new ones that would get him into the U.S. The passerby was a courier for the sleeper cell that Edhi created on Curacao years ago.

He inspected the fabricated passport, visa, credit cards, and driver's license in the taxi ride back to the airport. They were flawless in every way. Candenas physically altered a valid passport by changing the photo and altering the biographical data that corresponded to his cover story. It gave him a Swedish nationality, since Sweden enjoys a visa-free relationship with the U.S. The passport matched-up with the data on his driver's license, credit cards and visa, even though he probably would not be asked to show the visa.

Back at the airport, he blended in with the tourists, browsing through the shops offering duty-free perfumes, liquors, cigarettes, designer sunglasses, fashion watches and jewelry. Confident that there were no tails, he easily passed through security and boarded an American Airlines jet for a flight to Miami that lasted a little over three hours.

Edhi went through U.S. Customs at Miami International Airport without difficulty, not even a second glance by customs officials. Things went so effortlessly that he thought someone may be on to him and planned to track him to his final destination. He remained alert for any suspicious shadowing behaviors, but there were none on the flight to Philadelphia, nor on the final flight to Columbus, Ohio. In

Columbus, he was picked up outside baggage claim by the owner of the Dearborn safe house where he planned to recuperate from jet lag.

Hakim Ahmadi and his wife, Asma, followed the rules completely to remain under the radar of U.S. intelligence. Edhi didn't feel like moving from the comfortable chair in the living room of the Dearborn safe house. His upset stomach and feelings of nausea were symptoms of something more than mere jet lag. The queasiness began just after Hakim picked him up at the Port Columbus International Airport. Before they reached the Michigan border, they had to pull off the road several times for him to vomit.

The Pepto-Bismol tablets Asma gave him didn't help much. Hakim would arrive there shortly from his Muslim used-clothing and consignment store, named Ahmadi's. Edhi stared at the stacks of hijab caps and headbands, shawls, scarves, turbans, and children's prayer rugs piled in the corner next to an ironing board. Hakim didn't allow Asma to work in his store, so she spent the day at home washing, ironing and patching up the clothing donations.

Edhi stared at Asma as she obediently sewed, stitched and ironed at her living room workstation that Hakim set up for her. He admired her beauty from across the room and thought that she, indeed, lived up to her Quranic name. "Asma" meant sublime and superb. She was just that, beauty-wise, but remained abysmally low on the social and human-rights scale. She wasn't allowed to drive a car and respectfully walked behind Hakim while shopping. Outside the safe house, she wore a two-piece suit and Muslim hijab headscarf that covered her satin hair and tightly framed her face. Hakim believed, like most Muslims, that the hijab actually honored women by concealing their beauty. The American vision of her walking down the runway as a fashion model was remote, although she probably could become a highly-paid one.

In Dearborn, these religious and social behaviors go unnoticed due to the large fundamental Islamic populace. Outside Dearborn, heads were often raised and people wondered why such a beautiful woman wore a "beekeeping outfit" in public, so Hakim made sure Asma rarely accompanied him beyond the city limits.

That was fine for Edhi, who preferred that his safe house operators in Dearborn and elsewhere in the U.S. refrain from traveling, for they may be captured by pure coincidence. Border Patrol and Immigration and Customs Enforcement (ICE) agents have detention centers full of illegals from Afghanistan, Egypt, Iran, Iraq, Pakistan, Sudan and Yemen. Through experience and training, they remain alert for illegal immigrants from the Middle East just as much as they do for Hispanics entering from Mexico and Latin America. Much to the chagrin of the ACLU, racial profiling returned to the U.S., but the practice no longer focuses on Afro-Americans.

Edhi was deep in thought, planning his trip out of Dearborn to northwest Pennsylvania for the final attack preparations. Suddenly, the Salukis dog sleeping at his feet rose and in one bound reached the front door. They were used throughout the Middle East to run down and kill gazelles and hares. It must have heard its master drive up the driveway.

Edhi was pleased Hakim Ahmadi closed his shop and came home early. There was much to talk about, for he was obsessed with insuring that the pending slaughter of many American lives was impeccably executed.

Ahmadi entered the front door and sat across from Edhi. "Are you feeling better, my friend?"

"No. I'm afraid Pepto-Bismol tablets will not cure what's ailing me. We will talk about that later. For now, I want to make sure the safe house security measures are in place. I see you drove home from Ahmadi's in a nondescript Ford Fiesta."

"Yes, I keep the van parked at Ahmadi's and only use it for deliveries around Detroit."

"That is good. The apprehensive FBI and homeland security agents are alert for vans, pickups or small trucks that could be used to transport WMD's."

Ahmad stared over at his beautiful wife and said, "Asma, why don't you go into the kitchen and prepare us some kenafeh. It may make Edhi feel better."

Asma quietly arose and walked obediently to the kitchen, slightly bowing her head to both men as she passed.

Edhi nodded approval as she walked by, then continued. "Tell me about cell phone usage. You faithfully serve Allah by offering your home as a safe house and never discuss the planning of attacks or buying materials or chemicals that may alert the authorities. As I understand, you own one cellular phone in your name. Asma has none." "Yes, that's correct. I have one cell phone and use it for business purposes only. If the American spies are listening to me talk on it, they will be bored with what they hear. I take store orders over the phone and the number is advertised in the newspaper."

Edhi quickly grabbed the wastebasket next to his chair. He felt like vomiting again, but only dry heaves ensued. "Maybe I better pass on the kenafeh."

Ahmadi laughed. "Asma would be heartbroken if you refused it.

By the way, I do use my cell phone for another purpose."

"For what? Anything that might raise the eyebrows of DHS?" "Perhaps. I use it to order a home-delivered Arabic pizza every Friday from the local pizza gallery. If Satin's agents eavesdrop, they'll know what toppings I like on my pizza...Zaatar with thyme, sesame seed mixed with olive oil, and chunks of chicken and feta. Would that make them suspicious of me?"

Edhi laughed despite his upset stomach and headache, but quickly became deadpan serious again. "What about innocent purchases that might raise suspicion? I noticed a BBQ grill in the back yard. How often do you buy propane? Last year one of my attack cells in Colorado was taken down because the fools bought BBQ propane canisters from different stores over several months. They accumulated fifty canisters in their garage. Even though they paid cash and left no credit card trail, DHS got on to them."

"I buy maybe two canisters a year, no more than my neighbors buy."

"I'd advise you to not buy any more. Use pure charcoal from now on."

"Your advice will be carried out as you so desire."

"One more thing. The storage shed in the backyard has a padlock on it. I suggest you take it off. DHS agents have caught our martyrs hiding attack equipment in such sheds, in locked garages and even storage rentals. Do you use a storage rental for your business?"

Ahmadi pointed to the ceiling-high stacks of Mideastern toys and clothes at his wife's workstation. "No, as you can see, we store our inventory here."

"That's good, because if you were renting one, I'd have you discontinue using it. Also, I want you to keep the garage door up during the day. You can close it at night, but leave it open all-day long. If DHS agents do a drive-by, they'll not suspect you of hiding anything."

Sahbi, it will be carried out exactly as you say."

Edhi waved his hands and shook his head. "I appreciate your alle-giance to Allah and to the jihad. We have to be vigilant. You remember the Zazi sleeper cell in Denver was brought down after he bought too many peroxide and acetone bottles from a beauty shop supply store."

Ahmad shook his head despondently. "Yes, the FBI was alerted by one vigilant store owner."

"You'd be surprised how vigilant the average American infidel is. What about your financial transactions? American intelligence knows sleeper cells need funding and keep an eye out for checking and credit card fraud. Do you have more than one checking account or have you switched banks often for better checking account deals?"

"Why...yes, I just switched banks last month. Better interest rate paid and free checking."

"OK, keep the bank you switch to. But, do not switch accounts ever again."

"Yes, as you say."

"How many credit cards do you have?" "Two...Visa and Discover."

"Have you ever reported one of them lost or switched cards for better deals?"

"I never reported one lost or stolen, but last year I paid off my Master Card with the new Discover card account I opened up."

Edhi shook his head in disgust. "Once again, do not do this again. I want you to pay off the Discover card and terminate your membership. Just use the Visa card from now on. I have witnessed cell members...even lone wolves... arrested after reporting lost or stolen credit cards, opening up numerous checking accounts, carrying around separate checkbooks from different banks...total stupidity! An innocent move on your part may put you, your wife, and this home under surveillance...the FBI, CIA and NSA pigs will chronicle every person who visits here...until they arrest us all and send us to Guantanamo!"

La if laha il Allah, Muhammad a rasool Allah...there is no God but Allah and Muhammad is his messenger! I will obey your commands! *Astaghfirullah*...may Allah forgive me!"

"One more thing. I know you are dedicated to the destruction of the infidels and despise what America and the West does in the Middle East, but I urge you to keep your hatred bottled up inside."

Ahmadi looked confused. "But, many of my brothers that I meet at the mosque, in prayer meetings, and at the store feel the same as I. They express anger toward Americans and their way of life and they dislike what America does to their homeland."

"That is true, my dear friend, there is widespread anger, but most American Muslims do not support terrorist attacks inside America or anywhere else. Thanks to al-Qaeda and ISIS, they reject terrorism as a whole and view the 9/11 attacks as morally wrong."

Ahmadi fidgeted in his chair, then blurted out, "I cannot alter my beliefs! Muhammad himself declared I must follow the Qur'an... the words of Allah... and carry out the Hadith, the Muhammad's teachings...I cannot do anything less! The Muslims you refer to...the moderate ones...they deserve to be killed along with the infidels!"

Edhi waited a few moments for Ahmed to settle down, then spoke. "I admire your conviction. One cannot follow some of Allah's words while disobeying others. You are a true believer who obediently follows the ideology of Islam and would gladly give your life to the Qur'an, to Allah's words...to Muhammad's teachings. I recognized this years ago... that's why I recruited you to help in the struggle."

"Thank you...*jazakAllahu khair* ..may Allah reward you with good."

"You are so welcome Ahmad. But, you missed the point I'm trying to make. There are many brainless and ill-advised Muslims in America... moderate ones...who lack total allegiance to Islam. I don't want you getting hot under the collar at them... anywhere...anytime... whether it be in the mosque, at the corner store or during a chat across the backyard fence. Do not make threats and tone down your hatred towards America. I was wrong by ordering you to keep it 'bottled up' inside. You can engage in healthy debates, but you must refrain from blowing up when discussing politics or debating societal or religious issues in America. Don't send out red flags... a moderate Muslim may turn you in to the authorities."

Feelings of dishonor and ignominy swept through Hakim Ahmadi. He looked down and spoke softly. "You are so right, Edhi. One of my neighbors lost a nephew and niece in the World Trade Center on 9/11. He despises the violence of al-Qaeda. I told him they were both martyrs...and that angered him a great deal."

Ahmadi's words annoyed Edhi. "That's what I'm talking about! Your neighbor's loved ones were among twenty-eight Muslims killed in the twin towers that day. Unknowing American Muslims were also passengers on the two hijacked planes that crashed in a rural Pennsylvania field and slammed into the Pentagon. Most Americanized Muslims do not feel the innocent Muslims on these planes were martyrs. They view them as victims to a radicalized form of Islam. On 9/11, Muslims were killed from Pakistan, Bangladesh, Guiana, Sri Lanka, Gambia, the Ivory Coast, Yemen, Iran Ethiopia, Turkey, Burma, Albania, Greece, India and from Trinidad and Tobago.

American intelligence has no doubt approached those who were dear to these martyrs and redirected their sorrow and anger into an anti-radical Islamic cause."

"I will follow your instructions and no longer argue with the moderates. I understand our fatwa against the West. We wage an offensive jihad against America, not a defensive one. Decades ago we were bent on driving Western boots out of our Middle-Eastern lands, a purely defensive tactic. Today, we kill Americans on their own soil."

Edhi nodded his head in agreement and stared pensively at the attack cell safe house owner. "You know, Ahmadi, my friend...I will become such a martyr one week from today. Many Americans will die...maybe more than on 9/11...with stolen, hi-tech weapons. I am not afraid to die...*Allahu Akbar*

Episode 41

Nassau Love Beach contact

Love Beach
Nassau, Bahamas
(25.063261, -77.488458)
Corey held snorkel, mask and fins under his arms as he walked across the talcum-powdered sand lining the secluded Love Beach. He waded into the warm, gin-colored waters and began snorkeling among the jetties, rocks and patch coral reefs which lay a few yards offshore.

Things hadn't changed much since he was here a decade ago.

Love Beach is off the beaten track and during most of the day you have the beach all to yourself, the reason he chose it as the contact point to meet with Devon Ledard. Lounge chairs and beach mats lay stacked in piles by the Nirvana Beach Bar.

He took a deep breath and submerged to where the rock formations were. A large Stoplight parrotfish sought shelter from him under the shadows of the rock ledges. A seemingly never-ending school of Blue tang glided by, seeking safety in deeper waters. Audacious Banded and Foureye butterfly fish ignored him while flitting about the rocks, while a peacock flounder fluttered on the bottom, pitching sand over its iridescent blue-spotted back. Corey observed its bright speckled pattern swiftly transform into a plain, duller disguise, appearing like a seamless continuation of the sandy bottom, save two raised eyes protruding out. It could see everything while remaining hidden. *It's kind of how CBIF operates.*

Suddenly, the bold butterfly fish darted into the rock crevices just as a barracuda glided into view above the jetties. It seemed to sparkle as the sun reflected off its silvery sides, but once over the nearby sea grass beds, it descended into them. Its flashy body transformed into a gloomy form of darkness, making the predator appear as a harmless shadowy extension of the murky beds.

Corey thought how CBIF's counterintelligence teams inadvertently replicate the deception, camouflage, and surveillance activity that takes place among the reefs, between predator and quarry. His CI teams were accomplished in the art of countersurveillance. At that moment, four teams were positioning themselves in key choke points around Nassau.

As Devon Ledard passes through these predetermined places, they will observe to determine if he is being shadowed...perhaps hunted down to be killed. If Sandoval found out about Ledard's double agent activities, he would torture, then murder him, his wife and kids...in reverse order. The red mark Ledard scribbled on the Hibiscus Beach Inn welcome sign signaled he had an urgent message to deliver.

Since Corey flipped him, he seemed to be a relatively trustworthy double agent. Ledard was instructed to notify Corey immediately if a serious event was about to unfold at Abaco Poultry, LTD. Corey checked his diver's watch. It was 1pm. Ledard would be notified to begin his trek along the surveillance detection route to Love Beach about now.

The couple walked across the Paradise Island Bridge to East Bay Street, then strolled eastward until they came to a hand-painted sign that read "To Potter's Cay." They dressed like most rich Americans staying at the Atlantis Resort on Paradise Island...upscale casual, resort wear, like they just dined at the Café Martinique. Expensive Louis Vuitton chronograph watches were strapped to their wrists and the lady wore cultured pearl floral earrings with diamond halos.

They peered down the walkway which led into the area called Potter's Cay. Local Bahamians were buying fresh seafood from the day's catch and wandering about the stalls piled high with fruits and vegetables of every color imaginable: cabbage, cassava, hot peppers, plantain, pumpkin, sweet pepper, sweet potatoes, avocado, coconut, mango, sour orange and pineapple.

The man wanted to continue on down East Bay Street to the Poop Deck and enjoy a view of Nassau Harbor while sipping a few signature martinis and munching on their famous Andros Crab Cakes and conch fritters. His spousal facsimile, a fellow counterintelligence agent, pleaded with him to explore Potter's Cay. Their performance was magnificent and he reluctantly gave in to his beautiful wife with long satin-black hair.

They sauntered down the entrance walkway just as a mail boat full of passengers and freight arrived from some far-flung Bahamian outer island. Walking past Darnell Ferguson's fishing boats to view what was being unloaded off the mail boat, neither gave Devon Ledard a first glance. He was mending fishing nets on the bow of Darnell's boat, and immediately recognized them as the ones to contact. The instructions that Darnell gave him were to not stare at them, but to go to the next location they visited.

Fresh conch was off-loaded from the mail boat and heaped onto a table where it was sold to venders. Food and household goods on pallets marked "Destination Ragged Island" were hauled onto it. Ragged Island, population eighty-four, was one of many Bahamian out islands that is too small and too remote to receive airfreight. Seventeen mail boats operate out of Potter's Cay and they are, indeed, floating life- support systems for many of the isolated islets scattered through the 700-island Bahamian archipelago.

The well-dressed couple snapped some photos, then proceeded past Ledard again to a row of wooden food and fish stalls with handwritten names on them, like *Doc Sands Bethel Dem Bones Drift Wood Cafe* and *Old Q*. Many of the shacks were small, take-away joints, but they walked into a larger one with a kitchen and full-course menu, named *McKenzie's*

Having gone over the interior layout with Corey the night before in his room at the Hibiscus Beach Inn, the couple strolled past the small bar in the front room to a small balcony in the back that overlooked the water. They sat at one of three small picnic tables surrounded by a guardrail. The other two tables were occupied by tourists from one of the cruise ships. They were eating several plates of large grilled red snappers with the heads still attached, washing them down with Bahama Mamas and Nassau's Kalik beer.

The group of six talked loudly enough so the locals at the bar and anyone else close by could overhear them. Their ship docked in Prince George Pier that morning and they boasted of the great duty-free purchases they made in downtown Nassau. A few of them walked to *McKenzie's* from the cruise terminal, while their newly-acquired friends at the other table took a taxi.

The rich couple who walked over the bridge to Potter's Cay from the Paradise Island Atlantis Resort didn't have much in common with the cruise ship folks, so they sat in silence and admired the spotted eagle rays gliding by in the waters below, the fishermen bringing in boatloads of conch, and the cook expertly cleaning conch before them. As planned, Devon Ledard strolled into *McKenzie's* fifteen minutes after they did. He walked past the bar and stood by the tiny back patio, hunting for a place to sit down.

The only seating available in the cramped patio was at the table occupied by the well-heeled tourists from the Atlantis Resort. Seeing Devon, the woman lifted her Gucci handbag off the empty seat next to her and gestured for Devon to join them. This was an everyday behavior at *McKenzie's*, due partly to the cramped space but mostly due to the sociable and gracious nature of the customers and staff. Many enlightening conversations between locals and tourists occur here.

Devon gladly sat down and thanked them.

Corey finished snorkeling and sat at a barstool at the Nirvana Beach Bar. Love Beach lies directly under the final approach to the Lynden Pindling International Airport, so the tranquility is interrupted often by incoming jets. It is an airplane-spotter's paradise. He ordered a Kalick beer and French fries, then retreated to the shade under a Caribbean pine. Two of the local potcakes followed and sought shelter in the shade with him. He shared half his French fries with them while thinking about the countersurveillance operation and his pending meeting with Devon Ledard. *The Potter's Cay stakeout phase should be completed. By now, CI Team-1 from the Atlantis Resort made contact with Ledard at McKenzie's and notified him where he is to go next...to the first surveillance detection point. Team-2 and Team-3 from the cruise ship docks should be occupying the two other tables on the small patio-balcony, so no strangers can enter the picture. Team-4, a single guy who is sipping wine from a paper bag outside on a bench is observing for suspicious individuals hanging around ...especially Middle Eastern men. And, of course, my friend Darnell Ferguson is seated in his boat cabin scanning the area with binoculars. If any of Sandoval's thugs are shadowing Devon Ledard, they will be detected...and the contact meeting will be cancelled. Let's hope Ledard hasn't been compromised. He has something to tell me, something important. He should be proceeding along the surveillance detection route to the first detection point where Team-1 will be at. They've got to change their cover and get there before he does!*

CI Team-1 whispered to Ledard while they chowed down on a scrump-tious conch salad at *McKenzie's*, instructing him where he was sup-posed to go next. Then, they paid their bill and left without glancing at the cruise ship folks, who were actually CBIF's CI teams two and three.

Upon leaving Potter's Cay, the opulently dressed duo flagged down a cab which delivered them back to the Atlantis Resort where they walked to an adjacent parking lot and climbed into a worn-out dodge Durango SUV with tinted windows.

Inside, they quickly switched to a totally different dress and appearance. The woman agent climbed into the backseat while her male companion drove around Paradise Island. In about the same time it took a flashy peacock flounder to transform itself into a colorless, imperceptible creature, she removed her long, raven-black hairpiece, revealing short-cut, blond hair, and replaced her expensive earrings and watch with cheaper versions bought at the straw market. Next, she shed her expensive, tight-fitting resort-style garb and slipped a loose-fitting maternity dress over her head, inserting shoulder pads to make her physique appear larger. She strapped on a large-size bra with foam inserts and tied a pregnancy pillow to her abdomen.

Because pregnant women have a 'glow' due to taking extra vitamins and increased blood flow, she quickly wiped off her "sexy" makeup and proceeded to make herself appear as a maternal vessel of life bearing a child. She didn't overdo the makeup, since few pregnant women have the time to doll up. Instead, she merely added a pink blush to add a healthy 'glow' to her cheeks, then applied matching pink lipstick.

The man pulled into a vacant lot and crawled over to the front passenger seat while his "pregnant" partner took over driving to the surveillance detection point. He reached into the back seat, retrieved an electric razor and shaved off his stylish shadow beard. Then, he pasted on a pencil-thin mustache and donned a black baseball cap with attached pony tail that had a sprinkling of grey/silver hair. He opened a small vial of gel and applied the contents over the exposed hair on each side of his head under the cap. It dried immediately, tinting his hair to resemble that of the pony tail. Next, he quickly took off his three-inch elevator dress shoes with insole lift and Donald Trump slacks and shirt, and slipped into a cheap pair of jeans and a Bahamas Goombay Punch T-shirt.

Lastly, he reached into his disguise box in the backseat and retrieved two matching tattoos, peeled off the plastic covers and stuck one onto his right forearm and the other onto his female companion's forearm while she continued driving. They both applied even pressure to their tattoos with the opposite arm hand for several moments, then the male agent covered both with a wet towel until the paper was completely saturated. In thirty seconds, the water released the tattoos from the papers and he removed the wet towels and peeled the corners of the tattoo paper away.

The female agent looked at her tattoo, which displayed an arrow pointing to a comic-faced father smiling broadly under the caption, "He did this to me!" She looked over at her CI colleague and calmly said, "You bastard."

Both slipped off their Ray-Ban sunglasses and replaced them with a low-priced pair. Their masquerade was complete. If anyone shadowed Devon Ledard to the Potter's Cay stakeout and noticed the Team-1 couple there, they would not recognize them at the next surveillance detection point where Ledard was about to journey to.

As instructed, Ledard left *McKenzie's* after finishing his conch salad, walked out of Potter's Cay and headed west on East Bay Street. He turned left and proceeded on Dowdeswell Street, then made another left onto Burnside Lane. After a short walk, he turned right at Shirley Street, then made a left onto Elizabeth Avenue. There, he asked the security guard at Princess Margaret Hospital where the entrance to the Queen's Staircase was. They guard obligingly pointed up a hill to where the poorly-marked entrance was.

The Queen's Staircase was originally known as the "66 Steps" and is part of the Fort Fincastle complex. The admission was free, so Ledard walked directly up the steps which were carved out of solid limestone rock 250 years ago by over 600 slaves. The staircase can be reached from Fort Fincastle because, in days of old, the nobility needed an escape route if the fort came under attack. When Queen

Victoria ascended to the throne in 1837, she abolished slavery and the "66 Steps" were renamed the "Queen's Staircase" in her honor.

Lush vegetation lined the tall limestone walls. The place was much cooler than the streets of Nassau, and Ledard watched the tropical birds flitting about the palm trees and ferns that lined the way to the staircase. The shade, cool air and aroma of ancient limestone blending with fauna didn't lower his anxiety level.

He ascended the staircase, keeping a close eye out for suspicious bystanders while thinking about how Sandoval's thugs followed Sidney Fowler to Nassau from Abaco and gunned him down on Parliament Square in broad daylight. The same could happen to him...here...right now.

A couple climbed the steps ahead of him. The woman was pregnant and her pony-tailed husband assisted her up the steep staircase. Ledard scrambled past them and arrived at the top by a small straw market. His instructions were to buy a straw hat and intermingle with the shoppers there for five minutes, then proceed to Fort Fincastle. One sweet Bahamian lady was selling straw hats for twenty dollars each. Ironically, the well-heeled couple back at *McKenzie's* slipped him that amount as they left. During their conch salad dinner, they gave him instructions on how he was to proceed through the complex.

Ledard offered ten dollars for one of her hats, but she insisted on the full twenty-dollar price. He told her that was all he had on him, so she relinquished. While he hung around the straw market for five minutes, the pregnant tourist and her helpful husband walked to the nearby Fort Fincastle, where they found a volunteer guide to give them a "free" tour. Actually, the man was an opportunistic local who talked about the full history of the place for tips.

The local capitalist was well-versed in the many sagas surrounding the citadel's past. He showed the couple spectacular views of the entire city from the cannon battery, the highest point on New Providence Island. It was a stunning view of the cruise ships docked in Nassau Harbor, the government buildings in Parliament Square and of Paradise Island and Potter's Cay.

The pregnant lady appeared moved by the vista and pointed toward the new Baha Mar Resort on Cable Beach far below them on the left to the Atlantis Resort on Paradise Island on their far right.

The unofficial tour guide took photos of them sitting on one of the mortar cannons, then they tipped him five dollars and returned to the large courtyard to sit on a bench and rest. They were people-watching, as many tourists enjoy doing, and kept their eyes on Ledard as he strolled past them and paid a dollar to enter the fort.

Moments later, the three members of CI Team-2 followed Ledard into the fort. They wore different attire, appearing unlike they did a half-hour ago at *McKenzie's*. The only thing the five members of teams one and two had in common were the concealed Glock 30, .45 caliber semi-auto handguns loaded with hollow-points that they carried.

The serenity of Love Beach was again broken by a commercial jetliner flying low overhead on final approach to the airport. Corey observed a local band arrive and begin practicing in the Nirvana Beach Bar courtyard. Their music brought back memories of Danielle. Feelings of sadness mixed with distress surfaced.

He didn't feel sorry for himself, but the traditional songs they played were what Danielle loved to hear when they frequented the pubs and nightspots of Abaco and Nassau. She could have been with him here, right now. He knew her murder wasn't committed by a home burglar or serial killer. It had something to do with their profession... intelligence they knew or possessed that could be harmful to certain people in power.

So why didn't they kill me, too? Why just Danielle? Danielle was the best friend to Duane Collier's mother...Joan Collier. Joan was abducted from her home in the U.S. and taken to the Abaco poultry operation and used as bait to lure Duane there. They both were murdered...and Dr. Slesman's forensic report shows Duane etched

"Penumbra Database" on an aluminum gum wrapper, then swallowed it. Could the killers have thought Danielle had the Penumbra Database in her possession...that she was hiding it for Joan? Drew Collier, husband to Joan and father to Duane, was a CBIF mole working inside the Pentagon alongside the Defense Intelligence Agency. He was planted there by General Morrison and worked on some undercover assignment that Morrison would certainly know about. The Penumbra Database, whatever the hell it is, and Abaco Poultry, LTD are linked together in some way. That link holds the key to the mystery of my wife's murder.

The music flowing from the Nirvana courtyard was the Bahamian genre that Danielle enjoyed, a trace of African rhythm and Caribbean calypso. Since the Bahamians were under British rule up to 1973, the melody carried a tinge of European colonial influence and fast-paced Goombay as well.

I wish Danielle was here, with me. She'd love this band. It was a "rake and scrape" group that emulated the distant past when African slaves were too poor to create instruments. They beat on drums made from pork barrel and goatskin, scraped a carpenter's saw with a metal file, shook maracas, banged rhythm sticks, and plucked away on a bass violin made from a washtub and string. The five-member group carried on the tradition, mostly for show, since they also played modern instruments as well.

Corey ventured up to the Nirvana bar and ordered a Bahama Mama. The two potcakes followed him from the beach, sat on each side of him and stared pleadingly.

"Sorry, guys. I'm just ordering a drink...no more French fries." Monique, the bartender, laughed. "They be hanging out here fo' years. Don't worry, we fed 'em lots of stuff scraped off the bottom of our cookin' pots."

Corey smiled back at her. "Thus, the name 'potcakes'."

Just then his hidden ear peace buzzed, almost inaudibly. It was the pregnant lady from Team-1. "A cloudless day, clear day. Principle

ETA in five." It was code indicating that Devon Ledard was not being tailed and he would arrive at Love Beach in five minutes.

He thanked Monique and returned back to his lounge chair underneath the shady Caribbean pine. The potcakes didn't follow him, comprehending that snack time was over. They stretched out in the shade of the bar and patiently waited to curry favor from the next credulous visitor.

Corey had confidence in his CI teams, for he trained them well in countersurveillance. They skillfully observed the human activities at the Potter's Cay stakeout and retained images of suspicious individuals there. Instead of using different teams, he had the same operators at the initial Potter's Cay stakeout change appearance, then proceed to the next designated surveillance detection point, the Queen's Staircase.

The teams arrived at the Queen's Staircase ahead of Ledard and at the same time he did. Having different CI teams at each detection point would be manpower intensive and require them to take photographs to compare and ferret out if the same suspicious person appeared at the different locations. Using the same CI operators at different choke points enabled them to straightforwardly confirm if a suspicious suspect showed up a number of times at the unrelated locations where Devon Ledard was sent to.

Corey's agents left the initial stakeout before Ledard did, disguised themselves, and arrived at the next surveillance detection point before Ledard showed up. Since it was easier to take off a disguise than to apply one, the Team-1 couple appeared at the Potter's Cay stakeout elaborately dressed with ornate jewelry. When they advanced to the Queen's Staircase detection point, they quickly shed their rich attire and heavy makeup and quickly slipped into loose-fitting clothes and deceptive add-ons. It was much easier to dress down than to dress up.

Devon Ledard was puzzled that he didn't see the agents he met at *McKenzie's* show up at the Queen's Staircase or at Fort Fincastle.

Still, he followed their instructions. At the fort, he checked the rear leg of the rusty-colored howitzer mortar cannon. Sure enough, a folded candy bar wrapper was there with a note telling him to immediately leave Fort Fincastle, walk towards the Government House and walk the path at the far end of the fort.

He reached the end of the path at the bottom of a hill. A blue mini-van with tinted windows pulled up. The sliding panel door opened and he was beckoned in. He recognized the three occupants inside, but didn't know they were formally referred to as CBIF CI Team-3. They were among the cruise ship passengers seated at the tables next to his on the outside patio at *McKenzie's*. Unlike their fellow operatives, they didn't change disguises since their sole job was to stay inside the air-conditioned minivan and hide behind the windows that were darkened to a level that would violate most state tinted-window laws.

They earlier had parked the van along Shirley Street and observed the human activity around Ledard as he walked past them on the way to the Queen's Staircase from Potter's Cay. Their final job was to pick him up when he emerged from the path that led out of Fort Fincastle and deliver him to Love Beach. Like the six other agents working the countersurveillance detail, they also carried concealed Glock 30's loaded with .45 caliber hollow points.

Corey observed a Bahamian male wearing a straw hat and red T-shirt enter the far end of Love Beach and walk toward him. It was Ledard. Corey slid an empty lounge chair next to his and sipped the Bahama Mama that Monique so expertly concocted. He was confident that his double agent was not compromised and that no one tailed him. Proper countersurveillance is time-consuming and costly, but it as-sured that Ledard arrived at the contact point unharmed, and guaran-teed that his double-agent status wasn't compromised.

Corey was about to hear vital HUMINT about the narco-terrorist operation at Abaco Poultry, LTD.

Episode 42

Double agent

As he approached the shady Caribbean pine where Corey sought shelter from the glaring sun, Devon grew more anxious. Before he sat down, Corey said, "Get yourself a drink at the tiki bar and tell Monique to put it on my tab."

Moments later, he returned holding a Collin's glass of Goombay Smash and sat on the lounge chair. "Yes, I be nervous...indeed. Dem counter-whatever people you said would protect me ditched me. Dey were nowhere 'round da Queen Staircase. I be dere all by myself. All I could think 'bout was what happen to Sidney Fowler."

"Relax, Devon. They were all around you. You didn't see them because they're trained not to be seen. A Fowler incident wouldn't have happened anywhere along the route you took to get here. Now, what have you got for me?"

The coconut rum and apricot brandy drink seemed to soothe him a bit. Ledard stretched out on the lounge chair. "Well, I be at da Abaco Poultry place doin' some yard work fo' Cesar Sandoval when he tell me to get into my waiter outfit cause a guest was comin' to visit and he wanted me to wait on dem."

"Who was it?"

"Dat big banker guy I told ya 'bout at Nippers when ya busted me...Sean Branagh. Da Abaco constable, Turnquest, bring him to da poultry farm in a police car. Must a picked him up at da Marsh Harbor airport."

"He came by himself? Did his brother, the owner of the Irish Frenzy Pub in Nassau, come with him?"

"No. He come alone."

"Keep going. I know you've got more to tell."

Devon grew a trifle apprehensive again. "Well, while I was in my room in one of da empty barns switchin' out of my groundskeeper uniform, I hear Tougas and Cherestal talkin' outside as dey walk past da window. Dey talk 'bout bein' in Cali, Colombia at some swank restaurant protectin' Sandoval at a meetin' with a Colombian general. Dey talk 'bout mortars bein' stolen from da Colombia army."

"Did they say who stole them and what they're to be used for?"

"No... but I find out. When I go to da mansion and start servin' conch fritters to Sandoval and dat rich banker, dey stop talkin' wheneva I walk up to dem. So, I know they be up to no good...especially after I hear what Tougas and Cherestal say. It be a hot and humid day, so Sandoval tells me to start makin' frozen Rum Runners. After three rounds, dey start talkin' loud. I start addin' a bit more rum afta da first one, but dey don't notice."

Corey listened intently to what double-agent Ledard had to say. The day before, the CI team that tailed Sean Branagh around Nassau reported he abruptly left the bank and flew off to Abaco. Corey made a quick call to General Morrison on the secure sat phone, for he knew Branagh was most likely heading to Abaco Poultry, LTD. Morrison alerted the team of satellite image IMINT interpreters at the Key West Drywall Co safe house to reposition the image satellite and start photographing as soon as Sean Branagh touched down at the Marsh Harbor airport.

Branagh was recorded, from 110 miles overhead, being picked up by Tougas and Cherestal at the airport in their SUV and driven to Abaco Poultry, LTD. More images were shot of him entering the front door of the mansion, then strolling out onto the back patio with Sandoval and sitting down. Corey also viewed shots of Devon Ledard appearing in a waiter uniform, serving both men conch fritters and drinks. He thought how useful IMINT and ELINT is to complement HUMINT in order to confirm that Devon's critical human intelligence is on the level...so far.

Corey didn't tell Ledard that he already knew what both men drank and ate on the backyard patio. What he didn't know was what they were saying, thinking... feeling.

"So, Devon, what more did you find out. They didn't spout out top-secret matters while you were on the patio, did they?"

"No, Mistah Pearson....they..."

Corey interjected. "By the way, I'm your handler and we may be working together for years to come, possibly on other matters when the dust settles on this one. So, call me 'Corey'. Now, continue."

"OK...Corey. As I was sayin', dey get drunk but not careless. I could tell dey was talkin' serious stuff...hunched over the table, stern looks on dere faces, tryin' to talk quiet-like. I knew dat I could hear what dey say if I sneak closer...out o' site."

"I'm dying to hear what you heard them say, if you were able to." *The sat images had no indication of him on the patio or near it after he finished serving them. However, the photos did show Sandoval and Branagh leaning towards each other over the patio table, as if whispering back and forth*

"Well, dere's a long line o' yellow elders dat run from the kitchen to da patio. The table was only 'bout five feet from it. Da elder hedge was only three feet high, so I crawl on my belly. It be a thick hedge, so dey couldn't see me."

Good grief! Devon has bigger balls than a Brahma bull in a herd of estrus-ridden cows. The IMINT satellite images showed a line of coconut palms partially covering a yellow elder hedge. No wonder we didn't catch him sneaking up on them

"Tell me what you heard...and start with the stolen mortars." "Dey mention two men from Colombia army... Lieutenant General Castano and Juan Rojas. Rojas, he be retired but deals in arms stolen from da barracks in Cali. I neva heard o' them before."

"They never came to the Abaco Poultry operation?"

"I neva see dem two when waitin' on people at da parties. But, I hear Sandoval and da banker mention anotha party comin' up and a bunch of people comin' to it."

Corey made sure his hidden microphone was working. "Another party at the mansion?"

"Yeah."

"Give me some names."

"Most of the people who came to the last one...the names I give ya when ya busted me at Nippers."

"I want them all, again."

"Da two guys from da Middle East, you know, da Arabs...they comin'."

"How do you know that?"

"Cause Sandoval told da banker to make sure his brother Patrick Branagh brings dat shit drink they like...Arak. Remember, I tell ya I snuck a few gulps of it down in the kitchen. Sandoval even mention dere names to da banker...Eamal Batoor and Kassim Khoury."

"What else did they say about Batoor and Khoury?"

"Well, Sandoval and Sean Branagh get into a pissin' match, den Sandoval reminds da banker dat Batoor be keepin' his brother Patrick's pub afloat...dat da Irish Frenzy would a gone broke years ago if he, Sandoval, neva introduce Patrick to Batoor, who be keepin' da Irish pub floatin' good eva since."

It's beginning to make sense. My Mata Hari...ala honeypot 'Dona' who I called in from the Turks and Caicos and sent to visit the Irish Frenzy Pub and seduce Patrick Branagh...she reported the pub takes in a measly amount each day, but Branagh reaches into the safe and gives her a moneybag with no less than $15,000 cash to deposit in his brother's bank...on a daily basis. She's seen him pouring whiskey, wine and beer bottles down the drain...even throwing away good food, only to reorder and replace his "sold" inventory quickly. She also snooped around his office at the Irish Frenzy and found stacks *of fake invoices and made-up receipts. In one report, she stated she worked the bar all day for him and only eight customers came in, but a thousand food and beverage paper receipts miraculously materialized atop his office desk after closing time. What's more, Dona found out that Sean Branagh's bank fudges the numbers for Patrick's Irish Frenzy. These Irish dudes are worse than drug dealers...they're cleaning money for Middle Eastern terrorist cells...to secretly fund attacks on the U.S*

"Did you hear anything about Batoor depositing money directly into Sean Branagh's bank?"

"No, but I know dere's lots of money involved. Dat's why I scribbled the red mark on da Hibiscus Beach Inn sign. I saw Abner Orival's smugglin' boat arrive from Haiti and five more Middle Eastern-lookin' guys got off with a couple of poor Haitians."

"What's that got to do with 'lots of money'?"

"Da Middle-East guys... each one carry a large moneybag with drawstring ova his shoulder...bulging with money."

"How do you know they were moneybags full of cash?"

"Cause dey look like da sacks armored cars carry around Nassau to deposit in banks. And, one a da men trip and da bag drawstring must not a been fastened cause wads a bills fall out and slide down da dock...he pick it all up quick-like and dey all hurry into da mansion."

Fuck...talk about direct deposit into Sean Branagh's bank! I'll notify Morrison immediately. CBIF has several moles working in the Department of Treasury's TFI, the Terrorism and Financial Intelligence division. Sounds like dirty money cleaned through the Irish Frenzy is only a small part of the picture

"So, Sean and Patrick Branagh, Eamal Batoor, Kassim Khoury and Abner Orival will be showing up at the party. What about Laurent Rousseau, the Haitian Minister of Public Health & Population...you said he was at the last party. Is he coming?"

"Yeah, Sandoval say he comin' with Orival. And, I almost forgot, Mr. Moss, da Bahamian Minister of Agriculture...he be comin', too."

"Think hard. Anyone else?"

Devon thought for a second. "Oh...yeah... I hear Sandoval jokin' bout' dat bigwig from da U.S. comin'. He be arrivin' with his chief 'a staff...Mark Serwin. Sandoval say da guy likes da Colombian whores and dat he has him...what you say...compromised?"

"Are you saying that Sandoval has something over on the U.S. bigwig... something incriminating against him?"

"Incriminatin'...I think I know what dat word means. I hear Sandoval say he got a video of da U.S. VIP gettin' a blowjob from one of da whores at da poultry farm."

Holy Shit... Senator William Warren, the Chairman of the Senate Select Intelligence Committee is being blackmailed by narco-terrorists!

"Did you overhear when the party is going to take place?" "Yeah... Sandoval plans fo' me to be a waiter at it...in four days."

Episode 43

A terrorist on the move

It was 8am. A dozen Pepto-Bismol tablets later, Edhi thought he was getting better. The night before, he actually had a good sleep, but his improvement didn't last. Hakim Ahmadi had gone to work at his used- clothing and consignment store while his beautiful wife Asma tried her best to treat his worsening symptoms.

An hour after awakening, he felt dizzy and lightheaded. Stomach pains ensued and he began to cough up blood. If his ailment continued, Edhi feared he wouldn't be able to carry-out the suicide attack. He had to make it to northwest Pennsylvania to finalize the execution of Allah's campaign against the enemies of Islam.

Asma kept a close eye on him from her workstation in the corner of the living room while mending a pile of used hijab caps and headbands. He did not look well. She made sure he drank copious amounts of water and placed a tray of saltine crackers and a bowl of warm, clear broth in front of him.

He ate slowly, then got up and walked to the bathroom. A while later he returned and said, "I've got to see a doctor. It's getting worse...my stool was bloody. I must get some treatment so I can carry out Allah's decree. I can't go to a hospital. Is there a walk-in clinic nearby?"

Asma called the store and told her husband about Edhi. He immediately came home and drove him to a coffee shop on a busy side street, two blocks away from a free clinic. They definitely didn't want Ahmadi's personal car parked in the clinic parking lot while he waited for Edhi to be treated. With Allah's stanchion, he would walk on his own to the clinic.

The coffee shop served Arabic tea, so they ordered multiple servings with lots of sugar while quietly discussing the situation. The game plan was simple. Ahmadi's associate ran a used car dealership in Dearborn. He also rented cars and would quickly fill out the proper rental forms, using Edhi's forged driver's license and credit card. The dealership would provide auto insurance in case Edhi was stopped by the police on the way to northwest Pennsylvania, for both Ohio and Pennsylvania require drivers to have no-fault auto insurance coverage. When he was finished being treated, Edhi would walk back to the coffee shop. The rental car would be parked a few steps away. All the proper rental documents, his fake driver's license and credit card would be in the glove compartment. The fabricated passport, visa, credit card and driver's license that Cadenas passed to Edhi at the Willemstad's Curacao International Airport jived perfectly together.

An hour later, Edhi hobbled into the free clinic in Detroit. For a treatment center encircled by poor neighborhoods, it was remarkably well-staffed and equipped. The three doctors and support staff were aware that the funds of over $1.5 million per year came from a government grant provided by a nameless benefactor. However, none were aware that the original founder, Dr. Slesman, was approached by a shadowy figure representing a very wealthy, enigmatic organization. They did not know, through a quid pro quo agreement, that Slesman agreed to go back to school and obtain a Forensic Science degree while the organization took over the clinic operation...and saved it from bankruptcy.

The nameless organization hired all three doctors and Slesman mentored them while obtaining his forensic degree online. Upon obtaining the degree, to their stupefaction, Dr. Slesman simply vanished and they never heard from him again.

While seated in the waiting room, Edhi glanced at the other patients in the room. He didn't like the thermal-imaging security camera in the lobby or the fixed-dome camera in the waiting room. The clinic was in a high-crime area, but it seemed excessive so he pulled the bill of his Detroit Tigers baseball cap down to cover his eyes as best he could.

A picture of the three doctors hung on the wall. One looked Irish, one possibly Italian, and one appeared to be Arabic, named Dr. Amasi. He hoped Amasi would see him. In only a few minutes, a nurse opened the hallway door and called his name out. Apparently, the doctors judged him to be worse off than the others.

He waited in a small patient's room where a dome security camera protruded from the ceiling and after several minutes, Dr. Amasi entered and greeted him. "So, tell me what you are here for."

The doctor listened to him intently, showing concern when he heard about the headaches, burning stomach and coughing up of blood. After learning about the bloody stool, Dr. Amasi shook his head and told him they needed to do further diagnosis, immediately. Edhi felt the burning sensation return to his stomach upon hearing that he would be at the clinic for at least several more hours.

An RN and an anesthesiologist entered the room after Edhi slipped into a hospital gown and laid on the gurney. The RN attached an IV catheter into a vein in his arm and the mild sedative calmed his rattled nerves, somewhat. She sprayed more anesthetic into his throat to relieve the gag reflex as Dr. Amasi carefully inserted a thin, fiber-optic instrument into his mouth and slowly manipulated it down his throat. The images of Edhi's esophagus, stomach and duodenum appeared on the video screen for twenty minutes before the flexible tube was extracted. An hour later, Edhi had dressed back into his street clothes and slipped on the baseball cap. Dr. Amasi showed the photos taken of his innards and pointed to severe ulcers in both his stomach and duodenum. He added that they had to be taken care of, soon, less he ruptures an artery, which would probably prove fatal.

Amasi asked Edhi if there was any undue stress in his life. Instead of offering a diatribe of how he hated the U.S., that he spent months planning a vicious attack that will kill many Americans, and that he was going to die honorably as a martyr, he calmly looked at the doctor and replied, "Yes. I run a clothing business and it's not doing well. You know...dog-eat-dog business world." He told the doctor that he wanted an over-the-counter medication for his ulcers and didn't want to get a prescription medicine at this time. Dr. Amasi looked displeased with his patient's decision, but persuaded him to schedule an appointment for surgery in two days, reminding him that one ulcer was dangerously close to a major artery in the duodenum and if it ruptured, he would be dead in minutes.

Ten minutes later, Edhi walked ever so slowly down the streets of inner-city Detroit towards the rental car by the coffee shop. He entered a pharmacy and purchased Omeprazole, which he paid cash for. Upon leaving and continuing the arduous walk to his car, he didn't notice a man across the street inside a gas station, scrutinizing him from behind a tall display stand of sunglasses.

Corey waited twenty minutes after Devon Ledard left, then walked out of Love Beach and boarded a jitney on East Bay Street for the short ride back to the Hibiscus Beach Inn. Upon entering his room, he turned on the satellite TV and switched to a channel that was blocked by the channel blocker. He entered a code and it opened up, revealing a screen with an analog loop of green numbers speedily moving from zero to 3,000, then repeating the sequence.

He opened the small refrig, took out a Kalik and poured it into a glass of ice, then plopped down on the bed and stared at the screen. It would notify him if any listening devices or hidden videos were on the premises before he called General Morrison. A major terrorist attack against the U.S. was imminent and the funders and planners were about to congregate at the Abaco Poultry, LTD mansion. CBIF's special ops force must be in place and ready for a raid...in four days.

The green digital numbers flew past at an unbroken, uniform speed. If the number stream paused or stopped at or around 398, it detected a UHF-type listening device that someone planted close by. A break in the flow between 86.5 and 110 would indicate an FM listening device was concealed somewhere in the room.

He sipped the ice-filled glass of Kalik, remembering when he unlocked the TV-blocking device at the safe house in Montego Bay, Jamaica and turned on the anti-bug detector. The number flow immediately stopped between 900 and 2,400, indicating a wireless video was hidden somewhere in his room. A meeting with CBIF cell managers was about to take place, but was cancelled.

The IC team casing out the hotel premises found a man in the room next door watching a video screen of the meeting room. He was a member of Iran's terrorist proxy, Hezbollah, which was firmly imbedded throughout all of Latin America and the Tri-Border Area of Brazil, Argentina and Paraguay.

Satisfied that his room was secure from eavesdroppers, Corey called CBIF HQ in Key West on the unique satellite phone that Pinkston created. It had voice scrambling with a matchless twelve-digit security code that uses a digital encryption algorithm. It would be a long talk with the general about top-secret information that could prevent thousands of Americans from dying.

Corey programmed the twelve-digit code and the algorithm began rolling it over, up to over 50,000 times. Corey and General Morrison could talk for hours in complete privacy before the pattern repeated itself.

The general answered. Corey could tell he was chewing on the Montecristo. "Corey, you wouldn't believe what's going down."

"I think I would, sir."

"Try this on for size. Our CI teams in Port-au-Prince tailed Virgilio Cesar Sandoval to his plane. He took off with his two killers, Tougas and Cherestal, and flew an unscheduled flight to Cali, Colombia."

"He didn't fly the chopper this time?"

"No, but the CI agents were able to attach a GPS bug on his plane, which he kept at the Port-au-Prince International Airport in a hanger that Laurent Rousseau, the infamous Haitian Minister of Public Health and Population reserves for his 'guests'."

"No flight plan scheduled? Sounds like Sandoval and Rousseau have the air traffic controllers paid off."

"No doubt. To make a long story short, the CI teams photographed Sandoval meet up with three other men for lunch at a gourmet restaurant called Platillos Voladores in the Cuisine Corridor section of Cali. Security was tight inside and out, but the team snuck in the back of a store across the street and bribed the owner to take a long lunch break. They told him they were from the National Intelligence Agency of Colombia, ANIC...and to keep his mouth shut...which he did."

"The photos were run through the FBI's Next Generation Identification system, the NGI, and four of the men were identified."

"Who were they?"

"Sandoval, of course. But, his lunch mates were intriguing at the least. Juan Rojas, a retired Colombian Army officer who MI6 and CIA suspect to be an arms dealer, along with Javier Sanchez, a top lieutenant in FARC, the Fuerzas Armados Revolucionarias de Colombiationary. Lieutenant General Castano of the Colombian Army also showed up."

Corey grew uneasy. He had to move around to release the ill feelings cropping up, so he got up from his single bed and retrieved a couple of spiny lobsters from the mini-fridge. He'd grill them on the communal BBQ later on. "Didn't Castano recently speak to the Senate Select Intelligence Committee?"

"Yes, Chairman Senator Warren had him speak to the committee at Castano's request. He urgently needed hi-tech mortars with laser guidance and grid switches so he could launch precise firing operations against FARC."

Corey gulped down his glass of beer. "Isn't it a bit odd that he'd meet with the top leader of FARC, a person his army has been trying to hunt down and kill? I'm afraid Javier Sanchez and Lieutenant General Castano are in a plot to attack America's heartland with hi- tech weapons...the laser guided mortars that the U.S. shipped to him have been stolen."

General Morrison started chewing heavily on his superb cigar. "How the hell do you know that!?"

Corey relayed Devon Ledard's intel, including his daring belly-crawl behind the yellow elder hedge to just a few steps from where Sandoval and Sean Branagh talked at the Abaco mansion. He mentioned the imminent, euphemistic "party" which was actually a last-minute jihad reunion at Abaco Poultry, LTD of hardened Middle Eastern planners and funders with naive but greedy Western accomplices, some downright evil co-conspirators.

Morrison was silent for several moments, then gave his supposition. "Fuck...four days!"

"My exact words to Ledard at Love Beach, sir."

Morrison chewed his Montecristo to a pulp. "That explains another event."

"What's that?"

"Our stealth ELINT satellite picked up a signal from the transponder you requested our CI team in Haiti to place in the case of Arak booze. It's aboard one of Abner Orival's smuggling boats and is now approaching the Bahamian archipelago."

"No doubt headed directly to Abaco...to the mansion. I doubt if it's going to Patrick Branagh in Nassau, even though his name was on the Bahamian Customs declaration forms they found at the Hotel Montana.

Morrison tossed the tatty vestiges of his Montecristo into a near-by wastebasket. "In four days, Cesar Virgilio Sandoval and his henchmen Bolan Tougas and Pierre Cherestal, Sean and Patrick Branagh, Eamal Batoor, Kassim Khoury, Abner Orival, the Haitian Minister of

Public Health Laurent Rousseau, the bastard Bahamian Agriculture Minister Alfred Moss who no doubt was complicit in Duane Collier's murder..."

"And that of his mother, Joan Collier, too."

"Of course, Corey...her too. She was a good friend of Daniell's. We can also add RBPF's local constable on Abaco, Cecil Turnquest...and last but not least, our ignominious Senator William Warren, Chairman of the Senate Select Intelligence Committee, along with Chief of Staff Mark Serwin."

"Sounds like you're making a list of some sort."

"Indeed, I am. I'm calling an urgent meeting with President Rhinehart to place these thirteen individuals on a 'Capture or Kill' list...and I know he will OK it. In four days, CBIF is going to raid that fucking jihad party and all, including the small army of Middle Eastern gunmen smuggled in by Abner Orival from Haiti that are earmarked to be future attack sleeper-cell agents inside America...everyone there will be shot and killed or arrested and sent to Guantanamo. That's what OT Level is all about...and the American public will never know the difference."

"Nor will they know the harm we prevented from coming their way."

General Morrison was silent and Corey knew that meant he was about to share some ominous, fresh intelligence. He always saved the best, or worst, for last.

"I'm not so sure the assault will prevent America's heartland from being hit."

"What do you mean, sir?"

"The one facial photo taken by the CBIF CI team at the Platillos Voladores restaurant in Cali the other day...the one that didn't get a hit on NGI...it got a hit on that same photo several hours ago."

"How could that be, sir?"

"You recall the CBIF surveillance operation that you set up in Detroit, Michigan years ago, in the free clinic...when you recruited Dr. Slesman to work for us?"

"Yes, of course, we took over the clinic, sent Slesman back to school to become our forensic examiner and hired three doctors... one was named Dr. Amasi, a Saudi national I recruited to work there. His sister was obtaining U.S. citizenship, but still lived in Saudi Arabia, in the city of Najran, which is close to the Yemen border. AQAP attacked a market in downtown Najran and killed her along with forty other innocent men, women and children. Actually, he was a walk-in, he volunteered to work for the CIA, but you sent me to recruit him into CBIF."

"I'm sure you remember that the surveillance system set up in the clinic is directly tied in to NGI."

"Yes. The video streams taken there, just like the ones taken by our counterintelligence ground agents and CBIF stealth IMINT satellites throughout the Caribbean, are sent to Stacie, our CBIF mole inside the NSA. She has a separate key-in to the NGI system and the results are sent back to her without anyone else knowing, including the FBI."

"That's another way we remain completely anonymous. Stacie notified me that the same unidentified photo of a Middle Eastern man, believed to be Pakistani, who met with Rojas, Castano, and the FARC leader at the restaurant in Cali, just entered the free clinic. As we speak, a CI team is following him along the downtown streets of Detroit."

Episode 44

Domestic surveillance

It was a hot, sultry day in Detroit. Edhi turned the air conditioner on high in the rental car, a Ford Fusion, which idled near the coffee shop. He sat in the driver's seat, jotting down brief descriptions of suspicious persons and vehicles he just passed while walking from the free medical clinic- a man sitting on a bench reading the *Detroit Free Press*, a woman sitting in a parked Chevy Cruze, a couple walking a small dog on the sidewalk near the coffee shop, the seven vehicles parked along the street near him...he took no chances.

He stared at himself in the rearview mirror and shook his head in antipathy. The vibrant-tone polo shirt and gold necklace from which a brilliant stainless steel pendant hung of a three-dimensional Jesus with his arms splayed on a cross smacked of Western avariciousness and ignorance. His Western goatee was well-trimmed and allowed him to fulfill his duty to Allah without growing a full beard.

Edhi thought of the shame he and the members of his sleeper attack cells endured in order to blend in and remain under the radar of U.S. intelligence. The joy of entering martyrdom by crucifying thousands of Americans in a crowded stadium would make it all worthwhile.

A short time later he drove down Woodward Avenue and entered onto M-10, Jefferson Avenue, but ran into stop-and-go traffic congestion while passing the Coleman A. Young Municipal Center with its famous "Spirit of Detroit" statue. He chuckled to himself and praised Allah as several hundred members of the Islamic Society of North America (ISNA) were peacefully protesting around the bronze monument

The twenty-six-foot-tall sculpture of a seated male figure held a bronze sphere in his left hand which emanated rays to symbolize God. In the right hand was a family group of some sort and a plaque before it bearing the inscription, "The artist expresses the concept that God, through the spirit of man is manifested in the family, the noblest human relationship."

The protestors were attending an ISNA conference in Detroit along with thousands of others from across America. A week before the event, a local imam draped a Karim tunic over the monument in honor of the pending ISNA get-together. His reasoning for doing so seemed sound- he wanted to emphasize the importance of assimilat- ing Muslim-Americans into Western societies. After all, a Detroit Red Wings sweater was placed on the statue during the 2009 Stanley Cup playoffs. It was also dressed in a tuxedo honoring a visit by The Three Tenors, an operatic singing group.

The city officials disagreed and removed the tunic, causing quite a stir among the members of the imam's mosque and among other Muslim-Americans throughout the Detroit area. The number of dem- onstrators swelled as Muslims arrived from afar for the ISNA sym- posium. They joined the ranks of local protesters and spent the day surrounding the "Spirit of Detroit," giving speeches on their difficulties maintaining Islamic values in an un-Islamic American society.   To them, the tunic removal symbolized the isolation and ridicule that greeted them in their daily lives.

Edhi rolled his window down to listen as a megaphone was passed around. One woman wearing a hooded tunic complained about how her daughter of marriageable age couldn't find a compatible spouse. Another Muslim woman adorning a Jal-i-Niyaz prayer dress objected that the public-school principal insisted her young son had to dance and sing in music class, despite her pleading that such behavior is contrary to their strict beliefs. Even a letter from the local imam didn't result in her son's being excused from the class, so she was forced to transfer him to an Islamic school where he wouldn't be subjected to intimidation or forced to do things against his beliefs.

Alhamdulillah! Edhi was pleased. The loudspeaker was passed around and more complaints were voiced about the difficulties blending-in to mainstream America. A man dressed in a full dishdashi robe adjusted the egal that kept a red and white shemagh in place over his head. He spoke about how he works with Americans, completed his college education with them, and now sends his children to the same public schools with them. But, he still cannot adopt the American way of dressing, eating, speaking, worshipping a higher power, and making financial transactions.

The traffic congestion cleared and Edhi sped up, pleased to witness so much discontent among Muslim-Americans. *I hope none of you, my obedient protesters...ever adapt to the infidel's way of life. There are eight million of you living in America and you should live and stay within your own communities and remain totally devoted to Allah and the Muslim way of life. Have large families and multiply! Support our offensive jihad inside America and the West... support our growing numbers of sleeper attack cells! I'm about to demonstrate to you what we are capable of doing to bring the Great Satan to his knees*

He continued on M-10 then turned off on Exit 2A and merged into I-75 S to Toledo, Ohio. He checked his rearview mirror and noted several other cars that exited the M-10 behind him. It was fifty-four miles to Toledo and he would make sure they weren't surveillance agents of the Great Satan.

For the next twenty miles, Edhi set his cruise control at sixty mph, five mph under the speed limit. Dozens of cars passed him, including the cars that exited M-10 onto I-75 South just after he did. Noting that no cars lingered behind him, he sped up to sixty-nine mph.

A nondescript white Toyota Camry discreetly remained a mile behind Edhi's Ford Fusion. A man in the passenger seat of the Camry peered through hi-powered day and night-vision binoculars while a woman drove. Both wore invisible Bluetooth, wireless earphones with two-way communication.

The man snapped another photo of Edhi with the binoculars. "He hasn't made us, yet, but I think he's speeding up."

The woman replied, "We're far enough away not to arouse his suspicion. I sense he's gradually moving away, too. Check it out with the radar gun."

Her CI team trainee/partner checked to make sure no cars were behind or passing them, then placed the miniaturized gun on a small dashboard platform and hooked its cord into the cigarette lighter. The CIA's Directorate of Science & Technology division took a liking to the radar gun used in professional baseball to track pitcher release speed, plate speed, and batted-ball speed, all in one fell swoop. The DS & T engineers developed a new software and digital signal-processing algorithm that increased the range, sensitivity and accuracy ten-fold, so moving objects could be targeted and tracked over a mile away.

"Yep, you're right. He's sped up to sixty-nine miles per hour. We can either match his speed or call in support."

"Better call in assistance. He's obviously switching speed erratically to see what other cars behind him do. I'm sure he hasn't made us, but I don't want to raise his suspicions. Have team two pull ahead of him."

Her male passenger spoke into his hidden microphone. "Team two."

"Team two here."

"Target sped up to sixty-nine miles per hour. We'll remain stationary. Increase your speed to seventy-four mph and pass target, then slow down to his speed when two miles ahead of him."

"Roger that."

A minute later Team-2 drove past them in a Dodge Caravan and gradually narrowed the distance to Edhi, who remained at his sixty-nine-mph pace over a mile ahead. Team-1 would continuously measure Edhi's speed with the radar gun and notify Team-2 to match it and stay completely out of sight two miles ahead of him.

Minutes later, Team-2 passed Edhi's car and proceeded to exactly two miles ahead of him.

The Team-1 male CI agent spoke softly again into his hidden mike, "OK, team two...slow down to sixty-nine miles per hour to maintain a two-mile lead position ahead of target."

"Team two copies that."

Several times Edhi gradually oscillated his speed between sixty-nine and fifty-five mph, but with the hi-tech radar gun, the two teams were able to maintain their indiscernible positions. At one point, Edhi abruptly braked and reduced his speed by thirty mph. His brake lights didn't illuminate.

The female leader of Team-1 said to her apprentice, "Shit! We saw the brake lights light up in the traffic jam back in Detroit...that car must be modified. He has some sort of button that disengages them. He almost caused us to inadvertently close the distance and force us to unnaturally slow down behind him. They didn't tell us about this tactic at the 'Farm' in vehicle-surveillance training."

The CI novice replied, "I think one of my instructors did." "Smarty pants."

Her male colleague chuckled, then spoke while peering through the binocs. "Yeah, but the radar gun picked up his rapid deceleration, anyway."

The woman smiled confidently. "And even if he did trick us, we wouldn't have slowed down and continued to tail him from behind. We'd maintain our speed, pass him and call in team three, who is a half mile behind us, to take over our present position."

U.S. Navy amphibious assault ship
150 miles off Daytona Beach, Florida
(GPS: 29°14'46.1"N 78°50'38.3"W)
The captain of the USS Caribbean Sea scanned the ocean with his binoculars. He hadn't slept for over twenty-five hours and took another gulp of strong, black coffee. Yesterday, he was awakened by an urgent call on his secure phone just after midnight at his home in a middle-class suburb of Norfolk, Virginia. A voice ordered him and his full crew to steam out of the Norfolk Naval Base and proceed due south for 500 miles to a GPS position off the coast of Daytona Beach, Florida.

In less than three hours the captain, his officers, and 1,100 crew members set sail from Norfolk Naval Base. Just after rounding Willoughby Bay and sailing underneath the I-64 bridge, his ensign brought him a sealed envelope. A letter inside was signed "Robert Rhinehart, President of the United States" and stated that his mission, if successful, would save countless American lives and strike a blow against the heart of radical Islamic terrorists in the Caribbean Basin. The last word in the top-secret communiqué read "Godspeed."

He ordered the engine room to proceed full throttle. The USS Caribbean Sea's two steam propulsion plants generated over 70,000 shaft horsepower and moved the 21,000 tons of steel and 400 tons of aluminum at twenty-six mph. He would reach the GPS position well under the ETA.

Enroute, the captain received another communiqué ordering him to clear the flight deck around the aircraft elevators. His crew rolled the Sikorsky SH-60 Seahawk helicopters and MV-22 Ospreys away from the elevators. Shortly after, five UH-60L Blackhawk air assault choppers appeared on the horizon, followed by two AH-64 Apache attack choppers, then three UH-60Q Medevac choppers. The ten helicopters quickly converged on and circled the assault ship like

anxious bees returning to their hive. The commander of the ship noted the AH-64's were armed with laser-designated Hellfire missiles.

Landing on the dual aircraft elevators two at a time, the newly-
arrived choppers were promptly lowered beneath deck. In a half hour,
all ten of the CBIF special ops helicopters were concealed in the cargo
bay area. Fifty special ops warriors and a team of Medevac surgeons
and surgical RN's aboard were ushered through the 120,000 cubic-
foot cargo hold into private living quarters to await further orders.

It was the same CBIF special ops unit and Medevac team that
partook in Corey Pearson's Operation Salt Flamingo mission, when
they raided a FRAPH police station on the outskirts of Port-de-Paix in
northern Haiti and confiscated thousands of documents, video tapes,
and DVD's that documented the tortuous regime's atrocities. Then,
they took Corey's recruited mole inside FRAPH, Gesner Verdieu, back
to the U.S. along with his wife and four children.

The captain of the USS Caribbean Sea did not know that the new
occupants of his ship worked for an organization called the Caribbean
Basin Interdiction Force (CBIF), nor was he aware of their mission. He
simply followed orders, without question...especially when they originated from the Oval Office. He was now to proceed to a second GPS
position forty miles off the coast of Marsh Harbor, the capital of Great
Abaco Island in the Bahamas.

Counterintelligence Team-1 remained over a mile behind Edhi, who
had driven erratically since leaving Detroit. He passed Exit 208, which
led to the Ohio Turnpike. They presumed he would head east or west
on the turnpike, but just south of it he turned onto old Route 20, an
east-west, two-lane road that runs parallel to the turnpike. He proceeded east on U.S. Route 20 and drove through old, historic villages
and towns with names like Stoney Ridge, Lemoyne, and Woodville.

The woman agent spoke to her partner. "Our target may be wary
of the CCTV cameras at the Ohio Turnpike tollbooths. It would have
been quicker for him to get to wherever he's going at seventy mph

on the turnpike...but he chose this secondary road. What's another reason he would choose this old route?"

It sounded like a future test question. The male trainee thought, then replied, "Maybe he's just checking to see who got off Exit 208 onto this old route. Another of his checks for tails."

The woman, code name 'Tracker', smiled and said, "I'm training you well. So far, you and the trainees in teams two, three and four have done well. If your theory is correct, what might our target do next?"

"Probably get back onto the Ohio Turnpike, and see who gets on it with him."

"Exactly, contact team four and find out their location from the I-280 entrance to the turnpike."

He spoke to Team-4 through his microphone then glanced at 'Tracker.' "They passed it four minutes ago. They're two miles behind team three."

The seasoned surveillance agent stared at the GPS Google Maps screen. "Tell them to immediately turn around and get on the Ohio Turnpike. Proceed east and pull off onto the shoulder just before reaching turnpike exit eighty-one and await further instructions."

Her trainee looked over at her and said, "Now I understand the reason for having team four so far behind us, three miles behind team three, which is a mile behind *us*."

'Tracker' stared at the GPS full screen embedded into the dashboard. "Correct. Team four can pick up our target if he takes the next road north to tollbooth eighty-one and gets on the turnpike."

Sure enough, fifteen minutes later Edhi slowed down upon approaching County Road 7, Damschroder Rd., then turned left onto it and proceeded north to Tollbooth 81 of the Ohio Turnpike. Tracker instructed her apprentice to tell Team-4 to wait until the target retrieves his ticket from the machine, enters the turnpike and travels east for one mile. Then, they should drive back onto the highway and resume the tail. Meanwhile, teams one and two would drive past the Ohio

Turnpike booth on Damschroder Rd., then turn around and enter it when Team-4 notifies them that the target had traveled east on the turnpike for several miles.

The maneuver was skillfully executed. An hour later, Edhi was traveling at seventy mph east on the Ohio Turnpike, entering the Cleveland vicinity. During that time, Team-4 slowed down to sixty-six mph so Team-1 could pass them and take over the lead position, a mile behind Edhi.

The Team-1 male trainee made good use of the high-powered binoculars. He saw the target's Ford Fusion pull off Exit 142 of the Ohio Turnpike. It was a long exit ramp and Edhi slowed down, then pulled over onto the soft shoulder. To get back on the turnpike, he would have to put the car in reverse and back up for several hundred feet, then drive over the exit ramp back onto the main thoroughfare. That would be a poor move on his part, for it could easily attract the attention of the state patrol.

He said to 'Tracker,' "He must be planning to exit the turnpike."

She replied, "He's setting us up again...checking out the cars that exit just after him. He'll also note who passes him while he sits in the breakdown lane, then probably proceed through the exit tollbooth and merge onto Route 2 East."

Her male apprentice who was quickly learning the art of vehicle surveillance said, "It's almost as if he knows we're following him...kind of creepy."

"Don't worry, he has no idea four counterintelligence teams are watching his every move. He's just naturally paranoid...and a damn good sleeper-cell terrorist he is! The ACLU would file a lawsuit if they knew what the government is doing right now...on home soil."

"Yeah, like keeping Americans safe from monsters like this guy?"
"It's a balancing act. The government must keep the citizenry safe from terrorists while protecting their privacy. The more we reveal to the American public about our domestic surveillance programs, the less effective our scrutiny becomes. That's why the FBI is so

ineffective...their agents are spread paper thin...and they must operate within the legal framework. Thus, the creation of CBIF. What the American people don't know about us won't hurt them...and actually saves their lives. The cry for complete transparency within America's domestic spying apparatus opens up a Catch-22...a no-win situation, and people will die."

"So, what do we do now? Exit with him and pass him while he's parked on the shoulder? He'll make us if he sees us again down the road."

"True, my honorable but novice learner. But, that's exactly what we will do. Remember, there are three other teams. Call team four and have them slow way down, then pull over to the shoulder and stop before they reach the exit he's parked on."

Team-1 entered the exit ramp and as bad luck would have it, Edhi pulled off the breakdown lane onto the ramp just as they passed him. They slowed down to the posted off-ramp speed limit of forty-five mph and Edhi passed them and headed to a tollbooth with the longest line.

"Good move, my terrorist friend," Tracker said acerbically. "He's observing for any vehicles that enter the longer line and pull in behind him rather than go to the shorter ones. We will thus proceed to the shortest line as if in a hurry to get somewhere."

"But, we'll pull ahead of him."

"Spot on! Adjust your rearview mirror so you can keep an eye on him, since he'll be far behind us once we're both on the freeway. If he noted us passing him when he was stopped in the break lane of the exit ramp, then sees us nearby on the freeway, his paranoia will go into overdrive. We'll slow down to five miles per hour under the speed limit until we see him behind us, then speed up and maintain his exact speed. Get your high-powered binoculars and radar gun focused through the back window. When he's merged onto Route Two East, contact team four to drive back onto the freeway and proceed past Exit 142 and speed up until they're a mile behind him, then hold that position."

"But further on, he may have notice our car, the license plate....and us inside."

"Believe me, he will. Our description is no doubt jotted down in his notepad. We're going to get a new surveillance vehicle and put on some new clothes." The experienced CBIF surveillance agent dialed a number on her secure cell phone. "This is 'Tracker.' Do you copy our position?"

"Roger that, we have you on satellite surveillance from your vehicle GPS transponder."

"In urgent need of 'VC'. Please advise."

A few moments passed, then an official voice came back on. "Proceed to Park Place Airport Parking, 18951 Snow Road, Brook Park...just past the Cleveland Hopkins Airport. Lot 57."

"Roger that. Thank you."

The trainee asked, "You requested a 'VC'...what does that stand for?"

"Vehicle Changeover."

After discussing the new intelligence with General Morrison, Corey left the Hibiscus Beach Inn safe house in Nassau and flew HST Airlines directly to Marsh Harbor airport. When Morrison contacted the POTUS and informed him of the impending terrorist threat that Corey uncovered, he summoned him immediately to the White House.

Four hours later, Morrison was seated in the Oval Office across from President Robert Rhinehart.

Episode 45

Death lurks inside America's heartland

President Robert Rhinehart looked away from General Morrison and gazed at the Cleveland Indians photograph on his desk. It was a signed by Mark Rounds, Indians All-Star pitcher and dated last week. Rounds was honored as the best southpaw in the MLB. His incredible "drop ball" forced the best of batters to hit only ground balls, which the Indian team did an outstanding job in fielding.

Born and raised in the affluent suburb of Rocky River on the far west side of Cleveland, Rhinehart grew up to be a devoted Indian's fan. His father took him to Saturday double-headers since he was age five. He had a baseball and photo signed in 1952 by Cleveland Indians pitcher and Hall of Famer Bob Feller. After his father passed away, the POTUS remained a devoted Indians fan and loved the game of baseball. He became a star pitcher in Little League baseball, eventually attending Ashland University on a baseball scholarship. It was Rhinehart's privilege to invite Mark Rounds to the Oval House for a chat ... and to ask for his autograph.

Rhinehart looked back at Morrison, who was seated on a matching couch across from him. "As you know, our meetings never happen, especially this one."

"I understand fully, sir." Morrison knew the modus operandi well. All his meetings with Rhinehart go unreported, so to speak. A fictitious name appears on the White House visitor's log and the press release simply says that the president had coffee and a chat with an outside consultant over "domestic and foreign policy issues." The records lack identifying details beyond the fabricated name, and typos often occur by design.

On several occasions, Morrison used the name of someone who was cleared to enter the White House but never actually showed up. Since the surge in terrorist soft target hits on America intensified since 2018, the Supreme Court ruled that the White House can keep secret the records of visitors who enter the building. They're not subject to disclosure under the Freedom of Information Act (FOIA).

"The intelligence that Corey Pearson gathered is very disturbing, indeed. I have sent the USS Caribbean Sea amphibious assault ship on a training exercise off the eastern coast of Great Abaco Island in the Bahamas."

"I appreciate that, Mr. President. All ten of CBIF's special ops helicopters and fifty of our best fighting men, along with Medevac choppers and surgical crew landed on the Caribbean Sea without incident. They are hidden below deck."

President Rhinehart chuckled sardonically and said, "I'm not supposed to know that."

Morrison took a sip of coffee while smiling back. He understood the hullabaloo. Here they were, planning to keep America out of harm's way and having to do so deceitfully. It made no sense.

"Yes, sir. I understand. The special op troops are loaded for bear and the Blackhawks and Apaches are armed with Hellfire missiles. Your 'Capture or Kill' order will be carried out."

The president rose, walked over to his work desk and sifted through the top drawer. Morrison admired the antique, known as the *Resolute* desk. It was made from wood taken from the ship HMS Resolute and given to President Rutherford Hayes by Queen Victoria of England in 1880.

Rhinehart retrieved a document from it, returned to the couch and laid a military manual down on the coffee table. The title was italicized: *140mm Laser and GPS Precision-Guided Mortar* "I read through this and knowing that stolen ones are in the hands of a radical Islamic attack cell has caused me to not sleep well. Do you think these hi-tech weapons are in the U.S.?"

"They are either inside the U.S. or on their way." "How many were stolen?"

"Three, along with twenty live shells."

"How do we know they're not headed to that fuckin' chicken farm... the one you told me about last week...on Abaco?"

"Highly unlikely, sir. The planners and funders are meeting at Abaco Poultry, LTD in three days. They would never get near the weapons. Since the sleeper attack cell leader has been discovered in Detroit, it's assured that the mortars are close by him."

"In America's heartland?"

"As I said, sir...they're either on their way to or are inside the U.S. right now."

Rhinehart loosened his tie, took off his sport coat and poured a glass of ice water. "Just how lethal are they? I glanced through the manual. Their accuracy is what bothers me."

"We believe that's why they stole them from the Cali barracks in Colombia. Lieutenant General Castano of the Colombian army pleaded for them to Senator Bill Warren's Senate Select Intelligence Committee and, bingo, he got them."

The president chewed nervously on a few ice cubes, staring at the manual, then said, "Warren is one of the participants at this gathering at Abaco Poultry, LTD. You told me last week that this...what's his name, Cesar Virgilio Sandoval...a narco-terrorist... is blackmailing him?"

"We believe so. Corey Pearson recruited a reliable asset named Devon Ledard inside Abaco Poultry. He reported that Sandoval has a video of Senator Warren having sex with a Colombian whore at the mansion on Abaco."

"If he's at the mansion… at this fucking terrorist meeting in three days when your special ops team attacks, he'll be arrested and cuffed along with everyone else…or killed if he resists."

"According to Corey Pearson's latest update, there is a contingent of Middle-Eastern men at the place…dozens of them, well-trained and most likely brought in to protect the radical Islam planners and funders who will be there. They were smuggled in from Haiti."

The POTUS smiled and said, "They will all die. I'm sure you know what you're doing and have a good plan of attack."

"Yes, sir. From Devon Ledard's description of the place and our stealth IMINT satellite images, we have every square foot of the buildings and grounds mapped out. The CBIF ops team will hit hard and fast."

"I hope Warren gets it through the head…the bastard!" "Was that an order, sir?"

"No, just a wish. If he survives the assault, he'll face treason charges. With the intelligence that Pearson gathered on him, he'll be convicted and sentenced to life in prison, for sure."

Morrison shook his head in disgust. "It's hard to believe the Chairman of the Senate Select Committee on Intelligence has been compromised by a narco-terrorist."

Rhinehart said, "If this pending terrorist mortar attack that Corey Pearson uncovered kills any Americans…I'll fuckin' shoot Warren myself…. in the balls first, then in the head. Tell me about this hi-tech mortar. The manual mentioned a term APMI…what the hell is that?"

"Well, it's worrisome, simply because of its phenomenal accuracy from a great distance. The need for such a weapon arose during the war in Afghanistan when Taliban fighters engaged U.S. soldiers from well-hidden, ambush positions on ridges and mountain rims. They already sited in their weapons and knew where to aim them at our troops in the valley below."

"Sounds awful...you talking from experience?" "Yes, sir. I was caught in several such ambushes." "So, how did these mortars come in to play?"

"We didn't have them yet, and our direct-fire weapons were limited due to rules of engagement and bad weather. Our rifles were useless. Thanks for air strikes...that's what saved our asses. Our recon squads spotted Taliban moving along distant ridgelines or valleys but didn't have the range for the direct-fire weapons to target them. So, the Army began the Accelerated Precision Mortar Initiative...aka APMI...back in 2009."

"So, what we used on the Taliban in Afghanistan is going to be used on U.S. citizens somewhere in America's heartland.... fuckin' wonderful. Just what is it capable of? Just how accurate is it?"

"Because of the GPS-guidance, the 140mm mortar rounds can hit within eight feet of a mailbox from 7,000 meters...over four miles away."

Rhinehart shook his head out of total aggravation. "You're telling me this radical Islamic terrorist cell lurking inside the U.S. can slaughter Americans from afar, with pinpoint accuracy?"

General Morrison poured himself a glass of ice water. He wanted to chew on his Montecristo, badly. "Yes, the GPS was chosen in addition to the laser designation for the mortar guidance system for a reason. The Taliban would duck behind ridges and boulders, making the laser pointing designation limited...we couldn't zero in on what we couldn't see. So, the GPS was included in the guidance system. It provided accurate targeting even when the Taliban took cover behind obstacles."

"So, you're saying this weapon, which is about to be used on Americans... on U.S. soil...cannot be escaped from once the barrage starts?"

"Yes."

"And, your CBIF countersurveillance teams are tracking...as we speak ...the leader of the jihad attack sleeper cell, the person who will execute the attack?"

"Yes, sir."

"And last but not least, this radicalized Muslim asshole will lead us to the weapons?"

"We believe he is going to meet up with the rest of the attack cell members to make last-minute preparations for their suicide mission. Setting up and firing these mortars cannot be done by one person. They will go through final preparations with the actual mortars."

Rhinehart leaned forward and gave Morrison a worrisome stare. "We can't afford to lose this fuckin' monster. I take it they won't let him out of their site? He won't be able to elude them?"

"Unlikely, sir. The four teams were completing their last phase of surveillance tradecraft at the 'Farm'. Their leader is a CBIF instructor that Pearson recruited years ago. She specializes in foot, vehicle and aerial surveillance and is the best there is. Her code name is 'Tracker', and rightfully so. She was conducting foot surveillance with the teams at the huge ISNA convention in Detroit when we called her in."

"I was told about the convention by Walt Mason, the FBI director... one of the *Gang of Six* members. He assigned fifty agents to monitor the thousands of Muslims who are attending the four-day event. They came from all over the U.S., Europe and the Middle East."

"Yes, I'm aware. My CI teams are secretly photographing all five thousand attendees and sending them through NGI. They got a half-dozen hits at the Cobo Center alone and handed the photos and names over to the FBI to put them under surveillance. It's ironic that NGI, the *Next Generation Identification System*, got an unexpected hit on the Pakistani man who walked into the free clinic that Corey Pearson set up as a clandestine surveillance office. While he was in the clinic getting medical care, we called 'Tracker' and her four teams off the convention detail and ordered them to immediately begin tracking him."

"Where's are they now? Do you know where he's headed?"

Morrison took out his smartphone and looked at the GPS tracking device screen. "They are traveling east on I-90 on the east side of Cleveland, heading towards the Pennsylvania border. We do not know his final destination, but wherever it is, you can bet his attack cell suicide jihadists will be there."

"And, hopefully the mortars will be there, too. Don't fuckin' lose this jihadist bastard, Tom. You know how well-trained they are in shaking off whoever may be following them."

General Thomas Morrison spoke confidently. "I'm aware, sir. 'Tracker' and her four teams will follow him undetected. She trained them to constantly behave as if their targets assume they're being constantly followed. When they started foot, then vehicle surveillance on this attack cell leader after he left the free clinic, I assure you he never noticed the teams or what they were up to. Their tactics enable them to blend in naturally to the surroundings...their behavior is indistinguishable from that of the common citizenry around them. They blend in."

President Rhinehart seemed a bit more at ease. "Glad to hear that. Of course, our conversation is not to leave the Oval Office. I have the tape recorders turned off, for obvious reasons."

"Absolutely, sir. Nothing will be shared. The FBI, NSA...no member of the Intelligence Community will know."

"It's a sad state of affairs that we can't balance privacy with security. As we speak, your secretive CBIF agents are tailing a person without a FISA warrant, illegal government surveillance is being con- ducted on everyone who walks into the free medical clinic in Detroit, masses of Muslim-American citizens are being secretly photographed at an Islamic Society of North America, ISNA convention... can you imagine if the ACLU or the Electronic Frontier Foundation, the EFF ever got wind of what we're doing?"

"I hate to think of the lawsuits. Fortunately, CBIF's activities are kept secret from the seventeen agencies of the IC, the Intelligence Community. You have integrity and CBIF's mission is to strike preemptively to keep the American public out of harm's way. But, as

Henry Kissinger once said, 'Ninety percent of the politicians give the other ten percent a bad name.' Quite frankly, the ACLU is partly right. I don't trust very many officials in government."

A sardonic smile appeared on Rheinhart's face. "Like Senator Bill Warren, chairman of the Senate Select Intelligence Committee?"

"Precisely. Look at the harm he's done already by being black-mailed by radical Islam. He's a sociopath. Who knows what a future despotic government policy-maker or even president might do armed with the surveillance expertise we now use to fight terrorism. The ACLU and EFF may save us from such a possibility. Ironically, the domestic counterintelligence we do protects Americans from such people, I might add."

"And, that's why CBIF will continue to operate in total secrecy." Morrison nodded in agreement. "One other thing, sir. 'Tracker' con-tacted me several times, reporting that this jihadist they're following is especially difficult to conduct vehicle surveillance on. He knows every trick in the book, so I called in a drone. She's well-versed in vehicle and aerial surveillance coordination...and so are her trainees. Our at-tack cell jihad leader will not elude us."

After the VC, vehicle changeover at the Park Place long-term parking section near the Cleveland Hopkins Airport, 'Tracker' and her train-ee put on new clothes and hairpieces that were in the trunk of their brand-new tracking car, a Dodge Caliber. They quickly snapped the portable Google GPS Map screen into the dashboard, paid a $400 parking charge with cash upon exiting the car park, and in a half hour were once again tailing the attack cell radical Islamist, staying a mile behind him.

Then, it happened. Edhi abruptly turned off I-90 onto Exit 223. The off-ramp was long, with a slight incline.

The Team-1 male recruit, who was now driving, looked at the GPS map. "There's a Waffle House, McDonald's and Burger King off this exit. Maybe he's hungry."

'Tracker' responded, "I doubt it. Look at the view he'll get of I-90 from that off-ramp. He'll pull over and observe. This little maneuver of his was pre-planned before he left Detroit."

Sure enough, Edhi pulled over and stopped on the soft shoulder, pretending to look at a road map, as if he was lost. He noted every vehicle that passed below him on I-90, searching for anything that looked irregular. Brief descriptions of the next dozen cars and the occupants in them were jotted down. Then, Edhi continued through the Exit 223 off-ramp, crossed over Route 45 Center Road, accelerated quickly and drove down the 223 on-ramp and back onto I-90.

Team-1 and Team-2 didn't exit, but continued on along I-90, passing him when he parked on the off-ramp berm. They knew Edhi jotted down their descriptions along with other passing cars. They were "made," so to speak, but 'Tracker' intuitively instructed Team-3 and Team-4 to slow down on I-90, even pull off onto the berm, if they had to, before nearing Exit 223, so Edhi wouldn't notice them.

Team-3 assumed Team-1's position and followed Edhi from a mile behind when he drove back onto I-90. Team-4 resumed the end position a full mile behind Team-3, keeping a close eye out for a counter-surveillance team that Edhi may have employed to follow him.

'Tracker' answered a call on her secure satellite phone. It was from CBIF HQ in Key West. Morrison was still in Washington making plans with President Rhinehart, but before leaving Key West he instructed the satellite image interpreters masquerading as drywallers in the front company *Key West Drywallers* to stand by and to call in a CBIF drone if 'Tracker' requested one. She did just that a half-hour ago. "'Tracker' here...go ahead."

"The UAV you requested is overhead your position of 41.828513 by -80.765954 at 10,000 feet altitude. We have you under visual surveillance. Please guide to target vehicle."

"Exactly one point four miles behind us, traveling east on I-90, just passing Route 11 south of Ashtabula. Single male driver in green Ford Fusion, license plate BDE 68Q."

Her male trainee was dumfounded. "A drone? When did you call a drone in?"

She looked over at him. "Thought I'd surprise you. I requested it while you were taking a piss back at the rest area. It's a CBIF operated MQ-1B Predator, the same UAV we practiced with along Route 50 back at the 'Farm'. Just remember the lessons I drilled into you... this is the real thing, no more rehearsals."

A large square suddenly appeared in the upper-right hand corner of the Google GPS Mapping satellite screen on the dashboard. It was an overhead close-up image of Edhi's car. His fingers could clearly be seen through the windshield, holding on to the steering wheel. "This is 'Scout MQ-1B'. We have target locked in. Do you copy visual feed?" 'Tracker' replied, "Affirmative...clear image. Keep continual visual stream coming in to us."

"Roger that...Scout MQ-1B will maintain continual visual flow."

The Team-1 trainee glanced at the live image of Edhi's car. "I can't believe the clarity! That's taken from 10,000 feet?"

His attractive female surveillance spymaster, mentor and instructor agreed. "Yes, it is truly amazing. It's operated by a CBIF pilot at Creech Air Force Base in Nevada, over two thousand miles away. A team of image specialists working out of a safe house in Key West is also watching it. The pilot at Creech operates it, but there's a four-second delay because the instructions relayed to and the images received from the drone pass through a satellite link. That includes landing instructions, so just before touching down on the tarmac, the Creech pilot hands the controls over to the CBIF team at the landing site and they land it visually."

"Where does it take off and land from?"

"I don't know. All I know is that when I request a drone...I've got one overhead in twenty-five minutes. By the way, the image is much clearer from this drone than from the one you trained with at the 'Farm' simply because it's loaded with very expensive, hi-tech stuff."

"What's it carrying?"

"It's got a treasure chest of sensors in its bulbous nose...both color and black-and-white TV cameras, image intensifiers, radar, infrared imaging for low-light conditions, lasers for targeting. The color cameras run at almost two gigapixels so it can track and monitor any activity on the ground. Before you are transferred to the Caribbean, you will attend a week-long seminar on the Argus-IS surveillance- imaging system, which is what this drone uses. The drone you trained with at the 'Farm' used an outdated system."

They approached Exit 235. 'Tracker' told her trainee to get off I-90, then pull into the parking lot of a neat mom and pop restaurant called Kay's Place. "Another nifty thing about using drone surveillance, we can pull farther away from our target and still keep tabs on him."

She pointed to the blinking dot on the Google Map screen and the close-up image of Edhi's car, which was now approaching the exit they just got off. "The Argus-IS enables the drone to send us a continual stream of him at the rate of ten frames per second. It can track him from over 20,000 feet altitude across sixty-five square miles. If need be, it can carry two Hellfire II missiles and strike at a range of five miles."

"Is this one armed?"

"That's another thing they don't tell us. General Morrison at HQ in Key West, the CBIF pilot who's flying it from Creech Air Force Base in Nevada, the satellite image interpreters at the safe house in Key West, and the CBIF pilot who lands it and launches it from some covert airstrip... they all know if it's lethally armed or not, but we're kept in the dark. The images it's sending are watched, analyzed and recorded by all of the above. Morrison, after consulting with the POTUS, gives the order to take a target out. You and I will be the last to know...but we'll know, believe me."

"Has it ever happened inside the U.S.?"

"Yes, once. I led three CI teams at the time. We were five miles behind a target van in Georgia with seven radical Islamist suicide bombers inside. The drone was overhead, streaming videos to all three CI team vehicles. The intelligence we had indicated they were going to a final meeting to plan an attack, but the CIA interrupted the surveillance streams and reported that new intel indicated the actual attack was in progress.

My three teams were tailing these assholes on the crowded I-285 loop circling Atlanta. Turns out they were about to attack CNN world headquarters. The first suicide bomber would walk through the front door, then bolt past security and run towards the newsrooms and studios. When they opened fire on him, his hand would release the detonator button...and boom. Five more suicide bombers would follow in waves, using the stairwells to reach the upstairs offices."

"I never heard about it."

"Neither did the American public. The jihadi suicide bombers never made it off I-285. It was total chaos but we took them out on the crowded interstate without killing any civilians. We practiced the drill many time at the 'Farm'. When General Morrison gave the order, our three teams burned rubber until we were right on the heels of the van. We fanned out and blocked all the lanes, then slammed on our brakes. The terrorists panicked and sped up to over a hundred miles per hour, passing cars ahead. But, the drone struck when the van was clear of other vehicles. There were civilian cars nearby, but no innocents were hurt, although some cars got hit by shrapnel."

"Hard to believe no one was hurt."

"That's because CBIF uses a modified AGM-114M Hellfire II on home soil. It has a lighter warhead that takes out light vehicles, not tanks. It was used in Afghanistan, Iraq and Pakistan for urban warfare and to shoot into caves. The smaller explosive charge is a blast fragmentation and incendiary type, but when it triggered the six backpacks full of explosives inside the van, there was quite a bang."

"How come people didn't notice the drone attack?"

"The customized Hellfire leaves a smokeless vapor trail and travels at nearly a thousand miles per hour. No one noticed it hit. CBIF's secret press release gave the FBI full credit for saving CNN HQ from destruction. The explosion was blamed on the backpacks accidentally detonating.

"I'm still surprised there weren't civilian casualties...even with the protective maneuvers your teams did to keep nearby motorists away."

'Tracker' nodded her head in agreement. "The truth be told, I was surprised, too. But, think of the lives we saved. it was lunch hour and if they accomplished their goal, hundreds would have perished and the world would have witnessed CNN being taken out."

'Tracker' remained in the parking lot of Kay's Place. Suddenly, Team-3 alerted them. "Target getting off interstate at Exit 235."

The Team-1 car was only several hundred feet away from the exit ramp and would be visible to Edhi. 'Tracker' quickly opened her door and said, "Get out of the car and stretch, then stroll with me into the restaurant. Look straight ahead and don't even glance back towards the exit or I-90."

They sat at a booth inside the restaurant. A kind waitress mentioned their split peas soup, Reuben sandwich and ribs specials, but they settled on two cups of black coffee to go.

'Tracker' turned on her secure smartphone app. The drone stream came in clearly. "He's driving over Route 193 and is about a hundred feet from us. Now he's onto route 84 heading east. He passed the entrance to I-90 and pulled into a parking lot of the Kingsville Video store, which overlooks the interstate. A sign outside reads 'Truckers Welcome!'.

"We'll sit here for a while and see what's happening. He's probably cross-checking to see if any suspicious vehicles he's jotted down since leaving Detroit pass by or get off at the exit."

The waitress came with two coffees in a cardboard holder. The male trainee gave her five dollars and told her to keep the change. He asked 'Tracker', "The drone is circling overhead. How long can it stay up there without refueling?"

"Eighteen hours, unless its toting Hellfire's under its wings. It doesn't hang around directly overhead. The pilot at Creech will steer it a good eight miles away from its present overhead position and climb to 20,000 feet. Even with a good pair of binoculars, our jihadi target won't be able to detect it."

'Tracker' instructed her partner to instruct Team-3, the first CI vehicle behind Edhi to continue on along I-90 past the exit, then to tell Team-4 and Team-2 to pull off onto the berm several miles before exit 235 and wait for further instructions."

From eight miles away at 20,000 feet, the drone video stream came into her smartphone with amazing clarity. Edhi's green Ford Fusion was parked in the lot facing I-90. She looked at a close-up of him through the open, driver's window. He watched the cars that passed on the interstate below him. His arm rested on the window sill.

'Tracker' observed him repeatedly lift up a notepad laying on the passenger seat. He was checking to see if any of the suspicious vehicles he recorded along the way reappeared.

Suddenly, he grew nervous and bolted out of the Kingsway Video lot. Instead of turning right and entering the I-90 on-ramp, he turned left and continued east on Route 84.

They got back in their Dodge Caliber tracking car and remained in the mom and pop restaurant parking lot, calling in the drone to pursue from above.

"Shit," Tracker said. "He'll slow down shortly, probably even pull off onto the berm to see if there's a tail. We'll sit here for a while and watch the screen. That's one of the best benefits of drone surveillance...to avoid being set up by the target's countersurveillance tactics."

'Tracker' contacted Team-3 and Team-2, instructing them to pull off the berm back onto I-90, remaining a mile apart, then to get off Exit 235 and split up- one to drive to a Burger King to the left, the other turn right and immediately pull into a Subway lot.

Edhi didn't slow down as expected. He drove five mph over the speed limit on Route 84 Bushnell Rd. and sped past a perfect surveillance position in a small parking lot at the Bushnell Country Store facing the Route 84/Route 7 intersection.

Team-1 watched the Google GPS Mapping images streaming into the dashboard screen from the drone, which was now 13,000 feet directly over Edhi's vehicle. Her keen surveillance intuition kicked into gear; 'Tracker' sensed that he was satisfied no one shadowed him from Detroit and was ready to complete the final leg of his mission. She spoke to her teams. "This is it. I think he's about to lead us to the other sleeper attack cell members. Hopefully, the 140mm laser-guided mortars will be with them." Her gut feelings were rarely wrong.

Episode 46

Target evades surveillance

Seasoned boaters know that Lake Erie is a dangerous and often unpredictable body of fresh water. Because it is the shallowest of the Great Lakes, the waves swell up quickly during storms. Bad weather and squalls seem to come out of nowhere. Even NOAA, the most accurate weather predictor, misses some storm cells that arise suddenly and blast quickly along the lake shore before hitting land in northeast Ohio and northwest Pennsylvania. Many boaters have been caught in sudden surges of eight-foot waves and sixty mph wind gusts, despite listening to NOAA on VHF.

Occasionally, the perfect storm develops over Lake Erie, as was happening while the MQ-1B Predator flew overhead. The four CI teams followed Edhi along Route 84 as he crossed the Ohio/Pennsylvania border, where Route 84 changed to Route 226.

It was a particularly hot and humid day, spawning a warm front that rose off the waters of Lake Erie. The day had been cloudless since the morning hours, giving way to sunshine that allowed temperatures to soar throughout the entire Great Lakes region.

A strong low pressure area centered near Duluth, Minnesota expanded and moved south into Illinois and Missouri. It crossed the Western Great Lakes and into Lake Erie. As the cold front moved eastward across the lake and merged with the warm and humid air, conditions in the upper atmosphere grew favorable for an outbreak of severe weather.

While 'Tracker' and her CI teams stalked Edhi along Rt. 226 through a canopy of green eastern deciduous forests interspersed with open meadows, thunderstorms developed north of them in Ontario, Canada just ahead of the cold front.

As the afternoon progressed, this thunderstorm-spawning phenomenon gradually moved south into northeast Ohio and northwest Pennsylvania. The cloudless sky enabled Lake Erie's rising warm front to mature into an even more super-heated mass with rising humidity.

Route 226 merged onto state Route 6N, and Edhi continued east through the borough of Albion, population 1,550. The drone feed showed him entering a McDonald's drive-thru on the far side of the small town, so 'Tracker' and her three teams held back from entering the municipality. They would wait until the target picked up his order from the window, departed Albion, and continued east on 6N.

'Tracker' spoke into the secure satellite phone to her team. "He waited at the pick-up window a good ten minutes for the order, a rather protracted wait for a single customer. The drone feed showed eight medium-sized bags were handed to him through the drive-thru window. I believe we're about to meet the other attack sleeper-cell jihadists."

'Tracker' expected him to proceed on 6N to the next town of Edinboro, but as she and her trainee in the Team-1 car passed through Albion, the target pulled off 6N onto a side road called Crossingville Road. Team-1 followed him onto it, ordering Teams 2 and 3 to not turn off, but to proceed on 6N into Edinboro. Team-4 was instructed to turn onto Crossingville Road and stay a mile behind Team-1.

The speed limit on the side road was forty-five mph, but Edhi maintained a sixty-mph pace and didn't employ any countersurveillance maneuvers. He seemed bent on reaching his destination. After ten miles, he crossed over Cussewago Creek and came to Route 98, which he turned left on and drove through the village of Crossingville. On his left was a large gathering of worshipers on the front lawn of the SS Peter and Paul Church. A sign read "Chicken BBQ & Holupki Dinner- all welcome!"

He slowed down and stopped to let a group of parishioners cross the street. They carried casseroles and desserts to the feast. He stared at the women dressed in immoderate gowns and their children decked out in luxuriant attire.

Edhi stared at the bounty of food on the tables lining the front lawn and thought about children starving in Iraq, Afghanistan, Pakistan and Iran. He uttered aloud to himself, "You rich infidels! What an evil government you send your tax dollars to. You invade and obliterate Iraq to kill Saddam Hussein and kill a hundred thousand civilians in the process, but forget that your Donald Rumsfeld met with Hussein and became his ally in the eighties..."

He ceased his soft tirade inside the air-conditioned car, noticing a little girl in a pink dress pass in front of him. She stared at him while holding her mother's hand. After crossing Route 98 and walking onto the church lawn, she continued staring at him.

More of Allah's offenders continued to walk by. Edhi wanted to scream at them, but smiled politely instead. A few smiled back. "You are a crazy lot who will never reach what you call Heaven. Your tax dollars supported Moammar Gaddafi in Libya who tortured and killed innocent women and children...then you killed him. You stood up for Hosni Mubarak of Egypt for years, then demanded his arrest and conviction. Then, you backed and defended General Zia of Pakistan who ended up Talibanizing his country. You have no idea of your own stupidity...so worship your Christian god inside your churches and send yourselves to hell... unless I do it first."

Edhi realized he had to control himself. Despite his fake smile, passersby gave him a second glance. His loathing must have shown through. He bottled up his thoughts about anti-Semitism, drone attacks killing innocents in the Middle East, America supporting oil-rich dictators, the wars in Iraq and Afghanistan, and his belief that America is raping the natural resources of the Mideast and is trying to take over the entire region. He repressed his vengeful thoughts by closing his eyes and praying to Allah...by thinking about the thousands of Americans he will soon murder...by imagining himself ascending into the eternal garden paradise for Muslims where everything he yearns for in this world will be awaiting his arrival.

He opened his eyes when a car politely honked behind him. It was an elderly farmer driving a classic pickup truck. Edhi politely waved at the gentleman and sped on out of the village. The little girl in the pink dress asked her mother, "Mommy, did you see that man in the green car we walked in front of? He looked like a meanie!"

Her mother was busy setting her pasta-chicken-broccoli baked casserole on the table. "Don't worry, my dear. He was probably late getting somewhere he wanted to go."

It took Edhi thirty seconds to drive through the village of Crossingville, then he turned right and headed due east on county road 1008, also known as Irish Road. Shortly, he passed underneath I-79 and headed to Plank Road, which led to Edinboro.

'Tracker' and her partner entered the village of Crossingville, making sure they were far behind Edhi. She noticed that the snow-white cumulonimbus clouds in the direction of Edinboro had flattened out against the upper atmosphere due to wind shear. The anvil-shaped monster rose 65,000 feet above the countryside and, in minutes, the entire sky turned blue-black. She glanced at the dots on the Google GPS Mapping which represented Team-2 and Team-3.

Edinboro was eleven miles away and Team-3 passed through the downtown area while Team-2 was just entering it. She wanted them to pull over before taking Route 98/Plank Road out of town to allow her and Team-4 to continue as the two lead cars. They could then follow behind after the entourage passed the outskirts of Edinboro.

"Team two...team three...come in."

The reception was poor. "Team two here. Don't know what's going on but this storm came on quick! Winds strong...rain and hail are bad... large hail...the size of baseballs ...must pull over, visibility is zero!"

'Tracker' noted that Edhi sped up to seventy mph on Irish Road and drove for six miles until he came to Plank Road, where it veered off from Route 98. The storm hadn't reached her yet, although she could feel the warm, moist air cooling quickly and the wind beginning to pick up.

The target proceeded through the rural intersection outside Edinboro. Tall trees and dairy farm meadows bordered each corner. He drove onto Route 98 and headed to the borough of Cambridge Springs. The Predator drone feed was still clear since the Creech AFB pilot maneuvered it six miles ahead of the storm and looked down at the target from a 45-degree angle. No wind shear, rain, clouds or hail interfered with the satellite feed.

Cambridge Springs was ten miles away. Edhi raced along at seventy mph on the fifty-five mph stretch of paved road, trying to beat the storm and meet up with his attack cell before the storm hit.

Regrettably, it developed into a catastrophic climate event. The line of thunderstorms off Lake Erie strengthened and spawned several F3 and F4 tornadoes along the shoreline in northeast Ohio and Ashtabula County. The National Weather Service Office in Cleveland issued a tornado watch for Crawford County, which included Edinboro and Cambridge Springs. Within five minutes, the watch turned into a tornado warning. A five-tornado outbreak of unprecedented magnitude blasted the area. NOAA and the NWS Cleveland tracked them ripping through Edinboro, traveling at thirty-five mph towards Cambridge Springs.

All four CI teams were in the midst of the chaos as Edhi sped into Cambridge Springs. He was three miles ahead of Team-1, but it made all the difference in the world. Weather and love, the only two things no one can be sure of.

One of the five twisters intensified into a category F5 with winds over 260 mph. It roared over Meadville Street in Edinboro where the Team-2 car pulled over in front of the University of Edinboro campus. They never saw it coming due to zero visibility. The monster tempest lifted their surveillance car fifty feet in the air and catapulted it through the university grounds. Both Team-2 agents were killed, along with a dozen college students, when the airborne car smashed into the university's glass-enclosed elevated walkway. The steel-reinforced, raised skywalk connected the east and west sides of the campus and bridged a steep terrain so students could move freely between their classes and residential dorms. Ironically, it was essentially built to protect them from inclement weather.

'Tracker' noted that both blinking dots denoting the locations of Team-2 and Team-3 disappeared from the dashboard screen. One blip representing Team-4 shown on the screen, a half mile behind her on Route 98. She sped up to eighty mph, planning to reach Cambridge Springs in five minutes. There was no time to be concerned about the teams that vanished off the screen, yet she still tried to contact them. "Team two, team three...do you read me...team two, team three... come in...do you read me?" Silence.

The wind picked up even more and a few raindrops hit the windshield of the Team-1 car. Fortunately, the F5 tornado veered to the southeast after ravaging Edinboro and missed Cambridge Springs by a few miles. "Team four, come in."

"Team four copies your broadcast."

'Tracker' spoke with unaffected calmness. "Team four, put the pedal to the metal. Proceed to Cambridge Springs immediately."

"Roger that."

Next, the surveillance pro contacted the drone pilot at Creech Air Force Base in Nevada. "Creech, I'm seeing the satellite feed getting a bit blurred on this end. Am proceeding quickly to get a visual. We must not lose him in Cambridge Springs. How's your view?"

"Creech here. The image remains clear from this end. Your target drove into Cambridge Springs, turned left on McClellan St., proceeded across the main street/Route 19 and pulled into the parking lot of a large old hotel called the Riverside Inn. As we speak, he got out of his green Ford Fusion and is entering the front door of same."

Walking up the front steps, Edhi glanced at the huge wrap-around veranda lined with rocking chairs, old-fashioned sleighs and historic cane chairs. He walked through the lobby and took a step back in time, although he didn't feel its significance or value the remembrances of the bygone era.

Most guests stop and enjoy the ambience; it offered an escape from the hectic life of the 21st century. It was easy to imagine women of the 19th century strolling around the premises toting parasols and wearing simple dresses with flower trimmings, and gowns with puffed sleeves covering petticoats, corsets and chemises underneath.

The place was an oddity to Edhi. He returned a quick smile to the friendly but restless desk clerk who offered to show him the way to the basement where the staff and guests sought shelter. He declined and walked past her and the Victorian-style furniture, wall paintings and artifacts embellishing the lobby and adjoining Concord Dining room.

Momentarily, he paused to stare at old photos of women wearing hoop skirts and poke bonnets. The reign of Queen Victoria and her positive influence on American culture meant nothing to him.

As a child, Edhi briefly studied the Victorian era in madrassas in Pakistan. He studied Islamic subjects such as Tafseer, where he learned the full interpretation of the Quran; Hadith, where he memorized thousands of sayings of Prophet Muhammad; and Fiqh, the Islamic law itself.

In the Tafseer classes, his imam teacher compared the Koran's implications to the decadence of Western culture and actually blasted the Victorian age for pushing men into the background while women became the focus of fashion and home life. He remembered the moral warning of his madrasas imam, who preached that, because a woman rose to power and became the queen of England, women in the West surged to the forefront. Wives became the show of their husband's status and wealth, while the husbands continued to work hard to earn a living, but faded into the background of significance. The idea of women wearing anything but tent-like burqas and walking outside the home without their husbands escorting them was against Allah's teachings.

He fled the lobby in disgust. To him, the Queen Victoria era with its long period of peace, prosperity and refinement was an age of wickedness and irreverence to the God of Islam. It sickened him...his anger began to grow again. *I will have my revenge against all of this!* Edhi stomped down an adjoining hallway that led to the Riverside Pub.

Outside, the wind gusts were reaching sixty mph even though the F5 traveled southeast from Edinboro and missed Cambridge Springs. It was still on the ground, tearing through the countryside a full twelve miles away.

He sat on a barstool just as the electricity went out. The frightened barmaid announced she was heading to the basement level. She had been watching the local TV weather channel and heard that the tornado veered away from Cambridge Springs. But, without TV updates, she wasn't going to take any chances. She asked him to seek shelter with her and the others, but he again declined, telling her he loved storms and was going outside on the back patio to have a cigarette. She left the bar, giving him an incredulous look.

Plans had changed. He was supposed to remain in the bar for fifteen minutes and order some crab cakes and a beer, then go onto the back patio and smoke a cigarette. From the barstool, he noticed the wind-swept rain pelting the sliding-glass door that led outside.

A white utility van pulled up ahead of schedule in the back, gravel alley behind the inn. Edhi exited the empty bar, hurried down the wooden steps of the back patio, and jumped in the van as an attack cell member slide the door open.

Moments later, Team-1 and Team-4 sped down McClellan Street in Cambridge Springs and entered the Riverside Inn grounds. In the rain and gusty winds, they failed to spot a white utility van pull out from behind the inn. It turned right onto Route 6N and traveled a couple hundred feet, then veered off quickly and disappeared onto a back-country road named Miller Station.

'Tracker' ordered the two men in Team-4 to speed around to the back alley while she searched the parking lot in front. She and her partner located the abandoned Ford Fusion parked on Fountain Avenue, the inn's front drive.

Team-1 exited the car, ran through the heavy downpour and blustery winds, and entered the front door. They prowled through the front lobby while Team-4 entered the rear of the inn through the Riverside Pub's patio door. All four agents had their Glock 30, .45-caliber semi-automatics with sound suppressors drawn and pointed forward as they stalked through the darkened pub, lobby and hallways. No one was around.

Their orders to kill Edhi were sent minutes ago by General Morrison. He had been watching everything unfold in the Situation Room in the West Wing of the White House. President Rhinehart sat next to him. The two men sat alone in the 5,500 square-foot room which is normally used by Rhinehart and his advisors from the National Security Agency, Homeland Security and his White House Chief of Staff.

The secure communications system was turned on and the duo seemed lonesome in the midst of dozens of wall-mounted monitors. They silently watched NOAA broadcasts of the severe weather in Ohio and Pennsylvania. Several screens displayed Images of Edhi's face that were downloaded from the thermal-imaging security cameras at the Detrioit Free Clinic.

The two met sat in silence watching the severe weather broadcasts and the drone's last video stream of Edhi entering the historic Riverside Inn in Cambridge Springs. Then, the images blurred. A sixth tornado had spawned between the drone's 20,000-foot position and Cambridge Springs, making it impossible to employ it further. Morrison and Rhinehart agreed to call the $24 million UAV back to its covert base, but not because of the financial loss accrued if it were demolished by the approaching storm. They were concerned about what would be found amidst the wreckage, including two modified AGM-114M Hellfire II missiles.

The perfect storm saved Edhi and his fellow sleeper-cell jihadists from being blown to bits while traveling inside a white van along a rural back road in Pennsylvania.

Episode 47

Action, the cure for grief

Marsh Harbor, Abaco

Corey sat at the bar in the shade of the "Dilly Tree" at Sapodilly's Island Bar. Because a major operation was imminent, he didn't want to meet Constance at the Abaco safe house. He told her to call him when there was a lull in business, which she did when the lunchtime crowd left. A few bar patrons remained, but Corey sat far enough away so his conversation with Constance wouldn't be overheard. She turned up the music a bit before coming over to him.

He posed as just another hungry customer and ordered a Sapodilly Burger, the owner's specialty. While waiting for Constance to bring it from the back kitchen, he admired the Sapodilla Tree, aka "Dilly Tree," and its beautiful white flowers. The fruit has a natural sugary taste, somewhere between a ripe pear and crunchy, brown sugar. The bark has a latex material called Chicle that's used for a chewing gum base. *Chiclets chewing gum...clever name.*

Constance brought his order and began washing beer mugs in the sink in front of him. "So, what's the latest?"

"The Abaco Poultry mansion meeting is on. Morrison told me a signal from the transponder hidden in the case of Arak at the Hotel Montana in Port-au-Prince was picked up by our ELINT satellite. An IMINT satellite honed in and got some images. The Arak is aboard one of Abner Orival's smuggling boats. Half a dozen Middle Eastern-looking men are aboard, too."

"I thought the Arak was going to be shipped to that turd...what's his name...the owner of the pub in Nassau?"

Corey bit through the thick layer of hamburger stuffed with Danish bleu cheese topped with sautéed onions, mushrooms and bacon strips. "Patrick Branagh, and it's the Irish Frenzy Pub. I thought he was heading to Nassau, too, but Orival's boat bore west of Crooked Island and Cat Island. I notified two CBIF agents on San Salvador Island staying at Club Med Columbus Isle and they actually saw him heading north towards Abaco through their telescopes."

"So, the Middle-Eastern funders and planners of an imminent attack inside America are meeting at the Abaco Poultry mansion?"

"Yes. Who else would drink camel piss? Eamal Batoor and Kassim Khoury...both dangerous men that met with Sandoval in Port-au-Prince at the Hotel Montana. Batoor, a terrorist who was captured and spent time in Saraposa Prison in Kandahar before the Taliban freed him. They'll be there... and so will I."

Constance rinsed out another beer mug. Corey noticed the athletic and womanly body with plenty of curves underneath the side-tie skirt and spaghetti strap halter top. She smiled slightly, noting Corey's interest. She leaned up against the bar. "I remember Khoury and the FBI fuck-up on Curacao."

Corey reached over and placed a hand on her arm. "I remember sending you there with the eight other CBIF agents to monitor him. He was the ringleader of the large cell...sixteen militants. Your surveillance uncovered a link not only to drug trafficking and money laundering, but you stumbled upon Khoury meeting with Lebanese nationals linked to Hezbollah."

She noted Corey kept his hand on her arm. "Yes, we shadowed them and staked out his safe house...a luxury condo outside Willemstad. Four were Syrians, four from the Tri-Border Area, and four were Lebanese nationals. Our CI team did an *excellent* job...if I may so myself."

Cory caught himself holding her arm and slowly took it away. "Well, it looks like you're going to get another shot at him...along with all involved in the murder of Duane Collier and his mother."

Constance reached in the cooler and grabbed two Kaliks. "Here, it's on the house." She took a long swig. "We were just about to find out where all the drug money was laundered before they cleaned it and sent it back to Iran to fund Hezbollah cells in the U.S. Then, FBI Director Walt Mason sent in his good squad and arrested a Lebanese-American for cigarette smuggling."

Corey noted how fast she finished the bottle of Kalik. She retrieved another one from the cooler. He let her rant on...it was good therapy for her...for them both. He would support her a little more before disclosing the dreadful news that Morrison passed on to him... news that would pull the emotional rug out from under her.

He spoke softly. "Constance, don't beat yourself up over the FBI's blunder. You did everything right...documenting Hezbollah sleeper-cell agents at the Willemstad safe house, tailing them back to the Tri-Border Area in Argentina, Paraguay and Brazil...finding their Iranian contacts. True, we were about to smash a huge terrorist network, but it went underground after Mason's G-men stormed in and arrested one lowlife. But, your efforts weren't in vain."

She leaned against the bar again. "Thanks for that. We did gather a hell of a lot of intel. I'll bet they had plenty of leads to follow up on." Corey placed his hand on her arm again. "Morrison has a huge database incorporated into Jeannie in the War Room. The fresh info from your Intelligence reports out of Curacao was a treasure chest."

"Thanks again, Corey. I guess it's all in the family. My father is a former Naval Intelligence Specialist and my brother is completing his training at the 'Farm' and is soon to be a case officer for CBIF...   at least that's what you told me when you recruited him out of naval intel." Constance took another swig on her Kalik and gave Corey a tongue-in-cheek look. "Are you here to tell me that you're going to station my baby brother on Abaco so he'll be near his older sister?"

Tears formed in Corey's eyes. Constance's comical look vanished quickly. He put his other hand on her arm and looked remorsefully into her eyes. "Constance, your brother was in Detroit on a counterintelligence mission...recording facial recognitions at a huge ISNA, Islamic Society of North America convention and sending them through NGI. There was a hit on one. Your brother, with three other teams, tailed him through Ohio and into Pennsylvania. Their target was the leader of an attack cell that is going to hit America hard, with mortars..."

Constance interrupted him. She started to shudder, then whimpered, "Tell me what happened! Is my brother alright?"

Corey felt her firm grasp on his hands. "In a town called Edinboro, Pennsylvania, his team was hit by an F5 tornado...he and his female partner were killed instantly."

She closed her eyes, sobbed quietly and continued to hold Corey's hands. A long silence ensued before Corey continued. "Whatever you need, I'm here to help you...you can take time off and be alone with your son for a while."

Constance withdrew her hands, opened her eyes, wiped away the tears and stared at him with a determined look. "We're at war... radical Islam is waging war against the West...and we're losing. Not only do I *not* want to take a leave of absence, I want to go with you on the mansion raid. I feel heartache for my brother, but the only cure for how I feel is action."

Corey felt a surge of sentiment that he hadn't felt in a long while. It was a strange sensation he felt years ago, with Danielle...but it vanished when she was taken away from him. He never wanted to feel it again, but here it resurfaced. *Do I love this strong woman before me?* "But, what about your twelve-year old boy? What about your parents? It's going to be a dangerous raid. Remember, Sandoval has dozens of well-trained men smuggled in from Haiti."

Her resolute posture never wavered. She spoke with tearful eyes. "War is hell, ain't it? If this radical, attack-cell fuckhead that my brother was killed for while trying to track down succeeds...and if thousands of Americans die while I was mourning at some feel-good retreat...I'd never live it down. Yes, battling terrorism is an ugly business...that's why CBIF was created. This is one war worth fighting. I'd be morally wrong by taking a leave of absence. I want in on the raid!"

Corey felt a strong emotional surge. Was it admiration...respect... love? In moments of anguish and heartache, grief reveals who the sturdy people with integrity really are. He reached out and held her arm again. It was a natural impulse. All he knew was that the feeling he felt for her right now...this moment...was strong.

He looked into her eyes. "I understand...I just don't want you to be harmed. But, OK... you will be at my side when the raid begins. It will begin with a lightning-fast strike by CBIF's Special Ops. They'll rappel from six Blackhawks while two Apache choppers light the place up if the troops are fired upon, which they will be. I gave them a detailed layout of the entire grounds...out buildings and the inner-rooms of the mansion, including the large conference room where the meeting will take place."

"How did you get the plans of the place?"

"From one of our IMINT satellites, plus Devon Ledard described in detail the inner hallways and rooms. He knows the layout well... served Sandoval drinks and snacks in his office and den."

Constance placed bottles of Nassau Royale, 151 rum, grenadine and various fruit juices on the bar. "Time to toast our bringing down another terrorist plot. I can't think of a better drink to honor their downfall... have a 'Dilly Willy'."

The pokerfaced agent that Corey recruited and trained years ago handed it to him. "What's our part in the raid going to be?"

"After the shooting starts, it should be over within five minutes. When it stops, we're going in through the front gate and immediately search Sandoval's office and den. If we run into any of the surviving enemy, we shoot to kill."

"What will we be looking for?"

"Devon told me that Sandoval makes homemade DVDs and CDs. He's got a large library of them...all labeled. He's also got one file cabinet we'll unload. While we're confiscating everything in his library, keep an eye out for anything labeled 'Penumbra Database'."

Episode 48

The recovery

Edinboro, Pennsylvania

The events unfolded unexpectedly and rapidly. The path of death and destruction left by the F5 tornado appalled 'Tracker' and her partner. She had endured the misery of many victims in the battle against radical Islam, but not to this extent. They had to find what was left of the car driven by Team-2 and remove the surveillance equipment and, if possible, locate the bodies. The Team-3 members were on the outskirts of Edinboro and away from its direct path. Still, they were injured when a large oak limb fell on the hood of their surveillance car. They were rushed to a hospital in Meadville for lacerations and a few broken bones.

Team-1 took Route 99 out of Cambridge Springs and hurried to Edinboro, but the road was blocked by fallen trees and debris from leveled homes. They parked on the berm of Meadville Street and hiked a half mile into town. 'Tracker' downloaded the location of Team-2's blip into her smartphone before it disappeared off the Google GPS Map screen. It was dead ahead on Meadville Street at the intersection of Terrace Drive: location 41°52'09.9"N by 80°07'41.9"W.

Dozens of chainsaws cut through felled trees as hundreds of police, EMS and National Guard soldiers searched the debris and damaged homes for survivors. Reporters from all the major news media outlets captured the destruction on videotape. A team of meteorologists and engineers from NOAA snapped photos for further analysis to determine the intensity rating.

The Fujita scale or F-Scale is used to rate tornado intensity and is based on the damage inflicted on human-built structures and vegetation. The seasoned NOAA team would interview eyewitnesses and study ground damage and aerial ground-swirling patterns to make a final report. But, in their hearts and minds, they already knew it was an F5.

It was total destruction. While standing on the trunk of a huge maple lying across Meadville Street, 'Tracker' and her trainee looked to the northwest and got a good view of the tornado's path into Edinboro. They thought they were looking at a huge farm field until they noticed dozens of what appeared to be manmade excavations. It turned out they were the bare basements of residential homes- the furnaces, water heaters and all contents had been vacuumed out after the 280mph winds lifted the structures off their foundations before obliterating and flinging them southeast onto Meadville Street and through the Edinboro University campus. It literally looked like a squadron of B-52's carpet-bombed the entire area.

Upon reaching the GPS coordinates at Terrace Drive, they followed the tornado's path southeast through the campus, hoping to find remnants of the Team-2 vehicle. The asphalt was stripped off Meadville Street and muddy strips were all that was left of patterned-brick walkways that meandered through the once-beautiful campus. Even the verdant lawns and ornate bushes were shredded and flung miles away.

They walked through the barren campus, passing bits and pieces of the leveled 880-seat Louis C. Cole Auditorium. The violent whirlwind had shredded the seats and thrust the metal scraps deep into the surrounding earth.

The labs, lecture halls, classrooms and art gallery in neighboring Doucette Hall had all vanished in an instant with the exception of a mangled John Deer farm tractor that was hurled into its huge empty cellar from miles away.

Miraculously, they came across the lifeless bodies of only a few students. They expected to run into many more, but the tremendous blast of wind carried the victims far away. Dozens of mangled cars lay scattered along the tornado's path. They checked each one, but the CI Team-2 car was not among them.

After slogging through the wet dirt past large hollows in the ground where the Crawford Center and Ross Hall once stood, they noticed a green car embedded in the twisted metal remnants of the student walkway. The Team-2 car was green. They rushed up and were able to read the front license plate...they found it!

Both Team-1 agents wriggled through the wreckage of the steel-reinforced, above-ground walkway, which now lay collapsed and spread out over the lawn. The surveillance vehicle was sheared in half and the male agent was still strapped in his driver's side seatbelt. An eight-foot oak tree limb protruded through the front windshield and pierced his chest and car seat, and extended into thin air where the backseat used to be. His female CI partner was missing from the passenger seat, but tufts of her golden-brown hair were embedded with much brain matter into the dashboard window frame.

'Tracker' and her male trainee spontaneously vomited, then dutifully took photos and gathered DNA evidence from the remains of both agents. They removed the Google GPS Maps screen and location transponder from the dashboard and left.

On the way back to their car, the CI apprentice noticed his instructor was sobbing. He didn't feel like crying...only vomiting again. Finally, 'Tracker' spoke between sobs. "I know his sister...her name is Constance and she runs a CBIF safe house on Abaco, an out island in the Bahamas. Corey Pearson recruited both of us into CBIF from the CIA. We trained together at the 'Farm'. She always spoke highly of her younger brother... now deceased. We'll send the vials to Dr. Slesman for identification...but you and I already know who they are. I'll notify General Morrison and give him the bad news."

Marsh Harbor, Abaco, Bahamas After leaving Sapodilly's, Corey strolled down Bay Street in downtown Marsh Harbor to the Conch Inn Hotel & Marina where he reserved a room. He hated having to tell Constance the dreadful news that Morrison passed on to him. Although the DNA match wasn't completed by Dr. Slesman, the facial recognition by 'Tracker' was good enough.

Shianna, Sidney Fowler's younger sister, was working at the outside Sunset Bar, so he stopped in.

"Mistah Pearson, how are you?" She was genuinely happy to see him

"I'm anxious to continue my research."

Without asking him what he wanted to drink, she opened a Kalik and placed it in front of him. "You gonna study dat pod 'o dolphins out in da Sea of Abaco again? I see dem all the time...they visit the marina every day."

Good memory she has...remembers what I drank the last time I was here "Yes, I'm going to use the boat your boyfriend revamped for me to identify each one... age, sex, and so on. Eventually, if I get my grant money, I plan to attach remotely-deployed satellite tags on some members of the pod so I can track them."

"Dat sounds really cool. Ya need some help?"

Corey took a swig of the ice-cold Kalik. "If I get the grant money, I plan on hiring two people to help me...people who know these waters well."

"And dat mean you gonna hire Bahamians, right?"

"You bet. I want to examine their migration and movement patterns, including their diving behavior."

"Diving behaviah? How ya gonna do that?"

"The tags are depth-transmitters, too. They record how deep they dive in search of food and so forth." *This is my deep cover while on Abaco, but I'm not lying...I'd really like to get such a program going for the future. A perfect cover for CBIF operatives to use to gather intelligence and to help the spotted dolphin population as well*

"So, who care where dey go?"

"Well, the Abaco's are getting more populated by humans each year...more boaters, busier shipping lanes, people water skiing and racing around on jet skis. I can use the info to convince the government to expand the national marine sanctuaries so the pods can be better protected and..."

"Ya mean like da Fowl Cay Preserve?"

Corey finished the Kalik. "Yes, and with the research results we can also change shipping lanes and better regulate where and when speed boats and jet skis zoom through the Sea of Abaco and Atlantic Ocean."

"Shianna smiled and said, "You dun need none of dat research equipment. We Bahamians already know what our dolphin friends do and where dey go."

"If I get the grant money, you'll be the first one I hire! In the meantime, I'll be photographing the spotted dolphin pod here in the Sea of Abaco. I'll be able to identify each of them by the nicks and scars on their dorsal fins and tail flukes. In that way, I can keep track of each individual and learn their social structure and population status." *And record from offshore what's going on at Abaco Poultry, LTD! Your brother's killer may also be killed, two days from now*

Corey left a hefty tip and retreated to his room. His mission at the Sunset Bar was accomplished. By tomorrow morning, the entire populace of Marsh Harbor will know what he'll be doing...his deep cover, that is.

He had a bone to pick with Morrison, so he quickened his stride through the Curly Tails Restaurant on his way back to his room. The aroma of Bahamian cuisine hung in the air as locally-caught fish, lobster and conch simmered, fried and boiled in the kitchen. Inside his room, he turned on the air conditioner and cable TV to create background noise, then called Morrison on the secure satellite cell phone created by Pinkston. He could hear the algorithm begin to relay through the twelve-digit encryption code, which would continuously scramble through 50,000 possibilities while neutralizing all wiretap and electronic eavesdropping attempts.

Despite the technical safeguards, Corey turned up the TV volume. A few moments passed before the general answered. "Did you tell Constance?"

"Yes, sir. It wasn't an easy task, but she handled it well. She refused to take a leave of absence and demanded to partake in the raid."

"I thought she would...very dedicated person who also loved her younger brother dearly...let her partake."

Morrison was in the Key West War Room, chewing on his Montecristo. "That Edhi bastard dodged four CI teams and a drone, thanks to the fuckin' weather...an F5!"

"Yes, and now a terrorist is roaming at large and about to attack America with laser-guided mortars. Sir, I'm a bit upset that you gave the order to kill him with a drone strike."

The general sighed. "I thought you might be. I was in the Situation Room with the president. Once the drone was about to be pulled away due to the storm, we both called the kill shot to take Edhi out. He was trained by General Manuel Castano's men in Cali on how to operate and fire the mortars. Without training, the rest of the cell members won't be able to carry-out the attack. With him dead, the mortars are useless."

"I see your reasoning, but he's *not* dead and the mortars are still missing. We must find them! How do we know Edhi was the only one trained in operating them?"

Morrison began chomping on his exclusive cylindrical roll of first-rate tobacco leaves. "We don't know for sure, but it appears he was going to meet up with his sleeper-cell comrades to instruct them on how to fire it. It takes at least three to operate the damn thing."

"But, sir...If you blew Edhi to bits with a Hellfire it would have alerted Sandoval at Abaco Poultry and the entire meeting would have been cancelled...top terrorist funders, organizers and planners...dozens of Middle-Eastern illegals smuggled in from Haiti...we would have lost the chance to bust a huge radical Islamic terrorist network."

"President Rhinehart and I planned on raiding Abaco Poultry immediately after smoking Edhi. The CBIF special ops team on the USS Caribbean Sea amphibious assault ship is now patrolling only fifteen miles off the Abaco coast. The Blackhawks and Apaches would have landed at Abaco Poultry mansion in minutes...the armed guards brought in from Haiti would have been killed and Sandoval would have been captured and sent to the Dirty Tricks division guys on the *Queen Conch II*. They've got the EIT room all set up. He would have been continuously waterboarded until he told us where the mortars are. Remember, he's the one smuggling them into the U.S. from Cali along one of his clandestine human and drug-smuggling routes."

Corey walked over to the terrace and looked out over the Conch Inn's private garden, checking to see if anyone suspicious was lurking close by...a routine habit whenever he talked to Morrison. Everything was clear.

He walked back into his room. "And, sir, I would have asked your permission to fly immediately back to Nassau for a meeting with Deputy Commander Ellison Rolle to secretly show him the mounds of evidence we have against the Honorable...and I use the term loosely... Alfred Moss, M.P., Bahamian Agricultural Minister, Patrick Branagh, owner of the Irish Frenzy Pub and his brother Sean Branagh, the banker in Nassau who's funding the operation. Rolle would have arrested them in a heartbeat."

"I would have granted your request. Now, what about your back-up on the ground, for you and Constance."

"I called in seven agents from two of the four CI teams that are in place in Nassau. Team ten already arrived in Marsh Harbor via HST Airlines this morning and booked into The Lofty Fig, a small, family-run resort across the street from me. They posed as a cruise ship tourist couple in Nassau and are assuming that same cover here."

"The other team has five agents. Where are they now?"

"Yes, five agents... three men and two women. They pose as scuba divers... thrill seekers...aboard a registered diving yacht that cruises the Caribbean reefs. They're here now, docked in the Conch Inn's marina. They didn't book a room and will be bedding down on their yacht."

"What are the two teams remaining in Nassau assigned to do?"
"One is the other couple that also is posing as cruise ship tourists.

They'll continue monitoring Alfred Moss while Addie Kolmogrovov cleans his office, which has more bugs in it than the Everglades on a hot, steamy, summer night. The other team consists of two men and one woman. They'll remain under their assumed diplomatic cover in the U.S. Embassy on Queen Street in downtown Nassau. They could be recognized, so it's too risky to call them into Marsh Harbor. Besides, they're monitoring the Irish banker Sean Branagh and his brother Patrick."

"OK, but no cowboy antics, Corey. Wait until special ops secures the mansion and grounds before rushing in."

"Right. They'll be nine of us, including Constance. As planned, we'll hit Sandoval's office and den and confiscate everything in it. But we'll kill anyone who resists."

"No problem. Just make sure you take Sandoval alive. He knows where the mortars are and their final destination inside the U.S. Capture and send him to the Dirty Tricks team on one of the special op choppers."

"Yes, sir Dirty Tricks is on Ferguson's *Queen Conch II*. It remained moored off Nipper's on Great Guana Cay after we busted Devon Ledard. They will be anxious to have a get-together with Sandoval.

We'll be packing stun guns and tranquilizer rifles with scopes...we can dart him from eighty yards if need be."

"Glad you flipped Devon Ledard the way you did. He ranks among our best assets down there."

"Thank you, sir. And remember, Deputy Commander Rolle was in on Ledard's bust, too. He heard how filthy Constable Cecil Turnquest is on Abaco. Rolle will be rolling in shortly after the shooting stops and officially arrest Turnquest, the fuckin' Branagh brothers, Alfred Moss, the smuggled-in Middle Eastern men...all of them, except for Sandoval. Rolle will be a hero...probably become the Bahamian Prime Minister in the next election."

"He'll become our highest-ranking asset in the Bahamas, for sure. Good luck on the raid...be careful."

The Top of Abaco Bar is upstairs from the swimming pool and provides a full view of the Conch Inn Marina. It's a perfect location to enjoy the beautiful Abaco sunsets and a handy place to observe CBIF's CI Team-11, the three men and two women who cruised in from Nassau this morning. He sipped a Bahama Mama while peering out the picture window. The friendly barkeep ran down a list of their cool, tropical libations, but he stuck with his favorite.

Corey checked out the dozens of other boats docked around the Team-11 yacht. Nothing looked suspicious. One female agent was sunbathing on the bow while a male colleague sat sipping a Kalik beer in the captain's chair on the flybridge. His arms rested on the steering wheel and Corey noted he was staring at the quite large-breasted sunbather below. *I wonder if they're breaking policy and getting physically intimate with each other? Two beautiful women and three men in their 20's, cruising the Caribbean on a yacht...it has single state rooms with private washrooms for each of them...what am I, a friggin' dreamer? As long as they do their job well, I don't give a damn*

The forty-nine-foot yacht had no keel and a draft of about four feet. It could easily meander in the tight little cays and inlets throughout the Bahamian archipelago. Corey convinced Morrison that such a vessel was needed to move a CI team under deep cover, along with operational materials, through the 700+ islands in the Bahamas. CBIF bought the used craft from a French company for $226,000. The five- member team posed as spoiled and very rich American kids who went scuba diving and partied while cruising through the Bahamas, Turks & Caicos, Haiti, Dominican Republic, Puerto Rico and the U.S. and British Virgin Islands. *Tough job, but somebody has to do it.*

It had five staterooms. The dining room table with eight chairs was removed from the salon and replaced with a steel-reinforced, fake L-shaped settee with Alcantara cushions. It was actually a large, locked safe housing the weapons and safety gear the nine CBIF agents, including Corey and Constance, would use in the raid.

Digital photos of Sandoval were sent to all the agents. They were skilled in firing the specialized semi-automatic dart-gun rifles and pistols hidden in the settee. During CBIF's training curriculum at the 'Farm', they became expert marksmen in these holographic and laser-sighted weapons which could shoot day or night and used CO^2, not gun powder to propel the tranquilizer darts.

After reviewing the IMINT satellite images, Corey determined the distances from where they would enter through the front gate at Abaco Poultry to where they would position themselves around the mansion following the special ops assault. He sent the approximate measurements to Team-11 along with Sandoval's body mass and weight so they could adjust the CO^2 firing pressure cans and fine-tune the tranquilizer dosages for each of the eighteen weapons... nine semi-automatic dart-gun rifles and nine revolvers.

Each tranquilizer dart traveled fast and accurately. Wherever the laser dot appeared, the dart hit within one-eighth of an inch from thirty yards away.

An Azaperone and Fentanyl cocktail would immediately inject into Sandoval's muscle tissue. The dosage was strong enough to immobilize him within five seconds but weak enough to not kill him. Thus, the importance of Corey's accurate estimate of Sandoval's body mass and weight. Corey and his agents were to capture Sandoval alive at Abaco Poultry and take him on a rapid Apache helicopter spin to the *Queen Conch II* where the Dirty Tricks division planned a welcome party.

A local reggae band set up on the patio outside the Curly Tail Restaurant by the open-air Sunset Bar. From his barstool in the Top of Abaco, Corey heard Shianna holler out, "Play the 'Redemption Song' by Bob Marley!" The plan was for Team-11 to meet Team-10 fortuitously at the pub. Then, Corey would bump into them, whereupon they would all engage in friendly conversation about their Abaconian experiences.

The teams would grow fascinated by Corey's stories of his dolphin research in the Sea of Abaco. He would then retrieve from his room the spotted dolphin photos and documents that identified each one by tail and dorsal fin markings. Their camaraderie would account for why the nine of them boarded the yacht together, before the mansion raid. Corey walked down to the Sunset Bar patio carrying his Bahama Mama and sat on a barstool just as the band started playing Marley's 'Redemption Song'. Four of the Team-11 agents strolled along the dock to the patio and set down at a table by the band. One agent remained on the yacht to guard the weapons and gear.

The rhythm of the lead guitar player strumming a Fender Strat and the Rastafarian beat from the bass guitar player's Jazz Boss was far above average, bordering professional musician rank. The Team-11 agents started dancing to the music as the keyboard and bongo players joined in. Corey noted the keyboardist wearing a black T-shirt with the names *Jackie Mateo, Robbie Lyn, Pablo Black* and *Paul Crossdale* blazoned in fiery reddish-orange letters across the front.

In due time, the cruise ship couple, Team-10, strolled in from the Lofty Fig across the street. They sat down a few barstools away from Corey. All purposefully ignored each other while ordering frozen tropical fruits united with a medley of Caribbean rums. The Team-10 couple sipped a *Tail Curler*, which Shianna made heavy with mango fruit, three different types of rum and peach schnapps. It went great with the free conch fritters.

Corey enjoyed the music and was especially intrigued by one band member who added inimitable reverberations and an African feel with wind chimes, a cowbell, shakers...even bottles of water filled to different levels which he tapped with drum sticks. He listened to the band while making sure the entranceway from Bay Street, the dock area where Team-11's yacht was docked, and both CI teams around the bar were in his sight. *Nothing suspicious in the least.*

He eyed patrons who flocked into the Curly Tail. Most were locals, but a few were boaters from the U.S. who docked at the Conch Inn Marina while cruising through the Bahamas. The CI agents dressed according to their deep-cover roles. The tourist couple donned brand-name tennis shoes, polo shirts and cargo pants. The four thrill- seeking operatives off the yacht dressed like the natives: flip-flops, cut-off jean shorts and T-shirts with logos about local issues.

Corey dressed somewhere in-between, sporting a loose-fitting Hawaiian shirt that hung over calf-length, gabardine pants and concealed a .45 caliber Glock.

His secure satellite phone vibrated. It was Dona Anani Guanikeyu, alias Mata Hari, his honeytrap agent. The band played a loud version of Stone McEwan's "Hangin' out in Abaco." "What's up, Dona?"

"Where the hell are you...at a concert?" "More or less. Give me an update."

"I'm at the Irish Frenzy Pub here on Cumberland Street in Nassau. Patrick Branagh and I are hitting it off pretty good...so good that he trusts me enough to take care of the pub while he's gone. He told me he's going to a big meeting with business associates somewhere on Abaco."

Corey gulped down his Bahama Mama and signaled Shianna for a refill. "That would be the Abaco Poultry operation, but the meeting is not until the day after tomorrow. We've got the raid all set up and ready to execute. When's he leaving?"

"He and his brother, Sean Branagh, the banker who keeps the Irish Frenzy from going bankrupt are flying out of the Lyden Pindling Airport in one hour from now."

Shianna placed another Bahama Mama in front of Corey. He nodded in gratitude and waited for her to walk away to serve other customers before speaking. "OK, good job. While you're managing the Irish Frenzy in his absence, sift through his file drawers for anything that ties him to Abaco Poultry."

Dona took another swig of *Turks Head* stout from behind the Irish Frenzy Pub's bar. "Roger that. I'll have plenty of time to sift...only had one customer today. Over and out."

She folded up her secure satellite cell phone and stared at the empty bottle of *Turks Head*. It triggered another memory from her childhood. She imagined herself at age eleven, laying on her upstairs bedroom bed on Middle Caicos Island...listening to her father laughing downstairs at the kitchen table, snorting lines of "weasel dust" with the Colombian drug smugglers, chugging down *Turks Head* beer. Then, the ugly Colombian she called Scarface burst into her bedroom...dragged her by her ankles from under the bed where she was hiding...then began raping her. As usual, her repetitive nightmare always ended there...before she thrust the knife into his side and literally gutted him alive.

Corey looked on as several locals held a broom stick up to shoulder height. The band began playing "Limbo Rock" by Chubby Checker:

> Every limbo boy and girl
> All around the limbo world
> Gonna do the limbo rock
> All around the limbo clock

He thought about what Dona told him. *Patrick and Sean Branagh are landing in Marsh Harbor shortly. They're arriving early, probably to launder the money that came in from the planners and attack-cell jihadists, Eamal Batoor and Kassim Khoury. Devon Ledard saw bank bags packed with cold cash on the dock at the mansion... brought in by Abner Orival on his smuggling boat.*

Team-11 joined a limbo line that the Conch Inn guests and local Bahamians formed. One by one, they limbo-danced under the stick until the last person, an inebriated salesman from Ohio, finished unsuccessfully. He fell on his drunken full moon and was ceremoniously carried off to a nearby barstool.

The broom, a.k.a. limbo bar, was lowered to halfway between the shoulder and hips. The line began another dance while the band continued with Chubby Checker's famous song:

> Jack be limbo, Jack be quick
> Jack go unda limbo stick
> All around the limbo clock
> Hey, let's do the limbo rock

One of the female Team-11 members, holding a *Tail Curler* garnished with mango slices, beckoned the Team-10 tourist couple to join in. "Get off the barstool and limbo with us...see how low you can go!"

Corey watched the conservative couple pretend they were reluctant to do so, but then wave their arms in a 'what the heck, you only live once' gesture. The woman laid her straw hat embedded with fake tropical flowers on the bar, and they joined in. The six agents laughed it up in the limbo line while drinking their tropical libations.

Fifteen minutes passed. The broom had been lowered to just below the knees. Only two participants remained. Team-10 had joined the Team-11 members at their patio table. Corey watched the two remaining competitors, a local Bahamian known for his limbo prowess and 'Chop Chop', the female Team-11 agent who enticed Team-10 to chill out and join them in the limbo line. *Companionship established amongst CI teams. Thank you, Chubby Checker. Phase I completed.*

Despite the looming terrorist network raid, which would be the largest in CBIF history, Corey's anxiety was temporarily diverted by 'Chop Chop's' performance on the limbo floor. She was as limber as a dishrag while gyrating under the horizontal broomstick, which was now held even lower. Not surprising to Corey, she spread her knees out until they practically touched the floor, leaned her torso back parallel to and only inches off the floor without collapsing, then jerked her body through while waving her outstretched arms in rhythm with the band.

'Chop Chop' was one of Corey's recruits. CBIF needed to rejuvenate its hand-to-hand combat instruction at the 'Farm', so Morrison gave him the go-ahead to find an expert in the martial arts.

He found her working out of a karate school in downtown Chicago. She was a sensei, a martial arts teacher who reached the upper echelons of karate skills. Corey assigned a counterintelligence team to put her under surveillance for two weeks and learn everything about her. They interviewed several of her friends and family members before notifying Corey that she appeared "clean" and it was clear for him to make contact.

After interviewing her for two hours, she was more than pleased to join the mysterious organization Corey described, for patriotic reasons more than monetary ones.

At the 'Farm' she was more than an A-1 hand-to-hand combat instructor. He watched her go through incredible katas to hone her skills. She mirrored the kata moves, doing them on her opposite, non-dominant side. Then, she went through them backwards by starting with the last movement and ending up at the first.

Corey was amazed at her ability to do her kata, both mirrored and backwards, under full speed with her eyes blindfolded. Without vision, she was able to maintain focus because the practice built up her other senses of balance, proprioception, and hearing. Needless to say, her CBIF trainees learned how to physically disable an opponent for a long period of time, if not permanently.

The local Bahamian touched the broom stick, making 'Chop Chop' the winner as she passed under it effortlessly. He bowed to her out of complete reverence as everyone applauded her dexterous victory. "Not only ya beat me at my own game...ya was an inch under da broom stick at dat!"

Corey looked on as the gracious loser was invited over to the table where Team-10 and Team-11 sat. 'Chop Chop' bought them all drinks. *Rapport established, blending into surrounding environ, intermingling with the locals... mission accomplished.*

Corey's secure satellite cell phone rang again. This time it was the CI team watching Sean Branagh. They reported that he met his brother Patrick and both just boarded a plane in Nassau that's headed to Abaco. Corey thanked them and hung up. Dona already told him what the Branagh brothers were up to. *Greedy bastards! Maybe that's how they ended up in Nassau...someone back home in Ireland didn't like them. Why is it that modern-day pirates are attracted to the Caribbean? How heartless and greedy these Irish dudes are...to hook up with terrorists and give them support...all for money. A disgrace to the Irish nation... I can see why some animals eat their young.*

From his tactically chosen barstool, Corey kept a wary eye on his CI teams while scanning the surroundings for suspicious activity. The Curly Tail patio bar was growing crowded with an equal mix of locals and tourists, including boaters who docked in the marina and booked into a room for a brief stay. After weeks of cruising the Caribbean, they yearned to walk on terra firma for a while.

The phone vibrated a third time. It was from Pinkston on his PT boat in the Hurricane Hole Marina on Paradise Island in Nassau. "What's up, Pinkston?"

Pinkston was on the bow of the PT boat, scratching several of his potcake dogs and chugging down his third ice-cold Kalik. It was a squelcher of a day without much ocean breeze. The CBIF-trained attack dog, a potcake that Pinkston named "Balls" sat on the captain's chair, hoping an uninvited stranger tried to board the boat so he could earn his name. "Your idea of having Addie Kolmogrovov bug Alfred Moss' office in the Levy Building has paid off."

I'm glad I recruited this ex-black hat hacker, computer science genius and saved him from a prison stretch. Corey recalled how Addie, posing as a cleaning lady working for the CBIF's *New Providence Cleaning Services* installed a small, flattened step-up radio transmitter under the Agricultural Minister's desk. It was another of Pinkston's creations. The end receiver was on the PT boat. "Great...what did you uncover?"

"Well, the Honorable Alfred Moss...M.P. The one and only Bahamian Agricultural Minister himself just hung up his office landline phone after calling Cecil Turnquest, the most honorable Royal Bahamian Police Force constable on Abaco. He told Turnquest to pick him up at the Marsh Harbor Airport tomorrow at noon. I just listened to the conversation on my receiver in the PT boat galley."

The Abaco Poultry mansion guest list is growing. "Thanks for the update, Pinkston. Stay close to the receiver and continue monitoring Moss' office... and throw 'Balls' a dog biscuit for me."

"You got it."

"And, one other thing, Pinkston, lighten up on the Kalik until this op is over. I know what you're thinking...you hear the Reggae band in the background, people laughing. I'm, indeed, sitting on a barstool with a drink in front of me, blending in. But, I need you sober...can't afford to miss anything Addie's bugs pick up. "

"You got it, boss. Just remember, it was me who created these transmitters and the receiver for them in the first place."

"Pinkston, I will never forget what your technical genius has done for CBIF. You're one of the most valuable agents I have."

An incoming call signaled so Corey hung up the phone. It was from Washington, D.C. "Mr. Pearson, this is team six. Have important info. Are you clear to talk?"

The band was playing "Dragonfly" by Ziggy Marley loud enough to drown out his voice. Corey assigned the four CI agents of Team-6 to target Senator William Warren after Devon Ledard identified him as a visitor to Abaco Poultry and friend of Sandoval. "I'm clear."

"Sir, we tailed Senator Warren and Mark Serwin, his Chief of Staff out of D.C. on I-270 to I-70 north to Hagerstown, Maryland. He drove onto I-81 then immediately got off at Exit 10A and proceeded to the Hagerstown Regional Airport."

"Did they take a rental car or the fancy one?"

"He didn't drive his Mercedes-Benz SLR McLaren. We tailed Serwin to a rental agency in D.C. where he rented a Ford Taurus. Then, he picked up Warren at his residence and they drove to Hagerstown."

"What did you find out at the airport?"

"They parked the Taurus in long-term parking, then walked with suitcases to the terminal. It's not much of a walk at Hagerstown Airport." Corey was nursing his Bahama Mama. "So, he drives over eighty miles out of D.C. in a nondescript vehicle to Hagerstown, which is a couple miles from the Pennsylvania border. I bet you're going to tell me he did not fly out on a commercial airline."

"Exactly, sir. They flew off on a single-engine Cessna Skylane. Mark Serwin piloted the plane."

"What's the registration number...the "N" number?" "N618TC."

"Paint pattern?"

"All white with blue wings. Blue stripes on tail and front." "Did you find where they're going?"

"Yes sir, port of entry is Bimini, Bahamas."

"OK. I want your team to track down the Cessna's 'N' number and find out how they got a hold of the plane. Did they purchase it themselves?" *With fuckin' narco-terrorist drug money.* "Was it a gift? Did they simply charter it from someone? If so, from who? I'll notify our agents on Bimini to begin surveillance when they touch down. Good job, team six!"

"Thank you, sir."

It was roughly 800 miles as the crow flies from Hagerstown Regional Airport to South Bimini. Corey immediately notified the two CBIF counterintelligence teams- one in Alice Town on North Bimini and the other at the Bimini Sands resort on South Bimini- to begin continual surveillance upon arrival. *The sleazy senator is island-hopping. His next flight will no doubt be from Bimini to Abaco. The guests to the Abaco mansion are arriving. I'll will be greeting you there, Senator Warren... with a few of my friends.*

Episode 49

Romance among spies

Marsh Harbor, Abaco Bahamas

Corey stuck around Curly Tails for another hour, then retreated to his room and slipped into on a jogging outfit. He began running his usual trek on Bay Street in downtown Marsh Harbor. In his rental car, he measured the distance from the Conch Inn to Albury's Ferry Service on the eastern shore and back. It was just over six miles.

As he jogged past a large, undeveloped area full of native vegetation off Bay Street between the Island Breeze Motel and the Java Coffee Shop, he hoped he would not have to enter it on the way back. It all depended on what was waiting for him at Albury's Ferry terminal.

The temp hit the mid-nineties and not much of a breeze blew off the Sea of Abaco. Corey sweated profusely in his baggy jogging attire in which a Glock and two full magazines were inconspicuously concealed.

Thoughts of Constance sprung up again. He admired her for the strength she showed when he told her the awful news of her brother's death and her unwillingness to take a leave of absence. *It was more than admiration... I wanted to go home with her, to hold her. I think I love her. I always have. She mixed the "Willie Dilly" cocktail to toast the pending raid on Abaco Poultry...the same drink we had a decade ago, before I met Danielle...the night Constance and I made love...all night long at the Abaco safe house...beautiful sex. I held her hands yesterday at Sapodilly's because of the heart-wrenching news I had to give her. I'm fond of her spirit...No! I held her hands because I adore her...I love her. She made us both the "Willy Dilly" drink for a reason. It was a message she was sending me...about how she feels, too...it was a message about us.*

He continued at a steady pace along Bay Street until it merged into Eastern Shores Road where the Albury's Ferry terminal was. Corey walked inside the small terminal and greeted the lady behind the desk, then got a Goombay Punch soft drink out of the machine. He cooled down and sipped the Bahamian pop. It had twice the sugar content than a can of Coke and tasted like liquid bubble gum with a healthy helping of syrup.

The lady clerk spoke. "Hey...I know you. My cousin Shianna work at da Conch Inn. You be da man studyin' our dolphins."

"The one and only." Corey felt his electrolyte imbalance from the heavy job improving. The Goombay Punch was Gatorade on steroids. "I think dats so cool what you do. I see ya out in da Sea of Abaco weeks ago, patrollin' a certain way ta attract dem. Shianna say ya got all 'o dem photographed and named. I luv dolphins. Dey come and ride da wake of our ferryboats all da time. If you need help studyin' dem, let me know...I'd do it fo' free. I luv dem so much, ever since I was a lil' girl!"

"I just might take you and Shianna up on that someday. She wants to help the dolphins, too."

Corey strolled over to the bulletin board on the wall. Notes of things for sale and spiritual messages were written with scrap paper. Below a "Feast Upon The Words Of Christ" message was Devon Ledard's note advertising a bike for sale: "Used bike. Good condition- $23".

If Devon indicated a bike needed repair, then something was wrong at Abaco Poultry and on the jog back to the Conch Inn, Corey would hike into the large woods across from the Java Coffee Shop. Inside the woods was an abandoned archeological dig site where British citizens living in America fled to following the Revolutionary War. Good move on their part, since many patriots despised anyone still loyal to the Crown. At the edge of the dig was a pile of discarded stones and under one of them was the dead drop. Corey instructed Devon Ledard, during their Love Beach contact meeting in Nassau, to keep him updated if anything seemed even remotely amiss at the Abaco mansion.

Corey was glad he didn't have to hike through the underbrush to the dead drop. He removed Devon's ad from the board and turned to the friendly desk clerk. "I think I'm in need of a used bicycle. I'll contact the seller."

She looked up from her paperwork and smiled. "Oh, dat be from Devon Ledard. He was in heah yesterday and pinned that on da board. He live in the Great Guana Cay settlement."

Corey acted surprised. "Oh...you know him?"

"I sure do. He take da ferry heah from Guana Cay 'bout three times a week. He work at da Abaco Poultry place in dat big mansion. Dey pay him good money, too. He wear a fancy waiter's outfit when he git off da ferryboat, and two guys in a big SUV been pickin' him up heah at da ferry dock. Dey drive him down dere south a Marsh Harbor to dat chicken place off da GAH. Now, dat's what I call service. Before dis week, Devon took a taxi down dere."

Fuckin' Bolan Tougas and Pierre Cherestal driving that SUV, no doubt Sandoval's keeping a closer eye on Ledard since the big meeting is about to take place

On the way back to the Conch Inn, Corey seemed to have more energy. It wasn't from the Goombay Punch soda. He began thinking about Constance again. She was alone at the safe house. He wished he could be there with her. He thought about his dispiriting visit to Sapodilly's to tell her about her brother and the words she spoke just before he told her: *Are you here to tell me that you're going to locate my baby brother on Abaco so he'll be near his older sister?*

He stopped jogging and walked off the road into a stand of Caribbean pine. Tears came to his eyes as he thought about those words she spoke with a teasing look on her face. *Then I told her.*

She shuddered briefly... wept softly and absorbed the emotional pain. Making the "Willy Dilly"...like she wanted to relive past times, going back ten years to that night we spent together. The hike on the abandoned logging road off the GAH and finding Duane Collier's murder site...the tire marks...collecting evidence off the dock for Slesman to analyze...the comment she made on the way back before the confrontation with Tougas and Cherestal...what was that she said? When I climbed into her Land Rover, she didn't put it in gear even though we were anxious to get the hell out of there. She turned to me and said 'You know something strange, Corey? That hike brought back old memories. We sure had some exciting times together a decade ago, before you met Danielle.'

Corey recalled how he wanted to hug her, right there, on the GAH. But, he didn't. He just couldn't move on after Danielle's murder. He regretted only saying "Yes, we did" and leaving it at that. He recalled what he really thought, but didn't say: *I cared a lot about you, Constance, then Danielle suddenly appeared in my life. Now, she's gone and even though I miss her, I find the former feelings I had for you resurfacing...maybe they never went away.*

Then, an intriguing notion came upon him. *Wait a minute! It's not good to pretend to love someone when you don't actually feel the love. Isn't it just as bad pretending to not love a person when you actually do? Love is not mine to command.*

He walked back onto Bay Street from the grove of Caribbean pines and jogged with vigor back to the Conch Inn. He suddenly felt better. When this mission is over, he would tell Constance how he truly felt about her...that he loved her.

Episode 50

Touchdown in Bimini, Bahamas

Bimini, Bahamas
(GPS: 25°42'06.5"N 79°16'20.4"W)

The Cessna flew in low over South Bimini's eastern shore. Senator Warren and Mark Serwin gazed out at the vacant stretches of white sand beaches stretching from the Bimini Sands Resort southward to Port Royal and Neil Watson's Bimini Scuba Center. The scuba/dive shop looked like an old surfing hangout, reminiscent of the Beach Boy's era. A small group of tourists were lined up to go on a stingray tour.

Serwin banked to the east and a few minutes later touched down on the tarmac of South Biminis Airport. They walked into the tiny terminal, about the size of a single-floor house and were greeted by custom officials. The customs and immigration processing went quickly. Sherwin filled out the "Arrival Report" and "Inward Declaration & Cruising Permit for Aircraft Entering the Bahamas" forms. He wrote in their time of arrival, his name, type of aircraft, and registration number on form C-7A, a form that is familiar to honest and deceitful pilots alike. The only thing preventing further scrutiny of Serwin and his plane was not being able to pay the fifty dollars processing fee that the C-7A requires.

Senator Warren paid the fee in cash and took the form a few feet away to the immigration booth and presented it to them. It was instantly and unceremoniously stamped.

Warren and Serwin walked out of the airport where a waiting taxi drove them to the ferry dock, a tiny open-air shack. In several minutes, a small boat with outboard motor picked them up and cruised the short distance over pristine, turquoise waters towards the North Bimini dock.

A rusted-out hull of an old freighter lay exposed on the western shoreline. A huge yacht passed their ferryboat in the Bimini Harbor entrance. Warren stared at the man in the pilot house of the ninety-eight-foot luxury vessel, who donned a captain's hat and yachting coat. Three voluptuous women lay sunbathing on the huge bow while a fourth sat on his lap in the captain's chair.

Warren turned to Sherwin. "I bet she's cranking him off. Someday, I'm going to have a party boat bigger than that."

In five minutes, the ferryboat crossed Bimini Harbor and reached North Bimini. They rented a golf cart and drove to the Biminis Big Game Resort & Yacht Club. Warren paid the Bahamian concierge twenty-five dollars for carrying their suitcases up to a newly-renovated room with two king-sized beds. He turned the flat-screen TV on, making sure the volume was turned up high then motioned for Serwin to follow him out to the balcony. The two men sat down in silence while looking out over the pool, gardens and bonefish flats beyond.

Finally, Warren spoke. "Got a few questions before we start partying in Alice Town. Give me the specifics of the form that customs gave you. What does it enable us to do?"

Serwin smiled and said, "Nothing to worry about. Remember, we're in the Bahamas...don't worry, be happy!"

"I'm not going to be happy until I hear from you what we don't have to worry about."

"OK, OK. Relax boss. The form is called a C-7A. I've got it tucked in my shirt. We can fly anywhere in the Bahamas with it. There's sixty different airports spread out over seven hundred islands and it's good for each one. We just present it to any port of entry we land in, they stamp it and we're cleared."

"What about when we leave and go back to D.C., I mean back to Hagerstown Regional Airport?"

"No problem. We pay a twenty-five-dollar departure fee and surrender the C-7A form to customs, then off we go."

Warren seemed alleviated by the simplicity of entering and exiting the Bahamas by plane. "OK...let's party. Alice Town is waiting for us. Our contact said to meet him at Paradise Bimini Big Johns."

NSA Headquarters
Fort Meade, Maryland
(GPS: 39°06'31.8"N 76°46'18.2"W)
Stacey hadn't slept for twenty-nine hours and the lack of even a short catnap was beginning to take its toll. Ever since Corey Pearson notified her of the pending raid on the Abaco mansion, she stoked up the ECHELON program, code-named "Dictionary" and tapped in the four-digital codes for the Nassau - Abaco Bahamas region.

Since arriving in the Bahamas, Pearson's counterintelligence agents performed well. They obtained internet addresses, telex, cell phone and fax numbers of their targets by surreptitious means, and she embedded them into the Dictionary Program.

If Patrick or Sean Branagh, Pierre Cherestal or Bolan Tougas, Shianna Fowler, Devon Ledard, Bahamian Agricultural Minister Alfred Moss or his limo driver, Abner Orival, the Haitian Minister of Public Health & Population Laurent Rousseau, Cesar Virgilio Sandoval, Senator Warren or his Chief of Staff Mark Serwin, Abaco's RBPF Constable Cecil Turnquest, or Damballah St. Fleur electronically wrote or spoke keywords or phrases that were remotely associated with the murder of Duane Collier, the mysterious Penumbra Database, the theft of high-tech mortars from Colombia or the pending terrorist meeting at Abaco Poultry, LTD... Stacie would be alerted immediately.

Even if one of the targets electronically contacted another, the Dictionary program would alert her. It leveraged a huge database of info and quickly data-mined connections. There were 358,000 keywords, phrases, cell phone numbers, first and last names along with nicknames and aliases, computer passwords and personal e-mail addresses and fax numbers that were all connected with each other via the Dictionary program. Even the myriad of names and related info that Addie Kolmogrovov photographed on the 256 Rolodex files in Aldred Moss' office were converted to digital terminologies that would not evade ECHELON's prying electronic eyes

Stacey was playing pegboard on a vast electronic board in front of her with a pattern of 358,000 holes into which she inserted 358,000 pegs. She connected the pegs with digital rubber bands so they were all linked to each other. If one of the bad guys CBIF was targeting tugged at any one rubber band, it would exert much tension between the pegs directly connected to it. But, to varying degrees, lesser tensions would be exerted on outlying pegs as well. ECHELON and the Dictionary program measures the degree of "tension" or associations between the targets and the myriad of key data stored in Dictionary.

Even though Stacie programmed ECHELON to focus on the Nassau-Abaco sector, it was a synergistic, global interception and relay espionage system with ground stations in the U.S., Britain, Australia, Canada, New Zealand and in other nameless locations. They were at each other's disposal, so the 358,000 pieces of data extracted from the Nassau-Abaco region could be linked to what the other listening stations throughout the world pick up.

She had to take a break. It was her personal savior when the National Security Agency installed a Starbucks franchise in a section of their vast subterranean vault, just like the CIA did in their HQ.

On the outside, in her civilian life, she was an ardent fan of Starbucks. The branch in Tysons Galleria on International Drive in McLean, Virginia became her second home. A single girl in her late 30's, she met some intellectual-type men relaxing and reading in the soft sofas and chairs scattered throughout the lounge area. She had a few serious relationships, loathed having to lie to them about her dull life as a bookkeeper in the Department of Homeland Security. What was she to do, tell them the truth... that she worked clandestinely at the NSA as a mole for the secretive CBIF organization? Her male friends grew suspicious of her cover story, especially with the long hours and being called to work in the wee hours of the morning. She watched as the barista created a *Caramel Maccchato* with steamed milk, topped with dense creamy foam. The girl poured a rich espresso over and through the foam which formed a brown mark on the top after it blended with the milk. The barista signed her artwork with a crosshatch of sweet caramel sauce.

It was not business as usual for the NSA Starbucks franchise, code-named "Store Number X." Since it accommodated clandestine spymasters working for one of the most powerful spy agencies in the world, it operated much differently than the other 12,000+ branches spread across the U.S.

The barista finalized Stacey's *Caramel Macchato* order in silence and never asked for her name, which they normally write on the coffee cup to expedite things. Undercover agents became uncomfortable when someone asks them for their name. Stacey didn't give the server her a.k.a. handle either, for that nom de plume, if discovered by the wrong people, could get her killed or compromised in some way. Even the receipt the barista gave to her had "Store Number X" cryptically printed on it.

Each maître d' goes through a robust interview and background check *before* they are even told that they will be working at the NSA Starbucks. "Store Number X" has nine baristas working there and whenever they leave their work area, a NSA "minder" escorts them. All of them are briefed about security risks, forced to take annual polygraph tests, and must report if someone is overly interested in where they work or simply asks too many questions about their employment. They can't even toot their horn about working inside the NSA to family and friends. If asked, they can only say they work in a "federal building."

Stacie hated having to forfeit her wonderful Starbucks Awards program with all those loyalty deals she built up in the Tysons Galleria Starbucks. No more free drinks and food rewards, custom offers, early access to new Starbuck products or making easy payments with her mobile app. The program is missing at "Store Number X," for NSA operatives could be exposed if the data on their loyalty cards were hacked and fell into the wrong hands.

Stacie and the young barista chuckled at each other as she took her *Caramel Macchato*...they knew the protocol! The place would seem like an insane asylum to a civilian. They nodded at each other in silence, then Stacey retreated to a far table.

"Store Number X" was a cloak-and-dagger Starbucks operation and also one of their busiest, for the customers remain captive. The Engineer and math geniuses, computer science geeks, cryptanalysis masterminds, intelligence and language analysis whiz kids, and black, white, and grey-hat hacker brains couldn't leave the premises during working hours. They sat around Stacie- some remained silent, others talked in hushed voices.

She looked around and sipped her coffee, beginning to feel a slight caffeine buzz. *They look like groups of football teams in a huddle, making up the next game plan. No wonder the NSA brass doesn't let this crowd go downtown for a coffee break or for lunch. A "stealthy Starbucks" is the only thing appropriate for them...and me too, I guess.*

In five minutes, her cup of *Caramel Macchato* was empty. Stacey considered downing another one. The caffeine buzz rejuvenated her tired body and refreshed her mind, which was overwhelmed by innumerable bits of information-ties that ECHELON's Dictionary program connected from the Nassau-Abaco sector.

She was about to have the barista refill her cup when her pager buzzed in consecutive two-second intervals. It meant that ECHELON got a hit on something...a very significant one. Stacey almost collided with a cryptologist who was sauntering into "Store No. X" as she hustled back upstairs to her workstation.

Episode 51

Terrorist contact

Warren and Serwin parked their golf cart on the narrow dirt and lime-stone Queen's Highway, then walked the same path Anthony Hopkins strolled down at the end of the movie "Silence of the Lambs" after he called FBI agent Jodie Foster on the phone from Alice Town, North Bimini.

They strolled past the dirt-floored End of the World Saloon where the late New York congressman Adam Clayton Powell hung out during his exile to Bimini in 1967. Some locals still order the scotch and milk drink in honor of him, which the émigré sipped on often. Serwin wanted to go in and try a scotch and milk, but the senator reminded him they had a contact to meet at Big John's Bar & Grill.

A minute later, they walked onto the patio of Big John's and sat down at a table overlooking the gin-colored waters off Brown's Marina. They ordered two Kaliks and several helpings of cracked conch, pigeon peas & rice, and the renowned Bahamian mac & cheese.

The place was vacant, but several minutes later a tourist couple sat down inside the open-air lounge area next to the outside patio. They dressed casually, wearing shorts and T-shirts purchased at the Bimini Straw Market just down the street. Senator Warren observed them briefly. While munching down on cracked conch, Warren kept glancing through the lounge area, past the tourist couple, to the front door. His contact should be entering at any moment. Serwin ordered two more Kaliks and asked the cute Bahamian waitress about the remarkable taste of the cracked conch.

She was proud to tell him. "Dey take the conch and soak it in a special Caribbean sauce o' spiced rum with orange juice and lemon juice with a' sprinkle of lime juice and brown sugar. Dey put it on high heat until syrupy den add butter until real thick. Den dey dip the conch in flour, den in da eggs and in sweet Bahamian bread crumbs. Dat whole plate be pure Bahamian, the..."

The cute waitress was about to tell them how the chef, her cousin, made the Bahamian mac & cheese, but Warren saw his contact walk through the front door. He cut her off sharply, "Thank you...you're excused. We have an important business meeting to attend to."

The young waitress walked away, feeling slightly disparaged as the new customer, a man who looked Middle Eastern, sat down with them. He faced the Bimini Bay waters with his back to the lounge area. The young tourist couple were behind him.

In perfect English, he spoke. "Ahh...the waters are so beautiful here. I have never seen so many different shades of blue, green and turquoise in all my life."

Serwin wiped the crumps off his mouth with a towel. "Maybe you should have bought us a seaplane instead."

"What! You don't like the Cessna I bought you...are you ungrateful?" "No, my friend Shahid. Mark is just using American humor. I'm very grateful to you for the gift. I want to repay you in some way, perhaps even have your wife and children obtain U.S. citizenship...I can pull some strings."

Warren stopped talking and looked annoyed by the cute young waitress when she reluctantly approached the table and asked Shahid if he would like anything. He ordered a Bahama Mama. She managed to smile slightly, then left. The condescending atmosphere radiating from Senator Warren impeded her naturally-friendly disposition from showing. She couldn't comprehend why his demeanor bothered her so much...it wasn't the rudeness. There was something else about the man that she couldn't explain, something that alarmed her.

The Middle Eastern man went along with the small talk, which he was certain that Warren was only capable of. "Ha, ha...my friend. So, tell me Mr. Serwin, how did it fly? After all, I paid over $350,000 cash for that new plane."

Mark Serwin was enjoying the cracked conch and spoke while eating. "Perfectly. That 230 HP high-performance engine got us down here from Maryland in no time." He smiled and winked at both men. "We're gonna find out tomorrow how it lands on an unlit, short runway at nighttime."

Warren and Shahid chuckled at Serwin, a kind of forced giggle that hid their apprehension. Shahid said, "Well, landing on the Great Abaco Highway at night by the Abaco Poultry mansion should be a piece of cake for you. After all, you used to do it all the time in your drug-smuggling days."

Serwin licked the spiced rum and lemon sauce off his fingers. "You two are forgetting that I flew F-4 Phantoms north of the DMZ, in Viet Nam. I outmaneuvered five Russian Mig-17's in a dog fight. They were no match for me or the heat-seeking Sidewinder missiles locked and loaded under my wings. Landing the Cessna on the GAH ain't a problem, even at night. That's what night vision goggles are for...I used them many times when flying for Royal Airlines."

Senator Warren recalled why he hired Mark Serwin as his chief of staff. They had something in common... greed. After Vietnam, Serwin quit the USAF for more pay flying commercial airlines...money trumped patriotism. But, gambling and heavy drinking put him in debt and got him fired. Skipping out on scheduled commercial airline flights and showing up drunk in the cockpit of a jet carrying over a hundred passengers was frowned upon by management. He really fell from grace after vomiting over the autopilot control panel.

No possibility of second-chance pilot suspension until completion of a drug rehab program...he was fired on the spot. Actually, the airline manager charged in from the gate and physically threw him off the plane. It turned out that two of his granddaughters were passengers Jobless, heavy in debt, and losing his plush home in Miami along with a Mustang GT made him easy pickings for Cesar Virgilio Sandoval to hire to work for Royal Airlines and smuggle drugs into the U.S. from the Caribbean.

Warren gently patted Shahid's forearm. "Don't worry. The landing will be simple for Mark. I'll make sure he lightens up on the booze."

Just down the dusty and narrow Queen's Highway from Big John's was a local restaurant named Captain Bob's. A single agent from CBIF's CI team sat at a table overlooking the Queen's Highway, enjoying a lobster omelet with sweet Bahamian bread and coffee. He would pick up surveillance when the target threesome left Big John's and headed north. His secure cell phone rang. It was from his boss, Corey Pearson. "Yes, sir."

Corey was in his hotel room at the Conch Inn in Marsh Harbor, Abaco. He just got a call from Morrison and had to notify his agents on Bimini. "Hi, 'Frank'...did you get photos of the Middle Eastern man who Warren and Serwin met?"

"Yes. We tailed them to a nightclub named Big John's. Two of our agents posing as a tourist couple are there now and just sent them. The Middle Eastern guy came in and sat down with Warren and Serwin. He sat with his back to the team but the female agent snapped several good shots when he first walked in the front door where there was good lighting. I'm sending them to you right now."

A few moments later Corey downloaded the photos. *Holy shit! Our mole inside the NSA...our one and only Stacie...she's just reached Sainthood!* Recently, she tracked down "Radical Archer," who purchased shoulder-firing missiles that were stolen off a British army unit truck outside London. Stacie tracked him down to Tunisia where they arrested him and found matching voiceprints connecting him to a Trenton, New Jersey warehouse, which was raided by local police,

FBI agents, and a dozen CBIF agents wearing head and face scarves to cover their identities.

The CBIF agents had presidential authority to confiscate dozens of items from the NJ warehouse, including an encrypted cell phone that Stacie filed into the ECHELON Dictionary program. CBIF technicians had little difficulty unlocking the photos, emails, messaging info sent and received, and phone contacts stored inside the cell phone, including one voicemail the NJ warehouse owner received but forgot to erase.

That voicemail recording was placed into Stacie's Dictionary program, which taps into a highly-advanced VOICECAST system that enables her to target an individual's voice pattern. That's when she got the hit that interrupted her from enjoying a second cup of *Caramel Maccchato* at the Starbucks "Store No. X."

The Middle Eastern man sitting with Warren and Serwin at Big John's made the mistake of contacting Senator Warren on his wireless cell phone to tell him to meet him there. Stacie locked onto his voice pattern immediately. It matched the voice message stored in the cell phone confiscated from the New Jersey warehouse.

Corey told the CI agent at Captain Bob's, code-named 'Frank,' to standby, then placed him on hold. He relayed the photo 'Frank' sent him to Morrison, who forwarded it to the *Next Generation Identification* (NGI) system. It took only five minutes to sift through the 120 million facial photos before a match was found and sent back to Corey.

He took the CI agent off hold. 'Frank,' you still there?" "Yes sir, Mr. Pearson."

"Listen carefully, the man you photographed walking into Big John's and sitting down with Warren and Serwin has been identified. His name is Shahid El-Sayed. Do not lose track of him! If the three split up, keep him under tight surveillance. I want to know everywhere he goes and everyone he contacts."

"I'll keep our two-person team on Warren and the other three-person team on El-Sayed."

Corey walked out to the balcony of his room and looked around the plush tropical gardens outside. "Great. I also want to know when Warren and Serwin take off from the South Bimini Airport, and if El-Sayed is with them when they do."

"No problem, sir. After they landed and took the ferry over to Alice Town on North Bimini, we planted a transponder on his Cessna."

Corey went back into his room and took out a Kalik from the compact refrigerator. "I trained you well, 'Frank.' Just kidding...good job! I spotted that initiative in you when I recruited you in the bar in Gainesville, Florida. You've got a lot of...balls."

Balls! 'Frank' understood the meaning behind Corey's last sentence. "Thank you, sir."

Corey switched the cell phone off, and the young agent looked out the picture window onto the Queen's Highway. The CI couple would alert him when the targets leave Big John's. He looked around while finishing his lobster omelet. The big chunks of lobster were fresh, probably taken from the ocean that morning.

Being a sport fisherman and scuba diver, he loved Bimini and didn't miss the U.S. at all. He looked at the walls of the small mom and pop restaurant. They were cluttered with aged photos of Ernest Hemingway with his trophy White Marlin, Goliath Grouper and Yellowfin Tuna catches hanging from the dock at Bimini Big Game Club. An unknown fisherman wrote on a photo of himself showing off a huge marlin, "Largest Blue Marlin ever to be taken- June 23, 1969."

The young agent had little doubt as to why this tiny island was named the "Game Fishing Capital of the World." He paid the bill, hopped in his golf cart and sped down the Queen's Highway towards Big John's. He would personally shadow Shahid El-Sayed if the trio split up. He owed it to Corey for recruiting him and assigning him to Bimini...he hoped he never got transferred out of this paradise.

Twenty hours passed since Corey took a catnap. He lay down on the bed and closed his eyes. A mental break was needed from mulling over the pending assault on the Abaco mansion. He daydreamed about his recruitment of 'Frank' from the University of Florida, where he studied criminology. A bright student, he maintained a 4.0 GPA in his law, sociology and humanities courses. CBIF was looking to recruit and train agents with a deep understanding of the criminal justice system, a system it often circumvented when going to the *Obscure Transgression* level.

After targeting 'Frank,' his real name being Robert Hurley, Corey recalled following him around the large campus, seeing who he met and talked to, girls he may be dating, and what his hangouts were like. Everything checked out. After discussing his findings with General Morrison, Corey made the recruitment pitch. He tailed Robert Hurley to a bar called "Balls" in downtown Gainesville, Florida. He walked in and took a seat at the bar. The joint was appropriately named. An old bartender poured him a cheap draft beer and overfilled the glass. The foam spilt onto the bar as the barkeep walked away. After his eyes adjusted to the dark interior, he spotted Hurley sitting by himself in a booth, eating bar food.

Corey thought it must be the cheap drinks and day-to-day food specials that kept Hurley, who was up to his eyeballs in student debt, coming back to this dive.

He decided to use a direct recruitment approach. He called the bartender over and pointed to a full bottle of Drambuie on the dusty shelf and ordered two doubles with two more draft beers to chase them down with. Corey watched the bartender unsuccessfully try to pour two shots of the sweet, golden-colored liqueur into two separate glasses. It looked as if he poured three shots in each. He asked for a tray and carried the drinks over to the booth where his target sat wolfing down a plate of super-hot chicken wings.

He stood in front of Hurley and said, "Doesn't look like you're a vegan. May I sit down, Mr. Robert Hurley? I represent an upright organization you might be interested in working for."

After guzzling down three more draft beers chased down with Drambuie shots, posing a myriad of questions to Corey, and discovering that his student debt loan and remaining tuition expenses would be taken care of, the future "Frank" was recruited. Corey wanted to assign the code name "Balls" to Mr. Hurley, but General Morrison refused.

As Corey fell into a deeper slumber, he thought of Constance and her brother. *Killed by an F5 tornado...only a month away from finishing his training. I was going to assign him to Bimini so we'd have seven agents there, and promote 'Frank' to be chief of the two cells. Constance would have liked that, having her brother so close to her.*

His mind went into a complete restful state and he began snoring loudly. The cell phone clock was set to awake him in a half hour.

Episode 52

Meeting evil

The Sea of Abaco was Devon Ledard's childhood paradise. He leaned over the rail of the Albury Ferryboat and looked down through the clear, gin-colored waters to the pristine white, sandy bottom twenty feet below. He made out the tiny grains of sand. A small patch coral reef of elkhorn and staghorn passed by and he grew excited as a pair of hawksbill turtles slowly munched off the sea grass beds that grew right up to the edge of it.

As a boy, he used to spear spiny lobster hiding in the crevices of the coral reefs in the Sea of Abaco. He glanced back at Guana Seaside Village and could barely make out his home, where he just kissed his wife and two children goodbye. Only 150 people populated the narrow seven-mile long cay. Most lived along the empty stretch of pristine beach which stretched the entire length on the Atlantic Ocean side.

In the distance, Gumelemi Cay slowly glided by as the ferry proceeded to the dock on Great Abaco Island. As a teenager, he was paid by the Bahamian National Trust to help protect the nesting turtles on the small two-acre islet. Loggerhead, hawksbill and green sea turtles used it as their nesting grounds. Devon would sit on a mangrove tree limb on the isolated and densely thicketed Baker's Bay on the tip of Great Guana Cay, watching for poachers through binoculars provided to him by the trust. He was given a walkie-talkie to call in the game warden if any one raided the critical sea turtle habitat.

Devon had many memories buried in the remnants of the once pristine Baker's Bay and the barrier reefs lying offshore. That's where he met a young Bahamian girl who was trekking through the mangrove and Caribbean pine forests of Baker's Bay in search of land crabs. She walked directly underneath his mangrove tree limb perch without noticing him. He scared her to death by jumping off and landing in the soft sand next to her.

The Albury's Ferry dock approached and he stopped daydreaming. The Baker's Bay he used to cherish had vanished, bought by a U.S. golf and marina megadevelopment corporation that caters to ultra-rich celebrities. The bulldozers came and dug out the mangrove marshes, dredged the pristine barrier reefs lining its shores, and cut down the virgin forest where white-crowned pigeons and white-tailed tropicbirds thrived. The beautiful Bahamian girl he once frightened on Baker's Bay was now his wife. She and their two children were depending on him to bring home another nice pay check from the Abaco Poultry, LTD mansion.

His fond memories were interrupted by evil. He saw the Ford Expedition SUV waiting for him in the small ferry terminal parking lot. Bolan Tougas and Pierre Cherestal stood beside it, guzzling down Kalik beers while watching the boat come in.

The two thugs ushered him from the dock directly to the SUV, not allowing him to go inside the terminal. They sped back to the mansion. After a few minutes of silence, Tougas, who was driving, looked over his shoulder and asked, "So, how my coke traffickin' buddy doin'?"

Devon smiled and wanted to change the subject, "Glad to have a job and earn good money from Mr. Sandoval at da chicken place." "What? You dun like sellin' coke at Nipper's no mo'? You live in da Guana Cay settlement and walk 'bout two minutes away to Nipper's where ya sell da stuff we steal from Abaco Poultry. Last time ya made ova' $600. Ya don' miss that anymore?"

"No, I want to make money honestly. Don't worry, ya know I ain't gonna rat on you and Pierre. Sandoval would kill all three of us if did... in a heartbeat."

Cherestal kept quiet while his older cousin continued. "We got orders to take ya to meet him. He's waitin' fo' you now."

The threesome drove along Bay Street past the Java Coffee Shop and the Island Breezes Motel. They sped past the Conch Inn Marina where Corey sat inside at the Curly Tail Restaurant eating stewed conch with grits and Johnnie Cake. After breakfast, he planned to take his regular six-mile jog to the Albury's Ferry terminal and check out the bulletin board to see if Devon left him another coded message. There would be none, for Sandoval ordered Tougas and Cherestal to bring him directly to Abaco Poultry.

In several minutes, they proceeded onto Queen Elizabeth Drive and left Marsh Harbor, then headed south on the Great Abaco Highway past the airport. Devon trembled slightly, not enough to reveal his fear. The murderous duo seemed more hurried than usual.

They passed the small fishing village of Crossing Rock and Tougas turned on an unused side road. He drove up to the entrance to Abaco Poultry, LTD and slipped a plastic card into the lock. The gate swung open and automatically locked shut after they drove through.

The SUV stopped at the front entrance door of the huge 35,000-square-foot mansion of imported Alpine stone. A half dozen Middle Eastern-looking men armed with semi-automatic pistols walked around the grounds.

Tougas looked back at Devon. "Da bossman be right inside. Go on in."

Devon exited the SUV and two guards immediately frisked him, then motioned for him to walk through the front door.

Inside, he was greeted by an unarmed servant in the grand circular foyer. He expected to be escorted up the arched carpeted stairs that wrapped around both sides of the foyer. The twin stairs ascended to a second story hallway where Sandoval's office and den were.

Instead, the servant ushered him down a long, elegant hallway to the left. They passed an open door and he quickly glanced inside to a leather-paneled poker room where four men sat, smoking cigars and playing a card game of some sort. They continued down the long hallway past rooms he had never been to before. Usually, he would serve refreshments and drinks to Sandoval and his guest on the out- side patio or upstairs in his office and den.

The huge stone manor house was amazing. They passed a line of large windows and Devon peered into an atrium with a pool and exercise room complete with treadmills, Stairmasters, Precor bike, Cybex arc trainer and free weights. The next line of tall windows looked down onto a full basketball court.

Devon grew uneasy at this display of enormous wealth. It wasn't earned by law-abiding and scrupulous means, but epitomized Sandoval's world of violence, murder, bribery, sleaze and corruption. He wished he never met Sandoval and fell for the temptation to make quick money.

The servant stopped at a closed door and knocked. An armed Middle-Eastern man opened the door and motioned Devon to enter. He walked into a large billiard room with a wet bar and forty-foot vaulted ceilings. Sandoval was bent over a tournament-sized pool table, taking a shot. Devon knew not to disturb him, noting the table had diamonds embellished in the rails and ornamental platinum leaves embedded in the legs.

The man with the teardrop tattoos under his eye sunk the eight-ball, then grinned. He was pleased with himself. He motioned the Middle-Eastern bodyguard to wait outside in the hallway. Devon was alone in the billiard parlor with Cesar Virgilio Sandoval. His heart began beating faster.

The killer sat down on a cowhide barstool at the wet bar and told Devon to make him a Goombay Smash. He obeyed and walked behind the marble-topped bar to find the right ingredients. The bar was constructed from imported walnut from the U.S., as were the matching cabinets that had inlaid stain glass with images of historical Bahamian events.

Sandoval put his elbows on the bar. "I like how ya make da Goombay Smash...my faithful snitch."

"Thank you, sir. I use the original ingredients from da lady who created it." Devon trembled slightly as he opened the cabinet doors to search for the right ingredients.

"I want you ta listen careful-like to what I say. I got a big event startin' tomorrow and it will last through da weekend to this comin' Tuesday. Dere will be important men and women in dis room and da pool area ya just passed in the hallway. You gonna be heah da full time...fo' four days. You will be their personal servant, day and night... twenty-four, seven. You won't be leavin' until everybody gone...til' the meetings over. You won't be goin' home to dat beautiful wife and two kids o' yours in da Great Guana Cay settlement...got it?"

Devon's hands trembled slightly when his family was brought up. He placed a collin's glass on the bar with coconut rum, Captain Morgan spiced rum, apricot brandy and pineapple juice blended together. "Yes, Mr. Sandoval, I will take good care of your guests. They will be happy I'm here to serve them."

Sandoval noted the ice rattling slightly from Devon's trembling hands. "Did I say somethin' that upset you, Mr. Ledard? If you be worried 'bout yo' wife and kids...don't be."

Devon slid the drink over the bar. Sandoval guzzled half of it down. "If I may ask, how come I dun have to be worried 'bout my family?"

"'Cuz I got several of my men dere now, in da Great Guana Cay settlement. Dey be watchin' yo' wife and two kids in your absence... makin' sure dey be OK til' you get back next Tuesday afta da big meetin' is ova with and everybody goes home."

A feeling of helplessness overtook him. Devon slumped down into the bartender's stool behind the wet bar. A faint grin appeared on Sandoval's face. He enjoyed tormenting his vulnerable victim and decided to prolong the anguish a bit longer before revealing what the final threat to his family would be.

"You say you use da original ingredients to da Goombay Smash... you know da lady who invented it?"

Devon regained some of his composure but his voice still trembled slightly. "Yes, sir. Her name be Miss Emily and she ran the Blue Bee Bar right across the Sea of Abaco on Green Turtle Cay." He remembered canoeing with his wife over to Green Turtle Cay and meeting Miss Emily. It was the next cay over from Great Guana. She revealed her secrets to making the Goombay Smash, a drink frequently copied throughout the Caribbean and in the U.S., but never equaled.

Devon decided to reveal the secret to the man sitting across from him with teardrop tattoos under his eye...the man who was smirking at him... enjoying seeing him in emotional distress. He thought it might appease Sandoval, make him begin to feel some slight attachment to him and maybe not think about harming his family. "I'd like to reveal Miss Emily's secret to ya. You, me and Miss Emily will be da only three people in da entire Caribbean who know it."

"I'm all ears."

"First, as ya know, I order 'dirty rum' for your bar... rum dat can be dark, amber or spiced rums like da Captain Morgan I put in yours." He pointed at Sandoval's empty, who shoved it back across the bar for a refill.

Devon continued while he mixed the right combinations of ingredients for Sandoval's second Goombay Smash. "Da basic parts o' da Goombay be coconut rum, apricot brandy, pineapple juice and any one o' da dirty rums. Da mistake imitators make is dey get too creative wid da variations. Some put in apricot liqueur instead o' brandy...others don't even use 'dirty rum' or use coconut cream instead o' coconut rum, and dat make da basic Goombay taste like a pina colada. Dey try ta get fancy wid da variations and screw up da basic Goombay dat Miss Emily created. Dey end up throwin' all kinds a' things in, like addin' lemon or orange juice to da basic pineapple juice. Dis Goombay Smash dat I make fo' you is easy ta make...and casual."

He slipped the drink to Sandoval, who wolfed down half the glass with no intention of sipping it and savoring the unique taste. Devon pretended he was at Miss Emily's Bluebee Bar, a humble place with boating and business cards, and hand-written signatures covering the walls. He visualized the T-shirts, boating flags and sundry clothing items hanging from the ceiling. Dreaming of the good times he had on Green Turtle Cay with his wife during their courtship helped him escape the apprehension that the sociopath before him purposefully created.

Suddenly, Sandoval pointed to one of the large stain-glass panes adorning a cabinet door. It had "Boxing Day" engraved on the frame with colorful inlaid-glass pieces depicting slave children running around what appeared to be a pile of boxes. "What is dat all 'bout... are dey trainin' da Bahamian kids ta be boxers?"

Devon said, "Dat is da Bahamas 'Boxing Day.' It's da day after Christmas, on December twenty-six, when da slaves were given empty boxes left ova from dere master's Christmas gifts that were shipped to dem from England."

Sandoval had little appreciation for the Bahamian culture, so he had Devon explain the meaning of the native celebrations portrayed in each stained-glass panel. He told the building contractor to install them with some Bahamian theme. Sandoval absorbed Devon's tutoring lessons about the Junkanoo, the Bahamas Independence Day in 1973 when they gained independence from the United Kingdom, and the famous Family Island Regatta held in Elizabeth Harbour off

Exuma Island. He didn't want to appear ignorant if any of his guests inquired about them.

When Devon finished the history lesson, Sandoval leaned back in his chair and cupped his hands behind his head. In a totally calm voice, he asked, "Tell me somethin' Ledard, my loyal snitch and servant...do you know of anyting' dat could go wrong at dis big meeting dat's startin' tomorrow?"

Devon fought off the icy fear that took hold again. He thought of his wife and children. "No, sir...I will be an excellent servant. I will make everyting' go smoothly fo' you."

Sandoval replied coldly. "You know what I'm gettin' at...I ain't talkin' about da service. I be referrin' to da authorities...Bahama police, RBPF, American intelligence...CIA, DEA...have any of dem ever contacted you?"

A thought of his recruitment by Corey Pearson and the mysterious American spy organization he worked for raced through his mind, but he remained cool. "No, Mister Sandoval, of course not. Why would ya ask me such a question?"

Sandoval put his elbows back on the bar and leaned forward, looking directly into Devon's eyes. "Because, you and five other Bahamians are workin' here at da big and important meetin'. You betta keep yo eyes and ears out fo' any wrongdoings by any o' dem. If anyting' happen to disrupt dis meeting over the next four days, if the authorities raid da place...the two men I got sittin' right now in your home in da Guana Cay settlement will torture your wife and children. Den, dey will strangle all three a dem ta death. Now, tell me again... do you know of anyting' that might go wrong at da meetin'?"

Devon maintained his composure as best he could. "No, sir...I do not."

Corey's secure satellite cell phone vibrated, waking him before the alarm he set went off. He got only twenty minutes sleep. The call was from CI Team-6, the agents who tracked Senator Warren and Mark Serwin to the Hagerstown Regional Airport in Maryland and found out they were flying to Bimini.

Corey groggily answered. "Were you able to track down the 'N' number and find out who Warren got the plane from?"

"Yes, sir. It took several hours but the person you hooked me up to at FAA found the owner from the 'N' registration number of the Cessna. The 'N' number means it was registered in the United States, but the person tracked it further and found out that the previous owner, the person who sold it to Warren, had a C-6 registration number, which means the Bahamas."

Corey jumped out of the bed and paced the floor. *Another Bahamian connection to Warren* "OK, give me all the details!"

"The guy at FAA spent much time checking it all out. He knew you would want to know everything. The Cessna Skylane with registration N618TC that Serwin and Warren flew to Bimini was originally registered in the Bahamas under a corporate trust named Abaco Poultry, LTD. The FAA guy wanted me to tell you that it appears they tried to hide the original owner of the Cessna through a series of trusts tied to it. He also wanted me to relay to you that such aircraft trusts allow foreign citizens, who wouldn't otherwise qualify under FAA rules, to acquire a valid registration."

Corey walked out onto the patio and sat on a chair. A mild breeze off the Sea of Abaco refreshed him. "Was our CBIF mole in the FAA able to find out the name of the seller in the Bahamas?"

"Yes, Mr. Pearson, he said you would want to know that, too. He put me on hold and made a call to the Civil Aviation Department at the Lynden Pindling International Airport in Nassau, Bahamas. He talked to someone in the Flights Standard Inspectorate and found out that a man at Abaco Poultry, LTD had filled out an aircraft registration application several years ago. You have to list the names of all trustees on the form."

Corey closed his eyes and let the breeze calm him down. "OK, tell me the bottom line. Who is the present owner and who sold it to him?"

"The current owner is a man named Shahid El-Sayed." "And who sold it to him?"

"The trustee's name on the Bahamian registration form was from Abaco Poultry, LTD. This trustee who originally owned the Cessna goes by the name Cesar Virgilio Sandoval."

Holy shit! "Well done, team six." "Thank you, sir."

Corey flipped off the secure satellite cell phone then retrieved a Kalik from his Conch Inn motel room refrigerator cabinet. He took a swig while quickly pulling out Pinkston's twelve-digit algorithmic- encrypted phone and called General Morrison.

A few moments passed before he answered. "Morrison here." "Sir, are you clear to talk?"

Morrison sat at the Turtle Krall Restaurant & Bar on the waterfront of Key West's Historic Seaport District, savoring his favorite dish of crab cakes topped with mango chutney. He looked around the open-air patio. Only his four CI agents posing as business people were seated around him. No other customers. In five minutes, he could be back inside the War Room at CBIF HQ on Eaton Street, but the urgent tone of Corey's voice negated that action. He looked up and down the boardwalk that tourists often strolled along. It was vacant.

"I'm clear. What you got?"

"The Cessna Skylane that Senator Warren and Mark Serwin flew from Hagerstown Airport to South Bimini is owned by Shahid El-Sayed and he bought it from fuckin' Sandoval."

Morrison put down a crab cake and lit up his Montecristo Cuban cigar. "So, Senator William Warren, America's widely-respected statesman, the chairman of the Senate Select Committee on Intelligence... the protector of the American public, is cozying up to a radical Islamic terrorist who handles the end point of Sandoval's smuggling pipeline into America at the New Jersey warehouse."

"Yes, sir. Stacie at NSA linked El-Sayed's voicemail off the confiscated cell phone at the New Jersey warehouse with his call on Bimini to Warren to arrange a contact at Big Jim's."

Morrison blew a flavorful aroma of smoke into the air. "It's almost certain the stolen mortars out of the Cali Army barracks would have ended up at that New Jersey warehouse."

Corey took a healthy swig of Kalik. "I agree. We shouldn't have raided it. If we kept the place under surveillance, we would have grabbed the mortars when they arrived. Now they're headed somewhere in northwest Pennsylvania where we lost Edhi, the jihadist sleeper attack cell leader."

"Very true. Even though Stacie tracked down 'Radical Archer' and captured him in Tunisia, we still could have left the warehouse alone and put it under close watch, but the FBI and its law enforcement mentality couldn't hold back from raiding the place, arresting the owner."

"I'm sure the Special Agent in Charge got a promotion out of the raid."

The general chewed on the end of his cigar. "As a matter of fact, he received a commemoration from the director of the FBI himself, Walt Mason. But, look on the bright side, we're about to raid the largest gathering of radical Islamists and narco-terrorists in CBIF history."

Corey finished the Kalik. "Yes, and the list of attendees is growing. I'm sure that Shahid El-Sayed will fly with Warren and Serwin from Bimini to Abaco for the terrorist pow-wow."

Morrison replied, "That's why the only people who know about this are you and I, Stacie at NSA, the CBIF special ops commander aboard USS Caribbean Sea amphibious assault ship, and President Rhinehart. The FBI is being kept in the dark."

"Walt Mason won't be happy when this is all over. At least we don't have to worry about a repeat of Curacao."

"I don't give a shit about Mason."

"And neither do I. Mason exemplifies the dispute between the FBI's law enforcement mentality and CBIF's counterintelligence frame of mind in fighting terrorism. It's been going on for quite a while."

Morrison agreed. "The rift also exists in the counterespionage arena, too. Before 9/11, the FBI was bent on arresting or deporting foreign spies rather than turning them into double agents. Overall, FBI agents are unimaginative police officer types who either can't or don't want to master the finer points of counterespionage and counterintelligence work."

"They must think we're dilettantes who dabble in the terrorism fight... idiots! Mason's FBI agents think like bank guards while our CI agents think like bank robbers. Mason's cop approach makes the battle a black and white issue when it's really a global battle full of gray areas and asymmetrical clashes between different ideas and wits that have nothing to do with legal etiquette."

"Well put, Corey. Fortunately, President Rhinehart realizes this. He is aware that the FBI gathers intelligence for the short-sighted goal of putting criminals and terrorists in prison while CBIF's mission is more long-term, deeper and broader."

Corey took a gulp of the cold Kalik. The electricity had gone out and with no A/C the room temp was rising quickly. *God damn Bahamian Electricity Corporation...BEC!* "That's why I enjoy working for CBIF. The FBI is basically beer-drinking, cigar-smoking, door-knocking cops while we're..."

"If I may interrupt, Corey. I assume that liquid I hear you guzzling down over the phone isn't an expensive cabernet imported from the Napa Valley. We're not exactly fancy wine-drinking, pipe-smoking, international-relations types either. We're going to kill, capture and torture people at that friggin' chicken farm the day after tomorrow. As MI6 says, we have a 007 license to kill."

"Yes, sir. And we'll save thousands of American lives. I realize we have to waddle in the mud and become dirtier than our opponents, but you're correct about the short-term and long-term mindset differences. The FBI goes for one-time ops...you know what I mean, pay the informant, make a bust, go to trial with the informer as a witness, lock the bad guys up and walk away. I enjoy my work with CBIF because I spend much time and money planting long-term seeds... recruiting agents throughout the Caribbean Basin, collecting information about our enemies and preemptively attacking and destroying them *before, n*ot *after* they break the law."

"Yes, Corey, and talking about collecting information...you've got so much on Senator Warren that if we turned him in to the FBI he'd be charged with treason and probably get the death penalty."

Corey stared at the almost empty Kalik bottle. *Wish it were a cabernet imported from Napa Valley.* "That's why President Rhinehart agreed to keep the FBI out of the capture or kill operation that's about to take place. It's also why CBIF was created in the first place...a new kind of domestic security agency like the UK's MI5. We have no law enforcement function and lack the legal authority to make arrests, but we continue to track down and destroy narco-terrorist and radical-Islamic networks. We're like a hybrid between the FBI and CIA. The two cultures have never worked well together but both by themselves are vital to protecting Americans from harm. Putting law enforcement and counterintelligence under the same roof is like assigning the Secretary of State a seat on the Joint Chiefs of Staff."

USS Caribbean Sea amphibious assault ship North Atlantic Sea, off coast of Abaco (26°31'38.2"N 76°42'34.1"W)

CBIF's special ops commander sat at a table with his four squad leaders. They poured over the diagram Corey transmitted of the Abaco Poultry, LTD mansion and grounds. He created them from the IMINT satellite photos and Devon Ledard's detailed description of the entire layout during their Love Beach contact in Nassau. The assault was planned out in detail and each twelve-man squad had a unique function to perform. Everyone knew what everyone else was supposed to do so they could back each other up.

After finalizing and agreeing upon the attack plan, the five men entered the huge cargo bay of the USS Caribbean, which was supposedly on a normal naval exercise forty miles off the coast of Abaco. They checked with the mechanics working on the five UH-60L Blackhawk assault, two AH-64 Apache attack, and the three Medevac helicopters. Everything was in perfect working order.

The fifty special ops warriors were organizing their gear. Most carried M4A1 carbines, a favorite among U.S. Special Operations forces. Each carbine was fitted with an under-slung grenade launcher and optic red dot sight. A Rail Accessory System (RAS) was affixed to the front of each rifle, enabling each commando to quickly adapt to changing circumstances- a tactical light, laser-aiming module, forward hand grip, telescopic scope for distant targets, red dot sights for short-ranged targets, and an old-fashion bayonet could quickly be removed and replaced with another item.

Three special ops snippers checked their MK14's, making sure the bipods extended properly for stability and the telescopic sights were mounted securely. They would position themselves on the periphery of the mansion and pick off hidden opponents that were unseen by their comrades. All of them were were top marksmen recruited by CBIF from the Fort Benning, Georgia Army Sniper School.

The special ops commander and his four team leaders visited the four squads and gave encouragement to each man and woman while inspecting their weapons and equipment. The M2 .50-caliber machine guns were properly loaded and mounted on the four combat watercraft that would be launched from the ship's open stern gate. CBIF technicians double-checked to insure the GPS navigation, UHF/VHF and SATCOMM radio communications, and IFF transponders were all operating perfectly on each craft.

If some unexpected threat emerged during the assault, like armored vehicles, the M2 .50 caliber rounds could blast through the plates. They could also punch through the stone walls of the mansion or chew up the surrounding thick pine forests if the Middle Eastern guards tried to escape into them.

Each warrior's helmet, night vision goggles, and body armor plates were laid out in a sequence corresponding to the order they would gear-up before leaping into the choppers and combat watercraft. Also included were .45 caliber Heckler and Koch handguns loaded with ten rounds of hollow points. They preferred the .45 due to its reliable stopping power. It proved to be an excellent weapon for room-to-room combat.

M67 hand grenades, fixed-blade knives, and IR Chem lights hung from their military vests. After viewing the outer buildings and layout of the Abaco Poultry, LTD grounds, examining Corey's diagram of the many rooms inside the mansion, and seeing the satellite images of dozens of armed Middle Eastern guards, the commander and squad leaders believed the grenades would be needed to clear rooms and kill terrorists sheltered behind the stone fence and walls.

The razor-sharp knives would be used to take out guards patrolling the periphery of the compound, since they're quieter than firearm suppressors. Because the electricity will be terminated immediately, the IR Chem lights will enable the squads to see each other in the dark. The Infrared emits an invisible glow in the darkness that's outside the normal light spectrum of human vision. However, with the night vision goggles, the special ops troops will remain invisible to the enemy but will easily distinguish each other.

After the weapons and gear were checked, the squads attached suppressors to their assault rifles. Known for their quiet kills, they didn't want to give themselves away when their stealthy, nocturnal attack began. In past engagements, they had killed sleeping terrorists without waking up the guys in the next room.

The CBIF special ops commander was satisfied with the pre-assault preparations. He returned to his small quarters in the bowels of the USS Caribbean and laid down for a brief catnap. His secure satellite phone buzzed.

He answered. It was Corey Pearson. "Hello, commander. Will you be ready by tomorrow evening?"

"It's zero dark thirty time...just give me the word, my squads are locked and loaded... ready to rock 'n roll."

Episode 53

Sleeper cell safe house

A doe and her two fawns quietly tiptoed along the dirt back road in Crawford County in northwest Pennsylvania. Although the road was rarely used, she remained cautious, for black bears and coyotes occupied the deep woods and meadows surrounding it. If the need arose, she would quickly signal her young ones to flee.

The road meandered up an incline and veered to the right, cutting through a thick forest of hemlock, maple, oak and beech, then passed a lone farmhouse on the left. The mother deer paused to gaze at the home and grounds. Her sharp eyesight detected no human movement or vehicles parked in the gravel driveway. She raised her head and focused on the home, tipping her ears and rolling them around like tiny satellite dishes, locking on to minute sounds. Other than a few soft chickadee and nuthatch intonations, no human sounds were detected. Sensing no danger, she continued along the unused road and walked past the driveway entrance.

Inside the house, seven men of the sleeper attack cell sat around a large dining room table. Edhi stood before them, holding a mortar shell that was a meter long.

"The stolen mortars have arrived early from Cali, thanks to our friend Cesar Sandoval. Now, listen carefully because the success of our jihad depends upon all of you, especially you three laser guiders. "Shortly after we fire each mortar, fins will unfold from the tail of the shell to give it stability in flight."

One of the jihadists stood up. "We will fight and die for the cause of Allah. He hears and knows all things...that we are about to become his martyrs."

Edhi nodded in agreement. "With the lasers, you will paint the target for the mortars to seek. They will rain down on the infidels from *Janna*, our garden, our paradise...they will be guided by Allah."

Edhi continued. "As we fire the rounds, they will arc into the sky then fall upon the infidels." He laid the heavy mortar on the sturdy oak table made by a local Amish craftsman. "The warhead is stuffed with electronic gear." He pointed to each section of the shell as he explained further. "In this explosive warhead is an optical-electronic guidance mechanism, a disposable nose cap, the control assembly, the detonator and a flight correction motor with fin stabilizers. That's why you must work your laser-guidance mechanisms exactly right. With Allah's guidance, *you* will guide each round to the target. As the shell reaches the height of its flight and begins to fall to the earth, it will lock on to your laser-designator beam... *you* will guide it to rain upon the infidels."

A man chosen by Edhi to be on the mortar firing crew rose and said calmly, "This will be my life's mission. Ever since my sister and brother were killed by the Americans in Afghanistan by mortars. It is my...*our*...duty to kill Americans and their allies. I sentenced them to death on that tragic day when my loved ones were killed by the same weapon I'm about to use on them...it is my...*our*...duty to Allah to proceed."

All eight men shouted *"Allahu Akbar!*

Edhi placed the mortar shell in the corner of the room. It was painted in olive drab with yellow markings. He retrieved a laser target designator and laid it upon the table. "This is what you will use to guide the laser beam onto the target. The beam will reflect off the target and create an electronic echo which the optical-electronic tracker inside the incoming mortar will lock onto. The warhead will fall from the sky and explode within three feet of where you aim this."

One of the laser beam designator terrorists spoke. "So, we should be absolutely still...you know, not jiggle or move the beam at all?"

"Precisely, my beloved son of Islam. You may be nervous and tense among the huge crowd of infidels, but Allah will enable you to remain calm. Remember, you are carrying out his duty by guiding the reign of terror upon them...the rule of Allah is to kill these people and liberate yourself from America's domination. By keeping the laser beam focused steadily on the target, the optical-electronic tracking heads inside the incoming mortar shells will acquire the steady echo reflecting off the target and enable the flight-correction motor to continually adjust the four fins that unfold out of the mortar rounds after they are fired. They will home in to within three feet of the target. If you remember your mission for Allah...you will not waver...you will remain calm."

The terrorist replied back, "*Inshallah*." If Allah so wills.

Edhi held up the laser target designator. "As you can see, it is too large...twenty-five pounds...and easily recognizable. The security guards will grow suspicious. Therefore, we will dismantle it into three separate parts and disguise them so they appear like some innocuous item that won't raise eyebrows. Once inside, the team will reassemble them."

For the next three hours, Edhi instructed the three-member laser-designator team on how to take apart and reassemble each device. Each had their own and he recorded their time with a stopwatch. His goal was for them to perform the action blindfolded in less than four minutes.

The four other attack cell members observed them and gave encouragement by softly murmuring "*Bismillahir Rahmanir Raheem*"... in the name of Allah, the Gracious, the Merciful. Edhi had them recite the phrase before each training session.

Edhi was pleased the mortars and laser guidance devices arrived early. He silently praised Allah for allowing this to be, but the premature arrival had nothing to do with his Islamic god. It was due to

Sandoval's savvy knowledge of and ability to manipulate each segment along his smuggling pipeline into the U.S.

Retired Colombian General Rojas and Lieutenant General Castano connived to have the three mortars stolen from the Cali barracks and transported on an M35 army truck to a FARC hideout along the Ecuador border.

Along this volatile boundary between Colombia and Ecuador, Sandoval maintained 170 spots that he uses to smuggle drugs, weapons and people into the Caribbean and U.S. mainland. He never told anyone which pipeline would be used to smuggle the mortars along. The disassembled mortars, laser beam designators and shells were smuggled back into Colombia and stored in an Urabenos gang safe house in Buenaventura. It was the same gang that served as spotters for General Castano when he drove along the road to Cuisine Corridor in Cali to the gourmet Platillos Voladores restaurant to meet with Sandoval, retired Colombian Army officer and arms dealer Juan Rojas, FARC commander Javier Sanchez, and Asif Qadeer Edhi.

Sandoval took advantage of the mayhem the gang created in Buenaventura. He, along with Castano and Rojas, supplied them with weapons and cash. The Urbanos, in turn, targeted community leaders and court officials that threatened Sandoval's pipeline. The safe house was used to store stolen military weapons and to hold kidnapped victims where they were often tortured, murdered...then dismembered.

A dozen officials working at the Buenaventura Airport had been bribed and threatened by the Urbanos. A custom official readily stamped approval for the containers to be loaded onto a cargo prop plane owned by Sandoval. One of the gang members called him earlier that morning just as he left for work and described what his sons wore as they walked to the neighborhood elementary school.

The transport plane flew nonstop to the Haitien International Airport in Cap-Haïtien, Haiti. Actually, the airport was renamed the Hugo Chávez International Airport in honor of the late Venezuelan leader, President Hugo Chávez, after he contributed over $1 billion of assistance to Haiti. From there, the containers were loaded onto a small and swift cargo ship docked at the Port International du Cap-Haïtien and transported to Fajardo, a small city on the east coast of Puerto Rico. The containers were unloaded into a warehouse and repackaged into innocuous-looking containers, then reloaded onto a small feeder cargo ship.

The feeder cargo ship was equipped with a crane that lowered the containers down into the hold. The mortar shells were placed in concealed compartments inside the hull while the disassembled mortar and laser-designator parts were cunningly stashed inside a wide variety of shipping containers and cargo boxes packed with groceries for supermarkets, department store merchandise, lumber, and building materials. The large, more suspicious-looking mortar barrels were wrapped in cardboard boxes and placed inside special refrigerated containers underneath perishable, frozen food items. After a perfunctory custom check, the ship proceeded to the U.S.

The feeder cargo ship took advantage of the sheer volume of commercial shipments heading to Florida and ports along the eastern seaboard. It hugged closely to northbound ships heading to major ports in Jacksonville, Charleston, Wilmington, Hampton Roads and Baltimore. The captain bypassed the ports in New York and New Jersey, which he was originally instructed to sail to. But, when Stacey at NSA tracked down "Radical Archer" in Tunisia in her efforts to find the shoulder-firing missiles he stole, she uncovered connections to the New Jersey warehouse which was subsequently raided by 185 local police officers, FBI agents and dozens of unidentified CBIF agents.

The warehouse was sagaciously abandoned by Sandoval as the last link in his pipeline, so the small cargo ship headed further north. At 3am, it stopped fifteen miles off the coast of New Hampshire alongside a 100-foot super-yacht. The sea was relatively calm and the crane on the deck of the small feeder container ship lifted the boxes on pallets from the hold and lowered them onto the deck of the huge luxury craft alongside. The twenty mortar shells were removed from the concealed compartments inside the hull and lowered carefully onto the deck of the yacht, five at a time.

An hour later, the luxurious yacht sailed up the Piscataqua River and docked in a private marina nestled in a cove hidden by towering beech, birch and maples. Just before sunrise, all the hitech weaponry parts were loaded onto a U-Haul truck. Two men climbed aboard and drove for ten hours to Cambridge Springs, Pennsylvania.

Virgilio Sandoval spent much time, effort and money to piece together this particular pipeline. A steady payroll went to the dozens of airline pilots, harbormasters, boat captains, baggage handlers, local police, customs agents, shipping officials, and airline workers that he corrupted. Both the carrot and stick approach was applied and noncompliant accomplices faced intimidation or death.

After the three-man laser-designator team was able to take apart and reassemble their targeting devices in under four minutes, Edhi showed them how to disguise each separate part by making it look like a normal item allowed into the arena where tens of thousands of infidels would soon gather for the slaughter. The weapon's handle, viewfinder and fire button were cunningly attached to their Cabella stadium binoculars, Canon digital cameras, and Sony camcorders. Even the screws, nuts and bolts to fasten the laser-designator pieces back together were placed in zip-lock baggies and inserted into Minute Maid fruit juice boxes.

When Edhi was confident his attack cell jihadists would successfully pass through security and make it into the arena, he walked out the back door of the farmhouse and took a path around the pond to a long-forgotten barn that remained sturdy due to the huge butternut beams that refused to rot. It was surrounded by dense undergrowth and nestled in a thick grove of hemlock, oak and beech. A rusted-out '57 Chevy was nearly hidden in the underbrush to the side of the large door made from thick oak slabs.

One man standing watch holding an AK-47 with a suppressor greeted him from an overhead hay loft. *"Murhaba. Allah eazim."* Further inside the spacious barn, his three fanatic cohorts were inside the large U-Haul van unwrapping the mortar shells and storing them in the "Mom's Attic," the large space that protrudes outward above the cab. All twenty mortar shells fit snuggly into the compartment and could be quickly lowered to the floor.

The three mortars were installed and bolted down securely into the floor, which was over twenty-six feet long and over seven-feet wide. There was plenty of space to maneuver around after the live-firing began. Edhi summoned them back into the farmhouse.

Minutes later, all eight men reassembled around the antique oak dining room table. Edhi looked at them in silence, then stated, *"Nahn ealaa washk 'ann yusbahuu shuhada.' Fi sabil alllah.* We are about to become martyrs... for Allah's sake."

He went to the kitchen and retrieved a bottle of wine from the refrigerator, where three backpacks were stored. Each was less than 16x16x8 inches. The infidel's arena had templates at the entry gates and any backpacks or bags with greater measurements would be confiscated.

Each pack was filled with single-serve juice boxes and sandwiches, peanuts, chips and an assortment of other snackables in small, soft-plastic containers. Edhi hoped the bags and the myriad of items in them would distract the security guards so they focused less on the other items assembled with the weapon's parts.

The radical Islam sleeper attack cell leader remained standing and took a swig from the wine bottle, then passed it to the jihadist on his left. "We will pass this bottle around until it is finished. We drink the wine from *aljann*, for the Quran says Muslims will drink wine while in heaven, and we will all be there soon. Quran 16.67 says we may obtain alcoholic drinks and goods, for they are from the fruits of the date palms and grapes which Allah bestows upon us. Tomorrow, we will do our prayers...all day, while we perfect our training even more. Tomorrow, we will be completely sober during our martyrdom prayers. Allah won't approve of praying with a double tongue. For now, drink the gift our Islam God bestows upon us...and listen to me carefully, for I will reveal the details of our attack upon the unbelievers."

The seven militants remained seated and passed the bottle around while Edhi continued. "Our target is Progressive Field in Cleveland. The Cleveland Indians will be playing another MLB team in one of the playoffs for the World Series. We checked and the arena is filled to capacity with over 45,000 tickets sold."

One of the laser beam designator team militants rose and shouted excitedly, "We will guide the mortar bombs from *aljann* and kill them all!"

Edhi smiled in approval, *"Alttafani fi Allah*...Allah thanks you for your dedication, but you will *not* be pointing your weapons upon the masses of infidels. You will aim the laser beams to an exact position above the field... then you will press the laser fire buttons while aiming at the Champion Suite... a lavish safe haven inhabited by men of money and power. You will focus the laser beams upon the suite's spacious balcony and the large windows behind it. You will remain steady until the white brackets on the designator screen appear around the Champion Suite and then close together to form a tight, red box. Death will then rain down upon them from the skies of *aljann.*

The awestruck group of jihadists remained silent until one mesmerized martyr asked, "Who are these alkuffar we seek vengeance upon?"

Edhi calmly replied, "President Robert Rhinehart...the president of the United States...we are certain he will be there."

Episode 54

Curacao arrival

"Two more Guinness and take ya time pouring them," Sean Branagh said to Devon Ledard, who stood patiently behind the wet bar in the large billiard room of the Abaco mansion. Sandoval ordered him to take special care of the two Irish rejects. The pair flew out of the Lyden Pindling Airport in Nassau the day before and Abaco Constable Cecil Turnquest picked them up at the Marsh Harbor Airport and brought them to the mansion.

Devon obeyed the Irish Banker, who was playing eight-ball with his brother Patrick Branagh at the tournament-sized pool table, complete with diamonds set in the rails. He carefully poured two drafts, set them on a tray and brought them over to them.

Patrick held his up to the light. "Ah...a perfect pour Devon! The foamy head is just right and the effervescent bubbles are settling nicely, like silk poured into the glass."

Sean gulped a mouthful. "Ya know, my dear brother, our father said we were remotely related to Arthur Guinness himself...our great, great, great uncle. In 1759 he got a hold of four acres and signed a 9,000-year lease for the St. James' Brewery in Dublin. He started with dark ale and his followers kept perfecting the process over 250 years until the finest dark stout in the world was finally created...Guinness!" He gulped down another mouthful and took a shot at the eight-ball.

Devon smiled at both men and walked back behind the large wet bar. He assumed Corey Pearson and the mysterious organization he works for would launch an attack on the mansion after all the guests had arrived, which means his wife and children would be killed. He couldn't contact Corey because Sandoval confiscated his cell phone. Tougas and Cherestal picked him up at the Albury ferry dock, escorted him directly into their SUV and drove him straight to the mansion. He wasn't able to go inside the ferry terminal and leave a coded message for Corey on the bulletin board.

Sandoval's warning remained imprinted in his mind: *If the authorities raid da place...the two men I got sittin' right now in your home in da Guana Cay settlement will torture your wife and two children...den dey will strangle all three ta death.*

Lions Dive & Beach Resort, Willemstad, Curacao
(GPS: 12°05'08.3"N 68°53'50.3"W)
Kassim Khoury flew in on Rutaca Airlines from the Simón Bolívar International Airport in Caracas, Venezuela. The flight took one hour. He had been holed up in the Tri-Border Area of Brazil in a safe house run by Lebanese immigrants who were Hezbollah sympathizers. Curacao was a prized link in Sandoval's drug smuggling pipeline since it borders the Venezuelan coast...an ideal radical Islamic and narco-terrorist staging point for entrance to the Caribbean Basin nations.

He retrieved his suitcase from baggage claim, went through immigration and hopped into a taxi outside. Khoury told the driver to give him a half-hour tour of Willemstad then drop him off at the Lions Dive & Beach Resort which was five miles outside of town.

Upon arrival at the resort, Khoury looked out at the snorkelers enjoying the reef life as he strode along the private beach. The National Curacao Underwater Park lay offshore. He meandered inside a stand of palm trees and enjoyed the shade while holding his suitcase. Tourists from many nations sunbathed on lounge chairs, read books and relaxed under beach huts.

He glanced at his watch...2pm. As planned, he strode to the Hemingway Beach Bar nestled in the private, palm-studded beach, sat on a barstool and admired the gin-colored waters and fringing reefs of the underwater park.

A few moments later, a man sat across the bar from him. He was one of the couriers from the Curacao sleeper cell that Asif Qadeer Edhi formed years ago.

Khoury put a cigarette in his mouth and padded his pockets, pretending to search for a lighter. The courier walked around the bar and lit a match for him. "Here, looks like you need a light." He lit Khoury's dangling cigarette, then flipped the pack of matches on the bar. "You can keep 'em. I've got another pack."

Both men had a drink and made small talk, then the courier said he had to meet his wife in the nearby shopping plaza. He removed his sunglasses and shook Khoury's hand before leaving. It was a signal that his airport taxi hadn't been tailed as he toured Willemstad, nor during his walk around the Lions Dive & Beach Resort grounds. Khoury flipped open the matchbox. "Room 116" was written inside the cover.

Inside Room 116, Khoury was greeted by Francisco Cadenas of Venezuela's spy agency SEBIN, the Servicio Bolivariano de Inteligencia Nacional, and by his fellow terrorist financial backer Eamal Batoor. Batoor flew from Karachi, Pakistan to London, then directly into Curacao.

The fake documents Cadenas created for them were as good as the ones he prepared for Edhi. Batoor and Khoury inspected the immigration documents, visas, passports, credit cards, and driver's licenses. They were flawless. Just as he did for Edhi for his entrance into Miami, Cadenas took valid passports and changed the photo, then altered the biographical data so they were compatible to their cover stories.

Lying on one of the twin-beds were two Louis Vuitton suit cases packed with clothes and personal items. The initials for each man's fake name were monogrammed into a fancy brass plate under the handles. Airline tickets that matched the fake documents lay on top of each suitcase...the final destination was Marsh Harbor, Bahamas.

Khoury handed Cadenas an envelope containing 50,000 bolivars, worth $8,000 USD. "Here's a present I picked up for you in Caracas. Come on, Eamal...we have a plan to catch."

Sea of Abaco, Abaco Bahamas
Tahiti Beach
(GPS: 26°30'01.7"N 76°59'03.8"W)
Great Abaco Island is lined with a string of cays down its eastern shore. Hawksbill, Pensacola, Powell, and Nunjack cays protect the northern section of Abaco. Lying off Marsh Harbor in the central section are Green Turtle, Whale, Great Guana, Scotland, Man-of-War, Lubbers Quarters, and Elbow cays. This archipelago of small islets shelters the Sea of Abaco from the rough waves of the Atlantic Ocean and creates an ideal setting for snorkeling.

Corey put the old seventeen-foot Boston Whaler that Shianna's boyfriend overhauled for him on idle and stared at Tahiti Beach, a white talcum-powdered stretch of sand on the southern tip of Elbow Cay. The beach gave way to a verdant forest of breadfruit trees and coconut palms. *Danielle and I moored this same Boston Whaler in the shallows off Tahiti Beach and waded in. We laid in the sand, in the shade of the trees, relaxed and opened a bottle of wine and enjoyed the view...enjoyed each other...we walked into the forest and make love*

He reminisced as the boat drifted past Tilloo Cut, a narrow gap between Elbow Cay and Tilloo Cay that boaters use to reach the Atlantic Ocean. Then, he saw it. *There it is! The patch reef that Danielle and I used to snorkel in... the largest and most beautiful patch reef in the entire Sea of Abaco.* Corey set the boat on idle and peered down through the clear waters. He counted the queen conch and spiny lobster on the white-sand bottom fifteen feet below. A large Moray eel slithered into a crack in the hard coral. The patch reef appeared like a lush, multi-colored oasis in a vast desert of white sand.

A decade ago he explored the sixty-two-mile-long Sea of Abaco and studied the dolphin pods. The research was part of his deep cover. It is actually a saltwater lagoon separating Great Abaco Island, known as the "mainland" from the chain of barrier islands known as the Abaco Cays.

When the Boston Whaler drifted over the reef, he tossed out the anchor and made sure it landed harmlessly in a nearby sea grass bed. After quickly slipping on flippers, mask and snorkel, he dove down to it. A pair of spotted eagle rays glided past him while a large southern stingray erupted out of its sandy hiding place, creating a cloud of sand that fell like snowflakes. Hundreds of blue tangs swam over golden elkhorn and brain coral, then through a garden of red, blue and green sea fans that grew on top of a large formation of hard coral.

Corey swam past the eastern edge of the reef, passing a small hawksbill turtle grazing in the sea grass bed below him. It eyed him briefly as he passed overhead, but didn't seem concerned. He came upon tall pillars of elkhorn and staghorn coral where blue-stripped grunts set motionless, fairy basslet and butterfly fish darted, and parrot fish munched away at the choking algae, keeping the coral reef healthy.

After four minutes, he surfaced and was about to dive down again, but his cell phone that he wrapped inside a waterproof zip-lock bag vibrated in his swimsuit pocket.

He swam back to the boat and lifted himself up over the side, then sat on the captain's chair and checked his secure phone. It was the CI team casing out the Marsh Harbor Airport. "Go ahead."

"Sir, you won't believe this! Eamal Batoor and Khoury Kassim just landed aboard a plane from Curacao. Constable Turnquest picked them up and is driving them, presumably, to the Abaco Poultry mansion. We called in the IMINT satellite and are following a full mile behind."

"I copy, over and out." Corey toweled himself dry, turned on the motor and sped back to the Conch Inn Marina in Marsh Harbor. He imagined Danielle snorkeling with him in that beautiful patch reef, but with two of the most dangerous radical-Islamic terrorists on CBIF's list just landing on Abaco, it was back to business.

Corey wondered how Batoor and Kassim could have slipped off the radar shortly after the CBIF teams surveyed them at the Hotel Montana meeting in Port-au-Prince. It was assumed they went back to the Middle East or holed up somewhere in the Tri-Border Area in a Hezbollah safe house.

The terrorist pair troubled him a great deal. Batoor was freed from the Saraposa Prison in Kandahar by the Taliban back in 2008, and Kassim Khoury, who met with Sandoval in Medellin, had many Iranian Hezbollah contacts throughout the Tri-Border Area. They were about to smash his terrorist network at the luxury chalet safe house outside Willemstad, Curacao when Walt Mason's FBI goons moved in. Khoury ran the Curacao terrorist cell that had direct links to Hezbollah's entire terrorist organization throughout the Tri-Border Area of Paraguay, Argentina and Brazil.

Eventually, both men linked up with Sandoval in Medellin and transformed the low-level drug smuggler into the leader of a multinational narco-terrorist conglomerate. Batoor and Khoury are the financers of this hi-tech mortar attack on America and Sean Branagh and his unexceptional brother Patrick launder the funds. Islamic terrorist money is safely concealed in Sean Banagh's Nassau bank.

Corey recalled Devon Ledard's report of the bank bags full of cold cash being carried into the mansion, brought in from Haiti on Abner Orival's smuggling boat. *No electronic money transfers or deposits, no paper trail...nothing for the Department of Homeland Security to pick up on and track through the financial system. Everything is done by couriers carrying cash. Batoor, Khoury and Asif Qadeer Edhi*

*are working together. Edhi, who evaded us due to a fuckin' torna-
do in northwest Pennsylvania, is the attack cell leader and execu-
tioner while Batoor and Khoury are the financiers. Sandoval is just a
drug-smuggling killer. The pending attack on America's heartland...
the smuggling of Middle Eastern radicalized jihadist attack cells into
Haiti, then to Abaco, then into the United States...all take enormous
amounts of planning and money. I failed busting this cell in Curacao...I
won't fail again.*

HUMINT- human intelligence gathering

The IMINT stealth satellite verified that Eamal Batoor and Khoury Kassim arrived at the mansion. Constable Turnquest dropped them off at the front door then drove back to the police station in Marsh Harbor. The live stream video was sent to General Morrison at CBIF HQ in Key West and recorded into Jeannie's huge database.

Morrison called Corey immediately on Pinkston's inimitable twelve-digit security code satellite cell phone. "They walked into the front door of the mansion. Tell the agents casing out the Marsh Harbor Airport it was a job well done."

Corey was in his room at the Conch Inn Marina, studying a Google Map of the entire Abaco Poultry, LTD buildings and grounds. "Will do, sir. The stealth IMINT satellites do wonders. Our CI team was able to stay far back and reduce the chances of being spotted."

"Yes, but HUMINT is the bottom line. ELINT and IMINT are merely handmaidens for good HUMINT. Who all's at the mansion right now?"

"A conglomeration of selfish and heartless assholes meeting up with violent jihadists...Patrick and Sean Branagh from Nassau, Duane's murderers Pierre Cherestal and Bolan Tougas, the psychopath Sandoval, and now Eamal Batoor and Khoury Kassim. Constable Cecil Turnquest is running an airport shuttle service in his police cruiser between the mansion and airport."

Morrison felt an urge to chew on his Montecristo. "Who's still missing?"

Corey sat back down in front of the screen and studied the Google Map he set on satellite view. "The Bahamian Agricultural Minister, Alfred Moss. He'll no doubt be there with his limo driver, the guy who helped abduct Duane Collier from the Hard Rock Cafe in Nassau. The human smuggler from Haiti, Abner Orival and his associate, the Haitian minister Laurent Rousseau haven't arrived yet. Of course, our friends on Bimini...Senator Warren, Mark Serwin and Shahid El-Sayed haven't arrived yet."

"Our CI teams in Port-au-Prince have Orival and Rousseau under surveillance. We'll know when they depart to Abaco. How secure Is Bimini?"

"Our teams there are watching Warren, Serwin and Shahid El-Sayed. Team leader 'Frank' will personally tail Sayed if they split up. They put a transponder on Warren's plane at the South Bimini Airport. We'll know immediately when they fly to the mansion."

Just then Corey's other phone, the secure satellite phone, beeped. It was Addie Kolmogrovov. "Hold on, sir. I think I've got some important Intel coming in as we speak." He switched on the sat phone. "What you got, Addie?"

"I'm in the Levin building cleanin' out Moss's office. Just emptied his secretary's wastebasket in the greeting area. There's a note from Moss to her with instructions to make two airline reservations for a nonstop flight to Marsh Harbor."

"For what time?"

"That's why I'm calling you right now from his office. I inserted a mini-digital recorder inside the secretary's chair and played it from the time this morning when Moss's note was written to her. Her call to the Lynden Pindling International Airport was recorded loud and clear...Moss and his limo driver are taking off at 5:45pm today, a half hour from now on Bahamasair. It's only a thirty-five-minute flight, so they'll be touching down at Marsh Harbor at 6:20."

"Did she talk to the reservationist about the flight number or what kind of plane?"

"I checked into flights to Abaco from Nassau at that time. They'll be arriving on a De Havilland eight."

Corey gently hit the armrest of his chair with a fist. "Great! Addie, I remain thankful for finding and recruiting you on Andros. Our CI team at the Marsh Harbor Airport will be waiting for them. When this is all over I'm giving you a two-week respite to visit your folks in Nicholl's Town on a free flight aboard HST, High-Speed Transport Airlines."

Corey hung up the sat phone and switched General Morrison back on. "Well, sir, add two more guests to the list. Agent Kolmogrovov just reported in from Nassau...Moss and his limo driver are arriving in one hour."

Morrison made mincemeat out of the fresh Montecristo he inserted in his mouth. "That leaves Orival and Rousseau on Haiti and Warren, Serwin and El-Sayed on Bimini. What should we do if they don't show?"

"I'm certain they'll show. When they do, we'll attack in a lightning flash. It's our only chance to kill two birds with one stone...shatter the biggest radical Islamic terrorist cell in CBIF's history and find out where the hi-tech mortars are... and take down the sleeper attack cell that's lurking inside America."

CIA Starbucks Langley, Virginia
(GPS: 38.952102, -77.145165)
She couldn't believe it...once again, interrupted! Three short vibrations from her pager summoned her back upstairs to her desk. The Starbuck's *Caramel Macccchato* was nearly full. Since taking coffee out of Starbucks "Store No. 1" was forbidden, she took two gulps, tossed the rest into a wastebasket and strode out quickly, almost colliding with a computer science geek at the entrance. Echelon can't wait.

Two minutes later, Stacey found out what the alert was about. The NRO's "Evening Star" satellite, code-named "Mother Ship" was re-positioned to fly over the Nassau/Abaco sector. It was programmed to communicate with CBIF's IMINT and ELINT stealth satellites which flew in geosinc orbits over the Abaco Poultry, LTD region at coordinates 25° 5' N 77° 21' W.

The exchange just happened and "Mother Ship" received image and electronic signals emanating from pre-set coordinates delineating the perimeter around and everything within the Abaco Poultry, LTD grounds. The data stream was relayed to NSA and filtered through Stacie's Echelon's Dictionary program.

Part of Operation Invisible created a satellite communication network between CBIF's nine stealth satellites and the "Mother Ship," thus connecting CBIF directly into the global NSA Echelon surveillance system.

One of CBIF's ELINT satellites triggered the alert. It picked up two encrypted burst transmissions sent from a secure cell phone within the Abaco mansion. The NSA "Mother Ship" received the relay and filtered it through the ECHELON Dictionary program which contained key words typed in by Stacie.

It was the destinations that raised the electronic eyebrows of Dictionary. One was sent to a house in the shantytown of La Saline, just north of Port-au-Prince, and the other to an Internet cafe in Bimini, Bahamas. The burst transmissions were encrypted and the cell phone had no backdoor to skirt around the tricky encryption, so, HUMINT needed to be alerted. Counterintelligence agents, on the ground, needed to watch the suspected recipients.

Stacey contacted General Morrison, who alerted the CI teams in Haiti to watch Abner Orival. Then, Morrison gave the heads up to Corey, who alerted 'Frank' on Bimini that Warren, Serwin and Shahid El-Sayed may make a move.

Sure enough, the CI team in Haiti reported that Abner Orival walked out of his home in La Saline and loaded a suitcase into his van. He drove to the health department offices on Route de Tabarre in Port-au-Prince and sat in the van for a while. Eventually, Laurent Rousseau, the Minister of Public Health and Population walked out of the building, lugging a suitcase, and hopped into the van.

Two CI teams circumspectly tailed them. A half hour later they drove into a small, makeshift airstrip outside the coastal town of Léogâne. The airstrip was set up on a section of Route 9 after the 7.0 magnitude earthquake devastated Haiti. Small planes used it to bring in aid shipments. Orival and Rousseau boarded a waiting Rockwell Turbo-Commander 690 prop plane and flew off.

A quick check revealed it was a charter company plane and was scheduled for a nonstop flight to Abaco's Marsh Harbor Airport.

After receiving Corey's tip, the teams on North and South Bimini moved in closer to their targets. El-Sayed had booked into the Bimini Big Game Club in a room just down the hall from Warren and Serwin.

'Frank' took over personal surveillance on El-Sayed. He sat in the second floor of the Bimini Big Game Bar & Grill, enjoying their famous cheeseburger, the one that inspired Jimmy Buffet to compose "Cheeseburger in Paradise." He watched CNN News on the big screen TV and admired the navigational charts inlayed into the top of the bar. He had an exceptional view of the pool and penthouse suites where his three targets just returned to from a trip to the Alice Town straw market. He was glad Corey's nickname for him didn't become his code name.

El-Sayed, Sandoval's controller of the now defunct New Jersey warehouse, received a cell phone call while at the straw market. It must have been an urgent call, for he hung up after two seconds and hurriedly returned via golf cart to the Bimini Big Game Club. The other CI team members kept tabs on Warren and Serwin, who eventually walked into the End of the World Saloon.

Shortly, 'Frank' saw his target stride quickly out of the hotel complex and hopped back into his golf cart. He donned his cycling helmet, jumped on a fast mountain bike chained to a palm tree out-side the bar, and followed El-Sayed north on the Queen's Highway. The target's golf cart sped along at fifteen mph, an unsafe speed for the limestone and gravel main artery connecting Alice Town and Bailey Town. 'Frank' continued peddling past an Internet cafe that El-Sayed parked at.

Inside, El-Sayed left his fake passport at the counter and found an open computer cubicle. He sat down and opened his Lycos mailbox, finding a draft message from Sandoval. It was clear to fly to Abaco.

Sapodilly's Bar & Grill
Marsh Harbor, Abaco
(GPS: 26°32'44.9"N 77°03'09.4"W)
A Bananaquit flew into the "Dilly Tree" above Corey's table at Sapodilly's. He watched the colorful tropical bird as it eyeballed his tall glass of Bahama Mama. It had been feasting on the fruit of a nearby gumbo limbo tree and sipping the sugary nectar of the color-ful flowers growing all around.

It flew down and perched on the side of Corey's glass and began sipping his Bahama Mama. He emitted a soft chuckle at the cute, people-friendly and highly inquisitive little bird. *No wonder the locals call you the 'sugar bird.' Not too much, my little friend...you need quick reflexes to escape the many feral cats on Abaco.*

He gently shooed the little mooch away. It was 5pm and Constance was scheduled to work so he arrived fifteen minutes early and ordered a Sapodilly Burger to make it look like a chance meeting. She arrived, carrying a small duffel bag, and walked be-hind the bar as he finished the last tasty bite of the burger stuffed with bleu cheese and topped with sautéed onions, mushrooms and a strip of bacon.

Corey chose this time for the contact, for there was usually a lull in customer traffic. A local Bahamian lady cleaned up in the back kitchen. He picked up his backpack and sat at the end of the bar by the sink. Constance walked over and started cleaning beer mugs and cocktail glasses. *Damn...that feeling again when she's near me. I want to reach over and hold her in my arms. Fight it off!*

He spoke while she cleaned a tray full of empty glasses. "Just about everyone we're going to kill or capture is there, except for Senator Warren, his Chief-of-Staff Mark Serwin, and Shahid El-Sayed. They're still on Bimini, but the Bimini CI teams reported El-Sayed got an urgent cell phone call and immediately went to an internet cafe in Alice Town...probably read a draft message from Sandoval in an encrypted email account, then erased it."

Constance stood up and looked Corey in the eyes while drying off a glass. "When's the raid scheduled?"

"Tomorrow night...if Warren and his treasonous accomplices arrive or not. I instructed High-Speed Transport Airlines to land in South Bimini today. If they don't fly to Abaco, 'Frank' and his teams will abduct all three the moment the raid begins and fly them to the 'Farm'."

Constance spoke sarcastically, "Just wait until the ACLU finds out about *that* maneuver."

"I'm not worried. We have enough intelligence gathered on our two-timing senator to easily convict him and Serwin for treason. He already faces life in prison or the death penalty."

"Have you and Morrison finalized who's to be captured...or exterminated."

"Photos and names of all those we're going to dart are in my backpack. They may know where the mortars are and will *not* be killed... the Dirty Tricks division is waiting for them on Ferguson's ship."

Constance said. "Screw the enhanced interrogation technique etiquette. Skin 'em fuckin' alive."

Corey asked for a Kalick and she placed a cold one in front of him. He took a gulp. "There are hundreds, probably thousands of American lives at stake so CBIF went to OT level. They may do just that."

"Do just what?"

"Skin them alive. The Dirty Tricks division is a bunch of psychopaths using patriotism as a form of catharsis. I've seen them actually skin people alive, but the info they got prevented four snipers with Ak-47's from slaughtering children in Massachusetts on a crowded elementary school playground during lunchtime recess."

"I never heard of that op."

"Neither did the news media, American people or anyone walking the halls of congress. Only our CI teams, a small CBIF special ops squad, Morrison, myself, and President Rhinehart knew what went on. The four terrorists... who were radicalized American citizens... temporarily lost their civil liberties... mainly their freedom to *not* be tortured and to simply disappear forever."

"Holy Jimmy Hoffa! Thank you, President Rhinehart for allowing us to go to OT level...even if he looks the other way and will let us hang out to dry if the ACLU finds out. At least he knows we can't fight these radical Islamic monsters without going to it. Corey, we have to find out where the mortars and the attack cell are, quickly! The moment we raid the mansion the cell will be notified and launch an immediate attack... somewhere... in America's heartland."

"That's why they'll skip the normal EIT etiquette with those we capture at the mansion. Not enough time to subject them to prolonged stress positions or deafening noises, or to throw them in a cold refrigeration room, stuff them inside small coffin-like boxes or deprive them of sleep, food, or water. Once aboard Ferguson's *Queen Conch II*, Dirty Tricks will immediately strip them naked and start slapping and beating them in between waterboarding and wall-slamming."

"What if they're ready to visit seventy-two virgins?" "Then they'll start skinning them alive."

"I hope it works. Thousands of American lives are at stake." "We also have an additional trump card."

"What's that?"

Corey took a swig of Kalik. "Overseas CBIF agents embedded in the CIA worked with General Morrison and foreign intelligence to learn much about the private lives of Eamal Batoor, Khourty Kassim, Shahid El-Sayed, and Sandoval. They know who their wives, children, parents, brothers and sisters are...even took telephotos of them. The Dirty Tricks team will hang the photos of their loved ones on the walls of the EIT room for them to stare at when the torture begins. They will be told that their loved ones will be abducted and if they don't disclose where the mortars are, or if the mortar attack actually happens, they will be brutally tortured before their throats are slit."

Constance made herself a strong drink and let Corey's words sink in. After a few moments, she said, "Do me a favor...never bring your Dirty Tricks associates to Sapodilly's for a good time."

"Don't worry. I don't hang out with them. General Morrison and President Rhinehart operationalizes them behind closed doors *only* when the *Gang of Six* makes the decision to go to OT, *Obscure Transgression* level. The moment an operation is completed we go off OT and they go back into hiding. They're necessary at times but, yeah...they give me the creeps, too."

"Unfortunately, now is one of those necessary times." "You got the SAT-LC?"

"It's in the duffel bag. HST Airlines flew it in from Key West last night." She palmed something in her hand and slid it over the bar. "Here's the memory stick to it. I'm sure Morrison's satellite image interpreters at *Key West Drywall* embedded some interesting waypoints on it."

Corey put his hand on hers and kept it there. "When this is all over, I have to talk to you, Constance...I think about you all the time. I even thought of *not* letting you go on the raid. I don't want anything to happen to you. It's not because I'm lonely...have no family and go through life mostly by myself...it's simply because I feel a warmth inside when I'm around you. I think I'm in love with you."

She laid her other hand atop his and pressed gently. "Corey, I feel that warmth right now being near you...it's a shared feeling. I felt it long ago, then it resurfaced after our close call with Tougas and

Cherestal on the GAH after discovering Duane Collier's murder site on the abandoned logging road. Remember when you climbed back into the Land Rover and I didn't put it in gear, even though we had to get the hell out of there? I stared at you because I felt old memories... the exciting times we had over a decade ago...the way we worked together...related to each other...the night we spent together. I'm glad we finally revealed our true feelings. I kept something else from you after all these years...I'll tell you about it after the raid."

Corey took the memory stick to the SAT-LC. *I have to know what else she has to tell me! No, later...gotta get back to business* "I'll be looking forward to it. We have much more to talk about...plans to make, together."

Constance reverted back to her disciplined, counterintelligence demeanor. She didn't want to get maudlin when she or Corey could be killed in action tomorrow night. "What's the pre-raid game plan?"

"Tomorrow morning, team ten, the cruise ship couple, will call you from the motel they're staying at, the Lofty Fig. There's a landline phone there at the desk. They'll tell the desk clerk they want to tour the Abaco Parrot Preserve and to schedule a tour with *Natural World of Abaco*. You are to pick them up at 1pm and tour the preserve. It's twenty thousand acres and borders Abaco Poultry, LTD, so you can openly hike near it. An IMINT and ELINT satellite will hover overhead to record any responses from Sandoval or his guards. I want to know, since we will use the Parrot Preserve for our approach. We will do re-con and call in the special ops attack. I want you to find a good spot for it."

"What are the plans for the pre-raid rendezvous?"

"Out in the open, amidst normal civilian activities. Leave the parrot preserve and drive back with team ten to the Conch Inn's Curly Tail Restaurant at 5pm. They'll buy you dinner for the great tour you gave them. I'll be at the outside patio bar with four members of Yacht team eleven. Since we all met there and partied during the Limbo dance bash the other night, we'll simply reconnect and decide to go for an evening boat ride on the yacht."

Constance nodded to Corey. "Understood. Let's make the exchange."

Corey took a swig of his Kalik while gently shoving his backpack around the end of the bar with his right foot. Constance bent down underneath the bar and pretended to realign the liquor bottles in the bottom shelf. She quickly zipped open her duffel bag, took out the SAT-LC and placed it into Corey's backpack while retrieving a brown folder containing the photos of the men they would dart. She slid the backpack back around the bar.

After finishing his beer, Corey picked up his backpack and whispered. "See you tomorrow at five." Then, he left.

Episode 56

Capture or kill

Corey took a chance setting up the Sat-LC device outside his room within the verdant grounds of the Conch Inn Marina. Since it looked like an ordinary PC, he thought passersby wouldn't suspect anything. He placed it on an isolated bench underneath a stand of breadfruit trees to see if the thick canopy of leaves and the bulbous bread-fruits hanging overhead interfered with the reception or transmission. Tonight, he would lead his CI Team in total darkness through dense forests in route to the perimeter of the Abaco Poultry, LTD property under a similar canopy of Caribbean pines.

The Satellite-Link Connection was another Pinkston mastermind creation. He downloaded a variety of Google Map and other online topographic map overlays of the Abaco Poultry GPS perimeter co-ordinates, and their planned approach to it. Back in the hotel room, Corey would upload it into nine handheld mobile devices disguised as smart phones. Each team member will use one as a personal information manager.

Corey's handheld device was connected to the Internet, to the special ops commander and his team leaders, and to General Morrison via linkage with one of CBIF's COMMINT stealth satellites. He would receive fast-shifting circumstances from them and quickly relay adaptive-tactic maneuvers to each of his eight CI team members as the raid progressed.

He peered at the screen. The *Key West Drywall* image-analysis experts embedded key waypoints on the Abaco Poultry, LTD grounds into the SAT-LC. They were based on Devon Ledard's testimony and by the images gathered by CBIF's stealth IMINT satellite.

A red-blinking dot appeared where Sandoval's office was located in the mansion's second floor corridor. After the Middle Eastern guards were neutralized and the captured prisoners were transported to the Dirty Tricks team aboard the *Queen Conch II*, Corey and Constance would advance to the office and fill their duffel bags with Sandoval's computer hard drives, his library of videos, audio tapes and notebooks, and the paper documents in his file cabinet.

A curly-tail lizard startled him as it scampered over his bare feet. t had a cockroach in its mouth. *I will soon have some human cockroaches captured as well, my friend.* Corey noticed 'Chop Chop' and another female member of Team-11 strolling through the Conch Inn gardens. They toted a wildflower field guide, pretending to be identifying the native vegetation while casing out the grounds for suspicious activity.

Thanks, gals He looked down as the SAT-LC screen beeped. It began downloading a send from Constance, who was with the Team-10 cruise ship couple. While hiking through the parrot preserve, she marked coordinate waypoints of thick rock and brush formations where they could hide behind, as well as openings and trails made by wild boars that would make their advance to the grounds safer and easier.

The system worked perfectly under the dense overhead foliage. Corey embedded the waypoints directly onto the SAT-LC topographic Google Map that would be employed that night. With a flick of his finger, the topographical image of the combat zone and entire theatre of operations was sent via satellite to the CBIF special operations commander aboard the USS Caribbean and to General Morrison in the War Room in Key West.

Back in the hotel room, he downloaded it into the nine handheld devices his team would use. Then, he uploaded the transponder signals from the devices into the SAT-LC and they appeared as nine small green, blinking triangles on the screen. Everyone would be on the same page and know the whereabouts of everyone else.

When Constance slipped the SAT-LC into Corey's backpack from behind the bar at Sapodilly's, she also inserted nine body cams. He programmed their output ports into the SAT-LC. General Morrison would view the raid on a large video screen separated into nine smaller screens. Each Infrared night vision cam would be attached to each agent's shoulder, enabling Morrison to view live streams of the raid unfolding from nine different angles.

The miniaturized shoulder cams were water resistant and used 150-degree wide angle lenses. They had no memory storage; the video streams would be received by an overhead COMMINT satellite and forwarded in encrypted form to the War Room, where Jeannie would store them in her vast database. A built-in voice recorder would record each agent's verbalizations as well.

Corey planned the raid out thoroughly. He went over the list of people who already arrived at the mansion, then typed in a "K", "C" and "A" on a photo of each who were to be killed, captured or arrested. He texted the file to Morrison and the special ops commander:

Patrick Branaugh (A)
Sean Branaugh (A)
Pierre Cherestal (C)
Bolan Tougas (C)
Alfred Moss (A)
Moss' limo driver (K)
Abner Orival (K)
Laurent Rousseau (A)
Cesar Virgilio Sandoval (C)
Senator Warren (A)

Mark Serwin (A)
Cecil Turnquest (A)
Shahid El-Sayed (C)
Eamal Batoor (C)
Khoury Kassim (C)

Corey stared at the list, then embedded the link into the nine mobile devices. *The only ones on the list who aren't at the mansion yet are Warren, Serwin, and El-Sayed. What the hell's keeping them?*

Episode 57

Black hat hacker

North Bimini, Bahamas

The white beach sand contrasted with the varied shades of blue coloring the pristine waters and dark blue sky. 'Frank' parked his golf cart on a sand and limestone section of Blue Lagoon Road just north of the Bimini Bay Resort & Marina and took a seat at the Beach Club Grill & Bar. Goombay Smash drinks were on special for twelve dollars. He ordered a cold Kalik beer for eight bucks.

He sat on a barstool facing north so he could keep a visual tab on his target, Shahid El-Sayed. It was ninety-four degrees and humid, but the ocean breeze and shade in the open-air bar, plus the ice-cold beer soothed him.

Warren, Serwin and El-Sayed were on the move. They left the Bimini Big Game Club in two golf carts and headed north on the Queen's Highway through Bailey's Town. Soon they reached the Bimini Bay Resort & Marina, a maze of paved streets and condos where mangrove marshes once flourished. Several times inside the resort they split up and as the cart with Warren and Serwin proceeded north, El-Sayed backtracked to see if anyone suspicious was following.

Fortunately, 'Frank' earlier sent Team-5S from South Bimini ahead of them and they parked their golf cart and strolled around the complex while the targets made a rather rudimentary attempt to see if they were being tailed. 'Frank' and his team held back and refrained from entering the complex. When the targets were satisfied that the site was clear, they continued north along Blue Lagoon Road and exited the condo development while the CI foot-surveillance team signaled their comrades to proceed.

The three had been sitting in their two carts for twenty minutes, obviously waiting for someone. When 'Frank' gave the go ahead, CI Team-5S left the complex and proceeded north on a sandy side road and positioned themselves in a dense growth of Caribbean pine parallel to the targets. Since they may have been noticed inside the complex, they stayed well out of site.

A Boston Whaler was moored offshore in the Bimini Road and a single man snorkeled among the half-mile long limestone block formations. They were rectangular and perfectly set together. Scientists claim the road is a natural formation of bedrock, but 'Frank' believed they were man-made structures constructed over 3,500 years ago. Many times, he scuba dove and caught spiny lobsters between the equally-spaced, rectangular boulders. He believed the formations were remnants of a wall, road, pier, or breakwater that an ancient civilization once constructed.

While keeping one eye on Warren, Serwin and El-Sayed, he noted the snorkeler stayed under for over four minutes at times, and competently snorkeled through the entire area. He was in good physical shape.

'Frank' whispered softly into the microphone embedded into his sunglasses. "Get a few photos of the dude in the Boston Whaler. I noticed El-Sayed staring out at him once too often."

Then, the lone snorkeler climbed up the rear ladder and boarded his boat. He toweled himself off and slipped a Ralph Lauren polo shirt over his swim suit, put on sunglasses, started the boat and slowly moved towards shore.

In four feet of water, he set anchor and raised the outboard motor, then jumped overboard and waded in to the beach adjacent to the targets. He strolled along the beach for several minutes in the hot sun, pretending to search for shells while El-Sayed looked around as if trying to spot any overly-interested bystanders.

Finally, the man walked off the beach and up to the Blue Lagoon dirt road, then jumped into the golf cart with El-Sayed. Warren and Serwin started their carts and headed south with El-Sayed following. The entourage passed 'Frank' and headed back through the Bimini Bay Resort & Marina.

They may have made a 'make' on him, so he had Team-5N already in place ahead of the four targets. He and Team-5S waited until they disappeared, then trailed behind. "We'll use the same surveillance MO as we did coming here, but in reverse."

'Frank' was a little irritated that the snorkeler put on an outback shade hat and large sunglasses and that team 5-S probably was unable to get a good facial shot. "We'll try for another pic at Bimini Big Game Club. I have a feeling that's where they're headed."

Team 5-S replied, "Boss, you trained us better than that...we got good shots with the telephoto when he first got back into the Boston Whaler, before he put the hat and shades on. We're sending the pics now."

Ten seconds later, a series of perfect, full-face photos appeared on his satellite cell phone. 'Frank' was ecstatic. "Good job, guys and gals. I don't know who this dude is...will relay them to Corey."

Corey jogged to the Tiki Hut and sat at the table underneath the purple umbrella. Dillon was in the kitchen, behind the open-air bar making him the famous crabs and rice lunch. In three hours, Corey was to meet with Constance at the Conch Inn with CI Team-10, the cruise ship couple that she took on a tour through the Abaco parrot preserve. He would fortuitously, on purpose, meet them and the five members of Team-11 at the Sunset Bar. After a candlelight dinner, all nine would go on a moonlight cruise aboard Team-11's yacht.

Dillon brought the plate of steaming crabs and rice. He smiled, nodded his head indicating he understood that Corey wanted privacy, then walked back behind the bar. He knew Corey was reminiscing again under the same umbrella...at the same table he used to wine and dine his beloved Daniel.

The crab meat was delicious. Corey didn't know exactly why he came here just before the raid was to begin. Perhaps, it was to honor the relationship they had together. He thought that, tonight, he may meet up with destiny...with death. After all, he's been stabbed once, shot twice. There were bullet scars in his leg and forearm and a knife scar in his upper back. Corey pondered how he was almost devoured by the huge tiger shark but was saved at the last minute by 'Chop Tail' and the pod of spotted dolphins. Maybe he used up his good fortunes...maybe tonight, he'll catch a bullet to the head, and join Danielle.

Or, maybe my visit here is to pay tribute to Danielle and to let her know that I plan to start a new life...with Constance.

The secure satellite cell phone vibrated. It was from the two teams on North and South Bimini. "Sir, 'Frank' here. We followed Warren, Serwin and Sayed to the northern section of Bimini. They met up with an unknown then returned to the Bimini Big Game Club...am sending photos now."

The stream of five photos appeared on Corey's screen. He stared in disbelief at a man he instantly recognized. *Holy shit!*

Dillon came out of the kitchen and noted Corey was gone. He walked across the patio to the table to find only a few bites of his crab meat and rice delicacy were eaten. A $20 bill lay under an empty bottle of Kalik. *Dat Corey...he always be in a hurry! Everyting' is an emergency to him...I dunno what got to him dis time, but dere ain't nuthin' in life dat important.* He took the plate, walked back to the stove and scraped the remaining crab off Corey's plate back into the large pot. More customers would be arriving.

After a quick jog back to his Conch Inn Marina hotel room, he called Morrison and listened for several moments as the twelve-digit code opened the digital encryption algorithm. It kicked into gear and Morrison answered. "I'm counting down to zero, Corey."

"Sir, something's come up...you won't believe who met up with our targets on Bimini."

"Surprise me."

"The Black Hat Hacker, alias BHH."

There was silence for several moments before Morrison spoke. "He's the only person I regret that you recruited."

"Yes, sir. That was years ago. I recruited both him and Pinkston at the annual hacker convention in Las Vegas. They hung out together back then, but Pinkston never trusted him. He refused to work with BHH after we enticed them to work for CBIF."

Morrison already had the end of his Montecristo shredded. He was in the War Room. "We should have listened to Pinkston."

Corey grabbed an icy Kalik from the minibar. "It was a tough call, recruiting BHH. I liked his genius and the safety precautions he took at the convention. He paid the entrance fee with cash only, registered with a false name that passed the hacker convention's security check, and never carried a credit card. Your instructions were to go there and recruit cybersecurity experts to harden-up CBIF's computer networks."

"Well, I have to admit, after we hired BHH, I'm glad I assigned him to *Operation Jeannie*. He found security holes in Jeannie and devised strategies to safeguard her against cyberattacks."

Corey thought about the Jeannie operation involving BHH. His thoughts returned to pre-9/11 when Duane's father, Drew Collier, CBIF's mole inside the Pentagon, created the deep data mining algorithm, code name Jeannie. It was kept as a cryptic program in Drew's Pentagon computer and a duplicate was installed into the War Room computer at CBIF HQ. Morrison assigned BHH to ferret out any cyber threats to it.

Corey took another swig of Kalik. *And now the fucker's heading to Abaco with the Jeannie algorithm to meet with narco-terrorists.* "Not surprising he was able to do so, sir. At the Las Vegas hacker's convention, I decided to approach him after he won a game called 'Flag Village'. I couldn't believe what I saw. Dozens of hackers ventured out of this make-believe village and attacked each other's computers by solving complex codes. They attacked each other while defending their own computers. A flag was added or taken away depending upon if they attacked or defended successfully or not. At the end, BHH amassed a forest of flags while most of the others retreated back inside 'Flag Village' and refused to come out. He won a second contest by planning out how to break into an airplane's navigational system by using its own Wi-Fi signal and entertainment system."

Morrison lit up his classy cigar. "I don't blame you for recruiting him...it's just that I should have assigned Pinkston to *Operation Jeannie* instead."

"Well, sir...hindsight is always twenty-twenty. So, what's our next move? He probably stole the Jeannie deep data mining algorithm... and is about to give it to a bunch of radical Islamic terrorists on Abaco."

Morrison took a nervous puff and blew a ring of smoke. "We can't move in on him now, not with a sleeper attack cell hiding out somewhere in northwest Pennsylvania with a hi-tech mortar weapons system. We'd also lose our chance to bring down the largest narco-terrorist network in CBIF's history that's about to congregate at the mansion on Abaco."

Corey knew Morrison didn't like making snap decisions, so he didn't prod his boss further as to what to do with BHH. He remained silent for several moments, then offered a suggestion. "There is a good chance BHH is carrying the Jeannie database. He is either going to hand it off to Warren, Serwin and El-Sayed in Bimini, then fly back to the U.S. ..."

Morrison broke in. "Or, travel to the mansion on Abaco and take it with him. In either case, Jeannie will fall into the hands of the terrorist network. Let me do some thinking on this…I'll get back to you in one hour. In the meantime, cancel tonight's raid on the Abaco mansion."

"Yes, sir. I'll notify the special ops commander aboard the USS Caribbean Sea to stand down."

Morrison left the War Room after talking to Corey and decided a stroll to the Key West Historic Seaport area would help him think. He contacted his CI team next door on the secure sat phone. "I'm heading out now to the Schooner Wharf Bar."

He walked out onto the front porch and paused to light his Montecristo, then petted the two Key West cats lounging on the wicker chairs, allowing the CI teams to position themselves.

After several minutes, he strode west on Eaton Street. The aroma of searing Mahi from inside the Bien Caribbean-Latino Restaurant aroused his hunger. He smiled at a man seated on an outdoor seat of the quaint place, munching on sautéed prawns and Jasmine rice.

A bicyclist stopped at the corner of Eaton and Margaret Street and pretended to adjust his helmet as Morrison strolled by and headed north on Margaret Street. He was a counterintelligence agent.

Morrison thought about what he never revealed to Corey about BHH and the Hsin Chow connection. Chow set up the super-secret Chinese complex in Cuba that eavesdropped on U.S. satellite-based military transmissions as well as on private faxes and e-mails pouring out of America's homes and businesses.

Corey targeted him when he registered at the Sofitel Sevilla hotel in downtown Havana. He posed as a French businessman and befriended Chow, finding out that his son attended MIT in the states and his wife visited him in Cuba several times a year. Chow revealed that his son no longer wanted to return to China and had fallen in love with a fellow MIT student. They planned to marry.

Corey offered Chow a defection opportunity whereby he and his wife could defect. A CBIF exfiltration team would fly them clandestinely to the U.S. and unite them with their son. They would be given top-secret clearances, new identities, and two million dollars' cash. Both Hsin Chow and his son would become CBIF moles inside the NGA, the National Geospatial-Intelligence Agency. Chow promptly accepted the offer.

Morrison was satisfied that he held back no secrets from Corey about the Hsin family defection plans and about BHH's involvement n *Operation Jeannie*. But, as he strolled down Margaret Street, he thought about the rest of the story...what Corey didn't know. That's why he felt awkward when Corey contacted him about the two Bimini CI teams reporting that BHH met up with Warren, Serwin and El-Sayed on North Bimini. There were events involving BHH that he kept Corey in the dark on.

At age seventy-five, the ex-Marine and Director of CBIF operations thought his cognitive abilities may have been lacking when he appointed BHH to manage the $1.8 billion deep data mining project. Its purpose was to amplify Jeannie, which Duane's father originated inside the Pentagon.

Although the original Jeannie data mining algorithm was destroyed at the Pentagon on 9/11, Morrison had a replica earlier installed in the CBIF War Room's mainline computer.

The original Jeannie was invigorated beyond imagination, and he endured ignominy for not telling Corey the complete story about this black-funded pilot project. The mission was to determine its effectiveness when applied to CBIF's counterterrorism efforts through- out the Caribbean Basin.

A front operation business was set up in Silicon Valley. It was aptly named Cyber Security Sanctuary (CSS) and specialized in protecting businesses from cyberattacks and computer breaches. CSS blended in well with the hundreds of start-up tech companies operating in the shadows of Google, Apple, and Facebook. Morrison secretly appointed BHH to manage the operation and located him in a CBIF safe house outside San Francisco. He never mentioned any of this to Corey, for he knew he would vehemently disagree.

The black-funded project began. Chow Hsin and his son Cheng embedded a cutting-edge mathematical algorithm into Drew Collier's original Jeannie data-mining format. The Hsin's remained under the radar of Chinese intelligence while Cheng continued his studies at MIT and Chow remained in Cuba. A research facility was set up at MIT to enable Cheng, with his father's help, to surreptitiously develop a complete mathematical structure of terrorism itself. Father and son communicated via CBIF's secret satellite phone link, the same one Chow currently uses to correspond with Morrison.

As Morrison strolled further down Margaret Street toward Harpoon Harry's, he felt regret for not telling Corey about the San Francisco CBIF safe house. Through the CSS business, he instructed BHH to attempt to breach Cheng's MIT computer in Cambridge, Massachusetts and to devise new firewalls to patch up any cyber weaknesses in its defenses. After all, he had already perfected impenetrable firewalls around Jeannie.

Four men walked out of Harpoon Harry's just ahead of him. One of two CI agents across the street walking toward Morrison took off her sunglasses. That was a signal for him to stop, which he did. The general never questioned their street savviness. He stopped and pretended to have received a call on his cell phone. The CI couple crossed the street, walked right up to the four men who lingered outside Harpoon Harry's and asked them how the food was.

As Morrison stood there with the cell phone to his ear, he overheard the men tell the couple to definitely order "The Harpooner" and described the half-pound of ground chuck with cheese, bacon, grilled onions and mushrooms delicacy. While the woman agent discussed the menu, her male counterpart observed the loose-fitting Hawaiian shirts and camera cases the four toted.

The four guys bragged about how Jimmy Buffet used to do all night recording sessions just around the corner, then go to Harpoon Harry's for breakfast at sunrise. After several minutes, they parted.

The four men walked down Caroline Street. The female agent put her sunglasses back on, signaling Morrison it was OK to proceed.

He walked past the pink stucco restaurant, piecing everything together in his mind. Sandoval wanted to steal the original Jeannie database. He somehow found out that Drew Collier kept a duplicate in his bank safety deposit box, the reason why Duane Collier was abducted from the Hard Rock café in Nassau and Joan Collier was snatched from her home in Severna Park, Maryland. Duane didn't follow protocol and allowed himself to be abducted because they showed him a photo of his captive mother. He went with them willingly, to save his mother's life, but made it appear as an authentic kidnapping.

Morrison began chewing nervously on his lit Montecristo and spit out the tobacco bits into a row of pink ginger and red bleeding heart plants. A roused Key West rooster squawked, ran onto the sidewalk and strutted indignantly in front of him.

The general deduced that once Sandoval found out the stolen Jeannie database wasn't the enhanced version perfected by the Hsin's and BHH, he, along with Eamal Batoor, Khoury Kassim and Shahid El-Sayed bribed BHH to deliver the $1.8 billion-dollar deep data-mining database to them at the mansion on Abaco. Thus, his appearance on Bimini.

The aging ex-marine general felt culpable for trusting BHH and for carelessly allowing him to steal the upgraded database off Cheng Chow's computer at MIT. He would tell both Corey and Pinkston of his gaffe and how stupid he felt for ignoring their misgivings about him.

He strolled past the Turtle Kraal. Today, he would pass on their crab cakes and try something different. *A change of routine makes me more creative*

As he walked into the Schooner Wharf Bar, he noticed three CI agents already positioned inside. The couple who scrutinized the four unknowing men outside Harpoon Harry's sat at a corner table. A lone male agent sat on a barstool with a camera case placed on the stool next to him...a .45-caliber Glock 30 with two extra 36-shot clip nestled inside.

The informal, open-air atmosphere calmed Morrison down a bit. He sat at a small table and inserted his Montecristo back into the black, gold-trimmed snuffer, then gazed out at the classic yachts lining the Key West Historic Seaport. A few dogs lay patiently under the barstools their masters sat at.

His mind wandered back to BHH's unexpected appearance on Bimini. The guilt resurfaced... disregarding Corey's reservations about the hacking genius after he recruited him at the Las Vegas convention... overlooking Pinkston's distrust of the guy and his refusal to work alongside him.

A friendly waitress asked him what he wanted, interrupting his thoughts.

"A Key West Sunset Ale."

"Anything to eat?"

A fisherman walked past, toting a large net satchel of oysters. Morrison said, "I want that!"

The waitress laughed, "You can't get 'em any fresher! I'll throw in some extra cocktail sauce with your order...be right back with your drink."

Morrison's smile evaporated the moment the waitress walked away. He feigned being in a good mood...but felt miserable for not listening to the gut instincts of Corey and Pinkston. BHH was an opportunist with sociopathic tendencies.

On a daily basis, BHH called him from the safe house outside San Francisco. He found weaknesses in the $1.8 billion deep data-mining algorithm that Hsin and Cheng were devising and embedding into the outdated Jeannie database. Since BHH already perfected a failsafe firewall shield around the old Jeannie, why not have him perform the same function on Cheng's MIT computer?

The waitress brought a full serving of oysters on the half shell from the raw bar. Morrison dug in. He tried to keep his mind off

BHH's treasonous deception, but couldn't. The pleasurable atmosphere of the Schooner Wharf Bar- a place Charles Kuralt once called the "center of the universe" and what Mel Fisher, the treasure hunter who discovered the 1622 wreck of the Spanish galleon Nuestra Señora de Atocha, referred to as "a treasure," gave no comfort to Morrison.

He grew nauseous and stopped eating the fresh oysters. It wasn't the oysters that sickened him...it was the thought that BHH had conned him. He hacked into Cheng's MIT computer and stole the entire mathematical algorithm that boosted the original Jeannie's deep data mining capabilities a hundred times over...and now it was about to get into the hands of the terrorist network on Abaco. He left a fifty-dollar bill on the table and left.

Corey sat on the small patio deck of his Conch Inn Marina hotel room. He was anxiously awaiting General Morrison to get back to him. It would be terrible to lose the Jeannie data-mining algorithm. His secure satellite phone vibrated. He quickly went back into the room, slid the patio door shut, and answered. After several seconds of algorithmic noise, Morrison came on. There was a weary but resolute tone in his voice. "Corey."

"Yes, sir."

"I've thought about what we're going to do with BHH and the satchel he brought to Bimini. I want him killed and the stolen Jeannie database recovered. That's top priority."

"His photo has been sent to the special ops commander. I will relay your orders to him."

"Good. We can't allow that software to get into the hands of ISIS or Hezbollah in the Tri-Border Area. It will compromise CBIF's entire Caribbean strategy of identifying, hunting down and killing terrorist networks. The moment Warren, Serwin, El-Sayed and BHH land on Abaco, the raid is on."

"I agree totally, sir."

"And, one other thing. When this is all over, I have something on my mind that I want to tell you. Let's first murder BHH and reclaim the data-mining database, capture and deliver Sandoval, Shahid El-Sayed, Eamal Batoor and Khoury Kassim to the Dirty Tricks division on Darnell Ferguson's ship, the *Queen Conch II*...and find out where Edhi and his fuckin' terrorist sleeper attack cell is hiding out in north-west Pennsylvania. We've got to recover those mortars."

Morrison disconnected from Corey and sat alone in the War Room. In due time, he would reveal to Corey the real name of the most advanced data-mining algorithm the world has ever known. For now, he'd allow Corey to think that BHH was smuggling the stolen and outmoded Jeannie software to Abaco. Later, he would tell him its real name...the Penumbra Database.

Episode 58

The counterintelligence hunt for terrorists

Cambridge Springs, Pennsylvania

It was 8am and 'Tracker' had been up since sunrise. She sat in an antique wicker chair on the sprawling porch of the Riverside Inn, sipping a cup of coffee and pretending to read a copy of the Erie-Times newspaper she picked up in the lobby. It showed photos of the devastation the F5 left behind as it tore through Edinboro: battered bodies, huge oaks sheared to shreds, mangled automobiles and hollow basement cavities where houses used to stand. She thought of the nightmare both Team-2 agents went through…then felt sorrow for Constance on Abaco, who must have been told by now of her brother's death.

Revenge will come. Her head remained motionless while her eyes darted everywhere from behind dark sunglasses. Edhi's green Ford Fusion still remained parked on Fountain Drive, the inn's private drive. She and her male trainee, along with both agents in Team-4 booked into the historic inn. Morrison called in three additional teams with four agents each. They arrived, posing as golfers, bird watchers, hikers, and bicyclists.

Including Team-1 and Team-4, a total of sixteen CBIF counterintelligence agents registered at the quaint, Victorian-styled inn. Each carried a photo of Edhi and would spot him immediately. They pretended not to know each other, but by "chance" met and befriended one another in the inn's Riverside Pub and hallways. They blended in well. The nine rooms they occupied were unrelated in shape, size and décor, and contained dozens of Victorian-era antiques and artifacts. The only thing the rooms had in common were that TV's and telephones were absent.

Since there was no elevator, they used the beautiful carpeted staircases and hallways to travel among the three floors. One could hear them moving along creaky floorboards to meet up with each other and quietly discuss their plans. Old-fashioned sofas, tables and lamps adorned the wide hallways and spacious lobby, so the five teams had little difficulty finding a private nook somewhere to chat.

'Tracker' glanced at her watch…8:20am. The teams would resume their hunt for Edhi in ten minutes. Five agents would take a bicycle tour along the surrounding dirt, gravel and unpaved back roads; four would drive along the back paved roads while "birding" with binoculars and avian field guides; and the remaining five agents would split up into two hiking groups and trek through the 4,000-acre Seneca Division of the Erie National Wildlife Refuge.

She calmly sipped her coffee and feigned reading the newspaper on the wrap-around veranda lined with antique rocking chairs, passé horse sleighs and historic wooden cane chairs. One-by-one, the teams walked out through the wide, oaken entrance door to their respective cars and bicycles, then left to search for a white utility van, Edhi, or any persons of Middle Eastern appearance. He most likely would not show his face outside the sleeper attack cell safe house, wherever it may be. Seeing a person of Middle Eastern appearance in the rural roads of northwest Pennsylvania would be a rare occurrence When the last team left, 'Tracker' returned to her hotel room, hung a "Do Not Disturb" sign on the door and locked it, then set up a GPS Google Map screen on an antique desk. Each CI agent carried a transponder. She stared at the fourteen blips spreading out down Miller Station Road and onto adjoining country side roads off Route 6N.

She and her male trainee remained at the Riverside Inn. He strolled outside through the gardens and along the footpaths by the French Creek River, keeping an eye on Edhi's car.

The teams began positioning live-streaming camouflaged video cams in the underbrush along Miller Station Road and on each side road running off of it. When Team-1 and Team-2 approached Cambridge Springs during the F5 tornado, the last drone video stream showed Edhi walking up the front porch steps and entering the Riverside Inn. It also showed a white utility van pulling out from behind the inn, turning right onto Route 6N and traveling a couple hundred feet, then veering off quickly and disappearing onto a back road named Miller Station.

By the time 'Tracker' rushed into the front parking lot and Team-4 reached the rear of the inn…the van was gone, and so was Edhi. They missed him by thirty seconds. The trailing stream from the drone, although grainy due to the wind and continual lightning flashes, recorded a glimpse of the van entering Miller Station Road. They had something to go on.

'Tracker' looked at a yellow triangle on the GPS Google Map screen. It was the same surveillance drone, back in action, lingering in the air 8,000 feet above the countryside. Morrison called it back into service to back up the fourteen agents combing the rural landscape. It, too, searched for a white van and persons of Middle Eastern appearance

In the early morning shadows, Edhi's three-man laser guidance team left the farmhouse and walked past the barn where the U-Haul truck was hidden, then hiked into a large tract of Pennsylvania forest. They disappeared under the thick canopy of towering hemlock, oak, beech, maple, tulip and birch trees.

Ten miles away, John Dolan and his wife, Diane, awoke at sunrise. She made a pot of organic coffee while John scrambled the eggs he collected outside from their free-roaming chickens.

The aroma of freshly cut garlic, onions, green peppers, parsley, chives, basil and thyme searing in a pan of virgin olive oil permeated the small kitchen. John poured the scrambled eggs into the pan. In four minutes, they sat down and feasted.

Diane commented, "Amazing how your garden herbs and veggies kick up the flavor of scrambled eggs."

"Must be in my Irish genes. My father taught me how to cultivate a bountiful garden in our small suburban backyard outside Syracuse, New York. He learned the art of gardening from his father in Kailkenny County, Ireland. God bless their soles."

"What time is the contact?"

"In one hour. We better get ready."

The Dolans blended in well. They enjoyed nature and for the past fifteen years ran a hiking and canoeing business called French Creek Outfitters Both Irish Catholics, they remained active in church events and rarely missed a mass at St. Patrick Church in Erie.

No one would have guessed they secretly championed the radical Islamic cause and were part of an underground network of Muslim sympathizers. Edhi recruited them, years ago, when they trolled radical sites at an internet café in Erie, Pa.

For several years, Edhi sensed the Dolan's would never take the leap from being keyboard warriors to actually committing a terrorist attack, so he kept them isolated from his network of sleeper attack cells lurking inside America.

With Edhi's expertise, they stayed under the radar of the seventeen agencies comprising the U.S. Intelligence Community (IC). In their late fifties, they were U.S. citizens by birth and much older than the typical al-Qaeda and ISIS supporter, who was age twenty-five or less. They never traveled to the Middle East, donated money or supported terrorists in Syria or Iraq and remained distant from those cells plotting a domestic terrorist attack... except for today.

Their race, age, religion, travels, social class, personal interests and hobbies, shopping habits, education and family background were atypical of the typical Muslim sympathizer profile that the deep data mining systems in the IC constantly prowled for online.

Both John and Diane ran social media sites. Their Twitter account used nodes, amplifiers and shout-outs to promote their French Creek Outfitters business by spreading the joys of outdoor hiking, canoeing and bird watching. Their Facebook account, as well, shied away from any mention of Islam.

They loaded their Subaru Outback with snacks and drove down the long, winding driveway to Route 408. A beautiful meadow was on one side, a dense hemlock forest on the other. They stopped to look at the bluebirds that nested inside the nest boxes along their bluebird trail.

The serene and rustic living calmed John, who heretofore lived a life of pitiable self-image and poor social relationships. In his younger days, he was uncertain as to what his life goals and career choice should be. Now, pushing sixty, he felt as if he had firm roots and was grounded in a purposeful lifestyle.

But, along the road to finding himself, John had periods of extreme anger and violent thoughts. Coupled with substance abuse, his self-doubt and feelings of emptiness and boredom sent him searching for an identity.

He grew to dislike Christianity and Catholicism, for neither view of mankind's function on earth gave him purposefulness or ameliorated his feelings of estrangement from mainstream American society. When American right-wing religious extremists like Sarah Palin spouted hateful speeches against "angry atheists armed with attorneys who wanted to kick God out of the public square," he thought of the xenophobic and racist protests against building a mosque near the 9/11 site or the NYPD practice of profiling Muslims, and the growing number of hate crimes against Muslims across America.

As the right-wing evangelicals gained political power, the number of abortion clinic bombings and murdering of doctors, nurses and staff who worked in them rose. More and more homosexuals were roughed up, murdered and excommunicated from parishes and churches. His older brother, whom he worshiped as a youngster, announced one day that he was gay. Several months later, he committed suicide after his lifetime membership to a Baptist church was terminated by the preacher and church council.

John could care less if Jesus or Muhammad occupied every "fucking public square in America" as he once told his wife, who agreed. They first met each other at an out-patient psychiatric clinic. Both were diagnosed with Borderline Personality Disorder by two different psychiatrists. They soon fell in love.

Both were raised in strict religious families, John by devout Irish Catholic parents, Diane by a hallowed southern Baptist father. Her mother died giving birth to her. It was "God's will!" as her father rationalized. Her malleable and indoctrinated child's mind couldn't accept that fact and as teen she hated god for taking her mom away from her.

Their childhood memories were filled with corporal punishment and religious dogma and indoctrination: Sunday school, confirmation, reverent youth groups and saintly summer camps.

They rebelled against this proselytization as teens and both were shunned by their parents and ostracized by their respective god-fearing church community.

Now, fifty years later, neither Diane or John saw much difference between the religious brainwashing they once experienced and ISIS youth toting AK-47's and holding up severed human heads. They felt both were wicked, but the rationale for radical Islamic extremism seemed to make more sense to them. Little wonder that Edhi made sure they were taken well care of, financially.

Diane peered through her binoculars. "We've got bluebirds nesting in six boxes!"

"Great! We'll band the babies when the eggs hatch. Time for the meet up, then next stop... Cleveland."

They drove onto Route 408 and headed to the meetup site. After several minutes, they turned off on to a remote road that threaded through a tiny village called Teepleville that consisted of a large barn, Amish farmhouse and a church. They exited the hamlet and meandered through a section of the Erie Wildlife Refuge for several miles.

They passed several cyclists along the way, but didn't pay much attention to them. After their Subaru Outback disappeared around a curve, the bicyclists stopped and a woman spoke into a microphone attached to the inside of her collar. "Team nine here requesting a '10-37'."

'Tracker' stared at the blip on her GPS screen indicating their location.

"Go ahead."

"Pennsylvania plate F, V, R, seven, eight, eight...Frank, Victor, Robert, seven, eight, eight. Side paneling logo, French Creek Outfitters."

"Hold on." 'Tracker' called General Morrison on the secure sat phone and gave him the plate numbers. He taped them into Jeannie, which compared them to federal, state and local government databases which were updated every four hours.

A half-minute later the results came in. The Dolan's vehicle was clean- no fugitive wants or warrants, no suspended or revoked driver's license. Jeannie also checked into credit card expenditures to see if they made any suspicious purchases or travel destinations. Nothing out of the ordinary.

Jeannie also performed a check on their business, French Creek Outfitters, through the Better Business Bureau and local and state business databases. It was reported to have an outstanding reputation and was established fifteen years ago.

Morrison spoke to 'Tracker.' "NIF...nothing in file."

When 'Tracker' relayed the background check results to Team-9, they proceeded onward towards the village of Teepleville, trying to spot a white utility van or persons of Middle Eastern ethnicity. The law-abiding driver of the Subaru had red hair with the Irish name "Dolan" and ran an outback business in the area for quite a while...no suspicions raised.

Dolan drove for six miles along the backroads of Pennsylvania, then suddenly pulled over onto the berm of Teepleville Flats Road. Both he and Diane looked up and down the roadway for several minutes. No one bicycling or hiking, no cars approaching. He switched on the four-wheel drive and proceeded along a dirt and gravel path that meandered up a steep hillside. It was an old gas company road the crews used to check on a capped gas pipeline at the top.

The Subaru rocked back and forth as the wheels fell into eroded ruts and crawled over exposed rocks. Tree branches scraped down the side door panels as it ascended the timberland pathway. When the gas company bulldozed the trail through the forest to the hilltop summit, they must not have planned to maintain it. The forest seemed to be reclaiming its lost territory.

The laser-designator team hiked through the forest for an hour after they bid farewell to Edhi and left the farm safe house. It actually felt cool under the dense canopy of trees, even though the temperature was eighty-eight degrees in the open meadows. The three backpacks they carried contained the disassembled laser-guiding devices, each part disguised and appearing like a normal item one would take to a baseball game.

In the distance, the sun gleamed down through a clearing in the shadowy forest. As they approached it, they saw their contact car...a Subaru Outback. A red-haired man and his wife sat inside. The trio loaded their deadly backpacks and Cleveland Indians paraphernalia in the back, then placed an Indians bumper sticker on the rear fender and an Indians flag on the antennae.

There was ample room for the attack cell members to slouch down below the windows and remain unseen. As per Edhi's orders, they would remain hunkered down until reaching the Ohio border.

John Dolan drove slowly back down the gas pipeline road. His mission was to deliver the three men to a motel in Cleveland, then visit the famous Flats area and buy his wife dinner at Flannery's Irish Pub in the Gateway District. He was to use cash only and order Irish food: Flannery's famous *Shepherd's Pie* and their beef and lamb Irish stew. After the casual meal, they were to drive directly back to their Pennsylvania home.

Diane spoke to the Middle Eastern passengers. "From the looks of your dress, it looks like you'll be going to the Indians playoff game the day after tomorrow."

One of the terrorists handed her an envelope containing $15,000 cash and replied. "Yes, we will enjoy the American game of baseball." *But we will enjoy killing your American president and a thousand infidels much more.*

Bailey Town, North Bimini, Bahamas
(GPS: 25°44'28.6"N 79°17'13.5"W)
A rusted-out cargo van parked off the Queen's Highway in Bailey Town, a hundred feet north of Edith's Pizza. Although the van would be listed at a Blue Book value of $900, surveillance equipment worth over ten million dollars set in the back.

Two CBIF agents monitored the equipment. Corey and Morrison called them in to back up the two Bimini CI teams. They were CBIF moles inside the NSA and flew into South Bimini Airport an hour ago. 'Frank' had the aged cargo van waiting for them at the North Bimini ferryboat parking lot. The network tower device was housed in four large suit cases which Bimini Customs didn't bother to open.

The two reinforcements sat snuggly in the back of the van next to the miniaturized cell network "tower." Unbeknownst to the four targets sitting in an outdoor booth at Edith's, the tower emitted radio waves that sent a command to each of their cell phone's baseband chip, or antennae. Even though the targets believed their cell phones were powered off, they weren't. The tower remotely activated the microphones in all four cell phones and each phone automatically connected to it.

Senator Warren, Mark Serwin, Shahid El-Sayed and BHH leaned forward and talked softly to one another in the wooden booth while waiting for their conch and lobster pizza. Two of their cell phones lay face up on the table, the screens remained black since they had shut them off, but the microphones started running, picking up everything they said.

Fifty yards south of Edith's Pizza was a huge pile of empty conch shells lining a patch of mangroves. On the other side of it, 'Frank' stood in waist-deep water, fishing with rod and lure for yellow-tail snapper. He listened in through ear plugs to everything the tower recorded.

He recognized BHH's voice. "The deal is, I deliver the satchel to Eamal Batoor and Khoury Kassim at the fuckin' chicken farm and the moment I do, Sean Branagh agrees to deposit the cash into my secret account at his Nassau bank."

El-Sayed said, "Yes, that is the agreement. If the deep data mining algorithm and software you carry is what you say it is, we will compromise America's ability to hunt us down."

"Believe me. It does everything I said it does. When I see the ten-thousand bills with Benjamin Franklin's picture on each one, I forget everything."

El-Sayed replied, "Not to worry. The money was smuggled in by Abner Orival from Haiti and it sits in Sandoval's safe at the mansion. Sean Branagh will return to Nassau on Sandoval's yacht and deposit it in your account."

'Frank's' heart almost leaped out of his chest, not because a yellow-tail just hit his lure, but because of what BHH asked Warren: "So, what's the plans? When are we taking off for Abaco?"

Their conservation stopped as a lobster fisherman in a boat powered by a small outboard motor purred past them and stopped at Edith's. He waded on to the beach, toting a pail of freshly-caught spiny lobsters, and knocked on the back door of the restaurant only a few steps away from the outdoor bench where the four targets sat.

The cook opened the back door and 'Frank' heard the conversation picked up by the compromised cell phones. The fisherman sounded angry. "I make a deal wid you. Fifty dollars for da bucket a lobsta… take it or leave it!"

The cook replied, "Thirty-five and no mo'."

'Frank' heard the reply, "Ya go fuck yo' self. I got kids ta feed!" Moments later the outboard began purring again and 'Frank'

watched the lobster man speed away, his dreadlocks flying in the wind under the Rastafarian hat.

The targets began talking quietly again, totally unaware that their seemingly inactive cell phones had been turned into microphones and transmitted everything they said to CBIF agents.

BHH repeated his question. "So, when are we taking off? When we landing at the mansion?"

Senator Warren answered. "Tomorrow…Thursday at 9:45pm. It's a forty-minute flight from the South Bimini Airport. We'll touch down on Abaco at 10:25pm."

Bingo! 'Frank's' heart started pounding again. He remained outwardly calm and slowly waded back onto shore with his catch, then climbed back into his golf cart and slowly putted away.

When beyond sight of Edith's and the targets, he slammed the pedal to the metal and sped to the CBIF safe house to contact Corey.

Episode 59

The narco-terrorist alliance

The Abaco Poultry, LTD mansion
Abaco, Bahamas
(GPS: 26.128607, -77.195695)

Devon rolled the server cart down the plush carpet on the second floor of the mansion. He stopped at the closed door to Sandoval's office where Bolan Togas and Pierre Cherestal stood guard. They inspected the cart for bombs, guns and bugs. When satisfied, Togas gently knocked on the door, then opened it and let Devon in.

Six men sat around a Cherrywood conference table that looked like one a Las Vegas casino mogul would possess. Sandoval stayed quiet as Devon served drinks, including the Arak for Eamal Batoor and Khoury Kassim. When the case of Arak arrived from the Hotel Montana in Port-au-Prince, Devon stored it in the wine cellar of the mansion. Corey told him about the duplicate bottle containing a transponder that the Haiti CI team slipped into the case.

When Sandoval ordered the two Araks over the intercom, Devon stepped down into the basement wine cellar, found the bottle containing the transponder and brought it back up into the kitchen. He opened it and cleverly hid the transponder in a pile of fish innards lying on a newspaper on the counter.

After placing the drinks in front of each man seated around the conference table, including the two Arak "camel sweat" servings in front of Batoor and Kassim, Sandoval ordered him to place the bowl of conch fritters on the matching credenza and leave the room.

Sean and Patrick Branagh followed him to the credenza and quickly filled their plates with conch fritters. They knew Devon was skilled at preparing them. Both Irish rejects poured hot sauce on the fritters and returned to the table, enjoying the deep-fried balls of conch meat mixed with minced sweet peppers, onions and tomato paste. Devon placed napkins in front of them, then promptly wheeled the tray out of the room and returned to the kitchen. He had some malodourous fish innards, along with the transponder, to dispose of in the ocean.

Sandoval focused his attention on Sean Branagh. "We appreciate you launderin' the money for our operations. You hide it all nicely in yo' bank. This time you got more than ever to take back to Nassau."

Abner Orival said, "I'll say. My smuggling boat from Haiti was low in the water...ten bank bags full of cold cash. Da Royal Bahamian Defense Force...the RBDF...avoided stopping us as usual."

Sandoval replied, "Yeah, part o' my drug pipeline...I pay off one a da commanders well. Da drugs, money, and humans are smuggled through on his shift. And dat be why, Mister Branagh, you dun have ta worry about the Americans finding ya out...no electronic money transfers...no paper trail. It all be done by human couriers toting cash. You stayin' under da radar of DHS."

Kassim Khoury, alias 'John Doe-istan' raised his glass of Arak in salute to Sean Branagh. "We are indebted to you for laundering money for our Curacao operation. Our cell was large, sixteen members, and the luxury chalet outside Willemstad, our safe house, was paid for by you. The millions we raised in the Tri-Border Area was hidden in the bank accounts you so stealthily create. Paying off the local police, purchasing fake passports, buying the luxury condo, flying back and forth to and from the Middle East to Venezuela, then to Curacao...we couldn't have sustained that operation without you."

Sean Branagh seemed proud of himself. "Thank you. Me and my brother here know how to take advantage of the Bahamian secrecy laws."

Eamal Batoor said, "I hope so. The thought of prison scares me. I was freed from the Saraposa Prison in Kandahar back in 2008 by my Taliban friends. I'll never go back to any prison again."

Branagh replied, "You have nothing to worry about. If any court in any country, including your own nations...even if the U.S. law enforcement tries to get info on your accounts, you are protected in the Bahamas because of our bank secrecy laws. There aren't any tax or fiscal information-sharing agreements with any other country. You are the only ones who have the privilege to access your accounts in my bank."

Khoury asked, "As I understand it, my name is not on the account documents."

"Correct. There is a Code of Ethics that states I have to know who I'm dealing with...to prevent illegal activities."

The six men burst into laughter, then Sandoval asked, "We can trust that you consider us all upstandin' citizens, right?"

Sean Branagh knew what Sandoval would do to him if he ever divulged his illegalities to law enforcement. "Of course, Virgilio. I know all my upstanding clients by name...but all your accounts are numbered... you don't have names, you're all just numbers and that's the only thing my bank employees see."

Batoor asked, "How many guys like us have you set up accounts for?"

Sean Branagh swallowed the last bite of conch fritter. "Plenty. I get people from the U.S., Europe...all over. They hide their money from tax collectors, the DEA and other law enforcement dudes. Hell, there's over seven trillion bucks hidden in offshore accounts throughout the Caribbean."

Khoury asked, "Is that why you never have us visit your Nassau bank, so your employees don't associate our faces with the numbers?"

"Exactly."

Sandoval added, "And dats why I be sailin' him to Nassau on my yacht with money bags full o' cash in two days. He deposits it in each of your accounts his self."

Patrick Branagh spoke for the first time. "And, if we do need to have a bank meeting, we all meet here at the mansion or in Nassau at my Irish Frenzy Pub."

Sean Branagh said, "We don't cart the money directly through my bank's front door either. When Sandoval's yacht docks in Nassau, we'll carry it to the Irish Frenzy in suitcases and store it there in my brother's safe. When he makes nightly deposits from the day's receipts, he throws in thirty thousand from you guys. It adds up, a month of daily deposits from the Irish Frenzy totals one million bucks. I deposit it into your accounts, personally."

Sandoval was at the credenza making himself another Bahama Mama from the rum and mixes Devon left. "Yeah, we all be numbers wid no faces attached. Da Branagh brothers…dey make sure you guys never visit da bank. Ya submit a few pages o' paperwork by mail to da Branaghs and dey handle da rest."

Sean Branagh looked pleased. "Yes, when I received the paperwork that you guys sent me by snail mail, I wrote in Abaco Poultry, LTD as the company you're associated with. It makes things look good, just in case. In the Bahamas, a company isn't required to list the names of its officers and directors. You don't have to file financial statements here either. I write in the poultry operation because it's incorporated here in the Bahamas, a stable country which is a member of the British Commonwealth."

Sandoval chipped in, "Dat means deres no income tax, capital gains or inheritance tax. We keep it all."

Branagh added, "Nor is there a tax on the interest earned from the jumbo money market CD's I purchase for you."

Khoury, Batoor, Orival and Sandoval stared in silence at the Branagh brothers. They realized these money launderers were a narco/terrorist dream come true. Abaco Poultry, LTD was a legitimate shell company operating in the Bahamas, thanks to the Honorable Alfred Moss, M.P., Bahamian Agricultural Minister. The operation made a profit whereas many shell companies do not, since they don't do real business and are used as front operations by people trying to hide their wealth.

Sandoval noted Sean Branagh munch down the last morsel of conch fritters on his plate. It was time to excuse both Irishmen from the meeting before they refilled their plates again. "Yes, we all thank ya for your launderin' abilities. You can leave da meetin' now and join da others downstairs. Dey be enjoyin' da nice batch o' beautiful women I bring up from Cali. In two days, I will transport both of ya back to Nassau on my yacht. You will be totin' plenty o' cold, hard cash."

Sean and Patrick Branagh left the room with smiling faces. Sandoval, Batoor Emal, Kassim Khoury and Abner Orival sat in silence until Orival finally spoke. "Those two Irish bastards are greedier than all of us put together."

Sandoval agreed. "Yeah, dats why I hire people like dem along my drug pipelines. Dey'd turn dere grandmas into ashes fo' a fifty-cent piece. Neither knows dey be funding a mortar attack or helpin' ta bribe BHH to hand over da Penumbra Database...but even if dey did, dey wouldn't care. Dey'd still take our money, wash it clean through the Nassau bank...and let a few thousand Americans die."

Batoor Emal added, "They helped us get our hands on the most complex data mining algorithm U.S. intelligence has ever had. BHH has a numbered account in their Nassau bank and he'll be paid well... the infidel Americans are about to hand over their counterterrorism capabilities to us." He got up and poured himself another drink from the bottle of Arak that Ledard left on the credenza, then loaded up a plate of conch fritters and returned to his seat. He swiveled his chair around to face Sandoval and asked, "So, when is BHH arriving?"

Kassim Khoury chipped in. "Yeah, and while we're at it, let's review the complete timeline once again."

Sandoval appeared drunk and slurred his words. He waved his hand unsteadily and pointed at Abner Orival. "My money, human and drug-smugglin' accomplice from Haiti...why don you go over da master plan and answer both dere questions."

Orival stood up obediently and nodded politely to Khoury and Emal. He had smuggled dozens of their radical Islamic warriors into the Bahamas from Haiti and they had paid him well for it. He, too, had a fat bank account in Branagh's Nassau bank. "BHH is arriving tomorrow, Thursday night after ten. Senator Warren and his Chief of Staff Serwin, along with Shahid El-Sayed will be on the plane with him."

Batoor asked, "When are we going to get the Penumbra Database?"

Sandoval broke in. "Immediately...when BHH walks through da front door, he come up here to my office with Shahid El-Sayed. Warren and Serwin be kept in da dark bout' it. My Cali whores ready to suck dem off in da downstairs sauna." He pointed to Kassim and Batoor. "Both a you will be here along with Sean Branagh. I'll get da bag o' ten-thousand bills wid da picture o' Ben Franklin on each one and show it to him. Den, he hand ova da satchel containin' da complete Penumbra Database software."

Kassim asked, "What happens next?"

Sandoval slid open a hidden drawer, took out a 9mm Beretta M9A3 pistol and laid it on top of the polished Cherrywood conference table. The flat dark-earth cerakote coating made it look deadly. He then retrieved a silencer from the drawer and screwed it onto the threaded barrel. "Den I shoot him in da head and have Bolan Tougas and Pierre Cherestal dispose of da body. Dis beautiful weapon was given ta me by none other den Juan Rojas, da retired Colombian Army officer who Lieutenant General Castano gets ta supply me wid weapons."

Sandoval waved the weapon in the air then said to Orival, "Continue."

Orival stared at Sandoval briefly, then continued. He hoped he would never have to stare down the end of the M9A3. "Once all the transactions are made, Sean Branagh and his brother will board the yacht moored outside and sail to Nassau to make the deposits in the numbered accounts."

Sandoval broke in. "Branagh will be sailing to Nassau on my yacht before da attack in America goes down."

Batoor gulped down his Arak. "Me, my friend here, Khoury, and Shahid El-Sayed… we're dying to get the Penumbra Database, but the mortar attack against the infidel Americans is just as important. We planned and funded the operation with Asif Qadeer Edhi. Since he was trained by the Taliban in the Federally Administered Tribal Area, the FATA, he has helped us create and train jihadi sleeper cells throughout Europe and inside America. I don't want it all to go down in flames. We want President Robert Rhinehart blown to bits…along with thousands of infidels in the stadium. You will not fail us, will you?"

Orival replied, "We will not fail you. The Cleveland Indians will be playing in a playoff for the World Series at Progressive Field, in Cleveland. The game starts Friday, at Noon. Edhi's laser beam designator team will be inside the stadium. At 1pm the mortars will be fired from a truck parked in The Flats area in Cleveland. Edhi's laser-designator team will guide them directly into the Champion Suite, where President Rhinehart will be…with his son. The rounds are powerful and will destroy the entire balcony and blast through the windows behind it."

Sandoval said, "General Castano and Juan Rojas…dey both tell me how powerful dese 140mm mortar rounds are. Da entire suite will be leveled…and rememba, dere are twenty of dem. After the first four or five are fired at da Champion Suite, the rest will be guided to the 45,000 spectators…Edhi told me dats how many tickets were sold."

Eamal Batoor got up and retrieved the Arak bottle and filled his empty glass, then Kassim's. They stood up, faced each other and clicked their glasses together.

Kassim smiled and said, "Tomorrow is a big day for us, my friend. Months of planning and now the grand finale…we take possession of the most sophisticated deep data-mining, anti-terrorist defense the infidels have in their arsenal…"

Batoor finished the sentence. "…and at 2:45pm Friday, we will slaughter the president of the United States along with thousands of his infidels… *jazakAllahu khair* ..may Allah reward us with good!"

Thomas Bay beach, South Abaco, Bahamas
(GPS: 26.128607, -77.195695)
It was 9pm on a dark, overcast night. Corey stood with his eight CI agents a few yards inside a Caribbean pine and palmetto palm forest that looked out over the white sands of Thomas Bay beach.

Corey chose this landing spot because of the isolation, cover and shelter it provided. Large boulders jutted out into the bay from the forest and the small inlet they landed on was invisible from the north. It lay six miles south of the Abaco Poultry mansion.

They pulled two yacht rafts over the beach and hid them inside the forest, then swept their tracks like a greenkeeper rakes a golf course sand trap. Corey double-checked to make sure their footprints and the raft drag marks were erased.

Occasionally, the moon peeked through gaps in the clouds and illuminated the waters of Thomas Bay, making the gentle waves glistened. Team-11's yacht, moored a half mile offshore, was barely visible. The used yacht was a good investment that Morrison made, upon Corey's request. It moved operational gear, weapons and undercover agents throughout the Bahamas, Turks & Caicos, Haiti, Dominican Republic, Puerto Rico and the U.S. and British Virgin Islands.

The three men and two women of Team-11 were invaluable to CBIF. They masqueraded as spoiled American rich kids who scuba dove and partied everywhere they sailed. Corey recalled how, earlier, they started a limbo party at the Conch Inn Marina's pool, which he joined in on. Constance happened to stop in and ate a hearty meal at the Curly Tail Restaurant, then "accidentally" met the group and joined in on the poolside fun.

He thought about how expertly the pre-raid ruse was carried out. Chop-Chop turned up the boom box and set the makeshift limbo bar lower and lower while she shimmied underneath. A few unwitting on-lookers admired her body and agility while the other team members ordered beers that Shianna brought to them from the Sunset Bar. They feigned chugging them down and emptied the beer bottles and refilled them with water during frequent trips to the bathroom. They had to have their wits and reflexes finely tuned for the operation they were about to begin.

As prearranged by Corey, the Team-10 couple staying across the street at the Lofty Fig showed up for lunch at the Curly Tail Restaurant. 'Chop Chop' ran inside to greet them and insisted that they hold off from ordering from the menu and eat a large dolphin fish she caught in the Sea of Abaco.

She pretended to be a bit tipsy and yelled out to the poolside partiers for someone to walk back to the yacht and get the mahi mahi. The Curly Tail staff graciously agreed to prepare it for every-one. Team-10 joined the others at poolside while waiting for their mahi mahi delicacy to arrive.

Corey engineered the entire social gathering to create an illusion-ary shell to operate within. CBIF's tactics called for clandestine oper-ations to be openly visible to all, despite the underlying furtive intent. Shianna, the Conch Inn lodgers, the restaurant staff and patrons took it all in with amusement. No one imagined these partiers were about to bring down a large narco/terrorist cell that operated in their midst, nor would anyone suspect them when the raid was over and the dust settled.

Shortly, the staff brought out the dolphinfish meal to the nine agents, served in three ways: blackened, fried, and with a coconut mango recipe. Shianna made sure her friend in the kitchen added a side dish of johnnycake and conch chowder.

After finishing off the fish delicacy, they decided to take a joy ride on the yacht. They had little difficulty guiding the large boat through the shallow reefs, sand banks, tight little cays and inlets dotting the Sea of Abaco. It took four hours to reach Thomas Bay from the Conch Inn Marina in Marsh Harbor. Along the way, they retrieved the weapons and equipment from the locked safe in the yacht's salon.

Sailing out of the Conch Inn Marina, they motored due east to Elbow Cay then south to the Tilloo Cut on the southern end. The cut was between Elbow Cay and Tilloo Cay and allowed them to travel out of the Sea of Abaco into the Atlantic Ocean. While 'Chop Chop' slowly steered the yacht through, Corey stared at Tahiti Beach once again. Thoughts of Danielle resurfaced. *The white sand, verdant breadfruit tree and coconut palm forest that lay beyond where we made love, relaxing on the talcum-powdered sand, drinking wine...*

A male member of Team-11 yelled down to Corey. "Sir, we'll be at Pete's Pub in Little Harbor soon."

"OK, moor offshore and we'll take the two rafts in."

Once through the cut, Corey instructed them to sail south on the Atlantic side, using Tilloo Cay and Tilloo National Park to hide them from view from the Abaco mainland. They sailed past Lynyard Cay and moored in Little Harbor Cay, then took the rafts to Pete's Pub.

Two Team-11 members remained on the yacht while the rest docked at Pete's Pub and hiked around the remote, lush surroundings. They admired the works of the late bronze sculptor, Randolph Johnston. The bartender answered their questions about the Johnston's family, who settled in the harbor over seventy years ago and built a Bronze Art Foundry to cast their renowned sculptures.

They met Peter, the son of Randolph Johnston. He proudly told them how he continued his father's craft that depicted, in bronze and gold, the marine wildlife in the pristine waters around Abaco.

The masquerade continued while local patrons and several second homeowners sat inside the pub, eating mango grilled grouper and coconut cracked conch. Dolphin, yellowfin tuna and wahoo were on the menu, too.

Starting at five on Friday afternoons is Happy Hour at Pete's Pub. Locals, tourists and second-home owners come and enjoy five-dollar *Blasters* and special-menu items.

Corey timed the stop perfectly. He signaled it was time to leave.

Shortly, the Happy Hour began and he wanted to avoid the crowd.

They returned to the yacht and continued sailing south past Cherokee Sound, a boat building and smack fishing village. A few of their locally-built smack boats headed directly towards them from the village dock. Corey kept an eye on them to make sure they didn't follow. He trusted no one. He inspected each unique homemade boat through binoculars. The multi-sails on each vessel flapped in the brisk breeze. Only Cherokee fishermen were on board.

As the yacht made its way further south towards Crossing Rocks, the smack boats passed and continued out into the Atlantic. *Cherokee sound. Danielle loved to fish there. We'd drive down the Great Abaco Highway and get chum for bait, then fish for mutton snapper and hogfish. We'd trade a case of Kalik beer for buckets of "conch slop," the scraps left over after the Crossing Rock fishermen cleaned their conch. Danielle and I walked through the quaint village...so quiet and peaceful...the narrow streets, pastel-painted houses surrounded by ocean beaches. We'd go there often... an escape from our CBIF duties. Goodbye, my dear Danielle. I will continue my life with Constance, but will never cease searching for those who murdered you...and why they did it. I will find the answer... when we raid the mansion*

Corey had 'Chop Chop' maintain a due south course. The Abaco shoreline veered forty-five degrees inland past Cherokee Sound and by the time they sailed six miles further south, they were ten miles off the shoreline of the tiny village of Crossing Rocks. Corey instructed her to continue south for seven more miles, then steer directly inland and moor two miles offshore in Thompson's Bay at GPS coordinates

26.029883, -77.146159. Corey knew that General Morrison would position a stealth IMINT satellite along these pre-arranged positions.

Corey watched Constance and the others slip on their black special ops suits and daub black, green and brown patterns onto their faces with camouflage paint. They put on their backpacks, turned on the infrared goggles, shouldered their weapons, then gave him the "we're ready" sign. There would be no more talking.

Corey pointed at them with his left hand then raised the right one with all five fingers spread out vertically. It meant, "Let's Go."

They began their six-mile trek under a dark forest canopy of towering Caribbean pines and through thick undercover of thatch sisal, sword bush, thatch palm, wild coffee and century plants.

General Morrison sat in the War Room at CBIF HQ, staring at nine dots superimposed on his computer's satellite view of South Abaco. The group of dots, emitted by transponders affixed to their gear, began to advance northward through a thick forest. He began chewing on his Montecristo.

"Good luck, my brave friends."

Episode 60

Jungle reconnaissance

The nine agents moved slowly through the palmetto palm under-growth. Instead of spreading out, Corey decided to proceed in a single column. He led, with Constance a few feet behind him in case he needed her expertise. She knew the 20,000-acre parrot preserve better than anyone else. With their infrared googles, despite the total darkness, they could easily make out objects several hundred feet away. While Corey and Constance watched ahead, the other seven agents behind them watched the periphery and flank.

The deafening shrill from thousands of tree frogs drowned out any noise the agents made. Corey could hear the constant shuffling of land crabs moving out of their way through thick patches of low-lying palmetto palm and fern-like coontie plants. For some reason, the crabs made him flashback to the Tiki Hut. He pictured himself chugging down a Kalik beer while Dillon prepared his favorite lunch: land crabs and rice.

As Corey and Constance stalked past another patch of under-growth, a form exploded out from under a palmetto palm. Nine Glock 30, .45 caliber semi-automatics with silencers drew and were about to blast the attacker, but it veered away at the last second and fled. It was a large wild boar hiding underneath a large palmetto leaf. As they silently approached, the hog, with four-inch tusks, panicked. The urge to fight, then to flee passed through its mind.

The jungle turmoil silenced the tree frogs. The nine agents crouched down below the underbrush and remained still for a full minute. One could hear a pin drop. No other figures or movement were distinguished through the darkness with their infrared vision. After several minutes, the tree frogs resumed their cacophony of shrills. Corey held up five fingers with palm wide open. They proceeded.

The wild boar encounter startled General Morrison almost as much as it did Corey and his agents. The aging spymaster stared at the large screen in the War Room. The nine smaller screens around the edges of the main monitor displayed live streams of the happening. A hovering stealth satellite received the transmissions from the miniaturized video cams affixed to each agent's uniform and relayed them to him.

Morrison clicked on one and enlarged it, then rewound it to view the encounter. Sure enough, it was a large hog. The beast's white tusks showed clearly as it decided to halt the attack and flee at the last moment. *Fuck. So many unexpected things can go wrong on these ops.* He gnawed down nervously on his Montecristo.

Corey held up his hand with four fingers extended and thumb folded in. The eight warriors behind him halted and knelt down: "Pause, no threats ahead." Corey looked at the Satellite-Link Connection screen which was set on night vision with a greatly subdued light. Nine dots in a line marked their position. His first destination was the waypoint that Constance marked during her tour of the Parrot Preserve with Team-10. It was a thousand feet ahead.

He motioned for Constance to crawl up to him. She nimbly duck-walked the fifteen feet, despite the backpack, dart rifle and special ops gear dangling from her belt.

Corey eschewed airways communication between agents during special ops missions unless it was absolutely necessary. The enemy could be listening in. He preferred the old-fashioned way and whispered to Constance, "We'll head to the first waypoint and break for five minutes, take off our gear and recheck it, stretch some aching muscles, then proceed nonstop to your second waypoint bordering the mansion grounds. Let the others know."

They briefly stared at each other through protruding night vision goggles, making a potentially romantic encounter appear prosaic. Constance crept back to inform the others.

As she huddled with her comrades and relayed the plans, an overpowering uncertainty flooded Corey's mind. *I should have talked her out of coming. No, she insisted...to avenge her brother's death. She wants to bring Sandoval and his narco-terrorist network down, so her brother didn't die in vain. I'm being selfish, thinking of myself... of the hurt I'll feel if she gets killed. I will protect her with my life so we can spend the rest of our lives together...I love her.*

For the next half hour, they snuck through the jungle as inconspicuously as a jaguar on the prowl. The tree frog chorus blotted out any noise they made. In fact, they moved so quietly that the wary critters never stopped their shrill calls as they passed by.

Upon reaching the clearing, Corey remained vigilant as they checked their equipment. He listened to hear if a frog chorus stopped suddenly. That would mean human presence, for the frogs rarely grow silent if a raccoon, boar or other local animal slinks by them. It was possible that poachers could be in the forest and Corey would have to circumnavigate around them. The team had to remain invisible.

Corey checked the timeline on the SAT-LC. The yellow triangular mark from the transponder that Team-5 planted on Senator Warren's Cessna at South Bimini Airport flashed on and off. 'Frank' and his two Bimini teams were monitoring Warren, Serwin, El-Sayed and BHH. He'd report in if all four did *not* board the plane. The transponder will indicate when they fly out of South Bimini and their flight to Marsh Harbor Airport. Upon touchdown, CBIF agents, Deputy Commander

Ellison Rolle along with four uniformed RBPF officers and Milo's two detective sons would arrest them.

Rolle would become an instant national hero for making the arrests. The plan was for him to rush to the mansion after the airport arrests and arrest any surviving Middle Eastern guards along with Abner Orival for human smuggling.

The eight agents examined their gear. All thumbs went up. Corey signaled for them to proceed. The column of nine silently left the clearing and continued stalking through the dark jungle. The tree fog chorus grew louder as they skirted a marshy area. The night was hot and humid.

As they moved nonstop toward the mansion for the next hour, Corey thought about the furtive group meeting at the Hibiscus Beach Inn safe house in Nassau. Rolle met CBIF's mole working as an FBI attaché inside the U.S. Embassy, the embassy consular himself, and three CBIF agents who assumed diplomatic cover in the embassy and would accompany him when he arrested Warren, Serwin, El-Sayed and BHH at the Marsh Harbor Airport. They assured Rolle that he would become a national hero.

Despite the sweat beads dripping down his face and an occasional poke from a prickly-pear bush, Corey managed to smile. He admired Milo's two detective sons who would assist Rolle in the arrest. Milo was so proud that they were promoted to detective rank in the RBPF, but he didn't know Deputy Commander Ellison Rolle was a paid informant recruited by Corey and worked for the same mysterious organization as he.

Milo wasn't aware that Corey gave Rolle a hefty stipend for choosing both his sons for further schooling to become detectives. *Milo's sons unknowingly work for us. When I was in charge of New Providence-7 years ago, I had Rolle place individuals under surveillance that CBIF targeted... individuals we needed to gather intelligence about. Rolle assigned Milo's sons to partake in actual arrests of suspects that I considered "of interest." Now, I've returned to*

Abaco and am having them arrest a U.S. senator. It's a dicey assign-ment...that's why I had the U.S. consular attend the Hibiscus Beach Inn meeting. He assured Rolle that the arrest would be appreciated by President Rhinehart, who would meet privately with the Bahamian Prime Minister.

Rhinehart would announce on TV that a terrorist plot against America was thwarted with the help of Deputy Commander Rolle of the Royal Bahamian Police Force. Full credit for the airport arrests and mansion raid would be given to Rolle, in that he swiftly acted upon information given to him by the consular of the U.S. embassy in Nassau. Rolle and Milo's sons would become heroes for capturing a corrupt U.S. senator and arresting armed Middle Eastern terrorists smuggled into the Bahamas for a planned attack against the United States.

Corey came to the edge of the thick subtropical pine forest and held up a closed fist. The column behind him halted and knelt down. They wore tight-fitting, black cargo-style pants and black sweaters pulled over bullet-proof vests. Corey signaled for them to pull the dark balaclavas down over their faces.

The towering Caribbean pines gave way to a large area of low- ly-ing allamanda, aloe, bougainvillea and century plants. The last way-point that Constance selected, a large pile of boulders bordering Abaco Poultry, LTD, lay a hundred feet away by the GAH.

They crawled through the low-lying vegetation to the boulders, which shielded them from infrared sensors and provided cover if they were spotted and a firefight began.

A soft hum emitted from the SAT-LC. Corey pushed a button and the screen zoomed to the transponder blip on the South Bimini Airport. Senator Warren's plane just took off. 'Frank' didn't contact him, meaning all four men were aboard.

Corey timed the trek from Thomas Bay Beach well. His team reached the mansion just forty minutes before Senator Warren, Serwin, BHH and El-Sayed would land in Marsh Harbor and the mansion assault began. General Morrison and the special ops commander on the USS Caribbean Sea amphibious assault ship were monitoring the same SAT-LC screen. When Corey texted "STRIKE" on the screen, the fifty special-op warriors, helicopters and watercraft would swarm onto the grounds.

For now, his team performed recon. They scanned the clearing ahead with their infrared and night vision goggles. Everything was clear. Corey thought it strange that no patrols or sentries lay hidden around the edges of the grounds, so he took off his goggles and retrieved a special pair of binoculars with a softball-sized attachment on the bottom. When he switched on the lever and scanned the grounds, he knew why no lookouts or perimeter guards were needed.

The binoculars picked up dozens of electromagnetic laser beams pulsating from locations in the clearing ahead and from across the road along the stone fence encircling the grounds. The beams were no doubt controlled by a computer inside the mansion, probably in Sandoval's office.

He stared at the blinking red triangle on his SAT-LC, which indicated the location of Sandoval's office on the second floor. If all went well, he and Constance would soon be there, emptying his files and documents into large backpacks and duffel bags. Hopefully, the Penumbra Database files will be among them.

Trying to sneak under or around the pulsating laser beams to reach the boulders would be too risky. He tapped a quick message into the SAT-LC and texted it to Morrison and the special ops commander: "EM laser system detected. Too risky to sneak through. Will stay in place until raid begins, then will attack through front gate from current position. Can't risk setting off alarm before raid commences."

A few moments later a reply from the commander appeared on the screen: "No problem. Stay put. Apache's will compromise them."

Then, Morrison sent a text message: "I trust both your judgements. Proceed with modified plan."

Corey signaled his team to lay low and remain hidden. When the three CI agents accompanying, Rolle signaled that Warren and his three accomplices were arrested at the airport, he would text "STRIKE" on the SAT-LC. The Apache helicopters would arrive in less than one minute and compromise Sandoval's electronic countermeasures (ECM's). All hardware and software devices inside laptop and desktop computers, cell phones, iPads, GPS devices, security motion detectors and electronic sensors would be neutralized.

Corey put his night vision/infrared goggles back on, crouched low to the ground, and watched the soft red glow of the SAT-LC screen. His team's GPS position registered at 26.100484, -77.195675, exactly three hundred feet from the front door of the mansion. A triangular blip showed Warren's plane flying swiftly across the North Atlantic, then it headed over Castaway Cay at 250 mph. *They'll be touching down at Marsh Harbor Airport shortly.*

He observed four green blips representing the four combat watercraft that were launched from the open stern of the USS Caribbean Sea. They sped towards the mansion, about ten miles out, and would halt one mile offshore until the order to strike came from Corey.

Two blue blips appeared on the screen and moved swiftly toward their position. They were a pair of AH-64 Apache attack choppers that just left the USS Caribbean Sea. Twenty seconds later, five purple blips representing the UH-60L Blackhawk air assault choppers followed behind the Apaches. The three UH-60Q Medevac choppers were raised onto the ships deck and would remain there until needed.

Corey stared at the screen. Even though it was set on a subdued night mode, it lit up like a Christmas tree. He turned the brightness down even more. The hot, humid subtropical jungle rhythm continued. The tree frog chorus was about to be interrupted by the deafening thunder of war machines.

Suddenly, a RBPF patrol car appeared and stopped on the Great Abaco Highway just north of the Abaco Poultry, LTD grounds. The red dome lights were flashing and the headlights were pointed south down the GAH. Constable Cecil Turnquest got out and stood in the roadway.

Shortly after, a second patrol car sped past Turnquest and continued south, stopping a quarter mile further down the GAH. It, too, turned on its red dome lights.

Then, it hit Corey. *Serwin is an ACE Vietnam jet pilot...the potholes are filled along this section of the GAH and the forest berm is cut twenty-five feet wider as well. Fuck!* He peered at the SAT-LC screen to verify his hunch. Sure enough, the Cessna flown by Serwin veered east just south of Marsh Harbor Airport, then swerved south and was coming toward them. It dropped altitude quickly.

Twenty seconds later, spot lights appeared in the dark sky to Corey's left. A white single-engine Cessna Skylane with blue wings and blue stripes on the tail and front miraculously roared four feet over Turnquest and his police car and abruptly landed on the GAH with a screech of tires and brakes. It came to a rapid stop a hundred feet before the other patrol car.

Corey quickly texted his CI team at Marsh Harbor Airport to get to the mansion with Deputy Commander Rolle and his men ASAP. Then, he sent another text to the special operations commander aboard the USS Caribbean Sea amphibious assault ship … "STRIKE!"

Episode 61

Special operations blitz on Abaco mansion

The Cessna wheeled around on the GAH as a large wooden door on rails slid open in the stone wall. Serwin steered through it with five inches to spare off each wing tip and parked in a lot at the far end of the grounds.

The tree frogs and night insects grew silent after the plane landed. Silence is golden. There would be no whispering or airway communications until after the attack began. Corey held up a fist, signaling for Constance and the seven team members behind her to remain still.

Corey watched the SAT-LC screen as the four green dots representing the combat watercraft hit the beach behind the mansion. That was his signal to move, for synchronized hell was about to break loose.

Two Apache helicopters whooshed over the mansion roof and hovered over the front driveway. The crew of one switched on a strange electronic warfare antennae protruding from the nose. Instantly the grounds went dark.

Simultaneously, the combat watercraft landed on the beach and five warriors donned with night vision helmets and body armor leaped from each one. They took cover behind a stand of palm trees and began firing their M4A1 carbines at several dozen Middle Eastern guards, who quickly took cover behind a low stone wall along the spacious backyard patio.

The guards fired back with AK-47's, which were smuggled in by Orival from Haiti. The spotlights were out. A half dozen of the special ops soldiers fired grenades from their M4A1 under-slung grenade launchers. The projectiles bounced off the stone mansion, fell behind the low stone wall and exploded. Silhouetted images of bodies blown back over the wall and glass patio doors exploding into the mansion's interior flickered briefly. Rounds from the .50-caliber machine guns on each craft fired over the soldiers' heads and punched large holes through the stone barricade, killing more surviving terrorists.

The twenty CBIF fighters immediately advanced to the stone wall while .50 caliber bullets streaked inches over their heads. Four other special ops snipers positioned themselves several hundred yards away on the distant southern wall. They had snuck behind the wall to a GPS position that Corey and their special ops commander strategically marked as a waypoint on the SAT-LC.

When the fighting started, they mounted the wall and sat atop it, using palm trees as cover. They peered behind the low patio stone fence and picked off the surviving terrorists who took cover behind it. All four were top marksmen that Corey and the special ops commander recruited for CBIF from the Fort Benning, Georgia Army Sniper School. Within minutes, both able-bodied and wounded mansion guards were dead. The MK-14's fitted with telescopic sights did the job.

The four snipers and .50 caliber gunners on the combat watercraft ceased firing and watched the twenty IR Chem lights affixed to each of their comrade's backpack rapidly reach and jump over the stone fence. They met no resistance. No hand-to-hand combat was necessary. Twenty-four terrorists eventually bound to join sleeper attack cells inside America lay dead before them.

The special ops commander sat in his state room aboard the USS Caribbean Sea and stared at the SAT-LC. He watched in satisfaction as the twenty blips advanced to the back of the mansion. No glitches, but the assault was far from over.

Satellite image analysis of the grounds coupled with human intelligence gathered from Devon Ledard helped a great deal in the planning. The accurate and quiet sniper fire and .50 caliber suppression fire from the four combat watercraft reduced the enemy's morale and ability to fire consistently and in an organized manner at the advancing warriors. The IR Chem lights were invisible to the terrorists and protected his men from becoming close-in, friendly-fire casualties.

The special ops troops tossed flash grenades through the shattered back patio sliding-glass doors and knelt down. After several horrendous explosions, they swarmed inside.

During the commotion, Corey snuck through the low-lying palmetto palm ferns and crawled behind a boulder on the GAH. Cecil Turnquest stood by his police car, listening to the noise of battle on the other side of the mansion wall. While Turnquest stared in disbelief at the assault, Corey quickly snuck behind the patrol car and whispered, "Cecil!"

When the constable wheeled around with handgun in hand, Corey shot a dart filled with an Azaperone and Fentanyl cocktail into his neck. He collapsed immediately. Corey dragged his heavy frame around the back of the patrol car and quickly bound his hands behind his back with double zip-tie plastic handcuffs. He took the keys off his belt and opened the trunk, then dumped him inside. The limp but conscious body stared up with fear.

Corey showed no sympathy. "Sorry, my friend, you decided to join Mr. Sandoval's crooked empire. When the trunk opens, it will be Deputy Commander Ellison Rolle greeting you. Have fun in Fox Hill Prison."

Corey slammed the trunk shut and motioned his agents to join him on the GAH. They ran to the tall stone wall hugged it while making their way to the front iron gate, which was chained shut. Corey peered through the thick wrought iron bars and saw several dozen additional guards run out of a metal barn with AK-47's. They sought cover in the palm tree grove beyond the lot where Senator Warren's plane was parked.

They began firing at the Apache's. The gun battle lasted four seconds. Corey heard the electric motor on one helicopter begin whirring as the single barrel 30mm M230 chain gun on its lower side gun turret fired a three-second blast.

Simultaneously, the other attack chopper fired 2.75-inch Hydra 70 missiles from its rocket tube. The fins unfolded and the aerial rockets set the coconut palm grove, and the Middle Eastern terrorists, ablaze. Corey glanced quickly at his SAT-LC screen. All twenty blips were inside the house and moving swiftly through the first floor in a north to south direction. His team was to immediately enter the house when the outside guards were neutralized, which they were.

The chains were thick and fastened with a large padlock. No time for lock-picking. Corey motioned an agent behind him with a .12-gauge shotgun to blow it open. The blast was loud and the magnum slug shattered the lock.

They shoved the heavy gate open and ran up the circular driveway to the front door. A UH-60L Blackhawk chopper swooped in and hovered above them. A Thick rope dropped down and five special ops warriors rappelled onto the roof and ran to an upper gable sundeck door.

Corey watched the first warrior slide down and hold the rope steady for the second, and so on. Even though each carried a heavy load and slid down rapidly, their heat-resistant gloves and the thick, braided rope allowed them to descend rapidly without slipping or being burnt by friction.

The CI team reached the front door and stood ready with their .45 caliber Glock 30's drawn. A few moments later, as planned, a second Blackhawk materialized out of nowhere and hovered over them. A rope dangled onto the driveway and four more special op warriors fast-roped down and joined them.

Corey tried the front door latch. It was locked, as expected. He motioned for his agent with the shotgun to blow it open. One of the special ops soldiers handed the agent three Hatton rounds. Corey and the commander discussed the possibility of blowing the front door open with an explosive, but it may injure or kill someone inside that they were ordered to take prisoner.

A target they needed to capture could be hiding in the foyer near the door, so they elected not to use a shotgun slug either, for it would continue on after penetrating the door lock. The Hatton rounds, however, would disintegrate into dust after piercing the thick lock.

The heavy front door shook and swung open after the shotgun blast. The thirteen-member detail rushed into the foyer and halted at the base of the winding stairs that led up to the second-floor balcony and hallway that led to Sandoval's office.

Corey motioned for 'Chop Chop,' the yacht Team-11 leader, to take her squad down the first floor and join the twenty special ops soldiers in room-to-room clearing. A deck of cards dangled from her uniform, a packet of photographs of the sixteen individuals they were to arrest, capture...or kill.

After Team-11 disappeared down the first-floor hallway into total darkness, Corey peered up the winding stairway through his night-vision goggles. Everything seemed clear. He motioned for Constance, the cruise ship couple comprising CI Team-10, and the four special ops soldiers to ascend with him.

They moved stealthily down the long, carpeted second-floor hallway. Corey noted the paintings lining the walls, all originals created by the "fathers of modern Bahamian Art"- oil paintings of seascapes and landscapes by Don Russell and watercolor scenes of everyday life and individuals from Nassau's elderly community by Horace Wright.

They proceeded slowly and silently, pausing at each door. Corey and the special ops soldiers slid fiber-optic snake cams under each door and peered inside. In one room, he made out two men and several women. All of them were undressed. *Probably a few Colombian whores entertaining Sandoval's friends.* He couldn't make out who the men were, but wrote "X-4" on the door with a glow marker. *Sit tight and keep hiding, my friends, we'll be back for you later. Right now, we proceed to Sandoval's office and confiscate his files and computer hard drives.*

The hallway made a 90-degree turn to the left. Sandoval's office was thirty-feet down, the first door on the right. Even though it was pitch dark, the thirteen of them remained unseen as Corey knelt down and slid the snake cam around the corner and inspected the hallway.

Two male figures stood by Sandoval's office door, both holding handguns at arm's length. They were very nervous. Corey heard their heavy breathing.

Since they may be individuals to arrest or capture and not kill, Corey had to avoid a confrontation and gun battle. He motioned for one of the special ops to throw a flash bang grenade down the hallway, then held up three fingers to tell him the targets were thirty feet away.

The soldier glanced quickly around the corner then expertly lobbed one. They all squeezed their eyes shut and covered their ears.

Seconds later the flash-bang grenade exploded. A blinding flash and debilitating blast of intense sound pressure blew both men to the ground. The metal powder payload oxidized in the air in a way that prolonged the flash duration.

They rushed the disoriented duo and secured them with plastic zip-tie handcuffs. Corey pulled one up and slammed him against the wall. It was Bolan Tougas. He grabbed him by the neck and stared in his face. "You murdered agent Duane Collier...fed him to a shark. You know where the hi-tech mortars are and you're going to tell me where they are. Tell me!"

"I don't know."

Corey tightened his fist on Tougas' throat. "Devon Ledard overheard you talking to your asshole buddy, Pierre Cherestal, outside the window of the barn he was working in. You two were talking about mortars inside the U.S."

Tougas grew frightened as Corey's grip limited his oxygen flow. He was about to panic. "Please, we be talkin' about what we hear Sandoval say. He be talkin' about dem weapons being inside the U.S. but we dun' know where."

"I don't believe you. I want you to think about what you did to Duane Collier while you're being tortured by our pain-inducing specialists. You'll wish you could be eaten quickly by a shark. Tell me where Sandoval is and we'll forget about the torture."

Tougas whispered and nodded toward the door, "He be in da office. We was protectin' him."

"Anybody else in there with him?"

"Only Devon Ledard. He bring up some snacks and drinks fo' a U.S. senator, his chief 'o staff, and two other guys who just landed outside on da GAH. Dey run up heah in a hurry when da choppers come."

Corey released his grip and threw him on the floor next to Pierre Cherestal. "Just kidding…we're gonna torture the fuck out of you anyway." He signaled for two of the special ops troops to take them to a predesignated clearing in the back lawn, a space with enough room for a helicopter to land.

Corey slid the snake under the door. A body lay on the floor. *Shit! I hope it's not who I think it is!* The door was locked, so Corey took the shotgun and inserted a Hatton round and fired. The door burst open and as Team-10 and the two special ops warriors ran in to provide him cover, Corey ran to the body lying beside the conference table. Through his night vision goggles he recognized Devon Ledard. He was shot numerous times.

The five members of Yacht Team-11 made their way down the first-floor hallway of Sandoval's huge stone manor house. Three special ops warriors accompanied them. They crept past a long line of tall windows, peering over the bottom ledges into the atrium and pool area. No forms were spotted among the treadmills, Stairmasters or exercise bikes. They continued on, passing a full basketball court, then paused at a closed door.

'Chop Chop' slipped a fiber-optics snake under the door. She made out four men and four women. One man struggled in the dark to put his pants back on. The women and three of the men crawled underneath a large pool table. The man got his pants back on and crept over the carpet and disappeared behind what appeared to be a wet bar.

Two wireless laptops on top of the wet bar counter projected a minimal amount of light into the room, enabling 'Chop Chop' to recognize some of the men on her deck of cards. They were unarmed and no guards stood ready in the room. The eight must have been having a sex orgy, for bras and clothing items lay on top of the tournament-sized billiard table.

She whispered her findings to the special ops soldiers and decided to try a diplomatic room entry. One warrior with a deep and commanding voice yelled, "Unlock and open the door, then all inside stand with your hands above your heads!"

'Chop Chop' watched through the snake. No one moved. She nodded to the fighter to continue.

He bellowed even louder this time. "We know there are eight of you inside. Open the door immediately or we will consider you a threat. We will blast through the door with automatic weapons blazing. You have until the count of three...one...two...."

Two of the naked Colombian whores leaped from under the pool table and ran to the door, unlocking it. No one inside tried to stop them, but remained hiding.

'Chop Chop' grew impatient and yelled out. "We said to stand up and put your hands up in the air!"

She saw the two other prostitutes and three men crawl out from underneath the pool table and stand with their hands raised.

She yelled out, "The man behind the wet bar...join the others or we will toss a grenade behind the bar...move now!"

An image of a man with his hands held high moved from behind the wet bar and joined the group. She made out eight figures standing with hands raised in front of the pool table, facing the unlocked door.

A karate kick knocked the door wide open and they swept into the room. The special ops soldiers turned on the tactical lights affixed to the front of their M4A1 carbines, lighting up eight stunned and frightened faces. 'Chop Chop' and her four Team-11 partners trained their Glock 30, .45 caliber semi-automatics on the group. The silencers were no longer needed and they removed them.

The laser-aiming modules placed red dots on the chests of all. No one dared to say anything, save one narcissistic jerk who would make Donald Trump appear like an introvert.

"Do you know who I am? Do you realize how much trouble you are in, whoever you are? You have no right to arrest me. I am the Honorable Alfred Moss, M.P., the Minister of Agriculture of the Bahamas. Neither do you have the right to arrest my associate standing beside me."

'Chop Chop' asked, "And, just who is your associate and what does he do?"

"His name is Oliver and he be my motor car driver and personal bodyguard."

The Team-11 leader checked her card packet and whispered into the mic to Corey, who was in Sandoval's second floor office checking to see if Devon showed any signs of life. "'Chop Chop' here. We've got Moss' limo driver. Awaiting orders."

Corey whispered back, "We're at *Obscure Transgression*...OT level. You know what to do. Follow orders!"

'Chop Chop' ordered Oliver to step forward. She raised her .45-caliber Glock and stuck it in his face. There was no remorse in her voice. "This is for smuggling my colleague and friend...Duane Collier, out of the Nassau Hard Rock Café and then torturing and murdering him…and his mother." She pulled the trigger and a reddish-pink vaporous mist of blood and brains spewed out onto Moss and the others.

The Colombian whores screamed, then began whimpering uncontrollably. 'Chop Chop' told them all to shut up, turn around, and keep their hands held high above their heads. They immediately obeyed, including Moss.

One-by-one, the five Team-11 members grabbed each person and strapped their hands securely behind their backs with plastic double-zip tie cuffs. Both Irish miscreants were among them.

"Team eleven to Corey. Come in" "Go ahead."

"We neutralized the limo driver and secured Moss, the banker Sean Branagh and his brother Patrick Branagh."

'Chop Chop' noted vexation in Corey's voice. "Have the special op boys escort Moss and the two asshole brothers out front. Deputy Commander Rolle will place them under arrest when he arrives with our CI team from Marsh Harbor Airport. Have them tell Rolle that Cecil Turnquest is locked in the police car trunk on the GAH."

"Roger that. Sir, is everything OK with you on the second floor?"

"Could be better…I'm trying to save the life of our asset, Devon Ledard…Sandoval shot him. I contacted the special ops commander aboard the USS Caribbean Sea and requested a Medevac chopper…

it will be landing shortly outside." "Good luck, sir."

Corey inspected a bullet wound to Devon's chest and another in his upper right arm. Constance applied direct pressure to the chest wound and lessened the bleeding while Corey retrieved a pressure bandage from the first aid kit and placed it on Devon's arm. No large blood vessels were punctured, but the bullet caused an open-chest wound. When Devon tried to suck in oxygen, his right lung collapsed. Corey handed Constance an occlusive dressing, which she used to close the open wound.

Corey and Constance gave Devon a few more minutes of life. They heard the UH-60Q Medevac helicopter land outside on the makeshift helo pad. Hope remained!

Corey motioned for two of the special ops soldiers to carry Devon down to the chopper. As they positioned the carry straps and blanket underneath him, Devon feebly gripped Corey's hand and pointed to a door in an adjacent room. *That's where Sandoval is hiding.*

He noted Devon's lips were quavering...he was trying to speak. Corey put his ear to Devon's lips. He barely made out what he mouthed. "My wife...my kids...Sandoval's men at my home ...Guana Cay settlement."

Corey whispered in Devon's ear, "Your wife and those two beautiful children of yours are going to be OK. I'll make sure of it."

A faint smile appeared on Devon's face as they carried him downstairs. Corey's words lingered in his mind as the Medevac nurses and doctor placed him on a table and the helicopter rose into the night sky.

On the way back to the USS Caribbean Sea, the medical trauma team stopped the bleeding completely and began a blood transfusion. A tube was inserted into the open pneumothorax chest wound and it was sealed. Devon's chest began rising and falling regularly.

A nurse looked up at the doctor as she finished applying fresh dressings to Devon's chest wound, checked the IV catheter, and made sure the air flow into the oxygen mask moved freely. "I think he'll make it."

The doctor was finishing some minor suturing. "Yes, I think you're right. Thanks to the emergency treatment by the first responders, whoever they are."

The nurse said, "Did you see that huge stone mansion! And, what about the bodies lying all over the grounds that the helo landing lights exposed? I saw a few of the faces...they looked Middle Eastern, and what about..."

The doctor interrupted the trauma nurse. "I suggest you forget about everything you saw. We don't know anything about the organization we were chosen to work for and it would behoove you *not* to try and find out. Whoever they are, I don't know…all I do know is that the world has become a dangerous place for Americans, and they are keeping us out of harm's way."

When the two special ops warriors returned from the Medevac, Corey motioned for them, along with Constance and the two CI Team-10 members to follow him to the door that Devon pointed to.

He slid the fiber-optic snake under the door and saw an entire wall filled with videos. It was the library, and Sandoval was crouched behind a desk, aiming a large handgun at the door. *Sandoval's too dangerous for a silent lock-picking entry or blasting the lock open with the shotgun. He'd kill one of us for sure before we cleared the doorway.*

Corey motioned for all to be completely silent and to stay clear of the door and crouch low. He noiselessly attached a small magnetic C4 explosive onto the metal lock-frame and had everyone retreat back to the adjacent room and hide behind the conference table.

When the charge detonated, they stormed back to the open doorway and threw a flashbang into the room. The heavy door was blown inside onto the carpet.

A stunned Sandoval tried to crawl across the carpet to his 9mm Beretta M9A3 pistol which lay six feet away. He was about to reach it but halted when a red dot appeared on his chest. He looked up as Constance stepped on his hand and stuck her .45 Glock in his face, then picked up his handgun.

She pretended to admire his weapon. "Nice craftsmanship… cerakote coating, custom-made silencer…is this what you used to shoot our friend, Devon Ledard?"

The eyes above the teardrop tattoo showed no fear. They actually twinkled a bit, as if he enjoyed the raid.

Corey understood that psychopaths do not feel empathy, guilt or compassion. But, they do understand punishment. He stepped past Constance and grabbed him, lifted him up and slammed him against the luxurious wall of imported mahogany and walnut.

He stuck his face into Sandoval's, smiled and said, "Listen carefully to me, you piece of shit. The luxurious life you relish has officially ended. If you don't tell me...right now...where Edhi and his sleeper cell is hiding, you will be helicoptered to a secret location and meet my friends, the Dirty Tricks guys...they'll torture you to the limits of your tolerance...then pause just before you pass out from agony...then begin to physically brutalize you again. Tell me where Edhi is or I will throw you to them."

To the amazement of Constance, Team-10 and the special ops warriors, Sandoval spit in Corey's face, then smiled.

Corey smiled back. "You just don't get it, do you?" He turned Sandoval around and slammed his face into the wall and strapped the plastic cuffs on, then spun him around to face him again. "You are on your way to be skinned alive if you don't divulge where the terrorist sleeper cell and mortars are that you smuggled into the U.S."

"I be laughin' from my jail cell when da Edhi attack on America begin."

"No, you won't be in a jail cell...you just don't get it...you'll be dead, from intense torture. We know all about the Middle Eastern terrorists you and Abner Orival smuggled into Abaco from his house in that shantytown just north of Port-au-Prince. Our agents have been watching it. We know about your murdering one of our agents... Duane Collier, not to mention his mother, who you abducted from the U.S. We know you murdered Sidney Fowler on Parliament Square in downtown Nassau...we also know you murdered Bernard Knowles, the customs officer at Sandy Point. Did you know Bernard was engaged to Deputy Commander Ellison Rolle's daughter?"

Sandoval's eyes flashed a bit of angst, but it didn't last long. "You know lots 'bout me...how ya know all dis?"

"Because we have more resources and we're smarter than you. We also know that Senator Warren, his advisor Mark Serwin who you go way back with, BHH, and Shahid El-Sayed flew here from Bimini. We want the contents of that satchel BHH is carrying."

"What's inside da satchel dat ya want so badly?"

"You know how to play stupid, my teardrop-tattoo'd dumbass. We want the Penumbra Database. That's what you killed Collier and his mother for."

"I gots lots o' stuff to tell ya 'bout if ya go easy on me. I could tell ya 'bout all the narco-terrorists I know."

Corey smiled and said, "You don't know it yet, but you will be ratting on everyone you ever met. You have no idea how exceptional my friends are at the art of torture...getting scumbags like you to spill the beans."

"I not all dat bad...Devon Ledard...I got two men at his house at da Guana Cay village. I called and told dem not to murder his wife and kids."

"You're a lying sack of shit. The ECM's on our Apache helicopters knocked out all the hardware and software in your computers, iPads, GPS devices and cell phones...including yours. Even your laser motion detectors outside went dead. You tried to make a call to them but couldn't get through to order the murder of Devon's family. You're going to suffer for the rest of your short life. I believe in revenge, an eye for an eye. You are going to disappear...no one you know now or have ever known before will ever hear from you again."

He turned to the special ops warriors. "Take psycho-dumbass here down to the helicopter pad and shackle him to Bolan Tougas and Pierre Cherestal. Tape all their mouths shut so they can't talk."

As they carted him away, Corey said, "Bon voyage, Mr. Sandoval... you and your buds are about to take a whirlybird ride to meet my friends of the Dirty Tricks division."

Episode 62

A time to kill

CBIF HQ, Eaton Street
Key West, Florida
Bits of Montecristo tobacco lay on the floor around Morrison's computer chair. The general continued munching on the stub as he studied the nine blips on his forty-eight-inch, curved Wide Quad High-Definition computer monitor.

The CBIF agents activated the infrared night-vision body cams fastened to their black uniforms. Even though the balaclavas hid their faces, Corey knew who each one was by their corresponding names that showed underneath each of the nine smaller visual screens surrounding the large SAT-LINK display.

Morrison could communicate with them all at once or to each one, individually. He watched the live stream of them moving through the mansion, hoping that Corey finds BHH and recovers the satchel containing the Penumbra Database. He would remain silent and not interfere with Corey's momentum. The special ops troops outside had the grounds surrounded and no one could escape.

Jeannie whirred softly as all the encrypted auditory and visual streams were relayed by the COMMINT satellite high above the mansion into her Penumbra Database deep data mining algorithm.

He watched Sandoval being subdued and wondered what drove men like him to become so sadistic and brutal toward others. It had to be something beyond a need for power and control...they must be turned on by hurting others...by watching others suffer.

The four smaller visual screens of the second floor showed the CI team moving further down the hallway in a line...Corey, Constance, then the two members of CI Team-10. The four special ops soldiers behind them appeared as blips on the larger screen.

The general knew they would find the other targets hiding in the mansion. He especially wanted BHH apprehended. He couldn't stop thinking about Duane Collier's father, Drew, who created the initial Jeannie deep data mining algorithm which was immensely augmented by Hsin Chow and his son. Jeannie became the Penumbra Database.

Morrison regretted not telling Corey that Jeannie was renamed Penumbra Database and that he assigned BHH to search through it to find cyber-threat vulnerabilities. If he listened to Corey's reservations about BHH, none of this would be happening, that this incredibly advanced data mining algorithm may fall into the hands of a global terrorist network.

After the mission is over, he would tell Corey that the Penumbra Database is a pilot project being tested by CBIF in the Caribbean Basin and that it proved effective in anticipating terrorist plots and preemptively striking before they could be carried out. He would reveal to Corey what this successful project meant, that CBIF, CIA and NSA would take over from an ineffective FBI all counter intelligence responsibilities inside America.

He'd also tell him that when the decision is made by the *Gang of Six* to go to *Obscure Transgression* level, it isn't because of scanty FBI evidence that's problematically collected due to law enforcement restraints. It's because the Penumbra Database secretly analyzed and produced an incontrovertible PDF, Presidential Daily Brief, from the intelligence gathered by Corey and the thousands of CBIF counterintelligence agents throughout the Caribbean who operate uninhibited by legal restraints.

President Rhinehart is given justifiable reasons to allow CBIF to go to OT level. The PDB created by the Penumbra Database turns incoming raw intelligence data into intentions, probable plans, most- likely targets, and the sentiments and passion levels of terrorist suspects lurking at America's backdoor…not only their opportunity and resolve to kill Americans, but the how, when, and where are accurately forecast.

Morrison stared at the soft-blue tint emanating from the large computer SAT-LINK monitor before him. And now, he thought, BHH is about to place the most advanced anti-terrorism data-mining algorithm the world has ever known into our enemy's hands. He tapped the smaller screen, which was Corey's.

Corey answered, whispering, "Yes, sir?"

"Morrison said. I've changed my mind about BHH."

Corey paused along the dark hallway. They were approaching a final door at the end. "How so, sir?"

"Kill him."

"Yes, sir." Corey motioned for the others to follow him to the last door. He snuck silently past it with Constance while Team-10 and the four special ops soldiers readied themselves on the other side.

Downstairs, 'Chop Chop' and her four agents reached the end door on the first floor. They were directly below Corey. She heard a loud flash-bang go off on the second floor above her as the ceiling reverberated.

She slid her fiber-optic snake under the door. *Bingo!* Four men were hiding in the room, staring at the ceiling. It looked like a lounge or waiting room of some sort. One kneeled behind a small secretary's desk to the right, two others hid under a table directly in front of the door while another sat in a couch to the left. No signs of weapons.

She slowly, soundlessly pressed down on the door handle. It wasn't locked. They must have been in a big hurry to find a hiding place when the Apache's roared overhead and the special ops warriors hit the beach. She signaled the others where the locations of the targets were, then swung open the door as another agent tossed in a flashbang grenade.

A second after the blinding flash and intensely loud detonation, all nine were in the room, standing over the disoriented men. One lay wailing with pain on the floor, holding his ears. The 190-decibel blast apparently damaged his ear drums. They identified him as Laurent Rousseau, the Haitian Minister of Public Health and Population, a man bought and paid for by Sandoval. He was designated to be arrested and turned over to Deputy Commander Ellison Rolle.

'Chop Chop' picked up a handgun laying on the floor by another target who was sitting on the couch when the flashbang went off. Miraculously, he wasn't blown off it and was still sitting up, but staring wide-eyed into the tactical light affixed to the front of the M4A1 carbine held by a special op soldier.

She knew who it was, for she had memorized the photos of the sixteen targets on the deck of cards dangling from her neck. It was Abner Orival, Sandoval's recruiter in Haiti, the man who smuggled radical Islamic terrorists into the U.S. The flash over-stimulated the photoreceptors in his eyes, making vision temporarily impossible.

'Chop Chop' turned to the special ops warrior, holding up Orival's handgun. "He would have shot one of us with this if he wasn't temporarily blinded. He's on the cards...authorized by General Morrison to be killed. Do your job."

As she walked over to the two remaining targets who lay on the floor, the soldier raised his carbine and switched the lever from fully automatic, rapid fire to semi-auto, single shot. The suppressor reduced the sound of the muzzle blasts to loud thumps as three 5.56 mm NATO rounds tore through Orival's left and right lungs, then through his forehead at 2,900 feet per second.

The other Team-11 agents lifted up the two remaining disoriented targets. It was hard to believe the CBIF yacht team lived the life of young, thrill-seeking rich kids sailing and scuba-diving throughout the

Caribbean islands, living off their parent's money…a great buffer and firewall, a front that interred the real world they lived.

'Chop Chop' stared at the faces of the shackled terrorists. She smiled, knowing that Morrison would be pleased when her infrared body cam streamed their faces onto his screen in the War Room. She spoke, knowing that Morrison was listening in. "We've just captured Eamal Batoor and Khoury Kassim, two very dangerous men who our CI comrades in Haiti recorded meeting with Sandoval at the Hotel Montana."

Batoor glared at her, but the hateful stare didn't intimidate her in the least. She got in his face and said, "And you, the Afghani who was captured and thrown into Saraposa Prison in Kandahar, but was freed by the Taliban when they attacked the prison…there will be no one to help you where you and Kassim are headed."

She remained nose-to-nose with Batoor as she spoke to her team, "Tape their filthy mouths shut and cover their heads… they're going on a chopper ride to be tortured by the Dirty Tricks division." Then, she calmly said to Batoor, "Have a nice day."

Upstairs, Corey, Constance, Team-10 and the special ops soldiers had burst into the last room in the hallway. The flashbang disabled their targets for five seconds, enough time to surround them and hoist them up off the floor and shackle their hands firmly with plastic zip-ties.

The assault rifle tactical lights lit up the room. Corey stared at the stunned prisoners through the haze. The smell of burnt magnesium and potassium nitrate filled his nostrils. "Well, well, if it isn't the honorable Senator William Warren, Chairman of the Senate Select Committee on Intelligence…"

Warren interrupted him. "I…a United States senator…come to the Bahamas with my chief of staff for a fishing trip and get invited to this mansion for a party only to almost get blown up, then shackled. You realize the trouble you're in…the charges I will bring you up on when I get back?"

Corey replied, "Your egotism has blocked your perception of reality and your vanity has made you careless and oblivious to the cleverness of the intelligence agencies you oversee."

The senator's fake, flaxen hair and pearly-white, laser-bright teeth showed through the clearing haze. "We shall see when I get back to the Hart Senate Office Building. I plan on launching a full judiciary inquiry into your unlawful and downright criminal behavior."

Corey smiled at the senator. "You won't be returning to Washington … ever. Nor will you ever again see the insides of your Mercedes-Benz SLR McLaren. Deputy Commander Rolle of the Royal Bahamian Police Force will be arresting you shortly."

"On what charges?!"

"Impersonating a human being, for starters. We know that your friend, Colombian Army General Manuel Castano stole the hi-tech, laser-guided mortars that the Senate Intelligence Committee, that you so skillfully manipulate, furnished him with. You and Serwin flew here from South Bimini with BHH and Shahid El-Sayed on board."

Corey pointed to El-Sayed, who was standing next to Warren. "In fact, this asshole bought the plane from Sandoval before he gave it to you as a gift. We've been tailing you since you left your Mercedez behind in D.C., rented a Ford Taurus, then drove to the Hagerstown Airport in Maryland. Our CI teams documented your flight from Hagerstown to Bimini, where you met up with BHH and El-Sayed."

Senator Warren wasn't smiling anymore. "So, I hang out with people you don't like. You'll have to come up with a legal charge."

"Once the American public learns you 'hang out' with Shahid El-Sayed, the radical Islamic terrorist who operates the end point of Sandoval's smuggling pipeline into America at the New Jersey warehouse… the pipeline used to smuggle in the stolen mortars... you will be as good as dead."

Corey noticed Warren lost his haughtiness. The senator's stare grew unpretentious. He continued. "You will be charged with treason. We have collected volumes of evidence that will indict and convict you. We'll have even more when Sandoval is tortured and divulges the payoffs and bribes he's no doubt given to you and Serwin. What Sandoval and El-Shahid neglected to tell you is that those stolen mortars are somewhere inside America's heartland...in the hands of a jihadist sleeper attack cell planning to kill thousands of Americans. If the attack goes down successfully, you will be given the death penalty."

Corey turned to BHH and held up a photo taken by the two Bimini CI Teams which their leader 'Frank' sent to him. It showed BHH jumping into El-Sayed's golf cart on the Blue Lagoon dirt road in North Bimini with a black satchel strung over his shoulder. Warren and Serwin could be seen in another golf cart in the background. He also held up a second greatly enlarged photo of the satchel. "Where is it?"

BHH stared at the photo. "Where is what? I don't have any satchel like that."

Constance and Team-10 searched the room for the satchel, but shook their heads when Corey glanced over at them.

"You had it on Bimini. I should have listened to Pinkston when I recruited both of you at the hacker convention in LA. He never trusted you and neither did I. General Morrison made the mistake of hiring you to search the Jeannie database for security holes in her firewall."
"Which I did. It was my patriotic duty to god and country. I also devised safeguards to protect Jeannie from cyberattack. Shouldn't I be given a medal?"

Corey said, "You're a better liar than Sandoval, Tougas, and Warren put together. You brought the upgraded Jeannie database here...on the fuckin' plane...in the satchel. Our agents saw you boarding the plane with it in South Bimini. One more time...where is this satchel?"

BHH stared at the photo. "I honestly don't know."

Just then two special ops soldiers appeared at the door. One said, "Mr. Pearson, we're part of the sniper team positioned on the south wall. We saw these men land on the GAH and park the Cessna below us. They ran into the mansion when the Apache's arrived, but one stopped and buried this in a thick growth of yellow elders. He handed Corey a satchel, an exact replica of the photo he just held up to BHH.

Corey asked the soldier which man was carrying it. He pointed to BHH and said, "That one, sir."

Corey opened the satchel. Inside were a dozen flash drives, five hard drives, ten DVD's and a half-dozen CD's stored in a waterproof pouch. Corey retrieved one of the CD's and read aloud the inscription, "Transcript for Penumbra Database: 50,000-page word file text."

Corey handed the prize to Constance, then held up his stack of cards. Warren, Serwin, BHH and El-Sayed stared at the card photo. He held up one. It was a photo of BHH with the letter "K" written on it. He spoke to BHH, "You know what the letter 'K' stands for?"

A solemn silence permeated the room. Corey raised his Glock 30 and pointed the suppressor attached to its end a foot from BHH's face. He thought of the al-Qaeda sleeper cell attack on the elementary school in Boston…taking thirty-five kids hostage…holding them for a week in the gymnasium…taunting their parents and all of America, then blowing them up after leading everyone to believe negotiations might work. None were U.S. citizens. They all snuck into the U.S. through the Bahamas. *The Penumbra Database will make it harder for them to terrorize America again.*

He pulled the trigger, releasing a lightning flash and loud "thump" sound. BHH's head shot back, his body went airborne and smashed into the wall behind him, then collapsed in a motionless pile on the carpet.

Corey checked the SAT-LINK monitor. The countdown blip in the upper right-hand corner showed twenty minutes left to conclude the operation. He pointed at Warren and Serwin. "You two don't know where the mortars are, so you will be arrested by Rolle."

Then, he faced Shahid El-Sayed and held a card photo of his face with the letter "C" written below it. "Do you know what the 'C' stands for?"

"I hope it means you're going to offer me for *shahada*…martyr-dom, like you did BHH."

"Wrong. It stands for 'Capture'…then torture. Like your radicalized jihad, my organization wages its own holy struggle, too. But, we only kill and torture the guilty, not the innocent like you do. You, Sandoval, Tougas, Cherestal along with Kassim and Batoor who we just captured downstairs…all of you know where the mortars are. The six of you will be drugged, tossed on a helicopter and taken to a secret location where you will be tortured by specialists until you tell us where they are."

Corey and his team began to tape their mouths shut and place hoods over their heads.

Suddenly, Mark Serwin bolted out of the room and ran down the hallway toward a stairwell that led to the roof. Corey and Constance ordered Team-10 and the four special ops soldiers to continue taping and "hooding" the prisoners, then take them down to the helicopter LZ. His SAT-LINK showed a violet blip a mile away and closing fast. It was the Sikorsky UH-60 Black Hawk chopper coming to transport the prisoners to the Dirty Tricks division aboard Ferguson's *Queen Conch II.*

Serwin burst through the partially-opened door to the sunroof and ran to the ledge. Corey and Constance stopped ten feet away from the shackled man, holding their Glock 30's down by their sides.

Corey said calmly, "It's over, Mark. You're cornered…there's no escape."

Constance approached him, but when she was five feet away he jumped up onto the narrow ledge. A cement backyard patio lay forty-five feet below.

She stopped and looked back at Corey, who motioned her to stand down.

Serwin smiled as he teetered on the slippery tiles lining the ledge. His hands were tightly bound behind his back. "Am I being recorded?"

Corey patted the miniaturized infrared video cam on his lapel and replied, "Yes. Live visual and auditory streams are flowing into our headquarters."

"I've got something to tell you, Mr. Pearson...something that I know has been gnawing at your craw for years. But first, I've got something to say about the entire Sandoval organization."

Constance said, "We have an arrest order for you, not a kill, capture or torture order. Why don't we talk about it somewhere else...in private?"

"I'll save you the time of arresting me." He looked over his shoulder at the patio below. "We all die eventually...everyone does...but not everyone has lived...I've lived life to the fullest...and am ready to die."

Corey said calmly, "Tell us about the narco-terrorist network you work for and how you got involved in it."

Serwin began a one-sided eulogy. "It began when I engaged Mig- 17's in dogfights over Viet Nam and shot many of them out of the sky... I was a decorated ace Phantom jet fighter pilot. After my stint in the air force, I met Sandoval and worked as a pilot for his Royal Airlines... flying pot and coke into the Bahamas and the U.S."

Corey asked, "Did you do any human smuggling...like flying Middle Eastern terrorists into the U.S.?"

"No. Not back then...nor today. I drink too much booze and am a greedy son of a bitch, but I'd never smuggle terrorists into the U.S. I'd never do anything that would harm Americans. Eamal Batoor, Khoury Kassim, Sandoval and Shahid El-Sayed... they deceived me, Warren, and the Branaugh brothers into believing the stolen mortars were to be sold to the highest bidder on the global weapons black market."

Corey asked, "And what role do you play in all of this?"

"Warren gives all the classified info discussed in his Senate Select Intelligence Committee about the U.S. battle against narco-terrorism to Sandoval…via me…I'm nothing but a courier…a well-paid one at that."

Corey said, "Give me a specific example, for the record."

"Batoor and Kassim paid Warren off to have Colombian Lieutenant General Castano talk to the intelligence committee in the Hart Senate Office Building…to plead for the hi-tech laser-guided mortars to be used in his battle against FARC."

Constance asked, "How much was the bribe? Give us details about the payoff."

"Like I said, I'm a courier for Warren. I met Sandoval at Nanny O'Brien's Irish Pub on Constitution Avenue in D.C. Warren tape-record-ed Castano's talk during the meeting, including the vote to transfer the 140mm laser-guided mortars to the Colombian Army. I gave Sandoval the microcassette tape of it all. In return, he slipped me two envelopes. One had $25,000 cash for me, the other $50,000 cash for Warren."

Corey felt anger surging deep within. *I'd like to contact Morrison and request that the "A" on Warren's card photo ID be changed to a "K."* He commented to Serwin. "It's clear now why Sandoval's human and drug-smuggling pipeline stayed under the radar of U.S. intelligence for so long."

Constance asked, "What is it you know about that's been 'gnaw-ing at Corey's craw for years?"

Serwin looked from Constance over to Corey. "Ok, here it is. I've learned much about Senator Warren since becoming his chief of staff. He and FBI Director Walt Mason are in a plot with BHH over some big rift between the FBI and CIA."

Corey asked, "That dispute between the FBI, law enforcement, and CIA, counter-intelligence, has been going on for years. What does it have to do with me?"

"Because of the Penumbra Database…that's what's in the satch-el. BKK told Warren about the Jeannie database that your organiza-tion uses to hunt down terrorists. He knew all about it and what it could do."

"Yes, we know that. My organization hired BKK to search through it to find vulnerabilities and set up a firewall to prevent hackers and foreign intelligence from getting through."

Serwin smiled. "You've been kept in the dark. What you don't know is that a revolutionary update to the original Jeannie was created...called the Penumbra Database. Your boss...at whatever organization you work for ...hired BKK to embed this new trailblazing deep data mining algorithm into the original Jeannie database...that is what the satchel holds, not the original Jeannie databank."

Constance asked, "How does it connect to the murders of agent Duane Collier and his mother, Joan Collier?"

"President Rhinehart made the mistake of informing my psychotic boss, Senator Warren, that the secretive organization you both work for ran a pilot project. If it effectively keeps the growing Middle Eastern terrorist presence in the Caribbean Basin in check, it will, along with the CIA and NSA, take over all domestic surveillance responsibilities regarding the radical Islamic threat to America away from the FBI."

Corey said, "And, Warren told Walt Mason about this plan to demote the FBI."

"Exactly."

Constance repeated her question. "You still didn't tell us how all this is connected to Duane and his mother?"

Serwin almost slipped on the tiles. He regained his balance. "Mason wanted to get his hands on the original Jeannie database and stop the effectiveness of your organization in the Caribbean. I know as a fact that Warren told FBI Director Mason that you were about to break a terrorist cell in Curacao. Your organization's Jeannie database sifted through the intel your agents collected and linked this Curacao cell to a huge Hezbollah network throughout the Tri-Border Area of Paraguay, Argentina and Brazil."

Corey said, "I'm aware of why Mason preemptively struck the cell before we did. He issued an emergency arrest warrant for a petty Lebanese-American who was part of the cell, for cigarette smuggling.

Kassim Khoury was tipped off by one of Sandoval's moles inside the Curacao Police Department and fled to Venezuela. Mason didn't want us to get credit for making a significant narco-terrorist bust...like we did just now."

Serwin turned carefully on the ledge to face Constance. "Warren knew that Duane Collier's mother had a copy of the original Jeannie database, hidden somewhere. They broke into her house and kidnapped her, then sent a photo of her tied up with a knife to her throat to Duane Collier in Nassau. Duane had to fake the Nassau Hard Rock Café abduction and come here, or they would have killed her. They brought Duane Collier here, then sent a photo to Joan Collier of him shackled with a knife to his throat. She retrieved the Jeannie database in order to save her son."

Corey asked, "Where was it hidden."

"Drew Collier made a copy of the Jeannie database, years ago, and kept it in his bank's safety deposit box. Joan Collier obediently drove to the bank with her captors and got it."

Constance asked, "But, why did they go to such great lengths to get this obsolete Jeannie database created by Dean Collier if a newer, state-of-the-art one replaced it?"

"Because they didn't know about the Penumbra Database until BHH told them about it and offered to bring it here...for lots of money." Corey grew contemplative. *Morrison is recording all of this in the 'War Room' in Key West. At a minimum, Warren will spend the rest of his life in a prison...in complete isolation.* "So, who is 'they'...who kidnapped Joan Collier in the U.S.?"

"Sandoval has access to a sleeper cell inside the U.S. Kassim and Batoor funded and trained the cell in the Middle East, then smuggled it into Haiti, then to here by Abner Orival. Shahid El-Sayed controlled the final destination of the pipeline...a warehouse in New Jersey, but it was busted by the feds. He and Sandoval smuggled the mortars into the U.S., but I don't know where since they had to find another location after the raid."

Constance asked, "So, Sandoval's sleeper cell is lurking inside the U.S. but you don't know where?"

"Correct. The cell abducted Joan Collier and smuggled her here, to the mansion. It is a command and control cell that keeps other Middle Eastern terrorist cells inside the U.S. in line. Remember when I told you that I met with Sandoval at Nanny O'Brien's Irish Pub in D.C.?"

Both Corey and Constance nodded their heads. Corey asked, "When you met with him, did he reveal anything about them...how widespread they are? Their locations?"

"No, not directly, but I think the network is pretty large...and well organized. Before contacting him at Nanny O'Brien's, I picked up Warren at the Hart Senate Office Building after his meeting with Lieutenant General Castano. Warren told me to drive him to the National Zoo and on the way there, I thought we were being watched. I drove down Constitution Avenue NW and onto US-50 past the National Archives. He told me to slow down by the Natural History Museum and I noticed a parked green van with a white cloth hanging out the passenger window...like a signal of some sort. Warren looked carefully at it then told me to proceed directly to the western entrance of the National Zoo by the visitor center. I dropped him off and he told me to leave but to drive slowly past the visitor center on Connecticut Avenue at exactly 4:50pm. When I did, he was standing behind a sign by the roadway, pretending to snap photos of the grounds. He said to me through the fence, 'Nanny O'Brien's Pub'."

Corey said, "Sandoval's sleeper cell, or cells, were doing counter-surveillance, making sure you weren't being tailed. They preplanned the route with Warren before you picked him up at the Hart Senate Office Building."

Constance added, "He had to have met with one of them inside the National Zoo to find out where your meeting with Sandoval was." Just then, the roar of the Sikorsky UH-60 Black Hawk chopper interrupted them. Its spotlights lit up the backyard landing pad where Tougas,

Cherestal, El-Sayed, Eamal Batoor, Khoury Kassim and Sandoval lie shackled and hooded. It began to carefully descend. Nine special ops troops grabbed them and formed a line, preparing to transport them to the *Queen Conch II.*

Serwin looked solemnly at Corey and shouted over the noise. "The cell is controlled by Sandoval and is just as vicious and cunning as he. You know what they did to Duane Collier...and his mother."

Corey nodded his head in agreement. The noise and bright lights behind Serwin made his silhouette appear spectral as he continued. "Mr. Pearson, Sandoval knew that your wife, Danielle, was Joan Collier's best friend. He thought Danielle was guarding the Jeannie database for Joan...that's why Sandoval and his sleeper cell disarmed the alarm system at your Severna Park home in Maryland. My psycho-boss, the *honorable* Senator Warren, obtained the disarm codes from the FBI and gave them to Sandoval, who bypassed the security system and entered your home. While the cell members ransacked your home looking for it, Sandoval tied your wife up and began torturing her. She couldn't tell him where the database was because she didn't have it...or even know it existed...so he strangled her to death."

Constance glanced over at Corey. His Glock was hanging down by his side and his mouth was agape. She ran over to hug him, but saw Serwin turn around and dive headfirst off the ledge. She quickly peered over and saw his body crumpled on the patio far below. His neck was broken.

She wheeled around to comfort Corey, to hold him...he was gone.

The six prisoners were shackled to the floor inside the Sikorsky Black Hawk and one of the special ops warriors was sliding the door shut. The blades were kicking into gear and the wheels were just about to become airborne when a hand blocked the door from closing and shoved it back open.

Corey jumped into the helo as it took off.

The special ops soldier looked at Corey. "Sir, this wasn't in the plans."

Corey replied, "CBIF remains flexible, something came up…I have a meeting of destiny with Sandoval…and the Dirty Tricks division."

Episode 63

Safeguarding the POTUS

Oval Office, White House
Washington, D.C.
President Rhinehart stood in the Oval Office, peering out through the three large bullet-proof French windows behind his desk in the West Wing. He sipped a cup of coffee while admiring the Rose Garden and blossoming trees and shrubs that the Kennedy's planted in 1962. They must have thought the view was too exposed and desired more privacy.

He turned around and stared at the Cleveland Indians photograph on his desk that was recently signed by All-Star pitcher Mark Rounds. Memories surfaced of his childhood exploits in Rocky River, a suburb of Cleveland. He'd always remember the Indian games in the old Lakefront Stadium his father took him to in the 50's and meeting baseball stars like Jim Perry, Herb Score, Rocky Colavito, Minnie Minoso and Jimmy Piersall.

After his beloved father passed away when he was in his early teens, he remained a devoted Indians fan, became a star Little League pitcher, attended Ashland College on a baseball scholarship... he carried on the family tradition.

And now, he would do the same for his son, Billy. The presidential helicopter would take him and Billy, along with Billy's classmate to see the Cleveland Indians play the New York Yankees in a playoff game for the World Series.

It was a 330-mile flight to the Cleveland Hopkins Airport and the Director of the Secret Service, John Handley, literally went nuts when Rhinehart told him of his plans. The POTUS ignored the director's opposition and ordered him to make full plans for the visit to Progressive Field.

Rhinehart sat down at his desk and checked his watch. It was 6:15am. Handley would arrive in ten minutes. He thought about the raid his special forces executed with CBIF on Abaco and prayed that General Morrison and his agents would find out where the laser-guided mortars were. He would stay in encrypted communication with Morrison throughout the day and instantly react to any revelations, if the need arose. The trip to see the playoff game would be a great ploy that would distance him from the OT level operation.

Rhinehart was pleased that the mansion raid was successful. The captured terrorists would know about the mortars smuggled into the U.S. and would be interrogated. He prayed that the info would be gotten out of them and the sleeper cell lurking somewhere in northwest Pennsylvania would soon be neutralized and the mortars recovered. He would then appear on national TV and announce the monumental victory against terrorism to the American public, and the world. It would restore America's wounded psyche and demonstrate the ability of the counterintelligence community to keep them out of harm's way, He would deliver the Address to the Nation speech from the Oval Office and tell the world that the U.S. intelligence agencies brought down the largest terrorist network ever, one that was positioned to attack America's heartland.

He sipped his coffee and thought of past presidential addresses from the Oval Office: President Kennedy presenting news of the Cuban Missile Crisis, President Richard Nixon announcing his resignation in 1974, Ronald Reagan addressing the nation following the Space Shuttle *Challenger* Disaster... George W. Bush talking to the nation on the evening of September 11, 2001.

His secretary knocked gently at the open hallway door, then escorted Handley in. Rhinehart thanked her and motioned for him to sit down in a small couch opposite his at a coffee table.

"OK, John. Let me have the plans. I know you're uneasy about my trip to Progressive Field, but I'm sure you have the security figured out."

"Yes, sir. Let's start with phase one, the flight to Cleveland. Marine One will take off from here, on the South Lawn."

"How long is the flight? The game starts at 3pm."

"It's just over three-hundred miles. We've decided to use the smaller VH-60N 'WhiteHawk' instead of the large VH-3D chopper. It's less conspicuous. I called in four other 'WhiteHawks' from MCAF Quantico in Virginia. They're landing nearby, as we speak, at the Naval Support Facility Anacostia."

"Decoys?"

"Precisely. Shortly after you, your son Billy and his classmate take off from the South Lawn, the four identical choppers will congregate around you in the skies over D.C. Don't be alarmed, for they'll shift positions for several minutes while we're traveling at 180 mph."

"Is that necessary? Might scare the hell out of the kids."

"I'm afraid so, sir. We call it the 'presidential shell game' between the decoys and Marine one. Once north of D.C., the formation will spread out and remain fixed until arriving in Cleveland, but your chopper's location will be obscure to any potential enemy. There will also be an F-16 securing your airspace, but it will remain out-of-sight, fifteen-miles to the northwest."

Rhinehart chuckled, "Before you arrived I was rehashing childhood memories of Cleveland, when my father drove me downtown to watch the Indians play. It was such a simple thing to do. Billy won't experience such simplicity. What's the phase two plan?"

Handley wanted to remind the POTUS of his opposition to this venture, but he refrained. "Phase two involves your arrival at the airport and the drive to Progressive Field. The distance is slightly over thirteen miles and should take roughly twenty-two minutes. A C-5 Galaxy transport will land at Cleveland Hopkins Airport twenty minutes before your arrival and unload Cadillac One. When Marine One lands, you simply climb in and we drive you to the game."

"What have you done to lessen our presence while in route?" "Well, it's hard to hide the presidential state car, but I made it so people will think you are just some VIP arriving in town. The Washington, D.C. license plates were replaced with regular Ohio plates. There won't be a formal motorcade with presidential flags flapping in the breeze...only four nondescript Secret Service SUV's and two Cleveland Police patrol cars in front and behind you to clear a path in case of a traffic jam. Without a normal presidential motorcade with several dozen vehicles for security, healthcare emergencies, the press, and route-clearing... it should be easy to pull off."

"Good. What about the encrypted communications gear I'll need?"

"No problem, sir. It's installed in Cadillac One. You'll have instant secured communication with the outside world while being hermetically sealed inside...bulletproof, bombproof and chemical-weapons proof with a self-contained environmental system on board."

"How will the four SUV's be transported to the airport?"

"They're already in an undisclosed location in Cleveland, with five agents in each. They drove there yesterday."

Rhinehart thought to himself *Christ...all I want to do is go to a fuckin' baseball game with my son!* "How many more phases are left in your security plan?"

"Four, sir."

"Why not give me a short synopsis of them."

Handley sifted through the stack of papers he laid out on the coffee table. Rhinehart eased back in his couch and listened patiently. "Here's a quick rundown. I had a team of agents visit Cleveland last week. They met with Cleveland Hopkins officials and cleared airspace at the airport. We have a trauma hospital to rush you to if the need arises and worked out a secure safe location to take you to in case of an attack. They also met with the Cleveland FBI and local police to identify any possible 'Class Three' threats and..."

Rhinehart interrupted, "What are 'Class Three' threats? I forgot."

"We consider them potential threats by individuals. We have a list of persons who have threatened you, other presidents, congressmen or senators in the past by phone call, snail mail, e-mail, or over the internet on social media platforms...and have the capability of carrying out the threat."

"Did you identify any?"

"Yes, sir. Five individuals. Normally, when your visit is public knowledge my agents go to their homes and warn them that they'll be watched closely while you're in town. In this case, we won't make home visits or let them know that you're coming...but they will be kept under surveillance."

"Continue."

"A team of bomb-sniffing canines arrived in Cleveland yesterday with the SUV-escort agents. The dogs will clear streets and parked cars near where Cadillac One enters Progressive Field. A canopy will be set up by a rear loading dock door that you'll use to walk up to the suite, so you won't be seen exiting the vehicle. I didn't want you entering through Progressive Field's main entrance. The dogs will also clear the back stairway that leads up to the Champion Suite before you arrive. The suites and adjacent rooms will be cordoned off and occupied by Secret Service agents."

"What about secure communications while I'm in the suite, which should be roughly three hours, the length of a typical baseball game?"

"You will be able to communicate freely. A team will do a complete sweep of the suite for bugging devices. The dogs, of course, will sniff for possible concealed explosives. The phones and HD flat-screen

TVs will be removed to further insure against implanted wiretapping and eavesdropping devices."

"Anything else?"

"That's about it, sir. There will be three security perimeters. Cleveland police officers will be stationed below the suite and my general agents will stand guard outside on the balcony and in adjacent rooms. I think it best for you, Billy and his friend to stay inside the suite. I will remain with my Presidential Protective Division agents inside the Champion Suite with you."

President Rhinehart shook the director's hand. "You've done another fine job, John. That's why you'll remain Secret Service Director for many years to come. I can't tell you how comforting it is just knowing you're in charge of keeping me and my family safe."

"Thank you, sir."

Asif Qadeer Edhi sat in the back of the U-Haul van, making sure the twenty laser-guided mortar shells were securely stored in the space above the cab. He jiggled the three mortars bolted onto the floor boards. They didn't budge...all was secure.

He jumped out the back of the van and peered through the old wooden door of the barn. Everything was clear. Edhi walked back to the farmhouse where his four jihadi brothers were making final preparations. The three-man laser-designator team would soon pass through security and enter the stadium in Cleveland. It was a four-hour drive...time to get moving.

Episode 64

Partisans to wickedness

White House, Washington D.C.

South Lawn

The 'WhiteHawk' pilot eased down gently upon the South Lawn. He glanced at the north-south vista towards The Ellipse, then past the National Mall and across the Tidal Basin to the Jefferson Memorial. It was a memorable landing spot, one he would someday tell his grand-children about.

Two Marines opened the door and strutted down the helicopter steps onto the manicured grass of the South Lawn and stood at attention. One was in full dress uniform, the other acted as an armed guard.

When President Rhinehart, his son Billy and Billy's friend walked up to the chopper with four Secret Service agents, the Marines formally saluted the commander-in-chief. The president saluted back, then shook both their hands while the two excited boys pranced up the steps.

Inside, the pilot greeted them just outside the cockpit door. He was donned in a Marine Charlie/Delta uniform instead of his regular flight suit. He greeted Rhinehart and the children, then nodded at the four agents. The two Marines boarded last and secured the door. In seconds, the 'WhiteHawk' lifted off the South Lawn and headed North West to the Cleveland Hopkins Airport.

The Flats Cleveland, Ohio

The empty lot was a dreary place. John Dolan used the key that Edhi gave him to unlock the chain-link fence gate. He swung it open for his wife Diane to drive the U-Haul truck through. As per Edhi's orders, they drove it to this run-down warehouse on Scranton Road from their organic farm and canoeing business in northwest Pennsylvania.

A wooden sign with peeling paint covered a first-floor window of the aging brick building. It read "Cuyahoga River Warehouse." Vines had grown from around the corner of the once-booming repository and spread horizontally along the stained-bricks, covering an entire side. All the first-floor windows were boarded-up with thick wood panels. Corroded metal signs lined the discolored brick walls, advertising passé enterprises that seemed like headstones for once-great companies: *Fly Pan Am Shop Tower Records Polaroid Instamatic Camera Carnation Breakfast Bar.* A faded wood sign splattered in white paint that read *PARKING- 10 cents/hr., 50 cents/day* somehow remained affixed to the corroded chain-link fence.

A month ago, the Dolans parked the U-Haul in plain sight on the front yard of their farm after renting it from a dealership in Erie, Pa. They used the truck for their French Creek Outfitters business, loading canoes in it and transporting clients to various rivers and large creeks around the area. Normally, they towed an eight-canoe trailer behind their Subaru, but Edhi's orders were to be obeyed.

They left the U-Haul van and locked the chain-link fence, then strolled to the end of Scranton Road and crossed the Cuyahoga River. They came upon the four-story, redbrick Powerhouse building that lay directly over the river. It was a restored nineteenth-century structure, which at one time provided energy to power Cleveland's streetcars. Now, it houses a café, pub, Improv Comedy Club and restaurant, party rooms for rent, and the Greater Cleveland Aquarium.

The duo strolled through the structure, holding hands, acting like a happily-married couple on a tour of The Flats. They paused to admire the stylish arched windows and distressed brick walls, then walked into McCarthy's Ale House and ordered a few pints of Guinness and some pub grub.

Diane asked, "Why do you suppose Edhi instructed us to drive around Progressive Field for so long?"

John dipped a nacho into the spinach artichoke dip. "Beats me. He wanted us to drive in from Pennsylvania and get off the I-90 Innerbelt freeway by the Indians stadium, then circle the ballpark slowly a few times as if we were lost and trying to find directions."

Diane soaked a mozzarella stick in the marinara sauce. "It was peculiar how quickly the Cleveland Police stopped us when we turned off East 9th Street onto Eagle Avenue."

"Yeah, they were pretty thorough. That one cop read our rental contract suspiciously, then asked us why we had a month-long rental agreement for the U-Haul."

"Well, John, we had nothing to hide and the explanation seemed to assuage his suspicions."

He munched down another nacho. "A copy of our long-term parking rental agreement contract with Cuyahoga River Warehouse and our French Creek Outfitters business seemed to appease him."

"Yeah, but he still insisted on searching the entire van. I didn't enjoy standing on the sidewalk along East 9th Street while he slid open the back panel and a half dozen cops searched through the back."

John Dolan laughed. "All they found were eight canoes on racks, a bunch of paddles and comfort seatbacks and cushions. He bought our story about coming to Cleveland to trade-in our canoes to buy new ones."

"I suppose, but they seemed overly-cautious...somethings going down that we don't know about. Even if he didn't buy our story and pressed us further, we couldn't give him any more information. Hell, we don't know the real reasons why we do what we do. All we do is follow Edhi's instructions and never ask why."

The borderline personality-disordered couple instinctively reached across the table and held each other's hands. They realized the residual anger from their youth would never diminish. Rechanneling it was the only alternative. Simply holding the anger within and not doing anything about it wasn't an option. Before meeting Edhi, John Dolan's built-up ire caused tense muscles, severe headaches and a sore jaw from constantly clenching his teeth. It wasn't until the pent-up anger led to high blood pressure and a stroke that he sought group counseling... and met Diane.

The Dolans couldn't find forgiveness for their ultra-religious upbringing. They tried tolerance and reconciliation with the God-fearing church community and with their pious parents, but were nevertheless eschewed for their blasphemous existence. Organized evangelical religion had no room for exoneration, mercy, or understanding. Happiness and a sense of fulfillment remained a fleeting segment of their lives...until they met Edhi.

The overseer of terrorist sleeper cells lurking inside America targeted them when they trolled radical Islamic sites from an internet café in Erie. The relationship grew via social media interactions over several years until Edhi recruited them into his ranks.

Edhi appreciated their hatred towards the duplicitous Christian religion, but never trusted them fully. He kept them isolated from his network and ignorant of the ill deeds they planned on doing.

John and Diane Dolan didn't know that an exact replica of their U-Haul truck was hidden in an old, abandoned barn near their organic farm. It had matching license plates, similar dents above the left back panel, an identical half torn-off "Honk if you love Jesus" bumper sticker on the lower right side of the door just above the loading ramp, and harmonizing paint scratches, scrape marks and other scuff marks that were meticulously replicated.

Other than receiving a cash restitution at a dead drop, they had no personal reasons for renting the U-Haul truck. A white chalk mark appeared on a "Deer Crossing" sign down from their farm. It was a signal to proceed to the dead drop located at the summit of a neglected gas company path off Teepleville Flats Road.

It was the same location where they picked up the Middle Eastern trio carrying backpacks and Cleveland Indians souvenirs. At the base of a large oak tree near the capped oil well, they retrieved a waterproof canister with a detailed note specifying how they were to rent and operate the U-Haul truck. A stack of $50 bills totaling $5,000.00 was included in the cache.

As instructed, they rented the U-Haul truck in Erie, parked it in plain sight at their farm, and drove it often around Cambridge Springs and the surrounding countryside. They played into Edhi's hands by creating a smokescreen through which his attack-cell truck could sneak through.

Unknown to Edhi or the Dolans, a week prior, at 3am, four CI agents wearing jeans and dark hoodies emerged from the surrounding Hemlock forest surrounding the Dolan's organic farm. A dog accompanied them. It was an overcast and moonless night. They snuck to the back of the open U-Haul and crawled in.

As one stood outside as a lookout, the three inside swept handheld devices close to the van floor, walls and ceiling. They did the same to the canoes and camping gear. The dog sniffed items its handler pointed to. One agent held a strange-looking device that detected minute traces of radiation.

In ten minutes, they vacated the truck and disappeared back into the forest, then made their way back to the quaint, Victorian-styled Riverside Inn where 'Tracker' was eagerly waiting for them.

In her room, 'Tracker' and the agents analyzed the air samples they collected for traces of biothreat residue. Special strips were inserted into the hand-held devices that detected traces of Anthrax,

Plague, Ricin, Abrin...even Tularemia. The results came up negative. The radiation detector device computed zero emissions.

The dog handler reported his canine gave no behavioral signs of smelling explosives. It was trained to detect C-4 signatures, buried land mines, IED's, and explosives used in military-weapon warheads... including mortars.

When pressed by 'Tracker,' the handler assured her that his dog would have picked up a week-old scent if mortars had been in the U-Haul. Even an infinitesimal amount would trigger a nerve in its nose, the trigeminal, and be sent to a part of its brain that processes sensations, including smells. He told her, "If any of these hi-tech mortar shells had been in the van, my dog would have alerted me... she never forgets an explosive signature."

'Tracker's' sixteen CI agents initially reported the Dolan's U-Haul as suspicious. The decision was made to target it, for they spotted it passing them often as they bicycled, hiked and bird-watched along the back roads surrounding Cambridge Springs.

A thorough background check of John and Diane Dolan came up clean and their truck was free of biological, radiological and explosive residues. U.S. intelligence decided they were not a homeland security threat.

Several more Guinness drafts later, the Dolans were feeling their oats. They were having a pleasurable time. John gave a toast to his wife and held up a bloated wallet full of fifty-dollar bills. "Here's to us, my dear, and may our lives continue to prosper."

Diane chuckled, then checked her watch. "It's one now... we've got an hour left of shit food and Guinness. At precisely 2pm, our instructions are to walk back to the Cuyahoga River Warehouse and drive the van through downtown Cleveland, then back to our farm."

They didn't know that a replica U-Haul van would enter the warehouse lot and park in their vacant space shortly after they left.

Episode 65

EIT black site

The inside hull of the *Queen Conch II* was unnerving. Corey stood in the dimly-lit chamber, quietly staring at the six soundproof cubicles spread out before him. He contacted Constance and put her in charge of the remainder of the raid plans. She and the other agents would fill the duffel bags with everything in Sandoval's library: videos, note-books, manila folders in the file cabinet, and computer hard drives. Then, they would retrace their steps back through the six miles of thick forest to Thompson's Bay beach, recover the camouflaged rafts, get back to the yacht and proceed back to the Conch Inn Marina.

Each steel cubicle had one glass, see-through side. They didn't face each other so the bound occupants couldn't see or hear one an-other. Empty wooden crates and cardboard boxes used to smuggle in the IET equipment lay strewn in the corners of the hull. Ferguson's fish-ing boat had, indeed, been transformed into a CBIF rendition black site.

The Dirty Tricks team leader, code-named "Oppressor," weighed over 300 pounds and sported a menacing tattoo of a snarling were-wolf with blood dripping from its jaws on his forearm. Corey always felt an innate uneasiness around him. *A Hannibal Lector ambience radiates out from this guy.*

Oppressor checked his watch. Twenty minutes had passed since the Black Hawk lowered the captives onto the deck into the hands of the seasoned torturers. He nodded to Corey and his five comrades that it was time to begin.

Corey glanced at the wall monitors which displayed the blood oxygen content, blood pressure and heart rate of their six victims who sat immobilized, bare-assed naked, and firmly strapped into metal chairs.

During the twenty-minute period of silence, which was geared to heighten anxiety and fear, the blood pressure and heart beat of El-Sayed, Eamal Batoor and Khoury Kassim remained only slightly elevated. The speakers next to the monitor recorded them softly chanting *Subhannah Allah Allhumdolillah* and *Allahu Akbar* repetitively.

Oppressor whispered to Corey. "Fuck…maybe there's something valid to that Muslim meditation stuff."

Corey replied, "Only to them, not us. I'll stick with transcendental meditation and yoga to find inner peace and happiness." He looked at the vital signs of Tougas, Cherestal, and Sandoval which measured like they just ran a marathon. Their heavy and labored breathing could be heard over the speakers.

Oppressor announced, "Let's interrupt their chat with Allah." The five 'Dirty Tricks' agents entered a separate cubicle assigned to them. Oppressor entered Sandoval's with Corey right behind him.

Corey looked on as the dimmer lights were turned up so Sandoval could view photos of his wife, mistresses and a few of his children that were taped on the metal wall. Oppressor unstrapped him and slammed his naked body hard into the wall, then threw him back into the metal chair and slapped him repeatedly.

Corey calmly asked, "Where are the mortars? Where is Edhi and his attack cell? What, where and when are they going to attack?"

Silence. Corey nodded to Oppressor, who slammed Sandoval against the wall again then threw him hard into the metal chair.

Corey spoke softly again. "Look at the pictures of your family. We know where they are. We will kidnap, torture and kill each of them… unless you answer my questions. He tore a photo of a cute little four-year-old girl off the wall and shoved it in Sandoval's face. It showed him sitting on a luxurious patio deck chair in Medellin, playing the

Chutes and Ladders board game with her. "That includes her...we will slit her throat." He lied.

Silence. Both Corey and Oppressor grabbed Sandoval and slammed him onto a slanting wooden board next to the chair. His head lay at the bottom of a twenty-degree incline. While Corey firmly secured his elevated feet, Oppressor strapped his forehead down in between two viselike slats so he couldn't wobble his head back and forth.

Corey stood back as Oppressor placed a thick cloth over Sandoval's forehead and eyes, then poured lukewarm water over it in a controlled manner. When it was fully saturated, he slowly lowered the cloth downward until it completely covered Sandoval's nose and mouth.

After a few moments, his body jerked helplessly against the re-straints as his airflow was restricted. The water kept flowing...slowly, methodically. Oppressor kept pouring a continuous stream from a height of twenty inches over his head...ten...fifteen...twenty ... thirty ... forty...forty-five seconds.

Although the breathing passages were only sixty percent blocked, Sandoval's brain interpreted the experience as an actual drowning. Complete primordial fear engulfed him and he began gagging un-controllably. Vomit traveled up his esophagus as he experienced the sensation of asphyxiation.

"Aw, fuck!" Oppressor shouted as the vomit puffed up the cloth around his mouth. "He hurled some puke."

Corey checked the Pulse Oximeter attached to Sandoval's index finger. It read "70." Any reading in the "60's" could result in death. He lifted the cloth and wiped away the vomit. "We don't want him dead... yet."

Sandoval was gasping and hyperventilating wildly. They allowed him to take three full breaths before Oppressor placed a freshly-satu-rated cloth over his forehead.

Corey signaled him to stop. He leaned over the waterboard and whispered calmly, "If you tell me where the hell Edhi is this will stop and your family…including that little girl…will be left alone. Where is Edhi?!"

Despite the fear in Sandoval's eyes, silence ensued. Corey slapped him hard several times then motioned for Oppressor to continue.

Progressive Field
Cleveland, Ohio
(GPS: 41.496301, -81.685120)
After a perfunctory examination of the contents of their backpacks, the three laser-designator team members passed through security with little difficulty. The stadium security guards looked at their Cabella stadium binoculars, Canon digital cameras and Sony camcorders, never realizing that laser-targeting devices would soon be assembled from their attachment parts with the screws, nuts and bolts hidden inside the sandwiches in zip-lock baggies and in the Minute Maid fruit juice boxes.

Cadillac One drove into the back of Progressive Field and stopped under a canopy that was erected by the rear loading dock. President Rhinehart, his son Billy and Billy's classmate remained unobserved while four Secret Service agents escorted them up a stairwell to the Champion Suite.

John Handley and five of his agents greeted them inside the luxurious suite. Billy and his friend ran over to the large windows and peered down into the stadium while Handley showed the president to a comfortable couch that offered an excellent bird's-eye view of the playing field.

Rhinehart thanked him and retrieved an old pair of binoculars from a case he brought along. They were the same binoculars his father gave him when he was age nine, the same age as Billy. He planned on passing them on to Billy for his upcoming birthday.

The president scanned the Indian's dugout, trying to spot Mark Rounds, the Indians All-Star pitcher whose signed photo set in the Oval Office.

Off to his side, a Secret Service agent scanned the 45,000 exuberant fans with a telephoto binocular camera created by the CIA's Directorate of Science & Technology. Some fans painted Indian war paint on their faces and held up signs like "World Series WINDIANS!" and "You Can't Hate Us Too Much, We Beat The Yankees!."

He zoomed-in on the upper sections where parents sat with their children, single individuals sat alone, lovers cuddled together, and groups of friends excitedly chatted with one another.

Occasionally, he snapped photos of faces he deemed suspicious. The images were sent via satellite to the NGI, Next Generation Identification database for an instant analysis.

Three Middle Eastern-looking men sat munching on sandwiches from zip-lock bags and drinking Minute Maid fruit drinks. They wore Indians jerseys and waved Tribe pennants. He snapped their portraits and sent them in to NGI, but all came back NIF...not in file.

Suddenly, the entire stadium stood up and a huge roar from bellowing fans reverberated the windows of the Champion Suite. Mark Rounds walked out of the dugout onto the pitcher's mound. The game began.

Geneva-On-The-Lake, Ohio

Edhi was nervous, but didn't show it. He drove the U-Haul truck seventy-two miles from the abandoned barn along back roads to remain unnoticed. Once in Ohio, he continued west on county roads until he hit Route 534, then headed north towards I-90 which he planned to drive on quickly at seventy mph into Cleveland.

His terrorist friend sat in the cab next to him, wearing makeup and a female hairpiece to make him look similar to John Dolan's wife, Diane. The other four jihadi attack cell members remained hidden in the back with the mortars and live rounds.

As they drove north on Route 534, a storm front rapidly approached from the north over Lake Erie. The dark, blue-black clouds contrasted against the powdery-blue summer sky.

Edhi's female-impersonating passenger said, "Looks like a bad storm approaching."

Edhi looked at the Google Maps navigator on his smart phone. "It seemed to come out of nowhere...we better drive past I-90 and head to Geneva-On-The-Lake, just to play it safe."

They listened intently to the Indians game on the radio. The sport's announcer commented, "A storm to the east of Cleveland is passing through, but it should miss us. We don't have to worry about a game delay."

The rain started to drizzle down. Edhi switched on the wipers. The wind picked up and the drizzle became a shower. They continued north, through the city of Geneva towards Geneva-On-The-Lake.

By the time they reached the small town, the drizzle became a barrage of heavy raindrops and hail pelted the windshield. He pulled into the parking lot of a place called the Old Firehouse Winery. A wine-tasting event was taking place and people ran from the outside patio back inside.

They parked in the corner of the lot and waited an hour for the storm cell to blow over and the torrential downpour and winds to subside. The sun finally reappeared.

Edhi started the U-Haul, retraced his steps south on Route 534 and drove onto I-90. He checked the GPS Navigation app on his cell phone. "The storm delayed us an hour, a half hour each way getting to Geneva-On-The-Lake from the interstate. We're two hours behind schedule, but the Cuyahoga River Warehouse parking lot awaits us. It's only fifty-five miles away. We'll be there shortly."

His passenger spoke softly, "*Nahn ealaa washk 'ann yusbahuu shuhada.' Fi sabil alllah*...we are about to become martyrs... for Allah's sake."

Edhi smiled and replied, *"Alttafani fi Allah*...Allah thanks you for your dedication. The president of the infidel nation and thousands of his followers will soon die. Our laser-designator team is in place... they will guide a rain of horror down upon the infidels from the skies of alijann."

Episode 66

Torturing a psychopath

Corey noticed Sandoval actually finger-counting the seconds away as the waterboarding continued. He stared dubiously at Oppressor. "I've got to know where those fuckin' mortars are."

"Don't worry. I follow a certain sequence. Once my clients think the torture is predictable and bearable, I switch the routine and increase the intensity of pain. I will bring him to the point of talking, eventually."

"I hope so. We've got lives to save."

"I never fail." Oppressor took a wiffle ball full of holes and forced it into Sandoval's mouth, then he threaded a strap through the holes and tied it firmly to the sides of the waterboard.

He replaced the cloth over Sandoval's face and began pouring the water in a deliberate, controlled manner again.

Sandoval started finger-counting, but when the normal stopping time arrived, the water kept flowing, past forty seconds. It gushed into his open mouth and nostrils but didn't flood into the lungs and asphyxiate him because of the incline. Instead, the water streamed into his nasal cavity. Oppressor didn't stop pouring.

Absolute panic struck. The narco-terrorist's body jerked and tensed, trying to break the straps binding him down. The cloth wasn't lifted and the water stream kept flowing.

Corey heard a faint cracking sound and saw Sandoval's wrist bone stick through the skin due to his intense struggling against the restraints.

Oppressor said, "It's normal to have bone fractures. That's why we tie them down so tight... fear and adrenaline makes them gain superhuman strength."

The cloth was lifted and a wild-eyed Sandoval gasped for oxygen. Normally, Oppressor allowed him three full breaths, but he flopped the cloth down in the middle of the second inhale and started pouring again.

The routine was repeated, nonstop, for twenty minutes: waterboarding, slapping, waterboarding, slapping- until Sandoval gargled through the wiffle ball "I talk! I talk! Please, no more!"

Oppressor immediately removed the saturated cloth and whispered into a hidden mike on his lapel, "We got a squealer."

Two of his men left their booths and came to assist. Corey helped them unstrap Sandoval, cuff his hands behind his back and escort him to an adjacent room that was carpeted and well-lit. They wrapped a bathrobe around him while relaxation music played softly and a flat screen TV broadcast CNN news.

Sandoval was allowed to sit on a comfortable couch. His face was bruised from being smacked dozens of times. He had to lean forward because his broken wrists were handcuffed behind him The EIT routine sickened Corey, but he avoided feeling empathy by thinking of the thirty-five children slain in the Boston elementary school, his wife Danielle who Sandoval tortured and murdered, and the Americans who may soon be murdered by the deadly mortars he smuggled into the country. He stood over the murderous bastard. "Start talking...tell me where Edhi and the mortars are."

Sandoval stammered, in-between coughing and gasping, "I tell ya...I don't know where dey are. But, I can tell ya 'bout corruption at da highest levels of da RBPF...top men dat be on my payroll, men who gonna end da career 'o your friend, Deputy Commander Rolle and take ova da Bahamian government."

"I'm listening." *He's starting to talk…it's a start. Rolle's in political trouble and I can't afford to lose such an asset so high up in the police force.*

Sandoval spat water out of his mouth that drained down from his nasal cavity before he spoke. "I pay off da RBPF Commissioner o' Police…da guy at da top, eighty-thousand a year. He know all 'bout my smugglin' in drugs and terrorists from Haiti and he make sure my operation ain't interfered with."

"Do you have Rolle on your payroll?"

"No, I try to bribe and threaten him…but he don't budge. He place God's law above my offerings. Dat's why I murder his future son-in-law, Bernard, da young custom's officer at Sandy Point."

"For revenge?" "Yeah."

Corey felt like pulling out his Glock 30 and shooting him in both knee caps. *Fuckin' bastard! When I was arrested at the British Colonial Hotel, the old 'BC', for being suspected of murdering Fowler at Parliament Square. Rolle had his detective transport me to Carmichael Detention Center instead of the downtown police station. He interviewed me in private, tears in his eyes when talking about his only daughter, Shantel, who was engaged to Bernard Knowles the young Bahamian Customs agent at the remote Sandy Point Airport…who didn't take Sandoval's bribes. Rolle showed me the police sketch of the suspect…with teardrop tattoos under his eye…fuckin' Sandoval. That's why Rolle interrogated me in private at Carmichael and not at his downtown Nassau office…he wanted me to find this bastard sitting before me…and hand him over. Mission accomplished.*

"Tell me about the higher ups in RBPF who are on your payroll and how are they going to get Rolle." *Not only am I going to hand-deliver this psychopath to Rolle… I'm going to save his career.*

Sandoval grimaced, the tight-fitting handcuffs exacerbated the pain from his broken wrists. "Da police commissioner promoted his nephew from constable to some position just below what Rolle's be. Den, 'cuz I gots da Bahamian Prime Minister in my pocket, da nephew appointed to be Superintendent of RBPF."

"Prime Minister Nigel Lightbourne is a decent man, he wouldn't take your fuckin' bribes."

"Yeah…I know dat. But, da police commissioner invited him to da mansion fo' a weekend. One ting' led to anotha and da Colombian whores showed up with Abner Orival. I got video of Prime Minister Lightbourne havin' sex wid two o' dem."

Corey concluded. "So, when the Commissioner of Police asked the Prime Minister to promote his nephew, he did."

"You betcha…dere's more den one way to corrupt an honest man…da nephew got promoted five ranks immediately. Othawise… da videos o' da Prime Minister of da Bahamas gettin' blow jobs from da whores would be sent to da *Nassau Guardian*."

Corey checked his shoulder-mounted videocam to make sure it was working, then grabbed Sandoval and picked him up from the couch, slapped him and got in his face. "Where is Edhi? Where is his sleeper attack cell and the mortars? Where and when are they going to attack?!"

Silence. Corey slammed him back down on the couch. Sandoval screamed from the pain. He turned to Oppressor. "Continue with the waterboarding …and kick it up a bit!"

"That will be no problem." The big man and his Dirty Tricks comrades ripped the bathrobe off Sandoval, shuffled his nude body back into the booth and strapped him firmly back onto the board. A dolly with two car batteries was wheeled in.

Oppressor took a strange-looking wand with a bronze tip off the dolly and attached cables from a control box to it. He calmly looked at Sandoval, who was allowed to view the setup. "This box is called a rheostat and I can raise or reduce the voltage. Are you sure you don't want to answer Mr. Pearson's questions about Edhi and the mortars? If you do, we will stop the enhanced interrogation process immediately."

Silence. Corey said to Oppressor. "Proceed."

The 'Dirty Tricks' team grabbed Sandoval's inclined legs, spread them wide apart and re-strapped them to the outer edges of the waterboard. Oppressor held the wand by an insulated handle and a sharp "crack" sound and spark flashed when he pressed a button. He turned the dial on the rheostat to low. "We'll start with a low current."

His comrades placed the wet towel over Sandoval's head and mouth, and began pouring water over it again in a controlled fashion. They thoroughly soaked his crotch area. Sandoval began finger-counting, but when Oppressor stuck the bronze tip between his penis and balls and zapped him, all his fingers straightened out and trembled.

While zapping Sandoval, Oppressor glanced over at Corey and calmly said, "This is called a picana rod. I engineered it myself."

Corey stared in silence at the big, tattooed man. *He actually sounds proud of his perverted ingenuity.* After a few moments, the electrocution stopped. Sandoval squealed in pain while gasping for air through the saturated cloth. The pouring continued past the normal time of stoppage that Sandoval was accustomed to.

Oppressor stuck the picana tip between his penis and balls again, sometimes shocking him, other times not…making Sandoval's suffering completely chaotic and unpredictable.

Sandoval was allowed to take only one and a half gasps before the cloth was flopped over his forehead, nostrils and mouth. The pouring began again while Oppressor jammed the picana rod in his crotch and unpredictably zapped…or didn't zap him.

Sandoval's body writhed and tensed even when the wand didn't shock him. It seemed to amuse Oppressor, who chuckled faintly at the panicked reaction. "Watch this Corey, more unpredictability."

Corey watched Oppressor in amazement as he intermittently began shocking other sensitive body parts...nipples, mouth, arm pits. *How can he find enjoyment in this? Yes, a true psychopath who has found his calling.*

Nausea overtook him, so Corey walked out of the EIT booth and sought the bathroom in the adjacent lounge. He stood over the toilet and vomited several times. He gargled with water, stared at himself in the sink mirror and wondered how much longer he could endure being around Oppressor. *I live in a world that no layperson could ever understand. A deceitful Irish banker, pub owner and U.S. senator, dangerous Middle Eastern men controlling a terrorist network lurking somewhere inside America...the merciless slaughter of children at the Boston elementary school...a psychopathic narco-terrorist who I would gladly put a bullet through the head of, but can't stand to watch being tortured. His murderous bodyguards who fed Duane to a tiger shark... Sidney Fowler gunned down on Parliament Square...Bernard Knowles slain in Sandy Point...Devon Ledard shot and his wife and children ready to be tortured and killed. I hope my call in to Rolle was quick enough and the constables he sent to Devon's home in the Guana Cay settlement arrived on time. The murderous endings to Duane Collier and his mother... the killing of my sweet wife, Danielle... my unease over the possibility of Constance being harmed...the tears flowing from the eyes of Shianna Fowler at the Conch Inn Sunset Bar over her brother's senseless murder and from the eyes of Rolle over his son-in-law's demise...all caused by greedy, cold-blooded, evil people. Will I ever be able to shake these memories? I don't think so.*

One of Oppressor's men appeared at the bathroom door. "Mr. Pearson, Sandoval's ready to talk...to tell you about Edhi and the mortars."

Corey ran to the EIT booth and stood over Sandoval. "Don't waste my time. Tell me where Edhi is or I'm out of here and my friends will continue where they left off."

Sandoval's face was black, blue and green. Electrical burns covered his nipples, mouth, penis and scrotum. He was able to talk in- between gasps.

"I tell ya, but you gotta uncuff me and let me see my watch." Corey nodded to Oppressor, who unstrapped his arms and wrist, leaving his ankles, legs, hips, neck and forehead still firmly secured to the inclined board.

Another Dirty Tricks agent returned with the watch and handed it to Corey.

"What the fuck do you want me to do with this?"

"Give it to me and I tell ya where Edhi and da mortars be at."

Corey said to Oppressor, "I take it you cleaned this watch and all his clothes?"

"Yes, Mr. Pearson. No bombs, bugs...it's clean."

Corey handed the watch to Sandoval, who could barely lift it to his face for close inspection. One eye was swollen shut but he put it up to the good eye and pressed buttons. A mother of pearl dial and chronograph subdials with luminescent inlays showed against the rose and gold-toned face.

He held it up for Corey to see. "Dis watch never off a second. It cost fifteen-thousand dollars and Edhi got a matchin' pair...so does dat pervert senator 'o yours."

"Warren?"

"Yeah, I give one ta both 'o dem."

"You give Senator Warren plenty of gifts, like the Cessna Skylane he flew here from Bimini."

Sandoval looked curious. "How you know I give him dat plane?"

Corey was quickly losing patience. "Because we're smarter than you think, you arrogant dumb ass...where's Edhi?! Tell me now! We have enough intelligence to know if you're lying. If you are, I will walk out of here and let my friends here have their way with you."

Sandoval rambled on. "OK, OK, I tell ya, but ya gotta know dat dere's a big difference 'tween da watch Edhi got and da one Warren got."

"Tell me, I'm all ears."

Sandoval's good eye actually twinkled, as if a spark of life returned to his dismal future. "Edhi and me...six days ago, we set our chronographs for a four-hour count down dat begin today, when he leave da farm in Pennsylvania to attack." Sandoval held up the watch face. "Look!"

The chronograph was stopped at zero. His swollen lips grinned. "You too late, da attack be underway...President Rhinehart and thousands of Americans are bein' blown ta bits as we speak!"

"Tell me where...now!"

"At Progressive Field in Cleveland, Ohio. Da president be dere on a secret visit with his son and anotha kid. It all kept tight-lipped... only da Secret Service know 'bout it...and Edhi, me, El-Sayed, Eamal Batoor and Khoury Kassim, too. So, ya not so smart...ya commander-in-chief and a stadium full of Americans are dyin' right now cause 'o your ignorance. You be da dumb ass, not me."

Episode 67

The ultimate sacrifice

CBIF HQ on Eaton Street
Key West, Florida

Corey ran back into the adjoining lounge and called Morrison on Pinkston's twelve-digit algorithmic-encrypted phone. He answered immediately, "I heard and saw it all. I'm contacting the POTUS at the White House as we speak. Sit tight and listen in. I'll put us on conference call."

Rhinehart's secure White House phone rang twice, then transferred to the secretary's secure phone, which was rarely used. "Hello, this is President Rhinehart's secretary. May I ask who's calling?"

"I'm sure you know me by my voice. Where is the president? I hope you're not going to tell me he's at the Cleveland Indians playoff game at Progressive Field."

"Why, yes... he is, General Morrison. He planned this private trip weeks ago, and has complete Secret Service protection. He planned to attend the game unannounced then return immediately back to the White House. The departure to return time is seven hours and he has..."

Morrison interrupted. "Listen to me! Contact the Secret Service agent outside your door and have Rhinehart evacuated immediately from the stadium...that is, if he's not already blown to smithereens! We have reliable intelligence indicating he is under a deadly mortar attack...at this very moment!"

"Oh...dear! Right away!"

Morrison hung up. "Corey, you still there?"

"Yes, sir. I ordered the Dirty Tricks agents to resume torturing Sandoval for more details. He just revealed the attack vehicle is a large U-Haul van. Edhi must have slipped through 'Tracker' and her sixteen agents combing the countryside in northwest Pennsylvania. You mentioned there was a U-Haul van they checked out, but it came up clean."

Morrison began nervously chewing on his Montecristo. "We'll deal with that later. I'm contacting Stacey at NSA on the secure phone. A weary voice answered. "Yes, sir."

"Stacey, immediately send a dispatch to all CBIF operatives working in the Fusion Centers in Erie, Pennsylvania and Cleveland. Pearson will now tell you what to transmit. Go ahead, Corey."

As Corey spoke, Stacie typed his words into her classified Dictionary program. She noted his voice sounded tense. "Stacie. Send this out immediately to our moles in the Erie and Cleveland Fusion Centers... 'A terrorist attack is in progress. Broadcast APB for large U-Haul truck traveling from northwest Pennsylvania east to Progressive Field in Cleveland. Vehicle is now traveling to or is now already in Cleveland near Progressive Field. Vehicle operated by radical Islamist, terrorist attack cell headed by man named Asif Qadeer Edhi. Vehicle carrying hi-tech laser-guided mortars and mortar rounds. President Rhinehart is at Progressive Field now and mortar attack may be underway. Secret Service agents at Progressive Field evacuating POTUS now. Consider occupants armed and extremely dangerous.'"

Stacie pressed the SEND button. The encrypted message went to the underground workstation supercomputers of locally-embedded CBIF officers in both the Erie and Cleveland Fusion Centers. Corey did not reveal any of the cloak-and-dagger particulars on the sources or methods used to collect the information.

In thirty seconds, the message was received, shared with FBI and other high-ranking law enforcement officials at each center, then broadcast out to every state, county and local law enforcement agency in the northern sections of Pennsylvania and Ohio.

Village of Madison, Ohio

Trooper Tom Benson was retiring in one week. At age fifty, and after thirty years patrolling Ohio's interstates and back roads, he decided it was time to relax and spend more time with his wife. Their two daughters were both married and lived in the nearby cozy village of Madison, Ohio. He dreamed of teaching his grandchildren the art of fishing. Knowing the local fishing hotspots in the Grand River and Mill Creek, he hoped to get them addicted to catching smallmouth bass and steelhead trout.

The seasoned patrolman was telling the barista inside the Open Door Coffee House of his retirement plans while waiting for his customary order of coconut coffee and a healthy veggie wrap. His silver-gray, super-charged Dodge Charger was parked out front on Main Street. Each door-panel emblem was emblazoned with the words "Ohio State Patrol" in-between outstretched eagle wings that protruded from gold-treaded tires. A rooftop radar gun was attached just above the driver's door.

The owners of the coffee house and the baristas who worked there enjoyed Trooper Benson stopping in for a half-hour lunch or for his fifteen-minute breaks. His presence gave them a sense of security, for I-90 was only a few minutes away from the peaceful town of only 3,100 people. Last year, a passerby on the interstate robbed them at gunpoint.

The barista handed him his take-out order in a sturdy double-paper bag. She knew the routine. Both items were placed in one bag, for he didn't like to carry the sandwich bag in one hand and the coffee to-go cup in the other. Benson preferred having a free hand near his holstered Sig p-226, just in case.

He walked out and paused by his cruiser, quickly looking up and down Main Street, checking out the dozen shops and eateries. The brewery, sushi bar, martial arts studio, vintage doughnut shop, toy store and the tree-lined Madison Village Square Park across the street appeared secure, as usual.

Benson climbed into his cruiser and patrolled north on River Street past old Victorian, mansion-sized homes before he left the village. After several minutes, he pulled over at the top of the I-90 Exit 212 entrance ramp. He angled the cruiser in order to point the radar at oncoming cars in the opposite, east-bound lane while still being able to view westbound traffic approaching him below.

He enjoyed the coconut coffee and munched on the veggie wrap, being careful not to spill anything on his immaculate uniform. The day turned bright and sunny after the heavy storm passed through a half-hour ago. He was going to clean his windshield before starting on patrol again, but the heavy downpour washed it for him.

The traffic heading towards him was light and he routinely eyed each vehicle while enjoying his meal. A large U-Haul truck caught his attention. It was brand-new and freshly-painted, but had old, worn plates on the front. He learned much over the past thirty years by observing thousands of vehicles passing by, including the fact that older model vehicles can have new plates, but new vehicles seldom have old plates. He also noted that it sagged too much on the front springs below the cab as it passed underneath.

Trooper Benson secured his coffee mug, sped down the ramp and followed the suspicious truck. The back shocks didn't sag as much as the front ones. The cab and large "Mom's Attic" space that extended over it made the truck front-heavy with whatever it was loaded with. He decided to make a traffic stop. "Unit sixty-seven to dispatch."

"Dispatch, go head sixty-seven."

"Request Code twenty-three license check on U-Haul truck, plate number 'R' Roger...'A' Alpha...two-one-five-nine-seven."

A few moments later dispatch came back on. "Sixty-seven?"

"This is sixty-seven, go ahead."

"R-A-2-1-5-9-7... U-Haul out of Erie, Pennsylvania...long-term rental under John Dolan of Cambridge Springs, Pennsylvania...NIF... nothing in file on Dolan or the vehicle."

"Roger that. I'll be stopping same in I-90 westbound lane, one mile west of Exit 212."

"Ten-four, sixty-seven."

Benson turned on the flashing blue lights and switched on the siren wail sound for a second, then to a few attention-getting "yelp" reverberations. As the truck obediently pulled over and stopped on the berm, Benson stopped thirty feet behind, angled the cruiser and turned the wheels so they pointed toward the highway. In case a careless driver rear-ended his parked cruiser, it wouldn't lurch forward and hit him.

He exited and walked cautiously up to the rear of the U-Haul, looking into the large driver's side mirror. He could see the driver's face staring back at him. It didn't appear to be a man of Irish descent... Dolan...maybe someone of Middle Eastern lineage?

Edhi began to perspire as he stared into the outside mirror and saw the trooper disappear, then suddenly reappear in the passenger's side mirror, walking up to the cab on the passenger's side.

Benson stopped several feet behind the passenger-side door. He calmly issued an order. "Please place your hands where I can see them. Driver... place both hands on the top of the steering wheel. Passenger...place both yours on top of the dashboard."

Edhi whispered into a microphone he used to communicate with the six cell members in back. "Kill him when I say the word 'officer'."

Once all four hands were visible, Benson spoke calmly. "Passenger...take your right hand off the dashboard and open the door." The attack-cell member dressed like a woman complied. Once the door was slightly open, Benson opened the door the rest of the way and stepped into full view. "Driver...I'd like to see your driver's license plus the rental agreement."

Edhi looked out his side mirror. No vehicles were approaching. Now's the time. He replied, "Yes sir, officer. Did we do anything
wrong?"

Benson watched closely as Edhi reached over and opened the
glove compartment and shuffled through a stack of papers, pretending to look for the nonexistent rental agreement.

Two of the cell members in back carefully lifted the altered outside
release lever from the inside of the cargo hold and gently lifted the
well-oiled sliding door. It raised noiselessly. One man slid out.

Trooper Benson talked to Edhi while he searched for the form. "I
stopped you because I noticed the shocks bounce quite a bit. You
must be hauling something pretty heavy."

Perspiration formed heavily on Edhi's face. *My entire operation
may be blown by this infidel of American law enforcement.* He distracted Benson by holding up a form. "Is this what you're looking for?"

Benson had his right hand resting on the holstered Sig p-226. He
reached for the form Edhi handed to him with his left hand. Suddenly,
a loud two-second salvo shook the peaceful countryside. Five rounds
from the AK-47 tore through Benson's neck and torso, slamming him into
the opened door. He fell on the ground while the woman impersonator
jumped out and quickly dragged his body into the tall grass off the berm.
The shooter fired the Kalashnikov from behind the back corner of the
truck. He crawled back into the cargo hold and slid the door back down.

Edhi sped off the berm back onto I-90. He spoke into the microphone. "Can you hear me in back?"

"The leader of the mortar unit spoke. "Yes, what should we do
now? The infidels will be upon us when they find out about their dead
comrade."

"That is correct. I'm sure he gave the truck description before
stopping us. So, we must alter our plans. Allah has ordained us to
cast terror into the hearts of the nonbelievers... and that we shall do,
no matter what. We will cancel our plans to attack the stadium."

The mortar unit leader asked, "Do you mean the backup plan?"

Edhi spoke calmly as he sped up to seventy-five mph. "Yes. You must hurry and follow my instructions and do what I taught you to do, for we will reach the alternate attack site shortly."

The cell member retrieved a large suitcase from the corner of the cargo hold and opened it up underneath the "Mom's Attic." The twenty 140mm mortar shells were positioned so the warheads protruded outwards, towards him. He spoke lugubriously as he began the armament process. "You taught me well, my faithful leader, Edhi. Allah will guide me through your instructions...the mortars will be linked together to create a massive bomb...they will detonate together... instantaneously...and many infidels who wage war against Allah and His messenger will die. We avenge them for making mischief in our holy Middle Eastern lands."

Edhi replied, "Allah will guide us all through this glorious strike. Inside the suitcase are the trip wires and trigger switch. As we practiced over and over inside the Pennsylvania barn, you will make a daisy chain to link all twenty warheads together. Take out the detonating cord, attach it to the electric blasting cap and insert it into the hole drilled in the mortar warhead at the bottom-middle of the stack, the one I wrote the red 'X' on."

After a few moments, Edhi's student spoke. "OK, it's done... securely fastened."

"Good. Now follow through with the coupling-link technique I taught you. Extend the detonator cord to the other mortar shells in the sequence I marked on them...X-1, X-2 and so on. Make sure to connect them in the proper order!"

Edhi taught his bomb-making apprentice well. In fifteen minutes, the primary mortar shell warhead was joined to the designated others... separate warheads united into one massive bomb. After making sure it was properly attached to the large truck battery, he passed the switch activator through a small hole into the front cab.

Edhi took it carefully in his hands and placed it on his lap. He smiled peacefully as an inspirational feeling engulfed him. He knew the lethality of the weapon he created...and that it would not fail. He thought of his weapon's training by the Taliban in Pakistan's Federally Administered Tribal Areas (FATA), and how he became specialized in forming and training terrorist sleeper attack cells within the U.S. It all was about to come to fruition.

The Taliban taught him well. He envisaged his homemade IED's exploding under the vehicles carrying American and coalition infidels in Afghanistan. In a meditative tone, he avowed to the attack cell jihadist sitting next to him and to those in back through the microphone. "Allah's mission is almost completed...*lillaahi wa inna ilayhi Raaji'oon*...to Allah we belong and to Him is our return."

Sometimes the verdant-green field appeared, then it turned into a darkness, only to reappear again as a meadow full of life. Butterflies darted among the wildflowers by the highway fence, cows munched on lush grass in the distance, birds flew overhead, touching the blue sky, and a red barn and silo silhouetted the skyline.

Trooper Benson lay on his back in a grassy ditch off I-90. He tried to keep his eyes open, to shout for help...but couldn't. He sensed everlasting darkness approaching. The beautiful rural landscape he loved to roam was fading away from consciousness. He decided to stop fighting and allow destiny to prevail, as it always does. He wished he were lying in his cottage home in the village right now with his wife, children and grandchildren sitting by his bedside.

Patrolmen Benson barely heard the broadcast from his shoulder mic which lay a few feet from him. The jihadist ripped it off after dragging him down into the ditch.

A worried dispatcher was speaking. "Unit sixty-seven, reply immediately... unit sixty-seven, reply immediately!" Two seconds transpired. "Attention all units! Back up sixty-seen immediately! It stopped a U-Haul truck, plate number R-A-2-1-5-9-7 on I-90 westbound, one mile west of Exit 212. Just received Fusion Center Code-one alert. Terrorist attack in progress... repeat... terrorist attack in progress...

unit sixty-seven may need assistance… large U-Haul truck from northwest Pennsylvania traveling west to attack Cleveland Progressive Field… carrying laser-guided mortars… Unit sixty-seven may have stopped it and has not responded back to dispatch!"

The bright and balmy Ohio summer day grew dim. He couldn't force his eyes to stay open anymore. His vision plunged into gloomy shadows, but Benson fought back. A glowing aura replaced the darkness: He was sitting on the banks of the Grand River and Mill Creek fishing with his grandchildren. One of them held up a smallmouth bass and proudly shouted to him, "Grandpa, look what I caught!"

The first trooper arrived at the scene in two minutes after a speedy 126 mph response to the call. He found his fellow officer lying in the ditch and checked for signs of life. There were none…but a peaceful expression shown on Trooper Benson's face.

Episode 68

Penumbra Database warning

Tower City Center
Cleveland, Ohio
Jan was amazed at the unconventional shopping mall. Tower City Center was situated on Cleveland's downtown Public Square in the shadow of the landmark Terminal Tower. It was added to the National Register of Historic Places as the "Union Terminal" due to the busy railroad hub it used to be. She enjoyed *not* shopping in a typical box-type mall. The large ceiling windows, spacious main lobby and beautiful fountain exuded the ambience of a bygone era.

As she strolled past the shops in the colonnade-like arrangement, her preschool-aged children jumped up and down when they came to the Children's Place. A magician was performing illusionary tricks for a growing crowd of parents and children.

After the magic show ended, she bought some of the latest children's fashions, then took them up to the observation deck.

The Indians playoff game wouldn't be over for about three hours due to a storm front that roared through and caused a game delay. After showing her children a bird's eye view of the Cleveland skyline from the observation deck, she planned on taking them to the Tower City Cinema and watch a kid's movie. Then, they would return to their room at the Renaissance Cleveland Hotel, which was connected to the entire complex.

While taking the five-dollar ride to the 42nd floor of the attached Terminal Tower, she didn't notice the growing police presence in the streets below. Upon exiting the elevator, her children pulled her towards a large window facing north that overlooked Cleveland's Public Square. The vast expanse of Lake Erie spread along the horizon.

The trio walked to the opposite, southern section and looked out upon the long stretch of Ontario Street that weaved past Quicken Loans Arena and Progressive Field, then disappeared underneath the I-90 expressway. She pointed towards Progressive Field and told her children that was where their father was, watching the Cleveland Indians playoff game against the New York Yankees for the World Series.

She noticed throngs of people below walking towards them, north on Ontario Street. Others were gathering by the hundreds in a tree-lined cemetery across from the stadium, then being escorted north on East 9th Street...by police officers!

An orderly and steady stream of people continued down Ontario Street and East 9th. Suddenly, a calm, soft voice came on the intercom that broadcast throughout the Tower City complex: "May I have your attention please? As a precautionary measure, the management is requesting that all patrons evacuate the Tower City and Termnal Tower complex. Store owners, please make sure all your doors and windows are left open. Please leave the building by the nearest stairway or exit. Do not use the elevators. Please walk. Do not run. There is no need for panic."

Fifteen minutes later, Jan and her two exhausted children walked out onto Ontario Street and joined thousands of bewildered people. She thought it strange that all the stores were instructed to leave their windows and doors open. *They're supposed to be shut and airtight for a fire. Could this be a bomb scare?*

Police continually arrived. She glanced down Ontario Street. There must have been 20,000 people walking towards her in an orderly fashion. Hundreds of police now lined Ontario and East 9th streets, directing the throngs to proceed to Public Square where she stood with her children.

Jan scanned the crowd, hoping she would spot her husband. She tried to contact him on her cell phone but it was not functioning, despite a full charge.

Police officers with megaphones instructed the mass of people she was standing with to walk down West Superior Avenue. Others who gathered in Public Square were told to calmly walk in the opposite direction, down Euclid Avenue while officers directed a third section of people to proceed north on Ontario and West 3rd Streets.

A few in the crowd grew upset and panicky, afraid of the unknown, so the police broadcast in a fair but firm manner, "Follow the police officers' instructions as to where to go. We are here to assure your safety. For security reasons, we are evacuating the Progressive Field arena and Tower City Complex."

"Mommy, I'm scared!" Jan's four-year-old began to cry. She picked him up in one arm and clutched the hand of her older child, then strode quickly west down W. Superior Avenue as instructed, away from the area. She figured it out- windows and doors left wide open, huge police presence, dispersing thousands of people so they weren't clustered together...it had to be a terrorist bomb threat ...a serious one at that!

They continued walking briskly past W. 3rd and W. 6th streets where police at each intersection motioned for the crowd to continue on. She noticed every officer held a 12-gauge shotgun in ready position.

Before Jan and her children reached W. 9th Street, the police around her seemed to grow excited. They listened briefly to their portable radios, then yelled to the crowds to halt and lay flat on the pavement. Each unslung their shotguns and pumped a shell into the chamber. Two dozen cops formed a line across the wide street in front of Jan, some standing, some kneeling, but all pointing their shotguns down West Superior. Wailing police sirens and gunfire could be heard in the distance, growing closer.

Moments later, a large U-Haul truck sped out of W. 10th street onto W. Superior Avenue several hundred feet away and headed straight for them. A dozen police cars chased it, firing at the tires and through the rear sliding-door panel and both cab doors.

Even though the truck seemed to be rolling to a stop and the driver was slumped over the steering wheel, the line of police officers in front of her opened fire. The ear-splitting noise of dozens of riot shotguns blasting away with magnum loads made her ears ring. She quickly covered her four-year-old's ears with her hands, instructing her older child to cover his. She laid her body gently over both children, shielding them from her dreadful suspicion...*it may be a suicide truck-bomb!*

The intense firing continued. Both children cried hysterically and trembled from the horror, but she held them securely and whispered, "Don't worry...we're going to be OK...they are protecting us."

The thunderous salvo ceased. Jan looked up from her prone position. Children whimpered in the massive crowd behind her, which stretched all the way to Public Square and beyond.

A bullhorn came on and everyone was ordered to remain down on the pavement. The U-Haul truck was completely demolished. The 12-gauge magnum slugs blew the grill, radiator and hood into shredded metal fragments. The powerful loads even perforated the engine block. She could see skull pieces and brain tissue lining the back seat and dangling from the shattered windshield.

For ten seconds, an unnerving silence ensued. Jan tensed up as if expecting a huge explosion. She wrapped her body over her children tighter.

Then, she heard the word "Go!" A dozen cops dressed in SWAT gear surrounded the truck while the others stayed back to reassure the anxious crowd and to make sure they remained prone on the pavement. She looked to see what transpired. They raised the bullet-ridden back sliding door panel and leaped inside. Others jerked open both cab door panels and pulled out the mutilated bodies of a woman and man, letting the dismembered torsos fall onto the pavement.

A few moments later, the officers finished searching the truck and regrouped in front of it. She heard them speaking to each other and to the dispatchers over the portable radios. "Yes, it matches the truck in the trooper shooting on I-90, same plates, description of man driving with female passenger...but there weren't any mortars in back...only a bunch of fuckin' canoes on racks!"

CBIF HQ, Eaton Street
Key West Historic Seaport
General Morrison sat alone in the War Room, confident that he made the right decision. He took a mental break from staring into the pale-blue computer screens and gazed out from his soundproof space through the bulletproof glass that enveloped him.

The decisive climax to the counterintelligence operation was about to unfold. He thought of the events leading up to this moment: Duane Collier's abduction from the Hard Rock Café in Nassau and his decision to call Corey home from Jamaica and reassign him to the Bahamas to investigate it; Sidney Fowler's desperate flight to Nassau to tell Darnell Ferguson about the murder he witnessed on Abaco, his subsequent demise on Parliament Square, and Corey's arrest as a murder suspect; Stacie's ECHELON hunt for "Radical Archer" and the resultant New Jersey warehouse owner's link to Abaco Poultry, LTD; Addie Kolmogrovov's brilliant bugging of Alfred Moss' Agricultural Ministry office; the exotically-beautiful but pathological Dona Anani Guanikeyu, Corey's honeypot from the Turks and Caicos who seduced the Irish Frenzy Pub owner Patrick Branagh and helped to exposed the connections to his corrupt bank-owning brother and Sandoval; Corey's controlled drug bust of Devon Ledard and his recruitment as a vital CBIF double agent; the Cali meeting between Castano, Sadoval, Juan Rojas, Javier Sanchez, and Edhi; the raid on the Abaco Poultry mansion...

His thoughts were interrupted when Pinkston's twelve-digit algorith-mic-encrypted satellite cell phone creation sounded. Only two other people were sharing this frequency- Corey Pearson and President Rhinehart. It was Rhinehart. The Secret Service evacuated him from the Champion Suite at Progressive Field. He was calling from Cadillac One, which was speeding to the Cleveland Hopkins Airport, surrounded by several dozen Cleveland Police cars with lights and sirens on.

"Yes, Mr. President." "When is it going down?"

"Immediately, sir. I'm confident it's the right thing to do." "Very good." The president hung up.

Morrison stared at the large Penumbra Database computer screen. The soft whir could be heard as the vast amount of deep data mining results continued to be analyzed and conclusions drawn. So far, it printed out 189 pages of deductions, suppositions and assump-tions on Edhi's sleeper attack cell strike on America. He, the president and Corey didn't need to read any more predictions after the first sce-nario came through, which the Penumbra Database ranked as "Highly Possible":

Penumbra Database Algorithmic Prediction- Scenario 1

"Unaccounted nuclear material stolen from Iran nuclear power plant one year ago. Edhi has strong connections to Hezbollah sleeper-cell leaders identified in Tri-Border Area of Argentina, Paraguay and Brazil. Has strong link to Iran. STOP. Edhi may have constructed high-ly-enriched radioactive dirty bomb from stolen Iran nuclear power plant fuel rods. Iran's nuclear reactors produce significant amounts of plutonium-239 residue waste inside reactor cores and in spent nuclear fuel rods. STOP. Edhi sleeper attack cell exposed to radio-active material no concern...ready for martyrdom- radiation expo-sure would not stop them. Sleeper cell would chop up and dissolve nuclear waste in nitric acid to extract pure plutonium, then smuggle into U.S. by grinding the radioactive rubble into a dispersible powder form. STOP.

Edhi has training and expertise to construct such a super-dirty radioactive dirty bomb...Edhi trained in FATA region in Pakistan by Taliban. STOP. Bomb would contain plutonium-239, the most carcinogenic substance known. Possibility of U-Haul truck transforming into truck-bomb highly likely if initial plan of mortar attack fails. Backup plan almost certain...mortar shells would be incendiary material (thermite) which would vaporize the radioactive powder in downtown Cleveland. STOP. Twenty 140mm mortar shells stolen from Colombian Army Cali Barracks...if all detonate simultaneously... explosion would be massive. STOP. Sleeper attack cell leader Edhi's M.O. would not risk stealing lower-grade radioactive material from doctor's and dentist offices, x-ray labs, etc. or from highly-secured nuclear power plants with more-lethal material. Edhi would not buy from arms dealers or suppliers...Edhi personality is highly suspicious and paranoid- would fear CIA or CBIF undercover operatives."

Ten minutes passed since Morrison reported these Penumbra Database predictions to President Rhinehart and to Corey in a three-way conference call on Pinkston's tamper-proof and impenetrable phone. He queried the incredible database for "Predictive Consequences" for Scenario 1 and when the answer came, all three men grew solemn and spontaneously agreed to proceed. The costs were simply unimaginable:

Penumbra Database Algorithmic Prediction- Predictive
Consequences for Scenario 1
"Winds ideal for large super-dirty, radioactive bomb attack around I-90 and Progressive Field area in Cleveland. Southerly winds steady at 9 mph. STOP. IMINT satellite photo...five minutes ago...shows highly-dense human concentration- 57,000 people directly downwind after stadium and nearby buildings evacuated. STOP.

Note: U-Haul truck bomb with twenty 140mm mortars coupled with current winds, detonation location Progressive Field would instantly kill 3,000, injure 5,000. Knowledge of radioactive dirty bomb would create mass panic. STOP. Research studies of weapons-grade plutonium-239 inhalation toxicity on lab animals shows catastrophic human exposure level- one sniff will cause future lung cancer. Moving radiation cloud will produce inherent public horror and panic downwind. Radiation cloud would overwhelm safety forces as first responders care for wounded and respond to stress-induced heart attacks and traffic accidents by people fleeing the immediate vicinity and from miles away, downwind. STOP.

A dead zone would result. People couldn't live or work in downtown and surrounding Cleveland areas for possibly years. Restoring detonation and downwind vicinity would be painstakingly slow. STOP. Minimum of 1,000 de-contamination experts donned in protective suits needed to steam spray, vacuum, sandblast, and bulldoze tainted buildings, pavement, earth and vegetation. Many out of state visitors attending game at Progressive Field. STOP. Thousands of locals and out-of-state visitors needed to be quarantined in decontamination centers and not be allowed to return home."

General Morrison, President Rhinehart and Corey Pearson didn't need to see any more of the Penumbra Database algorithmic scenarios and predictive consequences that continued to be printed out. Rhinehart said over the encrypted phone, "Stop Edhi immediately… do whatever it takes."

He knew something was wrong, for there were no cars around. Vehicles appeared a few miles behind him but he couldn't make out if they were the police. Twenty minutes had passed since his revered cell member murdered the state trooper. Edhi gripped the switch activator in his right hand, maintaining a seventy-mph speed.

He neared the far east side of Cleveland and noticed that no cars passed him in the east-bound lane. He drove past Exit 200 in Painesville. No cars came down the entrance ramp onto I-90 from Route 44.

Then, he spotted them. After passing Braodmoor Rd. Exit 103, he quickly glanced back up the entrance ramp where a busy Route 306 normally has a line of cars merging onto I-90. Three Ohio State Patrol cars and two county sheriff cruisers had assembled at the top, partially concealed by a row of bushes. They did not give chase, but were obviously aware of his presence and what he had done to one of their own. The situation did not look good. He sped the U-Haul up to eighty mph. Progressive Field lie twenty-four miles ahead. He would be there in twenty minutes.

Edhi switched on the intercom and spoke to his warriors. "Our target is minutes away. We will seek the glory of death on the holy battlefield and all nine of us will receive the highest rank in paradise... the 'house of martyrs', *dar al-shuhada*. We will be near the throne of God... where Muhammad wants us to be. The battle scars we are about to receive will shine, our deaths as martyrs will free us from all sins and purify us all."

General Morrison watched the Penumbra Database computer screen. It linked in to the secure sat phones that Corey and President Rhinehart were watching. A live video stream appeared.

CBIF's satellite image interpreters masquerading as drywallers for the front company *Key West Drywallers* in Key West were in contact with a CBIF pilot at Creech Air Force Base in Nevada, over two thousand miles away. The satellite image team spoke to the pilot. "Strike point for minimum collateral damage is along Interstate ninety at 41°37'01.3"N 81°24'52.8"W. Low civilian population density and no bridge overpasses near."

"Roger that. I have target in sight...locked onto it...two point three miles from launch."

Morrison, Pearson and Rhinehart stared at the live stream event unfold. Morrison munched on his Montecristo. Corey stood in the lounge of the *Queen Conch II* watching with his fingers crossed. Rhinehart sat aboard Marine One, chewing on a fingernail while hurtling full-throttle towards the White House in the midst of four identical choppers.

The MQ-1B Predator drone flew out-of-sight at 9,000 feet above and a mile behind the U-Haul suicide truck bomb. Morrison ordered it airborne immediately after Corey informed him of Sandoval's confession about the Progressive Field attack...where the president was!

The drone started a slight descent but still remained above 8,000 feet. The two AGM-114 Hellfire missiles under its wings galvanized their active radar homing (ARH) missile guidance systems with the U-Haul's incoming target location data. Each missile contained a radar transceiver and was equipped with the electronics necessary to find and track its target autonomously.

At 8,000 feet, the MQ-1B cruised quietly and was soundless to anyone on the ground. It's Hellfire missiles flew supersonic. No one would see or hear them coming.

The more nervous Edhi grew because of the deserted highway, the more he preached the beliefs of Allah to himself and his comrades. "We are holy warriors...*mujtahids*...we will die in battle and receive seventy-two virgin maidens in paradise...we will reap heavenly rewards above the infidel Christians and moderate Muslims...throwing ourselves against the infidel enemy soldiers who outnumber us... that is the only way to Paradise."

The image specialists at the Key West safe house announced, "Firing location three seconds away. No other vehicles or persons nearby."

The Creech AFB pilot responded. "Roger that...missiles launched!" No further electronic guidance was needed. Both Hellfires operated autonomously and locked on to the U-Haul...the ultimate in "fire and forget" weaponry. The pilot at Creech and the specialists in Key West shut off all radar and communications, vanishing from the airwaves.

The predator ascended rapidly to 24,000 feet and abruptly turned toward the southeast, retracing its digital steps back to the clandestine airstrip from which it came. The lethal missiles homed in on Edhi and his sleeper attack cell members.

Edhi was continuing on with his homily. "I follow in the footsteps of my grandfather who was among the martyrs who killed the moderate infidel Egyptian President Anwar Sadat! For Allah's religion, we are about to offer skulls, we make ourselves martyrs...blood will flow...we are about to make the infidels into widows and orphans...hands and limbs will fly into the air so Allah's religion can stand on its..."

Both missiles hit the truck squarely and detonated their forty pounds of high-explosives. In a split-second, all twenty 140mm mortar rounds ignited. The instantaneous explosion was horrendous.

Episode 69

WMD threat response

South Lawn, White House
Washington, D.C.
The Marine One 'WhiteHawk' swooped in quickly from the northwest and landed on the South Lawn. Two Marines opened the secured door and saluted President Rhinehart as he clambered down the steps with his son and son's classmate along with four Secret Service agents.

Rhinehart had been working on his address to the nation since the chopper took off from Cleveland Hopkins Airport. He would deliver it live from the Oval Office to the nation and world in three hours.

Local CNN, MSNBC and Fox news affiliates were already on the ground in Cleveland. News teams were interviewing people along Public Square while TV network action cam vehicles rushed towards Willoughby, Ohio where a huge explosion occurred on I-90. Emergency vehicles responded to calls from nearby Gully Brook Park and from the River's Edge at the Nash Farm housing development, where a few nonfatal casualties were reported.

The tens of thousands who evacuated Progressive Field, the City Center and nearby office buildings were reassured by the police that they weren't in any danger and that a terrorist attack had been thwarted to the east of Cleveland. What the local authorities didn't know about was the possibility that the original planned mortar attack on

Progressive Field, if it failed, could be switched to a dirty bomb attack using highly-enriched plutonium stolen from an Iranian power plant.

After Morrison, Corey and Rhinehart discussed this possibility that was predicted by the Penumbra Database, they unequivocally called in special DHS anti-dirty bomb teams. Before his address to the nation in three hours, President Rhinehart had to know.

In fifty-five minutes, four customized leisure vehicles with tinted windows were allowed to pass through a police checkpoint on I-90, which was completely shut down. They sped on for five miles to the explosion site, where the pavement suddenly ended at a cavernous thirty-foot-deep crater. The detonation blew out the interstate east and west-bound lanes, plus the wide medium strip that separated them.

The eight men and women in each WMD team checked each other's hazmat suits, making sure they were airtight. The shelves in the large vans were stocked with both liquid and foam-spray radioactive decontaminants, and special showers that drained into hermetically-sealed tanks were at ready, just in case.

It was a strange site to view thirty-two people donned in odd-looking orange suits with attached hoods and three-layer Teflon face shields exit the vans and spread out around the crater and nearby woods. Their suits had double-taped seams and double flaps over rear gas-tight zippers. The double-exhaust valves protruding from the face shields that attached to oxygen tanks added to the mystique. Any conspiracy theorists who witnessed the event would no doubt believe an alien invasion was underway.

Public Square
Cleveland, Ohio
The Cleveland Police successfully evacuated Progressive Field, the City Center and nearby office buildings. Up to 75,000 people lined the downtown and surrounding streets when the U-Haul van shoot-out occurred on West Superior Avenue. Officers reassured the nervous throngs and continued to disperse them further north on Ontario

Street and east and west on St. Clair Street, away from the crowded Public Square.

After the mutilated bodies of John and Diane Dolan were removed, the police continued to split up the masses congregating on Pubic Square and disperse them further down West Superior Avenue, past the bullet-ridden remains of the U-Haul truck. Based on the info that Sandoval was divulging to Corey and Oppressor, it appeared a secondary suicide attack was highly likely. The intelligence was transmitted, via Fusion Centers, to local law enforcement without mentioning the sources or methods it was obtained by. The Cleveland authorities didn't want the populace packed tightly together.

In addition, a huge Galaxy C-5 touched down at Cleveland Hopkins Airport. Eight vans similar to the ones already in position at the detonation site were unstrapped from the 121-foot-long cargo hold. The nose and aft cargo-bay doors opened and the vans quickly drove down the full-width ramps in double rows onto the tarmac.

The pilot, copilot, two flight engineers and two loadmasters were familiar with the routine, for the crew of six were constantly on stand-by to instantly assist CBIF operations. Their last assistance occurred when two CBIF cells that Corey formed on the little-known island of Saba identified a narco-terrorist group that moved heroin into Latin America.

The leader of the group was almost as ruthless as Sandoval. He hated gays and lesbians, and began threatening Saba's commissioner, director of tourism and a few island council members, all who were openly gay. On top of his hatred towards them, they couldn't be bought off.

As Saba grew more and more LGBT-friendly, the threats increased and several council members were beaten by the trafficker's thugs. This island commissioner asked Corey for help when his wife and children received threats. One morning, he received an anonymous phone call. The rough-sounding caller described what his two little girls were wearing while they walked to primary school that morning.

Forty-eight hours later, at 3:30am, the Galaxy C-5 crew flew low over the volcanic island of 1,800 sleeping residents with the aft cargo door open. The 190-ton craft floated like a seagull over the small harbor and villages, then weaved around the dormant volcano and glided over the rolling green hills that faced Saint Marteen, which lies twenty-five miles to the northwest. Thirty special ops troops parachuted out and were on the ground in seconds. They slowly made their way towards a huge mansion that the narco-terrorist built.

As ordered, the crew then transported the remaining twenty special ops warriors, one AH-64 Apache helicopter, and four amphibious light armored vehicles to the Princess Juliana International Airport on nearby Saint Maarten. The four light armored vehicles weren't that light… twelve tons each…and the C-5 needed at least 4,900 feet of tarmac to land. It would have been suicide attempting to land on Saba's short runway built into its volcanic cliffs.

Seated in the cockpit on the tarmac of the Cleveland Hopkins Airport, the pilot watched the eight vans speed away with police escort. He knew this mission had something to do with the huge explosion on I-90 just outside Cleveland and the evacuation of Progressive Field.

Just like with the Saba mission, he and his five crew members would keep their mouths shut. *Follow orders and keep quiet about every aspect of the mission.* He thought back to Saba…taking off from Saint Marteen's airport with an empty cargo hold, leaving the special op warriors, armored vehicles and Apache's behind. The next day, CNN reported that a narco-terrorist leader was shot and killed on Saba and several dozen of his lieutenants were arrested and sent to Guantanamo. It also reported that the U.S. gave the Saba government four amphibious armored vehicles to help them battle future narco-terrorist intrusions. The news reported that the DEA had conducted the raid, but no DEA agents ever boarded his plane.

The pilot knew that the extemporaneous assistance missions he undertook involved deep secrets… dark secrets…that was the nature of the organization he worked for. *Follow orders and keep your mouth shut.*

The eight Hazmat Response Vans sped from the airport at eighty mph along the deserted I-90 Innerbelt into Cleveland. Four took Exit 171 onto Abbey Road, a side road that they used to approach the western edge of the masses along West Superior and St. Claire Avenues. The others sped further on and got off Exit 173A, then proceeded to the east end of the huge crowd that was dispersed along Euclid and East Superior Avenues.

They parked the vans in back alleys. Twenty agents departed each one and calmly walked into the crowds. The 160 agents were unlike those at the detonation site. Instead of wearing space-like gear, they dressed in casual attire. Some wore Cleveland Indians baseball caps and T-shirts. Each carried a handheld air-intake device or "sniffer" disguised as a cell phone, iPhone, or sports water bottle. The sniffers were wirelessly connected to radiation-detectors housed inside ordinary-looking satchels of some sort: pocketbooks, backpacks, large fanny packs, or shoulder bags.

A "super-dirty" radioactive bomb may have been constructed from stolen Iranian power plant nuclear material, so they searched for residue of highly-enriched plutonium and uranium. Morrison, Corey and Rhinehart were tipped-off by the Penumbra Database algorithmic conclusion-generating program, which they prayed was wrong.

In addition, they "sniffed" for toxic chemical and biological agents. A secondary suicide sleeper cell could have been activated in order to poison the masses with such deadly WMD toxins. Twenty of the agents strolled among the throngs with their "pet" dogs; i.e., highly-trained canines that could quickly and accurately sniff out explosives.

The agents separated into teams of two, then dispersed into the masses. Innocuous-looking pager-like devices that detected the presence of minute traces of neutron radiation were attached to their belts. Neutron radiation, even in small doses, is deadlier than other types and is a red flag for possible weapons-grade plutonium. It is odorless and invisible, but the keen devices would vibrate if any was nearby.

One team posing as a couple devoted to the Indians strolled calmly down West Superior Avenue through the oncoming multitudes. They smiled politely at people passing by, noticing their looks of quiet desperation.

Suddenly, both their devices started vibrating simultaneously. They immediately walked in opposite directions- the man to the north through the crowd and the woman to the south. After a dozen steps, his stopped vibrating while hers quivered even more intensely, indicating the source was nearby towards Public Square, in a group of about twenty people who just passed.

She put out an alert of a possible "hit." Before backup teams arrived, the duo discreetly walked into the crowd and split up. It looked strange as she quickly passed people with her sports water bottle facsimile held up in the air while her partner walked rapidly through the throng, donned in an Indians cap and shirt, with his iPhone held out in front of him. He heard an older man say to his wife, "Takes all kinds. We're in the middle of an emergency of some sort and he's taking 'selfies'...must a had too much to drink at the game."

A few moments later, the radiation monitor in the female agent's purse set out an audible alarm, soft enough so passersby wouldn't notice. She unobtrusively aimed her sports bottle at a man in front of her and held it close to his back.

He was emitting gamma rays, far above the preset level for normal background radiation. She whispered into her hidden microphone, "We have a definite hit!"

Her male partner joined her. They continued tailing the man while both their radiation monitors analyzed the incoming air samples. It was a radioisotope of some kind. A high-resolution digital camera in her purse took photos of the perpetrator and the surrounding area, including people nearby. Each photo was sent to an overhead SATLINK hooked into Stacey's Dictionary Program at NSA. The facial photos of the male suspect and of those near him were entered by Stacey into CBIF's *Next Generation Identification* (NGI) system and analyzed by its vast face and biometric recognition system. Stacie could find no links. She replied to the agents on the ground in Cleveland, "NIF... nothing in file."

Moments later, a half dozen backup hazmat teams arrived and mingled with the crowd. One, with a bomb-sniffing dog, walked next to the target. The canine would have smelt explosives if he was wearing a suicide vest. The female agent motioned to three policemen standing nearby as she and her companion made contact.

She tapped the man on the shoulder. He turned around quickly to see both agents holding up bright, silver badges with "Hazardous Materials Response Team" written in red over a bald eagle with spread wings and American flags under each spread wing. "Hazmat Agent" was written in red at the bottom.

The woman agent spoke authoritatively. "Sir, we have stopped and detained you because our radiation-detecting equipment indicates you may be a radioactive threat. We are going to search you."

The half-dozen agents who arrived formed a loose circle around the confused man while the two agents began patting him down. A dozen Cleveland Police formed an outer circle, motioning the approaching crowds to go around them.

The man was clean. No bulges, suicide vest or aerosolized device to spread anthrax or other biological/chemical toxins into the air.

The male agent spoke. "Sir, our instruments show you are constantly emitting radioactive isotopes. We have to determine where you have been recently."

The man said, "I was just having a barium stress-test at my family doctor's office on Euclid Avenue when they evacuated the building. He gave me this card to show to the security people, the TSA... at the Cleveland Hopkins Airport tomorrow in case they detect radioactive emissions comin' from me. I'm flying out to see my daughter in Seattle."

He looked at the card. It had the date and the location of the office on Euclid Avenue, the radioisotope used and its half-life, plus the potential duration of radioactive emissions. It also listed who to contact for verification. He called the number. Luckily, the doctor answered on his cell phone.

A few moments later, the agent hung up and nodded to his female partner. "He checks out." They apologized for inconveniencing him and resumed searching through the crowds.

Queen Conch II
CBIF EIT room
Corey Pearson sat in a comfortable chair in the lounge of Darnell Ferguson's cargo ship. Tears ran down his face. The five portable IET booths in the large room were down the hallway. Over his back, on a wall-mounted flat-screen TV, a five-minute home video was playing over and over again. He set it on continual replay.

When Constance and the CI agents confiscated everything in Sandoval's library, she came across a video marked "Duane Collier" and viewed it for a minute, then immediately ordered a special ops soldier to get it to Corey immediately. It arrived in minutes via Apache helicopter from the mansion.

The video showed Pierre Cherestal and Bolan Tougas beating the handcuffed Duane Collier on the secluded dock in the Abaco forest, then hoisting him by the ankles with a mobile lift and swinging him over the water...then Dagger Mouth severing his body in half.

At first, he grew angry and went into a rage as he watched them jokingly puncture his wet suit and fill it with chicken parts. He drew his Glock 30 and was about to run down the hallway and gut shoot both of them, but then he heard the sandy-haired young man speak in an unafraid and determined voice, while hanging upside down as the monster circled. "I want you to tell Sandoval something. The organization I work for has resources beyond your comprehension.

They will stalk you to the ends of the earth...and spend limitless resources to do so. They will exterminate Sandoval and both of you. You've made a grave mistake...your lives will go to the dogs after today."

Corey collapsed into the chair and sobbed for ten minutes, then regained his self-control and ordered Oppressor to release El-Sayed, Eamal Batoor and Khoury Kassim from their EIT cubicles.

Six special ops soldiers marched the trio into the lounge with their hands handcuffed behind their backs and their legs shackled so close together that they had to shuffle in. They were still calmly chanting *Subhannah Allah Allhumdolillah* and *Allahu Akbar* repeatedly.

Corey motioned for the soldiers to shove them down into the huge couch opposite him so they could view the video playing over his shoulder. They grew silent upon seeing it.

After a minute, Corey spoke. "You failed. The mortar attack at Progressive Field was thwarted, thanks to Sandoval. He ratted on your jihad attack... tipped us off about the U-Haul truck. We blew it up with Edhi and his sleeper-cell jihadists inside it. *I won't mention that Sandoval didn't know about the rain delay when he spilt the beans and that he thought the attack was already underway.* Neither did you get your hands on the Penumbra Database that you wanted so badly."

The end of the tape was playing and Corey used the remote to turn up the volume so they could hear Duane Collier's courageous warning before his miserable death. "It looks like he was right...your lives have 'gone to the dogs'. You three wouldn't be sitting here right now if Sandoval didn't murder this agent of ours. He was like a son to me."

Shahid El-Sayed said, "I never liked that bastard Sandoval! His cruelness would be his downfall."

"And yours, too, since you were his controller of the New Jersey warehouse which was raided and shut down. That's where the mortars stolen from the Cali Army barracks would have gone to."

El-Sayed noticed the Glock 30 laying on the armrest of Corey's chair. "Yes, you are right. But, after the raid we simply diverted them to another location in northwest Pennsylvania."

Fuck Walt Mason and his FBI cop mentality... swoop in, slap the handcuffs on, prosecute, make the headlines, get a promotion! Morrison and I wanted to hold off on the raid, keep the New Jersey warehouse under surveillance and capture the mortars when they arrived...and Edhi's jihadist sleeper attack cell, too. All this would have ended then and there. "You made a mistake by leaving your cell phone at the New Jersey warehouse. We found it during the raid and put a voicemail you left on it into our voice recognition system. It matched your voice when you called Senator Warren in Bimini to arrange a meeting with him. That's how we picked you up on Bimini." *Stacie, our mole inside the NSA did, that is.*

Eamal Batoor said, "We all hate your Senator Warren, too. He is a despicable traitor to your country. We used him because he has no morals, no integrity...he is evil!"

"Evil draws men like you together, my friend. Before we go on, let me tell you what's going to happen to you. You're going to disappear from the face of the earth...at Guantanamo. You'll each be caged in a concrete, windowless isolation cell that's smaller than a horse stable... no interaction with other prisoners... not even with the guards. You'll have food slid in through a slot in the door. The doors have perforations in them to allow small streaks of light inside. No reading materials, including the Koran. You'll stay in them all day long, except for fifteen minutes of 'recreation'... a door slides open and you can walk into an attached walled concrete pen that's smaller than a dog run. Agent Duane Collier was right when he said 'you're lives will go to the dogs after today'."

Eamal Batoor asked, "What's the alternative?"

Corey rose from his chair and retrieved four beers from the kitchenette. He handed three of them to the special ops soldiers standing nearby. They smiled and nodded in appreciation. "One alternative that won't happen is that of the Taliban attacking Guantanamo and freeing you, like they did at the Saraposa Prison in Kandahar back in 2008. The special ops fighters we have on Gitmo, like these three young warriors before you, would kick their ass. You'll be there for the rest of your lives, in total isolation...unless."

Corey remained standing and watched the video. He took a swig of beer as it showed Pierre Cherestal sticking the gun in Duane Collier's belly while stabbing holes in his wetsuit, then stuffing chicken parts into it. Corey's actions were purposeful- he wanted to convey to the three that the terrorist attack is all over...they failed in their mission... and nothing but trifling follow-up and tying-up loose end questions were left.

Khoury Kassim asked, "Unless what?"

Corey sat down. "Unless you tell me everyone behind the Penumbra Database algorithm theft and the deaths it caused." *Including the murder of my dear wife, Danielle.*

El-Sayed started squealing on Senator Warren, who he truly hated. "Warren was behind it all from the start. It also involves FBI Director Walt Mason and BHH..."

Batoor interrupted. "Hold on, Shahid. Before we tell him more, we must know how he is going to make it easier for us on Gitmo."

Corey took another hearty swig of beer and nonchalantly told one special ops guard to grab another beer for himself and his buddies, then replied to El-Sayed. "You will be placed in the regular prison population with your Muslim buddies. No solitary confinement. You can read, pray and worship the Koran and have access to a spacious outside area. I will also make sure that you have visiting rights with your wife and children. They will be flown to Cuba at my organiza-tion's expense...you will be able to have private, conjugal visits."

Kassim spoke. "Batoor and I used Sandoval to get to Senator Warren. The Jeannie database your organization uses was successful in uncovering our Caribbean operations and preemptively thwarting our jihadi attacks."

Batoor added, "We couldn't hack into the Jeannie database. The firewall protection was too sophisticated, so we had to steal it."

Corey asked, "How much did you offer Sandoval to steal it for you?"

Kassim said, "Four hundred and fifty thousand. That includes bribes to Warren. Warren told Sandoval that the creator of the original Jeannie was Drew Collier who worked for the Pentagon and was killed on 9/11, but he made a duplicate."

"So, Sandoval finds out from Senator Warren that Collier's widow has a woman friend, a best friend, who worked for your DOE's Office of Intelligence and Counterintelligence. He suspects she may be holding it at her home in Severna Park, Maryland."

That's Danielle! "So, what happened next?"

Batoor said, "Sandoval and his thugs broke into her home, tied her up and tore the place apart looking for it. They couldn't find it, so Sandoval tortured her but she wouldn't talk, so he strangled her to death."

My precious Danielle. I won't mention that Morrison recruited her out of DOE to work for CBIF. "If this woman worked for DOE intelligence, she would have an elaborate home security system. How could they have broken in?"

Kassim fidgeted on the couch. "That's when the story gets interesting. Your FBI Director Walt Mason wanted the Jeannie database, too. Warren told us at last year's Abaco mansion party that Mason was angry that the CIA was encroaching on his turf, making the FBI look bad...something about a rift between law enforcement and counterintelligence."

Batoor actually chuckled. Corey looked at him and said, "What the fuck are you laughing about?"

He replied. "Allah willing...don't you see? We radical jihadists, as you Westerners call us, bent on turning your democracy into a Sharia Law state...and the FBI, the premier U.S. law enforcement agency is fighting to get their hands on the same thing as we... the Jeannie database!"

Corey gave a fake chuckle back. "Yeah, I see your point. By the way, there are thousands of people crowded together in Cleveland after the Progressive Field evacuation. We're concerned about a possible secondary follow-up attack by suicide bombers...maybe even one of your sleeper cells releasing stolen highly-enriched radioactive plutonium into the crowd. Is that going to happen?"

Batoor, Khoury and El-Sayed looked at each other, then Batoor replied. "No, that was not in the plans."

Corey took another swig of beer and dispassionately said, "That's good, because if anything like that goes down while we're sitting here chatting, I'll shoot each of you through the knee caps then have Oppressor drag you back to your cubicles, strip you naked and do to you what you saw him do to Sandoval... all the way to Guantanamo, 'Gitmo'... where you'll spend the rest of your lives in solitary confinement. Now, think hard before you answer... are you *sure* there's no secondary attack planned?"

They knew he wasn't bluffing. Khoury said, "Absolutely...none was planned."

Corey looked at Kassim Khoury. "I'm sure you remember Mason's FBI raid on your terrorist safe house in Willemstad, Curacao."

Khoury replied, "Yes. How could I forget. I flew in from Pakistan to Venezuela, then to Curacao on a fake passport."

"I had sixteen of my best agents watching every step you made. Four of your cell members were from the Tri-Border Area. They hooked you up with Colombian drug lords and Hezbollah sleeper cells in Argentina, Paraguay and Brazil. We were about to bust you all."

"I'm well aware. I was tipped off by a paid informant we have embedded in the Curacao Police Department. I flew back to the Middle East the same way I got there."

Corey added, "And your cell members linked to Hezbollah and the drug lords fled back to the Tri-Border Area. Mason arrested one measly Lebanese-American with an outstanding warrant for cigarette smuggling."

"I didn't tell him about the pending raid and left him there on purpose...to give Mason and his FBI something to crow about."

You threw him under the bus, you two-faced bastard! "We learned enough to know that you made huge profits smuggling Middle East heroin into Europe and the U.S., and Colombian coke back to the Middle East. Where did you launder all the cash?"

"In Sean Branagh's bank, in Nassau."

Corey leaned forward from his chair. "We also know that you have close ties with Hezbollah sleeper cells in the Tri-Border Area. Tell me about them."

Silence.

Corey stared directly into Khoury's face. "My organization also knows that you and Batoor have funded sleeper attack cells inside the U.S., minus the one led by Edhi. How many remain and where have you positioned them?"

Silence.

"Is FBI Director Walt Mason on your payroll?" "No."

Corey leaned back in his chair and placed folded hands on top of his head, staring directly into the eyes of the three condemned men before him. "Were Walt Mason and Senator Warren in cahoots with each other to get the advanced Penumbra Database?"

Batoor answered. "Yes. Warren learned all about the research BHH had done with some brilliant Chinese spy. They took the original version of Jeannie that Sandoval killed the female DOE spy in Maryland for, and enhanced it over a thousand times. BHH approached us and offered it to us. That's why he suddenly showed up on Bimini with it while your agents were shadowing Senator Warren, his Chief of Staff Mark Serwin, and Shahid."

El-Sayed chipped in. "That's why they sent me to Bimini...to make sure BHH brought it to the Abaco mansion."

Khoury said, "BHH told us that the Penumbra Database made Jeannie totally obsolete. It was a top-secret, deep data-mining government project bankrolled with black funds... over two billion American dollars."

Corey asked, "So, you kidnapped Duane Collier at the Hard Rock Café in Nassau in order to force his mother to get the original Jeannie database from her deceased husband's safety deposit box, then smuggled her and the database to the Abaco mansion."

The trio nodded their heads in agreement, then Batoor spoke. "We had to get our hands on it. You and your organization make a good opponent. You thwarted many of our Caribbean plans. The technology you have, the data-mining algorithms on your software has stopped us many times in our tracks. If we could get our hands on the Jeannie software, we would compromise your ability to hunt us down."

Khoury added, "And then, along comes BKK with news that the Jeannie database has been surpassed by Penumbra. He offers Penumbra to us for $1 million. We agree. The rest is history...we don't have it... Walt Mason doesn't have it... you do."

Why didn't Morrison tell me about this new database? "How did BHH get his hands on it?"

Batoor replied, "He hacked into the Chinese guy's computer at MIT. Stole the whole thing."

MIT...has to be Cheng, Hsin Chow's son. I recruited Hsin when he arrived in Cuba to set up the secret Chinese electronic-listening station. We plan to exfiltrate Hsin and his wife out of Cuba and reunite them with their son in the U.S. "How much did Warren and Mason know about Sandoval's break in at the DOE operative's home?"

"They both planned it! FBI Director Walt Mason gave Warren the know-how...and he gave it to Sandoval."

Corey felt the anger and frustration he buried inside for years begin to flow again. *I knew it wasn't a home burglary by common thugs. The police report was wrong* He asked Batoor, "How do you know this?"

"Because Sandoval bragged about it last year at one of his mansion parties. He was full of pride that a U.S. senator gave him a wireless jamming device. Warren had Mason use his FBI resources to get the proper device tuned-in to the right frequency. Sandoval used the device to jam the woman's security setup and blocked the alert signal from reaching the base station. Sandoval simply lock-picked the side door to get into her home."

My poor, dear beloved Danielle. "Think hard and give me an honest answer. Did Warren and Mason know that Sandoval tortured and murdered this woman?"

Batoor hesitated, then spoke. "Senator Warren knew about the murder, but Mason did not. Mason only wanted to get his hands on the original Jeannie database."

The emotions swelled inside Corey. He wanted to go somewhere and weep. His muscles tensed up and a headache developed. His jaw was sore after clenching it tightly for the last twenty minutes. *Be tough!*

After a few moments, Corey felt he could talk dispassionately again to these monsters sitting across from him. He asked Khoury, "The abduction of Duane Collier and his mother, Joan...did Warren know about the abductions?"

"Yes."

"What about Mason?"

"No. Warren never told him anything about the means Sandoval used to get it. Mason simply wanted it for law enforcement use. He was patriotic, pour soul...he thought his FBI was the only way to save America from radical Islam...the name he calls us on TV."

Batoor added, "Warren has no principles...no ideologies to guide him. Too bad he hasn't found Allah. At least the FBI director is guided by something. I don't understand how people like Senator Warren get elected."

Corey thought of what his dad used to tell him when he was a child. *Son, never underestimate the stupidity of the American voter.* "Just a few more questions before we're done. The stolen mortars... did Mason know about them?"

They all shook their heads. "No."

"Second question, and this is for you, El-Sayed. How much did Sandoval get for smuggling the mortars into the U.S.?"

"Edhi paid him fifty-thousand up front at the Platillos Voladores restaurant in Cali when it was arranged, then two-hundred-thousand dollars when they were delivered to the Pennsylvania safe house."

"Last question. At the mortar smuggling exchange at the Platillos Voladores, who were the Colombians involved?"

Silence.

Corey stood up and motioned to the special op soldiers that he was done. One of them signaled for Oppressor and his men to come in. "The three of you gave me useful information. But, I lied to you. There are jihadi sleeper attack cells lurking inside America and you did not tell me where they are. If I sent you to Gitmo to join the regular prisoners and enjoy the freedom to worship the Koran and stroll around the open recreational area, I would be frustrated every time another terrorist attack occurred in the Caribbean or inside America's heartland."

Khoury piped up, "But Allah would forbid us from revealing to you where they are!"

Corey ignored him. "Therefore, these gentlemen are going to take you to Gitmo and you will disappear from the face of the earth. You will be placed in solitary confinement for the rest of your lives. Forget about reading the Koran or ever seeing your loved ones again. If Allah tells any of you to reveal where the sleeper cells are, you will be taken out of solitaire. Goodbye, and have a nice day."

While their mouths were taped shut and hoods were placed over their heads, Corey turned away and watched the video. Tougas and Cherestal were viciously punching and kicking Duane Collier to the ground. They tied chains around his ankles. Cherestal sat on the dock with a Beretta stuck in Duane's stomach, smiling and threatening to "gut shoot" him.

He walked out of the lounge and back into the IET room, opened Pierre Cherestal's cubicle and untied him from the slanted board. He grabbed him by the handcuffs and took him out into an open space in front of the opened cell door of Bolan Tougas, who was strapped down on the waterboard. The two cousins looked at each other, then stared at Corey's troublesome face. It bore a solemn look... a mien worn by someone who is duty-bound to do something that he has to do, but doesn't want to.

Cherestal began thinking back to his youthful life, living in poverty on the dirt floor of their shack outside Milot, Haiti. He closed his eyes and saw the Massif du Nord Mountains in the background. He regretted leaving the countryside and coming to Port-au-Prince...of meeting Abner Orival and Sandoval. He felt metal touching his abdomen and opened his eyes to see Corey's Glock 30 stuck in his gut.

"This is for Duane Collier, the man you and your cousin mercilessly murdered on Abaco. I saw the video of you taunting him on the dock with your Beretta stuck in his gut."

Corey pulled the trigger. Cherestal slumped to the ground in front of his cousin's cubicle. It would take ten minutes before he bled to death. Corey walked away.

Episode 70

America's domestic surveillance transformation

The Oval Office
White House
President Robert Rhinehart stood behind a podium that was mounted atop his desk. A plaque on the lectern read, "Seal of the President of the United States." Standing slightly behind him were Director Maxwell Gordon of the CIA's National Clandestine Service, Director Dr. Alex DuRoss of the National Security Agency (NSA), Director Col. Brent Burkin of the Defense Intelligence Agency (DIA), and Deputy Director Roger Hart of the National Reconnaissance Office (NRO).

The American flag and President's Flag stood behind them, in front of three large, south-facing windows with mute red-orange drapes hanging from them. It offered a presidential appearance to the American public and the world. The cameras zoomed in as the president began his address to the nation:

"Good evening, my fellow Americans. Earlier this afternoon a terrorist attack cell attempted to bomb, with sophisticated mortars, the Progressive Field baseball park in Cleveland, Ohio. They did not succeed, due to a robust counterintelligence effort performed by the CIA and NSA. The intelligence they gathered was instantly shared with law enforcement agencies. I give my heartfelt thanks to the FBI, Ohio

State Patrol, Ohio's county sheriff's departments, and to the local police departments involved. They saved thousands of lives today.

I commend the FBI Special Agents in Charge of the Cleveland, Buffalo, Detroit and Pittsburgh main offices, along with the brave FBI agents in their satellite offices in Erie, Pennsylvania and Painesville, Ohio.

These federal, state and local law enforcement officers shut down Interstate Ninety to keep innocent travelers out of harm's way, then engaged the suicide terrorist cell in a deadly firefight. The powerful 140mm mortar shells hidden in the back of the truck blew up in a less-densely populated area to the east of downtown Cleveland. The explosion was caused by the hail of gunfire from these brave law enforcement officers.

I give my condolences to Ohio State Patrol trooper Tom Benson who was gunned down by this sleeper attack cell during a normal traffic stop. May the nation pray for trooper Benson's wife, children and grandchildren as well. He was to retire in one week and planned to spend time with his grandchildren...teaching them how to fish.

Right now, due to the expertise and bravery of America's counterintelligence and law enforcement communities, I can confidently announce that Americans are safe...the threat has been eliminated. Specialized teams arrived quickly at the detonation site on Interstate Ninety. Other teams were sent to Cleveland's downtown area and crisscrossed through the entire congregation of people, estimated to number over 75,000, after they were evacuated from Progressive Field, the City Center and from surrounding office buildings.

These teams are trained in the use of specialized equipment which detect minute traces of weapons of mass destruction material. Upon receiving their findings after an intensive sweep of the bomb crater where the truck-bomb exploded and of the downtown Cleveland area, I can confidently say the public is safe from WMD's... no traces of radiological, chemical, biological or explosive material were detected.

I also want to give praise to the fifteen hundred men and women of the Cleveland Police Department who evacuated tens of thousands in an orderly and professional manner, and dispersed them away from the target area.

It was a sophisticated attack plan. The sleeper cell created a diversion using a second truck identical to their own. Alert police officers spotted it in The Flats area of Cleveland and gave chase. The chase ended in a gun battle in close proximity to a large crowd of citizens being dispersed along West Superior Avenue. Thanks to the professionalism of the Cleveland Police, the two radical jihadists driving the decoy truck were killed with no civilian casualties. It is my belief that this truck, although it did not carry explosives, would have driven full speed into the masses of innocent people being dispersed.

My apologies to those who tried to contact their loved ones by cell phone, but could not. I take full responsibility for this inconvenience, but this was a sophisticated terrorist cell. They could have set off explosives from afar with cellular phones and I did not want possible pre-positioned bombs to detonate in the amidst of the advancing crowds. We all remember the Boston Marathon bombing... my mind will always carry the image of terrorist Dzhokhar Tsarnaev holding a cellular phone in his hand minutes before the pressure cooker bombs exploded.

To protect the innocent people, the agents patrolling through the crowds carried cell phone jammers that cut off communication in this specific area. I would also like to commend the AT&T and Verizon phone companies. Upon my request, they willingly shutdown the local physical connection points that mobile phone services pass through.

Thank God it is all over and everyone is safe."

President Rhinehart paused in his address to the nation, then stared sternly into the cameras. He continued. "This is the most sophisticated and largest terrorist network that our counterterrorism forces have ever smashed. The planners, funders and supporters stretch from Haiti, Nassau, the Tri-Border Area of South America and the remote Bahamian out island of Abaco, to Colombia and the Middle East.

For several years, America's counterintelligence has been working with a high-ranking official in the Royal Bahamian Police Force named Deputy Commander Ellison Rolle. It was through the brave undercover work of Rolle and his detectives, plus his dedication to work with America's counterintelligence that led to the destruction of this network on the out island of Abaco.

The investigation is continuing by Deputy Commander Rolle and U.S. counterintelligence, so I cannot reveal the sources and methods of the operation, but here are some of the details.

A small army of well-trained Middle Eastern terrorists were smuggled into the peaceful Bahamian out island of Abaco, then to property owned by a front company, called Abaco Poutlry, LTD. This company was created by narco-terrorist Cesar Virgilio Sandoval and two very dangerous Middle Eastern terrorist leaders, Eamal Batoor and Khoury Kassim.

Deputy Commander Rolle did not have the manpower to raid the meeting of these high-ranking terrorist network officials, due to the small army protecting them. U.S. counterintelligence recommended he contact the U.S. Ambassador to the Bahamas for assistance, for the USS Caribbean Sea amphibious assault ship was conducting standard naval maneuvers offshore. Upon Rolle's request, Ambassador David Cromwell held an emergency meeting with me and Bahamian Prime Minister Nigel Lightbourne.

Upon hearing about the gravity of the situation on Abaco, based on the intelligence collected by Deputy Commander Rolle and U.S. counterintelligence, the prime minister gave me the go ahead to call in a special forces team aboard the USS Caribbean Sea.

The United States of America hereby honors Deputy Commander Ellison Rolle of the Royal Bahamian Police Force and Prime Minister Nigel Lightbourne for their competent intelligence-gathering and quick decision to raid this terrorist smuggling network which planned, funded and was about to carry out a mortar bomb attack on the Cleveland Indians ballgame at Progressive Field where over 45,000 Americans were enjoying the game.

Here is a summary of those who were arrested, wounded, and killed during the raid. Five U.S. special operations soldiers were wounded. They were immediately life-flighted by Medevac helicopters back to the USS Caribbean Sea amphibious assault ship. All of them are expected to survive.

Thirty-Five Middle Eastern terrorists were killed during a firefight with the special ops soldiers. They were smuggled into the Bahamas from Haiti by a human smuggler named Abner Orival, who worked for Cesar Virgilio Sandoval. Orival was shot and killed during the raid. As for Sandoval, the narco-terrorist who owned the property... during interrogation, he confessed to U.S. counterintelligence of the Progressive Field attack. At this moment, he is being transported to Guantanamo Bay Detention Camp in Cuba.

Sandoval had two personal bodyguards, Bolan Tougas and Pierre Cherestal. Cherestal was killed and Tougas is currently being transported to an unknown destination. Due to security reasons, I cannot reveal that location. All three men were involved in the undisclosed kidnapping and brutal murder of a U.S. counterintelligence agent.

Three high-ranking radical Islamist kingpins were arrested... Shahid El-Sayed, Eamal Batoor, and Khoury Kassim. They are the major planners and funders of the failed Progressive Field attack. All of them are being transported to Guantanamo Bay as I speak.

America's counterintelligence agents throughout the Caribbean learned that huge sums of money were made by Sandoval, El-Sayed, Batoor and Kassim by smuggling Middle East heroin into Europe and the U.S., then trafficking Colombian coke back to the Middle East. Hundreds of millions of dollars were laundered by a corrupt Irish banker and his brother in downtown Nassau. These funds were used to sponsor terrorist operations against the United States. Deputy

Commander Rolle arrested both these men, banker Sean Branagh and his brother, Patrick Branagh.

Deputy Commander Rolle also arrested the Bahamian Agricultural Minister, Alfred Moss, M.P. Rolle and his detectives had gathered much evidence against Moss that linked him to aiding and abetting the terrorist network, and of receiving hefty kickbacks from their drug-smuggling ventures. Moss' limo driver was killed in the firefight. Intelligence disclosed that this limo driver, along with Bolan Tougas and Pierre Cherestal, kidnapped a U.S. counterintelligence agent from the Hard Rock Café in downtown Nassau and took him to Sandoval's mansion on Abaco.

Also placed under arrest by Deputy Commander Rolle was Haitian Minister of Public Health and Population Laurent Rousseau, who accompanied Abner Orival to the Abaco mansion."

An angry look appeared on Rhinehart's face. The cameras zoomed in for a full-face view. "And now, what I'm about to reveal to you is most disturbing. Also present at the mansion, meeting with the leaders of this terrorist network, were U.S. Senator William Warren, Chairman of the Senate Select Intelligence Committee and his Chief-of-Staff Mark Serwin. Our counterintelligence agents gathered hard evidence that shows Warren had been compromised by the network for years and that he actually assisted them in the theft of the 140mm mortars that were about to be used earlier today to kill thousands of Americans.

The betrayal of America's trust does not end there. Unfortunately, there's more. Without going into the specifics, the U.S. counterintelligence community has been utilizing a trailblazing deep data mining algorithm throughout the Caribbean Basin, our vulnerable southern flank. It has proven to be invaluable in helping counterintelligence agents identify and preemptively strike terrorist cells before they can operationalize their attack plans.

This particular deep data mining procedure has kept the radical Islamic presence in the Caribbean Basin in check. Therefore, I plan to utilize it here, inside the U.S., for a new domestic surveillance and intelligence-gathering mission that will better protect the American people, to prevent a repeat of what almost happened today."

Rhinehart paused in his address, then stared even more lugu-briously into the cameras. "Our undercover intelligence operatives have gathered substantial evidence that proves Senator Warren and another high-ranking U.S. government official stole this deep data mining algorithm and sold it to the terrorist network. One of the origi-nal designers of this new data mining system, a traitor code-named Black Hat Hacker...BHH...hacked past the computer firewalls and downloaded it.

Our counterintelligence agents recorded BHH arriving in Bimini, Bahamas with a satchel carrying the algorithm and meeting Senator Warren, his Chief of Staff Mark Serwin, and Shahid El-Sayed. The four men flew to the terrorist meeting on Abaco and, thank god, the satchel was recovered during the raid, in which BHH was killed.

In sum, Deputy Commander Ellison Rolle of the Royal Bahamian Police Force arrested Patrick and Sean Branagh, Bahamian Agricultural Minister Alfred Moss, the Haitian Minister Laurent Rousseau, who was bought and paid for by the narco-terrorist Sandoval, Cecil Turnquest, a corrupt RBPF constable on Abaco, and U.S. Senator William Warren. Mark Serwin, Warren's chief of staff, was killed in the gun battle at the mansion. All six men, including Senator Warren, are currently jailed at the Carmichael Detention Centre in Nassau.

The Bahamian authorities will charge Senator Warren with aid-ing and abetting a terrorist network operating on their soil under the statutes of the Bahamas Anti-Terrorism Act of 2014. As president, I will charge Warren with treason. Prime Minister Lightbourne and I will discuss prosecutorial procedures between our two nations.

America's law enforcement and counterintelligence communities are searching for all those connected to Senator Warren's treason-ous actions. I am confident they will soon be found and brought to justice. As president, I make no distinction between the terrorists themselves and those who knowingly support them and make their evil mission possible.

Lastly, I will move to incorporate domestic intelligence-gathering by the counterintelligence arm of the CIA into the mainstream of American society. I will do this in order to aid the FBI and other law enforcement entities in the battle against terrorism. As you know, after the terrible 9/11 attack which killed 2,977 innocent civilians, a new cabinet-level position was created called the Secretary of Homeland Security.

Unfortunately, the CIA was not included in this newly-formed cabinet...it will be, starting now. I hereby create a new cabinet-level department called the Domestic Counter-Intelligence Operations Center, DCIOC. The DCIOC will be embedded within the Department of Homeland Security. I appointed Maxwell Gordon to the newly-created position of Secretary of the DCIOC. He will also be the Deputy Director to the current Secretary of Homeland Security."

Rhinehart turned and held his hand up toward Gordon who was standing behind him. Gordon nodded in acknowledgement. The president continued with his speech. "Maxwell Gordon has done an outstanding job as the CIA's Director of the National Clandestine Service. He has conducted robust intelligence collection on America's enemies and is a true spymaster. He has worked undercover and has never been identified in the news media or outside the inner walls of the CIA, until now.

Although congress and the American public are aware that the National Clandestine Service exists within the CIA, only myself and the Senate and House Intelligence Committees knew that Maxwell Gordon headed it. Hopefully, ex-Senator Warren didn't give Gordon's name away to our enemies.

There will be a seamless and robust sharing of information between America's law enforcement and counterintelligence communities through Fusion Centers. This rapid dissemination and sharing of vital intelligence via Fusion Centers prevented Progressive Field from being mortar bombed today and saved thousands of Americans from being killed. Interestingly, Senator Warren, who is now sitting in a jail cell in the Bahamas, was against the formation of the Fusion Center network across America.

In conclusion, I want to speak to you candidly...what I am about to say flows from my heart. During the post-9/11 period, I was upset when an ACLU lawsuit handcuffed America's intelligence services in their attempts to ferret out die hard radical Islamic sleeper cells lurking inside America. I remember visualizing people jumping off the tops of the Twin Towers. I wondered what they were feeling as they fell toward the pavement below.

The National Security Agency's interception of billions of e-mail, fax, cell phone, I-Pod, and other electronic messages seemed more like a personal security blanket that kept Americans out of harm's way and guaranteed their future liberty. Both the CIA and NSA spy *for* us, not *on* us.

Gordon Maxwell, Secretary of the new Domestic Counter Intelligence Operations Center, will ensure the blending of robust CIA domestic intelligence-gathering operations inside America will not infringe upon our personal liberties and rights to privacy.

Shortly after 9/11, the ACLU sued the government for conducting unauthorized domestic spying. Fortunately, the U.S. Court of Appeals for the 6th Circuit concluded that none in the ACLU suit could prove they had been monitored and, therefore, had no standing to bring the suit. I'd wager practically all of the loved ones of the nearly three thousand 9/11 victims sided with that court decision. Interestingly enough, today's thwarted terrorist attack would have killed and wounded even more.

The amount of information collected by the CIA and NSA is too vast to be recorded and personally read by a human being. Instead, a program called 'Dictionary' at the NSA will whiz through Library of Congress-sized data and zero-in on specific threats. Then, and *only* then, a real live human may read the targeted intercepts to uncover terrorist activity.

This robust DCIOC monitoring of American communications to and from overseas points will not violate your personal freedoms. Maxwell Gordon will insure that never happens. When trillions of bits of intelligence are narrowed down to a few potential threats, the FISA requirements will kick into gear.

It is my heartfelt feeling that both the FBI and our counterintelligence agencies are handcuffed and are unable to effectively uncover the radicalized homegrown sleeper cells lurking amongst us. I remember, years ago, ex-FBI Director Robert S. Mueller lament to Congress about these domestic counterintelligence shortfalls. His concerns hold true today.

For example, many of the 100,000 Chinese permitted to visit the U.S. each year must agree to specific technology collection requirements set by Beijing. Through no fault of its own, the FBI's 20,000 agents are spread paper thin shadowing Chinese diplomatic and business officials, students, delegation envoys and émigrés. They've arrested dozens of them as they fanned out across America, seeking to buy U.S. military technology, such as the newer AGM-129 cruise missile. They arrested one of the most significant Chinese arms dealers ever when he attempted to purchase one from undercover FBI agents. This missile has stealth technology and can accurately deliver nuclear warheads to targets 3,000 miles away.

The FBI is overloaded in protecting sensitive U.S. technology from illegal foreign acquisition, such as the once super-secret and advanced AGM-129 that is carried under the wings of our B-52 bombers. They are spread paper thin and cannot effectively uncover jihadist sleeper cells lurking among us, who believe martyrdom and certainty of paradise can be reached by mortar-bombing a crowded stadium of innocent Americans watching a baseball game.

What will be the next attack? Detonating a "dirty" radioactive bomb with weapons-grade plutonium stolen from Iran's nuclear power plants? Perhaps, a biological weapons attack... or worse?

The symbol of America's strength and security is the majestic Bald Eagle, but after learning of the treasonous activities of Senator Warren and another high-ranking government official, I believe the shaft of our enemy's arrow is feathered with one of the eagle's own plumes; we are giving our enemies the means for our own destruction. This is another reason I created the Domestic Counter Intelligence Operations Center and embedded it within the Department of Homeland Security. The need for the CIA, with the assistance of the NSA, to conduct broad domestic surveillance and for FISA-approved wiretapping on narrowed-down, specific threat targets is justified.

As President of the United States, I give thanks to the information sharing between our counterintelligence professionals and law enforcement. I can assure you that the terrorist threat has been eliminated at Progressive Field and in downtown Cleveland. America is safe, for now. Good night...and God bless America."

Episode 71

Patriotic victim

Conch Inn Marina

Marsh Harbor, Abaco

Corey strolled through the lush gardens and sat on an isolated bench under the shade of breadfruit trees. The gentle ocean breeze coming in from the Sea of Abaco felt good. He held Pinkston's satellite phone to his ear, listening to it run through the twelve-digit encryption algorithm.

After several moments, Morrison answered. "Well done, Corey. Mission accomplished. The *Obscure Transgression*, OT, level has been officially terminated by President Rhinehart. I just got off the phone with him. We now operate under the legal and policy constraints that the FBI and law enforcement follow…make sure you and your teams adhere to them."

"Yes sir, I will notify teams ten and eleven." "Where are they now?"

Corey glanced over a red bougainvillea hedge that separated the gardens from the Curly Tail Restaurant and Sunset Bar. He could see the heads of 'Chop Chop' and the other four members of Team-11 seated on barstools at the outside Sunset Bar patio. They were watching Wolf Blitzer on CNN cover Rhinehart's address to the nation and the Abaco raid. The Team-10 cruise ship couple sat with them. Many locals also sat around the bar. All eyes were glued to the TV screen.

"They're all gathered here, at the Conch Inn Marina, pretending to be shocked by the news of the raid. We didn't want to suddenly vacate the island and disappear all at once… that might raise suspicion. The team ten couple is checking out of the Lofty Fig tomorrow morning and team eleven is cruising to Bimini the day after."

"Good. Constance managed them well after you left the mansion to join Sandoval's interrogation on the *Queen Conch II*. They retraced their steps through the jungle with knapsacks and backpacks full of manila folders, DVD's, tapes and computer hard drives from Sandoval's office. One of our Apache's from the USS Caribbean Sea picked up everything once they were back on team eleven's yacht."

Corey took a swig of ice-cold Kalik. "Sir, did you notice FBI Director Walt Mason was absent from the Oval Office during Rhinehart's address?"

"I suspected he wouldn't be invited. The body cams on you and the other agents recorded the confessions by Sandoval and by Warren's Chief of Staff Mark Serwin…before he did a swan dive off the ledge. I sent them to President Rhinehart as he was writing his speech."

The ice-cold Kalik tasted good. Corey took another gulp. "Things don't look good for Walt Mason. Rhinehart never mentioned his name in the address, only praised the local FBI special agents in charge. He blasted Senator Warren as treasonous and mentioned 'another high-ranking U.S. government official' stole the deep data mining algorithm to sell to the terrorist network."

Morrison paused before speaking. "Mason is toast…and he knows it."

FBI Headquarters Washington, D.C.
The SUV with tinted windows drove down Pennsylvania Avenue, NW and stopped three blocks from the FBI HQ. The driver and man riding shotgun urged their boss to let them drive him to the secure

underground garage, but he calmly told them to drop him off. They obeyed and pulled over to the curb.

FBI Director Walt Mason casually got out and walked down Pennsylvania Avenue, stopping to admire the massive US Navy Memorial Plaza. The five fountains shot cool water upward from the large basin. He thought the plaza was a wonderful way of honoring Americans serving at sea in the Navy and Coast Guard. He wished he could receive a similar tribute for his twenty-eight years of service in the FBI.

He continued walking down Pennsylvania Avenue, past 9th Street, then paused in front of the FBI headquarters to gaze at the bronze statue with the words "Fidelity, Bravery and Integrity" inscribed on it. Mason walked through the front entrance without any bodyguards accompanying him and strode past the surprised security guards manning the front desk.

A minute later, he walked into his outer office. His secretary handed him a memo and said, "It's from President Rhinehart, sir. He wants to see you in the Oval Office in one hour."

He thanked her, told her he didn't want any calls for the next fifteen minutes, then walked into his office, shut the door and sat behind his desk.

Photos of his wife and children lined the upper right-hand corner of the desktop. He slid them into a semicircle in front of him then walked over to a wood-paneled wall and retrieved a shadow box with two medals inside. He placed it among his family photos.

For several minutes, he stared at the photos of his loved ones and at the shadow box. It displayed his FBI Medal of Valor and FBI Medal for Meritorious Achievement awards. He thought about the fun time it was meeting and dating his wife, getting married and raising three children.

He stared at the medals and reflected back into his prime, when he was an agent... the bank robbery where a young, pregnant woman teller was shot...his shooting of the two robbers, then jumping over the counter… stopping the woman's bleeding…preventing her from going into shock…giving her mouth to mouth resuscitation when she stopped breathing…saving her and her baby.

Mason unsnapped the FBI badge from his belt and laid it on the desktop in the middle of the semicircle of photos and medals. He drew his Glock 22, .40 caliber S&W, placed it on the desk and began thinking of his devotion to America…his belief that the FBI should remain the leader in using domestic surveillance to battle terrorism. He yearned to prevent the CIA and the ingenious Penumbra Database algorithm from usurping his agency's role in protecting Americans from harm.

President Rhinehart's address last night made him feel ashamed at how he allowed Senator Warren to lie to and manipulate him. Warren knew he wanted to get his hands on the Jeannie Database in order to save the future of the FBI. He thought about how he gave Warren the hi-tech wherewithal to bypass Danielle's home security system to steal the database … but not to murder her!

The secretary to Director Walt Mason finished making his favorite cup of coffee. She knew he said not to bother him for fifteen minutes, but he looked notably fatigued this morning. She needed to perk him up a bit before his meeting with President Rhinehart.

She was about to tap on his door with the coffee when a loud blast sounded. She burst into his office and ran up to him. The entire back of his head was missing. A red mist still hung in the air and droplets of blood trickled down the wall behind him. A note lay in the middle of the photos and medals he assembled on his desk. It simply read, "I'm sorry." She started sobbing.

Episode 72

Falling from omnipotence

Carmichael Road Detention Center
Nassau, Bahamas

The sun beat down unmercifully on the prison which sat in the middle of a treeless field and was bounded by razor wire. Inside, the stench of human sweat and mildew mingling with the aroma rising from full toilets that didn't flush properly was overbearing.

Senator William Warren, wearing an orange tank top and swimming trunks, sat on a metal cot that jutted out of the wall, scheming what his next move would be. He was allowed to phone the consular at the U.S. Embassy in Nassau to see if he could be bailed out of Carmichael, but the reply was cold and firm. "Any American who commits an offense within the Bahamas is subject to Bahamian criminal jurisdiction. I cannot help you."

Sandoval occupied the malodourous cell directly across the narrow hallway from his. Both men were initially placed together in a more sanitary cell upstairs, but Sandoval tried to bribe one of the guards. He recognized the guard as the cousin to one of the baggage handlers he paid off at Nassau's Lynden Pindling International Airport.

If the guard brought him and Senator Warren two guard uniforms and two "Cybercell" Bahamas prepaid SIM Card cell phones, left the jail cell door unlocked during his night shift, and left the keys in his car in the parking lot, he'd become a rich man. Sandoval promised to send $30,000 cash to his cousin for them to split.

Unfortunately for Sandoval and Warren, the guard was an honest man and reported their escape plan to the warden, who immediately shackled both men and placed them in separate cells in the grubbier first-floor section.

Senator Warren closed his eyes and dreamed he and Mark Serwin were driving along a beautiful country road in his Mercedes-Benz SLR McLaren. Then, he fantasized that he was sitting in his premium Italian black leather ergonomically-styled chair in the secretive room SH-219 of the Senate Hart Office Building, resting his hands on the conference table so the other members of the Senate Select Committee on Intelligence would notice his Cartier pasha Chronograph watch.

He stared down at his bare wrist where the luxurious watch used to be. All he saw were scars, residual reminders of the childhood he resentfully journeyed through. He remembered Corey Pearson slipping the timepiece off his wrist when he was arrested at the mansion.

Loud thwacking sounds jolted him out of his attempt to mentally escape the shithole he was thrown in. It was Deputy Commander Ellison Rolle, scraping his metal baton across the cell bars. Following him down the corridor was Corey and the consular from the U.S. Embassy in Nassau.

Corey looked at Rolle and said, "You go first."

"Hello, Mistah Senator Warren. I hope you havin' a good time in da Bahamas...it's bettah in da Bahamas, dey say. I want ya to listen carefully to the convasation I 'bout to have wid dis monster in the cell across from you. When I'm done, Mistah Pearson and your U.S. counselor will have a chit chat wid you, too."

The big man turned to Sandoval, who had a makeshift splint applied to his broken wrist and dirty gauze dressings taped over his festering wounds from the waterboarding experience. "As for you, Mistah Sandoval, I am a religious man and I feel bad 'bout hating you so much...the Bible says I shouldn't, but I do. I been carryin' a hot ember in my heart since you gunned down my daughter's fiancé, Bernard Knowles. Ya shot him in cold-blood at da Sandy Point Airport custom station...'cause he wouldn't take da bribe ya offer him. Da Bible says to forgive, but I can't...I only dream o' revenge."

Sandoval, despite his wounds was able to get up off his cot and hobble up to the bars. "I didn't kill him...I swear!"

Corey chipped in from behind Rolle. "You're a two-faced liar. My organization did ballistic testing and the same gun you shot Devon Ledard with in your mansion office was the same gun used to kill Bernard Knowles."

Rolle held up the sketch of the suspect who shot Bernard. Corey recognized it as the same sketch Rolle showed him after he was arrested at the British Colonial Hotel shortly after the slaying of Sidney Fowler in Nassau's Parliament Square.

"Yes, Mistah Pearson is right...you are a liar. Dis sketch was made from what da good citizens of Sandy Point say ma son-in-law's killer look like. Definitely not a Cuban o' Haitian." He thrust the sketch in Sandoval's face. "You be a Colombian, too, like it shows. And dese bloodred teardrop tattoos under da left eye...it be you."

Rolle continued talking while Sandoval grasp the bars to keep himself from collapsing. "You also be charged wid da murder of Sidney Fowler in downtown Nassau and da kidnappin' of Devon Ledard's wife and children in da Guana Cay settlement. By da way, Devon Ledard survived yo' gunshot wounds. My constables on Great Guana Cay, wid da help from da brave men on da USS Caribbean Sea...dey raid Devon's house and save his wife and kids from da two Middle East terrorist gunmen you send dere."

Sandoval held on to the bars, looked down at the floor and kept his mouth shut. Rolle ended his formal charges. "And, finally, dese murders didn't take place in isolation... you hereby be charged wid terrorism and treason. Yo directly participate in da offense of terrorism, of da financin' o' terrorism wid da knowledge dat thousands would be killed in the city of Cleveland. You will be stayin' here, in Carmichael, for several mo' years in da stinkin' cell you be in now while you be prosecuted. And, if you are convicted, which you no doubt gonna be…you will not get life in prison…you gonna be sentenced ta death… ya gonna be hung in da courtyard of Fox Hill Prison…and dat fo' sure is gonna happen!"

Rolle stepped aside and motioned Corey and the consular to come forward to talk to Senator Warren, but Sandoval went berserk. "No, no! Listen to me! It was dat bastard sittin' in the cell across from me…Senator Warren! He paid me to steal the Jeannie database…to break into dat women's home in Maryland. Warren, he get a high-tech device from da FBI director dat deactivated da home alarm system… Warren cause her death, not me."

Corey wanted to take out his Glock and shoot Sandoval right then and there. Sandoval started sobbing. "And, dat ain't all. It be Senator Warren who got dat dirty Colombian Army Lieutenant General Castano ta lie to his Senate Select Intel Committee…to have dem fund the laser-guided mortars dat was ta be used ta kill all the people in Cleveland, not me. I got tape recordin' of da spy committee meetin' dat Castano spoke at…Warren gave me da tape…it be in my library at da mansion."

Corey calmly replied, "We already know all that. Kindly go back to your cot and shut up." Then, he approached Senator Warren's cell with the U.S. consular at his side.

The consular spoke first. "I'll sum it up for you, senator…you're in deep shit. President Rhinehart called me at the embassy and I'm delivering his message, practically word-for-word. He consulted with the U.S. Attorney General, and after reviewing the quality, depth and breadth of the intelligence gathered against you by Mr. Corey Pearson here and the organization he works for, you will be charged with complicity to commit murder and…treason. Therefore, due process is nullified. The U.S. will allow Deputy Commander Rolle and the Bahamian judicial system to pursue accessory to murder charges against you. The process will take several years and during that time, you will remain here, at the Carmichael Detention Center, in the exact jail cell you are now in. In fact, the POTUS had Deputy Commander

Rolle *promise* that you will remain in this very cell until you are extradited to the U.S.

Since you are officially considered an enemy of the United States, FBI agents have, without a warrant, searched through your residence in Georgetown and seized your personal computer, cell phones, routers, and bank statements. Your computer drives are being copied and the agents have digitally photographed all the documents housed in your safety deposit box and home safe. Under the restituted Patriot Act of 2018, you do not have any due process rights. The reconstituted act supersedes the U.S. Constitution in cases like yours.

Because you already have tried to break out of this place, you are considered a flight risk. Since you are implicated in the largest terrorist plot ever thwarted by U.S. counterintelligence, you will not be allowed to talk with an attorney or to have any visitors until the investigation is completed and formal charges are brought against you... which they will be.

President Rhinehart wanted me to emphasize to you that he knows treason prosecutions are rare and there have been fewer than forty such prosecutions in America's history." The consular looked sternly at Warren. "But, he believes that you, as a U.S. senator and as Chairman of the Senate Select Intelligence Committee, have intentionally committed the most serious offense possible against the U.S. government and the American people. Therefore, he is seeking for your punishment to be death, not life imprisonment."

Corey spoke through the bars to Warren. "Your greed knows no limits and you fall into a new kind of criminal class. After you rot for a long time in this hell hole reeking of human sweat and feces, you will be extradited back to America...a country that can't survive your kind of treason...a disloyalty and betrayal from within, concealed in the halls of congress. You sacrificed your country's soul for money, but you inadvertently altered the history of America's counterintelligence battle against terrorism."

Senator Warren stared at the broken toilet in the middle of his cell. Without looking up, he asked, "How so?"

Because of you and the huge terrorist bust, President Rhinehart established a new cabinet-level position called the Domestic Counter Intelligence Operations Center. He appointed Gordon Maxwell to run it. We now have robust CIA intelligence-gathering capabilities operating inside America through Fusion Centers. Americans now understand that their protection must flow from the inside/out... because of people like you."

Corey looked at the consular. "Let's get the hell out of here, I can't stand the smell of this shithole any longer."

Episode 73

PTSD- Struggling to unwind

Sunset Bar, Conch Inn Marina
Abaco, Bahamas

Corey sat at the open-air bar talking to Shianna. She brought him a *Conch Bruschetta* of grilled conch, tomato, onion and cilantro on a toasted baguette with a caper aioli. He ordered it because it was Constance's favorite item on the Curly Tail's menu and she would be arriving shortly.

Perfect timing. She walked onto the patio and sat next to him. "Sapodilly's was busy as hell. I ran around waiting tables and serving drunks at the bar. I'm exhausted and famished. Thanks for the din-din!"

Corey stared at her beautiful tan legs flowing out of the cut-off jeans. "It's your favorite à la carte...dig in."

They spontaneously held hands and sat in silence, watching the TV. The Zephyr Nassau Sunshine, ZNS channel, was covering the Abaco mansion raid all day long. Photos of Deputy Commander Rolle and the remains of Sandoval's stone palace flashed on the screen while the TV anchors described how Rolle hunted down and arrested the murderers of two Abaconians: Bahamian Customs officer Bernard Knowles, who also happened to be his son-in-law, and Sidney Fowler, the supervisor of Abaco Poultry, LTD.

Shianna clasped her hands together and started crying. "Thank you! Thank you, RBPF man...Rolle is my star! 'Cause a him, I can rest in peace knowin' ma brother's killer is rottin' inside Carmichael."

Constance played dumb. "Oh, Shianna...we're so glad that you're able to cope...we know how much you loved your older brother. People like Deputy Commander Rolle in the RBPF, they know how to track down and bring such terrible people to justice."

Corey thought about capturing Sandoval at the mansion and having him tortured by Oppressor. The video of Duane Collier being tortured and fed to the tiger shark came to mind. He recalled pointing his Glock into the face of BHH...then pulling the trigger. He struggled to summon up the image of himself sticking his Glock into the stomach of Pierre Cherestal... then pulling the trigger. It was never easy for him to kill another human being, regardless of how wretched they were.

A solemn look appeared on Corey's face. He ordered another Kalik and Shianna brought him an ice-cold one. "You O.K., Mistah Pearson? You dun look very happy at da moment."

Constance noticed the stare. She saw it before. "He's fine, Shianna... just a little tired." When Shianna walked away she placed both her hands on his arm and said. "Just keep reminding yourself that these people planned, funded and were about to massacre thousands of people, including the POTUS...in Cleveland, America's heartland."

Corey looked into her green eyes. "Yeah, I know. That's why CBIF goes to the OT level, temporarily. I don't feel sympathy or guilt for those you and I shot or had tortured...I actually feel anger towards them for putting us in a position where we had to do so. I don't like hurting anyone...I want to have faith in humanity, to believe that mankind is basically good. These bastards denied us the comfort of having such faith... there's too much evil out there."

Constance said, "Yes, and evil draws such men together. It's spreading because of the ineffectiveness of law enforcement to battle radical Islamic terrorists."

"By 'law enforcement,' you're referring to the FBI. The new CIA-run counterintelligence cabinet with Maxwell Gordon working alongside Rhinehart and the Vice-President will change the battlefield.

I feel sympathy towards Walt Mason. He thought law enforcement, not counterintelligence, was the only way to protect Americans from terrorist attacks. He was deceived by Warren and broke the law to get his hands on the Jeannie database out of patriotism, not greed. I'm sure he thought Warren would do a Watergate-style break-in at Danielle's home… and not commit murder."

Constance nodded in agreement, then slid a toasted baguette topped with grilled conch into Corey's mouth. He smiled and washed it down with a gulp of Kalik. "Damn, that tastes delicious… I'm addicted to Bahamian cooking."

"I wonder what our terrorist friends are eating, right now…did they make it to Gitmo?"

"Yes, the *Queen Conch II* immediately set sail for Guantanamo Bay after the EIT's were completed. Upon arrival, Batoor, Khoury, and El-Sayed were immediately thrown into solitary confinement."

She offered another baguette to Corey. He opened his mouth wide like a baby bird and gulped it down. She laughed, then grew serious. "Do you think they will ever tell where the sleeper-cell networks inside America are?"

"I don't know. The Gitmo cells they're in are totally isolated. There's a chance El-Sayed may start talking, but we'll have to wait and see." "Why would they want to tell us? Wouldn't they commit suicide before doing that?"

"There's no chance of suicide. Each cell is under 24-7 watch. The plan is to let the effects of total isolation make them vulnerable to interrogation."

"I don't get it. These guys are so committed…so hateful of the West. Why would they tell us anything to ruin their global jihad?"

Corey spoke softly. "No contact with other humans, the very social context that makes us who we are is gone. They, hopefully, will lose their sense of self. It happens over time…the brain chemistry actually alters, morphs into a state where severe psychological symptoms surface… hallucinations, paranoia, delirium. You know Constance, I just want to forget about this world we're in."

Several wild spotted dolphins cruised into the Conch Inn Marina dock area and playfully zoomed under the moored sailboats.

Constance said, "There is a better world out there…all around us, waiting for us to play in. I wonder if 'Chop Tail' is one of them?"

Corey looked at the free-roaming mammals swirl under the hulls, then surface and rise up on their tails to the joy of the boaters. "He could be. When we get back from Washington, let's do some dolphin research, just like we did a decade ago."

"That'd be great! My son will be back from staying with my parents in Nassau…he could come with us."

"Sounds like a plan."

They watched as the dolphins grew bored with their human entertainment and cruised back out into the Sea of Abaco to begin some serious echolocation to find crustaceans hiding in the sandy bottom.

Constance asked, "By the way, Bolan Tougas was on the *Queen Conch II*. Was he sent to Gitmo, too?"

Corey took a swig of Kalik. "No, he was dropped off when the ship returned to Haiti… handed over to a man named Damballah St. Fleur."

"What's going to happen to him?"

"I don't know, but it will be something worse than what Oppressor did to him… something so terrible that I don't even want to think about it."

Episode 74

Damballah's revenge

Saut-d'Eau Village, Haiti
Voodoo sacred waterfall
His followers began to gather in the tropical forest around the Saut-d'Eau waterfall in the remote Mirebalais district of Haiti. They came from miles around for this special ceremony.

Damballah St. Fleur stood on a large boulder watching his followers, voodooists... "servants of the spirits." They gathered in a large semicircle around the sacred waters cascading down from the hillside. Many believed the water cured infertility problems of the womb and Damballah's sterile female voodooists often made offerings of their underwear in order to someday bear children.

At this ceremony, another form of offering, a sacrifice, was about to be made. Oppressor stood on the boulder beside Damballah. He was impressed by what he learned from this Vodou priest who wanted Bolan Tougas so badly. Spymaster Corey Pearson ordered Oppressor to make the delivery: "Sail the *Queen Conch II* to Port-au-Prince harbor and tell the dock workers that you've got Bolan Tougas, one of the FRAPH squad members on board. You'll soon meet a man named Damballah St. Fleur. Give Tougas to him."

Twenty minutes later, St. Fleur showed up in a Jeep Wrangler with two of his vodouist bodyguards and took Tougas away, shackled and hooded. He was thankful for the gift and invited Oppressor to come along with him.

The two men related quite well to each other. Damballah revealed how the spymaster Corey Pearson recruited him years ago, and that Bolan Tougas was a member of the murderous FRAPH squad that tortured and murdered his parents. He told the big man with the werewolf tattoo on his forearm that he gives Pearson vital information about Sandoval's activities in Haiti and, in return, Pearson tracks down members of the murderous FRAPH squad.

Oppressor told him the EIT methods they use to make terrorists divulge information they wouldn't otherwise. But, he said it's ineffective against many hardened Middle Eastern radical terrorists. Damballah asked if he ever heard of sorcery medicine techniques, to which Oppressor replied, "No."

"Come," he said. "I will reveal to you my technique. You might find it useful in getting these hardened people to talk."

Damballah walked with him down a jungle path laden with palm fronds. They walked half a mile, then took a narrow side footpath lined with heliconia, lobster claw plants and rare orchids of some sort. The path led to a clearing where a large bungalow stood on stilts, hidden by large fern-like leaves of large attalea palms. On the opposite side of the clearing were five rows of solar panels. They climbed a short ladder to a balcony, then he took Oppressor inside.

It was a large, single room with tall ceilings protected by layers of thatch palm. The walls and floor were made of bamboo and wicker. A hammock suspended from a large beam and several stools were positioned by a workbench that lined one entire wall.

Damballah sat at a stool and beckoned Oppressor to join him. "Come, sit and watch. I am making a special powdered cocktail that I will give to Tougas for the offering. You will see its effects... maybe you can use it for your line of work. Dat Tougas, he sounds like one *canaille* type of guy."

Oppressor took out a notepad and pen to take notes. "Thanks, I can't wait to learn from ya. Always perfectin' my trade. By the way, I dig your accent. I'm from Louisiana and you sound just like the Cajuns there. You don't look totally Haitian, either."

"Very observant you are. My great grandparents are from southern Louisiana and their parents were French settlers in Canada. Da English drove everybody out dat didn't want to give up da Catholic religion during da 'Great Expulsion,' so dey fled Canada and settled in southern Louisiana. From dere, my parents left and came to Haiti, and heah I be."

Damballah took three soup can tins out of a bamboo cupboard and sat them on the workbench next to a digital scale. "Watch carefully. Dese three cans be full of powder from plant, land animals and ocean creatures."

He picked up a blue measuring spoon and scooped out a grey-colored portion from the first can and put it on the scale. "Dis is ocean creatures, mostly fish...couvillion. Equal parts of powder from da pufferfish, porcupinefish and triggerfish. Dey all contain da potent neurotoxin the American doctors call tetrodotoxin."

"What will that do to Bolan Tougas?"

"It stop da nerves from firing, make him immobile...ya know, paralyzed... but he will remain aware of everything."

He took a scoop from the second can. "Dis is da land animals I learn about from my father. He taught me all I know about Voodoo. Before age six, I learned da chants and how to enter the trance. The vodun, the spirit came into my body from my father when da FRAPH squad killed him. Dat's why we about to offer Tougas as a sacrifice... the Voodoo spirits inside me will want that."

Damballah measured out exactly 4.87 ounces of the blue-green powder from the second can onto the digital scale. "Dis mixture contains newts, poison frogs, some human remains, a special breed of toad we have in our jungle, and land crabs. I raise da crabs in a pen outside and feed dem a special diet dat makes dem toxic, full of cardiac cardenolides, which are capable of stopping the heart from beating, but I put in just da right amount to slow it down."

Oppressor took copious amounts of notes. Stuff like this turned him on. "What do you feed the crabs to do all that?"

"Dis is a best-kept secret dat nobody knows about...jimsonweed. It grow all ova the place. I collect the leaves and seeds. Dey contain an important alkaloid dat causes hallucinations. Bolan Tougas will grow delirious, *pie-ahd* as my Cajun ancestors used to say...drunk. He won't know what planet he be on. He'll see spiritual visions and have plenty of paranoid delusions."

The sun set and the jungle surrounding the Saut-d'Eau waterfall grew dark. Several hundred followers grew silent and watched their Voodoo priest Damballah walk back atop the boulder as Oppressor stood amongst them. The vodouist throng was convinced the man standing over them had been chosen by his father and dead Haitian ancestors to receive the divination from the deities.

Damballah raised the asson, a calabas rattle, above his head and began shaking it. It was made from the calabasse ordinaire tree, covered with a web of porcelain beads and filled with pebbles and snake vertebrae. It was the sacred rattle of Voudoun and passed on to him from his father, thus giving him priestly authority. He also held a clochette bell. The combination rattling and dinging sounds resonated through the jungle as a yellowish glimmer from the bonfire lit up the ghostly scene.

As Damballah stepped down from the boulder and walked to the altar that Tougas was strapped to, a follower slid the hood off the terrified man's head. The masses began to dance and slowly encircle the alter while drums beat and Dambollah continued rattling his asson and clochette bell.

A vodouist put his hands over Bolan Tougas' mouth and nose for a full minute, until the wild-eyed man was almost asphyxiated, then Damballah nodded for him to let go. When he did, Tougas gasped for air and the Voodoo Priest blew a large cloud of dust into his gasping mouth and nose.

Oppressor watched from behind the crowd. He was tall enough to peer over the shorter Haitians. He watched in awe. It was repeated three times, and he witnessed Tougas inhale large amounts of the powdered cocktail created by Damballah. Then, he was unstrapped and made to stand.

Several times he panicked and tried to bolt, but the crowd shoved him back inside the circle. He began screaming for mercy until paralysis immobilized his mouth and lips.

The dancing, drum beats, chanting, rattling and dinging reverberations continued until paralysis took over his extremities and he fell to the ground and began vomiting. Then, he went into seizures that lasted five minutes.

Afterwards, they lifted him up and, to Oppressor's amazement, he could actually stand erect. He tried to scream, but couldn't. He grasped Damballah's arms and tried to plead, but he couldn't speak.

Then, the pain returned. Tougas sat on the alter, wild-eyed and groaning from an agony that overtook his entire body. An intense headache, profuse sweating and tremors overwhelmed him. He began drooling, then went into a coma and lay still upon the alter.

The dancing and music stopped and silence took over. A wooden casket with a glass window on the top was ceremoniously carried in and placed in front of their comatose sacrifice. Oppressor listened and watched. They knew what they were doing... Tougas wasn't their first victim.

For fifteen minutes, all that could be heard were the tree frogs and crickets singing and the soft crackling of the bonfire. Everyone had their eyes glued on the seemingly lifeless Bolan Tougas.

Suddenly, his eyes opened wide and he tried to move but couldn't. He was completely paralyzed. Several of Damballah's followers raised him to a sitting position on the voodoo alter. Damballah spoke to the terrified man. "Can you hear me? Blink your eyes if you can." Tougas blinked.

"Dat's good. You take in and understand everyting', but you are now in a state that you will remain in until you die, which may be a month…maybe a year or two from now. Until you die, you will remain paralyzed, completely conscious of all you see and hear. I made you into a zombie, and you will remain one. You are a member of da hated FRAPH squad, the same one dat killed my parents in front of me when I was a young boy. I feel no sympathy for you."

Damballah took Tougas by the hair and tilted his head down so he could see the casket with the window. It also had a hole where a pipe would be attached so he could have just enough air to continue breathing.

"You will now be placed in da casket and buried alive. We have a special graveyard for you where we bury da other FRAPH squad members. You will be dug up now and again so we can force feed you to keep you alive, so you can continue da life of being a zombie for a long time."

Several vodouist followers lifted his totally immobilized but conscious body and laid it inside the casket, then latched the top shut. Damballah walked away after instructing his followers to form a line and cast a spell upon him, one-by-one.

Oppressor stood in the long line and when it was his turn, he looked through the glass window and saw Bolan Tougas' face staring up at him… with the wildest-looking eyes he ever saw.

Episode 75

A call to come back home...
to Key Largo

Key Lime Café Highway 1
Key Largo, Florida Keys
Corey sat at the mom and pop bar/restaurant eating a homemade key lime pie, gazing out the picture window at the column of coconut palm and pink hibiscus. It was a déjà vu feeling, for he was here a month ago, when he was called home to Key Largo from the safe house in Montego Bay, Jamaica.

Some things never change, and this place was one of them. He felt as if he was starring in a Twilight Zone episode with Rod Serling giving his soft-spoken narration in the background. The same waitress was there, shoving coins into the same aged jukebox that was playing the Jimmy Buffett song 'Wastin' Away in Margaritaville'. The same Parrothead wannabe sat at the bar, watching the black and white TV with rabbit-ear antennae.

She inserted enough coins in the jukebox to fill the airways all day long with Buffett tunes. Her cell phone chimed and she walked into the back kitchen.

A few moments later, she walked up to Corey and asked, "Anything else, sir?"

"No thanks. I'll take my check and another receipt like the one you gave me last time… with nothing written on it." He stared curiously at her for a long moment.

She smiled and said, "Yes, I am. A spymaster like you knew it all along."

Corey glanced towards the Parrothead at the bar. "Is he one of Morrison's CI guys, too?"

The waitress looked around the room to make sure no customers were nearby. "Yes, he is. I just got the order to write down 'You're cleared, Come on home' with invisible ink on the receipt. I'll pass this time…congrats on the Abaco mission and bringing Duane Collier's killers to justice. I trained with him at the 'Farm'." She reached over and held his hand firmly. "Thank you…now run along….Morrison is waiting for you at the same place as last time."

They smiled at each other, then Corey left.

CBIF Safe House
Conch Inn Resort
Key Largo, FL

The Directorate of Operations of CBIF greeted Corey when he walked through the door with a hug and pat on the back, then sat him down at the desk across from him in the unpretentious cottage. Morrison got right down to business, as usual. "There's a number of items we have to cover, Corey. The first is Ellison Rolle. I just got off the phone with Bahamian Prime Minister Nigel Lightbourne and have good news."

"Deputy Commander Rolle is a man of integrity. I hope it's good news."

"It is. President Rhinehart and I talked to Lightbourne and told him the United States is grateful to Rolle. We shared our intelligence with Lightbourne…showed him evidence that his RBPF Commissioner of Police was being paid off and bribed by Sandoval and by his Minster

of Agriculture, Alfred Moss. He immediately promoted Rolle as the new Commissioner of Police of the Royal Bahamian Police Force."

"Wonderful! Kudos to Ellison Rolle."

Morrison stuck a Montecristo in his mouth and tossed another one across the table to Corey.

"Thank you, sir. What happened to the ex-commissioner?" Morrison chuckled. "Rolle arrested him. He's rotting in the Carmichael Detention Center with the rest of them."

Both men paused to take a puff on the prized cigars. The aroma of nutmeg and Caribbean spices filled the air.

Corey said, "I learned that Prime Minister Lightbourne plans on retiring next year, at the end of his term."

"Are you thinking what I am?"

"Yes, I am. I'll encourage Rolle to campaign to be the next Prime Minister of the Bahamas. We could deliver the fleet of go-fast boats to him, with salutations from the United States. I can picture the fleet lined up in Prince George Wharf with the U.S. Ambassador to the Bahamas giving a speech, praising Rolle for uncovering a terrorist operation that smuggled Middle Eastern sleeper attack cells into America and how he single-handedly swept corruption out of the Bahamian government and bravely took on Sandoval's drug cartel."

Morrison smiled. "Our New Providence-7 network will have much campaign work to do next year. Just think, we'll have a prime minister as one of our highest-ranking moles in the Caribbean."

"Yes, sir. America...and the Bahamas, will benefit greatly from it.

By the way, what happened to Lieutenant General Castano?"

"Last night, officers of the Colombian Ministry of National Defense, along with their National Police and U.S. DEA agents arrested him and that bastard Juan Rojas, the retired Colombian Army officer turned arms dealer. No problem getting their cooperation after we showed them the photos our CI team took of Castano's luncheon at the Platillos Voladores restaurant in Calle with Sandoval, the FARC leader Javier Sanchez, Juan Rojas, and Asif Qadeer Edhi."

Corey shook his head. "Fuckin' Edhi. Thanks to that Ohio State Patrol trooper, Edhi ended up in a thousand pieces scattered along Interstate 90 east of Cleveland."

"Yeah, with the remains of his other sleeper cell members. By the way, Sandoval ratted on Rojas at his jail cell at Carmichael. He revealed how Rojas used his drug pipelines to ship stolen automatic rifles to Mexican and Guatemalan drug traffickers and narco-para-military groups. He also gave details of Senator Warren's involvement. Castano and Rojas will be incarcerated for a long time...maybe executed."

The Montecristo piquancy soothed Corey, enabling him to relax a bit. It was difficult for him to unwind and accept that the mission was over and the *Obscure Transgression* level was terminated by President Rhinehart. "Did we get all of Edhi's sleeper cell members? Laser-guided mortars have to be guided, which means there were terrorists inside the stadium."

Morrison puffed on his exclusive rolled-up bundle of pricey to-bacco from the Vuelta Abajo region of Cuba. He blew a smoke ring. "That was the next topic I wanted to discuss with you. There were three of them. A Secret Service agent in Rhinehart's private suite was scanning the 45,000 people in Progressive Field, snapping photos of anyone suspicious. In the upper section were three men that aroused his suspicions, but not enough to call in the troops. None were identi-fied on the NGI."

"I think I know the rest of the story. After everyone was instructed to leave the stadium, they checked the area where the three were sit-ting and... bingo!"

"Yep. They were Edhi's three-man laser-designator team. The Secret Service and Cleveland Police found paper bags and back-packs stuffed underneath the seats they were sitting in. Inside were three assembled laser target designators, all turned on and ready to guide the mortar shells down upon President Rhinehart and the thousands of people below them. The pieces were cleverly concealed as attachments to stadium binoculars, digital cameras and camcorders. They snuck right through security."

"Did they catch them inside Progressive Field?"

"No. They mingled with the fans and evacuated to Public Square. However, thousands of local police and our hazmat agents carry iPhones coordinated with each other. Instantly, all received close-up digital facial photos taken by the Secret Service agent in the Champion Suite with his telephoto binocular camera. They were spotted in ten minutes and arrested."

"Where are they now?"

"Gitmo. In solitary confinement."

"What about 'Tracker' and her CI teams in northwest Pennsylvania? Is Edhi's car still parked at that historic inn?"

"Affirmative. His Ford Fusion is still parked at the Riverside Inn in Cambridge Springs. What a chase that was! Edhi escaped because of that dam F5 tornado. 'Tracker' and her trainee and the two men in team four were right behind him. They roared into the Riverside ready to capture him but the wind gusts and torrential downpour allowed him to slip away."

Corey took a puff of his cigar and grew contemplative for a moment. *Poor Constance. Her brother was part of team three...killed along with his female partner by the F5 in Edinboro while closing in on Edhi. I can't wait to get back to her.* "It doesn't appear anyone will come to pick his car up. Did you run it?"

"Yes. Edhi's sleeper-cell network did a professional job in concealment. False registration, bogus VIN numbers, fake license plates, and forged driver's license...they were all synched together. If a cop stopped Edhi and ran his registration, he'd come up NIF. 'Tracker' and her partner are still there, just in case someone tries to pick it up, which is unlikely. But, it really doesn't matter."

Corey looked surprised. "How so? Don't we want to find more sleeper cell members, or sympathizers?"

"We already did through the new Penumbra Database algorithm. It helped us ascertain who rented the Ford Fusion to Edhi. That man, his dealership and home are under surveillance by CBIF and the CIA as we speak. Penumbra also enabled us to link him to a radicalized Muslim couple named Hakim and Asma Ahmadi. They run a sleeper-cell safe house in Dearborn where Edhi stayed."

"How could it track them down so quickly? The original Jeannie database could never have done it. Why is the Penumbra Database so unique?"

Morrison arose and went to the refrig in the kitchenette. He came back with two beers and gave one to Corey. "For starters, it combines several radically new microchips that process nine trillion tasks per second. I regret for not telling you about the black-funded project that magnified Jeannie's capabilities a thousand times over. Hsin Chow and a team of Chinese computer scientists created the microchips in Beijing. He handed over the microchip blueprints to one of our CI agents, who began handling Chow after you left and went to Jamaica."

"Yes, I'm familiar with him…code-named 'Recon', very capable in espionage tactics."

"He is, indeed. After all, you trained him."

Corey puffed his Montecristo and took a swig of beer. "What are the eavesdropping capabilities of Penumbra Database?"

Morrison leaned forward. His eyebrows raised, giving his face a look of incredulity. "I regret having kept you in the dark about this. It's a pilot project throughout the Caribbean… and its aptitude to pick up and follow digital footprints that terrorists leave actually frightens me. Whether they buy gas, simply walk into a building, make a cell phone call, surf the internet, send an e-mail or text message, interact on social networks, use a credit card, get hospital care and generate a medical record, book a plane flight, make a financial transaction …whatever…it has the knack to identify them and put them on our radar."

"Millions of Americans do those things every day. Don't you get a lot of false positives?"

"You'd think so, but Penumbra can analyze and predict beyond one's imagination... the inimitable in artificial intelligence. It analyzes huge databases and unearths suspicious activities and connections between individuals. Its mass surveillance capabilities are enormous... I'm talking about instant access to millions of CCTV and surveillance cameras, for starters."

"Is that how you found Edhi's accomplices in Dearborn?"

"Yes. Haim Ahmadi drove Edhi to a coffee shop a few blocks away from the free medical clinic in Detroit, then left. Later on, he drove the rental car to the coffee shop and parked it there. Edhi simply walked from the clinic to the rental, a Ford Fusion, and drove to Pennsylvania. Penumbra accessed back histories of CCTV cameras in the coffee shop, from other stores, and a few on the street."

Corey asked, "Is it tied-in to the Next Generation Identification, the NGI system?"

"There's a direct link to NGI and to many more databases. This was a $1.8 billion black-funded pilot project dedicated to CBIF... to determine if it would enhance our counterterrorism efforts in the Caribbean Basin. We set up CCTV devices in airports and municipalities in Nassau, Marsh Harbor, Curacao and several dozen other Caribbean locations that Penumbra deemed ripe for terrorist infiltration. They're all hooked into a biometric identification algorithm that recognizes suspects from five hundred feet away."

"The information collected must be enormous."

"Yes. The new microchips and algorithms enable Penumbra to explore across heterogeneous databases with different types of data. It can sift through phone records, criminal, and foreign spy agency databases, then probe on the World Wide Web through blogs, emails, records of visits to particular web sites, and social media accounts..."

Corey interrupted, "...and distinguish potential terrorists from ordinary citizens."

"Precisely. It gathers and stores so much information from around the world from so many innocent people... and from terrorists who have already planned and carried out attacks... that it learns key demarcations between both populations, even though the subtle, commonplace behaviors appear similar."

"It's ability to discriminate sounds... almost magical." Corey took a swig of beer. "So, the predictive nature of Penumbra is accurate?"

"If I could use it for futures trading on the stock market, I'd accumulate more money in a month than Warren Buffett did in a lifetime."

Corey blew a sigh of relief. "I'm glad it's not correct all the time in its predictions."

"How so?"

"It's calculation that Edhi's U-Haul was a truck bomb, a super-dirty radioactive truck bomb made from stolen plutonium-239 from Iran's nuclear power plant."

Morrison nodded in agreement. "That 'Penumbra Database Algorithmic Prediction- Scenario' sent chills up my spine... and President Rhinehart's, too."

Corey looked pensive. "I guess the cost of it not being wrong is why it made the prediction...a false positive is better than a false negative, right?"

"Exactly."

Both men sat silently, thinking of the scenario it printed out: 57,000 people directly downwind, detonation would instantly kill 3,000 and wound 5,000...radiation cloud moving southwest into dense human population areas, causing mass panic...one whiff of weapons-grade plutonium-239 causes lung cancer... safety forces overwhelmed caring for wounded, responding to traffic accidents and treating stress-induced heart attacks...downtown Cleveland and surrounding areas turned into dead zone for years...thousands needed to be quarantined in decontamination centers.

Corey spoke after a full minute of reflection. "I don't think President Rhinehart and Maxwell Gordon will have difficulty implementing the new Domestic Counter Intelligence Operations Center, the DCIOC. Domestic surveillance using CBIF, CIA and NSA counterintelligence methods have been a long time coming."

Morrison began chewing on his Montecristo. "We have finally caught up with the Brits. MI5 has conducted intense domestic surveillance inside the UK since it was created in 1909 without infringing on anyone's individual liberties or privacy rights."

"General Gordon is an honorable man, sir. When he was head of the National Clandestine Service at CIA, he always quoted Benjamin Franklin's warning- 'Those who would give up essential liberty to purchase a little temporary safety deserve neither liberty nor safety'."

"I think this new cabinet-level agency will work out fine. Gordon will have daily briefings with Rhinehart in the Oval Office. The Penumbra Database will be up and running soon across America and Pinkston, believe it or not, along with Hsin Chow and his son, and *Key West Drywallers*, my team of satellite image interpreters, will be monitoring its day-to-day operations."

"But, sir. Wouldn't it be dangerous to involve Hsin Chow in Cuba? If he got caught, he'd be executed for sure."

Morrison smiled and took a puff from his Montecristo. "No, Corey. He's going to be exfiltrated to the United States along with his wife when she visits him next month...and you're going to carry out the operation."

"What will my cover status be?" *Not one with deep non-official cover, a NOC, I hope.*

"You will be based in the U.S. Embassy in Havana and have diplomatic immunity in case things go wrong. Your cover will remain the same...marine biologist. The U.S. is working closely with Cuba's marine scientists and conservationists to protect their coral reefs, sea grass beds and mangrove marshes. You will meet with them and scuba dive the reefs and snorkel the mangroves to determine the extent their fish stocks are declining."

"I know they're currently at a critical level."

"Yes, and since Cuba's economy depends greatly on fishing, you will be welcomed. There are three hundred Cuban employees at the U.S. embassy in Havana and agent 'Recon' has recruited eight of them as spies. Since we restored relations with Cuba, American diplomats can travel freely around the country, unlike before when they weren't allowed to leave Havana without government permission. You are skilled in exfiltration tradecraft. America will gain much if you succeed in getting Hsin out of Cuba."

"Indeed! A Chinese engineer who was senior member of their SIGINT program. I'll do everything possible to make it happen, to bring both Hsin and his wife to the U.S. and reunite them with their only child. Is he still attending MIT?"

"Yes."

Corey recalled Hsin Chow's words when he posed as a French businessman and recruited him at the Hotel Sofitel Sevilla in Havana: *My China is a communist dictatorship masquerading as a democracy. My son told me in private he no longer wants to return to China. He fell in love with a fellow MIT student and they want to marry. You showed me a most detailed plan to get my wife and I out of Cuba and into the United States to begin a new life. I will do it.*

Corey looked solemnly at Morrison. "Sir, I made a promise to Hsin and his family...a promise I won't break. I'm sure Beijing's MSS, the Ministry of State Security, will send agents to the MIT campus to hunt Hsin's son down. Will they get the protection you and I agreed upon if he defects?"

"I've got a good memory, Corey. That's why I honor promises made in the past. I'm aware of your empathy for Hsin and his family. Upon arrival in America, they will be given two million dollars along with new identities. CBIF will give both Hsin and his son top-secret clearances and employ them as our moles inside the National Geospatial-Intelligence Agency in Washington, D.C. They will become full-time, clandestine consultants to Maxwell Gordon's DCIOC in order to insure Penumbra's data mining domestic operation runs smoothly."

"That's comforting to know, sir. It will be a significant defection, indeed." *Now that the mission is over, where will he be assigning me? Will I be relocated out of New Providence-7 to another Caribbean locale...away from Constance?*

The general took a sip of beer, then swung his chair around and gazed out the same tinted picture window he looked out of during their last meeting, a month ago. It was déjà vu. Children frolicked in the shallow waters of the Florida Bay, under the watchful eyes of their parents who were lounging in the shade of coconut palms.

He always paused and gazed out the window before making a profound statement. *All I want to know is...am I going to be separated from Constance? Where's my next assignment?*

Morrison swiveled back around, leaned forward and placed his elbows on the desk top. "This new cabinet-level counterintelligence operation is going to be run by CBIF, the CIA and NSA. We'll be under the microscope of President Rhinehart and General Maxwell Gordon. CBIF will be heavily involved in domestic counterintelligence and can't afford to miss clues in identifying potential terrorist attacks. For this reason, I am promoting you to be CBIF's Station Chief for the entire Caribbean Basin."

"Thank you, sir!" Corey was thrilled by the endorsement.

"Now, I want you to listen very carefully. As President Rhinehart said in his speech last night, CBIF and the CIA, along with the NSA, are replacing law enforcement...the FBI...in its use of domestic surveillance to battle the growing threat from radicalized terrorists. With Penumbra, we will be continually developing a threat picture and eliminating threats before they become operational, *before* a law is broken, not *after.*"

Corey took a full gulp of his beer and puffed on the Montecristo. *Caribbean Basin Station Chief!* "It's been a longtime coming. Every Western democracy has counterintelligence agencies that are separate from law enforcement and conduct domestic surveillance. Not allowing the CIA, NSA or CBIF to do so has been a national security nightmare."

"I agree. The FBI is simply spread too thin performing both functions." General Morrison reached into his briefcase and took out two handsome shadow boxes. He slid one over to Corey. "Congratulations from the POTUS and from me. This is the 'Intelligence Commendation Medal' for your exemplary service in this operation that saved thousands of American lives."

"Thank you so much, sir. Tell President Rhinehart I am truly honored."

He slid the second box over to Corey. Inside was the CIA's 'Exceptional Service Medallion'. "I want you to return to Abaco and personally deliver this to Constance. It is to honor her brother who died in the F5 tornado while tracking Edhi. As you know, it respects those agents who are injured or killed in the line of duty." He gave Corey a letter. "I also want you to give this to Constance. It's signed by me, the CIA director, and President Rhinehart. She can share it with her parents, but then must give it back to you. The letter will be placed in the young man's file at CBIF headquarters."

"I will do so, sir. How long will I remain on Abaco?"

A twinkle appeared in Morrison's eyes. He tried to conceal it, but couldn't. "As newly-appointed Caribbean Basin Station Chief, I am basing you in Marsh Harbor, Abaco. You will be staying at the safe house...the one run by Constance, until further notice. You need time to rest your mind after what you've been through, so I want you to resume your deep cover as a marine biologist studying the pods of wild spotted dolphins in the Sea of Abaco until further notice...happy snorkeling."

Epilogue

Sunset Bar Conch Inn Marina

Marsh Harbor, Abaco

Shianna arrived early and began to prepare for the noontime crowd. She retrieved the master key from the manager's office and unlocked the small safe underneath the cash register in the Sunset Bar. It was full of one and five-dollar bills, plus coin packets to insure she had enough small cash to make change. A small box lay under the bills. She thought it odd, for it wasn't there when she closed down the bar last night.

Opening the box, she was astonished to see a luxurious Cartier pasha Chronograph watch with sapphire crystals. It was worth at least $9,000. A hand-written note was attached: *Dear Shianna- Please accept this gift from us, even though it will never replace the love you had for your older brother, Sidney. We witnessed you agonize over his death from the hands of evil men, but they are now paying greatly for their misdeeds. It's time to move on, to leave your anger behind, to let go of the hurt and grow beyond it. Play Bob Marley's 'Redemption Song' on the juke box for us and limbo forward...onward! Anonymous*

Sea of Abaco

(GPS: 26.494710, -76.984624)

The Boston Whaler slowed down and stopped just at the right location between Lubber's Quarters and Tilloo Cay. Scattered coral heads and patch coral reefs could be seen through the gin-colored waters below. It was the best-kept secret for snorkeling and he planned to share it with Constance and her son, Matt.

Constance lowered the anchor, making sure it took hold in the sea grass beds. Matt was proud of himself because Corey let him power the boat through the Sea of Abaco, solo. "Well done, Matt!"

Corey patted him on the back. "Now, let's see what kind of life there is below us." He handed the boy a waterproof fish identification guide to take with him. The trio put on their snorkeling gear and dove in.

It was low tide and Matt enjoyed exploring the patch reefs with his mom and Corey. He checked off twenty-five species on his fish ID guide. When high tide rolled in, Corey knew the spotted dolphin pods would return to hunt squid in the submerged sand banks.

Corey turned to Matt and asked, "Want to have a wild spotted dolphin encounter?"

The eleven-year-old yelled, "Yes!"

Corey and Constance chuckled as the excited boy leaped back into the boat. "Let's go, Mr. Pearson!"

Corey let Matt pilot the boat again and taught him the dolphin maneuvers. "Stay in twelve to eighteen feet of water, avoid shoals around Lubber's Quarter's Cay, cruise at eight knots, point the bow at 206-degrees M by 3.47-degrees NM."

Matt proceeded on the same course. The thumping sound of the seventeen-foot Boston Whaler and the same RPM rhythmic hum of the motor attracted the dolphins in no time at all.

'Chop Tail' had no difficulty recognizing Corey's signature, turning the familiar boat sounds into memorable visual images from the past. He freely allowed his pod members, including three mother dolphins and their babies, to interact with these particular humans.

They spent the rest of the day swimming with the same pod that saved Corey's life. Corey taught Matt how to use the digital underwater camera with zoom lens and hydrophone to record them. He learned rapidly and took dozens of photos of each dolphin, recording their unique clicks and buzzing calls.

Corey and Constance gazed at the distant shoreline where the Abaco Poultry, LTD mansion used to be. While treading water with her amongst the cackling dolphins that surrounded them, Corey said, "We'll have a nice talk tonight."

CBIF Safe House
Outside Marsh Harbor
Abaco, Bahamas

A steady ocean breeze blew across the front porch while Corey, Constance and Matt talked about their snorkeling adventure in the patch reefs and the dolphin encounter. The pod of wild ocean mammals amazed Matt and he wanted to grow up and become a marine biologist, 'Just like Corey.'

Matt grew tired after the sun set. It was a long day for an eleven-year-old. Before retreating to his bedroom, he picked up the loose-leaf folder of photos and hand-written field notes of the life histories of the dolphins that Corey and Constance took years ago, before he was born. He gave his mom a hug, then said to Corey, "I'm going to know every spotted dolphin out there...thanks for today." Then, he gave Corey a big hug, too.

Alone and in the dimming light, they pulled their Adirondack chairs closer together and held hands. They sat in silence for a few minutes, contemplating the day while listening to the tree frogs and crickets in the hedge of sea grapes lining the gravel and coral driveway.

After a few restful moments, Constance spoke. "Your promotion to Station Chief of the Caribbean Basin is well-deserved. You'll be doing a lot more traveling."

"True, but Morrison located my HQ here, in Marsh Harbor ...at this safe house, with you."

Constance took a sip of wine, then said, "I think our boss understands how difficult it is for someone to have a spouse, lover... whoever, working as a covert counterintelligence agent."

"Maybe that's why he had a twinkle in his eyes when he assigned me here."

"I think so. You have to be one to understand one."

"It's difficult to live a normal life. We work clandestinely, live a life of lies under a false identity, conduct surveillance on people suspected of having connections to terrorists, hide our true identities from everyone, including family members… I bet Morrison has seen a lot of his married agents go through marital breakups."

Constance nodded her head in agreement. "Maybe that's why you and I are so compatible. How many other couples know the art of surveillance and spy tradecraft… who can track targets without being noticed, avoid being tailed and lose those tailing them?"

Corey chuckled. "You're so right, Constance, although that's not your *real* name."

"I'm glad we agree on that…*Corey Pearson*…although that's not your real name, either. We're two peas in the same pod…I can see how such relationships fall apart. How can there be a trusting relationship between two people when one lives a routine, predictable life… the other shrouded in secrecy?"

He lifted her hand and kissed it. "It's much more than our career compatibilities. When you're not around, I feel something missing in my life. All I know is that I love you."

Constance leaned over and kissed him. "Corey, I feel that unexplainable warmth right now…I feel it whenever you're near. I felt it when we were thrust together for this mission, discovering Duane Collier's murder site and the confrontation with Tougas and Cherestal on the GAH. I felt it over a decade ago when we first worked together… when we spent that one night together. I love you… I want to share the rest of my life with you."

A tear ran down Corey's cheek. "We'll make a loving family… you, me and Matt. I love that kid already… he reminds me so much of myself when I was his age."

"There's a good reason for that."

"How so?"

Constance smiled. This time her eyes filled with tears of joy. "Because he's your natural-born son. Welcome back home… father!"

Author Biography

In his capacity as a member of the Association of Former Intelligence Officers, Robert Morton, MEd, EdS, regularly discusses intelligence matters with professionals in and around Washington, DC. He currently consults with intelligence scholars and field operatives for both his novels and newspaper articles.

In addition to the Corey Pearson—CIA Spymaster in the Caribbean spy series, Morton is the author of over a dozen editorials published in Gannett's Newspaper Network of Central Ohio, as well as in Ashland, Oregon, newspapers and California's *Press-Enterprise*

Made in the USA
Middletown, DE
17 September 2017